TERRORISM IN INDIA'S NORTH-EAST A GATHERING STORM

TERRORISM IN INDIA'S NORTH-EAST
A Gathering Storm
(In 3 Volumes)

(Volume - I)

Col. Ved Prakash

KALPAZ PUBLICATIONS
DELHI-110052

Terrorism in India's North-East
A Gathering Storm

Rs. 2500 (Set)

ISBN: 81-7835-660-0 (Set)
ISBN: 9788178356617

Published in 2016 in India by
Kalpaz Publications
C-30, Satyawati Nagar,
Delhi-110052
E-mail: kalpaz@hotmail.com
Phone : 9811692060

Laser Type Setting by: Quick Media, Delhi
Printed at : Singhal Print Media, Delhi

DEDICATED TO

My grandson, Aryan Sharma,
with
a fervent plea to the present generation to
render his generation the world over
safe from the scourge of terrorism

Contents

Preface

The humanity today is in the virulent grip of a pandemic—the scourge of terrorism. Several groups and outfits are engaged in this 'War through terror', a low-cost option for the inhuman desperados; but the most potent and wide-spread threat to the very existence of this world as we know it comes from this insiduous war being unleashed by the Islamist groups perpetrating this heinous crime against the mankind in the countries spread from the Philippines to the United States.

It is only apt that the then senior most servant of the world community, Mr. Kofi Annan, who served the UN as its Secretary General for eight long years (1998-2006), is quoted on the issue. He said on 4 Oct. 2002 :

> "Terrorism is a global threat with global effect; .... its consequences affect every aspect of the United Nations agenda from development to peace to human rights and the rule of law. By its very nature, terrorism is an assault on the fundamental principles of law, order, human rights and the peaceful settlement of disputes on which the United Nations is established. The United Nations has an indispensable role to play in providing the legal and organisational framework within which the international compaign against terrorism can unfold."
>
> [Terrorism Prevention Branch
>
> United Nationals Office on Drugs and Crimes
>
> Vienna International Centre, PO Box 500
>
> A – 1400 Vienna
>
> Austria]

We have just been though the human history's most violent century. Curious, if interesting, trends have marked the era. If in the early years of nuclear age, which commenced with the Hiroshima blast, the world lived under the shadow of a nuclear holocaust, by the end of the Cold War the probability of a nuclear war and exchange was lower than ever before. Likewise, after the Second World War the likelihood of the clash of arms between any two major powers divindled progressively. In a manner of speaking, the 1991 Gulf War may well be the last classical war for a long time to come. The 2003 US invasion of Iraq was hardly a conventional war. It was a case of technology defeating the 'mighty' Army of President Saddam Hussain. But what is more significant is that when the Iraq war is entering the fifth year on 23 March 2007, the US military machine and coalition forces are losing it—almost—to the practitioners of an unconventional warfare : War through terror.

So in the recent years, the nuclear and classical inter-state wars seem to be becoming less likely, and the phenomenon of sub-conventional war and transnational militancy and terrorism have been on the rise. The latter belongs to the genre of "Low Intensity Conflicts" (LIC). The term LIC has emerged only in recent decades, with the US Pentagon's description of the spectrum of conflict consisting of 'high', 'medium' and 'low' intensity levels, in Klare and Kornbluh (ed), *Low Intensity Warfare*, 1988.

Contemporary warfare has begun to lean extensively towards the 'low intensity' variety. Since 1945, the world has seen some 160 or so conflicts. Of these, three-fourths have been low intensity. 'Terrorism' is the most dominant and most widely practised form of the LIC today. It is perpetrated by the non-state actors and its targets mostly are innocent civilians, including women and children. The real tragedy lies in the fact that the victims even do not know why they are killed so mercilessly. Some other compelling facts and data are recorded here :

- Only four of the 82 conflicts recorded between 1989 and 1992 were of the classic inter-state character, and every year since 1991, there have been at least ten internal conflicts around the world that caused the deaths of more than 10,000 where the primary weapons of war mere light weapons—mostly used by the terrorists.
- Non-state actors appeared to have little difficulty in accessing either the weapons or the ammunition, as prices dropped to as little as $ 8 for an AK-47 assault rifle—a prized possession of a terrorist.
- In all of the intra-state conflicts being waged today, light weapons are the primary weapons of war of both the combatants—the State and the non-state actor.
- The rise in sophistication was accompanied by a corresponding increase in the casualty rate in most conflict areas. The path from the .303 to the assault rifles and rocket propelled grenades (RPGs) has been a bloody one.
- All wars in Asia and in some other parts of the world are funded wholly or in part by narcotics movements—popularly known as nacro terrorism.
- Besides an inordinate number of casualties suffered by the civil society, the terrorism also causes huge refugee movement. By the end of the 20th century, the various conflict zones the world over had over 120 million chronically malnourished people, while there were

over 28 million refugees and displaced persons, an eleven-fold increase since 1970 (Human Development Report, 1999).

- In more specific terms, in Sudan's Darfur region alone, an estimated 200,000 people have been killed and over 2 million rendered homeless in the terrorism-related upheavels during the past half-a-decade period.

What should be a matter of serious concern to the international community is its inability to craft a joint, concerted and effective policy frame-work to confront and defeat terrorism. A western scholar has asserted that what the world is witnessing and experiencing today is a "clash of civilizations". Radical Islam is not only pushing hard to dominate the ummah, but also bent upon destabilising the countries it deems as its 'enemies'.

Presently, terrorism is perpetrating mindless violence—horrendous killings and wanton destruction of property. A Pakistani Army Officer Brig S.K. Malik, *Quranic Concept of Work* (Wajid Alis, Lahore), 1979, P. 59, has put it like it is :

> "Terror struck into the hearts of the enemies is not only a means, it is the end in itself."

Besides the Islamic outfits, some other terrorist outfits are active in Sri Lanka, North Ireland, Europe, Japan and South America. Not to speak of a joint fight against the terrorists, the UN has not succeeded till date to resolve the definitional hurdle in the counter-terrorism stakes.

The Author has the hands on experience of fighting the insurgency and terrorism during his two stints of service in India's North-East. When he joined as a newly-commissioned officer his unit, an Infantry Battalion (3 Sikh), in 1957, he was blooded into the active battle, so to say, as the Phizo-led Naga insurgency was at its virulent worst. During this tenure (1957-61), as young officer he led his platoon in attacks on the rebel camps in the jungles and cavernous hills of Nagaland, then merely Naga Hills district of Assam. Once tragedy struck his patrol and he saw one of his men fall to a bullet fired by a Naga rebel. The patrol fought its way out of the ambush sprung by the ultras. It has been aptly said that no one understands the pains and pangs of the battle/war better than the soldiers. In counter-insurgency operations, the action is generally at the level of platoon and company. The operations, thus, are led by the junior leaders.

His next tenure was the Mizo Hills, 1984-87, when he was commanding officer of an Infantry Battalion (18 Assam Rifles), deployed in the area along the Mizo Hills/Burma (now Myanmar) border. It was during the active-phase of Laldenga-led Mizo rebellion. It was again a rewarding experience, involving as it did, planning counter-insurgency operations in various areas under his command and liaison with senior civil and police officers.

A word of praise is due to the Naga and Mizo militants. Not only were they brave and doughtly fighters, they observed a certain code of honour. They usually targeted uniformed men, soldiers and policemen, and seldom the civilians. Of course, the perceived 'informers' were indeed targeted. They indeed were worthy 'enemies'—far removed from today's mindless murderers.

It may not be out of place here to mention some 'trivia' which will be of great interest to any Indian interested in the subject. It, of course, relates to the Author's two tenures in the North-East. During his first (1957-61) tenure, his unit was headquartered at Khonoma, the village of the legendary Phizo, who was then leading the insurgency against the Indian state. Some details deserve a mention. The Officer's Mess of his unit, 3 Sikh, was occupying the Dak Bungalow once home to a Japanese unit commander. The Bungalow, 13 km south-west of Kohima Garrison, which stubbornly thwarted the advance of Japanese forces to Dimapur and Gawahati, marked the limit of their penetration into Indian territory during World War II. More interestingly, this Bungalow was skirting the base line of a 650-meter long ridge on the top of which stood Phizo's house, occupied by his wife and children. Ironically, the Assam police was guarding and protecting the family of the rebel leader, Phizo, while the soldiers of 3 Sikh were hunting his Naga rebel warriors in jungles. Phizo by then, of course, was comfortably ensconced in a safe house somewhere in Pakistan, arranged by its intelligence agencies.

During his second tenure (1984-87), the Author's unit, 18 Assam Rifles, was located at Lungleh (now spelt, Lunglei), the village of equally legendary Mizo leader, Laldenga. His house was located near the Headquarters of the Infantry Brigade. Needless to say, his family too was given security by the Indian State of Assam. Another 'trivial' detail may be of interest to the lay reader. One late might, when the Author was returning to his unit after attending some function at the Brigade Headquarters, his vehicle was 'nearly' ambushed by the insurgents near Laldenga's house. This he learnt next morning from an officer who was travelling in his own jeep some distance from Author's : "Well, last night it was a close call for you. There were a couple of Mizo ultras well-concealed and all set to spring an ambush. After all, a Commanding Officer is an attractive prize for them. As soon as they saw the lights of my vehicle, they melted into the jungle."

That the Indian State was guarding the families of the top Naga and Mizo leaders in the 1950s and 1980s is a tribute to Indian democracy and reflective of its innate strength! And the tradition continues till date. All the Kashmiri secessionist leaders are being provided security today while they are carrying out vicious campaigns to violate India's sovereignty and integrity. The latest episode in this saga of generosity displayed by India came yesterday (20 March 2007) when the most passionate, some would say, 'vicious' among the hard liners, was granted visa to proceed to the US for treatment of a serious medical condition. This is not all. An opponent of this secessionist leader, Prof. Bhim Singh, Chief of the Panthers Party, offered to bear all the expenses for this treatment! Three cheers for the Indian culture, civilisation and tradition!

We must remember that never before in the history of civilization were human beings so much exposed to terrorism as they have been during the last couple of decades. Extremist, fundamentalist, and disruptive forces the world over are focussed single-mindedly to destroy its peace and harmony through wanton violence unleashed by their foot soldiers, blinded and indoctrinated by religious and ideological passion. The mindless death dance is not only targeting mostly the innocent people including women and children but is also transforming the tender youth into hardcore terrorists—the unthinking killing machines. The suicide bomber is the latest and the most lethal addition to the armoury of the planners and perpetrators of the terrorism. It is beyond comprehension how the fanatic, fundamentalist clerics and the narrow nationalist ideologues can easily convert simple youngman into human bombs alluring them with an after-world of living with given number of virgin nymphs and other luxuries they could have only dreamt of during their sojourn on the earth. The counter-terrorism policies and strategies of the West (the USA, the UK etc.) and East (India and Isreal etc.) do not seem to have an answer to this unthinking robot-like machine—also known as the human-bomber.

Incidents like the attack on the Indian Parliament, the largest democratic institution of the world; repeated attacks on transport systems and commercial hubs of Mumbai, the economic capital and nerve centre of the largest democracy in the world; the destruction of World Trade Centre of the US, popularly known as the Nine-Eleven; blowing up of a hotel on a Bali beach in Indonesia; ruthless killings of passengers on Metro trains and stations in London; similar attack on Madrid (Spain) trains; and the tragedy in a Moscow theatre are only some examples to prove that we all are vulnerable targets of terrorist depredations at any time, no matter which part of the world we live in. The elder statesman of India, AB Vajpayee, put it succinctly this way when he addressed the US Congres as India's Prime Minister in September 2002 :

> "No country in the world could enjoy immunity against terrorism on account of distance or geograpphy."

Majority of the material in this book is from open sources : the print and visual media, the internet, and personal discussions with the reputed experts and journalists involved with the subject. I owe a deep debt of gratitude to the Institute for Conflict Management, headed by a great Indian who retrieved the Punjab for India when it had 'nearly' gone under. At a more personal level, I am grateful to a senior Research Scholar at this Institute who not only sent me a particular monograph, but also offered to download for me any data/material I needed for my book. I thanked him profurely and told him that I would not like him to give him so much bother and would ask my son/ daughter to download all I needed from the South Asia Terrorism Portal (SATP).

This book, a multi-volume, comprehensive study, aims at spreading the awareness among the civil society about the dangers posed to the international community by the ever-spreading phenomenon of the deadly pandemic of terrorism. It covers all aspects of terrorism in various corners of the world including India, West Asia, Asian countries to the east, Europe and America. It explains the ground realities in a lucid style sans any academic and professional jargons.

Encyclopaedic in scope, the book will have served its purpose if it enables the reader to see the issues relating to terrorism in perspective and appreciate the implications of the threat it poses in clearer terms.

With this, I rest my case, hoping that the reader would find the book worth a read.

Ved Prakash

Abbreviations and Acronyms

AA	Asian Age
AAC	Awami Action Committee (J & K)
AAJM	Anjaman-e-Auqafi Jama Masjid
AASU	All Assam Students Union
ABDR	Al Badr (J & K)
ABQ	Al Barq (J & K)
ABSU	All Bodo Students Union
ADC	Autonomous District Council
AEH	Ahal-e-Hadis
AESS	Anjuman-e-Sipah-e-Sahila (J & K)
AFF	Al Fatah Force (J & K)
AFIS	Automatic Fingerprint Identification System (USA)
AFSPA	Armed Forces (Special Powers) Act
AHAB	Ahl-e-Hadith Andolan (Bangladesh)
AIPRF	All India People's Resistance Forum
AJF	Al Jihad Force (J & K)
AJKEC	All Jammu and Kashmir Employees Confederation
ALI	Assam Light Infantry
AMF	Al Mujahideen Force (J & K)
AMFI	Al Mujahid Fil Islam (J & K)
AMLT	Assam Muslim Liberation Tigers
AMU	Aligarh Muslim University
AMULFA	All Muslim United Liberation Front (Assam)
AMUS	Al Mustafa
AMYA	Al Madad Yalgar-e-Ali
ANLA	Adivasi Nationalist Liberation Army
ANVC	A'chik National Volunteer Council (Megh)
APHC	All Party Hurryat Conference (also, KJHC)
AR	Assam Rifles
AS	Adam Sena (Islamic, Asm)
ASI	Archaeological Survey of India
ASR	Assam Secretariat Records

ATGR	Allah Tigers
ATI	Anjaman-e-Tablig-ul-Islam
ATTF	All Tripura (Tribal) Tiger Force
AUC	Al Umar Commandos
AUI	Ansar-ul-Islam
AUM	Al Umar Mujahideen
Baharistan	Baharistani-i-Ghaibi, a contemporary account of events in the reign of Jahangir (1605-27). It has information on certain Muslim invasions of Assam (Jadunath Sarkar's trans, 1905)
BDR	Bangladesh Rifles
BdSF	Bodo Security Force
BIMSTEC	Bangladesh, India, Myanmar, Sri Lanka, Thailand Economic Cooperation
BJP	Bengal Judicial Proceedings (also, Bharatiya Janata Party)
BKI	Babbar Khalsa International
BLT	Bodoland Liberation Tigers (Asm)
BLTF	Bodoland Liberation Tiger Force (Asm)
BNLF	Bru National Liberation Front (MR)
Brig	Brigadier
BSF	Border Security Force (India)
Capt	Captain
CBS	Central Broadcasting Service
CEM	Chief Executive Member (of the ADC)
CFR	Council of Foreign Relations
CHT	Chittagong Hills Tract
CI	Center-Insurgency
CIA	Central Intelligence Agency
CKRF	Chin-Kuki Revolutionary Front (MPR)
CNLA	Chin National Liberation Army (Myanmar)
CO	Commanding Officer (of an Army Unit) also, OC)
Col	Colonel
COMOA	Coordination Committee for Minorities of Assam
CPI	Communist Party of India
CPI (M)	Communist Party of India (Maoist)
CPI (ML)	Communist Party of India (Marxist-Leninist)
CPM	Communist Party (Marxist)
CRPF	Central Reserve Police Force

CRS	Congressional Research Service (USA)
d	Inactive, and perhaps, defunct
DEA	Drug Enforcement Administration (USA)
DEM	Dukhtran-e-Millat (J & K)
DGFI	Director General Field Intelligence (Bangladesh)
DHD	Dima Halam Daogah (Asm)
DoD	Department of Defence (USA)
DoS	Department of State (USA)
EAM	External Affairs Minister
EC	Election Commission
Ed/ed	Edited, Edition
EM	Executive Member (of the ADC)
Encyclopaedia	All references in this book are to the *Encyclopaedia Britannica,* 15th Edition, 1984
Epigraphia	*Epigraphia Indica*
Exp	Indian Express
FALN	Fuerzas Armadas de Liberacion National (Venezuela)
FAR	Fuerzas Armadas Rebeldes (Guatemala)
FATA	Federally Administered Tribal Areas (In popular imagination, these areas in Pakistan's NWFP are self-governing)
FLN	National Liberation Front (of Algeria)
FPC	Foreign Political Consultations (British Indian Records/correspondence with foreign countries)
Gen	General
GOC	General Officer Commanding (of an Army 'division' or a 'corps')
GOC-in-C	General Officer Commanding-in-chief (of an Army 'Command')
GoI	Government of India
GR	Gurkha Rifles
GWOT	Global War on Terrorism
HAJC	Hamin Al Jihad Commandos
HALC	Hynniewtrip A'chik Liberation Council (Megh)
HEI	Hizb-e-Islami (Gulbuddin Hekmat Yar's outfit in Afghanistan)
Hizb	Hizbullah
HKEI	Harkat-e-Islami

HKMN	Harkat-ul-Musalmeen
HM	Hizb-ul-Mujahideen
HMM	Hizb-ul-Momineen
HNLC	Hinniewtrip National Liberation Council (Megh)
HPC	Hmar People's Convention (MPR, MR)
HT	Hindustan Times
HUA	Harkat-ul-Ansar
HUJ	Harkat-ul-Jehad
HUJI (B)	Harkat-ul-Jihad-al-Islami (Bangladesh)
HUM	Harkat-ul-Mujahideen
HUT	Hizb-ul-Tehrir
HVC	Hmar Volunteer Council (MR)
IAEA	International Atomic Energy Agency
IAS	Indian Administrative Service (successor service to ICS)
ICG	International Crisis Group (Belgium-based)
ICI TAP	International Criminal Investigation Training Assistance Programme (USA)
ICS	Indian Civil Service (predecessor service of the IAS)
IDP	Internally Displaced People
IDSA	Institute for Defence Studies and Analysis
IED	Improvised Explosive Device
IIC	India International Centre (New Delhi)
IISS	International Institute of Strategic Studies
IJ	Islami Jung; also Islamic Jehad
IJET	Islami Jamaat-e-Tulba
IKL[d]	Ireiba Kanba Lup
Ikhwan	A counter-insurgency outfit in J & K, mostly of former militants and supported by the State Government. Its best known face and chief was Kuka Parrey
ILAA	Islamic Liberation Army of Assam
IMU	Islamic Movement of Uzbekistan
IOJ	Islamic Oikya Jote
IPC	Indian Penal Code
IRB	India Reserve Battalion
IRF	Islamic Resistance Force
IRP	Islamic Resistance Party
ISAF	International Security Assistance Force (Afghanistan)

ISFI	Islamic Security Force of India
ISI	Inter-Service Intelligence
ISL	(International) Islamic Students League
ISS	Islamic Sevak Sangh
ISYF	International Sikh Youth Federation
IUM	Ikhwan-ul-Musalmeen
JAH/JAEH	Jamaat-e-Ahl-e-Hadis (J & K)
JAKLI	Jammu and Kashmir Light Infantry
JEH	Jamaat-e-Hamdania
JEI	Jamaat-e-Islami
JEI (A)	Jamaat-e-Islami, Assam
JEM	Jaish-e-Mohammad
JHU	Jathika Hela Urumaya (Sri Lanka)
JKIF	Jammu and Kashmir Islamic Front
JKJEI	Jammu and Kashmir Jmmat-e-Islami
JKLF	Jammu and Kashmir Liberation Front
JKLT	Jammu and Kashmir Liberation Tigers
JKML	Jammu and Kashmir Muslim League
JKMLA	Jammu and Kashmir Muslim Liberation Army
JKPL	Jammu and Kashmir People's League
JKPL (R)	JKPL (Rehmani)
JKPL (S)	JKPL (Shabir) or (S. Hamid)
JKPPF	Jammu and Kashmir People's Political Forum
JKSF	Jammu and Kashmir Students Federation
JKSLF	Jammu and Kashmir Students Liberation Front
JKUPL	Jammu and Kashmir United People's League
JMB	Jamaat-ul-Mujahideen (Bangladesh)
JMJB	Jagruti Muslim Janata (Bangladesh)
JS	Joint Secretary
JUD	Jamaat-ul-Dawa
JUI/JUUI	Jamaat-ul-Ulemah-e-Islami
JUIH	Jamaat-ul-Islam-e-Hind
JUM	Jamaat-ul-Mujahideen
JUMA	Jamaat-ul-Mujahideen Almi
JUUI	Jamaat-ul-Ulamah-e-Islami (Pakistan)
KAB	Kashmir Awareness Bureau
KAC	Kashmir Action Committee

KAF	Kashmir Army Force
KBA	Kashmir Bar Association
KCF	Khalistan Commando Force
KCP	Kangleipak Communist Party
KDF	Kuki Defence Force
KDM	Kuki Democratic Movement
KFS	Kital Fi Sabilillah (= armed movement for Islam = Establishment of Islamic Rule)
KJC	Kashmir Jihad Committee (Pakistan)
KJF	Kashmir Jihad Force
KJHC	Kul Jamaat Hyrryat Conference (also, APHC)
KLC	Kashmir Liberation Cell
KLF	Kashmir Liberation Force
KLO[d]	Kangleipak Liberation Organisation
KLT	Kashmir Liberation Tigers
KNA	Kuki National Army
KNF	Kuki National Front
KNO	Kuki National Organisation
KNU	Karen National Union (Myanmar)
KNV	Karbi National Volunteers (Assam)
KRPC	Kom Rem People's Convention (MPR)
KSF	Kuki Security Force (MPR)
KYKL	Kanglei Yawol Kann Lup (MPR)
KZF	Khalistan Zindabad Force
LEJ	Lashkar-e-Jabbar
LET	Lashkar-e-Tayyaba
LITF	Liberation Islamic Tiger Force
LMG	Light Machine Gun
LOC	Line of Control
LSI	Linguistic Survey of India
Lt	Lieutenant
Lt Col	Lieutenant Colonel
Lt Gen	Lieutenant General
LTTE	Liberation Tigers of Tamil Elam
Maj	Major
Maj Gen	Major General
MBT	Main Battle Tank

MC	Muslim Conference
MDI	Markaz Dawa-ul-Irshad
MEA	Ministry of External Affairs
MeA	Mahaz-e-Azadi
MEI	Mujahideen-e-Islam
MG	Machine Gun
MHA	Ministry of Home Affairs
MIM	Majlis-e-Ittehad-ul-Musilmeen
MJAH	Markazi Jamaat-e-Ahal-e-Hadith
MJC	Muttehida Jihad Council (also UJC)
MJF	Muslim Janbaaz Force
MKM	Muslim Khwateen Markaz
MLA	Muslim Liberation Army
MLFA	Manipur Liberation Front Army
MLFA	Muslim Liberation Front of Assam
MLTA	Muslim Liberation Tiger of Assam
MM	Muslim Momineen
MM	Muslim Mujahideen
MMA	Muttehida Majlis-e-Amal
MMG	Medium Machine Gun
MNA/F[d]	Mizo National Army/Front
MOD	Ministry of Defence
Mohd	Mohammad/Mohammed
MoS	Memorandum of Settlement
MoU	Memorandum of Understanding
MR	Maritime Reconnaissance
MSA[d]	Meitei State Army (MPR)
MULFA	Muslim United Liberation Front of Assam
MULA	Meghalaya United Liberation Army
MULTA	Muslim United Liberation Tigers of Assam
MVF	Muslim Volunteer Force
n	Note/Notes

Muslim Terrorist Outfits in Assam

AS	COMOA	MULTA
HUJ	JEI (A)	MULFA
ILAA		
HUM		
ISFI	LITF	MVF
ISS	MLTA	SIMI
	MLA	URPA

NAM	Non-Aligned Movement
NC	National Conference
NDFB	National Democratic Front of Bodoland (ASM)
NECA[d]	North-Eastern Council Army (MPR)
NEHU	North-Eastern Hill University
NFG	(Also FNG) Naga Federal Government
NLFT	National Liberation Front of Tripura
NLG	Nagalim Guard (MPR)
NNC (A)	Naga National Council (Adino)
NNC (K)	NNC (Khodao)
NPC	Naga People's Council
NSA	National Security Adviser
NSC	National Security Council
NSCN (I-M)	National Socialist Council of Nagaland (Isaac-Muivah)
NSCN (K)	NSCN (Khaplang)
NWFP	North-West Frontier Province (Pakistan)
OC	Officer Commanding (also, CO)
NIC	Organisation of Islamic Conference
Op	Bluestar Operation Bluestar
PC	People's Conference
PCC(I)	Pradesh Congress Committee (Indira)
PEI	Pasban-e-Islam
PFLP	Popular Front for Liberation of Palestine
PISCES	Personal Identification Security, Comparison and Evaluation System (US)
PLA	People's Liberation Army (MPR)
PLO	Palestinian Liberation Organisation
POK	Pakistan-Occupied Kashmir (To Pakistanis, it is Azad Kashmir)
PPT	Pir Panjal Tigers
PRA[d]	People's Republican Army
PRE PAK	People's Revolutionary Party of Kangeipak (MPR)
PS	Police Station
PULF	People's United Liberation Front
QMC	Quranic Muttehida Council
R	Reprint (of a book, with the year)
RBA	Royal Bhutanese Army

RDX	Research Department Explosives. RDX, in fact, is the popular name for cyclotrimethyle netri nitromine compound.
RGM	Revolutionary Government of Manipur
RJC	Revolutionary Joint Committee
RL	Rocket Launcher
RPF	Revolutionary People's Front
RPFK[d]	Revolutionary People's Front Kangleipak (MPR)
RPG	Rocket-propelled Grenade
RSF	Rabha Security Force
SAARC	South Asian Association for Regional Cooperation
SAIR	South Asia Intelligence Review
SC	Scheduled Castes
SEJ	Shora-e-Jihad
SF	Security Forces
SICC	Somalia Islamic Courts Council
SIG	Special Investigation Group
3 Sikh	3rd Battalion of the Sikh Regiment
SIMI	Students Islamic Movement of India
SLFP	Sri Lanka Freedom Party
SLI	Sikh Light Infantry
SOG	Special Operations Group (of J & K Police)
SP	Superintendent of Police
SSF[d]	Special Sacrificc Force (Kuki) (MPR)
S/S capt	Self-styled Captain
ST	Scheduled Tribes
TADA	Terrorist and Disruptive Activities Act
TEHK	Tehrik-e-Hurryat Kashmir
TEJ	Tehrik-e-Jihad
TEJI	Tehrik-e-Jihad Islami

Terrorist Outfits: Arunachal Pradesh

ULAA	ULVA
ULMA	UPVA

Terrorist Outfits: Assam

BdSF	NDFB
BLT/F	ULFA
DHD	
KNV	UPDS

Terrorist Outfits: Manipur

CKRF	KYKL	RJC
HPC	MLFA	RPF
IKC[d]	MSA[d]	RPFK[d]
KCP	NECA[d]	SSF[d]
KDF	NLG	SSF[d]
KDM	NSCN (I-M)	THADC[d]
KDM	NSCN (K)	UILA[d]
KLO[d]	PLA	UNLF
KNA	PRA[d]	VNO[d]
KNF	PRE PAK	ZRA
KNO	PULF	ZRO
KRPC	RGM	ZRV
KSF		

Terrorist Outfits: Meghalaya

ANVC
HALC
HNLC
MULA

Terrorist Outfits: Mizoram

BNLF	HVC
HPC	MNA/MNF[d]

Terrorist Outfits: Nagaland

NSCN (I-M)	NNC (A)
NSCN (K)	NNC (K)
NFG	
(Also, FNG)	

Terrorist Outfits: Tripura

ATTF
NLFT
TNV
TUJS

THADC[d]	Thangjing Hill Area Defence Council
TMK	Tehrik-e-Mazahmat Kashmir
TNFJ	Tehrik Nifwa Fiqa Jaffaria
TNRF	Tiwa National Revolutionary Front
TNV	Tripura National Volunteers

TOI	Times of India
Trans	Translated, Translation
TUJS	Tripura Upjati Juba Samiti
TUM	Tehrik-ul-Mijahideen
UBGL	Under Barrel Grenade Launcher
UILA[d]	United Islamic Liberation Army (Asm)
UILAA	United Islamic Liberation Army of Assam
UJC	United Jihad Council (also, MJC)
ULAA	United Liberation Army of Arunachal
ULFA	United Liberation Front of Assam
ULFSS	United Liberation Front of Seven Sisters
ULMA	United Liberation Movement of Arunachal
ULVA	United Liberation Volunteers of Arunachal
UMFA	United Minorities Front of Assam (Islamic)
UNHCR	United Nations High Commissioner for Refugees
UNIMOG	United Nations International Military Observers Group (in J. and K.)
UNLF	United National Liberation Front (MPR)
UNO	United Nations Organisation
UNP	United National Party (Sri Lanka)
UPDS	United People's Democractic Solidarity (ASM) (The DHD, KNV and UPDS are mainly active in the two Hill districts of Assam)
UPI	United Press International
URPA	United Refermation Protest of Assam
UPVA	United People's Volunteers of Arunachal
USI	United Service Institution (of India)
VDC	Village Defence Committee (J & K)
VNO[d]	Vaiphei National Organisation
WKFM	World Kashmir Freedom Movement
WMD	Weapons of Mass Destruction
ZRA	Zomi Revolutionary Army (MPR)
ZRO	Zomi Re-unification Organisation (MPR)
ZRV	Zomi Revolutionary Volunteers

ABBREVIATIONS SPECIFIC TO THIS BOOK ONLY

Newspapers

AA	Asian Age
HT	Hindustan Times

Ind Exp	Indian Express	
TOI	Times of India	
North-Eastern States		
	ArP	Arunachal Pradesh
	Asm	Assam
	Megh	Meghalaya
	MPR	Manipur
	MR	Mizoram
	NL	Nagaland
	TPR	Tripura
PS	Police Station	
SF	Security Forces	

1

Insurgency/Terrorism in India's North-East: A Quagmire or an Opportunity

The insurgency in Kashmir (more correctly, in Jammu and Kashmir) occupies centre-stage in most of the security related studies concerning India, amongst strategic community both at home and abroad. This could be due to a variety of reasons: strategic importance of the region, involvement of Islamist terrorists from several countries; its impinging on India-Pakistan relations; and its concurrent spill-over into India's other regions, posing a serious threat to its stability. All these factors notwithstanding, what is generally not realised by most countries is that India also continues to face major security challenges in its North-East Region.

Some of the seven states in the region have faced a series of insurgencies since India's Independence. In fact, all the seven states presently are facing one or more insurgent movements within their borders. In some ways, these insurgent movements and homeland demands may prove even more intractable problem (compared to Kashmir's). Given the extremely complex political and social environment, river by sharp ethnic rivalries and aspirations, the competing political demands with the ostensible aims of preserving their individual identities, the sheer number of insurgent groups (over a hundred, according to the South Asia Terrorism portal), each with different agendas and inter-linkages of these groups, is proving to be a challenging task for the security establishment of India. Even more curiously, the counter-insurgency operations in the North-Eastern region have always suffered due to happenings in other parts of the country : be it the 1971 Indo-Pak War, 1989 Punjab insurgency; or the subsequent worsening insurgency situation in Jammu and Kashmir, and 1999 Kargil operations. Much needed troops engaged in counter-insurgency tasks in the North-East are shifted/removed to deal with security threats in other regions.

Observers have noted that there does not seem to have been any consistent application and continuation of counter-terrorism measures in the

North-East, with a result that the insurgent outfits in the region have expectedly taken the maximum advantage of this situation and have succeeded to spread their tentacles in all the seven states, as stated above through an effective network/linkages.

India's North-East, located in the extreme north-eastern corner of the Sub-continent, shares international frontiers on its North, East and South with four nations—Bhutan, China (Tibet), Myanmar and Bangladesh and is connected to the rest of the country on its west through the 28 km Siliguri panhandle. It lies, geographically, between 22° and 29° North Latitudes and between 89° 46′, and 97° 5′ East Longitudes. In political terms, the region comprises of 7 States of the Indian Union, popularly and affectionately called "Seven Sisters".

Essential statistical information about these seven states is contained in the table below :

North-East's Seven Sisters : Comparative Figures

		Population			*Area*		
S. No.	*Name of State /Entity*	*2001*	*Rank in*		*Sq km*	*Rank in*	
			North-East	*India*		*North-East*	*India*
1.	Arunachal Pradesh	1,097,968	6	24	83,743	1	13
2.	Assam	26,655,528	1	13	78,438	2	14
3.	Meghalaya	2,318,822	3	20	22,429	3	19
4.	Manipur	2,166,788	4	21	22,327	4	20
5.	Mizoram	888,573	7	26	21,081	5	21
6.	Nagaland	1,990,036	5	22	16,539	6	22
7.	Tripura	3,199,203	2	19	10,486	7	23
8.	North-East	38,495,089	2.69 per cent of India's	—	255,088	7.75 per cent of India's	—
9.	India	1,027,015,247	—	—	3,287,263	—	—

The region has external borders with Bangladesh (4096 km, including 2216 km between West Bengal and Bangladesh), Myanmar (1643 km), Tibet (1035 km), and Bhutan (515 km).

The North-East was always remote and distant. It forced its way into national consciousness when some of its more vigorous and restless ethnic groups refused to be part of the celebrations when India gained her Independence in 1947. The first daunting task the hastily-divided fledgling armies of two nascent nations handled was the supervision of 7-8 million people who crossed the newly-created borders in either directions. Perhaps 200,000 of these did not complete the journey, slain on the way by the frenzied partisans. The Indian Army was still strong on the borders as also stretched in internal security duties when it was called upon to fight the Pak invasion in Kashmir under the facade of tribal incursion. With cease-fire signed on 1 January 1949, it looked forward to a well-deserved interregnum for rest, refit and reorganisation. It was not willed that way, because not long after that, the tribal upsurge in the North-East demanded Army's deployment there early 1950s. If the external aggression fomented the troubles in Kashmir, the internal dissonance was behind the eruption in the North-East. Thus it was that men in uniform came into close contact with the region. "But to a common Indian, the North-East had a romantic ring about it; it was a rainbow country, extraordinarily diverse, colourful and mysterious"; and to the well-read and the cloistered academia, it was a troublesome frontier for all too many and a strange land where the 'wild tribes' still ruled the roost. But this was the picture soon after Independence. Thus it was not a happy augury to begin with. The nation had to send troops to cool some hot heads in the region. But that was unavoidable for the process of nation-building. But today, the picture is vastly changed, compared to those turbulent days. The region is on the march; even if the insurgency continues, it is much reduced in extent and virulence, barring perhaps in the case of Bodo insurgents. The change is discernible.

From this general, broad brush picture of India around the time of 1947 Independence, we move to the specifics of the region, known as India's North-East, starting with the number of terrorist organisations in the region.

Terrorist/Insurgent Outfits in North-East : Nov. 2006

The table below has the detailed information :

Terrorist Groups in North-Eastern States : Nov. 2006

States	*Number of terrorist, insurgent and extremist groups*
Assam	36
Manipur	39
Meghalaya	4
Nagaland	3
Tripura	30
Mizoram	2
Arunachal Pradesh	1

Source : *Frontline*, 15 Dec. 2006.

General

Few countries can claim to have faced problems of secessionism and insurgency as serious as those of India. She faced such problems right at its birth in 1947 in Hyderabad and in Naga Hills. Soon after that, the state faced the problem in the then Madras Province and Telengana. In the succeeding decades surfaced insurgency, terrorism, and militancy problems in the Mizo hills, Kashmir, Assam and Punjab. Before launching into specific details of the issue under discussion, it will be useful to view it in contemporaneous perspective. The immediate instrument available to the state at that point in time to combat those disruptive forces was the Indian Army. But the nation and Army then had no model to look up to, no precedent to follow, and no locus classicus to study and learn from. The most recent example was that of the British Army fighting Malayan insurgency. But that was a case of a colonial army dealing with a subject people and its harsh paradigm could not have been an apt model to be followed by a democratic disposition dealing with its own citizens. The goal was clear, but to reach it, the army had to work its own devices and determine its own parameters of operations against the insurgents. So was the National Government required to undertake on-the-job-training exercise. But first a focus on the area we are concerned with and its situation.

The North-Eastern region of India is strategically located. It has immense regional geopolitical significance. This importance stems from the fact that it is the eastern part of a region that is dominated by the head-waters of some major rivers like the Hwang Ho, Yangzekiang, Sinkiang, Irrawaddy and the Brahmaputra. A rough and fractured topography dominated by dense forests, its accessibility conditions are very limited. It is inhabited by large number of tribes, some well-known, others not so. Most of the tribes are known to history for their antagonism towards the established central authority and on several occasions have asserted their autonomy and independence. The 19th century political circumstances brought them under administrative control of major powers, consequently dividing them politically.

Post-1947, in keeping with their traditions, some tribes took recourse to violent means to express dissent. Thus in the first three decades or so of India's independence, the North-East was characterised by socio-political instability and economic backwardness. But New Delhi's policy of winning them over through politico-military means has been seen to be succeeding. Liberal economic packages also are helping the region to come out of its isolationist attitudes.

It is to be noted that the extension of administration and its systemization in the region was a post-Independence phenomenon. Even this spread was viewed suspiciously by certain extremist elements, and condemned as an interference in the social, political and economic mores of their tribes.

In spite of the sustained and sincere endeavour, India has not solved the problem of violence fully. Though some tribes have come round and settled to democratic ways within India, some others are still carrying out their movements. The Chapter examines the course of insurgency in the Region and its present status.

The Genesis and Causes of Insurgency

The roots of emergency in the Region goes back to pre-independence days. The British deemed it prudent not to bring the tribes under a strict regime of political control and rigid regulations. Their tribal policy and Christian education and influence were also believed to have queered the pitch for Independent India. But cutting back to Simon Commission days, the clamour for autonomy that greeted it during its visit to the Region in January 1929 should not have been a surprise to the cognoscente. 27 memoranda were presented to it at Shillong by various groups, including the (1) Bodos and other Plains tribals, (2) Goalpara groups, (3) Kacharis, (4) Naga Club of Kohima, (5) Nagas of Mokokchung, (6) Khasi National Durbar, (7) Representatives of Khasi and Jaintia Hills. Dr J.H. Hutton, long-serving Deputy Commissioner of Naga Hills District and author of several authoritative books on the tribes, submitted a memorandum on behalf of the Assam Government, which pithily demanded: "The Hills should not be tied politically to the advanced plains." The Naga Club went a step further, telling the Commission: "Just leave us alone!" Indians blame the Hutton ancestors and their ilk for sowing seeds of separation among the tribes. Expectedly, the Nagas refused to be a part of India on 15 August 1947, declaring their own independence on the preceding day; refused to accept an ADC under Schedule Six; and were the first to raise the flag of insurrection early 1950s. Government of India acted wisely by granting autonomy to many ethnic communities who perceived their ethnic and cultural identities threatened by a mega-identity called India, and thus doused some potential conflagrations. But Assamese political class displayed certain insensitivity towards the ethnic insecurities and sensibilities of the tribal minorities. Some inconsiderate measures—the Official Language Bill of 1960 foremost among them—aggravated those fears. The Mizos went the Naga way a decade later, the two posing the most serious challenge to India's integrity till date. The others were to follow in due course.

At another level, rising aspirations of the people did not match up with the pace of economic development, and the consequent frustrations fuelled the discontent. Administrative apathy and economic dominance of up-country businessmen (particularly in Assam) was the right breeding ground for the growth of militancy.

Justice for the Tribes Still Awaited

Ideologically inclined scholars assert that the rights of the tribals have been curtailed, even taken away in some cases, by the demands of progress of the modern society.

1993 was observed as the "International Year of the Indigenous People". Their plight was highlighted in 1992 during the 500th Anniversary of Columbus' voyage of discovery and colonisation. As an angry activist put it: "....Apart from a couple of national tribal conventions, the 70-million tribal community in India, the largest indigenous population in the world, has little to look back on."

"The tribals are yet to secure their full rights", feel the sympathetic activists. The origin of the conflict between the tribals and the State can be traced to the colonial times. "The advent of the British brought about major changes in the pattern of resource use as the natural wealth of India became cheap raw material for British industry." The setting up of "Reserved Forests" led to the loss of tribals' control over natural resources. The "Rights and Privileges" of the tribals under the Forest Act of 1927 were further reduced to "Rights and Concessions" by the Forest Policy of 1952. So the Governments, whether of British India or of Independent India, have always encroached on the rights, lands, and forests of the tribals, nay, on their very lives. The National Commission on Agriculture suggested in 1976 that these rights should be abolished. The latest Forest Policy promulgated in December 1988 retained the concept of exclusive state ownership of forests. While industrial requirements were termed "national needs" in the new policy, the rights of the tribals and other forest dwellers were reduced to "people's needs", rendering the tribals encroachers in their own habitat. The crisis has been acknowledged by the 29th Report of the Commission for Scheduled Castes and Scheduled Tribes.

The resolution[1] adopted by the Indian Confederation of Indigenous and Tribal Peoples during the International Year celebrations in New Delhi admirably sums up the Tribal psyche:

> "We do not want to be museum pieces for the enjoyment of the tourists. Efforts are made to integrate us, who have lived in an egalitarian and classless society, into the mainstream as a low caste. Our culture is looked down upon and the dominant culture with its caste-based inequalities is imposed upon us."

The above is a good picture of unjust treatment meted out to the tribals by their "civilised" brethren. Now a word on "civilised" and "uncivilised" people. It was natural for European officers and scholars to describe these "unkempt and unwashed" tribals living in the remote and isolated hills as "uncivilised" or "less civilised". The use of such terms must have pained Dr Elwin in his lifetime for he considered the tribals as much, if not more, civilised as the so-called "civilised". It is therefore no surprise that Guha's recent book on his life[2] has been aptly titled "Savaging the Civilised", which accurately sums up Elwin's ideas and philosophy on the tribal people. But Elwin's understanding and empathy for the tribals had distinguished ancestry. Jean Jacques Rousseau (1712-78) was the first to apply the much-celebrated and much-used phrase, "noble savage" to the tribal.

It is Universal Truth that in the newly-emerging nations, the tribal populations are adversely affected by Government-initiated internal migration, presence of bureaucracy and SF. The reasons for insurgency were a combination of ethno-cultural factors, faulty nation-building strategies, and an inappropriate development approach/path. All these factors generally reduce the tribals to "a hopeless minority not only in religio-cultural terms but also in the power structures at the Centre and States".

In India's North-East, insurgency is an ethno-cultural phenomenon, in the sense that perceiving their ethnic identity threatened, they seek political power to preserve it and then develop their lands by their own genius. So, the insurgency is a political war, and it is amenable to political solutions only. Initially, State power is essential to convince the insurgents that their unlawful violence would not pay. It is only then that they come to the conference table for a political dialogue.

Ethnicity and Tribal Revolts/Movements

There was an unprecedented world-wide upsurge of ethnicity in the 1970s and 1980s. Ethnicity and autonomy movements are closely inter-connected. Political anthropology was born as a branch of social and cultural anthropology only when Fortes and Evens-Pritchard published their classic paper on the African political system as a part of synchronic studies in 1940. Social and political movements can be described as collective action by people either to promote or resist a change. Many Indians look askance at the spate of tribal revolts and movements in the North-East, particularly the one with secessionist overtone, taking them to be unique phenomena. This obviously is a misperception, flowing from ignorance. V. Raghavaiah chronologically listed as many as 70 tribal insurgencies during 1878-1971 period in his "Tribal Revolts" (Nellore, 1971). Again, "Man in India", 125(4) of December 1945, had four papers on various tribal movements. But what is noteworthy is that both these references dealt with the tribal revolts in Central and East India, and not in the North-East; essentially because there was no information available on the latter. It is a fact thus, that very few studies were conducted on the subject in the North-East during the pre-Independence period. Perhaps earliest such studies were by Stephen Fuch whose "Kabui", 1965 is a rather sketchy study and by Gautam Bhadra in 1975, who contributed a valuable paper *"The Kuki Uprising (1917-19): Its Causes and Nature"* in "Man in India", 55(1), January-March, 1975. Before giving details of various other post-1947 studies on the Tribal Revolts in the North-East, a brief look at the tribal situation there and the attendant causes that gave rise to these movements should be of interest.

Many tribes living on the international boundaries acted as bridge or buffer communities and shared cultural and ethnic affinities with tribesmen across the frontier until the advent of colonialism. The situation underwent a sea change with the British take over of Assam in 1820s. Not only was the cross-border intercourse discouraged as a result of the Yandabo Treaty, even the Hills-Plains contacts got regulated through policy measures like the Inner Line Regulation II of 1880. What was even worse was the designation of most of the hill areas as "Backward" under the 1919 Act and then as "Excluded Areas" under the 1935 Act. Intended or otherwise, these measures broadened the gap between the Hill and the plains people. The spread of education and activities of Christian missionaries were largely held responsible for awakening of the people regarding their individual and ethnic identities, or "nationality consciousness". The growth of nationality consciousness among different communities inspired several movements. Even the introduction of money economy to replace traditionally self-sufficient economy of the tribes "proved disastrous as it shattered the very basis of the tribal society in the long run, since it was not at the same time accommodated in the modern economic system".

The pre-Independence revolts, in the main, revolved round the land: land alienation, usury, forced labour, minimum wages, land grabbing, etc. The tribal resentment forced them into violence and protest movements. The influx of non-tribals and advancing tea plantations made the situation intolerable. It needs to be understood in these circumstances that the occasional tribal raids on the plains men were not always actuated by rapine and blood thirst. So it was not surprising that during the British rule, several tribes launched movements demanding autonomy to manage their own affairs, since they were convinced that the alien administration and the outsiders were ruining their culture and economy.

Because there are meagre studies on the subject of Tribal Movements in the North-East, it would be misleading to conclude that there were none before 1947. If that was the case, why did they invite repeated punitive expeditions? The movements might not have been well-led and well-organised, but they were very much there, resisting every British advance into their lands in any form. Besides ethnicity, language became an important divisive issue to start and sustain a movement in the post-1947 India. The demands for secession and autonomy in India's North-East gained geopolitical dimensions because of creation of (East) Pakistan in its neighbourhood. Some of the studies carried out on the post-Independence Tribal Movements are detailed in the table below for the interested readers to make his pick and for a concerned scholar to launch on a comprehensive study on the subject.

Tribal Movements in the North-East

	Author	*Year*	*Title*
1.	Anand, V.K.	1980	"Conflict in Nagaland." Analyses reasons for the conflict, and found psychological factors in geo-political context to be mainly responsible for it. The insurgency acted as an effective instrument to fulfil their demand.
2.	Bhattacharjee, S.R.	1989	"Tribal Insurgency in Tripura." Various aspects of the subject discussed in the book are listed below: 1. Inequality of economic opportunities and matters economic. 2. Sharing of political rights. 3. Changing demographic profile, with the percentage of tribal population falling in each successive count. 4. Urbanization. 5. Immigration. 6. Land alienation. 7. Cultural and political domination by non-tribals.
3.	Bhattacharjee, Suchintya, R.	1990	"Genesis of Tribal Extremism in Tripura."
4.	Bhuyan, P.C. (ed)	1989	"Political Development of the North-East." It has 17 papers of which 5 deal with tribal movements for autonomy in Assam.
5.	Bhuyan, S.K. (ed)	1951	"Kachari Buranji" (in Assamese), Second Edition. Deals with Kacharis, a branch of Bodo race, under the following heads:

Author	Year	Title
		1. Legend on origin of Kacharis. 2. Their Kings and Kingdoms. 3. Comprehensive history of Ahom-Kachari relations from end of the 14th century upto the beginning of the 18th. The work is an important reference on the Kacharis.
6. Chaube, S.K.	1973	"Hill Politics in North-East India." It points out major factors and root causes behind the political turmoil in the North-East, as listed below: 1. Concept of nationalism that partially ignored the smaller identities. 2. Territorial boundaries that criss-crossed the ethnic consolidations. 3. Process of industrialization, unconcerned with or unmindful of the traditional tribal economy. Though the subject was essentially political, yet, the historical, geographical, and sociological aspects were given due importance.
7. Chatterjee, Suniti Kumar	1974	"Kirata Jina-Krti" (Second Edition). It is a profound work in the Indo-Mongoloid tribe, the Kiratas. It focuses on Kiratas in general and particularly on their presence in the North-East.
8. Daimary, V.K.	1986	"Boro Movement since Independence." (M. Phil Dissertation, North-East Hill University, History Department, 1986. Unpublished.)

Author	Year	Title
		A useful study on Bodo demand for a separate state, though limited in its approach and contents.
9. Datta, P.S. (ed)	1990	"Ethnic Movements in Poly-cultural Assam."
		It has four papers, three of which deal with the people of Mongoloid origin and question of identity crisis. Its strength lies in its emphasis on ethnic connotation inherent in their movements which has not as yet been analysed adequately.
10. Datta-Ray, B.	1989	"Tribal Identity and Tension in North-East India."
11. Endle, S.	1975	"The Kacharis".
		A monograph that comprehensively details the social and domestic life of the Bodos.
12. Goswami, B.B.	1979	"Encyclopaedia of Social Sciences (Vols. 11 and 12) The Mizo Unrest."
13. Guha, U.C.	1971	"Kacharer Itihritta" (in Bengali).
		It is an indispensable source book for Cachar and Kacharis.
14. Misra, Udayan	1988	"North-East India: Quest for Identity."
		It deals with contemporary development in North-East in two parts.
		Part 1: Nagaland question and typology of Naga nationalism.
		Part 2: Assamese national question.
15. Nag, A.K.	1984	"Mizo Dilemma."
		It draws attention to certain issues raised by the growing ethnic aspirations and how they pose a threat to national integration. It also focused on the role of the Church in the imbroglio.

	Author	Year	Title
16.	Narzi, Bhaben	1985	"Bodo-Kachari Samaj Aru Sanskriti" (in Assamese). An admirable work on social life and culture of Bodos. The demand for a separate state to secure an independent entity for Bodos has received little attention from professional researchers.
17.	Nibedan, Nirmal	1981	"North-East India: The Ethnic Explosion." It dilates on the ethnic and nativistic aspects and factors behind the explosive situation.
18.	Paul, M.C.	1989	"Dimensions of Tribal Movements in India: A Study of Udayachal in Assam Valley." It attempted to interpret the theoretical framework of the demand for a small state.
19.	Sanyal, C.C.	1973	"The Meches and Totos of North Bengal." Monographs on two sub-Himalayan tribes, believed to belong originally to great Tibeto-Burman Bodo race. The two are much influenced by the Assamese and Bengali cultures and are now making desperate effort to preserve their linguistic and cultural identity.
20.	Sarin, H.K.	1980	"Insurgency in North-East India: A Study of Sino-American Role." It studies the role played by these two foreign countries. The North-East will continue to remain vulnerable to foreign pulls and pressures because of its geography. The fire of insurgency first lit in Nagaland spread to other states in the area and the consequent unrest provides excellent opportunities to other nations to strike fires of

Author	Year	Title
		conspiracies against India on its own soil. The author seems to have overlooked facts and feelings that led the people into revolt in the first place. The outsiders can at the best only stroke the fire, not create it. A similar study was carried out by V.I.K. Sarin also.
21. Sarin, V.I.K.	1980	"India's North-East in Flame." The book stresses the geo-political importance of the region and clearly states that transition from traditional barter economy to modern economy created an upheaval in the tribal societies. The issue of immigration was examined with its consequent ill effects on the tribals, including their alienation from land. "Some groups chose path of insurgency with help from foreign powers." The author gives an outline of counter-productive efforts made by the Government of India to resolve the ethnic problems that further whipped up the parochial sentiments.
22. Singh, G.P.	1990	"The Kiratas in Ancient India." It is an admirable attempt to study this ancient tribe, widely spread in North and North-East India. They reputedly lived in the Mahabharata period. The author relies on the historical, anthropological and archaeological data to exhaustively deal with the origin, antiquity, identification, and expansion of the Kiratas in ancient India.
23. Singh, K.S. (ed)	1983	"Tribal Movements in India." Volume I covered all tribal movements in the North-East region, except the Kuki uprising, concentrating on the movements in post-Independence period.

	Author	*Year*	*Title*
24.	Singh, N.J.	1992	"Social Movement in Manipur, 1917-51." The author draws a conceptual framework of social movements and avers that the Kuki Rebellion (1917-19) and Zeliangrong movements (1930-32) were two of the foremost and well-organised anti-imperialist and anti-feudal tribal Movements.

These studies on different tribal movements in North-East India reveal broadly similar causes/factors responsible for these Movements, even if they seem to differ by nature and in matter of details.

In view of what has been described above, the causes of tribal unrest and consequent militancy/insurgency are easily understandable. The insurgency thrives when ethnic minorities see a threat to their identity from a "brute" majority. This threat could be perceived in cultural, economic, or political spheres. The perception is compounded if it is combined with a feeling of being neglected or discriminated against. Even imaginary discrimination can be exploited in the cause of insurgency through skilful propaganda. Lack of good governance, economic deprivation and large scale unemployment can be cited to support the neglect, and discrimination theory. If a hostile neighbour extends moral and material support to an insurgency, it can greatly strengthen it and prolong its life, if not ensure its success which would largely depend upon the quality of its leadership—steadfast and dedicated—and popular support.

A charismatic leader, of course, is a *sine qua non* for the success of an insurgent movement. Che Guvera's is one of the finest examples of such leadership in 20th century. In their own way, Phizo and Laldenga could be said to belong to this category.

The causes of the unrest may differ, but the process is similar. Some analysts feel that in one form or other, it is a reaction to the homogenizing state and control over livelihood. When the external control results in less land and fewer jobs, they are then reduced to fight among themselves, e.g., the NSCN factions, Nagas and Kukis, Bodos and Adivasis, *et al.*

Two Experts Speak Out

Two Indians' testimonials, who have dealt with the insurgency situations in their times, should be of interest. First, Lt. Gen. VK Nayyar, who while in service commanded Army formations engaged in active counter-insurgency operations in the North-East and after retirement was Governor of Manipur in the 1990s and resigned, nearly accusing his Chief Minister of collusion with the insurgents, says rather bluntly: "The problem here is about social, economic, ethnic and political deprivation. These people are not anti-India, only anti-establishment. They have been exploited by wily politicians in league with the rebels, and sense of alienation has deepened.... The money for development never reached the target villages. The corrupt politicians divert the public money to insurgents to buy security...." Now Ved Marwah, a distinguished policeman who served as IGP Mizoram during its worst phase of insurgency, speaking in 1999: "Things are worse than ever before as recent killings and blasts show. The NSCN and ULFA are never short of the recruits as educated youth is swelling their ranks.... All this coupled with infiltration from Bangladesh, drugs, role of the ISI, has complicated the problems." Then he gives some instances of display of insensitivity and ignorance about the Region: "Prime Minister Desai reprimanded the Mizo officials and lectured them about the naturopathy when they asked for more hospitals. It all ended in bruised egos. Expectedly, he was given a cool send-off. His Home Minister, Charan Singh, once asked a Chief Minister from the Region the name of the capital of his State...." Even Nehru seems to have gone amiss in the sensitivity stakes. To wit, here is what the former Nagaland Chief Minister Vamuzo says: "In 1953, Nagas turned their backs on Nehru after he refused to meet them.... This alienated common Nagas."

Role of Middle Class

Main feature of style of middle class politics is characterised by certain universalist ethos. The fact of being middle class becomes far more important in shaping the style of its politics than anything else (like its being affiliated to a particular ethnic group). Viewed in this light, the middle class politics the world over is seen to cut across the particularistic ethnic affiliations and loyalties.

But that does not seem to be the case in India, and more so in its North-East. Here, the middle class politics does not seem to be infused with such a universalist ethos, not in the long run in any case. Here the emergence of classes does not result in the obsolescence of ethnic communities. Thus in Assam, when we refer to a middle class, we invariably refer to an ethnically afflicted-middle class: an Assamese middle class, a Bodo middle class, and even a Bengali one at that. That ethnic difference there are so pronounced that they seem to be "at the root of separatism". So, it is not surprising that the middle class is not an homogenous entity here; it seems to be ethnically fragmented in character. The other striking feature of the middle class politics is its "movemental nature". The Assamese middle class is commonly designated as "agitationist" and sometimes, less charitably, as "xenophobic" (Das, A., 1991).[3] As per "recent studies, there are as many as 19 ethnic (10 in Assam itself) movements demanding further reorganisation (of Assam)" (Chattopadhyay, 1990). Obviously, the middle class ethos did not subsume various ethnic identities within its fold.

Rats are the Culprits

It is popularly believed that rats were responsible for the birth of the Mizo National Front (MNF), the progenitor of the Mizo insurgency. Mizoram experiences flowering of the bamboos (*Mautam*) once about every 40-50 years. The rats are known to multiply fast after feeding on these flowers. Subsequently, the armies of these rodents destroy the standing crops in the fields and then attack the granaries. This causes acute food shortage and famine. Mizoram experienced *Mautam* and consequent famine in 1957. It was Laldenga's Mizo Famine National Front (MFNF) that helped the suffering Mizos during those dark days. Subsequently, MFNF was converted into MFN by dropping one 'F' from it. The rest, as they say, is history. It took three decades of death and destruction before peace returned with the June 1986 Accord.

Scared of the *Mautam* and its consequences, Mizoram and Manipur had declared a war on the rats in March and April 1999. Mizoram Government had offered Re. 1 for each rodent tail. "Till 25 April 1999, 90,000 tails had been collected" (*Times of India*, 27-4-1999).

Insurgent Outfits in the North-East and their Aims

Every State in the Region has a number of insurgent groups, though not uniformly active. Some of them have been around for decades, others of more recent origins. Some may have been floated, as some hard-nosed journalists like to suggest, by Indian Intelligence, to encourage splits and create confusion. The table below is merely illustrative, based essentially on published sources.[4]

A new element in the murky politics of insurgency in Manipur is Kuki insurgency under an outfit called Kuki National Council (KNC) and its armed wing, the Kuki National Army (KNA) (both raised early 1990s), not to be confused with another KNA, acronym of a recognised regional party called the Kuki National Assembly. The KNC, which is engaged in bloody clashes with NSCN(I-M) is believed to be an ally of NSCN(K), a natural alliance, given the enmity between the two factions of the NSCN. Another Kuki-Chin outfit, called the Chin Liberation Front (CLF), which like the KNC is based both in Burma and Manipur, is believed to have links with the NSCN(I-M). The UNLF, the oldest insurgent groups in the valley, is formally a part of the IBRF[5] but supports closer coordination with all the insurgent groups. Other Valley-based insurgent groups like the RPF, the KCP, and PREPAK have close relations with the NSCN(I-M) but these must be viewed in the context of the complex relations between the Meiteis and the Nagas and the fact that the fulfilment of Naga Nationalist aspirations for Greater Nagaland, under any appellation, are predicated on the disintegration of the present geographical entity of Manipur—something no insurgent group in the valley can support.

Assam

Sl.No.	*Name*	*Abbreviation (Acronym)*	*Cadre Strength (2005-06)*
1	*2*	*3*	*4*
1.	**United Liberation Front of Assam** banned since 27 November 1990. Both ULFA and BdSF, which are closely linked to each other, also seek close links with all other insurgent groups. Indeed, ULFA is formally committed to the "Liberation" of the whole Region, not of merely Assam. But given the contradictions between and within the groups, the goal is highly unrealisable. The most lethal of the North-Eastern militant groups, and wild child of the Assam movement, ULFA is now linked to Islamist groups in Bangladesh. Over 5,000 have surrendered since 1992. Responsible for 15-8-2004 blast that killed 13 children. (Details in Chapter 19)	ULFA	1,600
2.	**National Democratic Front of Bodoland.** Some Intelligence report held it was formerly BdSF. Banned since 1992. Founded in October 1986 as Bodo Security Force (BdSF). It was renamed as NDFB in 1994. Responsible for the 2 and 5 October 2004 blasts that killed 60 people. Over 1,000 have surrendered since 1992. Demand: Sovereign state for Assam's Bodo people. (Details in Chapter 5)	NDFB	500

1	2	3	4
3.	**Bodo Security Force** Armed Wing of the NDFB (see Chapter 5).	BdSF	600
4.	**People's Democratic Front**	PDF	NA
5.	**Bodoland Liberation Tiger Force** (see Chapter 5) banned since 1997, but has declared ceasefire with the Government since early 2000.	BLTF/BLT	NA
6.	**Assam Tiger Force** Police claims it is ULFA's red herring.	ATF	?
7.	**Islamic Militant Outfits.** Police has dossiers on 25 such outfits, formed mostly by criminals and ISI-backed fanatics. Mainly based in Assam; some of them have tentacles reaching out to Nagaland, Mizoram, Manipur etc. 14 of them are named here:		
	1. Muslim United Liberation Tigers of Assam Believed to be backed by Pak ISI. It sends batches of young boys to Bangladesh for arms training. Circulates fake currency. **Strength:** Not known. **Demand:** Greater Islamic nation comprising the North-East and Bangladesh.	MULTA	
	2. Muslim Volunteer Force	MVF	

1	*2*	*3*	*4*
	3. Islamic Revolutionary Force	IRF	
	4. Students Islamic Movement of India	SIMI	
	5. Indian United Liberation Army	IULA	
	6. Assam Minority Liberation Army	AMLA	
	7. Muslim United Liberation Front of Assam	MULFA	
	8. Muslim Liberation Front of Assam	MLFA	
	9. United Special Return Army of Assam	USRAA	
	10. Minority Liberation Tigers of Assam	MLTA	
	11. Tiger Liberation Front of Assam	TLFA	
	12. Islamic Revolutionary Army	IRA	
	13. Saddam Bahini	SB	
	14. Islamic Sevak Sangh	ISS	
8.	**Bengal Tiger Force.** It was floated to protect the Bengali Hindus who were targeted by ULFA and Bodo militants.	BTF	
9.	**Dima Halam Daogah.** Founded in December 1995, it has its origins in the now-defunct Dimasa National Security Force (DNSF). Espouses the national aspirations of Dimasa people. One of the two Hill Tribes of Assam (other being the Karbi, mainly in Karbi-Anglong District), Dimasas	DHD	

1	2	3	4
	are mainly concentrated in North Cachar. Its demand is Dimaland based on Dimapur and comprising of North Cachar Hills and other Dimasa areas of Assam and neighbouring States. It has links with NSCN(I-M) and is currently honouring cease-fire with the Government.		
10.	**United People's Democratic Solidarity,** a corresponding outfit based in Karbi-Anglong District, is presently observing a cease-fire and engaged in negotiations *(Frontline,* 27-11-2002). Founded in 1997, it also has links with NSCN(I-M). **Demand:** UT status for their district, where they form majority.	UPDS	
11.	**Karbi National Volunteers** (Karbi Volunteer Corps) Perhaps armed wing of the UPDS, or allied to it.	KNV/KVC	

1	*2*	*3*	*4*
	Nagaland		
Sl.No.	*Name*	*Abbreviation*	*Cadre Strength (2005-06)*
1.	**National Socialist Council of Nagaland (Isaac Chisi Swu - Thuingaleng Muivah Faction).** Banned, but it has declared truce with the Government since August 1997. The cease-fire does not extend to Manipur, Assam and Arunachal Pradesh. Founded by the duo (Swu and Muivah) in 1989 in the wake of the Shillong Accord between New Delhi and Phizo's NNC. It split into two factions of (I-M) and (K). Presently talking to the Government. **Demand:** Nagalim comprising of Nagaland and other Naga-inhabited areas in the contiguous States of Manipur, Assam and Arunachal and in border areas of Burma.	NSCN(I-M)	2,000
2.	**NSCN (S.S. Khaplang faction)** Banned; Sibling arch rival of NSCN(I-M). It is based in Burma. Its demands area same as that of the senior and more powerful (I-M) faction. It is in ceasefire with New Delhi since 1999.	NSCN(K)	1,000
3.	**Naga Federal Government**	NFG (also FNG)	
4.	**Naga National Council (Adino)** Military wing of the NFG	NNC(A)	
5.	**NNC (Khodao)** NSCN(I-M) and NSCN(K) are presently active in the field, the former being more powerful of the two. The rest are irrelevant.	NNC(K)	

1	*2*	*3*	*4*
	Manipur		
Sl.No.	*Name*	*Abbreviation*	*Cadre Strength (2005-06)*
1.	**People's Liberation Army** Founded in September 1978 by N. Bisheswar Singh. Its political arm, Revolutionary People's Front (RPF) was born in 1989. It has bases in Bangladesh. **Strength:** 1,500 (2004). **Demand:** Wants a Revolutionary Front covering entire North-East, uniting all ethnic groups like Meiteis, Nagas, Kukis, to liberate Manipur.	PLA	1,000
2.	**Revolutionary People's Front.** Political Wing of the PLA.	RPF	
3.	**United National Liberation Front** The oldest (Meitei) insurgent group founded in November 1964. Initially took East Pakistani help. Supported Pakistan during 1971 war. Sent cadres for training in China. Floated Indo-Burma Revolutionary Front (IBRF) with ULFA, NSCN (K), and Kuki National Army (KNA) in 1990. **Strength:** 1,000 activists (2004). **Demand:** Independent Socialist Manipur	UNLF	1,500
4.	**UNLF (M Oken Faction).**	UNLF(MO)	600
5.	**Peoples Revolutionary Party of Kangleipak** was founded in October 1977 by R.K. Tulachandra who was killed by SF in 1986. Part of Manipur People's Liberation Front (MPLF) with PLA and UNLF. Got initial training from NSCM (I-M). Also has links with Kachin Independent Army of Myanmar. **Strength:** 1,000 (2004)	PREPAK	1,000

1	*2*	*3*	*4*
	Demand: Ouster of all "outsiders" from Manipur. (There are ten other groups, with an uneven spread of sophisticated weaponry and cadre strength from 200 to 500. These are listed below serials 6 to 15.)		
6.	**NSCN (I-M)**	NSCN(I-M)	
7.	**Hmar People's Convention**	HPC	NA
8.	**Kuki National Front**	KNF	100
9.	**Kuki National Council**	KNC	—
10.	**Kuki National Army.** Armed wing of the KNC	KNA	—
11.	**Kuki National Organisation**	KNO	500
12.	**Kangleipak Communist Party**	KCP	
13.	**Kanglei Yawol Kanna Lup** The name means "Organisation to Save the Revolutionary Movement in Manipur." Formed in 1994 by merger of three groups: Oken faction of UNLF, Meiraba faction of PREPAK, and Ibo Pishak faction of KCP. Has links with both factions of NSCN. **Strength:** 1,000 (2004). **Demand:** Cleansing Manipur of corruption, drugs and immoral activities.	KWKL or KYKL	250
14.	**United Kuki Liberation Front** It is the latest name to join the Manipur fraternity of militant outfits. May be a front of already existing groups, or could be a new outfit (*The Hindu,* 11-10-2002).	UKLF	
15.	**Manipur People's Liberation Front** It is an alliance in action of three of the oldest valley-based insurgencies of Manipur: UNLF, PLA and PREPAK (*Frontline,* 27-11-2002).		

There are about 14 other groups in Manipur, with an uneven spread of sophisticated weaponry and cadre strength between 200-500.

Tripura

1. Tripura National Volunteers (Extinct) TNV
2. National Liberation Front of Tripura NLFT 150

   Founded in 1989 by Dhananjay Reang, former Vice-President of TNV, has camps in Bangladesh. Currently (2004?) in talks with the Government. This averment is of doubtful value. In 2005, the outfit is continuing with its violence, killings and extortions. Only a faction (Nayanbashi) came overground.

   Demand: Independent Tripura, free of Bengali migrants.
3. All Tripura (Tribal) Tiger Force ATTF 300

   Founded in 1990 by the renegade TNV after its main group signed an accord with the Government in 1988. In 1997, about 1,600 surrendered, but the core group continues with its violent ways. Has 16 camps and HQ in Bangladesh. Has links with ULFA.

   Strength: 600 (2004)

   Demand: Expulsion of all Bengali-speaking migrants of East Bengal/ East Pakistan/Bangladesh origin who entered after 1949.
4. Tripura People's Democratic Front—TPDF

   After signing of an accord in August 1988, TNV ceased to exist. Some remnant of the TNV had organised themselves as NLFT under Dhananjay Reang. However Reang and some others surrendered in 1993. The remainder NLFT, renamed TPDF, is still a force to count within Tripura and has continued its links with NSCN (I-M).

Mizoram

1. Hmar People's Convention	HPC	Hmar issue
2. Hmar Volunteers Council	HVC	settled
(Armed wing of the preceding)		
3. Mizo National Front	MNF	(Defunct)

HPC was active in Mizoram, Manipur's Churachandpur district, and North Cachar Hills District of Assam. Militants of the HVC and the NSCN(I-M) were known to have engaged in joint operations in Assam's NC District. The demand of HPC for creation of a "Hmar Autonomous District Council' in North-East Mizoram was conceded by the State Government, and peace has prevailed in the area ever since. A rather peaceful environ prevails in Mizoram. The Mizo Accord of June 1986 remains the only accord till date that succeeded in bringing peace to the state and harmony between the high parties.

Having said this, it must be remembered that the Chakma issue keeps popping up off and on.

4. Bru National Liberation Front BNLF

Brus are a small group, which occasionally suffers ethnic violence at the hands of the majority Mizos. BNLF has potential to foment trouble as consequence. It has some ethnic links in Tripura. They are presently agitating for creation of an ADC.

Demand: An ADC for the Brus in Mizoram. They are akin to original tribes of Tripura.

Meghalaya

1. A'Chik National Volunteer Council ANVC

   Banned November 2000

2. Hynniewtrep A'Chik Liberation Council HALC

   Banned November 2000

3. Hynniewtrep Volunteer Force HVF
4. Hynniewtrep National Liberation Council HNLC

   Founded in 1992 after the split of the HALC, the first militant group of the Meghalaya, Hynniewtrep, draws its members from the Khasi and Jaintia tribes. Has bases in Bangladesh. Known to circulate fake currency at the behest of the ISI.

5. A'Chik Liberation Matgrik Army ALMA
6. People's Liberation Front of Meghalaya PLFM
7. Bru National Liberation Front BNLF
8. Meghalaya United Liberation Army MULA
9. A'Chik National Volunteer Council ANVC

   Formed in 1995, the outfit has links with NSCN(I-M), ULFA, NDFB. Signed a cease-fire agreement with the Government but armed acts are still reported. (2004)

   Strength: 500

   Demand: A separate state for the Garos in Meghalaya's Garo areas and adjoining area in western Assam.

The situation in Meghalaya can be described 'iffy' as the insurgencies go, but less so than in Arunachal Pradesh. Most of the above outfits, the Police see, as ganging up of the criminal elements; but the first two occasionally grab the headlines, with some violence against the foreigners. Understandably, given their location and geography, they have tried to link with the NSCN(I-M), earlier known as NSCN (South), or NSCN(S). But given its distant location and salubrious climate, Shillong have often played host to insurgent groups from Assam, Nagaland, Manipur etc., whose members occasionally come here, as per the Intelligence agencies, to rest, refit, and re-think their strategies and coordination. It is overall a peaceful State but for an occasionally anti-outsiders riots, an affliction not restricted to this State of the Union only. Larger States like Maharashtra and Karnataka and smaller ones like Assam and Arunachal have also suffered and are still suffering from it. The outfits at Serials 1 and 4 above are demanding a separate Khasiland. Little is known about the outfit's at Serials 6 and 7.

12 major militant/insurgent outfits in the North-East are ULFA, NDFB, UNLF, NSCN(I-M), NSCN(K), PLA, PREPAK, ATTF, NLFT, KCP, KYKL and BLT.

Arunachal Pradesh

1. United Liberation Army ot Arunachal — ULAA
2. United People's Volunteers of Arunachal — UPVA
3. United Liberation Volunteers of Arunachal — ULVA
4. United Liberation Movement of Arunachal — ULMA

Its long-serving Chief Minister (Apang) had justly claimed his state to be an "island of peace" in the region. But during the recent years in the late nineties the presence of the long-settled Chakma refugees did create some dissonance, even mild violence occasionally. The first two groups have some militants in their fold, but the latter two have remained on paper. Some members claiming to belong to both ULAA and UPVA had surrendered in early 1990s, but some still occasionally surface making claims on the parochial lines. ULAA did try to link with the NSCN(I-M) and UPVA with NSCN(K), but there has been no Intelligence confirmation. It certainly is peaceful State till the anti-Chakma riots spoiled the idyll. For the last couple of years, say since the 1999 or so, the State has become a safe haven for Assam and Naga militants.

It may be noted that the States have been placed in the descending order of the intensity and virulence of the insurgency movements, and the last three are once again largely free from the virus, particularly so, Mizoram.

North Bengal

1. Kamatapur People's Party — KPP

Active since the last 10 years, is demanding a separate state of Kamatapur, comprising of five districts of North Bengal and adjoining areas of Assam.

2. Kamatapur Liberation Organisation — KLO

Armed wing of KPP, has become almost sole representative of the Rajbongshis whose party KPP is, and more worryingly, the KLO has developed secessionist orientation.

3. Some Muslim outfits are also operating here, but these has been discussed elsewhere.

KPP

It was set up in January 1996 by Atul Roy who ironically heads a break away (minority) faction presently (2005). Nikhil Roy is the President of the

KPP. Both the factions share with the more militant outfit, KLO, the demand for a separate State of Kamtapur (also spelt Kamatapur) in the region, to be carved out of North Bengal, comprising essentially its five districts, and some areas of the contiguous Assam. This demand of late (since 2001 or so) has taken the shape of Greater Cooch Behar (GCB) spearheaded by the Greater Cooch Behar Peoples' Association (GCBPA).

They Want Greater Cooch Behar Now

Though in a different guise, separatist forces are "making re-appearance in the political foreground in North Bengal, stoking ethnic sentiments and threatening peace in the nation" (Marcus Dam, *Hindu,* 22-9-05). The emergence of a new political entity the GCBPA, was announced loudly, rather too loudly and even violently by the mindless violence perpetrated by the demonstrators ('mobs'?) at Cooch Behar on 20-9-05, in which three policemen were killed, including one whose eyes were gouged by the "irate"(?) crowd, as one daily put it as if to provide some justification. The agitation is obviously carried out by the Rajbongshis, a majority in the North Bengal area, and particularly in Cooch Behar, an erstwhile princely State which became a part of West Bengal in January 1950. For West Bengal State Secretary of CPI(M) Anil Biswas, the demand for a GCB is both "meaningless and unacceptable". As is typical of the Indian political class, for this very reason, the demand is "a debatable issue" for the TNC leader Pankaj Banerjee, who blamed the "trigger-happy" administration for the 22-9-05 violence. How one wishes the political class could rise above the party interests, even if to ask them to soar into idealistic orientation while dealing with such issues will be asking for too much!

Chief Minister Buddhadeb Bhattacharjee, "due to address a public rally at Cooch Behar on 24 September 2004, in the post-20 September violence context, will have to address the separatist forces of his State in the backdrop of the changing political scenario". On the 19th, he warned that the KLO was engaged in a fresh attempt at reorganising itself in the North Bengal. Having been driven out of its camps in southern Bhutan by the 2003-04 Royal Bhutanese Army, most of what remains of the KLO leadership is sheltered in camps in Bangladesh, evidence of which was supplied by the BSF to the BDR early in September 2005. But one Intelligence report should worry Bhattacharjee: Separatist forces in North Bengal enjoy the support of the Maoist rebels in Nepal.

Violence Unlimited: 20 September 2005

On 20 September 2005, thousands of agitators took to the streets at Khagrabari and Chakchaka, outside Cooch Behar town on the call of GCBPA, spearheading a Movement for a separate State. The situation went out of hand when the agitators tried to break through the police barriers to enter the town to begin a fast-unto-death outside the District Magistrate's office to press for their demand. Lathi-charged and tear-gassed, the enraged mob which outnumbered the SF, isolated "two constables (Jogesh Sarkar and Gour Chandra Dhar) and mercilessly tortured them to death. Two women Sub-Inspectors (Tanushree Biswas and Mumtaz Begum) were mercilessly assaulted by the mob and both of them are in critical condition" (Parwez Hafeez, AA, 22-9-05). Kalimpong ASP Mushtaque Ahmed too was lynched to death. He was buried at Bagmari in Kolkata on the 23rd with full state honours (The violence was alluded to in the preceding two paragraphs).

The killing of Ahmed reminded a newsman of killing of Kolkata (Ports) Deputy Commissioner of Police Vinod Mehta by a mob in Garden Reach area in 1994. Two agitators were killed in the police firing.

Profile of Leadership and Weaponry

The information on the five worse-affected States is given below:

Assam		
ULFA	1. Arbinda Rajkhowa, Chairman	AK Rifles - 200
	2. Paresh Barua C-in-C	RPGs - 20 (Rocket propelled grenades) Rifles Sundry - 400
	3. Pradip Gogoi, Vice President (In Guwahati jail since 1998)	
	4. Anup Chetia, Secretary	
		(was awarded a jail term in December 1997 in Dhaka, on completion of which, he was released in 2004. Dhaka has refused to hand him over to India, citing another court case pending against him.)
Bd SF	Ranjan Daimary (1999)	AK Rifles - 50 Rifles Sundry - 100
NDFB	Ranjan Daimary, Chairman (2003)	
Nagaland		
NSCN(I-M)	Isaac Swu, Chairman Muivah, General Secretary	AK Rifles - 400 RPGs- 50 Rifles Sundry - 900
NSCN(K)	Khaplang, Chairman	AK Rifles - 200 Rifles (Sundry) – 350

Meghalaya		
HNLC	Julius K. Dorphang, Chairman	AK Rifles - 200
ANVC	Dilash R. Marak, Chairman	
Manipur		
UNLF	Chairman - Rajkumar Meghen General Secretary - T. Sanachou	AK Rifles - 200
PLA		A K Rifles-150
PREPAK	Chairman - Achamba	
KYKL	Chairman - Achou Toijamba	
Tripura		
TPDF	Tripura People's Democratic Front, (Political face of ATTF) Ranjit Debbarma, (President)	AK Rifles - 50
NLFT	Nayanbasi Jamatia	AK Rifles - 50

Coordinating Their Activities: Insurgent Outfits

For better results, various groups have joined hands against the State. The linkages, not made public, are prised open generally by the Intelligence.

Being oldest in the business, and mother of all insurgencies in the area NSCN, presently split into two factions, is central to such coordination, and over the recent years, has been aided and abetted by the Pak ISI. For this reason, most of the insurgent groups have gravitated towards one or the other of the two factions.

Beyond this, there have been attempts to float broader structures to coordinate the insurgent activities. Early 1990s, S.S. Khaplang of NSCN and John Khaw Kim Thang, President of Chin National Front reached an agreement to bolster the insurgency astride the Indo-Burma border with the active support of KIA. On the same lines was born the Indo-Burma Revolutionary Front (IBRF) on 22 May 1990—its founder members being Khaplang of NSCN(K), Paresh Barua, C-in-C of ULFA, and Sama Yaima of UNLF. The IBRF forbade any individual constituents from holding parleys with the Centre or States. Several factors have conjoined to bestow a position of hegemonic dominance on these outfits on the Indo-Burma border in the Region: these are the strategic importance of this border area, favourable topography for guerrilla warfare, existence of ethnic affinities across the border, and long experience of running underground movements by so many insurgent outfits on either side. These Fronts offer best chance to fight their secessionist battles against New Delhi (and Yangon). Though NSCN(K) was the first off the mark, NSGN(I-M) was to follow soon and formed more than one front. Its first attempt, soon after the May 1990 formation of the IBRF, was to form

Indo-Burma Liberation Front (IBLF). Its members, besides the prime mover NSCN(I-M), were the Revolutionary Joint Committee (itself an apex body comprising of RPF, KCP and PREPAK, all of Manipur), HPC of Manipur and Mizoram, BdSF of Assam and surprisingly ULFA, with a foot already in IBRF. If the IBRF aimed at creating an independent nation comprising of territories astride the Indo-Burma Border, and the Brahmaputra Valley under the Bra-Chin (Brahmaputra-Chindwin) Plan, the IBLF merely planned a coordinated effort. But if the former died a premature death, the latter proved a case of still-birth.

In 1993, NSCN(I-M) formed the United Liberation Front of Seven Sisters (ULF-SS). Some assign 1992 as its date of birth in Bangladesh, under the guidance of the ISS. It too was a failure. Not giving up, the NSCN(I-M) then formed a Front, with the jaw-breaking acronym SDUFSEAHR (Self-Defence United Front of South-East Asian Himalayan Region), on 30 November 1994. Its 23 members include the new insurgent groups of the 1990s like HALG; KNV and NDFB; HPC of Mizoram; and some groups from Manipur like the KYKL, UNLF (Okan faction), KCP (Isopishak faction), and PREPAK (Khamba faction) leaving out other factions. Even the ULF-SS, though virtually split, is not with the Front, the excuse that its leaders could not attend due to logistics problems notwithstanding. With so many factions within and more outside of it, the Front fared no better than the earlier ones considering that the KNV and NDFB were reportedly 'anti-social' elements and that the HPC had already signed a memorandum of understanding with the Government of Mizoram (B. Pakam, at the North-East India Political Science Association, Fourth Session, 1995 and *The Shillong Times*, 3-2-1995).

Much earlier, there were reports of joint meetings for strategic cooperation, in Dhaka during the 1970s, of outfits like the MULA, PLA, ATTF, NSCN(I-M) and MNF. All of them had their training camps in Bangladesh.

Shillong: A good host and safe shelter. Perhaps largest cosmopolitan town of the Region, with large number of settlers from all its states and beyond and very little Army presence, Shillong proves a safe haven for the insurgents of all hues. "It is well-known that the ultras of various groups from major affected states, including ULFA, NSCN, UNLF and PLA meet here regularly" to plan their joint operations.[6] In addition, these groups also send their members for medical treatment to Shillong, and hospitals, mostly private and at times even Government, are forced to treat them free of cost.

The latest to join forces seem to be the ULFA and the much older UNLF of Manipur. The alliance, latest of several such constantly shifting and cross-cutting linkages, is indicated by the fact that the bandh and boycott call against the Independence Day 2002, which had been announced from Guwahati since the Republic Day 1968, emanated from Imphal.

Earlier in the year, about 12 banned armed groups of the Region, including ULFA and NSCN(K) had called for a general strike and boycott of the Republic Day celebrations on 26 January (2002), according to a statement published by them in *Freedom*, ULFA's mouthpiece *(Indian Express*, 18-1-2002).

Nexus: A Summary

Insurgency and militancy have ushered in greater co-operation, co-ordination and nexus between various insurgence groups both within and without the region. At times, the pact could be symbolic or ideological. The nexus often involves arms supply, financial support and logistical assistance. Prominent secessionist groups such as NSCN, ULFA, PLA , UNLF, BdSF and KIA have at one time or other have/had reached close understanding among themselves [See Table below]. Some even established links with outfits such as the Liberation Tigers of Tamil Eelam (LTTE). Capitalising on the geographic proximity, a number of extremist established base and support facilities in the neighbouring states of Bangladesh, Myanmar, Nepal and Bhutan.

Nexus Amongst the Rebel Outfits : Around 2004

State	*Militant group*	*Partners*
Assam	ULFA	ATTF, NSCN(K), KIA, LTTE
Assam	NESO	AASU, APSU, AMSU, NSF (Nagaland), KSU (Khasi Students Union), MSU (Mizoram)
Assam	Dima Halao Daagah (Cachar region)	NSCN(I-M)
Assam	Bodo	NSCN(K & I-M), KNA, PLA
Nagaland	NSCN(K)	ULFA, UNLF, IBRF (Indo-Burma Revolutionary Force), Indigenous People's Pact (ORG, Bangkok)
Nagaland	NSCN(I-M)	BdSF Camp in Bhutan and Manas Tiger Sanctuary, Asian Indegenous People's Pact (ORG, Bangkok), Hmar People's Convention (demanding autonomy in Mirozam); NLFT (North Tripura close to NSCN route)
Tripura	TNV	NSCN, MNF

Networking and Linkages of Insurgencies in North-East: Current Status

In this age of internet and advances in technological field, the simple nexus of yesteryears have graduated to sophisticated networking and linkages of/among insurgents operating not only in a particular country but also beyond its borders.

So the insurgents in India's North-East could be networking not only with their counterparts in the contiguous countries like Bangladesh, Myanmar etc. but also with Al Qaeda operating far away. Consequently, the insurgent groups in this region have taken the maximum advantage of this and have managed to spread their tentacles in all the seven states of the region.

Of late, analysts have been arguing that the linkages of North-Eastern insurgent groups are heading towards a dangerous direction. With the supportive and active role being played by the Director General Field Intelligence (DGFI) of Bangladesh and Inter Service Intelligence of Pakistan in North-East India, successful attempts have been made to link these groups with Al Qaeda network. This is something the Indian Intelligence must concern itself diligently and uncover the sinister conspiracy for the world at large. "Then, there is also an attempt being made inside Assam by external forces to create a situation similar to Jammu and Kashmir."

In a wider context, one can see a broken pattern of emerging insurgencies, violence and poor governance. Ultimately, the consequent uncertainty along with human destabilisers who exploit the situation for their objectives create a vicious circle of hate. The armed non-state actors/groups are undermining the nation-states' physical capability to govern, and ultimately question and challenge even their moral right to govern. Generally speaking, "the near chronic political chaos can be seen propagating its respective form of instability and violence in large parts of North-East presently. The two current instances of political instability, generated by personal ambitions of the rival state leaders and consequent stage-managed rebellions by their minions in the legislatures forcing the current Chief Ministers to resign, have just been seen in Meghalaya (March 2007) and in Arunachal Pradesh (April 2007). Both these States are facing ethnic terrorism and the politicians involved in these shenanigans are possibly not even aware that by their actions they are helping the terrorist outfits in their states to exploit the political theatre of the absured played out as consequence of their skullduggery.

The rise of new war-making entities, helped by a variety of narco-traders, economic offenders and trans-national non-state actors, should be a matter of serious concern to the nation-states. It must be clearly understood that as a result of this phenomenon, various insurgent groups in the North-East are much more than mere stateless gangs. These new network insurgents possess "standing armed groups, treasury, revenue resources, their own intelligence services and ability to make alliances with other non-state entities and intelligence agencies of other countries." They also promote a common vision by promulgating the policy, laws and most importantly, war against the state. Brain M. Genkins, in an insightful essay, "Re-Defining the Enemy : The world has Changed But Our mindset has not" (RAND Review, Spring 2004) describes the distinction between war and crime, which continues to result in a policy quandary where we underestimate the power of militarily inferior foes (insurgent), difficult terrain, unceasing hostilities, and other unconventional measures of power.

Indian security planners must factor in such advanced technological innovations available to the simple terrorist of the yesterdays, which multiply his already formidable capabilities, to work out more effective counter-strategies to defeat the combine of transnational terror, crime and drug merchants. It is not a call for pessimism and despondency. India has been fighting the terrorism/insurgency for the past half a century by employing its military in a responsible manner, seldom taking resort to gunships, bombing the insurgent strongholds, or endangering civilian lives. It is also reasonably certain to aver that insurgent, terrorist, or militant outfits are aware that they cannot defeat India by mindless murder and mayhem.

What is called for is India finding ways to counter the sophisticated networking and linkages created by several insurgent groups in the North-East as a whole. These related issues have been discussed above in their theoretical and conceptual aspects as far as they concern the North-East. The details of linkages and network in respect of individual states of the region will be discussed in the respective chapters dealing with the terrorism in those states.

It bears repetition that tribal communities in the region are all zealously guarding their ethnic identity. India's Northeast is one of South Asia's hottest trouble spots, not simply because the region has more than 50 active armed insurgent organizations operating and fighting the Indian state, but because trans-border linkages that these groups have, and strategic alliances among them, have acted as force multipliers and have made the conflict dynamics all the more intricate. These linkages could be tactical, operational linkages or for financial benefits, as will be seen with the linkages in different states.

The inter-group linkages and networking in this region are heading towards a dangerous trend. This will be obvious if one studies the pattern of networks of terrorist outfits in individual states constituting the North-East. Most of these groups have linkages with other insurgents groups in some way or the other. The smaller insurgent groups have joined hands with bigger groups for support in case of need. The smaller groups provide safe sanctuary and passage to the bigger groups whenever required. In case of operations by the security forces against bigger insurgent groups; these groups fall back on the support cover and safe havens provided to them via small groups and vice versa. These linkages prove hazardous to the security forces in their operations. Gaining information about the insurgents would not only become difficult but also confusing.

The *interest groups,* as brought out earlier have already entered Assam. Their attempt to pierce into other states should be prevented by immediately taking the appropriate counter measures. There is also an attempt being made inside Northeastern Region by external forces to create a situation similar to Jammu and Kashmir. Unless innovative steps are undertaken to address the issue, the process could prove irreversible. It is expected that the Government of India would address the question more forcefully. The imperative of development buttressed by a security angle for the North-East Region should be uppermost in the Government's mind. Unless a pro-active role is taken by the government, this region could be infested by networked insurgent groups, shaking the edifice of Indian democracy.

The construction work of the border fence along the Indo-Bangladesh border has to be completed on priority so that a check is imposed on the inflow of Bangladesh nationals inside India. Constant pressure has to be mounted on Bangladesh government to take appropriate action against the India's North-East insurgent camps inside that country. Nepal may also be informed to keep a look out for any new linkages being established by the North-East insurgent groups.

Demonstrative Show of Force: July-August 1999

Over the years, the insurgents in the North-East plan special death dance around the Independence Day for its demonstrative effect. The Intelligence reported a meeting of several outfits—ULFA, NDFB, NSCN (both factions), PLA, PREPAK, UNLF, KCP, NLFT, TPDF and ATTF—in July 1999 at a place in Burma close to Manipur border to plan attack on the SF and communication arteries and also on production units, around 15 August. The meet was also meant to revive the fortunes of the IBRF not so active over the years. The ULFA Chairman on 6 August called upon all rebel groups to boycott the Independence Day. The other groups likewise issued warnings to citizens not to fly National Flag on the day. Major incidents, including acts of sabotage are summarized here:

1. *14 July.* A JCO killed and 7 soldiers injured when PLA ultras ambushed an Assam Rifles convoy at Pundongbam in Imphal East District, Manipur.
2. *3 August.* 5 policemen killed in a NSCN(K) ambush in Karbi Anglong district, Assam.
3. *4 August.* Bodo militants blow up a portion of rail track between Barpeta Road and Sarupeta Stations.

4. *5 August.* An attempt by ULFA to blow up oil facilities foiled with the killing of Bablu Ingti, ULFA Action Group Commander for Gauhati and Kamrup districts, at Gauhati. Quantities of RDX seized.
5. *7 August.* Two Power Grid Corporation pylons collapsed in a blast in Barpeta district.
6. *8 August.* The Arunachal Express also targeted but had a narrow escape when the explosives planted in one of its coaches were detected and defused minutes before its arrival at Bongaigaon.
7. *8 August.* A bomb was detonated under Sapkata bridge on NH No. 37, but security men foiled an attempt to blow up a rail bridge at Salakati Station.
8. *8 August.* The passengers on Gauhati-bound North-East Express had a narrow escape when a bomb blast derailed a pilot engine between Bijni and Patildaha Stations, near Bongaigaon.
9. *8 August.* A possible case of mistaken identity saves the Gauhati-bound Rajdhani Express. A goods train, 15 km ahead of the Express, absorbed the impact of the IED explosion by Bodo ultras under a bridge between Kokrajhar and Salakati Stations; 5 persons including 3 RPF men, injured when the explosion derailed it.
10. *8 August.* Most prominent incident. The Assam Police arrested two officers of the ISI—Mohammed Fasihullah Hussaini and Mohammed Javed Wakhar—and two operatives of 1 Harkat-ul-Mujahideen (HUM)—Maulana Hafiz Mohammid Akram Mallick and the totally blind Qari Salim. Qari, hailing from Muzaffarabad, was one of the four founders of the Lashkar-e-Babri, UP wing of HUM, and "one of the most dangerous operatives of the LSI in India". The arrest of these four ISI men had its fallout in other spheres, with police nabbing 27 other members of various Pro-Pak outfits, subsequently. The following two recoveries were the result of these four arrest:
    (*a*) 16 *August.* The State Police recovered 14.65 kg of explosive AMFO (ammonium nitrate mixed with fuel oil), from Platform No. 8 of Calcutta's Sealdah Railway Station. The Police believed this explosive was part of the main consignment from Bangladesh which was delayed/diverted after the 8 August arrest of the ISI officers.
    (*b*) *16 August.* 6 kg of RDX seized in Phulbari in Jalpaiguri district of North Bengal. It also possibly was part of the main consignment mentioned above.

The arrests and subsequent seizures should show continuous nefarious designs of Pakistan and its agencies to destabilise India.

11. *11 August.* NLFT ultras kill a police officer.
12. *12 August.* NLFT rebels, coming from Long Larai hill ranges gunned down 6 non-tribals in Shib-bari village of Dhalai district, Tripura, with their AK-47s.
13. *12 August.* The NDFB blew up with IED, an Army vehicle at Rajgarh (Sonitpur district) on Assam-Arunachal border, killing 3 soldiers.
14. *12 August.* A CRPF convoy had a narrow (miraculous!) escape when the IED planted at Bilpara in Nalbari district of Assam by ULFA, went off seconds after the convoy crossed the spot.
15. *15 August.* 3 CRPF men killed when armed militants ambushed two vehicles of 82 CRPF Battalion at Khabirakpam in Bishnupur district of Manipur. 31 others, including 17 CRPF, were seriously injured.
16. The following two events may be part of the 15 August-related death dance:
    (a) A series of blasts in the first 10 days of August 1999 prompted the Railways to suspend train services after sunset in Assam from 11 to 15 August.
    (b) In August, NLFT ultras kidnapped M. Debnath, father of Ranjit Debnath, Senior CPI(M) leader and former Transport Minister, from his Bangalipara residence in South Tripura.
17. *15 August.* The Bodo-dominated Lower Assam remained strike-bound.
18. *15 August.* A happenstance or a design? Over 200 ULFA and Bodo ultra surrendered to the Army in different parts of Assam; and handed in their arms, including AK-47s, grenades and revolvers. Among the welter of explosions that disturbed the peace around 15 August, did these surrenders make a statement?[7]

Unique Bomb

A blast at New Jalpaiguri Station killed ten people. It was unique in the sense that a new kind of bomb, nitro-based, was used for the first time in India. This explosion, unlike the one caused by the RDX, "cause more deaths in covered and semi-covered areas".

Aims and Methods of the Insurgents

The insurgency movement generally aims at challenging a nation-state and undermining its sovereignty. The political propaganda barrage is mounted to subvert the loyalty of the citizenry and cause disaffection among the masses. Besides the political mobilisation, instrument of mindless violence is employed to target the ruling classes, SF, and elitist sections to create all-round panic and fear psychosis. Finally, the innocent civilians are targeted to cause social disharmony; and selective killings are resorted to for causing religious, communal, or sectarian tensions and conflict. But an equally effective mean to subvert the will of a nation-state is to hurt it economically by attacking its economic sinews and communication networks. That will not only cripple the economic growth of the country, but also cause security problems for it by hindering the movement of its SF from one part to another when required for strategic and operational reasons; and this indeed was done in the Kargil conflict in 1999 (for some reasons, the Government did not want to call it the Kargil War).

To cripple the economic development of the Region, the militants have been targeting the railways and roads, oil installations and refineries, and hydro-electric plants. Here is just one example of sabotaging hydro-power development. The North-East is estimated to have a hydel potential of 40,000 MW of which only 1 per cent has been harnessed so far. "The Union Government has already cleared development of 20,000 MW hydel capacity for the Dihang and the Subansiri Projects in Arunachal, by the NHPC" (Vinay Pandey in *Times of India,* 25-1-2000). This is billed as the largest hydel project in the world. But the killing of S.C. Sher, CE, NHPC Loktak (Manipur) Project by militants cast a long shadow on the successful completion of the hydel plans in the North-East.

The Loktak project has 1200 workers, of whom over 50 per cent are non-Manipuris. They were panic-stricken. Railway Board Chairman told the press on 6-2-2000 that rise in terrorist violence has resulted in low morale of the employees of the NF Railway. Some instances of blasts on the rail track and coaches have been given in the preceding pages.

Fighting the Insurgency and Hurdles in the Way

Fighting insurgency is a complex, time-consuming, and strenuous exercise, which needs patience, understanding, and political skill of the highest order. Economic measures and anti-insurgency operations must go hand-in-hand. Once considerable progress have been made in the twin tasks, and particularly when the militant leadership is convinced that the violence would not pay, it is the time to repair to the High Table.

Economic Development

Economic development is the answer to the sense of deprivation and neglect of the Region by the powers-that-be. Consequent employment opportunities should draw the educated youth away from the enticements and blandishments offered by the insurgent groups. Prime Minister's economic package and the Shukla Commission's Report are meant to put the North-East on way to economic recovery. The Government have already accommodated the micro-identities and sub-nationalities with finesse and dexterity, essentially through the instrumentality of Sixth Schedule and subsequent elevation of certain ethnic minorities' territories into statehood.

The States in the Region have too been taking certain policy decisions to ameliorate the lot of common man. They are discouraging jhum cultivation and offering incentives to develop alternate methods to minimize the degradation of the land and environment caused by the former. Horti-flori- and herbi-culture and plantation have potential with every type of agro-climatic zones available here. But some problems of land, labour, capital and marketing intrude, which are being addressed.

Counter Insurgent (CI) Operations

It is an over-wrought cliche by now to say that force alone cannot root out insurgency. Perhaps it would be truer to say that no political solution is possible till the insurgents are made to realize that they cannot have their way with the gun. And force is the only language they understand. Stage for political negotiations would follow. Some of the musts for a successful CI operations are:

1. The operations of various SF involved must be well coordinated to avoid duplication and wastage of resources.
2. A unified command set-up has proved a success in the recent years. It must be headed by an appropriate political leader.
3. An effective intelligence network.
4. The State Police and Para-Military forces must play their role in these operations, and not be reduced to secondary positions.
5. Politics and political interests of parties and individuals must not intrude into the scene.
6. The police must get improved weaponry and better radio sets.
7. No undue harassment/excesses against the locals.

Banning the Underground Outfits

Banning the secessionist groups is deemed helpful in fighting them. Some of the outfits so banned are NSCN (both factions), ULFA, PLA, UNLF, etc. They are declared "unlawful associations" under the Unlawful Activities (Prevention) Act, 1967. To facilitate the operations of the CI forces, the Government in a related move, has declared the whole of Manipur, Nagaland, Tripura and Assam as well as Tirap and Changlang districts of Arunachal as "disturbed areas" under the authority of the Disturbed Areas Act, 1950.

The last groups to be banned were ANVC and HALC of Meghalaya in November 2000.[8] Some feel it will only help to glorify these two ragtag outfits, which police think are nothing more than criminals posing as gun-toting patriots even if the ANVC is fighting for creation of a separate Garoland out of Meghalaya. The policy of outlawing a militant outfit in order to discredit it or smash it cuts both ways, argues the analysts. If on the one hand, it enables the State to take effective and prompt action against it, the banning bestows an aura of martyrdom on the outfit, elevating the 'extortionists' to 'freedom fighters', on the other. It seems the politicians are still able to maintain contacts with the banned outfits to safeguard their turfs. If a Nagaland Chief Minister (S.C. Jamir) had allegedly close relations with NSCN(K), his counterpart in the neighbouring Manipur (Rishang Keishing) had similar links with such groups in his State (*Times of India*, 26-1-1997), which prompted its Governor, a retired Lt General, to send his resignation to the President in disgust. Again in Assam, the AGP and the Congress have accused each other of nursing ULFA.

Need to Staunch the Flow of Funds to Insurgents

Insurgents are known to be flush with funds, with some of their leaders ensconced in luxury hotels abroad. When the State gets weak, the insurgent outfits collect large amounts through taxes, "Voluntary" contributions (read extortions), coercion and intimidation, and plain robbery. In the recent decades, the narco trade is filling their coffers. Worse still, the politicians, bureaucrats, and contractors/the wealthy are known to pay the security money to the terrorists. In some areas, the insurgents are reportedly running a parallel Government. To staunch this flow, the Government must ensure safety of its citizens and employees through effective governance. Then comes the time to win the battle of minds, first of its own people and then of those gone astray.

Political Parties and Insurgency

The process of integration and development has generated the subjective sentiment of relative deprivation among some ethnic groups in the region, and that in turn has created an objective material condition for ethnic unrest and militancy in those groups. Simultaneously, it is necessary to evaluate the contribution of different political parties for the growth and perpetuation of violent ethnic movements to further their own electoral prospects.

A close observation of political developments in Tripura during the eighties and nineties should reveal the unholy nexus between the insurgency and electoral politics. The comparative backwardness of the tribals and the consequent tribal militancy have skilfully been exploited by the parliamentary forces for their electoral benefits. It is widely believed that the genocide perpetrated by the TNV before the 1988 Assembly elections at the behest of the Congress (I)-Tripura Upajati Juba Samiti (TUJS) combine brought the latter into power (*The Statesman*, 27-10-1994). The signing of the Peace Accord between the Congress (I) Government at the centre and the TNV after the elections to create some political space for the latter is proof enough of a clandestine understanding between the two. Similarly, the massacre committed by the ATTF on the eve of the 1993 elections is believed to have helped the

CPI(M)-led Left Front to regain power (*The Shillong Times*, 9-9-1993). It was reported that while the ATTF and the Tribal Youth Force (TYF) were floated by the Gana Mukti Parishad, a CPI(M) tribal wing, the Tripura Tribal Volunteer Force (TTVF), the Tripura Tribal Development Force (TTDF), and the Sangrak enjoy the tacit support of the TUJS—an ally of the Congress (I) (*Statesman*, 9-9-1994).

Thus it appears that the opposition parties, in order to capture power, not only patronise the militant outfits, they, at times, even float such outfits to destabilize the ruling dispensation through disruptive incidents by the latter. Another ploy of the opposition parties, as soon as they come into power, is to stage a surrender drama with much fanfare which gives the surrenderees double benefits; general amnesty and economic rehabilitation. The Left Front assumed power in Tripura in April 1993, and over 2,000 ATTF cadres surrendered on 9 September 1993 (*Anand Bazar Patrika*, 21-9-1994). A similar incident took place during the earlier stint of the Left Front when the activists of the All Tripura People Liberation Organisation (ATPLO) led by Binanda Jamatia came overground. The play-acting enables the political party to claim credit for bringing normalcy and peace to strife-ridden socio-political environment, and for the cadres, it ensures the Government jobs, licences, permits and respectability.

In certain cases, political parties ensure the longevity and perpetuation of the insurgent movements for their own political security and survival. It is well-known that the possibility of a negotiated settlement was bright in early 1990s as a result of several round of talks between the Central Government and the ULFA. But the move was allegedly sabotaged by the ruling party under Hiteswar Saikia, since they feared the settlement might oust them from power as indeed had happened earlier consequent to the Assam Accord (1985) and Mizoram Accord (1986).

The analysts assert that had an accord been signed with the undivided ULFA, the insurgency problem in Assam would have been solved once for all, as it happened in Mizoram. Any agreement signed with a section of a movement has never been successful, as was seen in case of Shillong Accord with Nagas and Rajiv-Longowal Agreement. The ruling elite at Gauhati engineered a vertical split in the ULFA through large-scale surrenders, and followed the policy of divide and rule to secure their own political fortunes. They brought the movement down to such a level that it could remain under control but did not put an end to it. It was obviously aimed at perpetuating its presence to ensure their indispensability in state politics.

These may be partisan rhetoric, but it is widely believed.

Divided Communities

Colonial encroachments created artificial boundaries. The Singphos in India have their kin in Jinphos in Myanmar, South China, Thailand and Laos.

The Mizo-Kuki-Chin group of tribes, some of the Naga tribes and the Meghalaya tribes, several tribes in Arunachal Pradesh, and even the plains people, Meiteis have their counterparts across the borders. All of them had dual—sometimes, multiple—cultural orientations, social and economic linkages and shared political beliefs in customs, traditions and mores. The divided communities syndrome continued even in the post-colonial era in the sphere of domestic reorganisations of the political boundaries as a result of agitations actuated and fuelled by the ethnic aspirations and identity crisis, actual or perceived, and consequently, the tribes, like the Nagas, find themselves in more than one state.

Insurgency as an Industry[9]

Were Phizo and Laldenga, the archetypal rebels, men informed by ideology and fired by apocalyptic vision? After all, they too spent long years abroad. But it is perceived by some that militants in the North-East "were not strong on ideology". The insurgents there are ethnic-separatist by inspiration. If they have more staying power, it is because they can draw on a large reservoir of public support, as also on a 'benign' foreign hand. In course of time, it becomes an industry which thrives on regionalism, rather ethno-separatism.

The pattern is similar by now. Having attained power through 'deals'—a cynical expression for 'accords'—with the Union or State Governments, the leaders who once fumed about independence, sovereignty, self-determination, ethnic identity and colonial syndrome, are now content to live on the Central doles, called grants. Again, a cynical view is that not only do they get coopted into the system, but also get used by the Centre as regional satraps to control the region for the central leaders. But somewhat surprisingly, even when some such leaders get sucked into the system, whether through persuasion, cajolery, inveighment, or cooption, the insurgency has endured. It seems clear that the ideology, if at all, of ethnic identity, or the colonial mind-set of the ruling classes, are not the sole—or even the main—motives that sustain the appeal of the insurgency. There are perhaps more pragmatic and mundane causes for this phenomenon; namely, personal ambitions, personal gains not only of monetary kind or even ego-mania. But for these not-so-idealistic causes, the plethora of Accords[10] signed by the Centre and State Governments with various militant outfits should have rooted out the insurgency situation from the North-East. All these accords failed to bring accord between the parties at the high table, at least not as yet; the Mizo Accord being the sole exception which only proves the rule.

So, it may be a truism to say that after a certain stage, the insurgency continues, rather, is sustained, not for the idealism and original causes, but for other reasons. At this stage, it is insurgency for the sake of insurgency. Not only it has to be sustained for the benefit of the rebels, but also for the gain of those ranged on the other side—politicians, SF, bureaucrats and the police. So goes the cynical wisdom, or is it? The Press and the public write and read widely about the "games politicians play". But are they the only ones playing games in this theatre of the absurd? No, there are so many other players, as named above. It may be surrealistic, it may even be macabre setting, but it is true! If there is "leakage"—an innocent euphemism for crass corruption and crafty manipulation of Government money—in the development funds, it is not because it cannot be staunched, but because so many are interested to see that it is not plugged. It is here that they play games with the public money—so adroitly and so deftly. Is it any surprise that the insurgency at certain stage becomes an industry, benefiting multiplicity of "industrialists" on both side of the divide? It is no surprise that a resident watcher told a journalist in January 2000: "The goal here is not identity any more, it is money.... If a gun is pointed, it is for the good time, not for the separatism" (Verghese, 1996). The politicos too may have a case. The Chief Ministers of Nagaland (S.C. Jamir) and Arunachal (Mukut Mithi) claim they are under the threat from the NSCN(I-M). It has been pressing Jamir's ministers and MLAs to withdraw support from the former in the Assembly elections due next year and targeting ministers from Tirap and Changlang districts because its members are insecure with the new Arunachal Pradesh Control of Organised Crime Bill, 2002 (*The Week*, 22-9-2002).

A word on the splitting games. Splitting is a legitimate weapon in the political field. But when the politicians extended the tactic to the insurgent outfits, it resulted in disastrous consequences. If the aim of splitting was to weaken or decimate a movement, it does not seem to have happened in most cases. In fact, the end result has been quite the opposite: the faction that stays the course emerges even stronger and more virulent. Whether it is Saikia splitting the Bodos or Rajiv Gandhi playing footsie with a faction (Longowal's) of the Akalis, results were opposite of the desideratum. On the other hand, the militant outfits are frequently splintered by internal dynamics fuelled by some leader's self-serving ambitions. Often, the factions try to outdo each other through incremental and competitive violence. Somewhere along the way, today's moderates become tomorrow's extremists. So some critics dub this splitting game as sharp practice. They ascribe mushrooming of militant groups in the Region as an "inevitable result of Government's efforts to solve the North-East's problem on the cheap". Whether caused by the shrewd politicians or by internal skullduggery, perhaps more by the latter, there are too many splinters for comfort; *viz,* NSCN(I-M) and NSCN(K); NNC(A)[11] and NNC(K)[12], latter closer to NSCN (I-M); the Meiteis have half a dozen valley-based militant groups including UNLF, PLA and PREPAK; and the Kukis have KNF, and KNA and the latest UKLF.

Now to the leakage of funds. It is axiomatic that most insurgency movements in course of time come to thrive on political patronage. Perhaps rightly, analysts have seen a symbiotic relationship between the politicians and militants—each drawing sustenance from other. Some linkages have been mentioned above. One time Nagaland Chief Minister Vamuzo had accused S.C. Jamir of supporting one group and trying to eliminate the other. In Tripura, if the ruling Left Front is alleged to have propped up the ATTF, the Congress is said to be sustaining the NLFT. In Assam if P.K. Mahanta is accused of being soft on ULFA, the Congress is blamed for creating BdSF to counter the AGP (*Times of India,* 26-1-1997).

Over the years, insurgency movements in the North-East seem to be characterised by killings, extortions, rapine, money-laundering *et al.* It is mindless violence all the way, perhaps actuated by the lust for power, pelf and naked ambition. It is no surprise that presently in large measure the militancy came to be sustained by money power alone. They have found ingenious ways to ensure that cash keep flowing, filling their coffers: narco-trade, cuts and commissions from the contracts, selective taxes levied in their areas and extortions. "The ruling politician, Government officials and businessmen divert Government funds as their contributions into the kitty of the militant outfits. Insurgents never seem to be short of money. How often does one see advertisements in Nagaland dailies, wooing the youth to join militants on a monthly salary of Rs. 15,000?

What kind of money is involved here? One computation has it that in a period of 25 years (1970-95), the Centre has spent over Rs. 30,000 crore in Nagaland alone. That works out to Rs. 25 lakh per person for a population of 12 lakh. This comment by a local academic sums up the scandalous situation: "If in the rest of the country only 15 paise from each rupee reach the target people, in the North-East it is 2 paise!" Some leakages, this! This illustrates effectively how the politicians, rebels, officials, contractors, *et al.* sponge on the Central grants and development funds, leaving the common man high and dry. All this must change drastically if we are to win the war.

In June 2003, Arunachal also came under the scanner for the politician-insurgent nexus; when the Deputy PM Advani ordered an Intelligence inquiry into the allegations of nexus between 6 ministers and 5 ruling Congress MLAs and the two factions of the NSCN (*Express,* 30-6-03).

A Different Game

The then Assam Chief Minister P.K. Mahanta's ambivalent attitude on setting up of the Unified Command to ensure better coordination between the Central forces and civil authorities was publicly commented upon. This is what a reputed national daily wrote, editorially castigating him for his dubious ways to sideline the real issues: "Centre's decision to launch joint operations was long overdue. It would have done good for Mahanta and his party if he had taken charge of the Unified Command instead of leading an All Party delegation for talks with the Central leaders on 'law and order' situation in Assam—essentially a state subject. His equivocal attitude in dealing with the insurgency in the State is an embarrassment for Mahanta as he is also a member of ruling coalition at Centre". (*The Hindu*, 18-1-1997).

Making Surrender Worthwhile

The Union Home Ministry offered a worthwhile surrender-cum-rehabilitation package in April 1998 to persuade the militants in the North-East to give up the path of violence. The scheme offered a number of monetary incentives and benefits to the militants to ensure that they don't return to the jungle again, including the vocational training to equip them to start life afresh. Each weapon handed in will be paid for at a fixed scale, but not in cash but in the form of a fixed deposit in the joint name of the surrenderee and a nominee of a NGO/State Government. The surrendered militants would be paid a monthly stipend for a year at a graded scale, the minimum being Rs. 2,000 a month. The surrenderees will be lodged in a Rehabilitation Camp for a year, with free boarding and lodging, and provided training in a trade or vocation of their liking. Subsequently, effort will be made to settle them in civil society.

Till 10 November 1999, 714 militants from Nagaland, Assam and Tripura had surrendered.[13]

The table below indicates the payment for each weapon/equipment handed in by the surrenderee, under "give up-and-gain" criterion.

Cash for Surrendered Arms (1998)

Weapon/Equipment	*Payment Per Piece Rs.*
Rocket launchers	25,000
Sniper Rifles	25,000
Assault Rifles of AK 47, 56 and 74 Series	15,000
Pistols/Revolvers	3,000
Rockets	1,000
Hand/Rifle Grenades	500
Remote Control devices	3,000
IED	3,000
RDX etc.	1,000 per kg

Response by the Government

An important aspect that government might consider is about incentive that should be provided to a group that seeks to cease the hostilities. Whereas the latest rehabilitation package which came into force from April 1, 2005, provides for monthly stipends and a one time grant in the end of a monitored three year period for surrendered, nothing is being provided to an insurgent group that comes over ground after instituting a ceasefire. The government has to put in dedicated efforts at all fronts to counter the dangerous networks and linkages operating in the northeast region.

Costs and Means of Fighting Insurgency

The nation has paid a heavy price in human terms, leave aside the material and financial costs for fighting the scourge of insurgency in the North-East. Some relevant information on the North-East as a whole and state-wise break-up/tally for worst-affected States for 10-year[14] (1989-98) period are adduced on the following pages. The toll had crossed 8000 (lives) by 1998 and has been rising ever since.

Some Select Facts for the Entire North-East

1. In 10 years (1989-98), over 15,000 insurgents have been arrested and more than 6,700 weapons recovered.
2. In 1996 alone, 2617 people were killed, including 374 Army men. Of these, 734 were killed in extremist violence in Assam alone, of which 210 were the victims of the Bodo-Santhal ethnic violence in May 1996. The BLTF topped the list in Assam, killing 129 in 104 violent incidents.
3. The Centre gave a grant of Rs. 260 crore to Tripura to defray its insurgency-related expenses for 3 years (1994-96). The amount was meant to rehabilitate 5000 rebels who had surrendered and to provide them employment.

Assam

1. Over 2700 killed.
2. 385 killed in Bodo-Santhal clashes alone.
3. If the Bodos want a separate state, so do Santhals.
4. Bodo Accord of 1993 is stalled over the issue of villages/ area to be included in Bodo Autonomous Council Jurisdiction.
5. The abductions and extortions have never ceased.
6. Army has lodged FIRs against senior ministers for their nexus with the insurgents, for often giving them shelter.

   The officials and contactors are known to be passing money to the insurgent outfits.

7. Cases have been filed against some tea companies for funding some outfits.
8. ULFA will have nothing short of independence.
9. Both its hill districts, Karbi Anglong and North Cachar, are agitating for Union Territory status.

Nagaland

1. Over 1500 killed.
2. It is the longest-running violent but fractious movement. Ironically, the Naga Agreement of November 1975 itself caused a split among the insurgents.
3. A cease-fire agreed with NSCN(I-M) is in place since 1 September 1997 and periodic talks have been held with their leadership by the Government of India representative in some foreign capitals, and of late in New Delhi.
4. NSCN(K) too is observing *de facto* truce.
5. Both factions desire independence.
6. All factions also want the Naga-inhabited areas of Manipur, Arunachal Pradesh and Assam (essentially in North Cachar Hills) to be merged into a Greater Nagaland.

Manipur

1. Over 3000 killed.
2. In the Naga-Kuki clashes alone since 1992, over 750 people have been killed and 4100 houses burnt.
3. Since June 1997, 270 have been killed and 3550 houses burnt in the Kuki-Zomi clashes.
4. The Meiteis fear balkanization if their state in the face of the Nagas demanding merger of Naga areas of the state into the Greater Nagaland.

Tripura

1. Over 1600 killed.
2. NLFT and ATTF are still maintaining bases in Bangladesh.
3. NLFT depredations are on the increase, and 27 Police Station areas have been declared as "disturbed".
4. Abductions by NLFT are up by over 30 per cent during the last two years of the decade in question.
5. There is increased tension between the tribals and non-tribals.
6. The tribal militancy is gaining more virulent edge.
7. In August 1988, an Accord was signed with the TNV. Consequently, the TNV ceased to exist, but its die-hard core gave birth to NLFT.

8. The one-time majority tribal population is an aggrieved party after it was reduced to a minority consequent to a post-1947 influx of immigrants from East Pakistan/Bangladesh.

Forces Deployed in CI Role

1. The Army deployment is seldom made known to the public. The following seems plausible information from the published sources:
   (*a*) Tezpur (-based) corps is responsible for counter-insurgency operations in Assam. It has one to two Army Divisions at its disposal for the task; approximately 20,000 troops.
   (*b*) Dimapur (-based) corps has more onerous charge of controlling insurgency in Tripura, Manipur, Mizoram and Nagalard. Its main job lies in the last two states. Besides the two to three Army Divisions, the BSF and Assam Rifles contribute considerable strength for the task.
2. Unlike the Army, the Para Military Forces (PMF) generally keep announcing the quantum of their forces deployed in different states. Some illustrative figures of PMF deployed in Assam in December 1996 are given below:
   (a) CRPF - 138 companies
   (b) BSF - 20 companies.
3. A little earlier (July 1996) Chief Minister Mahanta had announced (*The Hindustan Times* of 29 July 1996) that there were 57 companies of PMF, 37 of Assam Police, 5 from Karnataka and 15 from Bihar. He also disclosed that during the elections (early 1996), there were in all 157 companies.
4. CRPF told the press (June 1997) that it had a total of 350 companies in the North-East, of which 156 were in Assam to operate against the ULFA and Bodo militants. Its force was divided into three sectors (their term was *clusters*): Gauhati, Agartala and Imphal.
5. Reality and Fantasy. On the poll eve in February 1998, there were 69 companies of PMF against the projected demand of over 600 companies! An angry Mahanta told the press on 12 February, four days before the poll: "No additional forces promised to us have come.... If the forces come 36 hours before the polls, they will be of no use."[15]
6. Additional Units Raised. Home Minister Inderjit Gupta informs the Lok Sabha in January 1998 of the Government decision to raise 12 India Reserve Battalions for anti-insurgency duties in the North-East. The figure was raised to 13, Home Minister L.K. Advani informed the

meeting of the Consultative Committee of his Ministry, in December 1998. The State-wise allotment indicated was:

Assam	– 4	Manipur	– 2
Tripura	– 2	Arunachal	– 2

Meghalaya, Mizoram, and Nagaland – 1 each

North-East : Post 2001 Scenario

New Delhi's attitude towards Engaging the Militants : A critique.

Two entities signing a ceasefire should usually amount to a commitment to talk. But New Delhi seems to be dithering in its resolve on this score. One instance that comes to mind in this connection is the Centre's invitation for talks to the National Liberation Front of Tripura (NLFT) in 2004 by the then NDA regime. In response to the call to eschew violence, two splinter groups of the NLFT surrendered, led by Nayanbashi Jamatia and Mantu Koloi respectively. But the dominant group led by Biswamohan Debbarman refused to fall into line and continues, alongwith the All Tripura Tiger Force (ATTF), its defiant posture. The common objective of these two outfits is to cleanse the hills of the non-tribals who settled in the region after 1949 when Tripura state was merged with the Indian Union.

So far the Centre has made no move to contact the leaders of two factions of the NLFT who surrendered and to talk to them. Is it any surprise that within weeks of surrendering, when he was simply ignored by the authorities, Jamatia reportedly went underground in Bangladesh.

The Garo Hills-based Achik National Volunteer Council (ANVC) is a major security risk because of its nexus with ULFA and Bodo militants and its objective of securing a Greater Garoland obviously after achiving the disintegration of the present State of Maghalaya. It had got its image tarnished because of abductions, extortion and murders. So it surrendered in 2003, coming clean in the bargain. After surrender, its cadres killed boredom by playing cricket and football with locals until the Meghalaya Government perceived it as a violation of ceasefire codes and isolated them. It obviously miffed them. And to know that they were said to have gifted an ambulance van to a charitable organisation and also contributed towards the tsunami fund. Why do the authorities have to be so supercilious in such minor matters?[16]

It is not suprising, therefore, that the Khasi-dominated Hinnietrep National Liberation Council (HNLC), formed in the early 1990s with the blessings of the NSCN (I-M) and responsible for killing a number of non-tribal traders in Shillong, has refused to sue for peace. Its leaders, too, are in Bangladesh. Surprisingly, when the smaller ANVC has been proscribed, the HNLC bears no such stigma.

Both the United People's Democratic Solidarity (UPDS) in Karbi Anglong district of Assam and Dima Halam Daogah (DHD) in North Cacher Hills are at peace with the Centre, consequent to a ceasefire agreement, since 2003, even if not between themselves. In 2005, as a result of clashes between the two, as many as 90 people mere killed. The figure for 2006 was not very different either.

It is not that New Delhi has easy options. Still it must have clear cut and transparent policy on the issues involved on such subject, NSCN(K) faction has truce with the Government for years but has not as yet been invited for negotiations. It is known that the NSCN(I-M) comes in the way of such talks. The latter has been talking to New Delhi for years all over the world but the two are nowhere near an agreement. How long will the NSCN(K) hold patience? To express its uneasy feelings it occasionally engages in bloody street fights with the NSCN(I-M).

Similar logjam exists in New Delhi's relations with the Bodo outfits. Consequent to an accord with the Bodo Liberation Tigers (BLT) leaders, they are presently controlling the leavers of power in the Bodo Territorial Council (BTC) set up under the 6th Schedule. But the National Democratic Front of Bodoland (NDFB), rival of the BLT, is still waiting in the wings after signing the truce in 2005.

As for the Centre concluding peace accords with the militants in the North-East, the 1986 one with the MNF in Mizoram was the only success story so far. As a result, Mizoram remained peaceful for years. But alas even that no longer holds true. That distinction stands shattered as the state Government did not display due sensitivity towards the aspirations and ethnic identity of the Reangs. The Mizos obviously have forgotten their oven struggle of the yore. But the smaller tribes have learnt their lessons from that very struggle. The Bru National Liberation Front (BNLF), spearheading the agitation of the Reangs for a separate state since 1996, also adopted terrorism to achieve its aims. Conceding its demand, Aizawl signed a truce with the BNLF in Oct. 2005. But unfortunately, a splinter group, Bru National Front of Mizoram, emerged to challenge the truce. The worse is that even after truce with the NBLF, thousands of Reang refugees are still living in the camps in Tripura.

It is necessary, even urgent, that the Government crafts a coherent policy to conclude agreements with the militant outfits in the North-East and have required machinery in place to ensure its implementation. New Delhi must find time for this implementation. Otherwise, the youngmen languishing in the camps will be facing frustration again and consequently may get sucked into the vortex of terrorism and violence.

North Bengal Situation : Still Violent and Worrisome

Peace seems to be nowhere in sight in this region. Only on 5 Feb. 2007, the Howrah-Dibrugarh Kamrup Express had a narrow escape when an explosion took place at Kamakshyaguri railway station neighbouring Aliduar in Jalpaiguri district within moments of the train leaving the platform. Seven people were hurt when a bomb kept in a stray bag on platform no. 2 exploded in the afternoon.

A similar blast suspected to have been triggerd by an ULFA/KLO chique late last year inside a passenger train at Belakoba station, also in Jalpaiguri district, snuffed out seven lives.

It is indeed a matter of deep concern that in a span of five months, Oct. 2006 to Feb. 2007, North Bengal has witnessed three bomb blasts. Of these two went off at two railway stations and one explosion occurred in a market place along the Assam-West Bengal border. The toll : Eight dead and many more injured.

All that indicates that a tumultuous time is set to disturb peace in the region, lying at the junction of Assam, fighting insurgency for the past 25 years, and North Bengal, centre of Kamtapur agitation. The vulnerability is only increased by the fact that the region shares international boundaries with three countries : Nepal (just coming out of the throes of the Maoist insurgency and the anti-king political agitation), Bhutan (ULFA and Bodo militants are again attempting to establish a foothold there) and Bangladesh (breeding ground for the ultras operating in the North-East).

The KLO is the main source of the violence in the area. A local outfit, it is spearheading a movement for establishment of a separate homeland for the Rajbanshis of North Bengal and four districts of adjoining Lower Assam. It had unleashed a massive spate of violence till 2003 when Bhutan carried out operation Flush Out against Indian terrorists camping on its soil. Since that year, the North Bengal police has taken its gaze off the KLO, as majority of its cadres had surrendered.

It was obviously a miscalculation on the part of the State police. Even if its backbone had been smashed, the KLO could hardly die this way. Besides the ideological motivation behind this outfit, the outlawed ULFA would never allow the KLO to die, after all, it is its strategic partner and it would sustain it for its own cause. Simply put, ULFA needs an ally in this part of West Bengal to provide its cadres all the logistic support they need. It also helps it to access the camps in the neighbouring countries using the North Bengal corridor. In the bargain, the KLO also gets reciprocal help to wage its own war for Kamtapur. KLO cadres are trained, equipped and lodged in the ULFA camps in Bangladesh. Intelligence reported that a new armed group of the KLO cadres trained in the Chittagong Camps sneaked into North Bengal in mid-2006.[17]

Intelligence inputs suggest that the renewed violence, mentioned above, indicates the strategy of "minimal risk, maximum gains". They avoid direct confrontation with the security forces, and instead target the public zones. Attacks on the two railway stations (Belakoba and Kamakshyaguri) and at Barovisha market stand testimony to the new strategy. Is the State, and particularly its police, aware of this changed policy adopted by the outfit? Their inaction so far shows it is not.

For effectively countering the KLO violence West Bengal must share intelligence with Assam as this outfit has partners-in-crime operating in the latter's territory, like the ULFA.

It is essential to convince such outfits that they cannot bend the state to their will and only offensive operations launched by its security forces can do this job. Only then will the KLO feel compelled to come to the negotiations table.

Besides looking at this region in the context of insurgency-related violence, there is also a foreign policy angle to it. The recent (around the close of 2006) spurt in the incident of firing from across the Bangladesh border aimed at aiding the intrusion of militants into North Bengal and Assam has made the security experts to sit up and take a serious look at country's threat perception vis-a-vis our existing foreign policy stance of reconciliation in regard to India's immediate neighbours. Unprovoked firing by the BDR in Assam's Cachar sector and along the North Bengal frontier encompassing the sensitive districts of Jalpaiguri, Cooch Behar and North and South Dinajpur will give sleepless nights to North Block officials dealing with the internal security.

The use of RDX in the 20 Nov. 2006 explosion in the Haldibari-New Jalpaiguri passenger train at Belokoba in North Bengal (already mentioned earlier) should persuade the MHA to reorganise the operational blueprint designed for the Eastern/North-Eastern region. It is worth remembering that the Chicken's neck located in this region is strategically significant for India's security as this 29 km panhandle joins the entire North-East to the mainland. A few dozens of determined terrorists, stiffened by some suicide bombers of whom there seem to be no shortage of late, could effectively disrupt this connectivity.

Even more worrisome is the fact of India having a long and porous international border with Nepal, Bhutan, Myanmar and Bangladesh, which only encourages our adversaries to try and dominate the region by sponsoring or helping the insurgent movements in the area. It has already been stated that situation in Nepal and Bangladesh can cause concern to India's security minders (The caretaker government in Bangladesh has taken some tough anti-terrorism measures in Feb.-April 2007 period, but they could turn out to be short-term palliatives). Even if the intelligence has held the KLO (in association with the ULFA) responsible for the Belakoba blast, there are other sources of worry as well. The leaders of groups like the ULFA, KLO, ATTF, NDFB and others are in touch with HUJI-B and Jamaat-ul-Mujahideen (Bangladesh) and are supported by Pakistani ISI. ULFA leader Paresh Baruah's recent (late 2006) visit to Pakistan only fortifies such claims. Yet again, it is believed that KLO Chief Jeevan Singh had taken refuge in ULFA training camps in Chittagong in order to arrange more recruits for his own outfit to spread terror in his "area of operations."

With terror groups like the LET and Al Oaeda having set up links with the insurgent groups, West Bengal has turned out to be a safe haven for jihadi outfits. The State has not taken seriously the advisory from the MHA to strengthen security apparatus at the railway stations and other vulnerable areas.

To prevent any further flare up particularly in West Bengal, counter-intelligence agents must be deployed in sensitive border districts, with back-up from the special forces. Observers feel "the ruling party in West Bengal must realise the harsh fact that a police force deployed in self-esteem and politically browbeaten can never be an effective tool against insurgency."[18]

MHA Worried over Violence in North-East : 2006 Report

The MHA report reviewing the internal security situation in 2006 says :

> "In Assam and Nagaland, the violence has gone up due to increased activities of the ULFA and factional clashes between the NSCN(IM) and NSCN(K). But the overall situation in the North-Eastern states has shown signs of improvement. There has been a decline in violence in Tripura, Manipur and Arunachal Pradesh. In Meghalaya, violence has been contained. Mizoram and Sikkim continue to be peaceful."

The report says after a temporary/unilateral suspension of operations against the ULFA, the counter-insurgency operations have been resumed because there was no direct response from it.

In Nagaland, fratricidal clashes between the rival NSCN factions have claimed at least 200 lives during the past five years.

Current Situation in North-East : A Review : March 2007

About 30 organisations described variously as terrorist, militant or insurgent, are active in Assam (presently 'Asom') and other states in North-Eastern India. The South Asia Terrorism Portal (SATP)[19] actually identifies over a hundred 'terrorist/insurgent groups' in the region. Most of them are admittedly little more than names and sign boards with poorly written constitutions, manifestos and charters of demands, engaged essentially in extortion and racketeering. Many of these are nearly moribund/defunct. Others, with a little more substance to them and boasting of 'greater autonomy' agenda are engaged sporadically in violent activities alternating with some kind of negotations with the State/Central governments.

About a dozen of the 30-odd active outfits are engaged in 'armed struggle' against the Union of India. The most prominent of these outfits are the ULFA and the NSCN. While the ULFA seeks to restore the sovereignty of Assam lost as a result of the 24 Feb. 1826 Yandabo Treaty, the NSCN (IM) demands an independent Nagaland, as "the Nagas were never part of India—British or Independent". In fact, the Nagas under ZA Phizo 'declared their independence on 14 August 1947, a day before India's'.

The oldest organisation engaged in 'armed struggle' in Manipur is the UNLF, even if 3-4 other outfits are engaged in similar struggles for restoration of Manipur's lost sovereignty as a result of 'the undemocratic and inequitable' Merger Agreement of 15 Oct. 1949.

But these sovereignty claims by various insurgent outfits on the territories they aspire for themselves are complicated by the district and state boundaries drawn and redrawn by the British India as dictated or demanded by the administrative convenience or constriants. As a result, the history and geography of the territories concerned being what they are, there are inescapably conflicting territorial issues involved in, and indeed integral to, the sovereignty aspirations. "Ironically this interface between sovereignty and territoriality impinges on all the states where these organisations are active, highlighting the fundamental contradictions of these sovereignty struggles.

The ready and an apt instance that comes to mind is the NSCN(IM) demand for Nagalim (= Greater Nagaland), which is the most intractable difficulty blocking the resolution of the long-outstanding Naga problem, as also any further progress in the sustained 7-year long negotiations between the NSCN (IM) and New Delhi. The conceding of this contentious demand will simply mean disintegration of the three Indian states—Manipur, Arunachal Pradesh and Assam—and the latter will just not hear of it. Nor is the Centre in a position to force it on them. The constituent states of India guard their constitutional and jurisdictional rights rather jealously. A remote and an indirect hint of New Delhi giving in on Nagalim demand some years back created a conflagration all over Manipur.

Can the leaders demanding sovereignty ever hope to succeed, considering their adversary is the Indian state? Sophisticated and well informed as these leaders are about history, the answer must be clear to them. India is too big and too powerful to be defeated in war, or allow foreign occupation. Their aim in continuing with these meandering negotiations is rather simple: To get maximum out of India for their 'dream lands'. They know India would not bend beyond a point. Negotiations in any case is their best bit—for the age-ing leadership in some cases. Even then, they want to continue nurturing the hope however slender the thread.

All human beings have a right to dream. The modest and continuing gains made by the Catalonian autonomy movement and rather more dramatic success by Montenegro, which in the May 2006 national referuendum voted narrowly for secession hold promises for separatist movements in the region. Neither the example of Kosovo is lost on them. But it is equally clear to them that India is neither the (now defunct) Soviet Union nor Yogoslavia. You cannot fault them for unrealisable dreams!

A mention must be made here of a new demand in Manipur : the current campaign for a plebiscite on the issue of Manipur's independence, proposed initially by the UNLF and since then taken by several 'civil society' groups. Some analysts have noted that it "followed closely, indeed almost coterminously, in the wake of referendum in Montenegro." Interestingly but surprisingly, if not omenously, it drew an assortment of eminent speakers for its 6 June 2006 meeting in Imphal. Some of them should have displayed more discretion than attending this meeting on plebiscite, opined a scholar. Some of those who addressed this meeting were the titular king of Manipur, a former Lok Sabha member, a former Human Rights Commissioner, the President of the Manipur Working Journalists' Union, leaders of political parties and several women leaders—always a potent force in Manipur.

Coming to the latter half of the year 2006, a ceasefire arranged through the exertions of a civil society group led by eminent author Indira Goswami collapsed as the ULFA refused to come to the negotiations table for the direct talks with the Centre. Subsequently, it resorted to doing what it is justly infamous for : killing innocent civilians, mainly non-Assamese Hindi-speaking Biharis. By way of reaction, the Government mouthed the usual, inane shiboleths—"culprits will be brought to book", "it shows the frustration of ULFA", "all necessary measures will be adopted to prevent the recurrence of such ghastly act", *et. al.,* which are best forgotten till the next outrage.

So after that brief lull of cease-fire period, Assam was in turmoil once again by Jan. 2007. An analyst put it rather bluntly on 19 Jan. 2007: "The killing of innocent civilians by rampaging insurgents, as a malleable' Centre desperately calls for a truce to rescue the forthcoming National Games (in Guwahati) from the scourge of terror, and reluctant to act tough on the illegal migrants, goes on to prove that the North-Eastern theatre is on the verge of ignition."[20]

The NSCN(I-M) held its latest round of talks with the Government of India at New Delhi in March 2007, which "made some progress", as Muivah put it.

Notes

1. *Times of India,* 26-1-1994.
2. Ramchandra Guha is the author of the book *Savaging the Civilised; Verrier Elwin—His Tribals and India,* OUP, March 1999.
3. These observations seems to be particularly applicable to the AASU agitation (1979-1985) in Assam.
4. Collated from the *Frontline* of 11-2-1994; *Times of India,* 1-1-1997; *Sunday Observer,* 19-1-1997; *Outlook,* 1-2-1999; and *Hindu* of 23-8-1999 and 25-11-2000.
5. Indo-Burma Revolutionary Front (IBRF) is a conglomerate of multiplicity of insurgent outfits in India's North-East and Burma's Eastern regions.
6. *The Indian Express,* 26-9-1999.
7. The details in 1-18 serials are from the *Hindustan Times,* 10 and 21 August 1999, and *Frontline* of 10-9-1999.
8. *The Hindu,* 25-11-2000.
9. This heading is inspired by a story penned by that indefatigable journalist (now a Minister at the Centre), Arun Shourie in the early 1980s on the politicians and their corrupt ways, on the front page of the *Indian Express,* under the heading "Politics as Commerce".
10. Here is the list of major accords signed in the Region: (1) 16-Point Agreement with the Naga People's Convention in 1960, (2) Naga Accord, Shillong, 1975, (3) Assam Accord, 1985, (4) Mizo Accord, 1986, (5) TNV Accord, Tripura, 1988, (6) Bodo Accord, 1993. Half a dozen minor accords signed within the Regional States are not enumerated here. Also not included is the first written understanding Sir Akbar Hydari had with the Nagas in 1948.
11. After Phizo's daughter, Adino, who leads this faction.
12. It is led by Khodao (K) Yanthan.
13. From the *Outlook Weekly,* 1-2-1999 and some dailies.
14. *The Hindu,* 23-11-1999.
15. *The Outlook,* 23-2-1998.
16. JB Lama, *The Statesman*, 26 March 2007.
17. Bappaditya Paul, *The Stateman*, 20 Feb. 2007.
18. Seema Sengupta, *The Pioneer*, 5 Dec. 2006.
19. MS Prabhakar, *The Frontline*, 22 September 2006.
20. Seema Sengupta, *The Pioneer*, 19 January 2007.

2

Foreign Nations are Muddying the Waters

If Russia and the now defunct Soviet Union were playing the great game with the British India before and till 1947 on the latter's North-Western frontiers, China quietly 'devoured' Tibet soon after that year. Post-Indian Independence period saw her neighbours—Pakistan, Burma (part of the erstwhile India), and later Bangladesh—nibbling at India's sovereignty and integrity by training, equipping and offering safe heavens to its insurgent outfits in the North-East.

Foreign Hand in Indian Insurgency

An insurgency movement challenges a nation-state and aims at undermining its sovereignty. When it finds an external (a neighbouring country usually) sponsor or supporter, it tends to become at one level a part of inter-state conflict. It is a form of an indirect aggression against the nation-state by that neighbour, made attractive for it by the inability of the former to use its conventional military power. For the neighbour, this war—popularly called 'low-intensity conflict' (LIC) is a low cost, cheaper option to destabilize, bleed and even defeat the nation-state. This in brief is the theory and reality of a foreign hand aiding and abetting insurgency in another country.

The extent of material and moral support by an external power is one of the important factors for the success of an insurgency. The geography of the North-East consequent to 1947-Partition of India, renders it eminently well-placed for the insurgent groups operating in the area to receive such help and support, sharing as it does its borders with four external powers—Bhutan, China (Tibet), Myanmar and Bangladesh (earlier East Pakistan).

Foreign Hand was always there Ubiquitous

So it should be no surprise that a foreign hand of one shape or the other has always aided and abetted the insurgent movements in the Region (and the country beyond) almost since 1947. If it was China in the North-East during the 1950s through 1970s, it was Pakistan to start with in Kashmir, later in Punjab, and finally (perhaps, post-1971 tragedy) in the North-East through its 'famous' ISI. Bangladesh and Myanmar too had added fuel to the insurgency fires at one time or the other.

It is no consolation to India if analysts ascribe racial and ethnic reasons for the external involvement. The North-East is inhabited by the Mongoloid tribes who have close ethnic and cultural ties with the tribes in China, Tibet, Burma (and even Bangladesh). Barring Khasis and Jaintias of Meghalaya, almost all hill tribes belong to the Tibeto-Chinese fold and to the Tibeto-Burmese family of languages. It was this affinity, they argue, which led some of the tribal groups to turn towards their own stock, across the border than towards the country they resided in. The strategic location of the North-East and the access of the disaffected groups to China, Burma, Bangladesh and Bhutan together with material and moral support of foreign Intelligence agencies have facilitated insurgency in the Region.

They also cite the historical reasons for the foreign interest in the Region. "Like India, its neighbours like East Pakistan (Bangladesh) and Burma, are bound to have 'permanent interests' in the Region with which all of them have had closer historical links." Assam, once invaded and occupied by Burma before British annexation, was an administrative part of Bengal Province (1826-74), and again of East Bengal and Assam province (1905-12). They might as well add that it was repeatedly attacked by the Muslim rulers of Bengal and Delhi. Again it was under a Muslim League Ministry during April 1937-September 1938 and November 1939-December 1941. The counter view is that these historical reasons for permanent interests are a mere sophistry for their nefarious designs on Assam by the Muslim fundamentalists. It needs to be remembered that Assam figured as an integral constituent of the yet-to-be-born Pakistan in the scheme of things vigorously espoused by the ideologues of the Muslim League. As if by way of wish-fulfilment, the Cabinet Mission Plan placed Assam and Bengal in Group C in 1946. Muslim League was not to be blamed if it had visions of Assam as part of future Pakistan "to act as a Lebensraum for its East Pakistan compatriots" (Assam was saved for India by fierce, stout and unceasing endeavour by her great son and a great Indian, Gopinath Bordoloi with unstinted support and blessings of Mahatma while the rest of the leadership of the great INC—including Nehru and Patel—had acquiesced). Another factor that placed Assam in an inextricable association with East Pakistan/Bangladesh was a continual influx of Bengali immigrants, legal and illegal, that started from Day one of its take-over by the British in 1826 and "continues till date in spite of the bitterness and political storms it has created over the years". Subsequent emergence of Bangladesh and consolidation in that country of a unilingual and virtually unireligious nationality which had historically been in an adversarial relations with the Assamese-speaking people, have only sharpened the anxieties and expectations arising out of these facts, on the respective side of the border.

That the Intelligence agencies of the countries of the Sub-continent, given the background mentioned above, would be active in the Region in a manner and with an intent going far beyond the legitimate intelligence gathering, was hardly unexpected. Specifically in the North-East, where several insurgencies have been active for over half a century, Pakistan has always been fanatically active, keeping track of them and extending full help. On the eve of emergence of Bangladesh, East Pakistan figured prominently as a sanctuary for both Naga and Mizo insurgent; their leaders were sheltered in East Pakistan and travelled to third countries on Pak Passports. The insurgents' camps located there came to light after creation of Bangladesh.

India Better Watch Out: Conspiracies Galore

Certain interests were already at work even before 1947. Some British officers, including the then Governor of Assam, were planning creation of a 'Crown Colony', comprising hills areas of both India's North-East and Burma's West and North-West which in due course would be an independence state—popularly called Coupland Plan.[1] Macdonald, Political Officer, Lushai Hills, mooted another scheme for carving out an autonomous state comprising of Lushai Hills and parts of Chin Hills of Burma, as a British protectorate, since "the tribes were not Indian—neither in origin, nor in language, nor in habits, nor in looks...and it would be unfair to allow this great body of non-Indian Animists and Christians to be drawn into the struggle between the Hindus and Muslims". The conspiracies have not ceased since!

India be better beware of the games the West want to play with and in its North-East. As early as 1966, the Agenda International de Prensa (International Press Service—IPS) circulated reports datelined Dhaka that there were efforts to create a united and independent Bengal, comprising East Pakistan, West Bengal, Assam, Nagaland, Manipur, Tripura, *Sikkim* and Bhutan.[2] An excerpt from the IPS Report: "The separatists are counting on USA and other western powers to give them necessary assistance. They are confident that these powers would be interested...in such an independent state in South-East Asia...which could provide shield against the Chinese aggression."[3] And there is more of the same designs!

The US International Communications Agency's June 1979 circular, entitled "Project Brahmaputra" is equally significant, perhaps sinister in its intent. Sent to all its branches in Delhi and Calcutta, it disclosed that the Special Research Cell of George Washington University, with the approval of the State Department, had detailed several teams of investigators to conduct research in the North-Eastern States, Sikkim and Bhutan. And pray, what was the purpose of research? "To throw light on the public opinion in the region to establish in what measure the present status of these states remain acceptable or whether there are indications that the formation of a 'New State' is a current problem."[4]

The above is somewhat elaborate picture of India's North-East and her neighbours' envy! It shows up the permanent interests of these neighbours! What follows is brief, very brief description of individual neighbour's perfidy to muddy India's North-Eastern waters. Briefly because it is recent, even current, history and facts are too well-known for detailing.

PAKISTANI SHENANIGANS

Pak abetment of the insurgency in the North-East has been blatantly direct. When Army was called out in 1956 to fight the Naga insurgency, Phizo crossed over to East Pakistan and was welcomed with open arms. After a 3-year stay in Dhaka, he was flown to Britain under a Peruvian passport (and he died there in exile on 30 April 1990). While in Dhaka and London, he was given all help to procure arms and raise the Naga issue at various international fora.

Between 1962-68, at least 10 underground Naga gangs, totalling over 2500[5], crossed over to East Pakistan and were trained in camps located at Rangamati, Ruma, Bandarban, Rangkhiang Ali Kadam[6], all close to Indian border in Chittagong Hill Tract. They returned with arms (including LMGs, RL, Carbines, and 2" mortars) and ammunition. The attempt to send any more batches for similar training did not seem to have succeeded. Mowu Angami-led band to East Pakistan was intercepted by Burmese Army.[7]

To show their solidarity with Pakistan, during the 1965 Indo-Pak war, the Naga leadership issued a statement calling upon Government of India "to take immediate steps to disengage the services of any Naga...".

The Pakistani help to Mizo rebels was even more crucial. Apart from the advantage of having a long, nearly unguarded border with East Pakistan/ Bangladesh that offered a choice of several infiltration routes, the Mizo rebels had an ideally-located sanctuary, just across the border, in the Chittagong Hill Tract (CHT). Laldenga, the Mizo leader, seemed to have done his homework rather well. He crossed the border in first week of December 1963 and was eagerly received by the Pak agencies. Quantities of Pak arms and ammunition were dispatched from Chittagong via the Dohazari Railhead to the CHT, whence the rebels moved them to safe places within Mizoram by January 1965. The Mizo uprising started on the night 28 February/1 March 1966 and the rebels made effective use of the Pak 'gifts'. Assam and India were taken by surprise and the Indian Army took more than a month to retrieve the situation.

After the Army crackdown, Mizo underground shifted their operational base to the safety of jungles in Burma and CHT. Interestingly, Laldenga's liaison officer on behalf of Pak Army in the late 1960s was a certain Capt Ershad, later General and Bangladesh President. At its peak, the MNA had over 7000 men and women under arms, majority ensconced in East Pakistan. Well supplied with weapons and victuals, they virtually had a free run of the land.

China and Indian Insurgents

Chinese entered the field late, but ever the pragmatic, their help to the rebels was comprehensive and they did not help the Nagas only; they took the Mizo and Meitei rebels also under their wings. For Nagas, the support from China, the inspiration for the revolutionary groups in many parts of the world in 1960s, would bring international spotlight on the Naga 'freedom fight' and consequently boost the morale of both the leaders and the led. The Chinese help was also a necessity "because, of late, Indo-Pak border had come under an increased surveillance". But China had its own calculations: A level of support to the Naga and other rebel outfits would keep some Indian Army formations engaged in CI operations which would cause some attrition in the process—greater, the better for the Chinese Army.

The Nagas started getting the active Chinese support from 1966 only. The guerrilla and subversive warfare training for their cadres was arranged in the Yunnan Province of mainland China, and later in Lhasa in Tibet.[8] Muivah, who had led the first batch in November 1966, had stayed back and was taken to Beijing and later to Hanoi to take some lessons on ideology as also in the art of guerrilla tactics against the modern weapons[9] (His batch had taken 3 months' arduous journey through jungles of Arunachal and Burma to reach Yunnan).

The Mizos and Meiteis also received some help and training from the Chinese. Three Mizo groups were sent to China during the May 1975-early 1976 period. Laldenga also visited Beijing and met Chou Enlai. The Meitei insurgents under Bisheswar took an unconventional route via Nepal to make it to Lhasa. The Meiteis were ideologically Left-oriented and were the first to bring with them the techniques of Urban Guerrilla warfare, aimed at engaging Indian troops in built-up areas in Imphal.[10]

In mid-1969, China and Pakistan evolved a joint strategy to train various rebel groups operating in India's North-East and to coordinate their activities to improve their functional and operational efficiency. A Guerrilla Training School was set up in East Pakistan with the Chinese instructors to train the Naga, Mizo, Meitei and Kuki cadres. A small air strip was also built at a place 15 Km off Rangamati.[11]

From the late 1970s, the Chinese support to the North-East Insurgents declined mainly because the cadres could be adequately indoctrinated within their respected areas by their own instructors and the realisation and emphasis on desirability and principle of sustaining a revolutionary movement with internal resources and mobilization at local level. A contributory factor for this decline in external support could be the Chinese concern at the large scale surrenders by the Nagas in the 1970s. Consequent to the Governor's call during his address to the Budget session of the Nagaland Assembly, 1049 Naga cadres surrendered in 1969 alone.

Bangladesh and North-Eastern Insurgents

When Bangladesh emerged from its travails of West Pakistani oppression and became a free nation in December 1971, with some help from India, it was expected all help extended to the North-East insurgents by the erstwhile East Pakistan would dry up and it indeed did for a time. The things started returning to the old ways after the assassination of Sheikh Mujib-ur-Rahman on 15 August 1975. The Mizo rebels regained some of the lost ground in CHT, not as an associate of Chakma militants but as collaborators of the local authorities, helping them in settling Bengali Muslims in CHT (at the cost of the interests of the indigenous Chakmas who had fled to India) and ensuring their own (Mizo rebel's) safe refuge in return[12] (The Mizos helping the enemies of the Chakmas is quite natural and logical, after all the latter were an unwelcome presence in Mizoram, and thorn in the flesh of excessively chauvinistic Mizo sections in Mizoram).

Besides the Nagas and Mizos, the cadre of Tripura Volunteer Force (TVF) also found patronage in Bangladesh. But the Bangladeshi help to Tripura insurgents was partially a *quid pro quo* to the support India was extending to the Shanti Bahini, a Chakma rebel outfit fighting the Bangladesh Government in CHT. Ashok Tandon, DG, BSF, in his annual press conference on 21 November 1997 asserted that both the ATTF and NLFT continued to get support from Bangladesh. Indian protests failed to persuade Bangladesh to close down rebel camps in its territory.[13] A 10-page Press Note released on the Raising Day of the BSF in November 1995 had details on the involvement of Bangladesh Government with the North-East rebel groups and help extended by it to them. It disclosed that most insurgent groups were obtaining sophisticated weapons from Thailand with the active connivance of Bangladesh Intelligence. It also talked of the nexus between Pakistan's ISI and Bangladesh Intelligence agencies. India's Home Minister at the time, Indrajit Gupta, disclosed as much in his reply to a starred question in Lok Sabha on 3 December 1996[14] (By this time, Sheikh Hasina had become the Prime Minister of Bangladesh).

The links of Manipur rebels with East Pakistan/Bangladesh go back to decades. The training camps of Manipuri insurgents were reportedly located in the Srimangal, Bhanugach and Dhamai areas in Bangladesh close to the border.[15]

Can Fencing be the Answer?

Foreign Secretary (FS) level talks held in June 2005 at New Delhi failed to bridge the gap between India and Bangladesh on the fencing issue. Bangla FS Mohammad Hemayetuddin reiterated his country's opposition to the border fencing that India is erecting as an anti-infiltration measure. India holds the fencing does not violate the 1975 border guidelines, with which Bangladesh disagrees. The two sides agreed to simultaneous patrolling of the border including the riverine stretches, by the BDR and BSF. The Bangla delegation provided details of recent operations against the Indian insurgents and criminal groups but the Indian FS Shyam Saran urged them to share the details of those killed and apprehended.

Bangladesh proposed three new bus routes: Dhaka-Siliguri, Dhaka-Guwahati, and Dhaka-Shillong *(AA, Hindu, Tribune,* all of 23-6-05).

Bangla FS said ULFA leader Anup Chetia, though he had served his term in jail, could not be sent to India as he had one more court case against him. The Bangla FS denied the existence of the Indian insurgents' camps in his country and assured the Indians that they would not allow any anti-Indian activities on their soil.

The work on fencing, and the road along it, has not been as per schedule, mainly because of poor funds situation. The target for completing the fencing along the Assam-Bangla border was fixed for 2003 but has been extended to 2006. Again, only 578 Km of fencing along the Tripura border was completed by 1996 against the target of 896 Km (*TOI*, 19-12-96).

Assam-Bangladesh Border Fensing : Status Dec. 2006

It is indeed a story of "another year, another target", as the Indian Express of 1 Jan. 2007 put it. Nothing illustrates this truism better than the mid-Dec. 2006 statement by Minister for Assam Accord Implementation Bhumidhar Barman in Assam Assembly : "on 31 March, 2007 a barbed wire fence will finally mark the Assam stretch of the Indo-Bangladesh border. It is the last and final target date for completion of this long-pending project." It is for record that at one stage, the fencing (and the accompanying road) was targeted to be completed by 2003, which, subsequently, through several changed target dates, was shifted to 2006. Now, as per the Minister, 31 March, 2007 is the "last and final target date."

But as of now, as Barman himself said, 17.80 per cent of the border length under the Assam Public Works Department remains to be fenced. In real terms; it works out to 43 km of the 263-km border in the state. The Centre however has sanctioned fencing of only 223 km, as the remaining part is across rivers including Brahmaputra. The total length of the Indo-Bangla border is 3,286 km

It may be mentioned in passing here that on 29 July, 2006 the Union Government had told a tripartite meeting (attended by representatives of the AASU, Assam Government and Central Government) that "the gaps (in the border fence) will be filled up by Dec., 2006."

As is well-known, it was AASU which made New Delhi agree to fence the Indo-Bangladesh border and had it included in the 1985 Assam Accord it signed with the latter in that year. The AASU has been sore with New Delhi for the tardy implementation of this urgently-needed project. On the Minister's setting a "last and final target date" of 31 March, 2007, Samujjal Bhattacharyya, Adviser to AASU, said: "We are happy that at least it is nearing completion... It will prevent further influx from Bangladesh, and put an end to the cross-border activities of the ISI and various fundamental Islamic militant groups which have their bases in Bangladesh."

Here is the Adviser's lament on the delay and changing target dates :

> "The saddest part is that the Government never had a time schedule for completion of the fence. Even when the Assam Accord was signed and the Government agreed to fence the border, there was no mention of any target. It was only in the first tripartite talks on the Assam Accord on 5 May, 2005 that the Government fixed a time frame, the target being Jan. 2006. But that was missed. The next tripartite meeting, attended by Home Minister Shivraj Patil, extended the deadline to Dec. 2006, which was reiterated in the next meeting on 29 July, 2006. We do not understand how the Government has now extended this to March (2007)."

One reason for the delay deserves a mention. Initially, the Assam PWD was assigned the task of constructing the border road and border fence. By the time it completed first stretch of 41-km of the job, its pace was found unsatisfactory, and the project was transferred to the NBCC.

The AASU, and for that matter, the AGP, BJP and all those who have been passionately vocal against the influx from Bangladesh, all are unanimous on the "irreparable" damage done by the delay in completion of the border fence. To wit, the state BJP President Ramen Dika: "The demography of Assam has already been changed, and no power on earth can revert it to the pre-Bangladesh times."

Now for the two statistical pieces of information :

- Rs. 198 crore have been spent on constructing the 179.91 km fence and the 263-km border road.
- Rs. 99 crore will be required to complete the remaining work according to government estimates.

Now this leaves only one question on the fencing : How effective will it be when completed to stop the influx of the Bangladeshis into India, especially Assam and West Bengal? To assert that it will make no difference and the infiltration would continue as hithertofore, as some analysts indeed do, would be height of pessimism, or conceding too much to human ingenuity. The more accurate answer will be : The fencing will definitely thwart, if not eliminate, the influx. It may be apt to mention here that the US is fencing its Mexican border as is Pakistan doing its Afghan border.

The Denials Notwithstanding

When the Indian Home Secretary Dhirendra Singh visited Dhaka in September 2004, he gave a fresh list of training camps being operated in Bangladesh by various Indian insurgent outfits: ULFA, NDFB, NLFT, etc. During his meeting with his BDR counterpart in August 2004, the DG BSF had given a list of 195 camps run on the Bangla soil. The September 2004 letter was an essentially updated version of the August list. India also demanded that Dhaka hand over fugitive insurgent leaders like Arbinda Rajkhowa, Paresh Barua, Anup Chetia (all of ULFA), Dev Burman (NLFT). Like the DG, BDR, Bangla Home Secretary also denied the existence of any such camps in his country.

In mid-2004, a 5-part article in a prominent Bangla daily *Prothom Alo* disclosed that the banned Bangladeshi Islamic extremist outfit, Harkat-ul-Jehad-al Islami (HUJI)—declared a terrorist outfit by the US State Department for its links with the Al Qaeda and Taliban—has established an active network through madrasas and local NGOs. The HUJI was also suspected to be "behind the recent attack on Sheikh Hasina at a rally in Dhaka". The article also said it "is imparting training to the insurgents from Myanmar and India" *(Hindu,* 9-3-04).

As an analyst put it (Exp, 3-2-05), "for several years now, India has been conducting a dialogue of the deaf with Dhaka, with bilateral relations deteriorating...". New Delhi has been consistently telling Dhaka to crack down on as many as 1174 terrorist camps housing cadres of not only of Indian insurgent outfits (Like ULFA, NDFB, NLFT, KLO) but also of Al Qaeda, Lashkar-e-Tayyeba (LeT), HUJI, Islamic Oikya Jote (headed by Mufti Fazlul Haq Amini), Jagrata Muslim Janata (JMJ) of Bangla Bhai.

By way of a smart riposte, Dhaka not only sought specific-addresses and telephone numbers of these so-called camps but also offered to ferry senior Indian officials by helicopter to the "alleged" sites to "prove" no camps exist. Unlike the more fixed structures in PoK, these camps are said to comprise hastily constructed bamboo structures that can be removed in minutes. In a constant denial mode, Dhaka has stubbornly refused to accept Indian Intelligence reports on the camps, countering them with the lists of criminals who, fleeing from the local criminal justice system, have sought refuge in West Bengal and Tripura.

After the 1992 Bombay blasts, operations by the extremist Islamic terrorists/jehadists have shifted from the western coast to the eastern regions—with the gun-running, camps, and clandestine anti-India activities concentrated along the CHT, the Siliguri Corridor and Myanmar.

There is enough evidence, if the evidence was required at all about the "cyclical rise of Islamic fundamentalism" since the return of the Khalida Zia's BNP to power in October 2001, followed by the familiar incidents like the mass exodus of Hindus from the villages and countryside; violence against the opposition leaders and minorities; and spate of explosions. All this should not come as a surprise as an extremist Muslim outfit is a partner in the Coalition Ministry as also Khalida's repeated anointment of India's North-Eastern insurgent groups as freedom fighters!

As for targeting the opposition, "there were over 100 blasts at political rallies with more than 200 casualties, the most recent being the killing of SAMS Kibria, a former diplomat and finance minister.... Blast within high security zone in Dhaka days before the (aborted) SAARC Summit further raised New Delhi's concerns" *(Exp/Hindu,* 3-2-05). 'Casual' violence aimed at political workers "has claimed over 1100 lives in the past three years (2002-04)." An analyst says "the present dispensation in Bangladesh is using Islamic militants to target their political opposition. On balance, it is absolutely clear the Government is involved." For the Indian Officials the 'Commando-style attack' on Hasina in August 2004 and the 'murder' of Kibria showed how "systematically the democratic, secular fabric of the country" is being eroded.

Inter alia the above para, the Intelligence reported July 2005 that "the ruling coalition in Dhaka has outsourced" the job of tackling its political rivals to the Indian insurgents it continues to shelter, all the loud disclaimers notwithstanding" (*TOI*, 5-7-05). Investigations into the recent attacks on Awami League (AL) leaders as also the 'huge arms haul' in April 2004 confirmed the suspicions of an unholy nexus between the ULFA and ATTF insurgents and the ruling coalition in Dhaka which includes the fundamentalist Jamat-i-Islami and has often been accused of intolerance of political rivals. This collusion got confirmed when the investigations disclosed that some of the grenades used in attacks on the AL leaders were supplied by the Indian rebels (Bangladesh's *Daily Star,* 29-5-05). Concerned about the fall-out of the disclosure on its ties with India and on its global image, in view of the post-9/11 heightened international anti-terrorism sensibilities, Dhaka ordered immediate suspension of the investigations. To deflect attention from its discomfiture and the real issue, the Zia Government resorted to the familiar ploy the governments the world over placed in such embarrassing, compromising situations often do: Launched propaganda blitz accusing the Awami League and the ubiquitous 'foreign agents' (read Indians) of engineering these attacks!

As for the denial of the Indian rebels' camps on Bangla soil, here is what ABM Mohiuddin Chowdhury, a senior AL leader and Mayor of the port city of Chittagong said at a press conference (10-4-04) at his office: "The Indian secessionists are running 50 to 60 training camps in the CHT and the huge cache of weapons seized on the night 1/2 April were meant to arm these rebels under a sinister conspiracy to create unrest in India and to destabilise the sub-Continent.

How come the Huge Arms Haul?

"The fire power involved may be enough to keep an army brigade in fighting fettle for a year." Another analyst thought "the largest ever illegal arms shipment in South Asia was enough to equip a division". They both were talking about the massive arms haul made in Chittagong on 2 April 2004. Its sheer size was mind-boggling.

AK-47s	1290	Rocket launchers	150
Rounds	1.1 m	Grenade launchers	2,000
Grenades (T-82/2)	25,020	Night vision devices (goggle sets)	3,550
Rockets	840		

The fact of Bangladesh coast emerging as a major avenue for arms smuggling is known, but the nature and size of this arms seizure has sent the *Intelligence* officials reeling: "We have never seen any thing remotely like this big before!" No one single insurgent group in the Region—not ULFA, not Nepal Maoists—could afford to pay for this shipment by themselves. The cache was obviously planned to be parceled out to different groups. The fact that this kind and level of coordination is being planned is itself worrisome. A radio intercept suggests a part of the consignment was for the ATTF, but then, who were the other recipients? The trucks hired to carry the cargo were due to go to Sylhet and Maulvi Bazar, bordering Meghalaya.

Even more worrying is the fact that the discovery was serendipitous. A policeman spots two trawlers pulling in at a jetty. Large crates are unloaded on to 10 trucks. Most superiors ignore his urgent calls but one inspector arrives with a large force at 4 AM (2-4-04). The consignment is seized but no arrests are made. Months after the seizure, no one knows who sent the arms, or for whom. Indian officials were rightly indignant: "These weapons were meant to be used in our country and we have a right to know who were involved. Until that happens, there will be little contact between us." In specific terms, the Prime Minister's (whosoever he or she may be post-April 2004 poll) visit for SARC Summit and others by the officials/ministers were no-no. But in the following months, Manmohan Singh did not go as the SAARC Meet was cancelled, but the rest did make the trips, viz the Home

Secretary in September 2004 and Union Ministers Kamal Nath (August 2005) and P.R. Dasmunshi (September 2005), even when the Indians are in the dark as to what all information Dhaka has provided to New Delhi. Going by the past record, the picture could not be too rosy. After all, India still docs not know what happened after the Bogra arms seizure in June 2003 when the Bangla police arrested Jogesh Dev Burman of the Tripura Cooperative Association, a front for the ATTF, along with 200 Kg of explosives and 1,00,000 bullets.

It is necessary to record that the Indian officials had been concerned at the possible involvement of leaders of the ruling BNP in the arms haul case. The Intelligence was then speculating about the involvement of some ships owned by BNP leader Salahuddin Qader Chowdhury's QC Shipping Lines which were in Chittagong port at the time. "We know the two trawlers received the weapons from a ship in anchorage." As the long arm of the ISI stood proven, knowing the past cases, the sleuths were worried that a part of the haul could be for the distant Kashmir-based terrorists (Siddharth Varadarajan, *TOI*, 10 and 12 April 2004). Here is what Chittagong Mayor Chowdhury says on the arms haul: "These arms were shipped from USA and Pakistan in sinister conspiracy to destabilise India by arming her rebels." A letter written in Urdu from Batsebawui in Pakistan was seized from near the weapons consignment, raising speculations about Pak connection with the incident.

New Islamic Outfit

India expressed concern over the emergence of an Islamic outfit, Jagrata Muslim Janata (JMG), led by one 'Bangla Bhai' in the country's northern region adjoining West Bengal. While secular politicians are blaming Khalida Government for its links with what they dub as "Bangladeshi Taliban", the press carries reports on the "unlawful activities" of Bangla Bhai, a trained middle-aged fanatic whose private army, JBJ, described as the "vigilante force to annihilate left extremists", has established its own administration in the Rajshahi region. Christina Rocca, US Assistant Secretary of State for South Asia, had expressed her concern at Bangla Bhai's activities "during her recent visit" *(Hindu,* 31-5-04).

Bangla Bhai, selfstyled 'commander' of the JBJ having thousands of volunteers, many of whom are the activists of the ruling alliance is operating with the alleged blessing of a powerful lobby in the Government. Despite an 'order of arrest' from the Prime Minister, Bangla Bhai "is still at large" and non-challantly commanding his 'army'.

Dhaka Acts, Finally

The BDR detained 18 suspected Indian militants near Habibganj town of Bangladesh on 4 October 2004, all newly recruited cadres of ATTF from

Tripura. The Bangla officials arranged wide circulation of the news, to extract political mileage from the first crackdown on the Indian insurgents, so long demanded by New Delhi. Some analysts see it as a cosmetic exercise to win Brownie points with India, and the world beyond *(Hindu,* 13-10-04).

"Tiny Packs Sniff of Big Terror Plan"

The *Indian Express,* (Sakkyasen Mittra), 22-6-03, carries a sensational news story under this headline. The Bangla Security forces seized 225 gm of "semi-processed explosive grade" Russian made Uranium. As this is not the first time that such a seizure has been made, and the seized material is Uranium, has put the West Bengal *Intelligence* agencies on alert. The explosive is packed in 225 gm protective packets complete with a user's manual, and has so far been seized from a particular zone along the Indo-Bangla border. If the recent catch was made in Puia in Bangladesh's Nowgaon district on 30 May 2003, it was identical to the one seized earlier in Balurghat in West Bengal's North Dinajpur district in August 2002. And Puia is 35 Km from Balurghat.

That the Uranium could be misused is clear from the 23 page manual accompanying each packet that provides details of how to extract its reactive quality to make explosives and charge them with nuclear tips. The officials are baffled as to how the Russian-made uranium made its way into India. But they are certain that the mineral is not from mines in Jaduguda in Jharkhand. The packets are marked from Kazakhstan and dated 1988. Earlier the agencies thought the uranium was being sent to Kashmir through Bangladesh. Now the Officials feel it is going to the rebel groups having bases in Bangladesh.

Bangladesh arrested two couriers of terror outfit Shahadad-ul-Hikma who allegedly confessed that the packets were coming out of India. Security Officials aver that the repeated arrest of ultras and hauls of incendiaries and arms have established that West Bengal is being used as a conduit by the subversives backed by the hostile operatives. They even claim to have discovered Pak plans to shift their focus from heavily guarded western frontier to the near-porous eastern and north-eastern borders.

ULFA's Foreign Hands Extend into Bangladesh

The ULFA first made contacts with the KIA and Naga rebels in 1986. By end-1988, it had established contact with Pakistan ISI operatives in Bangladesh. Going beyond, it established liaison with the Afghan Mujahideen in Pakistan. In March 1994, Assam Assembly was informed that ULFA cadres had been trained by the ISI of Pakistan, many of them in Afghanistan. ULFA had also established contact with Bangladesh FIU (Field Intelligence Unit) in Dhaka, and was allowed to establish bases in Bangladesh.

Top ULFA leadership was located in Bangladesh till the mid-1990s. They had training camps in Mymensingh district at Bhemugach, Nilfarmani and Dhamai, all located in Maulvi Bazar area.[16] The Sheikh Hasina Government came to power in 1996 and decided to freeze all help to the outfit. Subsequent to the crackdown, ULFA shifted its operational headquarter and bases to the jungles of South Bhutan, close to India's borders, and some camps in Assam's Manas Reserve Forest.[17] The situation could change adversely for India if an unfriendly and fundamentalist regime comes to power in Bangladesh, as many of opposition leaders including Begum Zia, have called the North-East insurgents as "freedom fighters".[18]

Situation did improve when Hasina took over in 1996. But in spite of her assurances, the Intelligence confirmed that there were 35 camps in 1998 of different outfits, operating in the North-East Bangladesh close to Meghalaya border. Later, she did initiate action against them.

Hopefully, there seemed some change in the hardline stance of Khalida Zia Government. At the February 2002 conference of their Foreign Secretaries, Bangladesh assured India of its commitment not to allow its territory to be used for any activity detrimental to India's interest *(Times of India,* 20-2-2002). "Whether the undertaking would be honoured is yet to be seen, as Indo-Bangladesh relations are subject to extreme fluctuations caused by the domestic situation, with the Islamic extremists often queering the pitch."

The porous nature of 4096 Km Indo-Bangladesh border makes things difficult for India, as the ultras can move across it without any serious difficulty. The situation gets aggravated along the riverine stretches of the border. Unless Bangladesh cooperates by stopping this cross-border traffic and closing the camps inside its territory, India's task of fighting insurgency in the neighbouring areas would become even more difficult.

The Narco-Arms Cartel

It is axiomatic that the most virulent form of insurgency is sustained with the weapons obtained from individual foreign countries. Over the years, the international cartels took over the role of major suppliers of the contraband; they perfected the art of gun-running and the lucrative narco-arms trade.

The LTTE over the years has come to occupy a leading position in the field because of its expertise in high-seas operations. Expectedly, the ISI joined hands with it to ferry arms into the North-East. The LTTE helps in transporting them upto the Cox Bazar and CHT ports from the sources in Golden Triangle. From there the ISI and Bangladesh agencies take over for their overland journey to the North-East. Interestingly, the arms-running through the sea off the Andamans, which had been reduced to a trickle by 1995-96, increased manifold since the late 1997. The US Intelligence Reports on the LTTE say that sea route from the Golden Triangle to Burma is a key conduit for arms and narcotics. "Almost 80 per cent of heroin in the world is channelised through this route", which is corroborated by the widespread drug addiction in large parts of North-East, especially in Mizoram. Most of the sophisticated weapons with the insurgent groups in the Region can be traced to the Far East market. The narco-arms dealers obviously have a free run of and an easy access to this arms bazar. That most of the arms consignments take this route and can be intercepted in the high seas off the Andamans was shown by the successful Tri-Service "Operation Leech"[19] in February 1998. The SF killed 6 gun runners, arrested 73, and seized a huge consignment of arms including 140 AK series rifles. The end-users of this particular consignment were NSCN(I-M) and ATTF in India's North-East and Chin National Army in Burma.

The Government of India were reticent for whatever reasons about the ISI activities in the North-East. But Dimapur-based Corps Commander had reportedly written to Army Headquarter in 1996 about the militants getting arms from the groups like Khmer Rouge.[20] His counterpart at Tezpur, heading the Unified Command in Assam, confirmed the elementary truth about the ISI, to the Press in October[21] 1997. By early 1990s, the LTTE had established links with the NSCN and ULFA, and in the recent years, perhaps by mid-1990s, the ISI had spread its tentacles in some North-Eastern outfits which came to light in case of BdSF during the Indo-Pak conflict in Kargil sector and of ULFA with the arrest of four ISI operatives on 8 August 1999.

The ISI, assert Indian Intelligence, is targeting the entire border belt from Kashmir through Nepal to Tripura. Having played havoc with India's national fibre in Kashmir, it is now hyper-active in the North-East. Besides arming the ultras for acts of sabotage and violence, the ISI is playing deep game of ensuring large scale bloodshed in the name of "ethnic cleansing", with the ISI pumping in arms and explosives for the insurgents on the one hand and the targeted non-tribals arming themselves for retaliation, on the other. Their prognosis came true in November-December 1999 when the ULFA ultras targeted the Bihari people in Assam.[22] "This should worry the nation" because the Intelligence circles foresaw "a hundred Nellie-type massacres". What should cause greater concern "is that even diplomatic bags are being used to ferry India bound RDX via Kathmandu while consignment of illicit arms have reached North-East through Bangladesh and Burma", as per the 1997-98 press reports.[23]

The Bodos and ULFA of Assam art not alone in letting the ISI in. The ultras in Nagaland, Manipur and Tripura too have discarded the abhorrence for the outsiders. The help from China and Burma till 1970s was welcome on the grounds of ideology and of ethnic affinity across the borders. Today, idealism is out as the golden triangle of cash-crime-corruption is in "in tune with the macho image of an insurgent". If foreign travels and luxurious, extravagant lifestyles are hall-mark of the leadership, the gypsies, girls, drugs, and a non-challantly strung AK-47 add upto a glamorous insurgent.

That ISI is planning subversion and mayhem is obvious from the interrogation of their four operatives arrested on 8 August 1999: Cause dismemberment of India's North-East through bloodshed incited by incendiary riots, communal and ethnic. Part of explosives, subsequently, were meant for blasting crucial Leh-Manali Highway, only alternative to the much-threatened Leh-Srinagar Highway, life line of troops fighting Pak aggression in Kargil. Imagine the explosives being shipped from Assam across the vast sub-continent for use in Leh.[24] Some confidence, this! The reach of the ISI is truly amazing. If Oari Salim is from Muzaffarnagar, UP, Mallick is from Kupwara, Kashmir. These operatives had flown from Islamabad to Dhaka and thence crossed into Assam through the porous border. Consequent to their interrogation, 31 Harkat activists were arrested from Assam. Though these are first arrests of actual ISI operatives in the North-East, the Agency has been involved in the area for at least a decade, when it established contact with ULFA and helped it to secure bases in Bangladesh.

It was long suspected that besides the ISI, Bangladesh Intelligence was also active in the North-East. On 31 December 1996, Home Minister Inderjit Gupta named the Directorate General of Field Intelligence of Bangladesh in this connection. On 16 December 1996,[25] Foreign Minister Gujral announced: "Bangladesh Prime Minister Sheikh Hasina has acknowledged the existence of the insurgent camps on her soil...and promised to throw them out."[26] It is obvious the Indian insurgents had the run of the country during her predecessor Khalida Zia's regime. In her second coming, things have only worsened, with the Time of USA reporting (October 2002) that Dhaka is den of anti-India extremists. The involvement of Bangladesh with the insurgents in the Region was detailed in a 10-page Press Note issued by the BSF on its raising day in November 1995:

> "Most insurgent outfits in the North-East (ULFA, NSCN, PLA, etc.) were getting weapons from Thailand with active connivance of its Intelligence agencies.... They were coordinating with ISI to ferry arms from Bangladeshi soil into North-East, bringing Kashmiri youth into the country to motivate its citizens to join Jihad in the Valley. Bangladesh is not doing enough to stop the exodus of its national into Assam. Are they trying to solve their population explosion on the cheap?... There are already 8-10 million Bangladeshis living illegally in India."[27]

Having studied the problem and alarmed by its dimensions—an annual influx of 300,000 as per Intelligence—"Gen Sinha, Governor of Assam submitted a report on the "Illegal migration into Assam" to the President in November 1998, suggesting among other measures, annulment of the IMDT Act.

One of the operatives arrested on 8 August 1999, Hussain, disclosed "that over 300 ULFA ultras had received training in Pakistan over the past few years. In addition, the ISI also trained over 100 youth recruited from Assam by the Harkat-ul-Mujahideen, Lashkar-e-Toiba, and Harkat-ul-Jehad".[28]

It is widely believed that a lot of the ISI subversive activities are funded by drug money. It is also given that the "Pakistani Drug Syndicate runs a parallel economy in Cahoots with political and military establishment to destabilize India. The Pak heroin industry, says a UN Report, in terms of turnover is estimated at Rs. 74 billion, i.e., 5 per cent of its GDP of 1992-93, which is 20-25 per cent of the total estimated shadow economy. Pakistan reportedly earned $ 1.5 billion from the heroin export in 1992 (For detailed account of drug economy, *See* Inam-ul-Haq's *From Hash to Heroin*, Lahore, 1991).

BHUTAN : A HELPLESS NEIGHBOUR?

The Hindu of 23-12-2000 published an evocative photo illustrative of changed times. It showed the Army men on bicycles patrolling the fields along the Indo-Bhutan borders in the Nalabari district of Assam, "where vigil has been stepped up and night curfew imposed". It is a sea change for an international, so-far-off border.

Whenever under pressure, the militants in India, Myanmar and Bangladesh simply crossed over to the jungle sanctuaries of South Bhutan. The first influx came when the Indian Army launched Operation Rhino early 1990 against Assam ultras. By early 1992, there were as many as 21 camps between Kalikhola and Daifam. There was spurt again when ULFA terrorists in Bangladesh came under pressure in 1996-97 following Sheikh Hasina's ascension to power. In spite of repeated requests Bhutan seemed reluctant to proceed against ULFA and Bodo terrorist, then numbering around 2000. Bhutanese Home Minister Lympo Thinley Gyamtsho held two rounds of talks with ULFA, on 20 November 1998 and 7 May 1999. In second round, Paresh Barua, ULFA's Army Chief, offered to reduce the camps but expressed his inability to leave Bhutan before another year and half (say, before end 2000). Barua and his Chairman, Arbinda Rajkhowa, invited for third round, simply failed to show up. Similar talks were held by the Minister with Ranjan Daimary of NDFB bur the latter turned down the request to leave, *citing security reason.*

The Bhutanese National Assembly (BNA) did not sanction the Indo-Bhutan joint operations against the rebels at its 78th session in July 2000, and wanted Royal Bhutanese Army (RBA) to do the job itself. The stance hardened when senior rebel leaders Rajkhowa and Daimary ignored invitation for talks in Thimpu. Consequent to July 2000 decision of BNA, RBA raised two additional battalions, and 8,000 troops were deployed by December 2000 in Kalikhola-Daifam area "on the east of which are located the rebel camps. 2,500 ULFA and Bodo rebels were reported to be in Bhutan, with a large arsenal. G.K. Pillai, JS, North-East, revealed that "2,000 soldiers of RBA have already been trained by Indian Army in CI operations. The Campus of the Royal Technical Institute at Demathang was got vacated, and taken over by the RBA. Security posts were located at Bhurkhola and Dholkhola to guard two vital bridges on Sarphang-Gelegphu highway. All supply routes to the rebel camps were blocked. Meanwhile, exerting pressure on the rebels in the manner of Burmese Army, RBA forced ULFA in February 2000 to shift a key camp near Phukapthong towards Tshelingkhar in North-East of Bhutan, near Arunachal border.

The Intelligence reported that ULFA leaders converged at their Central Headquarters in Bhutan on 15-18 February 2000 to plan series of attacks in Assam, to take advantages of "lack of coordination and cooperation" among the constituents of India's Unified Command structure there. But for the killing of Assam's PWD and Forest Minister Nagen Sarma, ULFA failed, it failed to notch any spectacular successes, mainly because of its troubles in Burma and Bhutan. If RBA forced ULFA to close/shift a major camp in Bhutan, joint operations by Dimapur-based 3 Corps and Burmese Army forced the militants to move towards south-west Burma, bordering CHT of Bangladesh.

During the April 2000 visit of Bhutan's Foreign Minister Lympo Jigme Y. Thinley, some Assam officials raised a controversy, saying "the Indian rebels have Bhutan Government's patronage". One source claimed the "king had breakfast with rebel leaders on at least three occasions". A Bhutanese official said at New Delhi on 27 April 2000 that if 700-2000 ultras do not leave the country peacefully as a result of talks underway, RBA will use force to evict them. On his return from New Delhi on 22 April 2000, Chief Minister Mahanta was not diplomatic: "...Government was helping the rebels.... Militants are being imparted training by the ISI in camps located in Burma, Bangladesh and Bhutan".

As a part of mindless violence unleashed by ultras of all hues, the outlawed NDFB killed ten Bhutanese nationals at Laki Bazar area in Barpeta district, close to the Bhutan border, on 21 December 2000.[29] The victims had come down from Namlang, 7 km inside Bhutan, to sell their merchandise in a weekly market. This attack came on the heels of similar attacks on Bhutan national at Kokrajhar, Barpeta and Bongaigaon on 19 and 20 December, in which two people were killed and two Bhutanese vehicles set ablaze.

Realising that militants had no intention of quitting its soil and singed by the heat of these attacks Bhutan signaled its readiness to India not only to act more vigorously against the militants on its soil but also for joint operations to flush them out. There was no immediate formal agreement with Bhutan for joint operations, but India "has formed at an informal level a 'Regional Initiative' with Bangladesh, Burma and Bhutan to check the influx of arms and narcotics and to destroy the insurgent havens in these countries.[30]

Long last, losing all patience with the Indian rebels, who had enjoyed, and even exploited its hospitality on her soil for the long 12 years, the RBA launched its operations on 15-12-03 against the Indian insurgent camps in its territory. Bhutan explained it had held final talks with the ULFA in October and NDFB in November, while the KLO had failed to turn up for the talks. The Bhutanese move was widely hailed. Indicative of its pride and self-confidence, the RBA did not seek any help, logistic or operational, from the Indian Army which as a matter of abundant caution, sealed the border on the Indian side.

The "RBA had gone to war after 138 years, for us", gushed the *Indian Express,* 21-12-03. Bhutan announced 20-12-03: "All militant camps dismantled. The number dead was between 120 and 150." Apparently, the ultras were on the run, helter-skelter. The RBA, personally led by king Jigme Singye Wargchuk and his son, went into action professionally. It handed over to India the first batch of seven captured insurgents. ULFA openly declared of its being surprised. Dealing a serious blow to ULFA, its adviser and think-tank, 70-year old Buragohain injured in the first day of the offensive, died on 18-12-03. Besides the ideologue, other senior leaders killed included Apurba Deka, Satish Hazarika and Ranjit Hazarika. Among those arrested was Bening Rabha, a top leader of the ULFA's military wing and in-charge of the ULFA camps in Bhutan. A Bhutan official said 20-12-03 that "19 of the 30 rebel camps have so for been destroyed". He disclosed that the King was in constant touch with Prime Minister Vajpayee and senior Indian Army officers.

Reeling under the offensive, and Thimpu rejecting their ceasefire appeal, the rebel groups (ULFA, NDFB and KLO) called for a 48-hour strike in Assam and North Bengal, which got little response from the public.

The operation had been launched after much planning and preparations for which it elicited ungrudging admiration of the Indian Government and its military. India viewed it as an example for other neighbours, particularly Bangladesh, where, too 110 camps of insurgents from India's North-East have been operating. Apprehending negative security and diplomatic implications, the Bangla media even blacked out the developments taking place in Bhutan.

It was all over within three weeks.

Three weeks after Bhutan had cadres of the outlawed ULFA, NDFB and KLO on the run from the kingdom, "Myanmar troops have begun targeting North-East insurgent camps in north-west Myanmar, responding to the pressure from New Delhi", said the *Indian Express* of 6-1-04.

There was domestic fall-out also following the RBA action in 2003-04. As ULFA ultras joined Bodo outlaws and carried out a wave of attacks for the second successive day on 3-10-04, killing another 13 in as many attacks, Assam sent an SOS to the Centre: "Get Bangla and Myanmar to do a Bhutan soon." They wanted India to lean on its two neighbours to act against Indian rebels, as Bhutan did.

Bhutan again Assures Assam : Dec. 2006

"It goes without saying that we will not allow any insurgent groups to set up camps inside Bhutan''.This is Mr. Dago Trering Wangda, Joint Secretary (Home), Royal Bhutanese Government speaking to the media after leading a delegation of Bhutanese officials to talks with the Assam Government. After assuring Guwahati that Bhutan will not allow the ULFA insurgents to smuggle themselves into its territory, it made it clear that there should be effective patrolling on the Indian side by the security forces in Assam and Arunachal Pradesh.

He said the presence of ULFA and other groups in eastern Bhutan between the 1991-2003 period had devastated the Region's economy because during the Dec. 2003 anti-terrorism operations by the Royal Bhutanese Army, the Bhutan-Assam border was closed due to security concerns. That led to a sharp escalation in the cost of goods since they had to be transported long distance to the main entry point in West Bengal.

But he said the captured ULFA leaders had been handed over to the Indian security forces. ULFA insists a number of their leaders disappeared after being held and has been demanding that New Delhi and Thimpu clarify their status. Wangda's statement puts the onus on India.

MYANMAR (BURMA)

India shares 1670 km land and 200 km maritime borders with Burma. People on either side share ethnic affiliations, and some are fighting their respective Governments. Going back in history, insurgent groups like the Naga, Mizo and Meitei, had bases in Burma at some point in time. Mid-1996, the NNC established contact with the KIA (Kachin Independence Army) in Kachin Hills, and Indian groups found sanctuary in the lightly administered border areas of Burma.[31]

Some Burmese tribals of Kuki Chin group have been fighting for the merger of their land with India.[32] Some other Burmese insurgents outfits are Arakan Liberation Party (ALP), Burmese Communist Party (BCP), etc. The underground Zoomi Liberation Front (ZLF) in Burma used to recruit its cadres for guerrilla war there. When the Military Junta cracked down on the Project-democracy supporters, many of these rebels took shelter in Manipur and Mizoram. To show its unhappiness, they started giving support to India's PLA. Moreover, it is easy for the outfits (like ULFA, NSCN, KIA, BCP and ALP) of either side to move across the Indo-Burma border as there is free passage between Moreh and Tamu. Expectedly, all these groups are involved in drug trafficking, using the money for purchase of weapons.

India's cool attitude to the Junta in 1988 put Indo-Burma relation on a downswing. This unhappy phase was reversed when the two nations launched "Operation Golden Bird"—a joint military action against the ultras on both sides. Things changed qualitatively when the two joined BIMSTEC, around the time Burma was admitted into ASEAN in 1997. The periodic interaction between the two sides was institutionalized in the annual national level meets between their civilian border authorities; 6th and 7th rounds were held in July (28-31) 1999 and August (28-31) 2000. An important subject in these meets has been insurgencies in the two nations, particularly the nexus among some of the outfits operating from the either side of the common border between two nations, particularly in Manipur and Nagaland. The mutual relations further improved when Gen VP Malik visited Burma in mid-1999 and July 2000 and Gen Maung Aye, No. 2 in State Peace and Development Council, received a red carpet welcome during his November 2000 Shillong visit. Gen Maung disclosed that 5 NSCN(K) camps had been eliminated during 1999. The inauguration by Indian Foreign Minister Jaswant Singh of the 160 km Tamu-Kalewa-Kalemyo Road marked an important milestone in Indo-Burmese relations. To be extended soon to Mandalay, second largest city of the nation, this road would link Moreh in Manipur to Central Burma.

It is well to record that large quantities of contraband (arms and drugs) reached India's North-East by the overland route through Burma, especially till the mid-1995 when the supplies shrunk because of Burma's crackdown on the illegal trade and her agreement with the 17 rebel groups barring the Kachins.

1643 km Indo-Burma border is sensitive area, as the ethnic groups on either side have been waging war against their respective Governments. Yangon's situation is not easy as it is fighting several insurgent groups like Chin National Front, KIO, Karen National Front, New Mon State Party, Wa National Organisation, BCP, NSCN(K), NSCN(I-M), etc. Two nations are tackling the insurgents by politico-military measures. India is already negotiating with the NSCN(I-M) since 1997, and trying to bring NSCN(K), ULFA, PLA and Bodo groups into the mainstream. The ruling SPDC of Burma has reached peace agreements with 15 armed groups including KIA (*Hindustan Times,* 13-2-2002). While this has brought peace to northern and eastern parts of Burma, it still has not been able to control Karen, Arakenese and Chin insurgents active on its border with India. It is these groups who provide shelter and arms to Indian insurgents. It is this North-West hilly frontier of Burma which is used to channel narcotics and arms to India via Cox Bazar.

Both sides are coordinating their CI operations. It is known that NSCN(K), whose cadres are Burma-based Hemei Nagas, have camps in Hongyat, Chamyu, Longko, Bonyo and Wayok areas across Nagaland. The NSCN(I-M), UNLF and PLA have camps around Tamu, Mintha, Somra, Namphalong and Chikka-Phaisat stretch across Manipur. The two Nations must coopt Thailand Government in their battles as that country "is centre of activity for the Indian and Burmese insurgent groups". Secondly, majority of arms purchases by these groups are made in Bangkok, Ranong and Chiang Mai in Thailand, and reach India via Bangladesh route. The two nations are sharing Intelligence to thwart the insurgents. In the past two years (2000, 2001) particularly, there have been efforts by Yangon to ensure that its territory is not used by the Indian insurgents. In fact, February 2002, Burmese Army conducted CI operations in Onamyu area, killing 6 NSCN(K) and 10 ULFA cadres. The things should improve in this field with the increased politico-economic interaction between New Delhi and Yangon.

Myanmar's Top Leader Visits India: October 2004

It was as a result of greater understanding shown by India towards the military leadership of Myanmar that the latter's top man, Senior General Than Shwe, Head of the Military Leadership and the State Democratic Peace Committee of Myanmar paid a 6-day (historic) Official visit to India in October 2004, the first by the Head of State/Government during the last 17 years.

The MoU signed between the two nations on the non-traditional security issues on the 25th October would tighten the noose around the North-Eastern insurgent outfits operating from outside the country. During their talks, Manmohan Singh expressed serious concerns about these groups, and Gen Shwe assured him that he would not allow Myanmar to be used for anti-India operations. He also said Myanmar was willing to mount offensive against these insurgent groups in concert with India, and beef up the vigil along the border with India. The two countries decided to exchange operational intelligence and personnel too.

Barely three months after the visit of Senior General Shwe, a high level delegation arrived in India in February 2005. The two sides agreed on measures to strengthen co-operation in combating terrorism, narcotic trade and arms smuggling under the broad rubric of non-traditional security issues.

The first action under this understanding was taken by India when it proceeded militarily against the Myanmarese militant outfit, Chin National Army, in the Jungles of the southern district of Mizoram, Saiha, on 5-7-05, under Phase II of "Operation Hailstorm". Subsequently, acting on the instructions from the MHA, Mizoram Government closed the Indo-Myanmarese border at Champhai in eastern part.

Myanmar Fights Indian Rebels : Dec. 2006

Myanmar launched a military crackdown against an Indian tribal separatist outfit, SS Khaplang faction of NSCN, camped in that country, with heavy fighting reported between its troops and militants, said NSCN(K) spokesman Kughato Mulatonu on 29 Dec., 2006.

"A brigade of the Burmese Army with heavy weapons launched the assault in Burma's Hkamti district of Northern Sagaing Division, targeting our cadres for the past three days (26-28 Dec.)". (This was conveyed by Mulatonu to the AFP by telephone from an undisclosed location).

There was no immediate confirmation of this offensive from Myanmar with which India shares a 1640-km unfenced border. The last crackdown on Indian rebel camps was in Feb. 2006. The NSCN(K) has at least 50 camps with a total of around 5,000 militant fighters in Sagaing, according to Indian estimates.

Incidentally, SS Kahplang, leading his faction of NSCN for creation of an independent Naga homeland in India's North-East, stradling the Myanmarese border, is a Myanmarese by birth!

Myanmarese Shadow over India's Domestic Scene : March 2007

Myanmarese refugees in India held a silent rally at Jantar Mantar—India's Hyde Park—near Delhi's famous Connaught Place on 26 March, 2007.

The rally was held as "Global Day of Action Against the Shive Gas Project in Burma", informed a banner slung high on a pole. Its sponsors called themselves : 'Shive Gas Movement—India'.

It was obviously a multi-purpose rally which brought together various groups among the Burmese refugees in India. The Kuki students in the rally were holding a silent protest—the demonstrators had a black band sealing their lips—against "atrocities being committed on Kuki villagers on the Indo-Myanmar border by the Myanmarese Junta" A banner held aloft was reflective of their 'cry of anguish' : "Lathis, Tear Gas, Jail Hospitals—what more?"

It is rather curious that some Myanmarese refugee groups in India still want to call their nation as 'Burma'.

NEPAL

The 1800 Km Indo-Nepal border is an open one, and hence poses no problem to insurgents or their friends like the ISI. In the recent years, there is an increasing evidence of the Agency expanding its anti-India operations in Nepal. Several subversives arrested in the recent years disclosed their flying into Nepal and then entering India over the land-borders. "The reverse route is also being used by the ISI to smuggle its agents to safe havens in Nepal after committing crimes in India." The most well-known case of this kind was of Yaqoob Memon, one of the 1992-93 Bombay blasts accused being tracked down in Kathmandu.

Reports of numerous new madrassas and mosques springing up in the recent years—mid 1990s onwards—in the Muslim-inhabited areas of Terai, near the Indo-Nepal borders, should be a cause of concern to the Indian agencies. Some extremist elements are suspected to make use of this situation to foment anti-India sentiment. The ISI agents operating from the Nepalese soil have been worrying New Delhi. The hijacking of an IA plane from Kathmandu on 30 December 1999 was an unpleasant reminder of that Agency's operational success in Nepal

THAILAND

Thailand seems to be the latest country to have provided succour and shelter to North-Eastern rebels, as also operational bases. The MHA Report on the insurgency in the Region speaks of Thailand's flourishing, clandestine arms bazars located in the 3-Pagoda Pass area opposite Burma's Karen State, and another along the Ranong Goast adjoining the Tennaserim Division of Burma. Both the areas on Burma's borders are controlled by ethnic rebel groups. In both the markets, arms and communication equipments of wide variety are available for the asking. The real worry for India starts when these arms are transhipped from the southern coastal strips of Thailand and Burma to the coastal areas of Bangladesh in fishing vessels operated by Burmese rebels. India's "Operation Leech" was launched to thwart this type of the deadly cargo. From the Bangladeshi coastal rendezvous, the gun-runners ensure it reach the end-users in the North-East through west and north Mizoram. At times, arms for ULFA are stored in Meghalaya. It is ironic but true that courtesy such markets, the insurgents have better arms and equipment than the SF fighting them.[33]

History of interaction between the insurgents of the Region and Thai arms dealers tells us that the NSCN was the first group to register its presence in Thailand in 1987; followed subsequently by the Bodo ultra to negotiate arms purchase.

The NSCN leaders seem to favour Thai 5-star and luxury resorts for rest and refit—spending considerable time there for business and pleasure. In a queer twist of fate, NSCN(I-M) leader Muivah was arrested by Thai police for travelling on false documents; and later it produced him before a court in handcuffs.[34]

The above explains why Thailand has to have a place in India's plans to fight insurgency and other anti-national forces at home. To re-emphasis, Thailand—and Bangkok in particular—has long been the staging ground for all kinds of operations impacting India. After all, almost all insurgent outfits have a presence here. The Nagas have an office in Bangkok. ULFA leaders lived here in exile and the Bodos made frequent trips to it and the ISI distribute fake Indian currency there. On the crime side, India's dons like Chhota Rajan (involved in a shoot out early 2000), Chhota Shakeel, Dawood Ibrahim *et al.* are involved in their gang wars there. Even more significantly, Chiang Mai has maintained its leading position in the international drug trade, and the Intelligence confirms that very large percentage of drugs smuggled into India through its North-East emanates from there. These facts were pressing enough by themselves for interaction between the two nations. With Thailand emerging as an important economy in the ASEAN region, the Indian Prime Minister making an early visit was on the cards. Manmohan Singh was in Thailand in July 2004, for BIMST-EC Summit, soon after taking over the reigns.

But the situation has changed after the 9/11 and the Bali bombings. Early 2004, Thai forces killed over 100 Muslim extremists in the country's south, near the resort town of Phuket, "and the Thais are intensely worried that Islamic Militancy could wreck the country's image as a tourist paradise" (Vir Sanghvi, *HT,* 31-7-04), and may even thwart its rising economy. So while the Prime Minister discussed high policy with his counterpart Thaksin Shinawatra, K. Padmanabhaiah engaged the Swu-Muivah duo in peace talks at the Thai hill resort of Chiang Mai, 500 Km from Bangkok, and consequently, the cease-fire due to expire on 31-7-04, was extended for another year on the 30th.

In spite of the 9/11 and the understanding shown by the Thai Prime Minister, owner of one of Thailand's largest industrial conglomerates, some worries remain. The drug-mafia in the Chiang Mai region still flourishes. "And there is evidence that the officers in Thailand's notoriously corrupt Army are still willing to sell arms to the separatist groups." It was issues like these that were addressed by India's NSA, J.N. Dixit, accompanying the Prime Minister, in his talks with his Thai counterpart.

Needless to say, India looks more optimistically at its future relations with Bangkok.

Some Latest Developments

Pakistan does not Relent

With the emergence of Bangladesh in 1971, the Mizo and Naga rebels lost the use of their bases there at least for the initial years. The Mizos travelled West via Rangoon to reach the rump Pakistan and developed future ties with it. The MNF also strengthened its ties with the BCP, and managed to reach Yunnan through the Kachin Corridor. Bhaumik (1996) opines that it is only after China's overt support of Naga rebels and concurrently of Mizo outlaws that the Pakistanis devised a strategy of linking up the rebel tribal outfits under one 'joint command'.

From 1980s, there has been a quantum jump in covert operations by the ISI. It has not only fostered the destructive power of ULFA and Bodo groups by giving them arms and guidance, but also spread its deadly tentacles in Bangladesh and Nepal with the sole, singular aim of weakening India's internal security system and to sap the nation's will to defeat Pakistan-launched terrorism-driven low-intensity war in Kashmir. For this purpose, Pakistan has effectively exploited the prevailing communal divide in the Region. At least 18 separatist Islamist groups[35] have so far been identified by the Intelligence. Islamic fundamentalists have targeted India in the recent years, and have managed to find willing accomplices/sympathizers from these outfits. It is time, warn Indian strategic analysts, to take Osama's threat seriously as published in *Jang* (of Pakistan) of 16 September 1999, calling for the first time, an all out Jehad against India: "India and America are now our biggest enemy...."[36] Recent interrogation of Harkat-ul-Mujahideed (HUM) activists revealed that the "ISI plans to train 10,000 people in Assam for jehad to liberate Assam and establish an Islamic country comprising Assam and certain other parts of North-East".[37] The HUM, based in Yatrabari, near Dhaka, is operating in Eastern parts of India. Their operational nerve centre is Noorani Madrassa where they 'train' acolytes from Assam and Bengal.[38]

The role of ISI in the arms-drug trafficking into India is well-known and documented, but its blatant extent can be judged from Nawaz Sharif's interview to the *Jang*, a reputed Pak daily, in its 13-9-1994 issue: "...3 months after my election as Prime Minister in November 1990, Gen Aslam Beg, then Army Chief and Gen Durrani, ISI Chief, told me that military needed more money for covert foreign operations and wanted to raise it through mega drug deals. Durrani said the blueprint was ready for my approval. I was flabbergasted...." A few days later he told the Army not to launch the drug trafficking plan. Incidentally, by 1999 "the so-called Golden Crescent which lies along Afghanistan, Pakistan, Iran, almost replaced the Golden Triangle as the world's biggest drug producing region." The 1994 Report of the US State Department says: "About 70 tonnes of heroin is produced in Pakistan annually, a third of it smuggled abroad, mostly to the West." The UN says 80 per cent of heroin in Europe comes from the region. It has been rumoured for years that the Pak military, especially ISI, is involved in the drug trade.[39]

Some reports suggested that the ISI base camp in Dhubri area was being used as a centre for smuggling of *ganja* and brown sugar *(The Sentinel,* Guwahati, Assam, 10-3-2000).

With a major blast at New Jalpaiguri Railway Station on 22-6-1999 (details discussed above), killing 9, including 5 soldiers, Pakistan signaled its success in penetrating West Bengal as well.

It seems Gen Parvez Musharraf does not play host to Kashmiri ultras and Afghan mercenaries only; he has extended his hospitality to the militants in the North-East also. The Indian Intelligence says he has hosted several batches of ULFA and NDFB taking them round the country and training them in terrorist camps in POK and Afghanistan run by the ISI. These terrorists have been flown out of Dhaka to Islamabad via Karachi, and thence to their allotted camps. Besides, activists of some Islamic outfits in the Region have also been to Pakistan, including 30 Muslim youths from Western Assam (*Hindustan Times*, 29-6-2002).

Can China be Friendly with India?

In the 17 April 2000 Note, Arunachal Government informed New Delhi and the Army about 2000 Chinese laying the road track opposite Asaphila area in Tawang district. If this was cause of concern, more ominous disclosures were made during their interrogation by Lohit Dewri, a senior ULFA commander and ULFA rebels who had surrendered on 14 August 2000, including the hitherto unknown ULFA connection. The Intelligence reports that the Chinese resumed/stepped up their anti-India activities after the May 1998 Pokhran Tests, including supply of arms to the North-Eastern rebels but carefully avoiding direct hand. "They operate through a mysterious entity, called 'Black House', which delivers the arms after erasing the Chinese markings."[40] But the trail goes to the earlier past. The ULFA leaders, who had gone to China in 1993 for arms and indoctrination, had met Chinese Army officers. The contacts were renewed in 1997. This in spite of the two so-called landmark agreements of 1993 and 1995.

Pakistan ISI : A State within a State

Perhaps no Intelligence agency in the world can match the freedom of action enjoyed by the ISI. It is not only autonomous but nearly sovereign. It is no secret that it formulated Pakistan's Afghan policy and drives all its moves in Kashmir. It was Pak IB's poor performance in the 1947-48 war over Kashmir that resulted in the decision to create the ISI with an Indo-centric focus in 1948. Its pivotal role in the internal politics of Pakistan can be judged from the fact that the ISI under Lt Gen Hamid Gul was the prime mover in the formation of Islamic Jamhourie Ittehad (IJI) or United Democratic Front (UDF), to counter Benazir Bhutto's PPP in September 1988. For first three decades, it concentrated more on the internal intelligence; with limited external agenda, largely Indo-Centric, essentially because Pak fought three wars with India. Consequent to the Soviet advent in Afghanistan, the ISI evolved a greater external orientation from the late 1970s. It was closely involved with the guerrilla warfare against Soviet troops. Even then, it retained its internal orientation due to compulsions of military rulers who wanted it to keep a tab on the civilian politicians for their "subversive activities"!

The proxy war launched by it in 1989 continues to take its toll in J and K. The haul of 30 kg of RDX from the Indo-Bangladesh border and seizure of 63 kg RDX in Delhi during the three weeks (14 August-2 September) in 1999 is indicative of the penetration made by the ISI-backed militant outfits in the post-Kargil situation. The MHA assessment says the ISI has established its network in Western UP, North Kerala, Tamil Nadu, some pockets in Andhra and Karnataka, Indo-Bangladesh border, especially the Siliguri Corridor, and North-East, besides Jammu and Kashmir. It trained and funded mercenaries from 14 countries and pushed them into Jammu and Kashmir. Authoritative figures show that of the 1037 foreign mercenaries killed in Jammu and Kashmir during 1990-98, over 400 hailed from Pakistan.

"Besides the sabotage and usual killings, the ISI is now planning to foment communal riots in the country, especially in the so-far-quiet South." A little known Muslim sect, Siddique Deendar Anjuman, ostensibly a religious organisation "committed to promoting peace and harmony", was found to be involved in subversion+causing series of explosions—12 in all—that "had rocked churches, temples and a mosque across the peninsula from Andhra through Karnataka to Goa since 21 May 2000". Its aim was to trigger communal violence and tarnish India's image. A serious act of sabotage was aborted by an accident on 9 July 2000, when a blue Maruti Omni exploded off the JC Road in Bangalore, killing two of its occupants."[41] The MHA gave the following information/statistics to its Consultative Committee of MPs, on the magnitude of the ISI sponsored terrorism for the 1989-1998 decade:

1. 29,151 civilians and 5,101 SF men killed.
2. Public/private property worth Rs. 2000 crore destroyed/ damaged.
3. Nation incurred an expenditure of Rs. 46,000 crore on Army and PMF employed on IS (internal security) duties.
4. Rs. 18,500 crore spent on awarding compensation to the victims, erecting border fencing, and raising counter-terrorist forces.
5. High grade explosives, mostly RDX, quantity 51,900 kg smuggled into the country, of which 43,750 kg was recovered (what this quantity means can be realized by the fact that in a chain of 21 blasts that wrought havoc in Mumbai in 1992-93, only 3.5 kg RDX was used).
6. During this decade, 7,125 Paki and foreign saboteurs infiltrated into India, and 19,800 Indians were trained by the ISI in Pakistan, POK and Afghanistan Camps.[42]

The White Paper on the ISI activities in India, promised by Home Minister L.K. Advani in 1998, was never published, due to a variety of reasons. But what worries experts is the level of success achieved by the ISI in networking the militant groups in different parts of India, exploiting their ethnic, communal and anti-establishment sentiments. The threat from such a wide network of recalcitrant groups can be assessed from the massive haul of 4000 kg of RDX from the suspected agents during 1999 alone. The extent of spread and reach of the ISI should be judged from the fact that India busted 161 modules, Home Minister Advani told the Press on 17-10-2002, during the last three years (2000, 2001 and 2002).

Siliguri Corridor and Demand for Kamatapur State

The 28 Km wide Siliguri Corridor, also called the Eastern Chicken's Neck, is a sensitive area which has drawn attention of the ISI in recent years. A serious internal disruption, fomented externally, can cut off the North-East from the mainland. The situation has taken a serious turn with the violent activities of the Kamatapur Liberation Organisation (KLO) for a separate Kamatapur State, over the last few years. KLO is the armed wing of the Kamatapuri People's Party (KPP), essentially of the Rajbongshis who constitute 31 per cent of 12 million population of 5 districts of North Bengal.

The Rajbongshis also comprise a substantial section of the non-Bodo population in the proposed Bodoland. So the KLO also wants parts of Assam contiguous to North Bengal to be part of their Kamatapur. The KPP has been demanding a separate state for over 30 years, but has not made much progress as they do not have an outstanding leader to guide them. For the last few years, the KLO has taken over the movement, and it seems to have developed secessionist orientation, after coming closer to the ULFA. They too have started extortions and looting. On 22 November 1999, the two jointly looted cash from the Railways, near Siliguri. The worst outrage was their killing of five CPI(M) activists at their Dhupguri office in a dusk operation on 17 August 2002. In July 2000, they had killed two supporters of CPI(M) in same area. Their first strike was in May 2000 when they killed CPI(M) leader Pranesh Pal at Barobisha in Jalpaiguri.

Since 1996, KLP ultras have been visiting ULFA camps in Bhutan. They themselves are reported to have set up camps in Bhutan, just 3 miles from the border. Of late, KLO has an alliance with ULFA, in turn allied with NDFB.

Christian Terrorism in India's North-East?

This is not something that is widely talked about, nor is the Christian terrorism known to have been discussed in the rarefied policy circles of India. But there is indeed on entry on the subject on the internet, which is re-produced at the appendix below without any comment, and for whatever worth it is.

Appendix

Christian Terrorism in Northeast India

In our attempt to help promote peace in the world for mutual and social spiritual development, there are nonetheless areas and organizations that are devotedly working against that goal. Because of their own allegiance to a particular ideology, usually based on a religion, they threaten the freedom and challenge the well-being of those of other religions. And one area where this is taking place is in India's northeastern states, such as Assam, Arunachal Pradesh, Nagaland, Manipur, Tripura, etc. Because of wicked terrorist tactics and even "gun point conversions", some people are being forced to give up their traditions. This is something that much of the world, and even many Indians, are not aware of. And since I have personally traveled in this area to give lectures to promote the preservation of the culture there and met many wonderful people, it is region in which I have a special interest.

Here on this page you will find several reports and news items on the shocking amount of terrorism caused by the Christian militant groups in Northeast India, how they operate, where they get their funds, and the thousands of people who have already died because of it. It is primarily due to those who want to make the whole region into a separate Christian state at the expense of those who would prefer to follow their own indigenous and Hindu cultures.

Christian Terrorists Massacre Eight Hindu Civilians in India

Christian Terrorists Kill 44, Wound 118 in Attacks in Northeast India

Baptist Church Backs Terrorism in North-East India

Terrorists in North-East India get American Support

Christ and North-East India

Mahatma Gandhi on Conversion

Thirteen Years of Killings in Tripura

My Northeast India Mission

Preaching in India's Northeast for Cultural Preservation

Save Your Culture

[Home] [The Books by Stephen Knapp] [Book Reviews]
[CD Slide Shows] [Order Form]
[The World Relief Network] [Articles to Read] [Seeing Spiritual India]
[A Little Book of Prayers Mantras & Gayatris] [Krishna
Darshan Art Gallery]
[Vegetarian Recipes and Resources] [Stay in Touch with Us]
[Links to Other Websites]
[Jokes and Anecdotes]

(Source: http://www.stephen-knapp.com/christian terrorism_in_northeast_india.htm)

The Naga Talks : Hopeful Signs

After decades of dark clouds, there is some hope on the horizon. The Centre has been holding talks periodically with the NSCN(I-M) and the cease-fire has been holding since 1 September 1997. The talks so far held in the foreign capitals like Bangkok, might be shifted to a venue within India. Mizoram Chief Minister said on 21 October 2002 that NSCN leaders "are ready to visit India if the ban is lifted on the outfit. The MHA sources indicated the ban, due to lapse on 26 November 2002, "might not be extended", to enable Muivah and Isaac to visit India *(The Hindu,* 22-10-2002). Their first visit to Delhi indeed came in January 2004.

In March 2001, Home Minister Advani visited the Region and met Government representatives and leaders of outfits other than NSCN(I-M). The operations against these outfits were suspended. Advani informed the Rajya Sabha that "militant outfits in the North-East have responded positively to the suspension of operations and the call for dialogue" *(The Frontline,* 13-4-2001).

September 2005. The press reported that NSCN(I-M) wanted a firm assurance from the Centre on the integration of the Naga-inhabited areas before the next round of talks, likely to be held in October 2005. They also expressed their willingness to hold talks with the Governments of Manipur and Assam to find a way out of their opposition to part with any of their areas for Nagalim *(Exp* 21-9-05). More details on the subject will be found in Chapter 16 and 17.

Five Militants are Lynched

Five militants of NDFB were lynched to death on 8-11-03 after they threw grenades at the villagers following a scuffle with them. The villagers were from Aikata, on the border of Goalpara and Dhubri districts and Sialkunda in the same area. The ultras possibly entered the district from Meghalaya. 3 villagers also lost their lives.

Abductions Halt Trade

A spate of abductions—one customs inspector and six coal exporters were abducted in Meghalaya by the armed militants in March 2003 belonging to various militant outfits in the State-brought trans-border trade between India and Bangladesh in the north-eastern sector to grinding halt by the end of the month. As many as 10 customs stations (two in Meghalaya, four in Tripura, one in Mizoram, and three in Assam) will be closed until these States devise adequate security measures *(Exp.,* 6-4-03).

Gandhi Jayanti 2004—Terror Strike : 7 Blasts, 48 killed

A series of explosions and militant attacks in the North-East— 5 in Assam and 2 in Nagaland—killed 48 people on 2-10-04. Details follow:

Assam: NDFB behind all five (1) At 5 PM armed ultras opened fire at the weekly market at Makrijhar, 25 Km from Dhubri, close to the Bangladesh border, killing 11 persons on the spot. (2) Two persons were killed in grenade attack at Abhaypuri in Bangaigaon district close to Dhubri. (3) 5-30 PM, grenades lobbed by the ultras at Baihata Chariali Police Station (PS) in Kamrup district left three people dead and at Jagi Road PS in Morigaon district injured two policemen. (4) Mid-day, IED explosion at Shantipur village market under the newly-created Chirang district left two dead and six injured.

"Tomorrow (3 October) is the raising day of the banned Bodo outfit (NDFB)," which has demanded a sovereign Bodo tribal state *(Exp.,* 3-10-04). It was only on 30 September that Assam Chief Minister Tarun Gogoi had offered to declare a cease-fire against the NDFB and ULFA from 15 October if they came to the negotiations table abjuring violence.

Nagaland: Two simultaneous explosions rocked Dimapur, the commercial hub of the hill State at 9.35 AM: (1) at the Platform No. 1 of the railway station when hundreds of passengers were waiting for the delayed Lumding-Tinsukia Passenger train.[43] It created a huge crater on the platform and left its roof collapsed; (2) at Hong Kong Market on Marwari-patty Road, just 200 mtrs away. The blasts left 32 dead.

It was the first major blast in any public place in strife-torn Nagaland in the last ten years. No wonder Nagaland Chief Minister Neiphiu Rio rushed to Dimapur.

Manipur: Far from Peace: 11 Jawans of 5/8 GR were killed and 6 others injured when they were ambushed by the KYKL on 19-9-05 at Upper Ngarian in Bishenpur district, 45 Km from Imphal. The next day, one havildar of the 26 Assam Rifles was killed and four others injured in an IED explosion set off by the PLA, near Jiribam/Jirighat tea estate along the Manipur-Assam border. Defence Minister Pranab Mukherjee arrived next day on his first 2-day visit to the North-East since he took over (on 20-9-05).

NOTES

1. It has been discussed in some detail in this book. Also *See* Urmila Phadnis, *Ethnicity and Nation Building in South Asia,* 1989.
2. The Cabinet Mission Plan had placed Bengal and Assam together in Group C. This here is the enlarged Version, with the addition of Bhutan and Sikkim.
3. Cited by Brig SP Sinha, "Insurgency in North-East India: The External Dimension", the *USI journal,* July-September 1998.
4. Urmila Phadnis, 1989, Note 1, and V.K. Sareen, "India's North-East in Flames", 1980. Sareen gives a lucid account of CIA activities in the North-East in the early 1970s.
5. The first batch of 200 ultras led by Kaito Sema, C-in-C, Naga Home Guards (the then name of the underground Naga Army) went for training to East Pakistan early 1962 through North Cachar Hills, and returned in March 1963. Another group of *500* under Dusoi Chakhesang trekked to Pakistan through Chin Hills of Burma in October 1963 and returned in May 1964. The largest

group of 1000 insurgents was led by Zuheto Sema in October 1964, after suspension of hostilities negotiated by JP-led Naga Peace Mission. The group reinfiltrated into Nagaland during August-September 1965 through Burmese Somra Tract.

6. The MEA Press Note dated 3-10-1968, cited by Parkash Singh, "Nagaland", 1972.
7. Hazarika, Sanjoy, 1995.
8. The first batch of 300 Nagas under Muivah and Thinsuelie crossed the border into Burma in November 1966 and trekking 1000 Km, reached Yunnan in January 1967. The second batch of nearly 500 strong was led by Mowu Angami and Isaac Swu in December 1967. Throughout 1968, small groups were trekking back into India.
9. Parkash Singh, *op. cit.*
10. For Naga, Mizo, and Meitei insurgents' links with China. *See* Nibedon, 1981.
11. Parkash Singh, *op. cit.*
12. *Times of India,* 1-10-1984.
13. *Hindustan Times,* 29-11-1997.
14. *Times of India,* "Will Bangladesh now cut off support to North-East Insurgent", 19-12-1996.
15. *Frontline,* M.S. Prabhakar, 11-2-1984.
16. Hazarika, *op. cit.*
17. Verghese, 1996.
18. For a detailed analysis of external factors in the spread of insurgency. *See* Urmila Phadnis, n. 11.
19. That some such operation did hand down polemical missiles to the doughty warriors—Defence Minister Fernandes and Admiral Bhagawat—to engage in a no-holds-barred duel, is a matter of recent history.
20. Nitin Gokhale in *Outlook,* 1-2-1999.
21. *Ibid.*
22. It provoked a sharp reaction from the Assam Governor, himself a Bihari, and a retired Lt General. He had asked the victims of the senseless attacks to defend themselves, using all means at their disposal. That the Governor's strong comment came under sharp attack from a spectrum of political parties—the usual Left-Centre Combine—is indicative of a fractured Indian polity.
23. This was happening in spite of our improved relations with Burma since 1995 and Bangladesh since "the Vajpayee Regime took over (February 1998)". India did get cooperation from these countries depending upon the hue of their Governments. In April 1995, Indian and Burmese armies jointly launched "Operation Golden Bird" on Manipur-Burma border when over 40 ultras of two countries' insurgent groups were killed and huge cache of arms recovered. Later years, India got necessary help from Bhutan and Bangladesh. Earlier years also had seen such collaborative operations—published or unpublished. Col PV, a contemporary of this Author during his 1975-78 stint in Mizoram, informed him of a joint operation carried out by the troops of the three nations in 1977 in the area around the Indo-Burma-Bangladesh injunction.
24. *The Outlook,* 23-8-1999.

25. It is important to note that on this date (16-12-96) the two nations signed the Indo-Bangladesh Treaty on sharing of the Ganga waters.
26. *Times of India,* 19-12-1996.
27. Cited by Dincsh Kumar in *Times of India,* 19-12-1996.
28. *The Frontline* 10-9-99 and *The Hindu,* 28-8-1999.
29. Assam and Bhutan got involved in a public spat over killing of these ten 'Bhutanese'. Mahanta claimed the culprits were NDFB ultras, ensconced on Bhutanese' soil, who killed the victims across the border and then dumped their bodies on the Assamese side. Bhutan claimed it was the handwork of the ultras of BLT (who were then negotiating peace with the Assam Government) who killed Bhutanese nationals on the Assamese soil, and "we want Government of India to pay compensation for these deaths".
30. For further details, *see Hindustan Times* of 24-7-1999, 12-3-2000 and 26-4-2000; *Hindu* of 28-4-2000 and 23-12-2000; *Indian Express* of 24-12-2000; and *Frontline* of 19-1-2001.
31. *Deccan Herald* of 25-10-1998.
32. Phanjoubam Tarapot, *Insurgency Movements in North-East India*, 1993.
33. *Assam Tribune*, 4-7-1999.
34. An over-sympathetic 'North-East expert' was moved to an angry outburst over a press photo of a hand-cuffed Muivah: "It is a matter of shame that a leader of a movement, of Muivah's stature, was shown in such pathetic condition, hand-cuffed like a common criminal...." It seems to be a case of misplaced, even wasted sympathy! One can't understand this expert's anger and piety on seeming such a photo, until he belongs to ultra-liberal and bleeding hearts brigade who just cannot countenance even mildest of the inconvenience suffered by the most hard-boiled of the anti-national insurgents, who have blood of countless innocent civilians, including women and children on their hands. I have seldom seen them angry on the death of the soldiers fighting these ultras.
35. Some of the names are MULFA (Muslim United Liberation Front of Assam), MULTA (Muslim United Liberation Tigers of Assam), PULF (People's United Liberation Front), SIMI (Students Islamic Movement of India), Adam Sena, Jehad Council, etc.
36. Cited in *India Today,* 4-10-1999, by Jason Burke and Harinder Baveja.
37. *Deccan Herald,* 16-8-1999.
38. The recruits from Assam, for training at their seminary in Bangladesh, cross the border at Karimganj, and reach Sylhet through Zakiganj; those from Bengal cross the border at Dinhat in Cooch Behar *(Asian Age,* 23-5-1999).
39. *The News of Pakistan,* 13-9-1994.
40. *The Hindu,* 19-8-2000.
41. For detail, *see India Today* of 31-7-2000.
42. Vinod Kumar in *The Hindu* of 5-9-1999.
43. Army men, more than any other professionals, love to live by fond memories. I vividly remember the contours and outline of this Platform No. 1 where I landed on my first commissioning on 12 January 1958, like the back of my hand.

3

Turbulence in Assam

Assam is the most populous state among the seven sisters, but has been pushed down to No. 2 position in area.

Key Statistics : Assam State

Date of formation	26 January 1950
Area	78,438 sq. km
Population	26,655,528
Capital	Dispur
Principal Languages	Assamese
	Bengali
	Bodo/Boro
Major Religions	Hinduism
	Islam
	Buddhism

Before going into other details, an overview of Assam's terrorism situation (Assam Backgrounder) and a brief look at the year gone by (Assam Assessment 2006) are considered useful for the lay reader.

Assam Backgrounder

The problem of militancy in Assam has its origin in the large-scale migration of refugees from East Pakistan—what is now Bangladesh— since India's Partition in 1947. A continuous flow of illegal migrants across the borders has disturbed the local demography and brought much of India's Northeast to the knife-edge of violence. In July 1979, the All Assam Students Union (AASU) and the All Assam *Gana Sangram Parishad* (AAGSP) launched a mass movement for the detection of illegal immigrants, their deletion from the voters' list and their deportation to Bangladesh. The agitators demanded that the process of detection should cover all migrants who had entered India since 1951. The Central government agreed to the policy of deportation, but insisted on a 'cut-off' date of 1971 for the identification of illegal aliens. Irrespective of the cut-off date, it is a fact that a minute fraction of the illegal migrants has actually faced deportation and the processes of identification have, even now, barely begun. However, talks between the Central government and the AASU-AAGSP agitators broke down on this point, and the agitation gathered momentum towards the end of November 1979, when the entire State administration was brought to a halt as government employees joined the movement. In December 1979, Assam was brought under President's rule.

The anti-foreigners agitation soon took a violent turn and began to display secessionist tendencies. A militant organisation, the **United Liberation Front of Asom (ULFA),** was established on April 7, 1979, under the leadership of Paresh Barua. While secession from India was the declared goal, the organisation adopted an anti-foreigner plank since this was the popular issue gripping the masses in Assam. Pushing its objective of secession to the background, the ULFA operated within the AASU-AAGSP's agitation.

On March 28, 1980, the army was deployed in the State to restore law and order. The entire State, with the exception of Cachar and the North Cachar Hills districts, was declared a disturbed area and was brought under the Assam Disturbed Areas Act, 1955, and the **Armed Forces (Special Powers) Act, 1958,** on April 6, 1980.

Several rounds of talks were held between the Central government and the leaders of the Assam agitation over the period 1980-83, but they failed to make any headway. Despite a call for a boycott by the agitators, the Central government decided to hold elections to the State Legislature in February 1983. On February 18, over 600 Bangladeshi settlers, including women and children, were massacred in Nellie, Nagaon district. Nevertheless, elections were held. The Congress (I) under Hiteshwar Saikia, came to power, and, while the agitation continued, a measure of order was restored in the State.

Talks between the Centre and the leaders of the agitation were resumed when the Rajiv Gandhi government came to power in Delhi, and on August 15, 1985, the **Assam Accord** was signed. According to the terms of the Accord, all foreigners who entered Assam on or after March 25, 1971, were to be detected and deported.

After the Accord, a new regional party, the Asom Gana Parishad (AGP) was created, bringing together many of the prominent leaders of the agitation. Elections to the State Legislature were held in December 1985, and the AGP was swept to power, with Prafulla Kumar Mahanta as the Chief Minister.

At this stage, the ULFA, emphasised its basic objective i.e., to 'liberate Assam from Indian colonial rule' and to form a 'sovereign, socialist Assam' through an armed struggle. As the Assam Accord and the subsequent political settlement were inimical to this objective, the ULFA continued with its violent activities even after the AGP assumed power in the State. By 1986, the ULFA had established contacts with agents of Pakistan's Inter Services Intelligence (ISI), as well as with militants from the National Socialist Council of Nagaland (NSCN) and the Kachin Independence Army (KIA). Its strength then was estimated at 3,000 militants with access to some 2,000 weapons of various makes. The ULFA created terror in the State, disrupting communications and hitting various economic targets, kidnapping prominent businessmen for ransom and killing government officials. Its activities escalated, reaching unprecedented heights in 1990. As the AGP government lost control of the situation, the State was, once again, brought under President's rule on November 28, 1990 and the ULFA was banned under the **Unlawful Activities (Prevention) Act, 1967.** The army had been re-inducted in the State and *Operation Bajrang* was conducted between September 1990 and April 1991. 209 hardcore militants were arrested during this operation and a large quantities of arms, along with Rs. 48 million in cash—the proceeds of extortion—were also recovered.

Operation Bajrang succeeded in restoring a measure of normalcy in Assam, and elections were held in June 1991 to the State Legislature. The Congress (I) defeated the AGP and Hiteshwar Saikia was, once again, sworn in as Chief Minister on July 1. ULFA resumed its violent campaign almost at once, and the army launched *Operation Rhino* in September 1991. Over the succeeding four months, 2,578 hardcore militants were nabbed, along with large quantities of arms and Rs. 780,000 in cash. The army also destroyed 15 ULFA camps. However, in January 1992, the Saikia government suspended army operations and announced an amnesty for all militants who were willing to surrender. By March 1992, some 4,000 ULFA militants had surrendered to the authorities.

The ULFA, however, proved extremely resilient and restored its strength and activities, acquiring new military hardware and establishing a chain of training camps across the border in Myanmar, and later in Bhutan. In April-May 1995, the Indian and Myanmarese armed forces jointly launched *Operation Golden Bird* along their border. 50 militants were killed during this operation and huge quantities of arms and ammunition were recovered.

The AGP returned to power in the State Legislature elections of May 1996. Counter-insurgency operations continued, and on January 20, 1997, a Unified Command structure was set up to co-ordinate the functioning of the various forces carrying out operations against the terrorists. Since then, continuous military and para-military operations have considerably weakened the ULFA, driving its senior leadership into exile. A disturbing trend, however, is the widening network of extortion, criminal and quasi-legal operations that this leadership-in-exile now commands in Assam, which not only fuels and finances militancy, but, more significantly, has had an extremely corrosive impact on democratic institutions and structures in the State and a deeply corrupting influence on increasingly collusive government officials and political leaders. With this, there has also been a continuous process of 'lumpenisation' among the rank and file of the ULFA cadres, as increasing numbers of criminals join in the extortionary and other illegal activities of the organisation.

The emergence of a Bodo insurgency in the State has become another major problem. The Bodos, a major tribe of plainsmen, are one of the earliest settlers in Assam. They have been demanding better social, political and economic conditions since independence. There has been a long history of tensions between the Bodos and the Assamese. The former feel that they have been neglected and exploited by the latter. The All Bodo Students Union (ABSU) was formed in 1967 to represent the Bodo cause. In the early 1980s, the ABSU emerged as a potent force under the leadership of Upendranath Brahma.

A militant organisation, the Bodo Security Force (BSF) came into being in 1989 under the leadership of Ranjan Daimari. The BSF, later renamed the **National Democratic Front of Bodoland (NDFB),** resorted to terrorism in order to secure an 'independent Bodo nation' north of the river Brahmaputra. A very large proportion of violent activities in the State, including killings, explosions, arson, and attacks on police stations, have been carried out by the NDFB. This is an organised and well-trained militant group with a strength of about 900. It has established a 'working arrangement' with the **NSCN - isak-Muivah (NSCN-IM).**

Another terrorist group, the **Bodo Liberation Tiger Force (BLTF),** headed by Prem Singh Brahma, has been fighting for a separate State of Bodoland within the Indian Union.

An accord was signed on February 20, 1993, between the Government of India, the Government of Assam and Bodo leaders, creating the Bodoland Autonomous Council (BAC) within Assam. However, since Bodo villages are not contiguous, the demarcation of the jurisdiction of the BAC has remained a problem. Both the NDFB and the BLTF have condemned the Bodo Accord, and have, since the mid-1990s, been engaged in a campaign of violence directed against other ethnic groups within 'Bodo areas'. Large scale attacks were carried out against Santhal tribals in May 1996, displacing tens of thousands of people. A second wave of attacks in May 1998 displaced another couple of thousand Santhals. The Santhals and other non-Bodo communities have also begun to arm themselves and fight back. This has resulted in significant displacement of the Bodo population from areas where they are a minority.

These trends in retaliatory violence are not restricted to the Bodos. Muslim migrants in Assam have also shown signs of incipient militancy. The

Muslim United Liberation Front of Assam has been constituted. A demand for a separate State bringing together the five border districts in Assam, which now have a Muslim majority, has been already voiced.

The recent history of the fissionary trend in which every tribal, linguistic, religious or cultural sub-group demands separation from the others, compounded by the rhetoric of ethnic sub-nationalism, radical demographic shifts and a long history of poor governance, make this State, perhaps more than any other region in the country, a potential source of increasing mass strife over the coming decades.

(Source: South Asia Terrorism Portal, SATP, of Institute of Conflict Management, New Delhi.)

Assam Assessment 2006

In the year 2006, a total of 86 people have been killed in militancy-related incidents in Assam, which includes 48 (55.82 per cent) civilians, 16 (18.60 per cent) security force (SF) personnel and at least 22 (25.58 per cent) militants.

Fatalities in Terrorist Violence - 2006

	Civilians	*Security Force Personnel*	*Terrorist*	*Total*
January	5	1	2	8
February	10	1	1	12
March	3	0	0	3
April	4	0	3	7
May	1	1	0	2
June	13	6	5	24
July	7	0	3	10
August	5	7	8	20
Total	48	16	22	86

Source: Institute for Conflict Management database.

Among the major incidents of terrorist violence in 2006 are:

January 20: Ten persons, including eight CISF personnel, are injured in a grenade attack by United Liberation Front of Asom (ULFA) at the entrance of Guwahati Refinery at Noonmati in Guwahati city.

May 9: Two SF personnel are killed in an ambush by the ULFA near the Borahibari railway station in Sibsagar district. Five persons, including the former State Transport Minister and senior Asom Gana Parishad leader Pradip Hazarika, are wounded in the attack.

June 8: ULFA triggers a series of grenade explosions, while targeting SF personnel, at various parts of the State leaving at least 25 persons wounded.

July 11: Two ULFA cadres, Pradip Rajbangshi and Mrinal Rajbangshi, are killed in an encounter with the SFs at Baglamari village in the Nalbari district.

On August 13, 2006, the Union Government suspended Army operations against the ULFA at a time when the militant group was engaged in a routine stepping up of violence ahead of Independence Day (August 15). Specifically, the announcement came hours after ULFA cadres shot dead a petty trader in the Joypur town of Dibrugarh district, hurled a grenade at the private residence of a senior Assam minister at Digboi in the Tinsukia district (the minister was present but there was no casualties), and made an abortive grenade attack on the Police in the western district town of Nalbari. In ten days, beginning August 4, 2006, the ULFA had launched several grenade or bomb attacks, killing a dozen people, including six SF personnel, five of them of the Assam Police, and injured up to 40 others.

The Union Government, subsequently, decided to extend the suspension of counter-insurgency operations against the ULFA by 15 days. A decision to this effect was taken at the meeting on August 23, 2006, between the Government and the ULFA-backed People's Consultative Group (PCG) to decide modalities for direct negotiations with the outfit.

There have, however, been several roadblocks thus far, obstructing a possible face-to-face meeting between the ULFA and the Government of India:

- New Delhi has asked ULFA to name its negotiating team. ULFA says the team cannot be named unless five of its top detained leaders are freed.
- New Delhi has asked ULFA to give its consent for the talks in writing. ULFA responded by saying the Government must also state in writing that it would discuss the group's key demand of 'sovereignty'.
- ULFA has demanded information on the whereabouts of 14 of its cadres 'missing' after the Bhutanese military assault in December 2003.

In 2006, the ULFA continued with its depredations, bombing markets, oil and gas pipelines and other installations. And it sent alarm bells ringing in the State's industry and security establishment by slapping an INR 5 billion (USD 112 million) extortion demand on the state-owned Indian oil major, Oil and Natural Gas Corporation (ONGC) in January 2006, forcing the authorities to intensify vigil on oil and gas installations. Also on July 3, 2006, the Reserve Bank of India, the country's central bank, was served an extortion demand for INR 1.5 million by the ULFA.

On the other hand, the first round of talks between the Union Government and National Democratic Front of Bodoland (NDFB) was held in New Delhi on May 27, 2006. Both sides agreed to extend their cease-fire agreement for another one year with effect from June 1. However, the group reportedly continues to carry on its extortion and violent activities in its areas of operations even as it indicates its willingness to resolve its problem through negotiations. The Centre and NDFB had entered into a one-year ceasefire agreement in May 2005.

On the political front, the election results of May 11, 2006, brought in new, though not unanticipated, power players into Assam's Legislative Assembly and into the State's Government; players, who were, not long ago, designated as terrorists, and had relentlessly waged war against the state and the democracy that has now catapulted them into the arguable position of 'kingmakers'. The Hagrama Mohilary faction of the Bodo People's Progressive Front (BBPF-H), with its leadership comprising principally of surrendered militants of the Bodo Liberation Tigers (BLT), secured an overwhelming victory in the Bodo Territorial Council (BTC) areas, capturing 12 out of the 18 seats it contested in the 126-member Assam Assembly. The centrality of this victory is underlined by the fact that Chief Minister Tarun Gogoi's Congress Party has returned to power with drastically reduced margins, and just 53 seats in the Assembly, well below the halfway mark, making it dependent on BBPF-H's support to form the Government.

Casualties of Terrorist Violence in Assam - 2006

	Civilians	*Security Force Personnel*	*Terrorist*	*Total*
January	6	0	3	9
February	1	0	7	8
March	3	1	7	11
April	3	0	9	12
May	5	2	10	17
June	3	2	15	20
July	1	1	5	7
August	12	1	2	15
September	10	1	5	16
October	81	0	12	93
November	10	1	4	15
December	14	1	4	19
Total	149	10	83	242

Source: Institute for Conflict Management database.

Comparative Levels of Violence, 2001-2005

Year	*Civilians*	*Security Force*	*Militants*	*Total*
2001	264	59	283	606
2002	138	32	275	445
2003	212	12	281	505
2004	194	24	136	354
2005	149	10	83	242

Source: Institute for Conflict Management database.

Following is the sampling of the major incidents of violence in Assam during 2005.

January 11: Fourteen civilians, induding a nine-year-old girl and four women, are injured when suspected ULFA terrorists trigger an explosion at the Marwaripatty area of Jorhat town.

February 23: Willingson Timung, the KLNLF 'commander-in-chief, is killed along with two other cadres by cadres of his own outfit inside the Langlakso forest area in Karbi Anglong district.

June 16: Four ULFA cadres, including three women, are killed in an encounter with the police at Doloni village in Dibrugarh district.

June 19: Four ULFA terrorists and one SF personnel are killed during two encounters in Nalbari district.

August 7: Four persons are killed and 12 others sustain injuries in an explosion detonated by the ULFA at a bus stand at Boko in Kamrup district.

September 14: Eight persons are killed and several others sustain injuries as suspected Kuki Revolutionary Army (KRA) militants open indiscriminate fire at Thekerajan village in Karbi Anglong district.

October 2: Five members of a family are killed by unidentified militants at Hemari Terang village in Karbi Anglong district.

October 8: Suspected militants kill five Karbi villagers at Borsing Bey village near Diphu town in Karbi Anglong district.

October 9: Unidentified gunmen kill at least six persons at Bura Fanchu and Longsing Engti villages in Karbi Anglong district.

October 21 : Suspected DHD militants kill nine UPDS cadres at Tamulbari under Diphu police station in Karbi Anglong district.

December 2: Four civilians, including a two-month-old infant, are killed by DHD militants at Sirkangnep village in Karbi Anglong district.

It was on September 7, 2005, that the ULFA announced the setting of the People's Consultative Group (PCG), a hand-picked 11-member team comprising journalists, rights activists, lawyers and academics. The group is led by writer Indira Goswami, who has been acting as the mediator between the outfit and the Government in New Delhi for some time now. Rebati Phukan, a former football player from the State, supplements Goswami's efforts. The PCG's mandate was to clear the roadblocks and prepare the grounds for direct talks between the ULFA and the GoI. The PCG has held three rounds of talks with the federal authorities in New Delhi so far, the first meeting on October 26, 2005, chaired by Prime Minister Manmohan Singh. The second PCG-Government meeting was held on February 7, 2006, and the last on June 22, 2006. However, the constitution of the PCG has had little impact on the continuing violence in the State.

During 2005, thc ULFA reportedly reorganised its units in its traditional strongholds, forming new 'battalions', and moving into hitherto unexplored territories, both within Assam and in adjoining States. On April 20, 2005, the Police demolished a well-equipped camp of ULFA's newly-formed '27th battalion' in Karbi Anglong district, an area where the organisation's traditional influence has been low. The camp was established in the first week of April 2005 and was led by a middle level cadre, Dandi Bora. On April 21, 2005, six ULFA leaders, including a woman 'sergeant major', were arrested by the Army at Sesupani in Tinsukia District as they descended into Assam from their Changlang camp in neighbouring Arunachal Pradesh. Movements of ULFA cadres drawn from its '28th battalion' have been noticed in the Jonai area of upper Assam's Dhemaji District and also in the Poba reserve forest area spread over a 100 square kilometers along the borders with Arunachal Pradesh. Each of these is a territory that has remained untouched by the group's terror and extortion in the past. Meanwhile, ULFA cadres continue to use the neighbouring State of Meghalaya's Garo Hills area for transit and as an arms dump. On May 14, Police recovered two universal machine guns, three magazines and 60 rounds from an ULFA hideout at Masuk in the West Garo Hills district.

There was a series of macabre killings spanning almost a month (October 2005) in southern Assam's Karbi Anglong District. An analysis of official statistics relating to the violence revealed unexpected dimensions of the violence, suggesting that a particular community - surprisingly the majority in the District - bore the brunt of the merciless raids, suggesting that this was not, as has been widely projected, an 'ethnic war' that has been witnessed. Rather, the attacks had the character of an organized expansionist campaign by a particular ethnic militia, capitalising on absence of pressure from counter-insurgency forces as a result of the prevailing ceasefire with the authorities. As on October 29, 2005, a total of 88 people were officially reported killed, of whom 76 belonged to the majority Karbi ethnic group. The others killed include nine Dimasas, one Bodo, one Nepali and one Assamese.

On its part, the Government has admitted the role of local insurgent groups in the violence. Two rebel groups operate in the District: the United People's Democratic Solidarity (UPDS), pushing for 'self-rule' for the Karbis; and the Dima Halim Daogah (DHD), primarily based in the neighbouring North Cachar Hills District, fighting for a separate Dimaraji State for the Dimasas. Incidentally, both UPDS and DHD had entered into a cease-fire with the Government - the DHD truce came about on January 1 , 2003, and the UPDS cease-fire on May 23, 2002. Obviously, the UPDS cannot be behind the slaughter of the Karbis. The slaughter of the Karbis is believed to be the work of the DHD and its supporters or some other shadowy Dimasa forces. Some of the major incidents of violence that broke out in the Karbi Anglong district in October 2005 are:

October 2: Five members of a family are killed by unidentified militants at Hemari Terang village under Diphu police station.

October 9: Six persons from the Bura Fanchu and Longsing Engti villages are killed and hundreds of houses are set ablaze by unidentified terrorists in separate incidents under Diphu and Bokajan police stations.

October 10: Six Dimasa civilians are killed at Kheroni village. Nearly 60 houses also set ablaze by the miscreants.

October 17: Suspected Dimasa militants waylay two passenger buses traveling from Zirikinding at Charchim under Kheroni police station and kill 23 persons, including nine women, belonging to the Karbi tribe.

October 18: Six persons are killed at Doyangmukh area under Diphu police station.

October 21: Suspected DHD militants kill nine UPDS cadres at Tamulbari under Diphu police station.

The high hopes of the Bodos following the formation of the BTC were quickly shattered when former BLT leaders fell out with the former leaders of the All Bodo Students' Union (ABSU) in their bid to control Bodo politics. The nascent BBPF, formed at Kokrajhar on April 12, 2005, at the behest of the ABSU and former BLT militants, underwent a sudden split on the eve of the Council elections held in May 2005. The divide in the BPPF came mainly as a result of Hagrama Mohilary's support to some former militant comrades who had contested the Council elections as independent candidates against official candidates of the BBPF. Manoj Kumar Brahma, one of Hagrama Mahilary's close associates, for instance, was pitted against Rabiram Narzary, the founding president of the BPPF, at Banargaon. Nevertheless, on June 2, 2005, an 11-member Executive Council headed by Hagrama Mahilary was sworn in at Kokrajhar, to run the 46-member BTC. Post-poll violence continued to rock the Bodo heartland of Assam with two rival BPPF factions engaged in violent clashes - attacking villages, torching houses and indulging in vandalism.

The split in the BPPF and subsequent clashes between the supporters of the two factions have been a boon for the NDFB, which has consolidated its lost position among the Bodos. Its cease-fire with the Government has also raised hopes that the outfit might be able to secure a better deal than the present BTC - though it is difficult to see what more the Government could offer. When the NDFB signed the cease-fire agreement with the Union and State Governments on May 25, 2005, there was jubilation within a large section of the Bodo community. However, the proposed negotiations are expected to be difficult, since the outfit is yet to give up its original demand for a sovereign state of Bodoland.

With the BPPF having secured dominance in the BTC and now gaining a stranglehold in the Governing coalition at Guwahati, its power in Bodo politics will be difficult to challenge for the next five years. Other political formations will, consequently, be increasingly tempted to violence to undermine this influence, even as the Government will have little to offer the surviving Bodo militant group, the NDFB, to secure its return to democratic politics.

Assam was gripped by both euphoria and fear after the country's Supreme Court, on July 12, 2005, struck down as unconstitutional an immigration law that was in force only in the State. While certain groups welcomed the apex court's verdict thinking it would now be easy to detect and throw out the 'hordes' of illegal Bangladeshi migrants, others fear the exit of the special piece of legislation could lead to genuine citizens belonging to the minority communities being victimized or harassed in the name of detecting Bangladeshi aliens.

The Illegal Migrants (Determination by Tribunals) (IMDT) Act, a federal legislation, was introduced in Assam on October 15, 1983, at the height of the 'anti-foreigner' (anti-Bangladeshi migrants) uprising spearheaded by the All Assam Students' Union (AASU). With the introduction of the IMDT Act, Assam became the only State in India where the Foreigners Act was not applicable.

Over the past two decades, just about 1,500 'illegal Bangladeshis' have been expelled, according to official records. Even for this number, however, there is no evidence that Bangladesh has officially accepted their return.

It was in 1998 that the All India Lawyers' Forum for Civil Liberties filed a public interest litigation (PIL) in the Supreme Court seeking a direction to the Centre and the State Governments in Assam, Meghalaya, West Bengal, Mizoram, Tripura and Delhi to deport all Bangladeshis living illegally in India.

Then, in 2000, former All Assam Students Union (AASU) president, and currently member of the Lok Sabha (Lower House of Parliament) from the AGP, Sarbananda Sonowal, moved a PIL seeking the quashing of the Act itself. After a five-year legal battle, the Supreme Court's verdict came on July 12, 2005. The Court's observations were interpreted by the AASU, AGP and the BJP as a vindication of their stand.

Significantly, however, the Supreme Court's order said: "All the tribunals and appellate tribunals under IMDT Act shall cease to function. All cases pending before (these) tribunals shall stand transferred to Foreigners (Tribunal) Order and be decided under Foreigners Act." The ruling Congress in Assam found this a great relief. "The positive aspect of the Supreme Court verdict is that it did not leave detection of foreigners to police and directed constitution of tribunals under the Foreigners Act," Assam Chief Minister Tarun Gogoi was quoted as saying. He said the Congress party was all along demanding that the foreigners should be detected through a judicial process and that the matter should not just be left to the police machinery. So, it seems clear that the exercise of detecting and throwing out illegal migrants is not going to see results overnight even under the new arrangement

Assam : Too many Autonomy Movements

In its diversity, Assam epitomises India. It is not without reason that it has been called an ethnic and cultural mosaic, embracing in its fold the *Ahoms, Bodos/Boros, Rajbongshis, Mishings, Miris, Deuris, Hojais, Meches, Lalungs (Tiwas), Kacharis, Rabhas* and several other smaller groups in its plains, with a significant presence of the *Bengalis, Biharis, Oriyas, Santhals, Punjabis, Sikhs, Nepalese, Bhutanese, Sikkimese;* and of late, a smattering of the people south of the Vindhyas. To complete the picture of this bewildering diversity, the two autonomous hill districts alone are inhabited by the tribes like *Chakma, Dimasa, Garo, Hajong, Hmar, Khasi, Jaintia, Synteng, Pnar, war, Bhoi, Lyngngam, Kuki* (tribes), *Lakher, Man* (Tai speaking), *Mizo* (tribes), *Mikir* (now, Karbi), *Naga* (tribes), *Powi*, etc. Physiographically, Assam is land of great plains, great hills, and verdant valleys. But unfortunately, this land of bounty and beauty has been wrecked by inhuman levels of continual violence unleashed by various militant and insurgent outfits since the dawn of India's Independence.

Differences: Natural and Man-made

The militancy in Assam did not develop suddenly, nor did it spread to all parts of the North-East simultaneously. But it certainly had its origins in Assam for a variety of reasons. The initial impetus came from the ethnic resurgence and identity assertion in the wake of our Independence, which ultimately led to the vivisection of the Region. Some analysts aver the downslide could have been addressed promptly and effectively when they initially raised their head in the *Naga* and *Mizo Hills.* Others feel that disintegrative forces and separatist proclivities were in-built in the history of the Region, and unraveling of the pieces was almost inevitable. Still others hold the huge influx of human beings into the State from East Bengal/Pakistan, later Bangladesh (foreigners) and other parts of the nation (outsiders) as a major cause of troubles in Assam today, and more potentially dangerous, tomorrow!

Then there was certain hiatus between the inhabitants of the *Hills* and the *Plains.* Some scholars blame the British for keeping the *Hill* people away from the plains people through the instrumentality of certain deliberate policy and administrative measures, already discussed. That restricted the social and political interaction between the two peoples (Singh, S.N., *Mizoram, Historical and Geographical,* 1994). This created and then widened not only the physical but also the mental hiatus between the two communities. The natural process of social and cultural assimilation at various levels came to be thwarted. The march of time and exposure to modernity, changing lifestyles, social ethos and political perceptions, all added to the chasm. *Mutual distrust* was the natural outcome. If the hill tribals were nomadic, uncivilised, and even barbarians to the plains people, the latter were dubbed as 'grasping' and 'rapacious' outsiders; and interestingly, most, if not all, tribes had their own nomenclatures for the outsiders, like the *Dokhar (Khasi), Vai (Mizo), Mayang (Manipur),* etc.; and all these terms were disparagingly dismissive pejoratives for these not-so-loved outsiders.

Man and nature, it seems, complimented each other in creating and nurturing an unhappy picture. Physiographic constraints, geographical distance and isolation, and inter- and intra-tribal hostilities of the early times were the realities of situation before the Ahoms and the British tried to extend regular administration to the hill areas. Subsequently, peripheralisation of the Region, yawning communication gaps, long years of neglect, indifference of the nation to the hardship and concerns of their compatriots in the strategic Region, "unimaginative" Government policies, and gross ignorance of the tribal ethos and susceptibilities, created among the Tibeto-Burman people a sharp awareness of their ethnic and cultural differentiation between the "so-called" mainstream and themselves—or so have written some analysts. It is only the natural next step if "they tilt towards making closer affinities in the Shan and Kachin States of Burma and in the Chittagong Hill Tracts of Bangladesh".

The *Assamese* middle class has been described earlier as fractious, and divided along the ethnic, communal, regional and linguistic lines. It was, perhaps justifiably, dubbed as 'movemental' and 'agitationist' and at times, less charitably, as 'xenophobist' (Das, A., 1991; cited in *Reorganisation of*

North-East India, 1996). A 'Study' (Chattopadhyay, 1990) established that there were as many as 19 (10 in Assam alone) ethnic movements in .North-East, all demanding further reorganisation and division of the Region.

Revivalist Organisations and their Variants

Assam has faced a number of revivalist organisations, including some revanchist ones, from fairly early times. Elites of ethnic groups, which lamented their sinking to insignificant positions from their erstwhile dominance, thought of reviving their old glories to reclaim their due share in the power structure, through organisations like:

1. Ahom Association 1893
2. Koch Rajbhongshi Sanmilan 1912
3. All Bora Chhatra Sanmilan 1918
4. Kachari Sanmilan 1921
5. Kachari Students Association 1922
6. Boro Maha Sanmilan 1924
7. Mattak-Moran Sanmilan 1937

What follows are a variety of literary, socio-cultural and students organisations.

Literary Organisations

1. Assam Sahitya Sabha
2. Bodo Sahitya Sabha
3. Rabha Sahitya Sabha
4. Deuri Sahitya Sabha
5. Mishing Sahitya Sabha
6. Tiwa Sahitya Sabha

Socio-Cultural Organisations

1. Tai Historical and Cultural Society
2. Mising Bane Keband
3. Banak Puplik Maung Tai
4. Chutia jati Sanmilan

Students Wings of most Ethnic Groups

1. All Assam Students Union—AASU
2. All Bodo Students Union—ABSU
3. Kachari Students Union
4. All Rabha Students Union

5. Moran Students Union
6. All Tai Ahom Students Union
7. Karbi Students Union
8. Tea Tribes Students Union
9. Mishing Students Union
10. Tiwa Students Union
11. All Tribal Students Union

Several Students Unions have played a leading part in various movements in Assam, e.g., AASU Movement against foreigners in Assam and ABSU's for establishment of Bodoland.

Another point of note is that till the late 1960s, there was no Minister of Cabinet rank in the State Ministries from members of *Ahom-Tai Mongoloid group*. This and other such 'neglects' are cited as evidence of discrimination against the concerned group or community and come handy as justification for starting an agitation or launching a revivalist or identity-related organisation or movement.

Political Platforms

The nature of middle classes and differences, natural and man-made, among the communities have given birth to a variety of dissonances, first in the entire Region and later (presently) in Assam as it exists today, giving rise to issue-based or demand specific movements and platforms, at one time or other. Some of these are listed here:

1. Ahom-Tai Mongoloid Rajya Parishad (Later, to be renamed Ujani Asom Rajiya Parishad); Ahom Movement
2. Plains Tribal Council of Assam (PTCA)
3. Bodo People's Action Committee (BPAC)
4. Assam Movement (against foreigners) led by AASU and (1979-85).
5. United Tribal Nationalist Liberation Front
6. ULFA
7. Assamese agitation leading to the Official Language Bill of 1960
8. The above Bill, declaring Assames as official language of Assam gave birth to two organisations in Bengali-speaking Cachar (Barak Valley) to safeguard its linguistic interests and to espouse the cause of its Bengali population:
   (a) Nikhil Asom Banga Samiti
   (b) Cachar Zila Gana Sangram Parishad

9. Medium of instruction movement launched by other linguistic minorities in 1972
10. Autonomous State Demand Committee (ASDC) for UT status for two Hill Districts of Assam
11. Tiwa agitation for an ADC for their tribe
12. Rabha agitation for an ADC for their tribe
13. Mishing agitation for an ADC for their tribe (The above three are respective Movements by Rabhas, Tiwas and Mishings)
14. Bodo Movements for autonomy and secessionism.
15. The agitations mentioned at Ser 8 above led to the Cachar Movement.
16. Bishnupriya Conundrum
17. Islamic Militancy

We have seen "larger Assam" being divided into Seven States, the "present Assam" being just one of them. If some have chosen to call this unhappy denouement as the end result of "the ethnicity run amok", others justified it as the logical culmination of a process set in motion by ethnic assertions and people's urge for self-identity. But this does not seem to be the end of troubles for the rump Assam. Its troubled history seems to be intent upon continuing on its perilous path, "bent upon causing further self-inflicted injuries to its soul. Its integrity is still under various kinds of threats: Some immediate ones of the ethnic variety; others medium-term, of racial variety; and third, long-term, of religious variety. If the demand for Bodo Land and UT status for two *Hill* districts belong to the first category, the demand for separation of Barak *Valley* from Assam, presently waiting in the wings, answers the second category.To the third category belong the two threats, which will cause grievous hurt to Assam with sinister implications for the Indian *Nation* as a whole: ULFA's desperate struggle for secessionism which in turn, will inevitably give a fillip, at a certain future stage, to the secessionist yearnings of sections of large Muslim population in the Region, which is increasing disproportionately due to natural increase and more dangerously, because of continuing immigration (some Assamese and Indian academics call it infiltration). The latter will no doubt be helped by Pakistan and other members of the "Ummah", as has been seen in the recent years in case of Chechen and Kashmir imbroglios. Some of these movements are discussed hereafter, bar the ones at Sers 6 (ULFA) and 14 *(Bodos)*, discussed in Chapters 4 and 5 respectively.

Militant and Insurgent Outfits Operating in Assam

What follows is the list (for record) of terrorist/militant/ insurgent outfits operating in Assam alone as downloaded from www.satp.org on 30 September 2005.

Groups Proscribed under POTA

1. National Democratic Front of Bodoland—NDFB
2. United Liberation Front of Assam—ULFA

Active Terrorist/Insurgent Groups

1. Adivasi Cobra Force—ACF
2. Dima Halam Daogah—DHD
3. Hmar People's Convention-Democracy—HPC(D)
4. Kamatapur Liberation Organisation—KLO
5. Muslim United Liberation Front of Assam—MULTA
6. United People's Democratic Solidarity—UPDS
7. Harkat-ul-Jehad—HUJ
8. Harkat-ul-Mujahiddin—HUM
9. Karbi National Volunteers—KNV
10. Karbi People's Front—KPF
11. Islamic Liberation Army of Assam—ILAA
12. Koch Rajvanshi Liberation Organisation—KRLO
13. Muslim Tiger Force—MTF
14. Muslim Volunteer Force
15. People's United Liberation Front—PULF
16. Rabha National Security Force—RNSF
17. Tiwa National Revolutionary Force—TNRF
18. United Liberation Front of Barak Valley—ULFBV
19. Dimasa National Security Force—DNSF
20. Bodo Security Force—BdSF
21. Kuki Revolutionary Army—KRA

Inactive/Dormant Outfits

1. Adam Sena—AS
2. Adivasi Security Force—ASF
3. All Assam Adivasi Suraksha Samiti—AAASS
4. Barak Valley Youth Liberation Front—BVYLF
5. Bodo Liberation Tigers—BLT
6. Gurkha Tiger Front—GTF
7. Islamic Seva Sangh—ISS
8. Islamic United Reformation Protest of Assam—IURPA
9. Muslim Liberation Army—MLA
10. Muslim Security Council of Assam—MSCA

11. Muslim Security Force—MSF
12. Revolutionary Muslim Commandos—RMC
13. United Liberation Militia of Assam—ULMA
14. United Muslim Liberation Front of Assam—UMLFA

Aasu's Anti-foreigners Movement (1979-85)

The Anti-Foreigners Movement had spawned a considerable amount of literature books, magazine features and newspaper articles, scholarly theses, *et al.*, which attempted to analyse its course, context and character as also the causes that led to it.[1] The agitation, launched and run by the AASU, with AAGSP as junior partner, can easily be termed as one of the greatest mass upheavals in the history of post-1947 India. It should be useful to mention briefly the causes that led to it.

The long-festering problem of continued influx of the immigrants and infiltrators from across the border, and consequently, the ever-increasing pressure on land, coupled with the fear of the Assamese losing their socio-political identity, seemed to be the immediate, motivating factors, or provocations for the Movement. But some analysts would like to think that the real reason lay deeper in the history of Assam going back even to the British days. In fact, the real cause of this popular outburst was the decades of economic neglect of the State by the Independent India, and even worse, its continuation of policy of imperial exploitation of Assam's resources followed by the British (1826-1947) period. It is significant that the most-recent popular movement that preceded the Assam movement was the one of the 1974 led by the AASU protesting the economic backwardness of the State. There was great paucity of productive capital in the State and its annual growth rate during 1970-1980 decade was a mere 0.4 per cent against All-India average of 1.43 per cent. The number of the unemployed rose at an alarming rate during the 1971-1981 period, with the applicants on the live register of the Employment Exchange increasing as much as 270 per cent. More significantly, during the same period the educated unemployed increased by 343 per cent. Of the total number of job-seekers in December 1980 (3,50,000), as many as 1,50,000 were post-matriculates and the ITI and Engineering Diploma holders. Against this rising demand, unfortunately, the job sector in the State Government was virtually stagnant, "while the PSUs under the Central Government were known for their discriminatory attitude in the matter of appointment of the local candidates, particularly, the Assamese and tribals".[2] This discrimination was certainly rankling the mind of the Assamese educated middle class, a class that really mattered. "Such feelings spread poisonous seeds, creating further socio-economic tensions." Some analysts wrote that those in authority were taken in by the stillness that preceded the storm and earthquake.

The theorists of discrimination cited the patterns of employment, as on 21 February 1976, at the NF Railway Headquarters at Maligaon, Guwahati. Of the total of 4,474 employees, 59 per cent had their birth-places outside Assam; and of these, 57 per cent came from former East Bengal (now Bangladesh) and 22 per cent from West Bengal. Only 41 per cent (numbering only 1830) came from within Assam. The Bengali factor always weighed heavily on the Assamese mind, and in this case, 79 per cent of the outsiders were Bengalis, and this does not include the Bengalis, within Assam. This was only the proverbial tip of the iceburg, they asserted, for the situation in the State's coal, tea, oil and plywood industries was even worse. In the 1970s, the realisation was dawning that barring the coal, the latter three industries seemed to be having little impact on the economy of the State, and consequently, on the economic prosperity of the common man.

One scholar[3] thought that the tea industry which had grown up with unduly large concessions from the British rulers had done almost nothing for the welfare of the people of Assam.[4] Enormous profits made by the British and Indian companies were invariably channelised outside the State. Even in the matter of sales tax, Assam got only about half the amount secured by West Bengal by virtue of the fact that head offices of most of the tea companies were located in Calcutta. The *Assam Tribune* (15 June 1980) reported that for the year 1979-1980, *Assam* got only Rs. 22 crore as sales tax on the tea produced in the State, against Rs. 42 crore that went to *West Bengal*. A quick survey of profits made by the tea gardens in Assam in the years preceding the AASU Movement showed that the 175 Agency House gardens which had foreign capital involved, posted gross profits ranging between 1 and 12 crore. Transfer of ownership of tea gardens from British to the Indian hands made no difference to Assam's economy as not only the profits kept flying outside the State but the new Indian owners also brought the outsiders to man the managerial positions. 82 per cent of the managerial posts in Assam tea gardens were held by persons from outside the State.[5] A recurring heartburn for the *Assamese* is that despite the fact that 756 tea gardens of Assam produces 55 per cent of the country's tea and earned an annual foreign exchange of over Rs. 500 crore for the nation, not only most of the head offices of the tea companies continues to be located in Calcutta but even the main office of the *Tea Board*, the highest authority of the tea industry, continued in that city. One estimate placed Assam's annual earnings during 1962-1976 at $ 5,250 million, with an average annual production of 250 million Kgs, at tea price of $ 2.50 per Kg. But the industry's "role in the State still remains predominantly colonial, with not even marginal investment being made to develop the economic infrastructure of the region".[6]

The situation was no different for the plywood extracted from the State. Assam's share of the proceeds was a mere Rs. 35 lakh against the Centre's Rs. 80 crore.

A look at the oil industry also presents a dismal picture as far as Assam's economy is concerned. *Assam's* only private sector oil wells at *Digboi*, operating since 1890, produced some 0.1 million tonnes of crude annually, till 1962. The production expanded sharply from the late 1960s, with discovery of oil in several areas of *Upper Assam,* when it touched an annual figure of 3.5 million tonnes. 1970s onwards, it was 5 million tonnes a year. But the royalty paid by the *Centre* for the *Assam Crude* on the eve of the popular upsurge of 1979 was a mere Rs. 42 per tonne. It was only in the mid-1980s that the rate was raised to Rs. 325, and subsequently to Rs. 578 per tonne. The *Assam Government* demanded much higher rates, 20 per cent of the posted price of equivalent *Middle East Crude* in India, but *Centre* did not accede. Even in the matter of sales tax on the Assam crude, the *State* got only Rs. 574 per tonne, whereas the Centre got Rs. 991 per tonne.[7]

It was an unhappy scene on the kerosene front as well. The sales tax on it amounting to several crores went to *West Bengal* till 1979 since the marketing division of the product was located at *Siliguri*, the kerosene from the *Assam* refineries was carried there by one of the world's longest pipelines. In the matter of natural gas, of which Assam has an estimated reserve of over 60 billion cubic metres, the *Centre* displayed an even worse sort of indifference. "Over 50 million cubic feet of natural gas are flared up daily in Assam's oil fields[8], whereas its proper utilization would have turned the *State* into one of the richest in India in the matter of power generation, and production of various industrial goods like a variety of rubbers, nylons plastics, polyester fibres, paints and dyes, lacquers, pesticides, and other sundry *Chemicals.*[9]

Considering the facts about tea industry the regional scholars aver that "there is much gist in the allegation that this industry in *Assam* is part of the overall colonial exploitation of the State by big industry and the Centre". They believe that with a little bit of sympathy and positive attitude towards the *State* and its economy, both the tea and oil sectors could have contributed substantially in achieving the desideratum of improving the overall condition of the people of the region, "thereby keeping both the growth of secessionist ideas and forces espousing them, in check".

Adding to the growing feeling of colonial exploitation was the problem of ever-increasing influx and consequent pressure on land. Not only was there some jugglery over the influx figures in the state, with scholars either exaggerating or underplaying the crisis caused by such influx, depending upon which side of the fence they stood, there was also an effort to over-paint the benefits accruing to the State from the labours of the immigrants. The influx from East Bengal had been a common phenomenon in the early decades of the 20th century; and undoubtedly, the migrants had added to the State's economy by opening up difficult waste tracts and riverine belts for cultivation, which the local Assamese had been unable or unwilling to do. The immigrants, land-hungry, hard-working, and hardy lot, did prove their usefulness in the initial stages. But beyond a point, their presence was bound to be resented, making them unwelcome guests. This is what exactly happened as the immigrant pressure on the reserved tribal belts and blocks and the grazing areas increased; and the Assamese public opinion swiftly veered against immigration. The immigrants were seen as encroachers on the lands of the Assamese cultivators and the Government lands, and the reserved forests. To stem any further tensions between the sides, the British Government introduced the line system in 1920 to restrict the immigrants, mostly Bengali Muslims, to certain areas. But the measure does not seem to have produced the desired results. The 1951 Census revealed that the number of settlers had risen from 3 lakhs in 1921 to 5 lakhs in 1931. Attempts by Assamese members to legislate laws to prevent any further settlement of immigrants met with little success during the 1920s. Consequently, during the 1930-1936 period, as many as 59 grazing, forest, and village reserves were thrown open, de-reserved, so to say, in Nowgong district alone to the immigrants under the Colonisation Scheme.[10] Citing data from Nowgong district, a researcher[11]! points' a grim picture of threat posed by the immigrants to the Assamese people:

> "Out of the District's total occupied area of 5,41,160 acres (sown and fallow) in 1936, 2,04,078 acres, or 37.7 per cent, were under the immigrants' occupation, as against 62.3 per cent still in the hands of the indigenous people. The cultivable waste lands other than fallow in the district amounted to more than 1.4 million acres. The land-hungry Muslim immigrants, segregated and pitted against all odds never appreciated the Assamese point of view. If all men were equal in the eyes of Allah, why should thousands of acres of land remain waste, particularly when men in search of livelihood and lebensraum were available to turn them into smiling fields.... They wanted the Line System to go."

This was the threat the Assam movement was to highlight during its agitation against the foreigners, for the simple reason that immigration from across the border had continued even in the post-1947 period. The land alienation was adding to anti-immigrants sentiment among the Assamese people. All immigrants were coming to be perceived as hostile presence.

Land is another emotive issue that impinges upon the common Assamese. Decrease in the average size of ownership holdings, very high percentage of households owning no land (and to know that there was practically no problem of landlessness in pre-1947 Assam), reduced forest cover, etc. and resulted in pressure on the land. It needs emphasis that the land question in Assam is an extremely complicated problem, and it is this question, which more than the "ethnic" dimensions and "threat to identity" invested the Assam Agitation with a measure of legitimacy.

It was only natural that in course of time the students' demand for economic development of the State would be shifted to the unwelcome presence of the foreign migrants who were seen as the ones mainly responsible for the present unhappy state of affairs. The Assamese people became even more apprehensive when it dawned upon their mind that the migrants, particularly the immigrant Muslims, constituting easily the largest single vote-bank of the State, were about to emerge as a viable political entity. The long-built Assamese fear of being outnumbered and out-voted in their homeland found official confirmation in the statements of the Chief Election Commissioner (CEC) Shakdher, who expressed serious concern over the fact that the foreign nationals, constituting a sizeable proportion of the voters, would be affecting the outcome of the poll verdict. It was an obvious and unacceptable infringement of India's sovereignty. To ensure that the foreigners do not participate in the polls, the CEC urged upon the Union Ministry of Home Affairs to issue Identity Cards to the genuine voters of the State. For reasons administrative, political, or whatever, the CEC's warnings fell on the deaf ears in New Delhi. The advocates of autonomy/Swadhin Asom saw the Centre's response as arrogant indifference towards Assam's interests and sensitivities. The Assamese intellectuals of the Independence period had come to associate such arrogance and insensitivity with leaders like Nehru, and they perceived the current crop as no different.

The final shove of the Assam movement on the foreigners' issue came from the event of updating the rolls for the Parliamentary bye-election to the Mangaldoi constituency caused by the death of a sitting member. The tribunal set up by the State Government for the purpose declared as many as 45,000 voters in an electorate of 6 lakhs as foreigners. The foreign infiltrators had thus finally emerged as a major electoral factor in Assam's polity. Something had to be done to stem the tide. It was this aim and under these circumstances that a plan for united action among the All Assam Gana Sangram Parishad (AAGSP) composed of some regional parties, the Asom Sahitya Sabha, and the AASU, was born at Dibrugarh on the initiative of the AASU in August 1979. Within three mnths, Assam Movement had begun.

It should be relevant to mention some of the salient features of Assam Movement, whose very success seemed to have helped the demand for Swadhin Asom, subsequently spearheaded by ULFA. The Movement was, by and large, a democratic[12] agitation. But for its wide popular base, the Movement could not have sustained itself for five long years, in the face of vigorous (repressive) measures adopted by the Government to suppress it, claim its supporters. They also postulate that given the scale of people's participation, it must be conceded that there was a great degree of "national" content in it. The Assamese middle class, no doubt, played a leading role in the agitation, but its success must be ascribed to "the strong degree of support it received from the rural masses, both Assamese and tribal". The "civil disobedience programmes", "Janata Curfews", oil blockade, and finally, the boycott of the 1983 polls would not have been possible if the rural population of Assam had not overwhelmingly responded to the call of the AAGSP (The counterview that the coercive measures and violence threatened by its leaders could have silenced the opposition, or even forced the reluctant to join in, need not necessarily be dismissed as untrue. The "Swadhin Asom" (=Independent Assam) exponents aver that certain organisations supporting secessionism were also active partners in the movement.

It is also averred that by the time the Assam Accord was signed in August 1985, people's confidence in the Centre had been shaken, "because of the excessive force used by the Government during the agitation to suppress it, creating a vacuum in the political space with the virtual nullifying of the Congress which had ruled the State almost uninterruptedly since 1947. The "Independent ..Assam" theorist posits that this vacuum was sought to be filled in by forces which propagated separation from India through an armed struggle. And this space and opportunity, ironically offered by the success of AASU, was exploited by the ULFA to strengthen itself and its secessionist platform.

Subsequent to the success of the Movement, certain yearnings for Swadhin Asom resurfaced when the realisation dawned on the section of the youth that despite the massive involvement of the people, nothing very tangible had been gained by them. The disillusionment was further strengthened when the AASU-spawned AGP Government failed to achieve any success on the issue it had waged the long, acrimonious war for. The number of illegal foreigners the Students Ministry expelled from Assam was negligible. It was not surprising then that the ULFA increased its influence among the people during the Mahanta (1985-1990) Ministry. Some analysts claim that the extremist and irreconciled elements of AASU were the ones who provided leadership to the ULFA!

The above is an account of the causes that led to the Agitation, in broad terms, and some views about it being democratic or otherwise. What follows are some additional information on the Agitation, fleshing out some details on the aspects already mentioned above.

Assam Accord: Some Prominent Features

Some prominent provisions of the *Accord* signed on 15 August 1985 are mentioned here:

1. For purpose of detection and eviction of foreigners, 1-1-1966 shall be base date and year.

2. Foreigners who came to Assam after 1-1-1966 and up to 24-3-1971 shall be detected as per provisions of the Foreigners Act, 1946 and their names deleted from the Electoral Rolls. After expiry of 10 years, their names shall be restored to the Rolls.
3. Foreigners who came to Assam after 25-3-1971 shall be expelled as per the law.
4. The Government will give due consideration to certain difficulties expressed by the AASU/AAGSP about the implementation of the IMDT Act, 1983.
5. International border shall be made secure against future infiltration by erection of barbed wire fencing and... construction of a road...along it.

Violence Indeed was Part of the Movement

The impact of demographic changes as an important conflict-generating cause had come to the limelight in the two decades of 1970s and 1980s. However, the resentment over the large scale unchecked migration into the region from foreign countries East Pakistan/Bangladesh in the main, and Nepal and Bhutan on smaller scale had been brewing much before the anti-foreigners' agitation burst out in the late 1970s, subsequently engulfing various parts of the State. But when the immigrant population impacted upon the electoral processes of Assam, it became an explosive mixture. When many non-Assamese were elected to the State Assembly in 1977, the indigenous Assamese got apprehensive about their position in their own home. It was this spark, say some analysts, that started the movement in July 1979 for the eviction of these foreigners from Assam. The joint AASU-AGSP agitation was indeed peaceful in the initial stages, "and they even appealed to the Army not to use its guns against the volunteers of the Movement, whose sole objective was to protect Assam, and hence, protect India's sovereignty and independence. The agitation gained momentum fast and by the end of November 1979, all organs of the Government were infiltrated into". The oil production and distribution had been taken over by them; NF Railway took order from them, transport was controlled by them; the AIR Gauhati was broadcasting their programme; and the local media was fully supporting their cause. "All being terror-stricken, nobody dared to challenge them in the State", said a contemporaneous report. "It was the stage when they ran a parallel Government, a la Sheikh Mujib in East Pakistan before its formal demise on 17 December 1971." The State Government being near defunct, President's rule was imposed in December 1979.

In January 1980, the agitationists resorted to mass violence and terrorism, in which many people were killed and about 15,000 rendered homeless due to fear and arson, who were moved into relief camps. It was about this time that the minorities started losing confidence and began to separate themselves from the students' agitation. The Army was called in and given responsibility for internal security from 28 March 1980. The entire State, excluding the North Cachar Hills District, was declared a disturbed area under the provisions of the Assam Disturbed Areas Act, 1955 and the Armed Forces (Special Powers) Act, 1958, which were promulgated on 6 April 1980. The Gauhati High Court stayed the implementation of this notification on 8 April. Later, the Court modified the stay order partially and enjoined that the stay order would remain in respect of Section 4 of the Assam Disturbed Areas Act, 1955 and Section 4A of the Armed Forces (Special Powers) Act, 1958. "This partial stay constrained the powers of the forces to a considerable extent and put them at a serious disadvantage."[13] Subsequently, the Government had to approach the Supreme Court for necessary relief. During this period, the Army was also charged with the responsibility of flushing and production of oil that they did successfully, which in turn affected the image of the agitators. Consequently, a popular Government was formed on 6 December 1981. Due to the loss of support in the Assembly, the Government resigned and President's Rule had to be once again imposed on 30 January 1982.

During the period 1980-1983, a number of rounds of talks were held between the Centre and the agitation leaders, but without any positive outcome. Election had to be held before March 1983 to fulfil a constitutional requirement. The Student leaders demanded complete revision of electoral rolls before holding of the elections in order to delete the names of the foreigner; from these rolls. That being not possible due to immensity of the task, the Government scheduled the elections for February 1983. The agitationists made every effort to thwart these polls, resorting to intimidation and assassination of the candidates, threats to the Government employees engaged in the poll process and the voters, kidnapping, rapine, *et al.* There was widespread violence, causing death and destruction. The worst was on 18 February 1983 when over 1700 lives were lost in the worst-ever acts of mindless violence in Nellie and some other places. The February 1983 Poll was most violent ever. Consequently a popular Government under Hiteswar Saikia came to power. The SFs were able to restore order, and Government initiated steps of prevent further infiltration.

The Rajiv Gandhi Government signed an Accord with the AASU-AGSP Leaders on 15 August 1985 (discussed elsewhere). An organisation, known as ULFA, had been formed in April 1979, which constituted the armed wing of the AASU-AGSP combine, and was raised to support their struggle, some analysts had suggested. Their activities assumed menacing proportions when the AGP Government came into power in December 1985, with Mahanta as Chief Minister, as a result of the said Accord in August that year. During the

AGP Rule, the minorities felt insecure and demanded greater protection. On the other hand, the tribal communities, viz, the Bodos, Karbis and Cacharis, started demanding autonomy and separation from Assam. A reign of terror and violence was let loose by the ULFA and Bodo militants in the latter half of the Mahanta Rule, and the worst hit were the tea plantations. Due to its utter failure to maintain law and order in the State, the Mahanta Government was dismissed on 28 November 1990, ULFA banned and President's Rule was imposed once again. The Army had launched operation Bajrang in September 1990 to clean up the mess. Consequent to the June 1991 Election, Hiteswar Saika's Congress came to power, and the Ministry was sworn-in on 1 July 1991. ULFA again resorted to its violent activities. The Army launched Operation Rhino on 15 September 1991 against the militants, this time achieving better results compared to operation Bajrang. Chief Minister Saikia was able to lure large number of ULFA cadres into surrender but Paresh Baruah succeeded in fleeing to Bangladesh with his considerable strength intact. In 1996 elections, Mahanta's AGP again came to power, for a second stint.

Students in Power and Foreigners Issue

Having won the victory, the AGP-AAGSP combine during their first stint in power (1985-1990) faced problems from the Bodos, their one-time acolytes. If the Bodos were proving most recalcitrant, other tribes too were picking up the ropes fast. Plains tribes by then were clamouring for autonomy. In the 1989 Karbi Anglong District Council Elections, Marxist-led ASDC eclipsed the AGP, the ruling party, spawned by the powerful AASU in 1985, after the conclusion of the 15 August 1985 Accord and on the eve of taking over power. AGP thus was the political wing of the AASU. But they were finding it difficult to find their feet in political management of the State they had taken over. For the "experienced agitators" but the "inexperienced administrators", it was even more worrisome that some of their erstwhile colleagues and the AASU hardliners were veering towards the ULFA, an outfit which later grew to menacing proportion and unleashed unprecedented violence on Assam; and it had to be finally banned for espousing secessionism.

The Students' Movement and its Government suffered crisis of confidence when they failed to come up to the high expectations raised by their victory, as also their failure to deliver on the provisions of the Accord. They also could not provide an honest and efficient governance to Assam. On the other end, Rajiv Gandhi himself was on the defensive beset by his own domestic problems: Punjab terrorism, Shah Bano case and Muslim Women's maintenance case, reservation issue in Gujarat, Bofors Gun scandal, etc. Mahanta Ministry's worst failure was its inability to achieve any success on the hot issue of illegal influx—the very subject on which the whole edifice of

Students' Movement had been built. The allegations of unabated influx continued to be made, despite the construction of border roads and fencing. Even the AASU was unwilling to buy the AGP Government argument that "it was not possible to man every inch of the border and seal it against the determined infiltrators", particularly the 180 km riverine sector. In face of the strident criticism, the AGP Government shifted the blame for their own failure to the existing laws and the regulatory procedures, particularly the Illegal Migrants (Determination by Tribunal) Act, IMDT Act for short.

The crunch came because of its failure to control ULFA and Bodo militancy, and its running amok among the tea gardens. Consequently, the first Mahanta Ministry was dismissed by the President in November 1990, and ULFA banned as an illegal organisation.

The power had corroding effect on the AGP leadership even before they completed their five years in office; it was an open secret that Mahanta and his No. 2, Bhrigu Phukan were pulling in different directions. It was no surprise when the AGP was handed down a humiliating defeat in the 1991 Assembly Elections, and Saikia-led Congress came into power (1991-1996).

During the 1985-1990 period, Mahanta Government "could not detect more than 347 foreigners, and what was even worse, could not deport even one of them". Chief Minister Saikia created a huge controversy early in his tenure (1991-1996) by declaring that there "are no (later amended to 'no new') foreigners in Assam". Possibly to spite the AGP for its loud and noisy agitation against the foreigners, he cited the 1991 Census figures to make a point: Assam's population grew by only 53 per cent during the 1971-1991 period, one per cent fewer than the national average. He even claimed to have pushed back 48,000 foreigners—"a figure too neat and trim for belief".

Another issue that invited notice (in 1994) during the Saikia term (1991-1996) was the revision of electoral rolls, again an offshoot of the contentious foreigners issue. The revision was to be carried out in 1994-95 with 1 January 1994 as the qualifying date for the next Assembly election, "then due in mid-1996." The Election Commission (EC) wanted extensive revision under its special Revised Instructions which classified the voters into List I (valid voters) and List II (suspect or doubtful voters whose names were to be marked as such on the Rolls). All Assam Muslim Students Union (AAMSU) and United Minorities Front (UMF) were stoutly opposed to these special guidelines. The revision was carried as per the EC guidelines and AAMSU and UMF have ever since been agitating to upgrade the names in List II to the status of valid voters.

Another issue belonging to this genre also cropped up in 1994-95. As per the 1985 Assam Accord, some 18,294 foreigners of 1966-71 category whose "names had been deleted from the electoral rolls for 10 years, would be re-eligible in 1995, rendering them qualified to vote in the 1996 polls. Both issues had to be put on the hold during those polls.

Mahanta with his AGP was back in power for a second stint (May 1996-May 2001). His second innings was not any the more happier experience. He was accused of having forgotten the foreigners' issue. "He is only interested in saving his chair", was another uncharitable jibe hurled at him, clinching the issue with the question: "Is not he holding on to power with the support of the very people who are even denying the presence of any foreigners in Assam"? The issue indeed seemed to have been put on a back-burner, if not forgotten, when Assam's energies were spent on combating the lawless violence unleashed by the ULFA and Bodo ultras. To cite statistics, the extremist violence had cost 1370 civilian and 2201 police lives in Assam in the 10 years (1986-96) following the 1985 Accord. Moreover, things have only worsened after 1996, as shown by the statistics cited elsewhere. Even at the end of their second stint in power in 2001, the main issue that spawned a fairly violent movement (1979-81) and put its protagonist in power, is no nearer the solution than it was at the start of it. It is an accurate indictment of and a sad reflection on the performance of the Students in power. In fact, it is worth examining if they were any different from other politicians in exercise of power. Did the one-time starry-eyed, idealistic Students use power to ameliorate the lot of the common man?

Students in Power: Were they any different?

Two student leaders, P.K. Mahanta and Bhrigu Phukan, who successfully led the movement, were the leading lights of the Government that came to power consequent to the December 1985 elections, being its Chief Minister and Home Minister respectively. The nation, celebrating the victory of the idealistic young people, had high hopes from them. They had shown their organisational and mobilisational skills during the long, bitter, and often violent movement, and captured political power in the geo-strategically important State in India.

Here are some heart-warming and interesting statistics on the leaders elected in the 1985 polls:

1. Mahanta at 32 became the youngest ever Chief Minister in India.
2. With an average age of a little over 30 years, the AGP was India's youngest ever legislature party to occupy the treasury benches in a State Assembly.
3. Only 4 of the 109 AGP MLAs had ever contested an election earlier. Only one, Atul Bora, whose father was once a Minister, lost narrowly from Marigaon.
4. There were 50 MLAs with Bachelor's degree or more; just two without any formal education.

5. By contrast, AGP members in Lok Sabha were a senior lot, headed by Dinesh Goswami. The youngest MP among them, Gokul Saikia, at 34 just fell short of becoming the youngest ever MP from Assam, yielding the honour to another Assamese, the "Venerable" D.K. Barooah who, had first entered the Lok Sabha at 33.

As is its wont, the Press went overboard; Mahanta was the idealist; Phukan, strong and silent, Sardar Patel II. But even before the mid-way mark, things soured, rivalry between the two coming out in the open. Then there were hints of corruption and nepotism taking over the idealism of the youth. Phukan accused Mahanta of not being serious on implementing the 1985 Accord, the very basis of AGP' ascent to power. Mahanta returned the honours, accusing his own Home Minister of failure to contain ULFA's demand for a Sovereign Assam. But somehow, they continued in an uneasy relationship. Two years in power, internal dissidence had become serious, compelling Mahanta to drop 12 ministers (1987). Then on, the Government was always teetering on the brink. It had failed to confront the ULFA head on; some even accused it of pro-ULFA leanings.

The crunch came on 29 July 1990 when Phukan resigned, owning moral responsibility for the killing of the Dibrugarh SP in an ambush. The real reason lay elsewhere, he believed Mahanta was spreading rumours about his links with ULFA. General Manager of the Gauhati Refinery had been abducted, along with his son and driver, and the word was going round that the Home Minister was negotiating with the militants secretly and in his personal capacity. "On a certain clarification, he decided not to press his resignation."

By design or otherwise, the Mahanta Government had failed to control and crush the militancy, and it was already in the last year (1990) of its first term. It had failed in the primary responsibility of ensuring safety and security of its citizens. It was disgrace abounding when unable to meet the rising demands of ULFA and Bodo militants, the Doom Dooma India, a subsidy of Unilever Group, airlifted its executives and their families out of Assam. It was this 'infamous' evacuation by air that highlighted the utter failure of the Government in fighting the insurgency which brought the Chandrashekhar Government to the end of its tether—and patience. In November 1990, the Mahanta Ministry stood dismissed.

Even the dismissal was not chastisement enough for the factious leaders. In 1991, Phukan revolted against Mahanta, and in an attempt to dislodge him from the Party Presidentship, charged him with corruption, nepotism, treachery and hunger for power—some charges, these! Mahanta hit back, by expelling Phukan and six other senior dissidents. The latter formed the Nutan (new) AGP (NAGP), and Party stood formally split. It helped Saikia-led Congress returning to power in June 1991 Poll, winning 66 of the 126 Assembly seats, with the AGP getting only 19 and NAGP just 5. The wilderness taught them a lesson, as the two factions united to win the May 1996 Assembly polls (some comments were unambiguous that the AGP captured power with the active support of ULFA, but more on it later). A 5-Party Coalition under Mahanta came into power. Phukan and his supporters did not find a place in the Ministry. At the Third General Convention of the AGP held at North Lakhimpur in October 1996, Phukan's marginalisation was complete when he was even dropped from the AGP Executive. Later in a clever move, he was suspended from the Party, rendering him unable to float a new party, because if he did, he would have lost his Assembly seat under Anti-Defection Act. If expelled, he faced no such handicap. So the students were no less adept in the art when it came to playing games. To embarrass Chief Minister Mahanta, Phukan had been stridently demanding scrapping of the IMDT Act which, it was generally believed came in the way of expelling the illegal immigrants; and also wanted opening of talks with ULFA, even if the latter was disinclined to do so till that time.

So this is the tale of two young student leaders who, having worked successfully together to lead a long movement, could not put their heads together even for five years for the common good of their cause and State, unable or unwilling to rise above their personal egos and petty quarrels. So, they too proved, that in politics there is place only for one on the top. With what high hopes their people had put them in power in December 1985! Having seen these students, should the public and press still be too harshly condemnatory of the professional politicians for their "hunger and lust for power"? But having finished his rival and challenger, did Mahanta give a clean, efficient governance to Assam?

AGP's Second Stint in Power: 1996-2001

The question of AGP's links with and soft corner for ULFA had always been a matter of serious speculation and comment. On 7 June 1997, Mahanta had a narrow escape when an IED exploded just as the Chief Minister's cavalcade passed by the much-revered Kamakhya Temple in Gauhati. He ordered a crack-down on ULFA. Within ten days, it was realised how tough and even embarrassing decision it had been. Surely, realised Mahanta could not have been unaware of ground realities in his own capital, where the ULFA had not only penetrated the administrative apparatus but also established a strong grip on the people by persuasion or coercion. Mahanta was scheduled to address a public meeting in his home constituency of Barhampur in Nagaon district within a fortnight. Then happened something providing a stunning proof of ULFA's influence in the State! On 17 June, the Nagaon Unit of the Ruling AGP had to sign an agreement with the Convener of ULFA's Kalangiri Council to ensure a violence-free meeting of the State Chief Minister!

Here are some interesting clauses from the Agreement:

1. ULFA, AGP, and AASU—obviously in the same order—will fight jointly against the Unified Command structure in the State and for the withdrawal of the black (read, anti-terrorism) laws.
2. The promise to struggle for the self-determination of Assam will be delivered. And this will also have to be done jointly.

Mahanta finally addressed his meeting on 20 June but not before the militants had rubbed his nose in the dust, and reduced his Party to the situation faced by the numerous tea gardens in the State—helplessly obeying the diktats of ULFA. The AGP's reaction? Same as non-combatant civilians: It acquiesced. The Press was very critical of the 'Agreement'. It was published in detail. It was widely commented that Mahanta was using the Tata Tea imbroglio (they were being blamed for helping the rebels) to obscure his own Party's links with ULFA, and his own Government's failure to fight the insurgency. It was an ultimate ignominy for the political class in general and AGP in particular that a Chief Minister had to seek permission from an avowedly secessionist outfit to hold his public meeting. But Mahanta told a Weekly that "such things (documents on Agreement) can be easily fabricated".[14] But he failed to explain why his Government flinched from taking legal action against these fabricators.

Nor was the Students' Ministry above the charges of graft and corruption. The 400-crore LOC (Letter of Credit) scam, regarding 12 cases of fraudulent withdrawals from the State treasury and subsequent disbursement of the money through the Veterinary Department without proper bank guarantees, hit the headlines in 1993, and case handed over to the CBI next year. 11 charge sheets had been filed by the end of 1997, and Mahanta was suspected to be involved in the 12th case. In 1998, the CBI approached the Governor, Lt Gen Sinha, for permission to prosecute Mahanta but Sinha rejected the request on 5 February 1999. But Mahanta's troubles were not yet over. Nabin Chandra Kalita, a poor cultivator from Hajo,[15] filed a public interest petition on 19-9-1999 in Gauhati High Court to reopen the case. The case had gone nowhere till date (November 2002).

There was a spurt of nepotism-induced dissidence in 1998 when Mahanta gave Lok Sabha ticket to his wife, Jayshree, for the General Elections that year. Mahanta somehow weathered the storm by parading a majority of MLAs at his press conference on 28 May.[16] Ironically, at the end of it all, Jayshree lost the election. But refusing to let up, Mahanta nominated Jayshree for a Rajya Sabha seat. Winning the seat, she was sworn-in in October 1999 as a member in the 197th session of that august body.[17] The following press comment should be an apt summing up of Mahanta's progress from a student leader to a politician:

"...what ULFA and Mahanta's closest colleagues now realise is that he has changed.... He is intent on keeping his chair. But like ULFA and Tata Tea, the Ministers now realise they are not dealing with a starry-eyed Mahanta. He is now Party's sole power centre, and Party's culture, once touted as revolutionary, has changed.... Staying in power takes a top priority now. Sycophancy and patronage have been imported from the Congress, Mahanta has kept all of 24 departments with himself, and with reason. 'When you have so many portfolios, it is that much easier to dole them out when people have to be won over', says a senior Minister.... As for implementing the main provisions of 1985 Accord on expelling the illegal immigrants from Assam, we can forget about it.... He is ruling Assam presently with the support of a party[18] which is fiercely pro-immigrants, legal or illegal."[19]

What was Mahanta's record in other fields? As for its financial health, Assam was virtually bankrupt. It owed over Rs. 7000 crore (till end 1997) to the Centre and PSUs. He pleaded with New Delhi for waving Assam's over Rs. 4000 crore debt and sought reimbursement of insurgency-related expenditure of Rs. 400 crore.

On the militancy front, ULFA was unrelenting in its depredations, even though the AGP had signed a virtual pact with ULFA in June 1997. Militants had killed till June 1997 over 1100 people since Mahanta took over in May 1996; the figure had climbed to 1490 till September 1997.

In view of the so-called 'Pact' AGP had with ULFA, Mahanta's attitude towards the Unified Command (UC) came as no surprise to the people. The UC was set up on 4 January 1997 under the Tezpur Corps Commander. Although Mahanta denied reports on the 8th that he was opposed to setting up of the UC but refused to acknowledge that such a Command has already been set up (four days earlier); he merely, blandly announced "that some proposals have been received". The Press reported his refusal to head the UC. In fact, he led an All-Party delegation to Delhi, met Prime Minister Deve Gowda and Home Minister Inderjit Gupta, discussed law and order situation of Assam (patently, the State subject) with them, and urged them to take necessary measures to control insurgency and find a political solution to ULFA's demand for independence. He was obviously politicking, and his Delhi visit was impelled by demands of the internal politics of the AGP—to impress the dissidents within his party. As a daily advised him editorially, "he should have followed Farooq Abdullah's example by taking over the UC", instead of an escapist visit to New Delhi.[20]

It all added up to a hopeless situation for Mahanta and his AGP. Out of 14 Lok Sabha seats for Assam, AGP did not win a single in the two general elections of 1998 and 1999. Then, the all-important question of illegal immigrants and their deportation seemed to have been forgotten. A 'cynical' question is: "Is any one interested?" The AGP was spending all its energies in retaining power. They could not get the IMDT Act amended/repealed. In two terms, the critics say, whatever number they claimed to have deported, which in any case, did not cross the three figures, "have already returned to Assam". This, in brief, is what the AASU Movement was all about, and what the AGP Government, spawned by it, had achieved in 10 years, split over its two terms of 5 years each, separated by the Saikia interregnum of 5 years (1991-96).

Finally, the inevitable question: How different were the 'Student' politician from the 'professional' politician? Does one need to give an answer!

Last Word on the Unhappy Situation

The last word on the AASU, AGP, and the present situation should belong to the two most eminent sons of Assam; one a poet and other, a historian.

In a 1998 Song, Assam's Poet Laureate, Bhupen Hazarika, asked in anguish and despair: "If we seek the sunrise, then why do we rush to embrace the sun-set?"

Assam's Historian Laureate, H.K. Barpujari,[21] is more direct if less poetical than the Bard quoted above. Says the Historian in an interview: "This phase since the Assamese movement began in 1978-79 is the worst I have seen.... The ruling AGP is its errant child, and ULFA the illegitimate grandchild ."

Mahanta's Fortunes: Ebbing

It seemed Mahanta had survived all the dissidence in his party when he was elected President of the AGP for the second time in a row since 1995 at the end of the Party's four-day fourth convention at Nagaon on 1 February 2001. When he was re-elected the AGP Chief for the second consecutive term, his wife too had been elected as one of the eleven Vice-Presidents of the Party.

The AGP came to power in Assam after signing the historic Assam Accord (1985) following a six-year agitation to flush out illegal Bangladeshi immigrants from the State. "It has been 15 years since. The AGP has ruled the State for two terms but seems to have forgotten about the Accord" *(Hindustan Times,* 29-4-2001). The Party's manifesto for May 2001 Assembly Poll released on 27 April made no mention of the unfulfilled clauses of the Accord! AGP lost the polls to the Congress.

Within three months of its rout in the Assembly Polls, the AGP, "which is the strongest regional party in Assam and has ruled the State for 10 years, suffered successive blows, with three of its former Ministers, including former

Chief Minister Mahanta, figuring in scandals involving women". In her interview published in an Assamese Weekly on 15-8-2001, Sanghamitra Bharali, a language officer in the Assam Assembly, claimed that she and Mahanta were married on 11 March at the Bigneshwar Ganesh Temple in Mumbai. Stung by the bigamy charge, Mahanta handed over charge of the party presidentship to Biraj Sharma, until October. The other former ministers involved in the sexual escapades were Rajendra Mushahary and Jatin Mali (For details, *see* the *Frontline* of 14-9-2001 and *India Today* dated 3-9-2001).

As if the bigamous scandal was not enough to make a dent in his personal graces, some months later, his wife lodged a FIR with Delhi Police that Mahanta had physically beaten her. Then came the unkindest cut of the political kind. The AASU accused Mahanta of "being the greatest traitor the State has ever seen" for betraying their agitation against the Bangladeshi migrant. AASU advisor, Samujjal Bhattacharya says "Mahanta has 'done nothing' to get the IMDT Act revoked when he was in power for two terms." Mahanta hits back saying his Government had filed petition in the SC in 1999 praying for revoking of the Act. Incidentally, the new Congress Government of Assam under Gogoi, after coming to power in May 2001, changed its stand and submitted a revised petition before the Apex Court, saying the State Government was against scrapping the Act (*Indian Express,* 22-8-2002). Incidentally, the betrayal charge came soon after the return (July 2002) of Mahanta from his 11-month self-exile consequent to the bigamy charge on 15 August 2001.

Once a darling of the Assamese people who led a sustained 6-year Anti-Foreigners Agitation of the AASU and twice was the Chief Minister of Assam Mahanta had—or, so it seems as of now—a sad end of his political career. After years of intra-party blood-letting, he was publicly called a 'betrayer' by his party, first suspended and then expelled from it in July 2005. Presently he heads his own party, a faction of the mother organisation.

ASSAM'S HILL DISTRICTS: THEY WANT AUTONOMY

(Karbi and Dimasa Movements)

Presently, Assam is left with only two Hill districts in its fold: Karbi Anglong (KA) (earlier, Mikir Hills district) and North Cachar Hills (NC, for short) district; the former has some distinction, located as it is at the junction of the two geographically undemarcated segments of Assam, popularly known as the Upper Assam (UA) and Lower Assam (LA). Further, this district, the largest in Assam, is formed of two discontinuous parts: the large one to the east (Diphu Sub-division) where the district capital, Diphu, is located, is separated from the smaller one to the west (Hamren sub-division), by a strip of NC Hills and a pan-handle of Nagaon district.

Mikir (Karbi) Hills were taken over by the British in 1838 and NC Hills in 1854. The Mikirs were the more active of the two, even as they are today. The Mikir-Dimasa (NC) Tract was designated as "backward" under the provisions of the Scheduled District Act, 1874. Again the two tracts, Mikir Hills and NC (Dimasa) Hills, were designated "backward tracts" under the Government of India Act, 1919. As recommended by the Simon Commission (1928-29), the two areas were given a slightly different status under Section 92 of the Government of India Act, 1935: NC Hills were placed in the category of "Excluded Areas" (EA) and Mikir Hills under the "Partially Excluded Areas" (PEA) category. Thus these two areas were treated as special categories, which was not the case, say, with the Bodo-Kachari areas. This special treatment in the historical context is cited as justification for autonomy by these two areas. As the two had shared a common history, hence the joint struggle for a place in the sun. But it needs to be noted as well that the Mikir (Karbi)-Dimasa demand for a separate entity came much later than the Ahom and Bodo aspirations raised in their representations to the Simon Commission in 1929.

Political aspirations grew as the Mikirs got the PEA status. They were allowed limited political activities, from which emerged some prominent leaders in the mid-1930s: Samson Singh Ingti, Seng Bey, Khor Sing, Terang, etc. In 1937, these leaders, in a memorandum to Assam Governor, Sir Robert Neil Reid, at Mohungodijua, demanded a separate hill district for Mikirs. To mobilize public support for their cause, they held two conventions, at Kathalguri in 1945 and at Hawaipur in 1947. At the latter convention, a regional political forum, called Karbi-A-Durbar, was formed to intensify the movement. These stirrings and consequent demand for a separate district with functional autonomy, can be deemed to be the genesis of the latter-day agitation for the UT status for the two hill districts of Assam. But the Mikirs failed to get their district under the Raj. The two, Mikirs and Dimasas, got their wishes fulfilled with the creation of a composite, United Mikir and NC (UMNC) Hills district on 17 November 1951. The new district covered the areas of Mikir Hills Tract and its contiguous Mikir-inhabited areas of the then districts of Nagaon, Sibsagar and United Khasi and Jaintia (KJ) Hills; and the NC Hills. Its total area of 15,237 km^2 was divided into two sub-divisions of Mikir Hills and NC Hills. The UMNC District got its ADC on 23 June 1952 under the Sixth Schedule. The Mikir and Dimasa Chiefs who had ruled till then in Mikir and NC Hills respectively, yielded place to the people's elected representatives.

The search for autonomy continued even after they got the ADC for themselves. The Official Language Bill of 1960 also caused some fears among the Mikirs about their own ethnic identity, and consequently the Bill gave a fillip to the autonomy demand in the two hill districts. The Karbi-A-Durbar, the ruling political party in ADC which had accommodated dissent in its fold till then, faced some turbulence in 1964. A section of the Durbaris began to speak the language of the opposition, which stood for: (1) Naga Hills and NC Hills merger movement and (2) Mikir and K-J (Khasi-Jaintia) Hills merger movement. This meant the Mikirs (Karbis now onwards) and Dimasas going their own ways—the Karbi-Dimasa unity was under serious threat from these dissenters. To counter this threat, a new body, Riso-A-Durbar was formed; it was a youth body raised by those opposed to the dissenters.

The hill leaders felt the ADC did not have adequate powers to develop the hills. On 1 June 1970, 30 development departments/subjects were transferred to the ADC of UM-NC District, in addition to the 29 handled by it under the Sixth Schedule.[22] The addition, meant to keep these hills away from the separatist movements in other hill districts, failed o satisfy the Karbi and Dimasa leaders, only whetting their urge for more. In a 1973 Memorandum to Prime Minister, they complained of continued Assamisation in the wake of "Medium of Instruction" order. The leaders demanded an autonomous state under Article 244-A of constitution which had been expressly added to it to create an autonomous/associate (Meghalaya) within Assam in April 1970. They also demanded "500 M^2 of contiguous areas from Assam plains".

2 February 1976, the UMNC district was split into two districts. It simply meant upgradation of the two sub-divisions, Mikir Hills and NC Hills, two separate geographical entities in any case, to the district status. Some relevant details on the newly-created districts are given in the table below:

Mikir Hills and NC Hills Districts Compared

Name of the District	*Area (Sq km)*	*Population (1971 Census)*	*Main Tribes*
Mikir Hills	10,332	6,55,415	Mikir (Karbi) in clear majority; Dimsa.
NC Hills	4,890	1,49,346	Dimasa in clear majority; Zemi and other Naga groups, Hmar and Kuki.

Both districts have mixed populations, dominated by a single, specific tribe; and both have substantial non-tribal populations. Needless to say, the two districts got their own ADCs after the split.

In October 1976, Mikir Hills district was redesignated as Karbi-Anglong (KA, for short in this part of the book) district.

It needs to be mentioned that these two hill areas did not join Meghalaya when it was created as an Associate State in April 1970. They were apprehensive of being swamped in a more advanced and Christianised

Meghalaya, inhabited as these two areas were by the more Hinduised and backward tribes. Or, may be, they were persuaded to stay with Assam, with promises of greater autonomy by the Assamese leaders. The fear of subsumption war fostered for ulterior motives, perhaps! After all, it does not need deep prescience to realise that their going out of Assamese would have physically severed the Barak Valley from the Assam Valley. In any case no one—a state or an individual—acts altruistically in political field. Both sides must have seen their own interest in the *status quo*. But this limited option available to the Karbi and Dimasa leaders—of either joining Meghalaya or remaining within Assam—rankled them. After all, all the hill districts of Assam had gained either statehood or UT status. Then why this discrimination against them. Their logic was simple and straight: Both Congress and non-Congress parties had supported their movement for autonomy. That is how they gained strength. No one can charge that their demand for a separate state was handiwork of some disgruntled elements since their leadership was essentially comprised till 1982, or loosely till 1985, of Congress or Congress-related political parties.

After the 1973 Memorandum, the next one came in 1980, in which the leaders complained to the Prime Minister that their identity was under threat from the AASU-AAGSP Agitation which was out to destroy the language, culture and traditions of the tribals and minorities. The protagonists of a separate State made a powerful statement when they scored a massive victory in the Hills in the December 1980 polls. Now follows the further progress of the movement:

1. *1981*. Separate State Demand Committee (SSDC) formed under Presidentship of Dhani Ram Rongpi; a memorandum submitted to the Prime Minister for a separate state comprising, the two districts.
2. Their 1982 Memorandum accused the Assam Agitation of preventing the conduct of 1981 Census in order to thwart the planned development of their area; and that the election to the two reserved Parliamentary seats too was not allowed for the same reasons. They went further: "Assamese Language Policy came in the way of the tribal students learning English and Hindi, so essential to forge links with India and the world beyond.... The tribals were also being prevented from joining the NEHU at Shillong."
3. By 1985, academics were praising the maturity of the SSDC Movement leaders for asserting their self-identity rather than railing against the Assamese hegemonism, as the ABSU and BPAC leaders were doing. But still, there was opposition to the demand within the hills, as will be seen shortly.
4. When the Autonomous State Demand Committee (ASDC) came into being in 1986 under the CPI(ML) leadership, the movement became mass-based. Expectedly, its 1987 Memorandum to the Prime Minister

was much more outspoken and jargon-ridden.[23] They demanded statehood for the two districts, together with the Inner Line restrictions.[24]

5. Karbi Students Association (KSA) joined hands with the ASDC, and the Movement became more strident in the post-reorganisation Assam (In February 1987, the Region stood divided into 7 States).
6. The joint ASDC-KSA Memorandum of January 1990 reasserted demand for a State; at the very minimum, a UT.
7. *March 1990.* Ultimatum to Assam Chief Minister: Concede demand or face agitation.
8. *1991.* United Peoples Conference emphasised a full-fledged State.
9. KA District ADC members' 1991 memorandum to the Bhupinder Singh Committee narrated its own litany of woes: (1) The ADC was dissolved four times in the past decade, and consequently development suffered. (2) Lack of police powers came in the way of maintaining peace. (3) Processing of all projects through the Deputy Commissioner gave him discretion to delay the decisions.[25]
10. NC District ADC memorandum to this Committee had a similar ring. It too had been superseded five times between 1978 and 1990. It accused the State Government of disbursing the Positive Hill Area Financial Assistance among all districts of Assam whereas it was meant for just two Hill districts.[26]

In 1992, State Government transferred some additional subjects to the two ADCs. The ASDC-KSA combine appreciated the gesture but refused to withdraw the State plank. Meanwhile the KA District ADC where the ASDC had huge majority, was dissolved by the Saikia Government in November 1992, provoking all-round resentment. But what was the level of support for the demand in each of the two districts?

KA District

Though the movement is on in both the districts, the ASDC is more active and influential in KA District. Of course, there is opposition to the demand within the district. But more importantly, the demand, though similar, has different ramifications for the two districts. The non-Karbi groups in this district formed a Citizen Rights Protection Committee (CRPC) and accused the ASDC of practising discrimination against non-Karbis and non-tribals who, they claimed, constituted a majority in the district. They also accused the ADC of collaring lands, appointments and funds, which led to the corruption and deforestation. The ASDC promptly dubbed the CRPC as Government agents and front for the Congress Party.

The religion also came in handy in this welter of accusations and counter-accusations. 40 per cent of the Karbis are Christians, the Church having played a major role in education and politicization of the community. The CPI(ML)-led ASDC, founded in 1986 as an offshoot of the KSA, has been accused of being anti-religious, despite having been sponsored by the missionaries. The ASDC dismisses the charges out of hand.

Violence was born about mid-1990s. Subsequently, the Karbi National Volunteers (KNV) and Karbi People's Force (KPF) have been active in the district since 1996-97. It is reportedly in cahoots with the NSCN. On the other hand, the Kukis and Bodos in the district are believed to have links with KNA and BdSF respectively.

NC Hills District

The situation here is more complicated because the district is home to large number of ethnic groups, and also because of its geography. The two factors render it prone to much ethnic activity and political turbulence. This district has come to occupy particularly the Jatinga[27] Valley (famed the world over for its mass suicide by the winged species) and Barail Hills, a geo-political significant place of its own in the current insurgency scenario in the Region. This is because the territory provides a corridor for the ultras from Nagaland, Meghalaya, Manipur and the Barak Valley districts of Assam to reach Bangladesh (Sylhet) areas. Even more importantly, the area constitutes a hiatus in the continuum of insurgency network spreading from Upper Myanmar to the CHT (of Bangladesh), covering most of the tribal pockets in Myanmar, (North-East) India, and Bangladesh. The NSCN is making clever, effective moves to fill this gap.

The ethno-religious political contradictions in the area offers a convenient, and ideologically suitable opportunity for the NSCN to make a success of its ethnic aspirations. It needs to be understood that the NSCN inroads in the North Cachar Hills are of different hue and intent from its exertions in Assam, Meghalaya, or Arunachal. In the latter areas, it is carrying out its operations to stretch the SFs and/or to secure a safe passage to Bangladesh; but in the former case, it has territorial ambitions. It is for this reason that the area North of the Railway Line in North Cachar figures significantly in the NSCN maps of Greater (Sovereign) Nagaland, or Nagalim. This move is a direct threat to the Dimasas, the dominant majority in the district. But it is well-known that the NSCN has been able to coopt certain Dimasa extremist elements to further its aims. So, the NSCN is able to rope in various ethnic groups of North Cachar Hills and Karbi Anglong districts under the promise that in the event of the creation of the Nagalim, their aspirations will be legitimately accommodated. The NSCN has been particularly solicitous towards Zeliangrong *(Zemi+Liangmai+Rongmai)* group of Nagas and others around Haflong, Mahur and Maibong—assuring them of a "Homeland of the dreams of their legendary Rani Gaidinliu."

The Nagalim ideologues are casting their gaze far beyond the immediate. Once the North Cachar Hills are incorporated into the rebel-controlled Nagaland-Manipur block, they will start exploring the possibility of a corridor connecting it to the sea via the Arakans. They do not see much difficulty in making Meghalaya, particularly its uranium rich areas, part of this dreamland; and they feel the incipient insurgency, that occasionally raises its head there, can always be reinforced for achieving their desideratum.

A word on the District. The dominant Dimasas are Kacharis, who speak Dimasa written in Bangla script, not a recognized language as yet. The medium of instruction here is Bengali, Assamese, or English, though the lingua franca is a pidgin, called Haflong Hindi, used by the local station of the AIR. The district has 500 km^2 under Reserved Forest and the remaining 4500 km^2 is unclassified State Forest which can be used or misused by various militant outfits operating in/throuph it. In the recent years, the district has become a transit for NSCN(I-M) and Meitei outfits movements to Bangladesh which has replaced Burma as a sanctuary, staging area/post, and conduit for arms and training.

Its contiguity with Nagaland poses threat to the integrity of the district, particularly because it has a considerable population of Zemi Nagas. The Zemis, also found in Nagaland, are ethnically allied to Liangmeis and Rongmeis, found both in Manipur and Cachar district. The three closed ranks to create a larger grouping, impressively designated Zeliangrong, the term coined by joining the first syllables from the names of these three tribes (ze+liang+rong). Thence, the three tribes demanded creation of a separate district by merging contiguous (Naga) areas from NC (Assam), Manipur and Nagaland, as these are inhabited by their kin. For form, the three states have rejected the demand as it would mean dismemberment of their territories; but those in the know believe the move is a clever plant by the NSCN(I-M) and even Nagaland Government to further the cause of Nagalim!

The district is presently in the grip of tribal extremism. The NSCN (I-M), historically powerful in Nagaland and Manipur, spread its wings here during the 1993-95 period. Surprisingly, the outfit found allies among the sections of the youth of the Dimasa tribe, largest in the district, "numbering 1,60,000, divided into a dozen communities".

It was not that the Dimasas needed any instigation from the Nagas to engage in violence. They were no novices at the game. In 1990, they had raised a militant outfit, called Dimasa National Security Force (DNSF), then the latest entrant at the revivalist stakes. It wanted restoration of the lost glory of Dimasa Kingdom, which once had its capital at Dimapur. It was reportedly demanding ransom from the rich. Not to lag behind, the students set up All Dimasa Students Organisation (ADSO), early 1991. It wanted

Dimaland and was "reportedly set up by Assam Congress to counter the ASDC". Wheels, within wheels, perhaps!

By mid-1990s, it had not gone beyond the wall-writing; and even subsequently, it was unknown beyond the confines of the district.

The NSCN(I-M)-Dimasa alliance suffered a set-back in November 1994 when most members of the erstwhile DNSF, led by Bharat Langthasa, surrendered. But subsequently, the NSCN(I-M) managed to bring together all those who did not surrender into a new outfit called the Dima Halam Daogah (DHD). Numerically a small force, its importance lied in the fact of it being a local agent of NSCN(I-M). The two joined hands to extort large sums as house-tax in their area and as security-money from the businessmen. It was reported that Assam's Minister, Gobinda Langthasa paid Rs. 7 lakh to buy the security of his family in late 1994. If some officers were known for not paying, a large number paid out willingly or otherwise.

There are easily discernible reasons for NSCN(I-M) focusing on this district: (1) Its border with "Nagaland and Manipur is porous, guarded now by only 4 check points against twenty in the 1970s and 1980s during the anti-Phizo drive" (A February 1996 Report in a weekly). When under pressure in Nagaland and Manipur, they crossed into North Cachar Hills: when things eased off they returned. (2) It is shortest and safest transit route between Upper Burma;and Bangladesh. It is also shorter route for weapons they received at Cox Bazar by sea or in Burma by land route from markets in some South-East Asian nations. (3) The Nagas, insurgents and moderates alike, have not stopped thinking of some areas of North Cachar Hills and Bhuban Pahar area of Cachar district, both of which have some Naga population, as parts of their dreamland, Nagalim (=Greater Nagaland).

But the North Cachar Hills are not an easy world for the NSCN (I-M). Several non-tribal groups, like Bengalis, Assamese, Nepalis, Hindi-speaking people, are not its friends. The Dimasas, its largest tribe, are Hindus and culturally close to Bengalis, who make up a vast majority in Cachar area. The NSCN's pronounced Christian identity cannot endear it to the Dimasas. The Kukis are Naga group's enemy, locked in lethal combat with them in Manipur. The Baites having a small number in the district, belong to the Kuki group, as do the Halams, Vaipheis and Khelams.

Who are the potential allies of the NSCN in NC Hills? Hmars, who struggled for a separate state in North Mizoram and later settled with the State Government with an accord in 1994, could join hands. Zeliangrgng Nagas, numbering 9-15,000 in the district, could be of help. But the Zemis, vast majority in the combine, are very different from the Tangkhul and Sema Nagas, the backbone of the NSCN. Being backward in comparison, they may not feel comfortable with the NSCN. Religion is another factor setting the Zemis apart from the NSCN, because only 40 per cent of the former are

Christian. Others suggest they are one with the NSCN, flaunting of differences is a put-on!

Besides the NSCN and Dimasa militants, the KNA and HPC ultras were/are also active in certain areas, often taking shelter in the respective village of their kinsmen.

The insurgent activity was on the rise from the end of 1980s, continuing through the 1990s. Insurgency-related crimes grabbed the headlines off and on, with reports of loyalty-tax payments, kidnappings, ransom killings, extortions, etc. The period 1992-95 saw, increased attacks on the SF. In a daring ambush, 13 BSF men were killed in Mahur area, near Nagaland border, in late 1992.

Chess Board Moves and Counter Moves

The Political Report of the CPI(ML) for 1993 had promised a broader front called North-Eastern Tribal Peoples Front as an ideological counter to the Indian ruling class's perception and solution of the problem of integration of the North-East with the mainstream of the Indian polity. The wider political alignment promised and envisioned by the ASDC in the KA District ADC in the shape of this "Broader Forum" proved a case of early death with the signing of Memorandum of Understanding (MoU) between Chief Minister Saikia and the leaders of ASDC (from both districts), KSA, Dimasa Students Union and NC Hills Students Federation, at New Delhi, on 1 April 1995. Under this MoU, the ASDC agreed to accept enhanced powers much beyond those available under Sixth Schedule and gave up its insistence on Sub-State, Associate State, or Autonomous State under Article 244-A of the Constitution, a la Meghalaya of April 1970. Not only were the two ADCs to be granted vast powers, they were also to be upgraded to the status of "Autonomous Councils". The MoU had generated high hopes: "New Councils would enjoy substantial devolution under the Sixth Schedule through a unique combination of powers vested in a Sub-State, UT, ADC and Deputy Commissioners: a degree of autonomy unknown so far.... The new experiment, granting the structure vast powers...including access to Governor and Planning Commission, will be watched with interest by many organisations and groups waiting in the wings, harbouring hopes of a State or UT status for their areas." The new AGP Government, that had replaced Saikia's in May 1996, handed over 30 additional subjects to the two ADCs on 31 December 1996. But as the respected daily *Hindu* was to) editorialise (31-5-1997): "This failed to satisfy the ADCs." But it all was to prove a false dawn. Move for Autonomous State was revived.

Events of May 1997

25 May. ASDC revived the demand for an Autonomous State within Assam under Article 244-A of the Constitution, at its General Body Meeting at Haflong.

28 May. Holiram Terang, Leader of 5-member ASDC group in Assembly announced withdrawal of his party from the 5-Party Ruling Alliance of Assam,[28] led by AGP (other three being CPI, CPM, UPPA). He accused the Chief Minister of not implementing the MoU. He grandly announced the formation of an alternative political front, Assam People's Front.

29 May. Dr Jayanta Rongpi,[29] MP and Chairman, ASDC, publicly announced revival of the old demand for a Sub-State, thus completing a full circle.

These are the games they play on the political chessboard.

They Want Two States Now—Not One!

The game goes on. The ASDC ascribes absence of the job opportunities and lack of economic development to the inadequacies of the ADCs and the Assamese machinations and manipulations! So it wants sub-State despite the opposition by the smaller tribes and minorities. And now comes the ultimate truth: Being conscious of their own deficiencies *vis-a-vis* the Karbis, the Dimasas have demanded two States, one for each district, and nor one which would surely be dominated by the more advanced Karbis.

ASDC Splits

The ASDC, ruling party in the two ADCs and having one MP, split on 25 July 2000. The followers of Dr. Jayanta Rongpi, MP and Chairman ASDC, adopted a no-confidence motion in the KA.

Council, against Jetson Bey, Chief Executive Member. Babu Rongpi, Council Chairman, was prevented from presiding over the session, which was conducted by Daniel Terang, a Dr Rongpi loyalist.

The crisis had been brewing for sometime. Most ASDC leaders are members of the CPI-ML (Vinod Mishra Group). Sometime before the October 1999 General Elections, ASDC decided to contest these elections in the name of CPI(ML) and that the ASDC would contest the District Council poll. It must be noted that "the CPI(ML) Karbi Anglong Party Committee is not affiliated to the Assam State Committee, but to the Central Committee" (*The Hindu,* 27-7-2000). The decision was not liked by the rank and file of the Party. In June 2000, Holiram Terang, Leader of the 5-member ASDC Group in Assam Legislative Assembly, raised the banner of revolt, accusing Dr Rongpi of corruption. On 21 July 2000, Terang and his supporters requested for postponement of the Standing Committee meeting that day at Diphu. When the proposal was rejected by Dr Rongpi group, they walked out of the meeting. The split on the 25th was the next logical outcome.

The events only show that the politics at the district level apes the politics at the State and national levels.

Mindless Violence Enters the Scene

We have read the comment about "maturity" of the Karbi and Dimasa leaders of ASDC in conducting their movement. Again a respected scholar/

political scientist praised the leadership for their sobriety. But alas, of late the idyll stands shattered in the late 1990s.

The United People's Democratic Solidarity, UPDS (a rather unlikely name for a militant outfit) and Dima Halam Dauga (DHD) are two outfits behind the depredations, murders, and mayhem, indicative of the latest recrudescence of violence in the two Hill districts, helped no doubt by the NSCN and ULFA, both long-reputed merchants of death and destruction in the name of their wars for the rights of their respected people—the Nagas and the Assamese. The UPDS was formed in 1999 when, two smaller outfits—Karbi National Volunteers (KNV) and Karbi People's Force (KPF)—merged to strengthen the Karbi Statehood Movement being conducted by the ADC for the last decade or so. The DHD, a militant outfit of *Dimasa* is in a manner of speaking, the counterpart of UPDS in NC District. Of late, as the Dimasas veered to have a state of their own, the DHD too stepped up their depredations during 2000 in demand of a separate Dimasa State.

Initially, these two outfits were aided and trained by the NSCN(I-M) as it was keen to make inroads into the area for its own strategic considerations. Since it signed peace with the Centre in 1997, UPDS turned to ULFA for help and guidance. Indicative of ULFA's desire to help the militants in this area were two Intelligence reports of its supplying arms to UPDS: 16 advanced model AK-56s in April 2000 and some small arms and ammunitions a little later. There had been periodical militant-perpetrated crimes in the two districts earlier also, particularly in KA District, but these killings assumed sinister colours in 2000. On 9 April, UPDS cadres shot dead timber workers at Langatso in KA District. All the victims were Biharis, that is, Hindi-speaking people. It did ring up alarm bells. On the 19th, UPDS, helped by DHD, struck again, mowing down 11 Nepalis—again non-Assamese people—in a remote village of the same district, under Baithalangso police station. So, the sinister ethnic cleansing was under way. Emboldened by its success, the UPDS forced the Government of KA-NC Hills Self-Rule Territory (GKN-SRT) to get rid of all outsiders. This violence brought the focus on UPDS which, it needs notice, started the ethnic cleansing in two Hill districts 6 months before the ULFA and NDFB started similar operations in other parts of Assam. After these two killings, the Hindi-speakers continued to be targetted by UPDS and DHD in the two districts till September when some unidentified gun-men killed relatives of two senior UPDS ultras. "The killings stopped immediately" (*Hindustan Times*, 30-12-2000). After a deceptive lull of two months, the troubled KA District reverberated with gun shots again when UPDS killed 8 Biharis again at Rangnagar village. It was obvious that NSCN-trained UPDS had joined hands with ULFA which "planned to target non-Assamese Hindi-speakers in some 2000 sensitive pockets of Assam". This dispersed area is unofficially referred to as "Hindi belts". The UPDS had reportedly divided the non-Karbis into two categories of affluence: rich and very rich, charging from them

Rs. 5,000 and Rs. 10,000 as taxes respectively. Clearly, there were no poor among the non-Karbis.

The non-Assamese selected by the militants for ethnic cleansing are attractive targets; Nepalis inhabiting the hills in Hamren Subdivision and the Hindi-speakers farming in Kheroni, Howraghat, and Baithalangso areas. So are the outsiders living in the foothills of the two districts. Besides being fertile, these areas have prospered because of their proximity to the markets in the plains. Unfortunately, the people in these Hindi belts had earlier been at the receiving end of the Naxalites who held sway in the KA and NC Hills, for refusing to toe their line, the officials told the media.

In December 2001, suspected DPDS ultras killed 8 persons of a polling party in an ambush near village Langlokso under Howraghat PS. The polls for the ADCs of the two Hill Districts "are due on 5 December 2001" (*Times of India,* 4-12-2001). 5 persons belonging to an ONGC drilling party, including a Senior Scientist and an Assistant Engineer were killed in an ambush by suspected DHD militants on 24 June 2002.

Ethnic Violence in North Cachar

Hmar-Dimacha clashes in April 2003 were worst in the recent memory. Eight persons were killed during sporadic clashes at several places on the 9th. Panic-stricken 3,100 families belonging to both tribes were either rendered homeless or fled their homes. Curfew was clamped in the entire district after hundreds of Dimachas, dominating tribe of the district, allegedly armed with 'lethal weapons attacked two Hmar settlement and set over a 100 houses afire. "The Dimachas and Hmars have been at war for more than a month now", *Express* 11-4-03. On the 10th, the leaders of the DHD and the Hmar Inpui and Hmar Church met for peace talks at Haflong. The officials accommodated about 1500 Dimacha and 1600 Hmar families in five relief camps. Besides, while 200 Hmar tribals took shelter in Lumding in the adjoining Nagaon district, another 200 had fled to Meghalaya who got shelter at the Evangelical Free Church of India campus in Shillong. It was only on the 7th that Chief Minister Gogoi had visited strife-torn tribal villages in the district following the massacre of 28 Dimachas and had announced a relief of Rs. 1 lakh to the next of kin of each of those killed. The 28 victims were abducted and gunned down by the HPC ultras in the neighbouring Cachar district on 3-4-03.

In the renewed ethnic violence in the disturbed NC Hills district on 12-5-03, Narmendu Langthasa, 35, son of senior minister and veteran Congress leader Gobinda Chandra Langthasa, was shot dead by suspected HPC ultras in the heart of Haflong when he had gone to pick up his son from his school. Narmendu's elder brother Purnendu, is the CEM of the NC Hills Autonomous Council. At 10.30 AM, a little before the murder of Narmendu, Phani Lal Liengjao, an accountant in the Haflong DFO's office, was gunned by the DHD ultras.

Violence in Karbi Anglong (KA) District

29 November 2003. Six Karbis, including a 5-year girl, were gunned down in villages Piti Atong and Jilangso under Bokajan PS by Kuki Revolutionary Army (KRA) militants. 116 Karbi houses were burnt.

There was violence as the anti-talks faction of the UPDS (re-named itself as Karbi Longri [NC Hills] Liberation Front, KLNLF, in 2004, and its armed wing as Karbi Long NC Hills Peoples' Resistance, KNPR; *see Sentinel,* Guwahati 16-5-04) gave a call for 120-hour bandh on 25-12-03 in the two Hill districts, in protest against clause 8 of the Bodo Territorial Council Accord which promises to "consider sympathetically" the grant of tribal status to the Bodos settled in the two Hill districts. Karbis are dead set against it. The UPDS, created in March 1999 with the merger of Karbi National Volunteers (KNV) and Karbi Peoples' Front (KPF) with proclaimed objective of purging KA of the Non-Karbi population (including Marwaris Biharis, Nepalis, Kukis and Bengalis), got split when a faction came out for talks with the Government in 2001.

3-12-03. The KRA was formed in December 1999, with the help of NSCN (I-M), with declared objective of creation of an Autonomous Kuki National Council for the Kukis in the KA district. Its three leaders are: (1) Thangkeng Hangshing, Chairman, (2) Zet Kuki, Publicity Secretary, (3) D.T. Haokip, Information Secretary. Its 50 cadres killed three people and burnt 30 huts when they attacked a remote Karbi village, Menterang.

5-12-03. The UPDS militants made an abortive bid on the lives of the DC (Anurag Goel) and the SP (Abdul Kuddush) at the village of Hidim Terang, KA district.

24-3-04. 31 Karbi villagers were killed by KRA militants in attacks on four villages during 36 hours: (1) Udematisso under Dilai police out-post, (2) Two adjacent villages Sarpoteron and Sarkhe-Engleng, 20 km from the first, (3) Jariteron, close to Diphu. Surprisingly, not a single woman or child was killed in any of these attacks. The men were called out, lined up, and gunned down or hacked to death. These killings "were in retaliation to the 19-3-04 incident when the UPDS gunned down six Kukis at the remote village of Thangbong, 45 km from Diphu".

This was the second major insurgent killing in the Hill District since it was rocked by a fierce gun battle between the KRA and UPDS which left nearly 50 people dead from both the communities (Kukis and Karbis) in October and November 2003. Several hundred people were injured, with over 1000 villagers from two sides rendered homeless.

The two hill districts "have been witnessing sporadic internecine clashes for the past one year, with the Kuki group that had entered the State from Manipur regularly targetting the original tribes of the two districts, the Karbis and the Dimasas (of late spelt as Dimachas)"— *Express*, 25-3-04 and *Hindu*, 25-3-04.

21-7-05. The police arrested 15 adivasis in connection with a clash on the 18th which left 5 Biharis dead and over 40 houses torched in the KA district.

The Cold Statistics: Karbi Anglong District

A study disclosed that the clashes between the KRA and the anti-talks faction of the UPDS(K) during Oct 2003-Mar 2004 killed 85 persons mostly men, which included at least 23 Kukis and 54 Karbis. Again, Guwahati's *Assam Tribune* said on 28 Dec 2003 that the UPDS(K) and KRA had killed 35 persons, including 17 Kukis and 15 Karbis since Nov 2003 in KA district.

The 24-3-04 incident (mentioned above) is an instance of the highest civilian casualty (the later toll stands at 34 killed) in Assam in a terrorist incident in a single day (Praveen Kumar, Strategic Analysis, Apr-Jun 04, an IDSA publication. Again it is the largest civilian casualty in the district since the Pro-Talks UPDS faction under Horen Singhey Bey signed the cease-fire agreement with New Delhi on 23-5-2002. H.E. Kathar, the UPDS General Secretary, opposed to the talks, leads the anti-talks fraction: UPDS(K).

A word on the KRA- The outfit claims a cadre strength of 540 (2004), 180 of these being in KA district. Based in the Saikul area of Manipur's Senapati district, the KRA claims to have linkages with UKLF and (KNF-MC); NSCN, both factions of (I-M) and (K); and NDFB and DHD. It is the sole militant Kuki outfit claiming to safeguard the Kuki interests in the KA district.

Ethno-political dynamics and desperate endeavour to control the underground economy of the KA district have pitted the KRA and UPDS against each other. The Karbis are the largest tribe in the district and th« Kukis claim to be in majority in its Singhason hill area. The Kukis roam in pursuit of Jhum cultivation in the district, but their main (largest) concentration is in Manipur (15 per cent), says the *Shillong Times* (Internet Edition) of 3-12-03 (Its "Demand for Regional Council could aggravate Kuki-Karbi Clashes"). Karbi groups, including the UPDS, dispute KRA's projection of the 'indigenous' population at more than 35,000 in the Singhason hills [*See* "UPDS says No to KRA's Peace Proposal", *North-East Enquirer* 2(18), 22 Dec 03-6 Jan 04, at http://www.nenanews.com/ NEE/20/Dec 22-Jan 6/2004/ oh11.htm]. They say the Kukis are no more than 2,000 in that area, and the hugely exaggerated figure of 35,000 is KRA's 'tactic'—just a clever ploy—in justification of their demand for a Kuki Autonomous Council in the district. In a manner of speaking, both are vying for a place in the sun: if the Karbis demand a 'State' to be carved out of Assam, specifically from its two hill districts, the Kukis want an Autonomous Council for themselves to be carved out of this 'State'. Then intervenes the 'foreigners question' in this imbroglio.

Citing the examples of foreigners displacing the indigenous tribals in Tripura and threatening to do the same in Assam, the UPDS ideologues express fears that the Karbis would be outnumbered in the district by the Kuki influx that started following the Naga-Kuki clashes in Nagaland and Manipur in 1992 (For details *see* M.S. Prabhakara, "Outrage in Assam", *Frontline* at http:// www flonnet.com/fl2025/stories/ 2003 121 9006800800.htm and "Karbi-Kuki Imbroglio: Ultras Blamed for Clashes", *Assam Tribune* 30-12-03).

There are differences between the Kuki National Assembly (KNA), the apex political organisation of Kukis in the KA district and the ASDC which is fighting for a Karbi state. The KNA had first demanded an Autonomous Regional Council for the Kukis in 1992 through a memorandum to the State Government. Two rounds of talks were also subsequently held in 1997 and 1998. The ASDC split in July 2000 due to differences within the local leadership that allowed the Congress to control the Karbi Anglong Autonomous District Council. Later a faction called ASDC-United (ASDC-U) endorsed KNA's demand for a Kuki Council, obviously to widen its support base against the rival faction of ASDC-Progressive (ASDC-P), an ally of CPI(ML) that represented the area in the 13th Lok Sabha. But interestingly the ASDC(U) is now against the KNA's demand.

Besides the ethnic factors, another reason for both the outfits—KRA and UPDS—fighting for supremacy over the Singhason hill area is 2000 MT of high quality ginger it produces annually. While both the outfits lean on the local tribal populace to extort their share from this lucrative trade, the UPDS considers the area as its exclusive turf. Hence the bloody rivalry.

Stirrings Among the Rabhas, Tiwas and Mishings

It was but a matter of time before other major plains tribes like Rabha, Mishing and Tiwa would follow the path traced by the Bodos. All these three tribes are predominantly Hindu, and speak Assamese, though Mishings and Tiwas have their own Tibeto-Burman languages, the former being of the Bodo group. Here are some other relevant information:

1. *Rabhas.* Mostly found in Goalpara and Kamrup districts on the south bank and in the Darrang district on the north, they constitute a minority in Bodoland. There were 1,38,630 Rabhas in 1971, including those in Meghalaya (No census was carried out in 1981).
2. *Mishings* (Miris). One of the larger tribes on north bank, it is concentrated in Dhemaji, Lakhimpur, Sonitpur districts and Majuli Island. They enumerated 2,59,551 in 1971.
3. *Tiwas (Lalungs).* Mainly inhabiting Nagaon and Marigaon districts, they counted 95,609 in 1971.

There are some other smaller tribes also in Assam:

1. *Deuris.* Mostly inhabiting Dibrugarh district, they enumerated 23,000 in 1971.
2. *Sonwal Kacharis.* They are a larger group, but scattered over the Eastern parts of the north bank.
3. *Meches.* They belong to the large Bodo-Kachari group and are found in certain areas of Assam and North Bengal. In Assam, they are a miniscule community, generally inhabiting Goalpara district and Hojai area. They number a mere 12,919 (1971).

The Assam Government feels local autonomy to the Rabhas, Mishings and Tiwas should go a long way to assure their cultural identity. Each of the three tribes has its Student Union and Sahitya Sabha. These tribes presently feel discriminated against and suffer from a sense of deprivation and exploitation. Formation of District Councils would allay discontent through a variant of Panchayat Raj introduced under the 11th and 12th Schedules (Amendments No. 72 and 74) of the Constitution. This measure, introduction of local self-rule, will ensure socio-economic development, and more importantly, direct popular energies from agitation to constructive pursuits, with insecurity yielding place to self-assurance. Conceded in time, and that is important, such politico-administrative measures should stem any fears of fragmentation, revivalism and balkanization. The Government is not willing to grant them certain concessions earlier bestowed on the Bodos. For example, in Bodoland, minority villages with as low as 10 per cent population were included in the jurisdiction of the Bodo Autonomous Council (BAC) to provide contiguity to the adjacent Bodo majority pockets. Government's unwillingness to extend the same understanding attitude to these smaller and more scattered tribes is resented by them. The powers prescribed by the Bhupinder Singh committee, however, have been adapted within 2-tier structure.

The Government constituted a ministerial committee to process formation of the three District Councils. The Rabhas, Mishings and Tiwas, meanwhile, have pressed their claims to 862, 1600 and 371 villages respectively. All three are demanding some intervening villages to establish contiguity, especially because these areas were initially tribal belts and blocks, surreptitiously usurped by others (read "outsiders" or "foreigners") or diverted for other purposes. One cannot put the issue more succinctly than Verghese (B.G), 1996: "There is a weight in these arguments, in spite of some exaggeration and inflation of figures of tribal population. Whatever be the truth, unscrambling of the omelette can be debated, but not undone."

The Rabhas

Rabhas have been politically more conscious and active among these three tribes. Their movement demanded Rabha Hasong (Rabhaland)

Autonomous State within Assam on south bank, extending from Joyrasmukh in Goalpara to Rani in Kamrup. Their other demands include:

1. An autonomous district in Darrang on the north bank,
2. District councils in yet four other districts with Rabha pockets,
3. Rabha village councils in several districts, and
4. Five reserved seats in BAC.

They seem to have flirted with violence and nurtured ambitions of organising some terrorist outfit. The press had reported the existence of Rabha Security Force (RSF), which reminded the observers of the depredations of the BdSF. The former seems to have made to the pages of the newspapers, with an occasional act of terrorism. To wit, the RSF kidnapped a Construction Engineer (Naresh Lalwani) on 24 December 1998 while working on a site on the 142 km second broadgauge line from Bongaigaon to Gauhati along the south bank of the Brahmaputra. Panic-stricken labour fled, rejoining only when RPF was deployed in the affected area between Goalpara) and Mirza for its protection. Because of such attacks, the project could not be completed as scheduled by 31 March 1999. This is just one instance of militancy adversely affecting the economic development.

The 7th Annual conference of All Rabha Students Union (ARSU) in 1994 demanded more Rabha Primary Schools and concerted measures to promote Rabha language and culture.

10 March 1995. A Memorandum of Understanding was signed, constituting Rabha Hasong Autonomous Council, an apex body, with "discontinuous satellite areas" and Rabha Hasong village councils in rural areas with not more than 50 per cent tribal population. The villages in the reserved forests were to be included after clearance from Ministry of Environment and Forests. Interestingly, Meghalaya issued a cautious warning against inclusion of disputed villages on the boundary. An interim Rabha Hasong Council was set up pending elections. The village councils were to have executive powers over 29 subjects (Shades of District Councils under 6th Schedule), and the Apex Council, over 39 subjects.

Understandably, similar Accords were signed with the Tiwas on 13 April 1995 and with the Mishings on 14 June 1995.

The Tiwas

The Tiwas were fast learners. When the Assam Students were running their anti-foreigners campaign in early 1980s, "a tribal community in the Centre of Assam was airing its own grievances from their house-tops literally", wrote a journalist in a Gauhati Daily. Travelling through Nagaon district, a visitor could see some posters on any likely place available (tree trunks, walls of the houses, telephone poles, way-side shacks and shanties), loudly protesting the neglect of the Tribe by the Central and State Governments and consequent lack of economic and social development, "more than three decades after the Independence". They seem to have been the first to learn from the AASU Movement the practical ways of registering their protests and grievances. It was an effective PR Job! Though they seemed to have started their protest about the same time as the Bodos, happily, they did not go the Bodo way! Even more happily, they seem to have shunned the example of the Rabhas too, who did register their presence in the field of violence through desultory acts of terrorism, like kidnappings and killings.

In 1967, the Tiwas first demanded autonomy around the same time as Bodos. They were generally peaceful apart from that frenzied outburst at Nellie in 1983 against the immigrant settlers. They demanded 3264 km^2 area for their "homeland". Their complaint: "The Assamiya chauvinists had under-enumerated us." Here is the famous outburst by Tulsi Bordoloi, convener of All Tiwa Students Federation (ATSF): "Bordoloi is not my real name. In our schools, Assamiya teachers changed our names without discussing anything with us" (Biswas, Ashish K., 1995).

Two-tier Tiwa District Council comprises of 144 villages, with the Autonomous Tiwa District Demand Committee claiming additional 175. The Tiwas Sahitya Sabha (TSS) wants acceptance of the Roman script only for Tiwa language, presently written in both Assamese and Roman scripts. This is perhaps to ensure that their language is not at some distant future subsumed by the Sanskritised Assamese language. This is the best way, feels the TSS, to ensure the continued existence and autonomy of their language.

The Mishings

Mishings felt aggrieved at non-inclusion of certain forests and other villages in the Mishing District Council. They rejected the majority-village principle insisting on inclusion of all villages with more than 33 per cent Mishing population. The proposition is unlikely to be accepted, going by the reaction in BAC areas, where non-Bodos resented being sacrificed in the interest of greater Bodoland.

AHOMS: YEARNING FOR PAST GLORY

The Ahoms, having been the rulers for 600 years, had always nursed a grievance during the British Rule that they had been marginalized in favour of the Assamese and Bengali Caste-Hindus. A section of the Ahom elite had been insisting that the Ahom identity had been under threat from Hindu Aryan culture. But unfortunately, their representative body, the Ahom Association, formed as early as 1893, was unable to make much headway among the Ahom masses, since they had largely integrated with the broader Assamese Community and accepted Sankardev's Mahapurusia Vaishnavism.

The Ahom Association, which till 1910 was known as Ahom Sabha, continued its efforts to claim a separate identity for the community. When the national movement spread in Assam, gaining greater momentum and larger adherents the Ahoms felt further marginalized and jittery, since the Congress leadership was largely drawn from the caste-Hindu sections of the Assamese Society. Dubbing the Congress as a caste-Hindu organisation, a section of the Ahom elite started demanding a separate, sovereign status for Assam, where the Ahom would once again be the major cohesive force in the Assamese society. They firmly believed that only through an independent Assam could the identity of the Ahoms be safeguarded and strengthened. In its meeting in September 1944, the All Assam Ahom Association (AAAA), Sibsagar declared: "In view of the peculiar position of Assam, both geographically and otherwise, and the great preponderance of the Mongolian races with their distinctive languages, cultures and religions in the population of the Province, Assam without Sylhet, has a legitimate claim for free and independent existence in the event of India being divided territorially into Pakistan and Hindustan Zones.[30] The demand for a sovereign Assam was also raised in several other Ahom-dominated areas of Province. It is obvious that the Ahom demand for a sovereign Assam and the Swadhin Asom demand by other segments of Assamese population had a lot in common. In either case, the protagonists harked back to a glorious, independent past: the former to their recent 600-year rule and the latter to the legendary Kamarupa days. It was also consistently maintained that Assam belonged ethnically to the Mongoloid race and that its culture and civilisation were a part of the glorious heritage of South-East Asian region, the Province sharing little with the rest of India. (But the matter did not end there. Today also, this argument forms a major plank of the thesis offered by the ULFA's ideologues who assert vehemently that Assam should look East, and not towards India, for inspiration and sustenance, as it historically forms a part of the great Mongoloid fraternity.)

But there is an inherent contradiction in the stance of organisations like the Ahom Association demanding an independent Assam, fearing the Hinduisation of their culture and polity. It is that Hinduisation in the first place was brought and promoted in Assam by the Ahom rulers themselves. Like the Ahoms, the protagonists of Swadhin Asom too could not wish away the Hindu connections of their "glorious" past, so fondly referred to, and repeatedly. The Kamarupa empire was well-known for its cultural and civilisational links with the rest of the Indian Sub-continent with its predominant Hindu ethos. If the Ahom separatists tend to completely sweep part of their own past under the carpet while pleading their case for independence, the proponents of *Swadhin* Asom do the same, intentionally failing to see that Pragjyotisha and Kamarupa were not only part of wider India civilisationally, but also politically, it would seem. After all, Bhagadatta had participated in the Epic war, and Bhaskar-Varman was an ally of the Great Harsha, the powerful King of Kannauj. These strong cultural and historical links, which both pre-Ahom and Ahom Assam had maintained with the rest of the country, goes a long way to explain the quick acceptance of Gandhi and the Congress in the Province. Ahom's stress on Assam's Far- and South-eastern connections, especially with Burma, was bound to evoke the frightful memories of the Burmese occupation of the land. The pro-British and occasionally, even pro-Muslim League posturings of bodies like the Ahom Association,[31] alienated them from the broad mass of the Ahom people, who, in any case, having joined and become indistinguishable from the Indigenous Assamese, went along with the Congress in the fight for freedom from the British Raj.

Failing to see any possibility of success, Ahom Association climbed down from its high horse of "Independent Assam", and started demanding creation of a separate Ahom State comprising the Upper Assam districts. They were also exploring the possibilities of establishing contacts with the Shan States beyond the Patkais.[32]

Having never been a powerful body, and failing to battle the Congress on the election front, the Ahom Association lost much of its relevance in the recent years.

Now, to flesh out some details about marginalisation of the Ahoms.

Degradation/Fall of Ahoms

It is a fact of history that the Ahoms had been enervated due to a long stay in the fertile, humid and luxury-inducing Brahmaputra Valley. Additionally, the self-destructive, internecine civil war among the Princes during the last 50 years of their rule nearly emaciated the ruling class and middle classes. The Burmese occupation subsequently completed the ruin of the masses. The abolition of the *paik* system by the British ruined the land-owning classes as they were unable to cultivate their lands. All this spelled their economic ruin. The aristocrats became destitutes overnight, so to say. The British policies reduced the Ahoms to penury, kept them away from power and position, and simultaneously ensured the emergence of a new middle class. It is recorded that most of the noble families were compelled to sell or mortgage their properties to meet their revenue arrears. Part of the property of Kandarpeswar Singh, the Ahom King was auctioned at Jorhat.[33] The British recruitment policy also contributed to the economic backwardness of the Ahoms. The Ahoms, erstwhile ruling class, unable to reconcile to the loss of power, tried to regain it through local rebellions and conspiracies. Consequently, the British distrust barred their entry to any important position—bureaucratic and political. They mostly imported clerks and officials from Bengal.

Their situation became even bleaker when the British made the formal western education a pre-condition for entry into jobs because during their rule, education was never considered important or even necessary as their livelihood depended upon their status.

Thus, the Ahoms deemed it derogatory, or at the very least, unnecessary to educate their children unless their forefathers were the class of Kakotis.[34] For these reasons, the Ahom society was conspicuous by absence of any formal education till 1826. Even after the British take-over, they did not take corrective steps almost till the end of the 19th century. It is on record that in 1851-52, there were only 39 Ahom students in a population of over 150,000. The picture was hardly encouraging in the last two decades of the 19th century as can be seen from the comparative positions of various communities in the two tables (on the following page) based on the Census Reports of 1891 and 1901.

The inadequacies and disadvantageous position of the Ahoms *vis-a-vis* some other communities, illustrated by the two tables, goaded their elite into organising themselves to articulate their grievances and demands for a better future. That is how the All Assam Ahom Association was born in 1893.

Ahoms Organise Themselves

AAAA was the first endeavour by the down and out Ahoms to ameliorate their socio-economic status. It was also indicative of the first revivalist stirring of an agitated community. It is also tempting to see it as something of a movement for an identity assertion. It may be a far-fetched proposition (or, may not be so), these end-19th century stirrings showed that the community realised the value of formal education for their socio-economic-political advancement. The 1921 Census figures in the table below prove the point.

The 1921 Census did show that the Ahoms registered some advance, but they were far outdistanced by other sections of the upper caste Assamese, as admitted by Gurdon: "In educational matters, Ahoms are more backward than even the ordinary Assamese Hindus, which is saying a great deal." The fact was further confirmed by the British Census Commissioner, C.S. Mullan, in his Report on the 1931 Census: "Looking at the 1931 figures, we see at once that the Baidyas and Brahmins show a long lead over all other Hindu castes in the matter of literacy, as they did in 1921. Among the Ahoms, 24.6 per cent of their males are literate but only 1.4 per cent of their females can read or write." This was possibly because of their 'royal vanity' and indifferent attitude towards education.

Literacy Ratings: Ahoms and others: 1891

Caste	*Male*			*Female*		
	Total	*Students*	*Literate*	*Total*	*Students*	*Literate*
Ahom	78840	990	4559	74673	17	57
Baidya	2600	545	1279	2066	39	249
Brahmin	52934	6157	23498	44042	224	506
Kalita	115978	2284	7498	106621	93	327
Kayasth	48731	5832	16346	43619	398	1226
Dom (Patni)	101139	1264	3155	100914	6	4

Source: Report on 1891 Census.

Literacy Ratings: Ahoms and others: 1901

Caste		*Literate in Non-English Languages*			*Literate in English*		
	Population	*Total*	*Male*	*Female*	*Total*	*Male*	*Female*
Ahom	178049	4588	4461	127	893	882	11
Baidya	5154	1401	934	467	757	740	17
Brahmin	109446	28941	27652	1289	3616	3577	39
Kalita	203108	9227	9062	165	865	858	7
Kayasth	86918	19967	17740	2227	4287	4250	37
Dom (Patni)	194852	3752	3587	165	97	97	–

Source: Report on 1891 Census.

Literacy Ratings: Ahoms and others: 1921

Caste	*Population*		*No. per 1000 aged 5 and above who are literate*					
	1911	*1921*	*1911*			*1921*		
			Persons	*Male*	*Female*	*Persons*	*Male*	*Female*
Ahom	197000	216000	73	136	4	109	197	11
Baidya	5609	7210	654	833	437	704	817	570
Brahmin	137000	160000	375	623	64	438	721	111
Kalita	222000	235000	95	174	6	145	255	20
Kayasth	82000	12000	413	644	138	429	629	187
Dom (Patni)	63281	18000	45	85	4	41	78	4

Source: Report on 1921 Census.

It is to be noted that even a section of Ahom elite believed that apart from the British policies, the Ahoms themselves were to an extent responsible for their degradation, attributing three factors for the same: distorted

Hinduism, false pride, and excessive use of opium. One opinion is that the 55 years, from the disappearance of Purendar Singh's Kingship (1838) to the first stirrings of awakening among the Ahom elite symbolised by setting up of the revivalist AAAA (1893) was the most despondent period for the community. It was not only poverty in abstract economic terms, but also a drain of their moral, physical and intellectual resources as a whole that relegated a race with six centuries of dynastic rule to utter insignificance—socially, economically, educationally and politically. This collapse awakened them to the realisation that the development and prosperity of their own community must rest in their own hands, and for that they must establish and maintain a distinct identity within the larger Assamese society. Hence the birth of AAAA, with the aims explained above. This was the beginning under the leadership of a great Assamese litterateur, Padmanath Gohain Baruah. Subsequently came some other organisations into being to fight for their rights.

The Ahoms had been presenting their case before the concerned authorities. Some of their demands were conceded, and included in the 1909 and 1919 Reforms. It is for note that the British considered them a backward community within the Hindu fold. The Ahoms had asked for recognition as a separate, distinct entity and pleaded for a separate geographical area and autonomy for themselves before the Simon Commission (1929), like so many others in the North-East. The Commission did not accept their case, though it included them in the list of high caste Hindus. It is indeed ironic that because of being exalted to higher classification the Community did not find a place in the list of Excluded Areas of either of the two categories, as did the backward communities of the Lushai, NC, Mikir Hills, etc. Consequently, the 1935 Act excluded them from the list of minority communities (and consequently they did not receive any privileges under the Communal Award). So, it was during the 1930s that the need for political activism dawned on them. That is how the AAAA aligned with the Indian National Congress (INC) to fight for nation's independence; and after it was achieved, it merged with it, almost in the manner of the Tribal League (TL) of Assam. Both had unhappy experience of joining hands with nation's premier political formation. So, when the Government announced its decision to set up the SRC in mid-1950s, so the two, AAAA and TL, revived themselves under new names, All Assam Tai Sabha (AATS) and Plains Tribal Council of Assam (PTCA), respectively, to fight for the socio-cultural development of their communities, though deep down, the aims were political. If the PTCA pleaded for a separate state for the Plains Tribals, AATS wanted a separate state for Ahoms in Upper Assam comprising the districts of Dibrugarh, Lakhimpur and Sibsagar. The Commission even-handedly, rejected both!

From the late 1960s, several Ahom organisations are in the field, striving to achieve what they call their "legitimate share" in the administration of the State; an aim considerably watered down from the one they originally set for themselves, viz, "identity assertion"—a phrase that has unfortunately come to gather sinister connotations in the North-East. Some of the organisations—important, not so important, and even defunct presently—that worked at different times with the express aim of safeguarding and promoting the ethnic, cultural, social, and so far undeclared, political interests of the Ahom are mentioned below:

1. Ahom Tai Mongoliya Rajya Parishad
2. Ban Puplik Mioung Tai
3. All Tai Ahom Students Union
4. Tai Ahom Council
5. In 1960s, an attempt was made to revive AAAA, but it never could be revived to be a force to be reckoned with.
6. In 1970, the nearly defunct AATS was revived and re-christened as Ujani Asom Rajya Parishad (UARP), again aspiring for a state of its own within the Indian Union. It did engage in some political activity in the early 1970s, but without any singular achievement.
7. Another organisation formed by a section of the Ahoms is Phuralung Buddhist Council of North-East India. It obviously seems to be a religious platform.

The North-East has remained a battlefield, to put it tersely, ever since our Independence. Nagas even declared their independence 24 hours before India's. Luckily for the nation, the others did not follow their lead as violently and as single-mindedly as the Nagas, even if they concealed and carried a hurt. The Ahoms kept along the path of peaceful agitation. But their attempts to regain their ethnic identity through several organisations formed for the purpose did not succeed.

But unfortunately for them, their identification with the larger Assamese identity is nearly so complete that none of their several movements aimed at identity assertion really took off.

Their last attempt at tribal revivalism was in the 1970s when they rechristened AATS as UARP to espouse their cause for a separate state within India. It also turned out to be a tame affair, like the earlier ones. It was also in character that when in the wake of violent Bodo agitation, Chief Minister Saikia (1991-96) was bestowing (some cynics thought "forcing" was the right term) autonomy on other ethnic groups like the Rabhas, Tiwas and Lalungs, and also the Karbis, perhaps as a pre-emptive move to dissuade them from adopting the violent ways of the Bodos, the Ahoms were kept out of his bounties. It should cause no surprise if a casual observer to the area finds that the Ahoms are reconciled to their present situation—almost.

BISHNUPRIYA CONUNDRUM

The Vaishnavite influence which spread from Bengal to the North-East centuries ago—it possibly started spreading even before the putative date of the 15th century—has left scattered Bishnupriya communities in Tripura, Manipur and Assam (mainly in Cachar valley). This community has become a cause of tension in Assam in the recent years, with implications far beyond its borders since it is also found in certain neighbouring States as mentioned above. For the present, the Assamese-Manipur row over the subject is very prominent, threatening to vitiate the relation between the two neighbours.

The "Bishnupriya Manipuris" in Cachar have been seeking official recognition for their language, which they have started teaching in Silchar along with some other minority languages like Dimasa and Karbi. They have been carrying on this campaign for years. Interestingly, but not surprisingly, the Manipur Government has been objecting to the Bishnupriyas of Assam using the suffix 'Manipuri' with their community's name, harbouring some apprehensions and even forebodings flowing from this association. The issue has been causing some uneasiness in relations between Assam and Manipur.

"Assam Chief Minister P.K. Mahanta has invited more trouble by recognizing the Bishnupriya language as 'Bishnupriya Manipuri'. This has led to strong resentment being expressed by Manipuris in the State and in Manipur" (Kashyap, Samudragupta in the *Indian Express* of 2-6-1999).

It all started with the Assam Government announcing its decision in May 1999 to recognise Bishnupriya Manipuri as a language of instruction at the primary level acceding the longstanding demand of the Bishnupriya community of the State. The Manipur Chief Minister, W. Nipamacha Singh, reacting strongly, criticised Assam's decision, asserting that the Bishnupriya community was not part of Manipuri community. He emphasised that Manipuri and Bishnupriya were two distinct and separate linguistic groups, as the former belonged to the Tibeto-Burman family of the languages while the latter language was part of the Indo-Aryan linguistic group.

The scholars did not lag behind the politicians to safeguard the interests of their language and the State. Manipuri Sahitya Parishad of Assam threatened to launch an agitation against the decision. The Manipur Government has lodged a protest with the Centre and urged it to press Mahanta to drop the suffix Manipuri from the term.

Sounding reasonable, Nipamacha Singh said that while his Government and community had no objection to the Assam Government recognizing

Bishnupriya as a language of instruction, the suffix Manipuri should be immediately dropped. Sensing strong sentiments, Mahanta was compelled to hold discussions with leaders of both communities and assured the Manipuris of an amicable solution, which is still to see the light of the day.

But why this strong position on the issue by Manipur? Is it only born out of unwillingness to confer the privilege of Manipuri identity on the false claimants? Or, is it something deeper and more sinister that troubles the Manipur State and its people? Is it the fear of disintegration of their State that is looming large in the Manipuri psyche? Already facing claims to the northern parts of their State from the Naga insurgents and Nagaland Government to fulfil their dream of Greater Nagaland, do the Manipuris perceive the Bishnupriya's insistence on the suffix (Manipuri) as a ploy for use at some future date? The unstated fear is that the Bishnupriya Manipuris could be thinking of laying claims on western part of Manipur, on the plea of it being inhabited by their compatriots. A worse scenario is also imagined. If the Barak Valley succeeds in achieving the UT status/statehood somewhere in the future (say, Purbanchal of their dreams), thence they might start clamouring for a Greater Purbanchal a la Nagaland — greedily eyeing areas in western Manipur. The fears might be far-fetched, but the scenario envisaged here is within the realm of possibility. Manipuri fears are not unfounded; and in any case, the fore-warned is fore-armed!

Islamic Militancy and its Implications for Assam

Of recent years, a new kind of religious threat has raised its head in the North-East, report certain concerned Intelligence agencies. While the official agencies and the Government have been busy fighting and controlling politically and ethnically-impelled insurgency/militancy in the North-East, Islamic militancy has been unobtrusively consolidating itself there. In Assam, the Muslim community and Bangladesh infiltration/immigrants are sensitive subjects, more so than the rest of India. Again, as in the rest of the country in Assam too, according to the analysts who study the subject, the Militancy and Islam have been used, misused, or exploited for political purposes by most political parties, if not all, but ironically each party blames the rest of them for the sin. The issue is especially contentious during the election time. And the question of presence of "illegal immigrants" on the electoral rolls makes the situations explosive at the elections, sometimes even "unmentionable". The related issue have been discussed elsewhere in this book, here only the limited question of newly emerging threats to India's sovereignty and integrity from the Islamic militancy will be looked into briefly.

SFs for some years have been reporting the existence of Islamic militants in Assam, as discovered by the Intelligence agencies, but the analysts aver the Governments and political parties have been smug about the subject for reasons of their own. The "blatantly blunt" Hindutva formations are blaming all "secularist" parties for playing politics of appeasement. A large number of Muslim fundamentalist organisations are now active in the region and the SF and Police have been arresting some of their members for anti-national activities. But more importantly, "what has been an open secret for a decade or so," received official confirmation when Chief Minister Mahanta admitted during the Budget session of Assam Assembly, 2000, that "the Islamic militancy has been menacingly active in Assam". For years the SF have been pursuing these extremists to control the situation in Assam, "it is now that the Chief Minister admits the growth of Islamic militant organisations in the inaccessible Char (riverine) areas of Muslim-dominated districts of Central and Lower Assam". "They grow away from the civilisation and scrutiny of the SFs." What is of greater concern to the State and its security agencies is that aided, abetted, guided, rather manipulated, by the ISI, this religion-driven militancy is on rise, and has become a potent force for spread of extremism and fundamentalism of obscurantist variety. Large number of youth belonging to these outfits have visited Pakistan for armed training under Harkat-ul-Mujahideen and Lashkar-e-Taiba, the two most rabidly fanatical, anti-India formations.[35]

The gravity of the Islamic fundamentalism and the existence of the ISI controlled and operated network in the North-East hit the media headlines and Indian public alike when Chief Minister Mahanta announced the arrest of four militants including two Pakistani militants in Gauhati in July 1999, viz, Mohammad Fasih Ullah Hussain from Hyderabad Sind and Mohammad Javed Wakhar from Karachi. Arrest of the ISI argent, Qari Salim Ahmad alias Abdul Hamid with three others, revealed that their mission was to hand over a large quantity of RDX to the Assamese insurgents to carry out subversive activities on the eve of Independence Day, 1999 *(India Today,* 23 May 1999). Further investigations disclosed even more sinister aims of the Pak Intelligence. Part of the deadly cargo was to be taken to North-West India to blow up bridges on the Kulu-Manali-Leh Road to disrupt the only alternative artery to the much-threatened Srinagar-Kargil-Leh Road. If successful, the plan would have completely cut off and isolated the Indian SF in Ladakh, "to be starved into submission", the expression used by the Pak think tanks. Need more be said about the long arm of ISI and Pakistan's morbid anti-India intent, obsession and hatred.

Some 17 of the Muslim fundamentalist organisations working in region are listed here:[36]

1. Muslim United Liberation Tigers of Assam (MULTA).
2. Muslim Liberation Tigers of Assam (MLTA)
3. Islamic Liberation Army of Assam (ILAA)

4. Muslim Liberation Army (MLA)
5. Students' Islamic Movement of India (SIMI)
6. United Reformation Protest of Assam (URPA)
7. Jamaat-e-Islami, Assam (JEI, A)
8. People's United Liberation Front (PULF)
9. Muslim Volunteer Force (MVF)
10. Muslim United Liberation Front of Assam (MULFA)
11. Adam Sena (AS)
12. Islamic Sevak Sangh (ISS)
13. Harkat-ul-Mujahideen (HUM)
14. Islamic Security Force of India (ISFI)
15. Harkat-ul-Jehad (HUJ)
16. COMOA[37] (Coordination Committee for Minorities of Assam)
17. Liberation Islamic Tiger Force (LITF)

The objectives of these organisations, as analysed by the Intelligence, are two-pronged (1) To spread the fundamentalism in the entire North-East and thus prepare and use the immigrant Muslim community for Pan-Islamisation of the region. (2) To foment serious political and religious riots in the area, compelling the Government to rush the SF, especially Indian Army, to control the situation. It will not only create anti-Army and anti-India sentiment when Army was forced to suppress the riots, thus giving further scope for creating disquiet and disafetion in Assam, but also weaken India's anti-terrorism capability in Jammu and Kashmir, giving greater opportunity to Pak-trained foreign immigrants to convert the situation in their favour, to sever the valley from India. This in simple terms, is the dimension of the threat to India's sovereignty and integrity, both in North-East and North-West. Reports with the Intelligence agencies indicate that almost all these organisations operating in Assam are working for a common cause, spelled out here, and have approached several Muslim countries and organisations like the OIC, with the active connivance/even help of the ISI, and they are getting material help of all kinds to achieve their aims. Of the fundamentalist organisations listed above, HUM and HUJ are most fanatical in their ideology and functioning, hence most diabolical and dangerous, having been directly raised as they have been, by the ISI. The members of these organisations are reportedly trained by the ISI personnel at their Bangladesh Camps, located in Cox Bazar and in Rangpur district. Though the activities of some of these camps are reported to had been scaled down under pressure from the Hasina Government, but the stranglehold of the fundamentalist elements in Bangladesh's political, economic and social fields, is so strong that it will need much bigger reserves of endurance, determination and patience than employed so far to break it. The Government's job is extremely difficult if not impossible in view of the opposition's known soft-corner for these anti-India forces; in fact, while in power, Begum Zia had not only spectrally supported these powers in their anti-India work and plans but had indulged in anti-India tirade herself.

It seems more than likely that there will be a spectrally shift in militancy profile in Assam, when the neighbouring countries like Bhutan, Myanmar and Bangladesh throw out Indian insurgent outfits from their soil as a result of India's diplomatic initiatives and they in turn are controlled, reduced and finally eliminated by the Indian SF. But meanwhile, the Islamic fundamentalism and militancy would have considerably added to its strength. Afghanistan supported world-wide Islamic extremism in the past, in concert with various similar organisations in several Muslim nations. But for the cliched nine-eleven, the macabre game would have continued. The recent recrudescence and mobilisation of Islamic Jehadis the world over to support the ongoing Palestinian resistance will provide a fillip to the fundamentalist mobilisation in Pakistan, Bangladesh and Bangladeshi migrants in Assam (And let woolly-headed Indians be warned that a similar mobilisation of Islamic Jehadis could take place on the issue of Kashmir in not too distant a future, if Indians do not wake up to the dangers). All these developments will have anti-India ramifications, positively inimical to its integrity and sovereignty. It will be an ideal situation for the ISI to fish in the troubled waters of North-East by fomenting subversion and terrorism in the Region. Given the population mix of Assam, it will be a sure-fire formula to generate communal conflagrations in India that could lead to its destabilization and ultimately, to its disintegration, a desideratum the ISI is working for. This might appear to be an over-drawn picture of dangers posed to the Indian State, "impelled by fervid imagination of some Intelligence hands", as some scholars, particularly of Left variety, are sure to assert, but Islamic fundamentalism in Assam is something the Indian security apparatus must devote sometime to. The DG, BSF was not exaggerating when he said on 7 April 2000 that "5 to 10 km belt (in depth) in West Bengal along its border with Bangladesh has already become a Bangladeshi and Muslim-dominated territory. This area is being exploited by the ISI for infiltration of subversive elements into India". A surer foothold could not have been asked for by a foreign Intelligence agency.

It bears re-emphasis, in the context of the foregoing, that some years back, the far-seeing Henry Kissinger spoke of one or more Muslim nations emerging from the North-Eastern region of the Indian Sub-Continent.[38] Within the country, tremours have been felt far-away from the North-East.

DGP of UP told a daily in October 2000, disclosing the role of SIMI in anti-national activities, that time bombs had exploded in the State for the first time on the eve of Independence Day 1999, and "the plan was hatched in Aligarh in which SIMI's role has been established[39].

Some of the Movements/insurgencies in the North-East are externally helped and New Delhi is close to bringing them around. The.Islamic militancy is the only one externally-generated and guided, essentially, by the ISI, and hence should be a cause of serious concern to India.

Current Scenario : 2005-2007 Situation

The presence of Islamic militancy in the North-East and dangers inherent in its further spread has been discussed in the preceding pages. It also shows that certain extremist outfits are already active in the region and are spreading their wings under active guidance from the ISI. The Islamist threat to the North-East is assuming more serious proportions as there are elements among the Bangladeshi migrants who are bent upon spreading disaffection among the Assamese Muslims. The growth of multiple Islamist organisations in the North-East and their metastatis are a cause for serious concern. The Government does not seem to be paying adequate attention to the security threat to India's North-East due to continuing ingress of foreigners, even when some of the Islamist outfits have, of late, started demanding creation of a Muslim nation in the region. Sounds of the Kissinger warning, mentioned earlier here.

Meanwhile, Islamist organisations like the MULTA, HUM, MULFA, MLA, MV, ILAA, LITF, MLTA, USRA (United Social Reform Army), ISS, URPA, SIMI, PULF, SIO (Students' Islamic Organisation) and ILA (Islamic Liberation Army) have spread their tentacles across the North-East. These groups are known to have been entrusted with the job of creating instability in the region.

Four of these outfits are seen in a little more detail in the pages that follow :

• MULTA

It was raised in 1993 with the objective of protecting the interests of Muslims in Assam, especially the illegal migrants from Bangladesh who continue to be its main support base. "It must endeavour towards carving out a 'rightful place' for Muslims in Assam. The outfit is attempting to have a separate Islamic homeland in Assam comprising the districts of Nagaon, Dhubri, Kamrup, Karimganj and Hailakandi. There are reports of MULTA cadres getting training for its assigned tasks.

A group of 13 MULTA cadres were trained by the ISI in Bangalmara, North Lakhimpur district. A joint group of 160 MULTA and MULFA cadres underwent three months training at Chetak and Jayantipur in Bangladesh under the supervision of two ISI officers (Maj Nizamuddin Shah and Capt Iqbal Ali) during the period 1999-early 2000.[40]

Besides training the MULTA cadres, Al Qaeda and Bangladesh are also channelling arms and ammunition to Islamist outfits from the temporary headquarters set up by the ISI in a mosque at Hathijan in Cox Bazar.

In early May 2002, nine Islamist groups assembled at a camp near the Bangladesh town of Ukhia and created the conglomerate Bengladesh Islamic Manch (BIM). The new umbrella organisation, in a bid to expand/ strengthen Islamic solidarity in the North-East, has also admitted non-Bangladeshi fundamentalist groups like the Rohingya Solidarity Organisation (RSO) and Arakan Rohingya Islamic Front of Myanmar (ARIFM).

Incidentally, MULTA is also a member of the BIM whose declared aim is to create a Brihat Bangladesh (= Greater Bangladesh) by merging areas of Assam and Myanmar's Arakan province. BIM has been formed at the initiative of HUJI-B and is reportedly being chaperoned by the usual suspects ISI and Al Qaeda.

Here are interesting nuances to MULTA's duplicious intentions. It does not qualify its stand on the issue of "separate homeland", refusing to clearly state whether it is to be a sovereign state or the one within the Indian Constitution. But because the Constitution does not cater for/ allow an Islamic state within its ambit, it is, therefore, reasonable to assume that MULTA indeed desires to carve out a sovereign state in India's North-East! Shades of Kissinger's prophecy, once again.

- HUM

It was formed in 1998-99 with the objective of fighting anti-Muslim forces for the creation of an Islamic state and safeguarding the interests of Muslims in Assam.

- MULFA

Formed in 1994, it demands the creation of a separate Muslim state, protection and preservation of Muslim Personal Law and 30 per cent reservation for Muslims in government services and educational institutions. The outfits has a well-accentuated link with the ISI.

- MVF

It was formed with the objective of safeguarding the interest of Muslims in Assam and fighting anti-Muslim forces.

Now to the looming dangers for India's security and sovereignty in the not-too-distant a horizon. After its ouster from the Bhutan soil, it is not too happy a situation for ULFA which by force of circumstances was compelled to break bread with anti-Indian Islamic outfits. After its request to China for sanctuary in its territory met with a curt rejection, ULFA shifted its base and camps to the jungles of Bangladesh. Presently, it is not only a welcome guest there, it is running an affluent empire of commercial and industrial enterprises.

Hence its compulsions of supporting anti-India Islamic outfits, whose support base is essentially among the Bangladeshi (illegal) immigrants (After all, it is well-known fact that the Assamese Muslim, long-settled there, have lived peacefully with their non-Muslim compatriots). As a consequence to its changed circumstances, it should come as no surprise to the cognescenti that ULFA's (new) definition of real 'illegal migrants' does not include the Bangladeshis! Some late wisdom, this!

It is time that Indians realise that it is already too late to stem the tide of Islamist foot soldiers belonging to various militant/terrorist outfits coordinating with each other and facilitating the spread of anti-India sentiment in North-East unless the Government at New Delhi and in the North-Eastern States show some stead fastness and take counter-measures to stem this tide. One is not optimist of such a thing happening in a hurry, as Indian polity's record of acting fast on countering terrorism in the country has been rather dismal. We are still to see our Government crafting an effective, no-nonesense anti-terrorism policy, especially the current dispensation, dominated by the left and weighed down by 'political' considerations on the issue.

An analyst says : "The entire North-East has become a seething-cauldron on account of persistent insurgency and the menance of illegal migrants has further compounded matters.[41]

If security fraternity and academics are worried on this score, they have a reason to nurture a degree of pessimism : "unfortunately, the Indian State has a habit of letting a problem fester to such an extent that it becomes intraceable in course of time."

If the security scenario remains unaddressed indefinitely, political, social and economic instability will follow in its wake. This is the law of the nature. By then, national security would have been damaged irreparably.

CACHAR MOVEMENT FOR A STATE

Cachar[42] is predominantly Bengali-speaking area, essentially because of its cultural affinity and physical contiguity with the Sylhet region of East Bengal. The two valleys, viz Cachar/Barak and Brahmaputra, have been in proverbial rivalry from day one when Cachar was merged, along with Sylhet, with the newly-separated and created Chief Commissioner's Province of Assam in 1874. Till then, Assam had been a part of Bengal as a Commissionership. For these 50 years (1824-74) since the advent of the British, Assam had been dominated by the Bengalis because of their ruling the roost in its administration and professions. To make matters worse for the Assamese pride, Bengali was made, on the advice and insistence of the well-placed Bengali-elite, the language of the courts and administration in mid-1830s. By the time the British undid the injustice in 1874, the anti-Bengali sentiment was already well-entrenched in Assam. The hurt and rancour was to continue for long, long-time—perhaps never to be forgotten or forgiven.

Because of its majority, the Bengalis dominated the administration in Cachar, even when merged with Assam in 1874. That was enough to cause a sense of an unease and jealousy among the Assamese, and an open display of arrogance and racial superiority by the Bengalis only made the matters worse. And some thought the Bengalis of Cachar and Sylhet, post-1874, were even more supercilious in their attitude. So the two valleys not only remained antagonistic throughout the British rule, the rivalries continued even after Independence. Occasional anti-Bengali riots continued after 1947, in spite of the fervent appeal by the much respect Governor Sir Akbar Hydari (1947-49) during his address to the State Assembly in November 1947:[43] "Please give the strangers in our midst (Bengalis) a fair deal." The anti-Bengali sentiment continued just beneath the surface to erupt in worst riots in 1960 which left many innocent dead and houses and property burnt/destroyed.

It is not only geography that separates the two valleys, the two hill districts separating the two. The physical separation is further accentuated by cultural and linguistic differentiation between the two entities. The Cacharis simply could not see them as part of the larger Assamese family. Not welcome in Assam, the Bengalis of Cachar pleaded before the SRC for creation of the Purbanchal State, that was rejected by the latter. But they did not give up. In 1967, their then representative body, the Jan Mangal Parishad demanded that Cachar be made a federating unit in Assam, echoing the one-time sentiment of hill districts of Assam under the leadership of the APHLC. Six years later, the Cachar Gana Parishad in their memorandum (1973) to the Prime Minister sought UT status for their area. Strangely enough, it made use of the Governor's words—"strangers in our midst"—cited above, to justify separation. The 1980 and 1986 memoranda cited the reasons proffered by the less developed hill tribes around the Assam Valley to demand separation, viz, discrimination in language, employment and development. Further, they asserted that all the promises and concessions made in the Assam Accord were in favour of the Assam Valley, constituting a positive discrimination against the Barak Valley. But the Centre rejected the proposition, asserting that (1) Bengali was an associate language in Cachar; (2) there were regional Medical and Engineering Colleges; and (3) "recently, a Central University has been sanctioned for them".

It is no surprise that they have been harbouring separatism for long. Months after Independence, they drew up a scheme for separate administrative unit, nomenclated Purbanchal to include the two districts of the valley (Cachar and Karimganj), NC District, and sub-divisions of Hojai and Hamren. The 1948 Memorandum on the subject adduced the following reasons for separation:

1. Cachar did not form part of the mainland of Assam. British took it over in 1832, eight years after their occupation of Assam. It remained a part of Bengal till 1824.[44]
2. After its merger with Assam in 1874, it was administered by a separate Divisional Commissioner, with his headquarters at Silchar.
3. The 100-mile long Barail Range severs it from the mainland of Assam.
4. Number of Assamese in the Cachar region of Assam was rather small.

The protagonists of separation have not succeeded as yet. But they are still optimistic, watching with keen interest the Movement for UT status being carried out by the Karbis and Dimasas of the two Hill districts of Assam. If they succeed, Assam will find it very difficult to keep the Barak Valley within its fold, disconnected as its would then be from the Brahmaputra Valley.

NOTES

1. Among the prodigious writings in the contemporary press, regional and national, the most interesting, well-informed, and deeply-reasoned, debate was the one that figured on the pages of *The Economic and Political Weekly (EPW)*, Bombay.
2. Barua, Srinath, *Employment Problem in Assam,* 1983.
3. Borgohain, Homen, *Aupanibeshak Soshamar Biruddhe Asomar Sesh Sangram* (Assamese), 1980; cited, Misra, Udayon, 2000.
4. The Assamese authors assert that till the ULFA came on the scene, extorting money from the tea industry or forcing them into launching some measures to improve the lot of common Assamese, this industry had done almost zilch by way of social responsibility towards the Assamese citizens. If at all anything was attempted in this direction, it was more of cosmetic in nature than substantive.
5. 5th Report of the 'Employment Review Committee' of the Assam Assembly, 1976.
6. Misra, Tilottoma, "Assam: A Colonial Hinterland", *EPW,* 9 August, 1980.
7. *Ibid.*
8. A part of such arguments and assertions must be ascribed to an overheated partisan rhetoric. If gas for years was flared or head offices of tea companies were not shifted to Guwahati, it was not just because the Centre was being cussed, or imperialist in its approach to Assam, as many of them like to believe. The inability or delay flowed from reasons of economics, non-availability of requisite technologies in some fields, or even political. The Centre itself was hamstrung due to the resources crunch. Even then, it must be conceded that a more sympathetic-approach could have moved the things a little faster.
9. Misra, Tilottoma, *op. cit.*
10. Under the Colonisation Scheme, 20 bighas of land were given to each immigrant family against the payment of a nominal sum.
11. Guha, Amalendu, *Planter Raj to Swaraj: Electoral Politics in Assam,* 1826-1947, 1977.

12. Certain reservations have been expressed by social analysts and scholars about the democratic content of this Movement. Midway through the Movement, the non-Assamese constituents of the AAGSP, namely the Plains Tribals, the Hillmen, the minorities, ethnic and religious, were disenchanted by the way the Assamese majority was conducting the movement. Much before its end, the former had practically dissociated themselves from the Movement. Then, despite its Gandhian claims, anti-foreigners Movement was not without its communal outbursts of violence. Even if the killings at Nellie might have been immediately provoked by the kidnapping and rape of tribal Lalung girls by the immigrant Muslims, yet the large-scale nature of killings where women and children "were mercilessly butchered, should clearly reveal strong communal overtones." Communal violence on large scale also took place in several areas of Kamrup and Darrang districts. In these outrages, not only the immigrant Muslims were attacked Bengali Hindus also became the target of mindless violence.
13. Gen (Retd) KV Krishana Rao, PVSM, former COAS, in his National Security Lecture, 1997, delivered at the USI, New Delhi, on 12 December 1997; excerpts from it were published in the *USI Journal,* April-June 1998.
14. In the interview Mahanta gave to *India Today* (20-10-1997) staffer Avirook Sen.
15. But Kalita, who engaged a Supreme Court lawyer, is an unlikely politician, and "appears to be a mere pawn in an elaborate game of chess being played between Mahanta and senior AGP dissident leaders Phukan and Atul Bora. "How does one otherwise account for the lawyers' frequent trips by air to Gauhati to pursue the case?," asks a Fortightly dated 30-9-1999. The Petitioner would have to field some uncomfortable questions, such as where did he get the funds from to engage an expensive lawyer and pay for those frequent trips. "The distraction, Mahanta's friends hoped, will lead the case where they want it to go: Nowhere!" And, they were right (For details, *see The Frontline,* 30-9-1999).
16. Taking advantage of Atul Bora's opposition to Jayshree's nomination, Mahanta stripped him of his PWD 'fiefdom', and Bora quit in a huff. Thence, Mahanta sacked another Minister for supporting Bora. It was a dangerous mix when Thaneswar Boro, Party's venerated stalwart and Education Minister, resigned and the Phukan-led dissidents proposed him as Chief Minister. But Mahanta won the day with his press conference.
17. She will be member till 2005, as the member of Rajya Sabha has 6-year term compared to Lok Sabha's 5 years. So she got an extra year as a MP, without going through the hurly burly involved in fighting the Lok Sabha election.
18. The hint is for the United Minorities Front.
19. *India Today,* 20-10-1997.
20. *Times of India,* 9-1-1997.

21. At 86 (in 1999), he is the oldest historian of the North-East with 50 books and over 50 years of research to his credit. He has the distinction and honour of having learnt his craft at the feet of that famed teacher of Indian history, R.C. Majumdar. In an article in a periodical, the Historian has lamented the fact that no library in India has the oeuvre of his works for study or reference but the Library of Congress (in USA) has deemed it necessary and worthwhile to have all his books on its shelves! He clearly implies through this statement a certain neglect and unconcern for the North-East and Assam in particular in the rest of India. My own personal experience confirmed this unconcern. I had read a review of *Comprehensive History of Assam* by H.K. Barpujari (ed) in some daily. All my persistent, even frantic efforts to obtain in a copy of this book (Vol. 1) from several Delhi colleges and universities, including Delhi and JNU, through some students and professors bore no results. The frustrating counter query was: "A book on Assam's history? Is there one? Never heard of it!" I had given up all hope when finally and luckily I secured a copy from an important functionary in the Lok Sabha Secretariat through a well-placed Army officer, and "strictly for one week, that is 7 days!"
22. The subjects that still remained outside the jurisdiction of the ADC were law and order, supplies, excise, elections, census and District Rural Development Agency.
23. The ASDC "castigated the arrogance of the plainsmen, their condescension towards the Indo-Mongoloid tribes of the North-East. The Hill areas have been turned into the sanctuaries for overflow of job-seekers, contractor and businessmen.... The locals were discriminated against" (Datta, P.S., 1993).
24. Datta, P.S., 1993.
25. Bhupinder Singh, *et al.*, 1992.
26. *Ibid.*
27. Jatinga is 8 km from Haflong, the District capital.
28. Chief Minister Mahanta was unfazed. After all, his coalition had 77 MLAs in the 126-member Assembly, excluding the five of the ASDC.
29. Dr Jayanta Rongpi belongs to the Vinod Mishra group of the CPI(ML).
30. In a resolution passed by the AAAA, at Sibsagar in September 1944. *See* Proceedings of the Executive Committee, Sibsagar, 1944.
31. Bhuyan, A.C., ed, *Political History of Assam,* Vol. I, II, III, 1977-78; and Phukan Girin, *Assam's Attitude to Federalism,* 1984.
32. Barpujari, H.K., ed, *Political History of Assam,* Vol. II, 1977.
33. Fort William Archives; Judicial Proceedings, 24 July 1859.
34. During the *Ahom Rule*, class of people who were entrusted with the responsibility of keeping written records of land and of revenue administration, was called Kakoti.

35. *North-East Sun*, "Threat Perceptions: Assam's Concern" 15-31 August 2000.
36. *Hindustan Times*, "Pakistan's Dhaka Mission has links with ULFA: Mahanta", 8 April 2000; cited by Dinesh Kotwal, in his "The Contours of Assam Insurgency", in the IDSA monthly, 'Strategic Analysis'.
37. Coordination Committee for Minorities of Assam (COMOA) is a political organisation. It has several affiliated bodies, some of the prominent ones being UPPA, UMF, Linguistic Minorities Forum (LMF), and All Assam Nepali Students Union (AANSU).
38. Henry Kissinger in his "White House Years".
39. *Hindustan Times*, "The UP DGP Hits out at SIMI", 15 October, 2000.
40. Seema Sangupta, *The Pioneer*, 19 Jan. 2007.
41. *Ibid.*
42. Presently, the Cachar Valley stands divided into three districts of Cachar, Hailakandi and Karimganj.
43. Datt, P.S., 1993.
44. In fact, the Cachar district was transferred to the Dacca Division of Bengal in 1836, and stayed as such till restored to Assam in 1874.

4

ULFA : A VIRULENT OUTFIT (But a Financially Rich 'Corporation')

ULFA presently is the most virulent terrorist organisation, espousing secessionism. With the NSCN(I-M) honouring cease-fire since 1997, this outfit remains most potent threat to India's integrity, with the NDFB being a distant second.

Origin, Growth and Objectives

ULFA was formed on 7 April 1979 at a meeting of its initial think-tank at the Rang Ghor; the 17th century amphitheatre of the Ahom Royalty, near Sibsagar. The group that morning included Arbindo Raj Khowa, Golap Barua alias Anup Chetia, Pradip (Samiram) Gogoi, and Paresh Barua. Their professed aim was liberation of Assam from the "Indian Colonial rule" and setting up of an independent State, through armed struggle if necessary. The slogan of "sovereign, socialist Assam" lent certain intellectual underpinnings to their ideological dreamland which did bestir the rural masses and a section of the intelligentsia. Most leading lights of the leadership at that time were of Muttock origin, belonging to Upper Assam. Could anyone have imagined at that point in 1979 that the event staged by these starry-eyed, young idealists would give birth to a major, secessionist force in Assam? By November 2002, after three spells of President's Rule and ten Chief Ministers, Assam and the country were still groping in the dark for reigning in the monster it has become for the last two decades and more. At its birth, Assam was passing through a spell of instability. The post-Emergency Janata Party Government of Golap Barbora had fallen, whence followed three Governments within a short span of 28 months.

The founders blamed exploitative policies of New Delhi for Assam's troubles. Like any ideologically-driven movement, they stood for a revolutionary purge of society. They had convinced themselves that Assam was never a part of India. It had forcibly been made a part of Indian polity by some Hindu and Muslim rulers at various periods of history. Till then the Assamese nationality grew in isolation and the people of Assam are proud possessors of a heritage—historical, racial, ethnic, and cultural—totally distinct from that of Metropolitan India. Assam was annexed by the British under the 24 February 1826 Yandabo Treaty, and it came under the unified Indian administration. But the Treaty itself was bad in law hence, the annexation under it itself became null and void as it did not have concurrence of the people of Assam, nor was it ratified by the Ahom rulers. So ran the ULFA argument. So on 15 August 1947, Assam reverted to its status of an independent country; the Indian Independence Act of 1947 only joined it artificially with India through a narrow strip of land (Siliguri Corridor). Moreover it contends that various laws and constitutional prohibitions and bindings about the migration of foreigners have by default been rendered inoperative, resulting in illegal in-migration of millions from the neighbouring Bangladesh, which has destroyed the distinct ethnic character of Assam. Therefore, as an ULFA publication explains, "to create an exploitation-free society, our next step (must) be a national war of liberation.... We have no alternative to armed revolution".[1]

ULFA objective, therefore, was and still remains the creation of an Independent Assam, intended to resuscitate the glory of the ancient Assam and Ahom civilisation.

It should be of interest to trace the lineage of sovereignty from earlier times, even if nurtured by a section of intelligentsia. In that sense, ULFA is not the progenitor of the *Svadhin Asom* (=Sovereign Assam) as it had already been dreamt of by earlier generations. The peasant struggles in Assam in the latter half of the 19th century were unique in the sense that, unlike the similar struggles in the rest of India, a common front was put up against the British Rule by both the land-owning class and the middle and poor peasantry. This was possible due to various factors: (1) nature of land settlement under the long Ahom Rule; (2) strong tribal content in the Assamese society; (3) predominance of the small land-holding farmers; and (4) absence of the zamindari system.

Different struggles during the period of British Rule by themselves were not a fight for "Assamese identity" or "Assamese nationality"; they were simply stages in the mobilisation of a people, who would in years to follow be involved in a larger national struggle where the peasantry would play the pivotal role. The different ethnic groups, which constituted the social fabric of Assamese society on the eve of British advent, were yet to be brought together on the common platform of the Assamese linguistic nationalism. The struggle against the British Rule led by the Assamese middle class, which had got a head-start over the other smaller nationalities of the Region, gave it a position of hegemony that was to continue till 1960s, and 1970s when the emerging middle classes of these nationalities started asserting their rights, and a schism began to appear in the facade of a monolithic Assamese nationalism. It was during the initial years of consolidation of Assamese nationalism in the 1920s and 1930s that the idea of *Svadhin Asom* began to fire the imagination of a section of the middle class. Incidentally, that ULFA ideologues claim to take the inspiration for their movement from this period.

Modern political consciousness in Assam may be deemed to have commenced from around 1853 when Maniram Dewan and Anandaram Dhekiyal[2] Phukan submitted their memorials to Moffat-Mills. It would take another 70 years or so for this consciousness to develop and give shape to the Assamese nationalism, with the INC establishing its unit in Assam in 1921. "By 1870s, non-indigenous element constituted at least a quarter of the population of Assam proper."[3] Added to this was the serious imbalance between the fast-growing modern sector of tea and extractive industry (oil and coal) and traditional agricultural sector. Almost the entire surplus from the former was being remitted to Britain. The colonial exploitation was on the rise. It was against this background that the Assamese students in Calcutta formed the Assamese Library Society (ALS) in 1872, supplanted by the Asomiya Bhasa Unnati Sadhani Sabha (ABUS) in August 1888. It published the catalogue of Assamese manuscripts in 1897 and the journal, *Jonaki* which ushered in a hew era of Assamese literature. The articles in Jonaki harked back to the glories of the past when Kamarupa held sway up to the borders of Bihar and bemoaned the loss of economic autonomy. Kanak Lal Barua[4] blamed the British for the decay in Assam's handloom industry. An argument for economic independence is but one step away from advocacy for political independence, given the socio-political scenario at the beginning of the 20th century. Kamala Kanta Bhattacharya[5] insisted that Assam should constitute an independent self-reliant nation and warned that with the development of transport and communication means, foreigners would pour into fertile soil of Assam and jeopardise our "distinct identity". Lakshminath Bezbarua[6] did not plead for political emancipation but worked for cultural resurgence of the Assamese. Noting the non-mention of Sankaradeva in the histories of Indian/ Bengali saints, Bezbarua says: "It only proves that Assam was till the other day an independent country." Although Bezbarua's Assamese nationalism (Asamiya Jatiyatabad) was part of broader Indian nationalism, still in his writings *Assam Desh* is an autonomous socio-cultural and political entity. His poem, *Mor Desh* (= my country) written in 1910, today is Assam's Jatiya Sangeet (national anthem), and sung on all public occasions along with India's National Anthem. The writings in *Jonaki* and other journals of the period show the existence of two types of nationalism, regional and national, side by side, in Assam. Scholars posit "it was a common phenomenon throughout India".[7] But in the case of provinces like Assam, not to speak of its hill regions which came under the British Rule much later than most of other parts of India, the Regional brand of nationalism got the better of pan-Indian nationalism whenever the Region and the Community faced a crisis—cultural, economic, or political. Geographical and historical factors often counted for pan-Indian nationalism to be overshadowed by regional nationalistic emotions in Assam and other regions in the North-East. Thus, for the understandable reasons, the struggle between the two strands of nationalism have formed an important part of Assam's history right from the days of the advent (1921) and consolidation of the Congress politics in Assam to the post-independence period when cries of "Colonial exploitation" of Assam rich natural resources by the Centre started becoming increasingly strident.[8]

As the Assamese joined the 1920-21 Non-cooperation Movement in large numbers, it resulted in swift politicisation of the masses. Consequently, a variety of socio-political organisations sprung up in Assam, ranging from the Assam Sangrakshini Sabha (ASS) founded by Ambikagiri Roy-Choudhury[9] (later, Asom Jatiya Mahasabha, AJM) to dozens of Krishak and Ryot Sabhas, dedicated to voicing the peasants' demands. In May 1920, Chandranath Sharma, virtual founder of Assam Congress, voiced his concern on the threat to Assam's identity from the unchecked infiltration, particularly from (West), from Bengal. It was in these circumstances that the Assamese middle class intellectuals like Roy-Choudhury and Jnananath Bora wrote on the need to defend Assamese homeland against "foreign" incursions. As mentioned above, Chandranath Sharma also harboured similar apprehensions about the fate of the Assamese nationality. Roy-Choudhury, who was no Assamese chauvinist (as he is often made out to be) and in fact was a senior Assam Congress leader (1926), initially advocated the concept of an Indian Federation of (equal) linguistic nationalities. But in the later years, it was the failure of the Indian National Congress (INC) to take an unequivocal stand on the issue of continued influx of foreigners threatening the very identity of Assam and its attempt to force Assam to accept the Cabinet Mission Plan[10], that would have resulted Assam going to Pakistan, were the reasons that pushed Roy-Choudhury and his AJM to express sentiments bordering on a demand for an independent Assam. As early as November 1937, he had submitted a memorandum on behalf of the ASS to Nehru, emphasizing the following:

1. If the line system segregating the autochthons and immigrants was withdrawn, it would lead to fresh tensions emanating from further occupation of Assamese-held lands by the immigrants.
2. A considerable section of Assamese intelligentsia feels that if the full leadership of the Congress did not view their fears regarding Muslim influx seriously, then Assam should secede from India.
3. The support for the Congress in Assam would depend upon the two issues that deeply trouble the Assamese: one, Sylhet and Cachar be separated from Assam; two, mass immigration into the Brahmaputra Valley be stopped.

In the June 1946 Memorandum to the All India Congress Committee, Roy-Choudhury's AJM accused it of not seeing the threat caused by the Grouping Plan[11] to Assam's identity and "the Assamese were prepared for a desperate struggle for national existence and emancipation. He even built up Asom Atmarakashi Bahini to save Assam from the designs of Muslim League, which had caused the widespread riots in the East Bengal districts, and "the victims of the Noakhali disturbances are entering Assam".

When after Independence, Assam's Congress Government failed to provide adequate checks against the infiltration from the newly-created East Pakistan, the AJM in a meeting on 1 January 1948 declared that "Assam should come out of Indian Union and become independent like Burma". It must be noted that the AJM's (Asom Jatiya Mahasabha) consistent demand that Sylhet be separated from Assam and opposition to the CHT being incorporated into it (Assam) were motivated by an urge to have a homogenous Assamese territory "distinct from the Indian mainland". But luckily for the nation, Roy-Choudhury, and others of his ilk, remained a lonely voice in the first two decades or so of the post-Independence Assam which, dominated by the Congress ideology and politics, veered sharply towards the pan-Indian nationalism. The success of Bordoloi in thwarting the Grouping Plan and separation of Sylhet (bar its Karimganj sub-division) had largely eased the Assamese fears of losing their identity. Thus, from 1947 till the 1960s, regional nationalist forces had to take the back seat. "It was from the early 1970s, that Roy-Choudhury's ideas started finding favour with sections of the post-1960 generation of Assamese who had become increasingly aware of the colonial pattern of exploitation of Assam by the Centre as well as the growing threat posed by the influx of foreigners into the State." Jnananath Bora was another intellectual who advocated for a sovereign Assam during the 1930s. He asserts the British forcibly incorporated Assam into British India and on that basis, "the educated amongst us have been trying to prove that Assam is a province of India."[12] This argument is very similar to the ULFA's present stance regarding the role of the intellectuals in Assam, who are dubbed by it as the 'Indian agents'. Bora's writings, forgotten for decades, have now been resurrected by the proponents of the *Svadhin Asom* who have been trying to use them to garner people's support for the ULFA's cause.

In spite of their large scale participation in the 1942 Quit India Movement, the Assamese felt let down when the Congress Working Committee accepted the Grouping Plan on 10 August 1946. Assam's fears were not unfounded as Bengal with its huge majority could/would impose its will on it.[13] In view of this betrayal by the Congress, some scholars ask as why the *Svadhin Asom* proponents did not push their case more aggressively. One of the main reasons for their low profile during this period could be the fear of Muslim domination resulting from the inundation of the indigenous Assamese in the flood of in-migrants from across the border and hence the need to stay with India. It was easy to see, given the demographic realities and the experience of the recent past with the Saadullah Ministries,[14] that a *Svadhin Asom* would be even more vulnerable to and fall an easy prey to the machinations of the Muslim East Pakistan. The Hill leaders too were well aware of the need to stay with India to avert a Muslim take-over. Nichols-Roy,[15] the eminent Khasi leader declared: "We know what the policy of Muslim League is in Assam. Even now, the Muslim League in Bengal wants to send thousands upon thousands of immigrants into Assam."

It may be fair to say that the fear of Muslim Pakistan and the demographic challenge posed by it through an aggressive migration policy pursued by the Muslim League and supported by it, attenuated the fervour of the *Svadhin Asom* proponents. Moreover, once the Muslim majority district of Sylhet voted itself out of Assam, the CHT did not get tagged to Assam, as some had reared, and Assam joined India on 15 August 1947; all existential fears of the Assamese seemingly evaporated and the concept of Svadhin Asom also petered out.

This is a brief, broad brush survey of *Assamese* 'nationalism', and urge for 'sovereignty', during the British days. The ideas on sovereign *Assam* may not have been widespread, but the germs were always there all be it just below the surface. Happily for us all, its espousal was restricted to a few eminent individuals, academics, intellectuals and leftists. The feelings of separateness persisted till the 1930s and even 1940s. To cite just one instance, a mere one month prior to the Independence, one of the leading intellectuals of *Assam*, Birinchi Kumar Baruah, a known authority on Assamese literature and culture, who subsequently became the Dean of Faculty of Arts, Guwahati University, said in a public lecture: "culturally, socially and linguistically, every non-Assamese is a foreigner, in Assam"...It speaks of India's strengths that all such individuals are happily doing their duty by India's cause. It is a tribute to *Indian* civilisation's all-encompassing nature that India exists as a multi-cultural, -linguistic, -religious and -ethnic nation, a pulsating democracy amidst a sea of autocratic and fundamentalist regimes.

The demand for autonomy—nay, sovereignty—was to resurface some forty years after it had subsided (if not died) at Independence. But this time around, it was to be backed by an adequate infrastructural support in the form of an armed outfit (ULFA) to wage the battle violently and on an en otive, sensitive issue of "colonial exploitation" of Assam (and the North-East) by the "Imperial India"; it was a war in the field of ideas and ideology.

The above should sum up the ideological and motivational basis in history that the ULFA leadership has intelligently, if cleverly, used to build and sustain their case for secessionism.

Graduating into a Virulent Movement

The ULFA remained rather dormant for some years after its formation in 1979. During the AASU Agitation (1979-85), some militant groups like the Assam Fighters Union (AFU) and Assam People's Liberation Army (APLA) came into being which lent some belligerent touch to it, from the sidelines. Subsequently sprang up some parochial organisations like Assam Jatiyabadi Dal (AJD) and Purbanchaliya Lok Parishad (PLP) which also occasionally shouted some belligerent slogans for effect. ULFA was, besides these four groups, another outfit that played on the sidelines of the Assam Agitation, but with a difference. Some saw it as B team of the AASU during the Agitation. With its brazen advocacy of Assamese Chauvinism, ULFA represented the extremity of xenophobic ideology, the bedrock of this Agitation. The AFU, APLA, AJD and PLP declined and fizzled out after the Assam Accord was signed in 1985. But the idea of forming a violent underground with the sole objective of liberating Assam did not die down. It stayed alive and was nurtured by ULFA.

There are interesting speculations on the AASU-ULFA relationship. Some feel the ULFA had watched the AASU Movement from close angles and learnt some lessons in organising and conducting such movements. In fact, the ULFA had ingratiated itself with the AASU hierarchy. It was not an unexpected development or difficult task, as the leadership of the two organisations was comprised of the idealistic, educated youth, having similar social and economic background. This was but a simple fact of life, even if the analysts have engaged in semantics on the issue. If some posited that ULFA was an offshoot of the extremist fringe of AASU, others counter it by saying that it was born at least 6 months before the AASU Agitation took off. A certain symbiosis between the two during the agitation is widely acknowledged. But once the AASU ascended to power as AGP, the chasm between the two was inevitable. Hence the postulation that the AGP lost the 1991 Assembly poll due to ULFA's antagonism, and returned to power in 1996 with its support. Some analysts assert that even when the two organisations are firmly pitched on the opposite sides of the fence, there is a degree of mutual admiration and kinship of ideas and interests between certain identifiable sections of the two camps.

The 1983 Assembly polls were excessively violent because they were held in the wake of the boycott call by AASU, since it alleged that the electoral rolls prepared in 1979 contained the names of over 4 million aliens who, if allowed to participate in the polls, would vitiate their sanctity. AASU deemed the Saikia Government that came into power as a result of these polls as illegitimate. It was during these un-popular elections and the tenure of the Saikia Government (1983-85) that rose to power in consequence that ULFA cut its teeth in agitational politics and made significant inroads into the body politic of Assam. It assiduously built its case of exploitation theory: India was not concerned with Assam's interests, but only in its resources. Hence its stubbornness in holding polls against fierce opposition of the Assamese. Spreading this sentiment adroitly, it built and expanded its support base among the educated, unemployed youth.

ULFA had infiltrated some departments of the Mahanta Government. Mahanta did not act even when he knew that the ULFA activities were harming his Government. By 1987-88, their depredations had reached menacing proportions. Towards the end of 1980s, situation reached a point of no return. AGP Government not proceeding against the ULFA cadres was understandable, "after all, they were our boys", but even the V.P. Singh Coalition at the Centre failed to act, hobbled as it was by its internal troubles; and in addition, AGP was part of the Coalition. Then came the infamous airlift of the Doom Dooma Tea Executives and meanwhile Chandrashekhar had taken over who dismissed the Mahanta Ministry on 27 November 1990. The Union Minister of State, Subodh Kant Sahay put it tersely: "The whole State machinery is with the ULFA".[16] ULFA was banned the same day. The next day (28-11-1990), Army launched operation Bajrang. The ULFA leadership escaped the dragnet as the word had leaked about the impending operation. The first camp to be struck was at Lakhipata, a short distance from both Digboi and Dibrugarh. It was the case of Army reaching and searching the just-abandoned camp. The same story was repeated elsewhere. The mass graves in some of the camps told their own story of gory torture and death. ULFA was in disarray, but far from being broken, as the educated youth was available and willing to join it.

"The elections of 1991 were completed despite ditching by those charged with responsibility to conduct them." These elections were completed courtesy ULFA, as some critics asserted. Though ULFA was seen as a half-brother of AASU, but it reportedly helped the Congress, covertly. The Saikia Ministry was sworn-in on 1 July 1991 and perhaps to remind him of the promises, it struck the same day. 14 officials and some others were taken hostages. In the ensuing negotiations, the Assam Government agreed to the following: (1) Amnesty for ULFA leaders and cadres. (2) Over 400 cadres released. (3) Operation Bajrang was called off much against the Army's advice. With a single stroke of pen, Saikia undid what the SF had achieved at some cost to them. All his was done against a mere promise of release of hostages. Paresh Barua went to Bangladesh to persuade Arbindo Rajkhowa, Anup Chetia and Pradeep Gogoi and their cadres to join the peace process. Not only they did not return, they issued a call from Dhaka for renewing the armed struggle. In a perfidious move, they killed some hostages and went on a rampage. Utilising the peaceful interregnum, they regrouped and rejuvenated their outfit and unleashed an orgy of violence. Within a period of 11 weeks, 166 innocents were killed and another 252 kidnapped. Singed by their perridy, the Government called out the Army again. Operation Rhino was launched on 14-15 August 1991. This is the story of ULFA during the first decade of its existence.

It needs re-emphasis that its initial success in building up and sustaining its mass base was because of its ideology-driven motivation. In its letter to the UN Secretary General dated 20 October 1990, it shunned all forms of disruptive violence. When the ISI wanted ULFA to "disrupt communications and economic targets like oil refineries and gas fields, and create chaos to pave the way for a general uprising against the Government", both Paresh Barua and Sunil Nath, two of ULFA's top leaders, expressed strong opposition to any major attacks on Government property, "as that would alienate us from the people...." This was early stage. The streak of idealism was still intact and they were keen to retain the sympathy of masses. The success in the initial stages could be seen in the way it was able to infiltrate the police, AGP, and other branches of the State administration. That should explain the fiasco in which Op Bajrang had to end, as ULFA had been tipped about it a week in advance. But this should not have been a surprise for the people in the know. After all, ULFA was the brain child of the extremist section of AASU and a certain symbiotic relationship must have continued to exist between the two. An analyst was not far off the mark to say: "AGP had become a cloak for ULFA's activities." Even more significantly, ULFA was able to create a space for itself in the public life viz, civil society, independently of the overwhelming State apparatus. That should explain the birth of organisations like Manav Adhikar Sangram Samiti (MASS) and hydra beaded growth of newspapers like Budhbar and Sadin, generally acquiescing in ULFA's violence but loudly protesting the State's so-called excesses.

So, initially at least, ULFA had ideological moorings, even if mixed with nationalistic cliches. At that stage, it indeed was ideologically-driven movement. But all that was given a go-by when, mid-1990s onwards, its leadership under pressure from Army, resorted to mindless violence. Its mass support really suffered with its pro-Pak stance during the 1999 Kargil war and communal killings in end-2000 period. It was simply violence for violence, sans any ideology.

Political Games

It is an accepted fact that ULFA came into its own only after its cadres were put through their paces in the NSCN training camps. It opened its account in the violence trade with a bank robbery at Namrup in Upper Assam in 1985. Saikia was in power then (1983-85). Some observers feel the wily Chief Minister built up ULFA to even out with AASU, which was then in the mid-course of its own agitation. In such situations, it is always difficult to know the "facts". But it does seem true that they gained strength during the first Mahanta Ministry.

Several batches of ULFA recruits got trained in Nagaland and Manipur in the NSCN camps. Subsequently, senior leaders began establishing camps within Assam as Mahanta, a youthful tyro, was struggling to pick up ropes as Chief Minister. As already discussed, he was unwilling or unable to confront ULFA in this term. ULFA Chairman Arbindo Rajkhowa (real name, Rajiv Rajkonwar; a school teacher and son of a freedom fighter from a place near Nazira) appointed Paresh Barua (a football player and a railway employee) the chief of ULFA's Military wing. It was around this time that the killings began, slowly but steadily. The Chairman of the United Minorities Front, a pro-migrant Muslim outfit in 1986, was among the first targets.

The initial training in Burma was arranged by ULFA for its cadres from the KIA in 1986. This needed hard cash which set in motion a train of extortions, kidnappings, and demands for ransom. The message was soon to reach a wide circle of traders, businessmen, tea garden executives, and Government employees/officers with a mixture of hype, effrontery, and selective strikes. Thus, it was that ULFA became a dreaded name by the closing years of the 1980s. "During 1989-90, they managed to extort Rs. 20 crore from traders in Jorhat alone." They had arrived on the scene with a big bang. But far more impressive were their pickings from the tea industry (details later):

> By 1989 the ULFA was a grown-up! It had started taking journalists to its hide-outs to draw some publicity mileage. Meanwhile the killings increased as did the extortions. They established links with the ISI, enabling them to obtain the Pakistan and Bangladeshi passports for travels abroad. It was only when their depredations reached tea gardens that the Centre sat up. In the latter half of 1990, Surendra Paul, Director, Assam Frontier Tea, was killed and many others were abducted. When the Doom Dooma executives were airlifted to safety outside Assam, the Chandrashekhar Ministry dismissed Mahanta (November 1990) only weeks before completion of his term. The press reports said he was compelled to take this step by the Congress which, angling in the troubled waters, had espied a political opportunity.

If Mahanta during his first term (1985-90) in office failed to see the threat posed by the militants to the nation's integrity, the Saikia Government (1991-96) proved even worse. The split engineered by him in 1993 proved counter-productive. The residual faction turned stronger and even more ruthless and SULFA proved an obstreperous child even to its own parents, indulging in its own little games of revenge and extortions. While Saikia spent-more and more time guarding his political flanks, thousands of SULFA cadres turned out to be a new pack of anti-socials. The fiasco was mainly because not only Saikia failed to make them surrender their weapons but his Government was lacklustre in providing them any worthwhile alternative employment as promised and planned. The slip-shod policy resulted in huge amount of money given as loans for rehabilitation, remaining unrecovered. And to imagine that 50 per cent of ULFA's cadre strength—amounting to about 3500—had surrendered by 31 March 1993 and Saikia had publicly said that "ULFA stood neutralised and as a result it would now call for peaceful negotiations". The subsequent events showed that Saikia's remained a vain hope, and there never was greater hiatus between hope and reality! In the end, ULFA emerged stronger, since it became more selective and stricter in recruiting the youth; and going by reports, over 600 joined its ranks and received arms training in Bangladesh, Myanmar and even Bhutan during *Saikia's* term. More unfortunate was the anti-SF sentiment resulting from the vociferous human rights activists. Large-scale corruption helped ULFA to fill its coffers with large amount of money resulting from the leakage of development funds.

The anti-Army sentiments was so strong during the 1996 electoral rhetoric that Mahanta had promised to send the Army back to barracks and withdraw the black laws.[17] There are two views about reasons for this unwise promise. One, his pro-ULFA leanings led him to this statement. Two, quite to the contrary, others felt he did so under direct pressure from ULFA. It is an irony that Mahanta had to eat crow, and call out the Army urgently to bail him out as the ULFA unleashed a vicious violence on the very day he was sworn-in (15 May 1996) for his second term. Midway through this term, he felt threatened enough with ULFA's depredations and fearing the fall of his Government, that he even wanted to requisition the services of K.P.S. Gill to help him weather his battle against ULFA.[18]

What are the political leanings of the ULFA? It is a difficult issue to tackle. Its support to the AGP resulted in Mahanta winning 1985 and 1996 Assembly polls; or so says the grapevine. The party lost to the Congress in 1991 elections due to its opposition. On similar grounds, it lost the 1998 and 1999 Parliamentary polls. But all this may be too simplistic, as if the AGP's own performance in power had no role to play. But there is another view to the scenario. Public pressure was seen to be building up against ULFA by 1997-98. Particularly after the cold-blooded murder by ULFA of Sanjay Ghose, a dedicated social worker who had brought hope and light in the lives of the Mujuli Islanders, there was a groundswell of anger against the outfit. If the political class had acted in national interest, the Mahanta Government showing the will to act and the Congress Party resisting the temptation to pull it down by fostering dissensions in the *AGP* ranks, ULFA might have openly come forward for talks.

All said and done, the AGP suffered due to its proximity to ULFA, perceived or otherwise. It was perceived to be pro-ULFA. After all, Mahanta had accused his own Home Minister (Bhrigu Phukan) of pro-ULFA stance during his first Ministry. Mahanta's own flip-flops could hardly assure the people of his hands-on determination to confront the secessionist outfit squarely. His anti-Army rhetoric in the run-up to the 1996 poll and subsequently eating his words, belong to the pages of history. It is also widely believed that he held a public rally in Guwahati in the 1998 elections after an agreement with the ULFA. Again, it is well-known that he dragged his feet for months after taking over as Chief Minister in May 1996 on setting up a Unified Command structure for efficient and coordinated conduct of CI operations in his State. "Even when forced down his throat early 1997, he refused to take command",[19] as some news reports claimed, and only agreed to a convoluted structure for Unified Command: a Strategic Group under his Chief Secretary and an Operational Group under the local (Tezpur) Corps Commander. But his distaste for the Unified Command did not end with the creation of a frayed and truncated structure. Late 1997, capital of Dispur (along with Jorhat) was taken out of the purview of the Unified Command. Was it any surprise that Guwahati witnessed a series of violent incidents in the months following this decision, asked a concerned citizen? It is also held that Saikia was no different from Mahanta for playing political games of his own. He had reportedly reached a tacit understanding with ULFA on the eve of 1991 Assembly poll (Did this ensure his victory?). It was his failure to deliver on some unwritten promises that forced the outfit to resort to large-scale kidnappings on the very day he was sworn-in on 1 July 1991. His soft-corner for ULFA was obvious from the so-called conciliatory offerings he made to it during the ensuing negotiations for release of hostages. The perfidy of ULFA, in killing some hostages, including the Russian Engineer, did not seem to have overly dismayed Saikia as he continued dealing with it "to persuade it to come to table for peace talks". As for the post-Saikia Congress' relations with ULFA, Chief Minister Mahanta (1996-2001) persistently accused it of a clear nexus with the outfit. After the October-December 2000 minority massacres unleashed by ULFA, Mahanta claimed in the Assembly that he had documentary evidence on this nexus, and claimed it was aimed to destabilise his Government.

Having said it all, how is the following news item as dessert?

"The ULFA has decided to help the Congress (I) in the (September 1999) Lok Sabha elections, like in 1998. It has already issued instructions to this effect to its units, reliable sources said here today." (*The Hindu*, 10 September 1999, Guwahati). The sources hinted that some Congress (I) leaders, mainly in Upper Assam, were in touch with the ULFA. An affluent former MP was likely to provide the necessary "inducement" to the ULFA to help the Congress (I).

It is an issue where no analyst can talk in terms of certainty. There are shades and shades between black and white. May be, it is fair to say that in this game, no political party can be pure evil or milky white. It is good enough to mention the possibilities and potentialities, and let the matters rest there. It is Herculean task to draw conclusions from the unedifying mud-slinging indulged in by different political parties.

VIOLENCE BY MILITANTS

1991

1 July	The Saikia Ministry was sworn-in this day and it was the day when ULFA kidnapped 14 people from different places in Assam. Most of them were officials from the oil industry, including a Russian Engineer. They were kept in captivity for long period. They killed three of them in cold blood, including the luckless Russian. How Chief Minister Saikia walked into the trap of negotiations with ULFA has already been recounted.

1993

5 Oct.	Rs. 2.34 lakh looted from the employees of Agricultural Training Centre at Amoni Tenali, near Tezpur.
17-18 Nov.	ULFA took away Rs. 50 lakh in cash from the ONGC central workshop, near Sibsagar.

1994

28 May	Kokopathar Tea Estate (TE) under Dibrugarh Police Station receives an extortion notice for Rs. 20 lakh.

1995

30 Dec.	15 militants sprayed a volley of bullets on the convoy of Assam Health Minister Bhumidhar Burman, killing 10 and injuring 3 policemen.

1996

7 Jan.	SP Nagaon's caravan fired at indiscriminately.
20 Jan.	Lachit Kalita, President of Assam Youth Congress shot dead in Guwahati.
12 Feb.	Two passengers on a Guwahati-bound bus shot dead near Golaghat.
21 Feb.	Mohd Haque son of Assam Minister R. Haque, kidnapped along with his three friends and his driver.

All set free, except the Minister's son, who was released much later, at 10 PM on 5 April, probably after taking ransom.

29 Mar. A.K. Brahma, a SULFA cadre, gunned down near village Balabari.

25 April Binu Chetia, Congress candidate in Assembly Election (due in May) along with his 3 PSOs (Personal Security Officers) shot dead, 3 km from Margharetta.

28 April Lt Col Devan Tyagi shot dead and Lt Col AD Ghosh injured at the Kamakhya Temple.

6 May Assam Minister Nagon Neog shot dead along with 9 of his security men while returning from Golaghat.

15 May Bodo and ULFA ultras unleashed an orgy of violence on this day. Mahanta is sworn-in second time as Chief Minister.

16 May SP, Tinsukia and 4 others shot dead.

31 May Rs. 5 lakh snatched from the Union Bank of India Manager (The loot from different incidents during the month totalled Rs. 12,65,780).

9 Sept. IGP, S.K. Deb, shot dead in the heart of Guwahati city from a point-blank range.

28 Nov. Oil pipeline to Baraumi blown up by ULFA, near Bijulighat in Nalbari district. The blast completely damaged the pipeline over river Pagladiya. The impact was heard as far as Nalbari town, 10 km away.

30 Dec. The Brahmaputra train blast.

Parag Kumar Das, General Secretary, Manav Adhikar (Human Rights) Sangram Samiti (MASS), was murdered brutally. He was the Editor of a Guwahati Daily and a ULFA ideologue. "Army had no hand in his murder, nor did the Police for that matter, particularly so after an ignominious departure of senior Police and Civil officials like DGP Ranjan Das, IGP Ashim Roy, and Chief Secretary Arunoday Bhattacharya, by the first available flight."

1997

16 March Lt Col KS Kalra shot dead at Tezpur where he had gone with his family for worship at the Ganesh Temple.

8 June ULFA tried to eliminate Chief Minister Mahanta by exploding an IED while he was on his way to the city from Guwahati airport.

23 June	A CRPF vehicle going to town from Guwahati airport ambushed; 4 men were killed and 5 injured.
3 July	Rs. 1.26 lakh snatched from the accountant of the Purabi Dairy in Kamrup district.
August	The re-charged ULFA and Bodo militants staged a death dance on the eve of Independence Day, 1997.
6 August	ULFA confirms the death of Sanjoy Ghose, claiming he slipped from a cliff top in Arunachal Pradesh.
8 August	Brig TDS Vishakhan and his staff officer are gunned down in Guwahati, with his daughter witnessing the killing.
8 August	The Bodo rebels blow up two bridges. 7 BdSF rebels killed. Army recovers 8 Kg of RDX.
11 August	A powerful blast 10 metres ahead of the Rajdhani Express near Sarupeta in Lower Assam, over 300 lives lost.
12 August	Bengalis lined up and shot dead by BdSF at Rangiya.
14 August	A bomb blast derails a passenger train near Siloni in North Lakhimpur district, killing 7 and injuring many more.
	Violence in Tea Gardens. The acts of ULFA violence during the period 1988-90 and 1992-96 are covered separately, on the next page.
1998	
11 February	ULFA targeted many AGP candidates during the 1998 Parliamentary Election. Its Vice-President Biraj Sharma is attacked, but escapes with serious injuries.
1999	
August	ULFA and Bodo militants launched a number of subversive attacks on the trains, bridges, and SF personnel (discussed in detail separately).
2000	
Oct.-Dec.	A reoriented ULFA, moving away from its ideological moorings, launched vicious violence against the non-Assamese Hindi-speaking minorities (also discussed separately).
27 February	The Assam PWD and Forest Minister Nagen Sharma and 4 others were killed around 1.45 PM when the ULFA militants blew their vehicle by a remote-controlled IED at Nij Bahjani village in Nalbari district. The village is considered one of the strongest bastions of ULFA, though the district itself is dominated by this outfit. Sharma, a senior AGP leader, was its seniormost General Secretary.

Summarised Information on Violence. ULFA violence claimed the lives of 1370 civilians and 20 SF men during the 1986-95 period. Details of killings and kidnappings for three years follow:[20]

Year	*Killed*	*Kidnapped*
1995	30	29
1996	107	36
1997	118	40

Here are the official figures[21] of human cost of violence perpetrated by ULFA.

Persons Killed by ULFA

Period	*Incident*	*Total*	*Persons Killed*	
			Civilians	*SF*
1996	141	107	59	48
1997*	79	60	41	19

*(1 January to 7 May 1997)

Poor Show by MHA

Fuller accounts of incidents of killing, kidnapping, and extortion are available in the 36-page pamphlet distributed by the MHA officials during the 16-17 October 1998 meeting of the NEC at Shillong. Coming from an exalted Ministry, it is a shoddily document; with poor grammar, poorer syntax, and careless editing. More surprisingly, it singularly lacks felicity of expression, generally a strong point with the IAS/IFS community, which must have drafted the document.

Assam Tea Tastes Bitter

If Assam tea has made a name for itself for its quality and flavour the world over during the last 150 years, it also made news in the recent years but for different reason. By the end of 1980s, it had become a milch cow for terrorist outfits like ULFA and BdSF. Crores of rupees had been extorted from the executives of various Tea Houses on the pain of death threats. Anyone daring to be defiant was dispatched without remorse. When extortions crossed the limits of forbearance, one company (Doom Dooma) decided enough was enough and flew its executives out of Assam. How this resulted in the dismissal of the first Mahanta Government in November 1990 has already been discussed. Subsequently, for some years, the tea did not boil over, even if it was simmering below the surface. But when a tea major (the Tata Tea Limited-TTL) got enmeshed in a major controversy in 1997, Mahanta again was in office and this time around he was determined to make political capital out of that company's discomfiture. Being recent events, they will be discussed in outline only.

The TTL vs Assam Government controversy grabbed the headlines following the arrest of ULFA's Culture Secretary Pranati Deka at Bombay on 22 August 1997. Her interrogation revealed TTL had defrayed her medical expenses after she had given birth to a baby boy a fortnight ago at Bombay's upmarket Jaslok Hospital. DGP, Assam told the *Frontline:* "Deka was living with her husband, C. Hazarika, Finance Secretary of ULFA, in a safe house in Bhutan. She boarded the flight for Bombay from Bagdogra in Siliguri district on 22 May, accompanied by Dr Brojen Gogoi, a manager with TTL." TTL had paid for her air tickets. The Assam Government adopted a tough stance against the Tea Companies, particularly the biggest of them all, TTL (with interest spread over 21 estates, employing 170 managers and 20,000 workers), following the allegations that they aided and funded militant outfits in the State. It was revealed that the tea companies were making regular payments to ULFA, NDFB, etc. How did it all start? The State CID disclosed that the whole thing resulted from the recovery by the Army of copies of the audited balance sheets of the NDFB for 1994-95 and 1995-96 in course of a CI operation in Darrang district in December 1996. The Army had lodged an FIR on 2 January 1997. The Mahanta Government never explained as to why it waited for full 9 months (till 2 October 1997) to hand over the case to CID. But critics argue it is easy to blame the tea companies but did they have a choice? ULFA had gained strength 1987-88 onwards, as did the violence unleashed by it. Killings in tea estates had started early 1989 for extortions and taxes. The brutal murder of Surendra Paul in June 1990 had completely unnerved the industry. The, Mahanta Government was unable or disinclined to protect its employees. ULFA and to an extent, BdSF were running parallel Governments in their respective areas of influence. So when ULFA summoned in June 1990 representatives of tea companies to a meeting at a garden outside Dibrugarh, leading lights of the industry responded. Under a compromise, they agreed to 'contribute' to ULFA's war chest. It should be no surprise that Assam's tea industry, with an annual turn-over of over Rs. 2,200 crore, had been prime target of militant groups like ULFA and NDFB. Some reports said the NDFB levied 'tax' at Rs. 2,500 per hectare. With 2,30,000 hectares under tea cultivation, their rakings-in must be staggering. And competing demands by different outfits must have squeezed these companies to unbearable limits. The faithfully-maintained balance sheets revealed that the fear of insurgents had penetrated deep in the official hierarchies. Various department officials manning the Srirampur check-post at Assam-West Bengal border were making regular monthly payments to the banned outfits since 1994, ranging from 3 to 5 lakhs. A list of 100 such officials was prepared who were thus funding the militants. The CID had arrested 6 such officials who had subsequently got bail from the High Court (1995-96). The payments made by various entities are given below:[22]

In Lakhs

1. Bhergaon Tea Estate (TE)	—	25
2. Willamson Magor TE[23]	—	24
3. Nandan Nayar TE	—	10
4. Badlapur TE	—	9
5. Chandana TE	—	5
6. Ambika TE	—	3
7. Motor Vehicles Department	—	4.5
8. Forest Department	—	4
9. Sales Tax Department	—	3
10. Heavy Industries	—	3

Now follow two tables listing the persons from the tea companies abducted and killed since 1992 and 1989 respectively. Reading the lists, can one fault the Tatas for adopting a certain course in dealing with the insurgents to safeguard their interests and save the lives of their employees in tea estates? Some comments commended the Tatas, India's largest industrial group with a combined net turn-over of Rs. 31,000 crore, for adhering to a principle (of not paying cash) in dealing with the insurgents. Two Tata executives,[24] who had attended the Dibrugarh meeting, and as they disclosed later, had guns pressed against their heads as they were served a notice to pay a tax of Rs. 95 lakh. Tatas refused to yield (as did the Doom Dooma). Three years later, Bolin Bordoloi, TTL's Deputy GM, was kidnapped by the BdSF, who slapped a ransom demand for $ 15 million (Rs. 54 crore). The Company chose to stick to its policy of not paying up. This angered the then Chief Minister, Saikia, who was under pressure from Bordoloi's mother, widow of Assam's first Chief Minister, G.N. Bordoloi, to secure his son's release. It was during the Bordoloi incident that B. Gogoi, a doctor serving the Tatas since 1975, gained prominence as a negotiator. Known to ULFA C-in-C, Paresh Barua, who always referred to him as an elder brother, he established contacts with BdSF through ULFA channel. BdSF finally lowered the demand to Rs. 5 lakh, passed off as "the expenses incurred in maintaining Bordoloi in captivity". Even that demand was refused. But significantly, the TTL decided to set up a Rs. 7 crore, 65 + bed hospital at Chabua Tea Estate for the good of the common Bodos. This crisis helped creating a working relationship between the TTL and IB. The former are believed to have kept the IB informed on their contacts with the insurgents. The Tatas troubles were not over yet.

Tea Estate Persons Abducted Since 1992

Sl. No.	*Name/Particulars*	*Date of Abduction*	*Date of Release*
1.	Subir Ray, Manager Dimakshi TE (Williamson Magor)	18-3-92	7-4-92
2.	K.K. Mital, MD, Manabari TE	Dec. 92	No trace
3.	S.K. Barooah, MD, Bhergaon TE	23-3-94	30-3-94
4.	Bolin Bordoloi, Deputy GM, Tata Tea (He is younger son of Assam 1st Chief Minister, Gopinath Bordoloi)	8-4-93	11-3-94
5.	J. Choudhuri, MD, Fatemabad TE	12-6-93	13-7-93
6.	R.K. Gohain, Asst Manager		
7.	D.V. Singh Manager and A. Datta, Asst Manager, Nonoi TE (TTL)	17-10-95	Rescued Next day
8.	O.P. Siwal, Asst Manager, Tyroon TE	19-10-95	26-10-95
9.	N.N. Kilpadi, Manager, Saola TE	26-1-96	30-1-96
10.	D.K. Baruah, Bhergaon TE	17-9-96	3-4-97
11.	Arup Bhaduri, Owner, Sonapur TE	29-1-97	26-9-97
12.	P.K. Chowdhary, Menoka TE	29-7-97	8 Aug. 97

Tea Estate Persons Killed Since 1989

Sl.No.	*Name/Particulars*	*Date*
1.	D. Chowdhary, Asst Manager, Ledo TE	15-2-89
2.	Amal Baruah, Field Clerk, Corramore TE	5-8-89
3.	P.C. Scaria, TTL	13-3-90
4.	Surendra Paul, Director, Assam Frontier Tea	7-6-90
5.	Jawahar Lal Jain, Manager Dheria TE	19-10-90
6.	D.K. Choudhury, Manager, Romai TE	12-2-91
7.	C. Chakrabortty, Manager, Panbari TE	4-4-92
8.	Rameshwar Singh, GM, Assam Frontier Tea	15-2-94
9.	Koilee Baisnav, Worker, Attrekhat (case of Mistaken identity)	15-10-95
10.	Tejinder Kaur, wife of S. Singh, Manager, Nagrijuli TE	3-3-97

On 15 December 1995, an ULFA letter demanded a supply of 100 Walkie-talkies. The Tatas refused and informed the Home Secretary of Assam of the

ULFA demand in their letter dated 1 January 1996. Meanwhile, they continued talking to ULFA through B. Gogoi and B. Bordoloi. After repeated warnings, the last one on 17 June 1996, the Tatas evolved a Medical Aid Scheme under which the Company would pick up the tab for hospital costs of people recommended by ULFA. Gogoi was selected to sell the package to ULFA chief in Dhaka at a July 1997 meeting. Again, Gogoi it was who had accompanied Deka. Hence the ire of Assam officials against him. IGP of Assam (Int) was convinced: "Gogoi is an active member of ULFA." He was arrested on 24 September 1997. Another damning charge was that TTL had made payment in foreign currency to the banned outfit in London in 1997. Mahanta was firm on crackdown on tea companies. Had he found a whipping boy for his party's and his own soft corner for the ULFA? But when Assam Government was riding a high horse against the anti-national activities of tea companies, the Army engaged in CI operations in the State lodged an FIR at the Mangoldoi PS on 23 October 1997, suggesting links between a senior (Revenue) Minister/colleague of Mahanta and ULFA. "Law will take its own course" was all that Mahanta said by way of response and refused the Minister's offer to resign.

To cut it short, the story took a murky twist when the *Indian Express* 5 October 1997 published transcripts of "illegal tapes" of telephone conversations among Ratan Tata and some of his corporate friends. It had some indiscreet remarks. Some wrote the Tata's troubles with Assam Government were the result of intercorporate rivalries. Others thought Mahanta had some interest in intra-Bombay House battles? Some asked who was behind the tappings, and why did the Express indulged in 'despicable' act of publishing the tapes? In an open letter, Ram Jethmalani asserted that successive Governments had failed to rid Assam of curse of terrorism. Some even doubted his sincerity of purpose. Lt Gen KS Brar, Eastern Army Commander early 1990s, handed down a stinging criticism of political class, Mahanta and his successor and predecessor Saikia included: "...By early 1992, we had captured top ULFA leaders and literally broken the back of the movement.... The Government got the leaders released as the IB and RAW had contacted them for talks.... It was a trap and Saikia Government walked into it.... Against our advice, operation Rhino was called off.... They regrouped and resumed fighting. As for the AGP, while in opposition, it used ULFA against the Government, like the Akalis (in Punjab).... AGP was born of AASU agitation, as was ULFA. Problem arises when those who hobnob with terrorists come to power" (*Sunday Observer*, 21-9-1997).

Finally an ominous truth and potential reality which cannot be ignored by those, including the businessmen, who are confronting the insurgents. Today's terrorist could well be tomorrow's Chief Minister, a la Laldenga. Can

TIL be hanged even if they had given cash to the ULFA, which in any case they deny? At the end of it all, it is fair to say that in such complex situations, the truth cannot be monopoly of any particular player. Either or both sides could be acting too pious![25]

After the 1997-98 events, things remained comparatively quiet on the tea front. The ULFA seemed to have gone into lower gear. In fact by 2000, SF had started talking rather loudly about their success in having controlled, if not defanged, the monster. It all proved premature when ULFA struck with a vengeance at the non-Assamese Hindi-speaking people in the last quarter of that year. But the militants had opened a new front in Cachar area in 1999. From the speeches made at the 99th AGM of the Surma Valley Branch of the Indian Tea Association on 4 February 2000, it seemed the tea gardens in the south were facing the troubles its counterparts in Upper Assam had gone through in the earlier years of the 1990s. Several terrorist outfits had been active since 1999 or so killing, abducting, and extorting. The abduction and killing of Rajat Banerjee, a manager with Pathemara TE sent shock wave in the Barak Valley tea gardens. There were 9 cases of abduction of managerial staff in 1999 alone, including that of Banerjee. The depredations continued throughout 2000. The outfits involved are DHD, KNV and NSCN(I-M); in that order. Most of the affected TEs are near the Manipur-Cachar border, totally isolated; giving the desperados a free run over them. Early 2000, a new militant outfit of Manipuri and Bengali Muslims, calling itself 'People's United Liberation Front' (PULF), appeared on the scene.

Important CI Operations

To ensure cooperation between the SFs fighting the ultras as also between them and the Intelligencies agencies, a United Command was set up in 1997. Three operations are discussed here:

1. *Op Bajrang*. Launched on 28 November 1990, it yielded less than satisfactory results as the timing had been leaked to the militants. The troops mostly found just-abandoned ULFA camps.
2. *Op Rhino*. Launched on the night 14-15 September 1991, the Army was able to achieve a surprise this time, leading to a great success. In the bag: 431 hard-core cadres, including 46 top and middle rung leaders, besides the 299 supporters and trainees. Army destroyed 16 ULFA camps, recovering quantities of arms and ammunition and some important documents. The latter established ULFA's links with KIA, NSCN and even LTTE; and its sanctuaries in Bangladesh. The Army landed Rs. 5 crore in cash and 32 gold bars some of it certainly from the narco-trade, fruits of illegal transactions. The records showed purchase of weapons and equipment: automatics at Rs. 50,000 a piece, pistol at Rs. 40,000, and VHP radio set at Rs. 45,000.

- During Op Rhino, Army launched a civic action drive, to win back the hearts and mind of the people.
- An Inf Bde organised an Army Samaj Seva Mela at Naharkatiya, 80 km from Dibrugarh, in August 1994, providing medical facilities in various disciplines to the people at their doorsteps.

3. Joint operations, code named 'On Golden Bird', launched by the Indian and Burmese Armies (April-May 1995). As a result of major engagements in the Chimtuipui and Champhai sectors of Mizoram borders, 52 ULFA and PLA cadres were arrested and 45 killed.

Surrenders, ULFA vs SULFA and Peace Talks

The surrender by one-time ruthless and lawless insurgents makes for an interesting subject. And there are surrenders and surrenders. Reasons? Any of the following:

1. They are induced into it (surrender) for political or economic gains.
2. They find themselves unequal to facing continued hardships and privations of an uncertain life.
3. They have realised the futility of their battle against the State apparatus, and hopelessness of it all.
4. Some might have seen the wrongness of their cause at some stage. Horrendous blood-letting caused/witnessed by them could hasten the day.
5. Dissensions within leadership and consequent in-fighting within the ranks.

The phenomenon of surrender by ULFA ultras really started during the Saikia tenure (1991-96). ULFA had gained strength during Mahanta's first stint (1985-90); and became notorious for killings, abductions and extortions by the end of 1980s. Moreover, they had no reasons to surrender in this period; after all, they were half-brothers to AASU/AGP. Their excesses in the tea gardens had led to Mahanta's dismissal in November 1990 and Saikia knew it. On taking over in July 1991, he started working on it and shrewd as he was, he achieved early success, creating factions within ULFA. With Saikia announcing amnesty in March 1992, Sunil Nath, ULFA's Publicity Chief, led over 3,500 youth overground. Later, outfit's Dy C-in-C and Foreign Secretary also surfaced to swell the ranks of the surrendered, popularly, SULFA. It was a singular success, and there is no reason to deny credit for it to Saikia, even if the success turned sour subsequently. His critics castigated Saikia for splitting the ranks of ultras, as if it were a cardinal sin. It was a success story gone awry. The Army had broken its back (during Op Rhino) and ULFA was pushed to the wall. It was at this precise moment that Saikia got the ULFA cadres released from the Army custody and the latter rightly accused him of playing into ULFA's hands, acting credulously on its promises. How the perfidious ULFA was subsequently dealt with has been discussed above. Returning to surrenders, it must be acknowledged that at the time, ULFA had as yet not lost its sheen accruing from an ideologically-driven movement and made up its losses quickly through a vigorous recruiting drive and returned to its violent activities with a renewed vigour. But in spite of the setback, Saikia did not give up, garnering even larger successes in the following years, through liberal terms offered to the surrenderers: a cash incentive of Rs. 50,000 and a loan of Rs. 200,000 per head. By end-1995, 4,860 ultras[26] had surrendered, of which 4,015 had chosen to avail of the incentive scheme.

Following the loss of its cadres, ULFA rewrote its constitution to re-energise itself, laying greater stress on the civic aspects of its policies and operations to win over the common Assamese to its side. Its leadership reiterated in October 1993 its demand for an independent Assam outside the Union of India. After re-working its philosophy and rejuvenating its cadres, it started working from its sanctuaries in Bangladesh and understandably became even bolder in its depredations. It was in this period that ULFA created and reveled in its image of Robin Hood, robbing the rich to help the poor. The image, actions and ideology gained it popularity and a constituency for sometime. But it started losing people's respect and sympathy when its cadres launched on a course of mindless violence May 1996 onwards. It suffered further decline when a popular social activist like Sanjoy Ghosh was killed next year. Towards the end of 1990s, its image stood tattered for several reasons: (1) the Robin Hood was dead; (2) Youth's enthusiasm to join ULFA flagged; (3) lack of funds; (4) Lavish style of living enjoyed by its leaders, ensconced in 5-star hotels abroad, their children studying in expensive colleges in these countries, and people seeing the pictures of these leaders wallowing in luxury and affluence splashed on the pages of the dailies; and (5) the success of the CI operations by the SF. To repair the dented self-image and to restore the sagging morale of their cadres, the leadership decided on an expedient short-cut. Discarding their ideology and ideals, they launched vicious attacks on minorities to divide the Assamese (last quarter of 2000).

As for the SULFA (surrendered ULFA) cadres, they were an Intelligence asset in the initial stages, say during 1993-95 periods. Then came the time when they were a cause of serious concern to civil and military authorities, becoming a law unto themselves. They indulged in looting, extortion and even killing to settle personal scores, all made possible since they had been allowed to retain their arms for reasons of personal security. But the things became really dangerous with the ULFA-SULFA clashes, which were not unexpected, as SULFA were the main source of Intelligence on their former colleagues. The fratricidal clashes assumed horrendous dimensions in the late 1998, with 25 ultras from two sides fell to one another's bullets during the two months' period of the year, mid October-mid December. Some analysts thought the

Government/SF were encouraging these clashes, which had started when ULFA felled Tapan Datta in the heart of Guwahati on 10 August 1998. He was a prominent Dibrugarh businessman and a SULFA activist who had surrendered in 1998 and had been accused by ULFA of misappropriating huge amount of outfit's funds. The SULFA retaliated by killing relatives of top ULFA leaders. In August itself, Arbindo Rajkhowa's brother and five relatives[27] of ULFA's Publicity Chief were done in. Some of the prominent killings on either side during November-December 1998 are listed here:

- *13 November.* Prominent SULFA and ex-Assistant General Secretary of ULFA at Guwahati. Not only had he criticised ULFA leadership for betraying the original ideology, he had also led 195 cadres into surrender in early 1998.
- *21 November.* Key ULFA hitman, Alok Goswami, in Silchar.
- *3 December.* Prominent SULFA, Diganta Barua and his two bodyguards in Guwahati in a well-planned operation.
- *8 December.* An ULFA unit commander, in an encounter, near Guwahati.

Reworked Surrender Package

The extravagant surrender package did not prove a success; and moreover it was "misused and exploited by certain non-genuine persons, in connivance with some smart operators, including politicians and officials". In particular, bank loans advanced to the SULFA were hardly paid till 1998. The Tezpur Corps Commander suggested in August 1998 that "the first two batches, totaling 210 militants, who recently came over ground, must be given jobs in the Central Security Forces as promised".[28] On 2 April 1999, Union Home Secretary B.P. Singh announced the new rehabilitation package, that included cash incentives[29] for militants surrendering with weapons. It was to start with the two batches of 400 and 150 militants "who had surrendered recently".

Cash Incentives for Different Weapons

1. Rocket Launcher	Rs. 25,000
2. Rifle AK-47	Rs. 15,000
3, Pistol/Revolver/Remote control device	Rs. 3,000
4. Wireless sets (short to medium range)	Rs. 1,000 to Rs. 5,000
5. Explosive (Each Kg)	Rs. 1,000
6. Rocket	Rs. 1,000
7. Grenade	Rs. 500

Cease-fire and Hopes

SULFA did create problems at times, but "it seemed to be the only hope for the nation to do business with the still powerful ULFA", went one line of thinking. The cease-fire observed by ULFA during the festive season of Bihu in April 1999 was in response to an appeal made by the SULFA leaders led by Sunil Nath, ex-Director Publicity, who had surrendered in March 1992. It turned out to be the first positive sign of peace in the bloodstained saga of a long-running militancy in Assam. More heartening was the news that ULFA was in touch with the Centre. GOC4 Corps at Tezpur, Lt Gen DB Shaketkar, told the press at Guwahati that "a top ULFA functionary had contacted him on 14 April,.... And if they take one step for peace, Army would take four."[30] Besides suspending its operations, Army also sent gifts to the kin of some top ULFA leaders.[31] Army also announced on 16 April that as a goodwill gesture, the troops had been ordered to allow safe passage to the ULFA militants who came unarmed to meet their kin during the Rangoli Bihu. Gen Sinha, Assam Governor also promised a safe passage during the Bihu and Diwali (7 November 1999). Mahanta did one better announcing a "millennium offer to the ULFA cadres", allowing them to meet their families between 21-31 December 1999.[32] Certain optimism was in the air.

ULFA leaders were not keen to sit with Mahanta, who asked for tripartite talks; they wanted to talk to the Centre only. "They opened a line of communication with New Delhi in June 1999." It was a significant first! Later, the Government officials reportedly met ULFA leaders outside India for informal talks; "Arbindo Rajkhowa in London, and Paresh Barua in Karachi were in direct contact with Home Ministry officials." Having earlier spurned all such offers of talks, why did ULFA had a change of mind in mid-1999? Likely reasons: (1) People were losing respect for it. ULFA cadre Amit Bhuyan was lynched by villagers of Kukrachara in Sibsagar district when he came to extort money on 7 July 1999 and threatened to blow up the locality if his demand was not met. They were really sick of "our boys"; (2) A spate of armed surrenders in the recent months, particularly since mid-1998 possibly unnerved the leadership, compelling it to clutch at the BJP's offer; (3) "ULFA's close liaison with the ISI and its support for Pakistan during the Kargil War made it extremely unpopular."[33] (4) It was under tremendous pressure from public, Army and Government; and (5) Bangladesh and Bhutan had possibly taken action against ULFA cadres who were in camps and hide-outs on their soil.

Spate of Surrenders

There was certain disillusionment discernible among the lower ranks, as indicated by certain events. The surrender by 22 activists, some with AK-47s, and led by Sgt Maj Khirod Gogoi in August 1999 at Joysagar in Sibsagar district was significant. Gogoi said they returned to the mainstream, realizing that the "attainment of sovereign Assam was impossible.[34] ULFA leader Akash Bora, in his letter of 28-7-1999, told the SP Sibsagar: "Leaders are only interested in mortgaging the state to the ISI and Pakistan.... They lived luxurious lives while the cadres were forced to lead a life of hardship."[35] But it is obvious that no forward movement was discernible till the end of 1999, even though some initial contacts were made during the year and some informal talks about the talks were held. Two relevant stories from a respected daily are excerpted below to indicate the realities of life at that stage.

The Hindu, 11 September 1999

> "Pressure is mounting on ULFA leaders from their armed ranks to start a dialogue. In Nalbari, many ULFA extremists are planning to surrender. Apparently to prevent this, some middle-rung activists were summarily executed by the outfit a few days ago. Gunning down of a prominent AGP leader yesterday at Barama in Nalbari district is believed to be a warning to the Party not to encourage surrenders."

The Hindu, 25 March 2000

> "18 ULFA cadres have deserted the outfit, come over ground, and are seeking 'to live freely'. The process of disillusionment with the ULFA started long ago, but the killing of the PWD Minister, Nagen Sharma, at Nalbari on 27 February, was the breaking point."

Before examining the talks front during 2000, a look at the surrenders front (1998-2000) should be useful.

1998

1. *24 July.* 51 at Thakurbari
2. *14 August.* 133 at Mariani.
3. *31 December.* 36 at Dispur.

1999

1. *21 January.* 159 at Tamulpur in Nalbari district.
2. *25 May.* 102 at Nagaon.
3. *16 August.* 178 in total, at nine different locations.

2000

1. March. "A spate of surrenders in the recent weeks has hit the outlawed ULFA", reported *Indian Express* of 28-3-2000. The General Council was alarmed enough to convene its meeting after a gap of 3 years to discuss the issue at its Bhutan hide-out on 4-5 April. These leaders had converged on the hide-out to take part in the Foundation Day Celebrations on 7 April. On 27 March, a group of 13 senior functionaries of ULFA, belonging to Nalbari district announced their decision to shun violence. They included Mintu Dutta alias Nagon

Haloi, Chief Political Advisor (Commissar) of ULFA's units in Lower Assam Zone, and Bikash Dutta, Organising Secretary in the same zone. The former, with ULFA for over 14 years, accused the leadership of straying from its ideology.

14 senior cadres at the zonal and Anchalik levels had surrendered during first two weeks of March. The total figure for the month rose to about 52, including Abinash Bordoloi, Chief of the Armed Wing for the three Lower Assam districts of Nalbari, Dhubri and Kamarupa.

2. 532 surrenders on 4 April. They laid down their arms before Gen Sinha at Rang Ghar, the very venue where ULFA was born 21 years ago, on 7 April 1979.

It was the largest surrender on any one day. The Governor assured them that the inadequacies in the Rehabilitation Package would be removed. Chief Minister Mahanta asked the ULFA and NDFB to come forward for talks, as the NSCN(I-M) was already talking to the Government. The leader, Lt Phukan charged that Paresh Barua was dictatorial, and using ULFA to serve his own interest. The breakdown of 532 ultras who surrendered on 4 April: ULFA-436, KNV-77 and NDFB-19.

3. 288 surrendered before Chief Minister Mahanta at Guwahati on 14 August. It was the 15th such ceremony in the State since the Unified Command came into being mid-1997. Their leader was ULFA Capt Lohit Deuri, who had served as General Staff Officer at ULFA's GHQ in Bhutan. He had been with the police for a while, helping them to track down ULFA activists. Joining ULFA in 1985, he had set up the first ULFA camp in Bhutan in 1992. The 288 had been under police protection for a long time, were getting monthly stipends, and had undergone training in different crafts under the Centre's Rehabilitation Scheme. This figure of 288 surrenders on 14 August brought the total number of surrenders since April 1998 to 1994.[36] Mahanta told the surrenderees that State Government had earmarked 300,000 bighas of land for distribution among them.[37] The break-down of the 288 surrenderees: ULFA-242, UPDS-25, RNSF-12, NDFB-5, DHD-2, and MULTA-2.

4. How vastly different was the Independence Day eve of the year 2000, compared to the one of the year before! In 1999, ULFA had unleashed an orgy of violence, killing many innocents, blowing up several rail and road bridges, dynamiting sections of railway tracks, bombing industrial plants and oil refineries, etc.

ULFA Surrenders: Official Figures

Yearly Surrender of ULFA Cadres

Sl.No.	*Year*	*Number*
1.	1998	227
2.	1999	970[38]
3.	2,000 (Till October)	1186[39]

1998-2000: ULFA at the Cross-roads

Beginning 1979, by end-2000, ULFA seemed to have reached at a certain cross-roads in its quest. It must have had its highs, troughs and lows during this journey. Its first test came in November 1990 during Op Bajrang but it escaped with minor losses since it was able to get advanced information of it. But was not so lucky during Op Rhino, launched in September 1991, suffering grievous losses consequently. But the crafty leadership earned a reprieve when Saikia Government, in power since mid-1991, 'forced' or 'persuaded' Army to suspend operations against it on a mere "assurance that it would abide by the Indian Constitution and abjure violence". But it then took advantage of the situation, regrouped and rethought its strategy, and then cocked a snook at Government of India. In May 1992, Chairman Rajkhowa announced that "ULFA never committed itself to talks on India's terms". By end of the year, it was ready for the fight. But then it was defeated not by the might of Army, but by "the guile and shrewdness of Assam's Chanakya (Saikia)"'. In 1993, he had lured close to 5000 ULFA cadres, perhaps majority of its strength at that point in time, into surrendering to join the mainstream. The main reason for that singular success might have been the fact that large part of the cadre then was of fresh recruits enlisted during the suspension of Op Rhino in 1992. This time again, ULFA was able to make up its losses quickly; and relaunched on its violence trajectory. Subsequently, it grew in size and strength, with the hardline leadership expanding its base of operations from Upper Burma to Bangladesh, and still later to Bhutan.

This accretion to ULFA's strength made it most feared outfit in the Region. Through skilful negotiations, it strengthened its ties with other such outfits in the North-East. Expectedly, at a certain stage, it struck an equation with the ISI, becoming a bigger headache for India. Some analysts assert it is totally under the thumb of the ISI and somewhere along the way, it has lost its moorings in the ideology of ultra nationalism. Once the ISI started training its cadres on the Bangladesh soil, peace eluded the Region. With its violent movement, ULFA cannot continue to remain popular and retain people's sympathy for ever. From mid-1990s, it seemed to be indulging in mindless violence. Of late, Bhutan and Bangladesh have taken initiatives to flush out its cadres from their soil and Unified Command has been closing in on ULFA; and consequently, it has been on the downslide. In the 1997-98 period, it had been fast losing people's support as the sole aim of its mindless violence seemed to be killing of people. If the killing of Sanjoy Ghose cost it the sympathy of socially-conscious common man, the killing of Assam's PWD Minister Nagen lost it the support and understanding of the intelligentsia and politically conscious class. In this situation something had to give in. It came in the shape of spate of surrenders, particularly April 1998 onwards. Consequently, by August 2000, with large scale surrenders and desertions, ULFA was certainly standing at the cross-roads. In the past two years or so, a number of senior posts at zonal and Anchalik levels had fallen vacant. The Army's CI Operations too had taken their toll. It was a frustrating period for the leadership. It was a discomfiting situation to be in. It must stem the rot or go under. The latter option does not come easy to the coarsened outfits like the ULFA. Having lain low for about two years, or so the SF thought, barring some attention-grabbing, high-profile killings, it decided to resort to something drastic to boost the sagging morale of its cadres, as also to announce the arrival of a reoriented ULFA. Forsaking the moral high ground claimed on the strength of its ideology, the desperate leadership unleashed the vicious killings of the non-Assamese Hindi-speaking people, to divide the society on communal lines and then to regain the support of the ethnic Assamese. This was the re-oriented ULFA, sans ideology, sans nationalistic philosophy! The October-December 2000 orgy of violence was meant to convey a message to the Government: ULFA was well and alive, and back in business. This was the route chosen for immediate gains and immediate attention for itself. The other way led to the peace talks. Having taken some halting steps in this direction in 1999, and registered its presence by end-2000, will it now seriously smoke the peace-pipe?

So, the question really is: will they come to sup? Gen Sinha and Mahanta, and now Gogoi (2001-) have been trying to create situation conducive for talks. The Government had offered safe passage to the ULFA cadres wanting to meet their kin, particularly during the Bihu festivities in 1999 and 2000. Their cold response notwithstanding, Mahanta repeated the good gesture during the period 21 December 2000-17 January 2001, as a millennium offer. Mahanta told Prime Minister Vajpayee during his 23 January Shillong visit that "the offer was availed by many militants". Similar offers were made by the two during 1999.

A back grounder to the 1999 offer is of interest. Gen Sinha flew into Lakuma, a small village in oil-rich eastern District of Sibsagar in October 1999 to call on the ailing Umakanta Rajkhowa, a veteran freedom fighter, recipient of the Tamrapatra and father of ULFA Chairman Arbindo Rajkhowa. It was after this visit that he announced the safe passage offer, and Mahanta followed suit. ULFA had rejected both. In spite of the October-December 2000 communally divisive carnage, Gen Sinha repeated the offer of a free passage on 9 December 2000 at Guwahati. "Gen Sinha feels it-is right moment for talks". He said on 23 January 2000 at Shillong that the middle and lower level cadres were in favour of talks but "the top levels are yet to respond. On 16 July, reverting to the theme, he said: "There was attitudinal change among the people, as they are now opposing the militancy." He claimed that "there has been marked improvement in security scenario; people are taking part in large numbers in the peace rallies and processions". On the economic front, Assam achieved foodgrains sufficiency for the first time in 2000. The Army, through the Unified Command experiment, has done its bit to chastise ULFA. In the three years (mid-1997-2000) 700 ultras were killed, over one crore rupees seized, and 2,000 weapons recovered. Now what was ULFA's response to this peace overtures? ULFA's three pre-conditions for the talks are well-known and oft-repeated:

1. Talks should be held in a foreign country.
2. They should be held under the UN supervision.
3. They should focus on sovereignty only.

In November 1999, Paresh Barua called up newspaper offices in Guwahati, and voiced his demand for a UN-supervised plebiscite in Assam on the question of sovereignty, outrightly dismissed by the Government as preposterous. The timing of demand was ill-considered, coming as it did within a month of the Lok Sabha poll (September-October 1999) in which 70 per cent of Assam's 1.4 crore voters had exercised their franchise in defiance of ULFA's call for its boycott. This was Assamese way of expressing distaste and disapproval of ULFA's support for Pakistan during the Kargil War earlier in the year. Thus ended 1999 and the year 2000 hardly saw any movement on the talks front. The next year began with some interesting stories. In his interview to a local daily in January 2001, ULFA C-in-C said if New Delhi's talks with NSCN(I-M) succeeded, he too would fall in line. He further mouthed standard vocabulary: "Government of India is only interested in bringing peace to Assam and not in solving real problems of its people.... We too want solution but not the one dictated by the Government.... The discussions must have some 'scientific basis', whenever they are held."[40] In the second interview to another local daily (cited by *Indian Express,* 15-1-2001), ULFA dropped first two of the three demands listed above and it was ready to discuss the issue of sovereignty alone. Barua disclosed "this stand has been conveyed directly to the PMO in December 2000". The Centre's pre-condition that ULFA must give up violence before the talks start was not acceptable to Barua. On 16 January 2001, at Guwahati, G.K. Pillai, JS, NE, in MHA, offered unconditional talks to ULFA.[41] So did Home Minister Advani at a public meeting at Nagaon on 5 February 2001, but asked the "banned outfit to lay down arms".

ULFA Leadership

The contrast between the living standards of the leaders and the led, even in Bhutan has been commented upon. The cadres in jungle camps of Samdrup Jongkhar, Deothang, etc. and hide-outs along the Manas Forest Reserve "are facing acute shortage of food and medicine, often leading to low morale. But their leaders are staying in classy hotels and well-appointed guest house in Thimpu and Phuntshoeling, with foreign cars and mobile telephones.

Recent mindless violence (1998-2000) inflicted on the people reportedly caused a certain dissent among the top leaders. Paresh Barua, the C-in-C, is leading the hardliners, and is often dubbed a 'dictator'. He is supposedly holding out on the issue of talks with the Government. The recent surrenderees (of 1998, 1999 vintage) have also commented on the wallowing-in-luxury lifestyle of the leaders, which has surely disillusioned the Assamese intelligentsia. And to imagine that four or five top leaders of today were among the youthful, starry-eyed, intellectual group which had met in April 1979 at the 300-year old pavilion of the Ahom Royals, to speak about establishing a "sovereign, socialist Republic of Assam". The details of leadership as known is given here.

What was the identity of members who joined it initially? Several of the founding members of ULFA belonged to the Asom Jatiyatabadi) Yuva Chhatra Parishad (AJYCP), having close links with AASU as well. The ULFA leaders actively participated in the anti-foreigners agitation, and the first Chairman of the outfit, Bhadreswar Gohain, was later elected Dy Speaker of Assam Assembly as the AGP nominee.

The AJYCPP roots of ULFA should tell their own story. Formed in March 1978, it quickly made its mark in Assam's public life because of its good organisational network and dedicated workers.

Essentially a secessionist outfit, it termed Indian Constitution as a tool for colonial exploitation of Assam and demanded right to self-determination. All this obviously had informed the thinking and philosophy of the ULFA leadership, whose profile follows.

High Command

1. Arbindo Rajkhowa (Real name, Rajiv Konwar)—Chairman.
2. Paresh Barua (Barua and Chetia hail from the same village)—C-in-C.
3. Anup Chetia alias Golup Barua (In Dhaka Jail since December 1997)—Secretary General.

4. Manoj Hazarika—Vice Chairman (Till 1994).
5. Pradip Gogoi (in Jail since April 1998)—Vice Chairman.
6. Raju Baruah, Dy C-in-C.
7. Sashadhar Choudhury—Foreign Secretary.
8. Raju Baruah alias Hitesh Kalita—Deputy Commander-in-Chief.
9. C. Hazarika—Finance Secretary.

Senior Officers

1. Mithinga Daimary—Publicity Secretary (Relieved of his charge in mid-2000. Paresh Barua personally handling the media.)
2. Ashanta Baghphukan—Organising Secretary.

   (He was ULFA's Senior-most leader in Bhutan who rose to become Organising Secretary in 1999. He took over the post after the arrest of Pradeep Gogoi.)
3. Pranati Deka (in jail since September 1997)—Cultural Secretary.
4. Babul Sarma—Chief Medical Officer, ULFA units in Bhutan.

Middle Level Officers

1. Dhrishti Rajkhowa—Appointment unknown.
2. Tapan Barua—Commander, ULFA's 28th Bn.
3. Capt Lohit Deuri—General Staff Officer, GHQ, ULFA, Bhutan (Surrendered).

It seems equations among the top leaders keep changing. The Chairman, C-in-C and Foreign Secretary decide on all important issues. The trio, known as the Group of Three, constitute the Central Core of ULFA leadership. Rajkhowa is believed to be a moderate, with his C-in-C being a hardliner, who had ordered attacks on the non-Assamese Hindi-speaking people in October 2000. The fourth important man Ashanta Bagh Phukan, is considered a theoretician. Raju Baruah, who is the Operational Commander, issues orders to the lower ranks for specific "acts".

So three of its top leaders are in jail. Pradeep Gogoi, Vice-Chairman, was arrested on 8 April 1998 at Calcutta, third important leader of ULFA to be held in the recent past. Its Cultural Secretary, Pranati Deka, was arrested in Bombay in September 1997. Her arrest gave rise to the Tata Tea-Assam Government controversy. She is wife of C. Hazarika, ULFA's Finance Secretary. Its Secretary General Anup Chetia alias Golup Barua, was arrested in Calcutta on 21 December 1997. Chetia's arrest followed a red corner notice issued by Interpol. Exact circumstances leading to the arrest of Gogoi are still shrouded in mystery. Was it a surrender dramatised as an arrest?

Gogoi, known to be in favour of talks for quite sometime now, "reportedly told his interrogators that ULFA was at the moment not interested in escalating violence. Occasional acts of violence committed by ULFA were only to keep up the morale of its cadres. ULFA leaders arrested earlier told their interrogators that C-in-C Paresh Barua was dictatorial and was trying to take over the entire organisations. Some reports suggested a rift within the outfit between the Ahoms and non-Ahoms. The reported move by Barua, an Ahom, to oust Chairman Rajkhowa, a non-Ahom, acquires credibility in this context.

Gogoi, who is in-charge of recruitment of cadres and their training in Bhutan camps told the police that for the past few months he was thinking of severing his ties with the outfit. He also admitted that the General Secretary of the Association of Voluntary Agencies for Rural Development (AVARD), Sanjoy Ghose, who was abducted by ULFA fron Majuli on 4 July 1997, was killed in captivity.

Foreign Hand

The subject of some neighbours muddying the waters of Indian insurgency has been discussed in some detail in Chapter 2. Here only a few selective facts will be mentioned in brief.

Pakistan, India and Bangladesh have been uneasy neighbours. If Kashmir issue has bedeviled relations between the former two, the in-migrants influx has done the same for Indo-Bangladesh relations. All three carry the load of problems left over by the Partition. Indian rebels have traditionally been given shelter and succour by these two neighbours, who in turn suspect India to be doing the same for their rebels. Given the realities, it is obvious that each country maintains hyper-active Intelligence presence in the other two. But as some would say, history, memory and ideology, however powerful their motivation, by themselves do not constitute facts. Therefore Indians assert that their claims about the involvement of these two nations and their Intelligence agencies, are based upon interrogation reports of captured insurgents and on documents recovered from them as well as during the raids on their camps.

It is certain that some ULFA militants had crossed over into Bangladesh by end-1988. The link and liaison work was possibly mediated initially by the PLA militants whose own links with Bangladesh go back decades.[42] The Dhaka authorities were certainly not unaware of the goings-on. The links with ISI were possibly forged almost immediately after securing access to Bangladesh. A senior ULFA leader claimed credit early 1992[43] for mediating links with the ISI[44]! Indian Intelligence is fairly clear on the broad profile of the movement of scores of ULFA cadres from small towns and villages of Brahmaputra Valley to somewhat similar environs of camps in the rural Sylhet; and then finally to a totally different world of the ISI in Pakistan, and in some cases also to Mujahideen camps in Peshawar and to some Afghan areas under Mujahideen control. Thence, the methods employed to test and break-in the new recruits were exactly the ones laid down in any textbook on classical terrorism and insurgency. A recruit was received by an Intelligence agent, lodged in a Dhaka safe house, given a Muslim name, and after confirming his credentials and suitability for the tough and risky job, found a local job. The initial training also included familiarisation with Islamic rituals and learning of Bengali, Assamese, or Urdu, as demanded by his future employment. A number of them are employed in India's North-East, and the brighter ones and fluent in Urdu are flown to Pakistani.

The first batch of 10 ULFA ultras was taken to Pakistan mid-1991. Subsequently, 5-6 batches of 10 to 15 militants each, were sent annually. By 1996-97, estimated 310 had been trained by the ISI. But subsequently, there were some problems, mainly "because it was difficult for anyone to manipulate ULFA", even if initially, it allowed itself to be used by some foreign agencies.

A photograph in *Sunday Observer* of 22-9-1991 hardly left any doubt about ULFA-Bangladesh linkages showing as it did the top ULFA leaders (Chairman, his Deputy, Manoj Hazarika, and Partha Bora) in a building adjacent to the Parliament in Dhaka. (Sheikh Hasina coming to power later broke the idyll but temporarily.) Paresh Barua possessed a Bangladeshi passport, as did many others who stayed in that country. Rajkhowa and Anup Chetia cultivated links with Islamic fundamentalists in Bangladesh. ULFA set up several profitable companies in Dhaka (covering media consultancies, soft drinks, manufacturing etc.), enabling them to make a lot money for luxurious living as also for sustaining their outfit. When Chetia was arrested on 21 December 1997, he had on him a state-of-art satellite telephone, three passports under different names, and large amounts in foreign currency: $ 65,000, Rs. 28,500 (Indian), 32,500 (Bhutanese) and 2,390 (Pakistani).

ULFA had started income-generating projects in Dhaka (grocery shops, drug stores, etc.), Mymensingh (Poultry farms) and Narsangdi. Chetia was in-charge, as CEO, ULFA Enterprises, Bangladesh before his arrest on 27 December 1997 by Hasina Government. The arms and ammunition (procured from Thailand and Myanmar) purchased with money thus earned was cached in several madrasas and mosques in Sylhet and Cox Bazar areas for subsequent use in India for its anti-India movement.

Its Dhaka connection forced ULFA to forget the very *raison d'etre* of its movement. Having built it up all on an anti-immigrants plank, it changed course mid-way when its leaders sought sanctuary in Bangladesh, and put all its money in Dhaka banks. Obviously, they could not keep all their cash in Bangladesh and still continue to inveigh against it and its nationals for whatever reasons. They were losing their autonomy. Final betrayal came when

ULFA allowed ISI agents to operate its fortnightly magazine Freedom on website. Freedom's 15 June 1999 editorial strongly supported the intrusion of Pak troops and Afghan Mujahideen into Kargil hills. Obviously, ISI was editing Freedom from within Pakistan. "ULFA had sold itself to Pakistan.... I cannot accept its complete surrender to the ISI", was the comment of a disillusioned ULFA supporter on 8 November 1999. He, a former rebel, further added: "...A camp in Bhutan was out of bounds for cadres from other camps. The ISI agents were imparting training to brainwash the specially-selected activists there. Only Rajkhowa, Paresh Barua, Raju Baruah and Munna Mishra could visit that camp." Some instances of the ULFA-ISI-Bangladesh-Pak nexus are cited here:

1. "Pakistan's ISI has now spread its tentacles to Nepal to carry out its anti-India activities in North-East" (Home Minister Inder Jit Gupta in Lok Sabha on 14 May 1997). So ISI had started operating from most of the countries in India's neighbourhood. ULFA, of course, continued issuing its proforma denials.
2. ULFA turned a blind eye to infiltration by Jamaat in the Sylhet-Cachar border areas.
3. "State Ministers and bureaucrats are paying taxes to ULFA which has stashed away Rs. 500 crore abroad" (Tezpur Corps Commander, Lt Gen RK Sawhney, March 1997).
4. "ULFA, which has shifted base from Bangladesh to Bhutan, paid Rs. 50,000 per head for training its cadres in Myanmar" (SULFA leader to Nagaon Police in May 1997).
5. Before Kargil conflict, a 80-100 strong batch was sent to Afghanistan via Bangladesh, thence by air to Karachi on Bangladeshi passports, and finally driven to camps in Afghanistan, for training in hilly terrain. ISI charged substantial sums for this training from ULFA, possibly over a crore. ULFA was also warned that any anti-Pak stance could rupture this link. That should explain ULFA pro-Pak stance during Kargil War, which lost much of public support for ULFA. ULFA even asked Indian Army not to fight the "freedom fighters in Kashmir" (A SULFA leader).
6. "I first went to Pakistan from Bangladesh in September 1990...and later to Afghanistan. ISI offered us money to blow up refinery and rail tracks.... While in Afghanistan, I was getting copies of reports published in Guwahati that very day. There are a large number of agents working for the Pak and Bangladeshi Intelligence, not their nationals but Assamese people who regularly transmit information to these countries from Assam...when we were translating our

> Constitution from Assamese into English, the ISI people said, Give us the Assamese version. We have people who can translate the document'. ...It was all so sad" (An ex-ULFA militant who had made initial contact with the ISI).

Bangladesh was not the first country ULFA established contacts with; that distinction belongs to Burma. It contacted KIA initially in 1986, as also NSCN. The KIA charged heavily for training the ULFA cadres, which initiated it into narco-trade network. It was the time Burma was engaged in CI operations against its own insurgent outfits, numbering over half a dozen. When KIA camps got raided, ULFA came under pressure to shift base. It was then, around 1989, that ULFA contacted ISI and Afghan Mujahideen. It was still later that ULFA made contacts with Field Intelligence of Bangladesh, and less successfully with the LTTE. Later it deepened its cooperation with the LTTE and at a certain stage became recipient of arms from the LTTE's clandestine narco-arms network, though the Naga and Meitei rebels remained its major beneficiaries. When NSCN was training ULFA cadres in its Burmese Naga Hills bases, Indian and Burmese Armies launched a joint operation, code named Golden Bird in 1995, which nearly ended ULFA presence in Burma.

But there is an interesting off-shoot to the active phase of the ULFA-Burmese relations. From their Burmese bases, ULFA had, through the good officers of NSCN(I-M), established a number of safe houses and liaison offices in Thailand, essentially for arms procurement. Senior ULFA leaders frequented Changmai (hottest arms market for illegal arms trade then, and even today) to augment their arsenal from the Khmer Rouge elements operating on the Ranong Coast and Bangkok for rest in the 5-star resorts. They also developed links with ex-drug baron Khun Sa's disbanded Mong Tai Army, both for arms and for a narcotics conduit.

As a result of joint operations and improved economic relations with Myanmar since 2000 (India helped in construction of Tamu-Kalewa-Kalemyo Road), ULFA came under pressure to move out. Hasina Government, coming to power in 1997, put pressure on ULFA to wind up its camps and as a first effective step, it froze its bank accounts. In the latter half of her tenure, even the Hasina Government went soft on ULFA due to the domestic politics. New Delhi kept pressure on Begum Zia also against ULFA. Some reports suggested ULFA shifted its Operations and General Headquarters to the base in thick jungles of Bhutan's border areas around mid-1995. Others say it was by end-1997. But Chairman and C-in-C continued staying in Dhaka, visiting Bhutan periodically; e.g., all senior leaders converged to Bhutanese camps for Raising Day Celebrations in April 2000. From Dhaka, Paresh Barua used to visit Bangkok frequently, but discontinued these peregrinations after the arrest of the NSCN(I-M) leader Muivah in Bangkok. Later reports talk of nearly all leaders shifting to their Bhutan camps. "Bhutan Government have talked to the ULFA leadership to move out, as a result of the Indian insistence, but so far majority of ULFA cadres are ensconced in their Bhutanese sanctuaries". No doubt Thimpu is putting pressure on ULFA and Bodo outfits to vacate their soil. But this is easier said than done. Some observers feel the Royal Bhutanese Army does not have the fire power and the logistics to force the ULFA and NDFB out of their bases in Bhutan. It did not seem keen to seek help from India. It is also possibly true that Thimpu has some genuine difficulties. The economy of many villages in Southern Bhutan revolve around the militant camps at places like Kalikhola and Noglang. Moreover, the ULFA cadres have been good guests, under instruction never to be high-handed towards the locals. Moreover, ULFA has nowhere to go. It seems inevitable that ULFA-Bhutan problem will have to await the solution of ULFA-India problem!

All this notwithstanding, Bhutanese Army finally acted in December 2003 and smashed all the ULFA (NDFB and KLO) camps in three weeks.

It is to be noted that ULFA was not content in ingratiating itself with the immediate neighbours of India. Casting its net far and wide, ULFA wrote to the Secretary General of the UNO, in an effort to influence the international audience. In its letter dated 26 October 1990, it urged him to declare Assam a colony of India (Phanjaubam Tarapot, Insurgency Movement in North-East India, 1993, p. 12.

It is Ethnic Cleansing (October-December 2000)

ULFA giving up its ideological plank and resorting to ruthless killings of non-Assamese Hindi-speaking people have been mentioned earlier. Without giving details of individual incidents, their date-wise victims are given here:

October 2000

22(15), 27(10), 27(3, by NDFB), 31(4)

November 2000

8(8, by NDFB), 17(7), 24(8), 25(4), 26(8), 28(3), 30(19), 30(3, by UPDS).

December 2000

7(28), 28(8, by UPDS),

By September 2000, the situation in violence-ridden Assam had appreciably changed for the better. The SULFA were claiming that three years of CI operations under the Unified Command (set up, mid-1997) had broken the back of ULFA. After all, 1500 of its cadres had surrendered since 1998 (*The Hindu*, 24-11-2000). It was in this circumstance that a re-oriented if not re-vamped ULFA resorted to attention-grabbing killings for short-term gains. The first casualty was DGP, Assam, P.V. Sumant, given marching orders. Harekrishna Deka replaced him.

The most worrying aspect of October 2000 killings was that it was for the first time that ULFA had resorted to targeting unarmed civilians of a particular community. It had followed in the foot-steps of the Kashmiri terrorists who had cleansed the valley of the Kashmir! Pandits. This was the start of the ethnic cleansing in Assam.

It is to be noted that ethnic killings were started in Assam (Karbi-Anglong district) by the UPDS and DHD militants' six months before the ULFA resorted to it in October 2000. In April 2000 in two incidents, UPDS and DHD had killed 11 timber dealers of Bihari origin and 11 Nepali-speaking people on the 9th and 19th respectively. The Hindi-speakers continued to be targeted periodically in the two Hill districts of Assam till September 2000 when unidentified gunmen killed relatives of two senior UPDS militants. "The killings stopped immediately", wrote the Press. But the very next month, ULFA picked up where the UPDS had left, mowing down 15 Biharis in two incidents on 22 October 2000. That is how ULFA launched on a new course. Here are some press comments of the period:

1. The Sadiya massacre, where 28 non-Assamese were killed on 7 December was 8th such incident since 22 October, taking the toll beyond the 100 mark in less than two months. The victims have been Biharis, Marwaris, Nepalis, and Bengalis (*Hindustan Times,* 9-12-2000).
2. Assam never had it so bad, not since 1500 Muslims were massacred at Nellie at the height of Assam Agitation in 1983. In less than two months since 22 October this year, 'a reoriented' ULFA killed over 105 non-Assamese. Most of them were Biharis, a few Marwaris, Nepalis, Oriyas and Bengalis (*Hindustan Times,* 12-12-2000).
3. At least 80 people were killed in seven weeks between 21 October and 7 December 2000 (*The Hindu,* 15-12-2000).
4. Nearly 150 people belonging to non-Assamese and minority communities have become victims of such massacres in Assam this year (*Hindustan Times,* 30-12-2000).

Predictably, the tremors of the killings reached as far away as Rajasthan. In Bihar, some Assamese passengers were roughed up in the trains going to Assam from Delhi. Some Assamese youths pasted notices on shops owned by Biharis and Marwaris, asking them to quit Assam. If the situation had gone out of hands on this front, it would have been what ULFA desired. Luckily, it did not go that far.

A little known outfit, Assam Tiger Force (ATF), claiming to have been raised in January 2000, owned responsibility for these killings. In a statement issued on 30 October 2000, it not only made the claim but also added further:

"All non-Assamese must leave the State. We agree with ULFA's struggle for Assam's sovereignty, but not with the view of AASU and AGP that only Bangladeshis be expelled from Assam.... The attacks against Hindi-speaking people in Dibrugarh and Tinsukia districts, followed by one in the Nalbari were only first acts of violence...." The police said the ATF was a non-existent, fictitious outfit. K. Sarmah, DIG Police, said two of the 159 ULFA militants who surrendered at Dispur on 6 December 2000 (Romen Nath and Suresh Bora) had admitted that they had been sent to Assam from an ULFA camp in Bhutan to execute these communal killings.

Various theories were doing the rounds about the real culprits behind these killings. A "Senior Minister" said he had heard it suggested that a Central Intelligence Agency was behind it all, to get the Governor's rule imposed in Assam. The AGP and Congress blamed each other, for being "allies" of ULFA. Mahanta said the Congress was helping and being helped by ULFA to destabilise his Government, aimed at winning the Assembly elections barely 6 months away (these were due in May 2001). Mahanta claimed to have documentary proof, and wanted Congress barred from contesting the elections. BJP blamed both these parties. Shortly after his surrender (He was one among 159 who surrendered at Dispur on 6 December 2000), Romen Nath (mentioned above) said he and two other ULFA leaders Drishtri Rajkhowa and Raju Baruah had been asked by Paresh Baruah about three months earlier in a Bhutan hide-out to make plans for these killings (He had a change of mind and surrendered). ULFA's objective was to have Governor's rule imposed in Assam which would afford a free hand to SULFA whose unchecked excesses would alienate the people. That would give an opportunity to ULFA to try and win back people's faith it had lost over the past few years, especially after its support to Pakistan during the 1999 Kargil War. To beat it all was the strange spectacle of a senior Assam Cabinet Minister Abdul Muhib Mazumdar (Irrigation) sitting in *dharna* near the State Secretarial to protest against the Administration's role as a silent spectator after these killings. He had forgotten the principle of "collective responsibility of the cabinet".[45] Mazumdar, Chairman of UPPA, a constituent of 4-party Ruling Alliance, sat in *dharna* along with leaders of various religious, linguistic and ethnic minority groups like those of Biharis, Nepalis, etc. The *dharna* was organised by the Coordinating Committee for Minorities of Assam (COCMOA) to which were affiliated 9 organisations including UPPA, UMF, linguistic Minorities Forum, and All Assam Nepali Students' Union. All this is sad commentary on the political class, and no comments are deemed necessary.

Speaking in the Lok Sabha on 18 December 2000, Home Minister Advani said, *inter alia:* "....One major impediment in containing insurgency in the North-East is the fact that pursued by SULFA, the militant often slipped into the neighbouring countries like Bhutan, Myanmar and Bangladesh.... Bhutan has already taken decision not to allow insurgents to take refuge in their territory."[46] Taking an overview of the situation in the entire North-East, Advani said: "Of the 8 States in the Region, 4 were largely peaceful. The situation in Assam, Tripura, Manipur and Mizoram has caused some concern. Assam in recent past has taken a turn for the worse."

Revenge Killings of ULFA Kin and Sympathy(?) Wave!

Assam witnessed a string of mystery killings of ULFA kin in the wake of end-2000 communal killings by ULFA (and UPDS) ultras. It led to an ironic situation where on the one hand, militants are engaged in a war with the SF, and the relatives of these militants are forced to seek personal protection from these very SF against the unidentified who seemed to be after their lives, on the other! The police had to post a picket at the house of Paresh Baruah, in Dibrugarh district, after a group of people fired at it early hours of 6 December 2000 (*Frontline*, 5-1-2001).[47]

'Mystery' gunmen continued targeting ULFA activists' kin apparently in retaliation to the communal massacres since 22 October. SULFA was suspected to be the mystery gunmen. The people killed/injured in the deadly ULFA-SULFA combat are listed here.

Lethal Duel: ULFA Versus SULFA

December 2000

- Paresh Barua's ancestral home attacked, his aged parents being the obvious targets. Both escaped unhurt.
- Deepak Choudhury, brother of ULFA's Foreign Secretary, Sasadhar, killed on 8 December at his residence in village Halosa in Nalbari district, a hot bed of ULFA militancy; obviously an act of avengement as Deepak was shot dead hours within ULFA militants butchering 28 people in Tinsukia on 7 December.
- Angry people torched the shop at Borbori in Nalbari, belonging to a relative of Tapan Barua, Commander of ULFA's 28th Bn.
- Houses of two senior ULFA leaders, Babul Sarma (in village Ghoghrapur, Tinsukia district) and Sailen Sarma, fired at on 6 December.
- House of ULFA's Sashi Phukan at Baihata in Kamrup district, blown up on 23 December, with two powerful hand grenades. None injured, as the house lay abandoned at the time. It was the 8th assault on this house.
- ULFA militant shoots at the dreaded SULFA member Monikut Kalita alias Tarzan (and his associate) in Mangaldoi, on 29 December. Kalita had gone to a nursing home to visit his pregnant wife when he came under attack.

January 2001

- SULFA's Avinash Bordoloi alias Sailen Haloi and his two associates (Ridip and Jabrang) were killed on 2 January at their agricultural farm at village Borbhag-Sholmara in Nalbari district. Avinash's two other friends sustained serious injuries. Interestingly, Mahanta and Agriculture Minister Chandramohan Patowari with senior officials, had visited the farm on 28 October 2000 to take stock of the good work done by the former militants led by Bordoloia, a top former ULFA leader, who had quit the outfit on 15 August 2000 to start this farm.
- Dwijen Haloi and Pulin Haloi, Kin of ULFA Dy C-in-C Raju Baruah, killed on 3 January.
- Jyotish Sharma, brother-in-law of ULFA militant Subhas Sharma abducted from Guwahati and killed on 4 January.

(*Source: Hindustan Times*, 4 and 8 January 2001.)

"Retaliatory killings by unknown assailants have killed at least 6 family members of ULFA leaders", wrote *The Outlook* of 25-12-2000. These retaliatory attacks were a replay of a similar wave of killings witnessed in 1998 when ULFA Chairman Rajkhowa's brother (Umakant Rajkonwar's eldest of the 9 children, Dimba Rajkonwar was killed in August 1998) and the entire family of the outfit's Publicity Chief Mithinga Daimary, were killed.

A surprising, perhaps not all that surprising, aftermath of these so-called mystery killings of the ULFA kin was an anti-SULFA sentiment across the state, and a series of protests against the 'eliminator Government' and SULFA in Nalbari and Guwahati. On 4 January 2001, over 8000 people took out a funeral procession with the bodies of Dwijen and Pulin Haloi, kin of ULFA Dy C-in-C. Their anger was against the Government "blind to the high-handedness of the SULFA activists". On 5 January 2001, protestors joining the cortege of Jyotish Sharma, kin of ULFA militant Subhas Sharma, killed the previous night, initially about 1500 swelled to 5000. Instead of proceeding to the cremation ground, they went to the DC's Court where members of various political parties and AASU joined them and expectedly, made "political speeches". Some protestors even threw stones at the police. In addition, an East Guwahati *bandh* was called in protest and consequently, educational institutions and business establishments in half of the town remained closed. All this should compel one to ponder over several questions. Why this excessive sympathy over the death of the kin of ULFA insurgents? All wanton violence and killings are abhorrent. How was it then that all these protestors remained ensconced within their houses when the innocents were being murdered over the years by the ruthless ULFA ultras? Why did not any of these leaders, who made passionate anti-Government and by extension and implication, anti-SF political speeches on the 5th, muster people for rallies and processions to show sympathy for the relatives of the victims of the long-running ULFA death dance in Assam? Or, coming to the recent past, why did not these politicos bring even a small number of sympathisers to commiserate with the families of the hapless Biharis and Marwaris killed in scores by the ULFA and UPDS during October-December 2000, in the plains and hills of Assam? Were these processions actuated by the genuine sympathy for the slain, or by the fear of ULFA gun? A kind of insurance policy for tomorrow! Or, is AASU still sympathetic towards ULFA, its half-brother, and its objectives? Will Assam's—or, for that matter, India's—political class conduct themselves with national interest in mind, ignoring the sectional, selfish, or party interests? Could the Indians, at least a vast majority of them, think national rather than provincial? Could they rise above their ethnic, linguistic, regional and religious puniness?

The officials had reasons to be apprehensive about these ULFA-SULFA clashes, and the consequent killings. The clashes which left 21 dead during December-January (2001) period alone, could have helped the ULFA to regain some lost ground. The analysts felt the ULFA whose mass base had eroded rapidly over the last half a decade, had every thing to gain from the chain of such mystery killings, particularly so if these were perceived to have been initiated by the police-backed SULFA. If there are certain ULFA-specific gains in the situation, a cynical counter-poser to ULFA leadership could be: Could some calculating, desperate elements, within the outfit, themselves have played some part, directly or indirectly, to foment, or even initiate, these killings?

ULFA on the Decline?

The analysts ascribe the 'success' of ULFA's attention-grabbing end-2000 communal killings spree to a complacency among SF top brass, flowing from the sustained CI operations by the Unified Command since 1997 and large scale surrenders by its cadres during 1998-2000. Bhutan's threat of evicting it from its soil, gradual dwindling of its mass base, and cool response to its recruitment drive to replace the losses through mass surrender were adding to its woes. It was a frustrated leadership that ordered the communal killings, abandoning its ideologically-driven philosophy, for short-term gains. But even that seemed to have back fired. Instead of retrieving some lost ground, these killings further made a dent in its image, particularly losing the support of certain intellectual quarters. ULFA leadership, through these killings, had intended to give its cadres an issue. After all the Biharis were outsiders and Marwari businessmen had long since been identified with exploitation of the locals. But it seemed to have back fired. It is a telling commentary on the morale of the ULFA cadres that even the spate of the killings during October-December 2000 did not staunch the stream of surrenders by its activists. Till 6 December 2000, over 160 of its cadres had surrendered with their arms since these killings began on 22 October 2000. Things had not been well, not only among the ranks but also with the leadership, with rampant dissensions over the years. The divided leadership had not held a joint meeting for several years, as revealed by the Intelligence. Its top leaders, the Chairman and C-in-C frequently changed their hide-outs in Dhaka, Karachi and Bangkok. "With most of its leaders living abroad, the estimated 2500 ULFA cadres, mostly the unemployed youth from the lower middle class, are rudderless and are coming under the influence of the ISI." Adds a confident Intelligence officer: "Despite brave front put up by its leaders, ULFA activists are on the run." *Times of India* of 29 November 2000 wrote: "In the past three years, 863 ULFA cadres have been killed in encounters, 2425 weapons seized, and over 1 crore in cash recovered from the militants."

An important indication of dissensions within the leadership surfaced with the reports that Publicity Chief Mithinga Daimary was stripped of his prestigious charge in December 2000. In a peremptory move, Paresh Barua disbanded the Publicity wing and took over the responsibility himself.[48] Perceptible erosion of ULFA's mass base and large-scale set-backs during 1997-99 period had made Paresh Barua edgy. He held Daimary responsible for these negative developments and deprived him of his charge, though his falling health (liver sclerosis) was given out as the ostensible reasons for the change. Barua personally started ringing up the press offices to pronounce ULFA's positions on various issues. The communal killings were ordered by Barua to regain some lost support, in the face of opposition from Rajkhowa and Choudhury (the two with Barua constituted the Core Group of ULFA leadership, called Group of Three, or Ruling Group), and Baghphukan.

All this and other contemporaneous events showed that all was not well with ULFA, which gave "credence to the reports that it has been sending feelers to the Government for talks but only in some foreign country". It was not a surprise then that even when the ULFA continued on its bloody trajectory, there were good news coming from the countryside which bode ill for the outfit. The villagers had stopped providing succour and shelter to the ULFA militants. "In the past year and a half (1999-2000), there have been at least 30 incidents in which the villagers either lynched the militants to death or handed them over to the SF." Even the local newspapers have stopped giving the rebels the kind of splash they used to do 3-4 years back (say, during the 1993-98 period). All this, and the continued dissensions among its leadership, and large-scale surrenders go to show that all is not well with the outfit. The next logical question can be: Is the ULFA on the decline? Some events and signs, as mentioned above", do seem to point towards it. But it cannot be immediate!

Distraught by large scale surrenders, the disconcerted ULFA leadership launched a recruitment drive in the Lower Assam districts in July 2000. "But to its dismay, the outfit received lukewarm response from the unemployed youth who were no more eager to join it." Thus wrote a well-known local Daily, *The Sentinel* of 26 September 2000. It seemed as if the people of Assam were tired of the mindless violence for the last two decades, including the milder variety of it during the latter part of the AASU Agitation (1979-85). There is a kind of yearning for the peace. Assam Governor highlighted the fact that the ULFA Raising Day on 7 April 2000 witnessed the common people openly joining the peace rallies all over the state for the first time.[49] To its chagrin, even the newspapers carried editorials condemning ULFA's violence. DG, BSF added his bit while speaking at New Delhi on 16 October 2000: "ULFA has finally broken up since people are no longer with it".[50] In October 2000, hundreds of followers of Assam's 15th century saint, Sri Sankaradeva, undertook a peace march from Sadiya in the extreme east, through its heartland, culminating in a rally at Dhubri in its west. The Rally was significant because it was organised by the *Satras* of Assam (numbering over 800), set up by the greatly revered Sankardeva and family members of several ULFA leaders and cadres participated in it. For the first time since its inception in 1979 the ULFA leadership was losing control over its cadres, as indicated by large-scale surrenders. The recent surrenderees, who were members of ULFA over long years, expressed disillusionment with it as "it has become a terrorist organisation devoid of any revolutionary image".

Paresh Barua was in the total grip of the ISI, obeying all its dicta without a murmur; and part of money collected by ULFA was also controlled by the ISI. "The ULFA cadres fighting the Indian Army along with the Pak Army during the Kargil War alienated vast majority of people of Assam."[51] ULFA leaders calling the Kashmir terrorists 'freedom fighters' was not only thoughtless but also anti-national provocation that further angered the ULFA cadres and common Assamese like. ULFA might reject the Indian Constitution and boycott the elections held under it and ask the Assamese not to exercise their franchise, but 70 per cent of them much above the nation average of 59 per cent, defying the call, went to the polling booths and cast their vote, during the 1999 Lok Sabha poll. More hearteningly and surprisingly, in a number of cases, the immediate family members of top ULFA leaders voted in the 1999 Elections, as they did in some earlier ones.

Aware of attenuating mass support and need to dismount the high horse, ULFA dropped two of its original demands and offered to talk to the Centre on the sole issue of sovereignty for Assam, with its C-in-C directly conveying its stance to the PMO. Expectedly the Government rejected it out of hand and refused to invite ULFA for talks—denying them any illusions of respectability. Where does the movement go from here? Will it repeat the vicious, mindless communal killings of end-2000? Will it dish out more of the same: extortions, kidnappings, retributions, killings, et al to add to the people's woes and sufferings? Will it continue to seek for the soft targets to spread terror among the masses in order to 'win' them over to their side? Will it continue to seek meanings in methods and motives other than the ideological and intellectual high-mindedness with which it came to be on 7 April 1979? If that be so, what a great fall it would be for an organisation founded to bring *aikya* (unity), *biplab* (revolution), and *mukti* (deliverance, freedom or sovereignty) to the Assamese! The only other option for ULFA is to open constructive, realistic talks with the Government to restore peace and prosperity to Assam which it desperately needs and deserves by right, and its people fervently hope for. We will have to wait for the coming years.

At the end of it all, where does the outfit stand today *vis-a-vis* the objective realities? To repeat, in the 3-year (1998-2000) period, over 700 of its cadres had been killed in encounters and over 2500 surrendered. During 2000 alone, about 1300 militants, mostly of ULFA, had surrendered. An overview of the militancy-related statistics (1997 to 2000) should be useful to assess the ground realities.

Militancy-related Statistics: 1997-2000

Head	*1997*	*1998*	*1999*	*2000 (Till August)*
Incidents	427	735	447	210
Militants killed	167	180	212	312
Militants arrested	587	742	812	510
Militants surrendered	—	227	970	1186
Arms looted	28	125	168	08
SF killed	85	72	77	56
Civilians killed	285	531	214	179

To be realistic, the preceding should not be read as an obituary notice on ULFA's times and life. It will be an act of naivete to treat all the above adverse and negative development concerning ULFA as anything more than the straws in the wind. The ULFA leaders can still muster resources to strike at the soft targets selectively, even at the SF through the IEDs. All efforts must be made to bring the recalcitrant outfit to the high table, whatever the difficulties and means necessary for the purpose.

Events and Trends: 2001-2002

What follows is a brief look at the events and situation after the end-2000 communal killings.

Violence by ULFA

The ULFA militants killed two AGP leaders in Bongaigaon district on 25 April 2001, and two again in Nalbari district on the 28th. This was during the run upto the Assembly poll, held in May 2001 (*Hindustan Times*, 29-4-2001).

The murder of 6 AGP workers on 3 May 2001 at the Party's office at Bogorihati in Nalbari's Belsor Police Station created strong anti-ULFA sentiment in Nalbari, a district which has contributed maximum cadres to the banned ULFA. "We want justice", "Bury ULFA rebels alive", and "ULFA murdabad". It was possibly the worst shock for ULFA in its stronghold.

People Indifferent to ULFA Deaths

The Frontline of 25 October 2002 has listed 15 cases of individual killings of ULFA militants at the hands of the SF between 13 May and 11 September. How the public sympathy for the banned outfit is gradually drying up is best summed up by the headline assigned to the story by the respected Fortnightly: "Increasingly, public opinion in Assam is much less exercised over the killings of 'suspected militants' than it was a decade ago." Here is telling excerpt from the story:

> "In contrast to what used to be the case a decade ago, there is not even a ripple of reaction to similar incidents now. Public opinion.... Could not care less, it seems."

Groundswell against ULFA seems to be palpable. The people seem to have had enough of the violence. There is an obvious yearning for peace. Does the outfit have its ears to the ground? Will it heed the warning signals? The next incident is even more pregnant with meanings and warnings, for ULFA.

ULFA Insurgents' Kin Sue the Outfit

Families of 202 ULFA cadres filed petitions before the Assam Human Rights Commission (AHRC) at Guwahati on 7 June 2002 against the ULFA C-in-C, Paresh Barua for either forcing or luring their family members into joining him. Among the complainants are the families of the ULFA's Foreign Secretary (Sasha Choudhury), its Cultural and Public Relations Secretaries. The petitioners demanded that Barua return their children to their homes. Sasha's father, Dinabandhu Choudhury, has alleged that Barua forced his son to join ULFA.

Among the petitions received, 80 are from Nalbari district, an ULFA stronghold, 51 from Barpeta, 21 each from Marigaon and Kamrup, 12 from Goalpara, 10 from Bongaigaon, and 5 from Tezpur districts. A Guwahati-based NGO, took the initiative to bring the families before AHRC.[52]

Peace Talks Initiatives

During his 5-day trip to the North-East in April 1998, Defence Minister George Fernandes failed to make contacts with ULFA leaders, though he had offered unconditional talks to them. He had claimed "some private parties were already meeting militants on my behalf". Rajkhowa rejected the proposal same day, 6 April 1998, dubbing India as "terrorist" for occupying "our country". But morale of the cadres seems to be low. The *North-East Daily* says: "Resentment among ULFA cadres currently in Bhutan has been brewing for some time.... Several of them have been writing pessimistic letters to their relatives, lamenting the way they have to live and face hardship."[53]

Nothing was heard on the issue till Rajkhowa made the offer on 27 November 2001, "provided Government of India is ready to accept our pre-conditions". The statement faxed to newspapers in Assam came on the 11th anniversary of the ban on the extremist outfit. Assam's Chief Minister Tarun Gogoi welcomed the offer of political settlement of "Indo-Assam Conflict", made for the first time by ULFA Chairman? The Government has adopted "wait and watch" policy on the offer, as they did before opening talks with NSCN(I-M). ULFA is obviously under pressure from Bhutan as well.[54] New Delhi's move to tighten the vigil along the Indo-Bhutan border "by deploying 10 battalions of BSF"[55] prevented the possibility of ULFA cadres sneaking back into India.

ULFA has not sent any feelers to the Government expressing its willingness for negotiations, Gogoi said on 7 December[56] 2001. He said it was "welcome" that ULFA had expressed publicly its desire for negotiations. He again said on 13 June 2002 that the Centre should initiate talks with the ULFA, as it was doing with the NSCN(I-M).[57]

The opposition AGP on 11 July 2002, asked ULFA to shun violence and come forward for a negotiated settlement. The Legislature Party Secretary, Dilip Kumar Saikia, made this appeal to "brother" Arbindo Rajkhowa in a 3-page open letter.[58] The Press reported (in June 2002) that Governor Sinha deputed a state civil servant to open talks with ULFA's Foreign Secretary Sasha Choudhury at Singapore. He denied the report.[59]

The way Arbindo Rajkhowa's father, undoubtedly a freedom fighter of some eminence, has been treated with respect and extra consideration, also seems to be a part of the Government's plans to facilitate peace talks with ULFA. Umakant Rajkonwar, the oldest freedom fighter of Assam, turned 100 on 11 January 2001. His birth centenary was observed in a big way, with senior ministers participating and planting saplings as a part of ceremonies to honour him. Laudatory references were made to his contributions in the freedom struggle. He was the Chief of the 9th Unit of the Shanti Vahini in Upper Assam during the Quit India Movement of 1942. Arbindo Rajkhowa is the 6th child and youngest son of Umakant. Chief Minister Gogoi released Rs. 30,000 for medical treatment of Umakant Rajkonwar in April 2002.[60]

Ban Extended: 2003-05

"In a setback to peace hopes in Assam, the Centre extended ban 7-2-03 on ULFA (as also on NDFB) under the Unlawful Activities (Prevention) Act, 1967 for two years" (*HT*, 8-2-03). ULFA was first declared an unlawful organisation on 27 Nov. 1996 and the ban has been extended every two years ever since.

With New Delhi engaged in extended talks with NSCN(I-M) over the last 6 years, there were hopes of some such understanding with the ULFA also, especially when it has expressed a desire for such peace talks. But ULFA's preconditions seems to have come in the way.

Sanjoy Ghose Murder Verdict

The murder case came to a close with P.K. Phukan, additional sessions judge, awarding life sentence to accused (Moni Neog and Kania Hazarika). Six others, including C-in-C Barua were declared absconders. They had abducted the social worker on 4-7-97 when he was on his way to village Mekheliga on Majuli, and killed him the same evening.

When Ghose, INLAK scholar, founder of URMUL, Rajasthan, and CHARKHA, New Delhi, and winner of Sanskriti Award, landed at Majuli, his friends and family thought he had gone crazy as the Island was infested with the ultras of ULFA and the latter took him as an Army spy. For the first three months of their stay, Ghose, head of the AVARD-NE and his volunteers stayed at the Islander's houses. Subsequently, his work at the grass-roots level made him so popular with the locals that he became an 'enemy' of the contractors for whom Majuli was a milch cow, where last year's imaginary works could be shown as having been washed away by the current floods of the 'wicked' Brahmaputra. The things became worse when Dweep-Alok, mouth piece of AVARD-NE, started exposure of cases of corruption in the money for development allotted by the centre. When the locals saw the benefits of 'his work' in contrast to the 'work' done by ULFA, the outfit was bound to do to him what it indeed did on 4-7-97, having told him repeatedly in talks to leave the island, the 'advice' obviously falling on the deaf ears. In his short stay, Ghose has shown that "if the youth could be helped to see the path of constructive work and development, much of the problem would end", he had written in his diary, which his wife later published in a book (Exp., 28 Aug. and 2 Sep. 2003).

It was no surprise that his abduction and murder caused widespread resentment. Records show 20 ULFA cadres were lynched over 7 years. There is hope even if there is one Ghose heading a NGO against the ten fraudulent ones in the field only to make a name and money; of course the latter must be tolerated and kept under strict scrutiny.

ULFA: 2002-2005

Now a brief look at the outfit in the first half of the first decade of the 21st century.

ULFA Rebel's Kin Killing: Fresh Probe

Inter-party politics is the bane of the Indian polity. Assam's Congress Government, after rejecting the report of a commission headed by a retired Guwahati High Court Judge, constituted 27-8-05 a new commission headed by a retired Supreme Court Judge (Justice K.N. Saikia) to probe the "secret killings" (mostly relatives of ULFA militants) in Assam, since 1998. All the cases referred to the commission, including five specific ones, took place when Mahanta-led AGP was in power. Critics dubbed it as politics of vendetta.

ULFA: Post-Bhutan Scenario

Two weeks after Bhutanese action against ULFA, its Chairman Rajkhowa addressed a letter to the Chairman of the PRC, seeking "temporary shelter" in view of the Bhutanese offensive. "We will request you to permit our cadres enter your territory extra-legally to save their lives. They have no other option. Your people should extend them minimum temporary hospitality necessary for their survival." The letter was e-mailed to Guwahati newspaper offices 28-12-03 (*Exp.*, 29-12-03).

Meanwhile, NSCN(K)-controlled-Naga Hills of Myanmar became an operating base for ULFA by mid-2004. These Hills "are now home to close to 4,400 ULFA cadres" (*Tribune*, 13-10-04) Spate of attacks on oil installations and civilian targets in upper Assam (Jul-Oct 2004), closer to Myanmar Naga Hills, came from ULFA cadres ensconced there. "Central Command Headquarters of ULFA is now based in Bangladesh."

Paresh Baruah, lodged in a BDR camp at Srimangal "has been actively reorganising ULFA ranks after the Bhutanese offensive. He hosted a meeting of 9 groups like NDFB, PLA, ATTF, ANVC, HNLC, etc. in March 2004 in Gulshan II, a Dhaka locality, in a house belonging to an important Bangladesh politico. His task of re-building ULFA is not easy because of low morale of the cadre after the Bhutanese crackdown, "while the gap between him and Rajkhowa has widened." *The Indian Express* of 27-6-03 had reported "Barua is alive and in Dhaka". He was injured in 27-5-03 shoot out. "In an interview to BBC, Baruah denied any rift with Rajkhowa."

Again, the press had reported a shoot-out when a major meeting of anti-India insurgent groups was taking place at a North Shamoli safe-house under the joint auspices of the DGFI and ISI. "Sources said food for 160 participants was specially catered from the Golf club" (*TOI*, 30-07-04). Besides this safe-house, three other ULFA camps were also attacked that day by gunmen. "Needle of suspicion behind these attacks, that left 21 dead, points to the rival group led by Rajkhowa." Intelligence suspected among the dead at North Shamoli could be Baruah. Among the other dead identified as top ULFA cadres close to Baruah more Paramjit Saikia, Lalit Hazarika and Biju Deka. "The bodies are lying at the Dhaka Medical College mortuary and efforts are on identify the other person killed."

Dhaka denied the incident but the press reported it widely. Bangladesh has consistently maintained that there were no ULFA training camps on its soil. Indians however "point out to the existence of ULFA locations at Mack Towers, Glove Pharma and Asia Hostel, while the DGFI safe-house is located in North Shamoli.

Like on some similar occasions earlier, an e-mail from Baruah a week later showed that he was alike.

In his e-mail statement in Assamese of 16-12-04, Rajkhowa said "Paresh Baruah is seriously ill and shifted to a safe place for an urgent medical operation." He said because of his illness, Baruah would, for now, not maintain his usual regular communication with the *literature* Indira Goswami and other intellectuals, media persons, and other organisations, and requested the latter to forward him their suggestions and advice through the e-mail address: rubybhuyan@yahoo.com.

Meanwhile, the unified command decided 17-12-04 to step up CI operations in the wake of a fresh spurt in violence by the ULFA.

ULFA Violence: Continues

Feb. 2003. Three mortar attacks in 5 months. In all the three attacks, the ultras used 60 mm mortars with 10 tailfins "used by the Chinese and Pak armies". Indian Army 60 mm mortars have 8 tailfins. The last such attack was on the IAF base near Guwahati airport on 23-02-03. The earlier such attacks came in October 2002 when similar mortar bombs landed at the Dispur Secretariat Complex, followed by five more exploding on 25 December near the Bishop House.

March 2003. ULFA blew up a storage tank (containing 5000 KL of motor spirit) of Assam Oil Division, barely a km from the Digboi Oil Refinery on the 7th. Its ultras blew up two pipelines the same day near Duliajan.

2 April 2003. A SULFA leader Nayan Das alias Guli was lynched to death by irate residents in Dibrugarh for his misbehaviour with a woman.

15 August 2004. The IED explosion triggered by ULFA at the Independence Day celebrations venue, Dhemaji College, killed 16 people, including 2 women and 10 children. "It was the worst in the recent months.

The 7-month peace in Assam following Operation Flush out in Bhutan in December 2003, thus proved to be a proverbial lull before the storm." Going overboard, Tarun Gogoi had declared that ULFA's back was broken. Analysts felt certain amount of complacency could also have crept in as Assam Government had possibly ignored several sporadic incidents of militant violence prior to the 15 August blast.

2 October 2004. Gandhi Jayanti was marked by several blasts, in a widespread operation spanning 48 hours. The Government obviously did not learn a lesson even from 15 August blasts, said the critics, "as reports of possible militant strikes on 2 October were taken lightly". ULFA was believed to be regrouping in Bangladesh and Myanmar after its Bhutan discomfiture, and every one seemed to have forgotten NDFB after many of its top leaders including Vice-President Dhiren Boro and Publicity Secretary B. Erakdao were arrested. Obviously biding its time, NDFB decided Gandhi Jayanti was convenient, being a day prior to its 19th Raising Day.

Beyond the capability of a single outfit, ULFA and NDFB were obviously involved as the two are known to have had a strategic alliance and specific areas of operations. They were two of the 9 outfits that had banned Hindi films across the Region from 15 November 2003. The NSCN(I-M) did not figure in the list while the NSCN(K) had later dissociated itself from the ban.

2 Oct. 2004. Twin blast at Dimapur kill 26 persons. "Dimapur, kissing the Assam Nagaland border, has also been a convergence point of other outfits of the Region like ULFA, NDFB and DHD", after essentially being the den of NSCN(I-M). The latter being in peace mode since July 1997 and engaged in serious peace talks with New Delhi cannot be remotely linked to these blasts. "After promptly announcing a reward of Rs. 5 lakh for information leading to the capture of the culprits, the NSCN (I-M) blamed a non-Naga outfit and a Naga ally for the blasts" (Rahul Karmakar, *HT*, 5-1-0-05). The identity of the latter is obvious, NSCN(K), it is the former phrase which draws the ULFA into its ambit, howsoever irrational it might sound. Hence the inclusion of Dimapur blasts in this list. The non-Naga outfit could either the ULFA, NDFB, or DHD. The ULFA has an alliance with the NSCN(K) for a toehold in Arunachal as also in Myanmar, and why would it risk both by purposeless strike at the Naga Civilians? Both NDFB and DHD belong to the Bodo-Kacharis stock, and Dimapur was the capital of the last Kachari Kingdom. And to wit, the DHD had staked claim to the Nagaland town some time back. So the Region "appears poised for a never-before showdown between the NSCN(I-M) and "culprit outfit".

June 2005

After lying low for some period, the banned ULFA sprung into action in June 2005.

20th. Threw a grenade inside the high-security zone of the new Secretariate building complex in Guwahati.

25th. A grenade thrown at a police station at Sibsagar injures 6 persons.

26th. CRPF Group Office at Guwahati comes under grenade attack, injuring 12, including 6 CRPF men.

"Recently invited for talks by New Delhi, ULFA had demanded the release of its 10 jailed leaders", to enable it to take a decision on the talks offer. Flexing its muscles through these June 2005 attacks, ULFA was sending a message to New Delhi against its dilly-dallying on the release of the jailed leaders, some analysts felt.

ULFA Attacks: Run-up to the Big Day (15 August) 2005

It has been the normal practice for these North-Eastern outfits in the (recent) past to unleash an orgy of violence before and on the Independence Day, often acting in concert. It was no different for 15 August 2005.

2nd: CRPF-Police team ambushed in Tinsukia, killing one sepoy and injuring five others.

6th: Grenade explodes in Guwahati, injuring two.

7th: Blast in two pipelines at Sibsagar and Dibrugarh.

8th: (1) Explosion in oil pipeline in Tinsukia. (2) Bombs defused near two schools in Jorhat. (3) Explosion at an ASEB powerhouse.

9th: (1) Gas pipeline explosion at Desaiborha in Sibsagar. (2) Explosion at a steel plant along Assam-Arunachal border. (3) Convoy of trucks carrying food items fired at in the KA district, killing one man. (4) Assam's MOS, Home, Rockybul Hussain told the Assembly 9-8-05 that "the ULFA has exploded 17 bombs and grenades since 6 August".

10th: (1) IED blew up railway tracks near Tihu railway station in Lower Assam, cutting rail links between Assam and the rest of India. (2) A police-station in upper Assam attacked. (3) Assam Government called the Army in aid to civil power.

SOME IMPORTANT EVENTS

ULFA Hits out at its 'Mentor'

In a statement, e-mailed on 7-12-04 by its C-in-C Baruah, ULFA lashed out at the NSCN concept of Nagalim, timing its outburst with the prolonged visit of the (I-M) leaders Swu and Muivah to India for sustained talks with the Central leaders, and asserting that the Nagas never in history had any control over Assam. Its incarcerated Vice-Chairman Pradip Gogoi, presented before the TADA Court at Guwahati 8-12-4 was more direct in attacking the NSCN: "We will not give an inch of Assam to fuel the Greater Nagaland dream of the NSCN."

US puts ULFA on Terrorist List

The US State Department in its "2004 Country Reports on Terrorism" released 28 April 2005, added ULFA to the Other Selected Terrorist Organisations (OSTO) List. The outfits on the OSTO List are the entities that do not target the national security of the US or its citizens.

ULFA Leader Released

A Guwahati Sub-Divisional Judicial Magistrate released 2 June 2005 Ramu Mech on bail.

"Major Player in Real Estate Business"

BSF claimed the ULFA leaders are running seven upmarket hotels (Surma International, Hotel Mohammadia and Hotel Padma International are in Dhaka; Hotel Keya International and Hotel Yamuna in Sylhet; and Hotels Basundhra and Rajking in Chittagong) and some nursing homes in Bangladesh. The MHA reports indicated Barua's business interests in Bangladesh (*Exp.*, 4-6-05).

ULFA Setting up Bases in Nepal

Intelligence culled from various sources disclosed ULFA setting up five camps in Nepal in the areas under the Maoist leader Pushpa Kumar Dahal, likely located in the districts of Bara, Dang, Syaganja Chitwan, Sagarmatha, and even Solok humbu, whose claim to fame is the Mt Everest.

Barua's trusted aide Rana Deuri, from Darrang district, is in-charge of these Nepal Camps, housing about 150 cadres. Deuri is close to the CPI (Maoist), which has for the past few years figured in the ULFA's "Golden Triangle" plan for the movement of the cadres between Bhutan, Bangladesh and Nepal. The ouster of the ULFA set-up in Bhutan following "operation All-Clear" in Dec. 2003 necessitated these camps, which might not be exclusive to ULFA, but possibly shared with the Maoists. In any case, analysts have long suspected an ULFA-Maoist nexus.

The report of ULFA shifting base from other adjoining countries come at a time when some intellectuals are trying to bring ULFA to the negotiations table at New Delhi.

ULFA-Centre Talks: Long in Coming

There were reports of Defence Minister contacting ULFA leaders during his April 1998 visit to the Region. Then for the first time since it was outlawed in 1990, its Chairman offered to talk to New Delhi on 27-11-01 if it accepted his pre-conditions (*Frontline,* 04-01-02). Both proved abortive.

From early 2004, noted Assamese writer and Jnanpith awardee Indira Mamoni Goswami has been active in bringing ULFA and New Delhi to the table. On 15 Nov. 2004, she submitted a 'petition' (nivedan is her choice for the term) to the Prime Minister's Special Advisor, M.K. Narayanan. She met the PM on the 16th. She told the press that PM agreed to her suggestion to initiate the process to open dialogue with ULFA by Jan. 2005. She thought the centre should have no problem talking sovereignty with the ULFA, since the former is in sustained talks with the NSCN (I-M) whose plank once was sovereignty.

7 Dec., Narayanan conveyed to Goswami Centre's willingness for talks with ULFA. Barua says 'No' to PM's offer as his letter made no mention of 'sovereignty'. 9 Feb. 2005, Goswami, who offered her services as mediator, handed over Rajkhowa's letter to Narayanan, pleading for an "agreement with honour and dignity". AASU welcomed the PM's letter, and wanted the Government to declare a unilateral cease-fire.

A MHA official handed over first formal letter to Goswami on 26 May 2005 for Rajkhowa (AA, 29-5-05). It was signed by Narayanan which, Goswami said on 28 May, expressed Centre's preparedness to hold "unconditional talks" to discuss "Assam's sovereignty", described by ULFA as the "core issue", an obvious contradiction in terms. In his telephonic conversation with her on the 28th, Goswami, the "go-between" informed the press at Delhi that Barua told her that some points in the letter such as abjuring the violence prior to talks required clarification.

The Hindu of 3-05-05 says the centre has chalked out a course to enter into a peace dialogue with ULFA, even when the US has put it on their terror list. Security analysts feel the US declaration would put pressure on Bangladesh to curb ULFA "activities at a time when Dhaka itself was being seen as a hub of Islamic radical outfits, which numbered 31 in January 2005. Scenario in Bangladesh is worrying with rising attacks against journalists, left and secular elements in the recent past. All this shows that the extremist groups are gaining ground in Bangladesh. No wonder the extremist fundamentalist groups are seeking, says the leading strategic journal Jane's Intelligence and Insight, formation of a greater Islamic territory, covering some areas in India also.

In a letter handed over to Narayanan on 30-6-05 by Goswami, Rajkhowa says "we can talk if focus is on sovereignty" (*Exp.*, 02-07-05). Four days after Narayanan wrote his 27-05-05 letter to the Chairman and C-in-C, the latter called the newspaper, demanding that the Government release 10 of its top leaders lodged in different jails "before they could discuss the letter".

In the editorial of their mouthpiece, *Freedom* of 15-7-05, Rajkhowa says their quick response to the letter from the PMO has not been reciprocated by the latter.

ULFA threatens 14-09-05 to withdraw from the peace process unless the Army stops its operations inside the Dibru-Saikhowa (National Park) Reserve Forest in Tinsukia district (AA, 15-9-05). Goswami said the ULFA wanted the

Government to mellow down its military operations. The stalemate continues as the Army refused to concede, reasoning that all earlier cessations of operations were utilised by ULFA to re-equip, rest and augment its strength. On the 20th, two ultras were killed inside the Reserve Forest, one of them identified as Achinta Saikia, Financial Controller of the outfit's 28th battalion.

On 21-09-05, a delegation of the People's Consultative Group (PCG) was barred from visiting villages inside the Reserve Forest. The Army stopped them at Bhuijanghat, informing them that the boats to ferry them to their destination were not available as these had been requisitioned by the Army due to operational reasons.

Given the circumstances, it is unlikely that the meeting between the ULFA appointed 11-member PCG and the NSA, M.K. Narayanan, "scheduled for the first fortnight/week of October 2005 will take place" (*Exp.* and *Hindu*, 21 and 22 Sep. 2005).

Talks were held but to no Avail

It must be put on record that the first round of talks between the PCG and the PMO indeed took place in Oct. 2005 and Prime Minister Manmohan Singh put in a brief appearance. Second round too was held at the PMO while the third round was held on 22 Jun. 2006 at the MHA by Home Minister Shivraj Patil. Talks broke down subsequently as ULFA insisted on release of its five senior leaders under detention.

ULF Depradations: No let up

After the failure of talks, the Government annulled cease-fire on 24 Sep. 2006 and resumed counter insurgency operations. The secessionist outfit to continued with its vivious ways. Some of the atrocities committed by ULFA are put on record here.

Editors tell ULFA: "Media gag must go"

Media persons hit out at ULFA on 14 June 2006 for the recent threats issued to four city-based journalists and asked it to withdraw it immediately. The threat was issued by ULFA C-in-C Paresh Barua through an e-mail on 8 June.

Speaking at the meeting organised by the Journalists Union of Assam (JUA) affiliated to the Indian Journalist Union at the Guwahati Press Club, DN Chakravarti, Editor, *Dainik Assam* (the oldest Assamese daily) came down heavily on the outfit and said: "The ULFA has lost its ability to identify friends and foes.... It is pursuing a meaningless philosophy which is proving to be self-destructive as well as harmful to the Assamese society."

5 Jan 2007: ULFA Kill 16 Non-Assamese

Six migrant brick kiln workers – mostly from Bihar and UP – were shot dead by ULFA militants in four separate incidents in Upper Assam's Dibrugarh, Tinsukia, and Sibsagar districts. 5 labourers were killed at Tingri Chariali, 35 km. from Dibrugarh; three killed and five murdered at Borhapjan (Tinsukia); and three killed at Gobindapore brick field at Borhat near Kamrup (Sibsagar).

5 Jan 2007

"95% oppose ULFA's demand for independence". A civil society group, Assam Public Works (APW), claimed that more than 95 per cent of nearly 2.6 million people, interviewed by its 1800 volunteers in nine (Bongaingaon, Goalpara, Guwahati (metro), Dhubri, Darrang, Sonitpur, Lakhimpur, Dhimaji and Nalbari) of Assam's 27 districts, rejected the demand for independence by the outlawed ULFA.

The APW, known for its anti-ULFA stance, claims to have several relatives of the separatist group as its members. Abhijeet Sarma, General Secretary of the APW said only 5 per cent of the people surveyed in the opinion poll to elicit public response to ULFA's demand for independence/ sovereignty, supported its demand and the rest thoroughly rejected it.

The opinion poll for the remaining 18 districts "would be taken up soon", he said on 5 Jan 2007.

Army Seizes 43 ULFA Weapons: 10 Jan 2007

Defence sources on 10 Jan 2007 said that "the Army is all set to launch air strikes by helicopters in some of the most inaccessible hideouts of ULFA militants."

The Army, on its first day of counter-insurgency operations, got a major success by seizing 43 weapons including a sophisticated Universal Machine Gun (UMG), besides unearthing an ULFA militant's plot to ambush the Convoy of GOC, 4 Corps in Upper Assam's Tinsukia district.

The UMG, recovered from an overground ULFA activist, was used in the killing of Bihari labourers in Tinsukia district on 5 Jan 2007, the first day of the 5 day violence (5-9 January) in Upper Assam's three districts that killed 71 non-Assamese migrants in Assam. The UMG has the capacity of firing 1,000 rounds (bullets) in one strike.

The over-ground ULFA activists were also instrumental in providing all necessary logistic support to outfit's militants belonging to its 28th Battalion.

This self-styled (SS) 28th Battalion of the secessionist ULFA was found to be responsible for these (recent) killings of migrant Bihari labourers in Upper Assam. Sources confirmed that "this unit has been entrusted with the responsibility of carrying out insurgent (violent) strikes in Upper Assam. While the 28th is active in the Upper Assam, the ULFA leadership has entrusted the same task of spreading insurgency in the Lower Assam to its 27th Battalion.

It was revealed that the ULFA has also patterned the structure of its fighting units on Indian Army's. "They have similar sepoy and officer ranks for their cadres. Each battalion of theirs has also four companies."

The ULFA's top leadership, known to be leading a life of luxury in their hide-outs in Bangladesh, is coordinating the insurgency strikes and extortion drive of these so-called battalions.

Extortion Drive by ULFA Continues: Jan 2007

Apart from continuing the targeting of innocent civilians, the latest being thc rccord killing of 71 Bihari migrant labourers in 5-day (5-9 Jan 2007) murderous spree in three districts of the Upper Assam, the ULFA has also continued with its old modus operandi of collecting ransom money by writing extortion letters – couched in ideologically appropriate terminology – to representatives of various companies in Assam to raise funds for its operations and other nefarious activities.

One such letter, recently written to the manager of a tea estate in Assam, was recovered by the troops during their operations against ULFA ultras after their early Jan 2007 killings of the non-Assamese labourers in Upper Assam. The extortion letter written by the ULFA's SS Lt Prabal Neog of the 28th Battalion to this manager reads: "Revolutionary Congratulations, we the ULFA, do hereby ask you/your company to contribute Rs. 30 lakh for a just cause and hope that you will comply with our proposal as soon as possible."

Post-Talks Situation: Early 2007

24 Sep. 2006: ULFA Cease Fire is called off in Assam

New Delhi called off 6-week ceasefire and resumed military operations against the ULFA following stepped up attacks and extortions by the rebels. Peoples Consultative Group (PCG), a civil society team appointed by the ULFA to mediate with the Centre on its behalf to get the two on the negotiations table, failed to get a written commitment from the rebels that its leadership would come for talks if their jailed comrades were released. The release of five of their senior leaders was the pre-condition they laid down for the initiation of talks with the Centre. Knowing the ULFA to be on elusive customer as shown by their past experience in dealing with it, the government interlocutors told the PCG that they were willing to consider their demand if rebel would give a written commitment as mentioned above. When ULFA decided against yielding to this demand, the Government expectedly called off the cease-fire. Surprisingly, the PCG feigned surprise at New Delhi's move, which was utterly inexplicable as they had been kept informed of the developments.

Peace talks between ULFA representatives and the Centre formally broke down first week of October after PCG pulled out of the peace process and ironically, blamed the Centre for calling off the truce.

Army steps up Operations: 8 Oct. 2006

Army launches anti-insurgency operations in parts of eastern Assam, close to the Myanmar border, to flush out rebels of the outlawed ULFA, soon after the ceasefire was called off. At least four ULFA rebels were killed and six more captured during this offensive. The cadres of 28th Battalion of ULFA were the main targets as they were active in eastern parts of Assam. The rebels were reportedly holed up in the thick forests of this area.

Movement of troops in these jungles is slow and risky. The best option is to air drop soldiers in specific locations, guided by intelligence inputs. A fleet of helicopters was on stand by for this purpose.

"The ULFA too stepped up its attacks in the past fortnight with a string of grenade explosions and blasts, killing three people and mounding another 33, including 10 soldiers". Intelligence reported a large group of ULFA guerrillas armed with explosives and sophisticated weaponry had sneaked into Assam from bases in Myanmar's North Sagaing Division in the last fortnight.

Analysts aver civil society groups like the PCG are best advised to avoid acting as mouthpiece of rebel outfits like ULFA. A stage comes when they get to be used by these outfits. They cannot hope to affect the thinking or attitude of the ultras, and in due course, start criticising the government for one reason or other. The worst, after a time, they start exerting pressure on the government to accept one demand or other of the rebels. But on the other hand, they can not persuade or pressure the rebels on even a very minor concession.

The PCG got the government to declare a ceasefire to enable it to persuade the ULFA to move to the talks table. One extension after another failed to move the ultras. Even when the government agreed to consider their demand for release of the in jailed leaders, they refused to give a written commitment for joining the talks. After all this, PCG ends up blaming the government for calling off the ceasefire which it had declared unilaterally and in the face of the strong opposition of the Army. Army had reasons to oppose this truce. It is wiser by the earlier experience. The ULFA has always used such truce periods in the past to reorganise, re-equip, re-coup and strengthen itself.

'ULFA used the Talks to Regroup'

The Army was opposed to any cease-fire agreement with ULFA because it is aware of this outfit's tactic of using all such interragrums to re-equip and regroup itself. ULFA has been active for over two decades, and no one knows its history better than the Indian Army. But once the political decision was made, Army simply has to fall in line.

But after the outfits' outrage on 5 November 2006, when it killed/injured 14/53 in two blasts in the heart of Assam's capital, both politicians and civil officials seem to be wiser to the truth told to them by the Army. If Chief Minister Gogoi admitted security failure, Union Home Secretary VK Duggal had somewhat similar message for his political bosses at the centre.

Duggal, accompanied by Joint Secretary, North-East, DGP BSF Mitra and DGP CRPF JK Sinha, visited two blast sites and later met Chief Minister Gogoi. "The meeting concluded on a note that ULFA's senior leaders had bought time on pretext of 'peace talks' with the centre."[61]

"ULFA was completely destroyed. Its senior leaders intiated the peace talks, which we now feel was a *tamasha.* They actually used this time to mobilise themselves to carry out the attacks like this"? Sinha told a daily.[62]

During the meeting, the intelligence inputs revealed that ULFA went on a recruitment drive and also strengthened itself monetarily, while pretending all the time that it was serious about talks.

A day after the ULFA killed 14 in two blasts, the Congress Party, which had been engaging the banned outfit in talks, "ran for cover, drawing plans for peace campaign in Assam's ULFA strongholds", wrote political analyst.[63] The campaign, of course, will not name ULFA. How carefully the political parties safeguard their party interests even in grim situations where national security is threatened. It is difficult to understand, much less appreciate, such squeamishness.

The UPA government and the ULFA have been in contact through a People's Consultative Group (PCG) since September 2005, but the violence continued in the State. Congress policy makers, clearly alarmed by the latest mindless violence perpetrated by ULFA, were inclined to give up the 'peace initiative'. Now they concede that the ULFA's peace overtures were not genuine. Between September 2005 and June 2006, there were 52 blasts and 41 civilian deaths. Now it was realised that the extremist outfit merely used the truce to regroup, recruit, and extort.

Indians are Migrants, Bangladeshis Could Go later: ULFA

Finally, the ULFA has shown its true colours. For the outlawed outfit, it is the migrants from the Indian sub-continent, and not the Bangladeshis who are the "real infiltrators into Assam". They must go first because these "illegal migrants to Assam from the Indian sub-continent have threatened the very existence of the state, created a chaotic situation in the social formation and occupied the political and economic spheres at the expense of the indigenous people.

There views of the outfit have been reflected in the Dec 2006 issue of Freedom, its monthly mouthpiece. It reminded the readers about the beginnings of the Assam Movement led by the AASU in 1979 when the focus was on "outsiders" and not necessarily Bangladeshi infiltrators.

The ULFA might have said so in so many words for the first time by putting its creed in cold print. The terror trail drawn here leaves nothing to imagination. Its main enemies are Indian. In the last few years, especially after its ouster from the jungles of Bhutan, the outfit has repeatedly said that the illegal migrants into Assam/North-East do not include the Bangladeshis. They are obviously paying back the debt they owe to Dhaka for offering them sanctuary and shelter in their post Bhutan second life. Here are the cold statistics.

- Oct 2000. ULFA guns down 15 people in Tinsukia and Dibrugarh districts.
- Dec 2000. 26 non-Assamese massacred in Upper Assam.
- Nov 2003. Over 100 Hindi-speaking people killed in retaliation for rape of a North-Eastern girl in a train in Bihar.
- 9 Jun 2006. 6 killed, 16 injured in a blast at Machkowa, Guwahati.
- 5 Nov 2006. 14 killed, 40 injured in blasts in Guwahati.
- 23 Nov 2006. 3 killed, 9 injured in blast at Guwahati railway station.
- 6 Jan 2007. 48 killed, mostly from Bihar and West Bengal, by ULFA in a 3-hour orgy in Upper Assam, including some places on Arunachal Pradesh border.

Army to take Baton from Police in Guwahati: Dec 2006

The last Assam Police bastion against the ULFA is likely to make way for the Army. Ever since the Operation Bajrang, the full-fledged offensive agaiinst the ULFA in 1990, the Army troops have been handling security almost everywhere in Assam except in Guwahati.

But the outlawed ULFA seems to be "getting too hot to handle by police with limited fire power", offered a police officer by way of on explanation—or perhaps justification. Soldiers in battle fatigues may soon make the men in Khaki play second fiddle.

The threat by ULFA to disrupt the 33rd Natural games, scheduled to be held at Guwahati in Feb. 2007 might have hastened the decision of the police to "cede territory."

The decision to deploy the Army in Assam's capital seems to have been taken on 24 Dec 2006 at the meeting of the Unified Command which, set up in 1997, is a coordination body of the State administration, the Army, the Police, para military forces and the intelligence agencies. Its success in Assam persuaded New Delhi to replicate it in Jammu & Kashmir to combat insurgency.

ULFA's 'B 'Force' in Army's cross-hair: Jan 2007

"B company spells terror in Assam", reads a news headline as the Army and other security forces continue its offensive launched on 9 Jan 2007, in the jungle areas adjoining the Assam-Arunachal border. Army's prime target will be ULFA's elite fighting unit, the 28th Battalion, who are killers of the 69 Hindi-speaking migrants in eastern Assam. They used cell phones to keep in touch. Intelligence disclosed: "Intercepts revealed that the massacre was carried out by the 'Bravo' or the B company of the ULFA's 28th Battalion." It has been trained at camps in Myanmar.

The Battalion, with an estimated strength of 350 plus is reported to have masterminded and executed some of the worst massacres in Upper Assam, including the latest round of serial killings.[64] "The unit also serves as the nerve-centre of ULFA for planning, kidnappings and extortions", said a senior officer of HQ, 2 Mtn Div. He also showed a ransom note for Rs. 30 lac sent to a tea estate manager and signed by 28th battalion commander, self-styled Lt Prabal Neog.

Its headquarters, earlier called 'Camp Kashmir' in Myanmar's Sagaing Division, moves among six locations in the country, two of which it shares with the NSCN(K).

Defence Minister AK Antony, accompanied by Chief of Army Staff Gen JJ Singh and Defence Secretary Shekhar Dutt, visited Dinjan on 10 Jan 2007 to take stock of the situation.

The Army has been targeting the 28th Battalion leadership since the end of the cease fire in Sep 2006. "Nearly 15 top-notch operatives have been eliminated in a string of counter-terror operations by crack teams. But the outfit continues to regroup and re-arm itself."

Car Bombs Arrive in Assam: 4 Feb 2007

The car bomb that exploded outside a police station at Guwahati in Assam on 4 Feb 2007 has understandably rattled the security establishment. The bombing planned and executed by ULFA and first of its kind in Assam, signals the advent of a deadly form of urban terrorism. If the banned ULFA and other terror outfits in the region, assisted, trained and armed by agencies like the Pak ISI, have decided to use car bombs, then it is only a matter of time before suicide bombers are deployed to further the separatists' agenda. Till now, the insurgents would carry explosives on bicycles and plant them in crowded areas, or they would hurl grenades from motor-cycles. The 4 February bombing opens up a fearful possibility of insurgents changing their tactics. This obviously points towards more troublesome days in the North-East.

Forces Strike Back After Outrage by ULFA: Jan 2007

Thousands of Armymen, para military forces and police from Assam and Arunachal Pradesh continued raids for the third day on 11 Jan 2007 on ULFA strongholds and bases in a jungle terrain described as "hostile and thickly wooded in Assam and adjoining border areas of Arunachal Pradesh."

A source put the total strength of the security force about 20,000. The counter-insurgency offensive came after a wave of attacks by ULFA ultras which killed 72 Hindi-speaking migrant-workers (mainly from Bihar and West Bengal) in the state during the last week. These attacks were Assam's worst violence in years and came after New Delhi called off a 6 – week ceasefire in Sep 2006 and resumed military campaign against the militants for stepping up violence and extortions.

Army is backed by the helicopters in its simultaneous operations in two states.

They have not Given up on Talks: Mar 2007

Nine months after the talks between ULFA-appointed People's Consultative Group (PCG) which was headed by Indira Goswami, and the Government of India broke down, there is a fresh move to revive the process. Interestingly, it is Goswami again who is behind the initiative, though this time she is going to press the ULFA to come forward for the direct discussions with New Delhi. Obviously the lady is wiser for her last abortive attempt to bring the devious ULFA on the negotiations table.

Goswami, who along with a group of eminent citizens of Assam recently floated the Citizens Peace Forum (CPF), said on 19 Mar 2007 there was every possibility of re-opening the negotiations especially if the society as a whole wanted it.

Goswami is not the only one working to see the talks between ULFA and New Delhi becoming a reality. There is another 'Curious' group working for the same aim. A platform of ULFA sympathisers, named People's Committee for Peace Initiative (PCPI), has been formed for the purpose.

The PCPI convened a conclave on 22 March, 2007 to revive Assam peace talks, starting a public debate on resolving the issue. Some interesting participants shared their thoughts.

- If Naga Human Rights leaders mooted the idea of a plebiscite to resolve the conflict, other rebel leaders holding ceasefire with New Delhi proposed peace talks without any pre-conditions.
- Political leaders like AGP President Brindawan Goswami and Praful Mahanta also favoured unconditional peace talks, with the former

saying the sovereignty issue should not be a stumbling block in starting these talks.

- The CPI also attended the peace conclave and demanded the suspension of the Army operation. How one wishes the daily[65] should have named this worthy.
- DHD leader Dilip Nonisha, who was among the prominent rebel leaders invited to the conclave reiterated that the agenda for the talks could not be decided without an initial round of direct talks.

ULFA's Condition for Talks: Still Acting Tough

ULFA on 16 Feb 2007 nipped the speculation that time was rife about a "track-II negotiations" with the government in the wake of the insurgent group's decision to call off the boycott of National Games. In the latest internet issue of its mouthpiece, Freedom, ULFA C-in-C Paresh Barua denied having entered into any sort of "track-II negotiations with New Delhi." His only condition was that "restoration of Assam's sovereignty should be on the agenda for talks". He further clarified: "In principle, ULFA is ready for a plebiscite, not referendum, under international supervision."

ULFA chairman Arbindo Rajkhowa on 29 Mar 2007 rejected Assam Chief Minister Tarun Gogoi's offer for unconditional talks and threatened to step up violence by suicide bombers.

In a hardhitting statement, he ruled out the possibility of budgin from their demand of sovereignty.

He also criticised the Congress MP Kirip Chaliha for his remarks against Indira Goswami who played the role of mediator in 2006 peace talks between New Delhi and ULFA, which never took off.

Can ULFA be Trusted? Or, Should it be?

It is a sad saga of murder and mayhem. For nearly three decades, ULFA has proved a tough, and often slippery customer. Should New Delhi call off all attempts at the negotiated settlement and go all out for a military solution? Should another chance be given to the sincere lady, Indira Goswami, to persuade the recalcitrant ULFA leadership to come forward for direct talks with the centre? Should another group of ULFA-friendly citizens, People's Committee for Peace Initiative (PCDI), also be given a chance to try their hand at peace-making? These are all inter-related questions, with no easy answers.

Some aspects of possible talks with ULFA are discussed, with a glance at the past events, with the aim of weighing the future options.

Tarun Gogoi offers Unconditional Talks

He has been criticised for offering talks and another truce to ULFA. Will the politicians, particularly at the state level, ever make an effort to learn from the past experience? Having himself said that "ULFA took full advantage of the temporary ceasefire in Aug-Sep 2006 to recruit, regroup and initial", how does he offer another truce to that outfit? It is obvious that Gogoi simply refuses to learn! He should have known that the ULFA's appointment of the 11-member People's Consultative Group (PCG) in Sep 2005 was a ploy to save, rather extricate, its leaders holed up in the Dibru-Saikhowa reserve forest. Expectedly, the first action of the PCG was to demand the immediate suspension of the anti-insurgency operations. The centre conceded the request in good faith, in spite of stiff opposition from the Army, as the latter knew better.

The rulers have short memories. A shrewd leader like the late Hiteshwar Saikia regretted the "biggest" mistake of his life when he allowed the pro-talks ULFA leaders to move about freely after Operation Rhino in 1991, hoping that they would persuade their peers in exile to come to the negotiations table. What happened actually? A volte-face and massive ULFA build up in Bhutan.

Whither the current anti-insurgency operation (Jan-Apr 2007) launched after the yet-another abortive (and futile) cease-fire in Aug-Sep 2006 will be taken to its logical conclusion is not certain. The future holds the answer. What is certain is that the most powerful ULFA duo of Rajkhowa-Barua would continue to be elusive. Gogoi must be wiser after two of them administered a snub to him through their internet mouthpiece Freedom. They questioned his authority even to offer talks to ULFA. Yet again, both declared defiantly that the issue of sovereignty must be/have to be on the agenda of talks. More than all this, C-in-C Barua demanded pebiscite under international supervision.

There is no hope of ULFA relenting until India can nab its most powerful leader, Barua, which is unlikely as he is ensconced in a safe, palatial house in Dhaka. But that is possible only if Dhaka cooperates, which again is unlikely, Bangladesh's neutral, transitional Government's tough action against its own terrorists notwithstanding.

Is ULFA Losing Public Sympathy and Support?

There are people who indeed are convinced that the ULFA is losing public sympathy because of its blood-thirst. In continuing to write chapters into its time on violence, it remains blind to this fact. The slide began after the killing of 13 innocent Assamese, mostly women and children, at Dhemaji on Independence Day in 2004. And now, with most sections of the civil society, including the Asom Sahitya Sabha, AASU and even the AGP opposing secession—for them peace is the priority— the ULFA seems to be caught up in the downward spiral of its own making.

What could be the cause or reason for its persistence and stubborn refusal to read the times? Some feel it could be a NGO's recent opinion poll which showed 95 percent Assamese rejecting the ULFA demand for sovereignty. Does it hope to change the trend by its ruthless Jan 2007 murder of 71 Hindi-speaking Biharis? Venting its anger in such an inhuman way is unlikely to constitute the means to what is now a largely unacceptable end. The poll ridiculed Chairman Rajkhowa's oft-repeated claim that sovereignty is not ULFA's demand but people's mandate.

There are some other related aspects of ULFA's tactics that demand attention. As early as in 2005 the official thinking was, and perhaps still is, that it is pointless making overtures to ULFA because its demand for "Swadhin Asom" will die a natural death.[66] It is possibly to counter this thinking that the ULFA adopted the oft-tested tactics of serving notice on the non-Assamese Hindi-speakers to quit Assam. It is obviously aimed at keeping the sagging morale of its cadres high.

At another level, this would amount to openly welcoming migrants from Bangladesh, something not entirely unexpected not only because it has enjoyed the hospitality of that country for years but also because ULFA can hardly afford to antagonise its foreign host that has for all these years been invigorating it. But this open-arms policy for foreign Bangladeshis has implications for its standing with the common Assamese citizens. They had run an intense, passionate and often violent anti-foreigners movement under AASU. It will seriously dent ULFA's much-vaunted 'popularity'. At a more practical level, the ULFA could not be unaware of the fact that if the so-called outsiders stop work even for a day, Assam's entire economy would crumble. But then, is ULFA really concerned with the well-being and prosperity of Assam and its people?

Some opine ULFA alone cannot be blamed for the continuing mayhem. Despite all caution by the security establishment, militants continue to trigger blasts. May be, a more vigorous anti-insurgency campaign is the answer. The Unifiled Command, of course, has launched just that in Jan 2007. But ultimately, political solution is the way out. But that will remain a distant dream till ULFA is forced to sit on the negotiations table.

But what is more worrisome is the blast reported from the Bodo region of Bongaigaon, which is suggestive of agents provocateur. It is obvious that the need of the hour is to stand united against the communal virus? Is that a tall order?

Wealthy ULFA Bankrolls Bangla Parties $ 6 m: Feb 2007

The banned ULFA is reported to have pumped in over $ 6 million to fund major political parties (like Bangladesh Nationalist Party, BNP, and the Awami League, AL) in the forthcoming Bangladesh elections, said a leading US think-tank—Strategic Foresight Inc, popularly Stratfor.

The funds have gone to at least 15 candidates belonging to both the BNP and AL. "ULFA is hedging its bet in order to protect its militant and business operations in Bangladesh should either party win." Some other comments and observation from the Stratfor report:

- The ULFA's core leadership is believed to have been living in luxury in Bangladesh for 15 years "under the protection of its political allies in Dhaka. As long as the ULFA can continue funding the appropriate candidates, it can ensure that Bangladesh government will resist caving into Indian demands to crack down on the militant group."
- Observing that $ 6 million was a "handsome contribution coming from an Indian militant outfit, the report said ULFA was no "ordinary organisation". Its chief, Paresh Barua, was "an enormously wealthy racketeer worth approximately $ 110 million" with business operations throughout India, Bangladesh and Persion Gulf. The business interests included hotels consultancy firms, driving schools, tanneries, department stores, textile factories, travel agencies, investment companies, shrimp trawlers and soft drink factories.
- Barua's businesses in Bangladesh is handled by a senior government official in Dhaka.
- The ULFA funded its militant activities "through a sophisticated extortion network". Major tea companies in Assam continuously faced "pay or die" threats but preferred to stay quiet, both out of fear as well as business interests. ULFA has increasingly become more concerned with its financial interests.
- ULFA is aware that New Delhi would not budge in its refusal to give in to the outfit's demands and therefore "is focusing its military operations to bleed the security forces in order to strengthen its negotiating position. That explains "its recent attacks on the migrant workers – mostly from Bihar – in Assam. Besides ULFA, Bangladeshi Islamist groups and Pakistan's ISI are other players having stakes in Bangladesh.

ULFA issue in Assam Assembly: 6 Mar 2007

Assam Assembly was informed by the Government on 6 Mar 2007 that the outlawed ULFA has not as yet responded positively to the efforts of the Centre and State to hold direct talks, while formal talks with the NDFB, holding a ceasefire with security forces, have not started because of the failure of the outfit in submitting its charter of demands.

Speaking on behalf of Chief Minister Tarun Gogoi, Assam's Forest Minister Rockybul Hussain clarified: "Three rounds of talks were hold with the ULFA-appointed People's Consultative Group (PCG) but in the later stages, the militant outfit did not look sincere for talks, and, in fact, taking advantage of the situation it started regrouping itself, besides launching violent attack."

The other points that emerged from the Assembly proceedings are given below:

- Prime Minister Manmohan Singh has made it clear that doors for talks are still open provided the ULFA abjures the path of violence.
- As many as 87 persons, 83 civilians and 4 security personnel, were killed in violence by militant outfits in Assam in the month of January (2007) alone.
- In Jan 2007, ULFA and KLNLF militants triggered 28 explosions in the different parts of the Karbi Anglong district of the State, killing 12 civilians and four security personnel.
- The police, Army and paramilitary forces, operating under a unified command, played a major role in containing acts of violence by the militant outfits.
- Altogether, 459 persons have been killed and nearly 13,530 injured in ULFA related violence since 2001 in the State.

ULFA Threatens to Step up Attacks: 8 Mar 2007

In a statement issued on 8 Mar 2007 in Guwahati, the outlawed outfit has threatend to step up attacks as the Centre and the State are reluctant for a political solution to the decades-old conflict in Assam. "We are compelled to continue our armed struggle to achieve our goal of sovereign Assam," it said. Referring to the initiative of the noted Assamese author Dr. Indira Goswami, ULFA alleged Government was not sincere to resolve the conflict through dialogue.

Ironically, the outfit was brazen enough to reiterate that it believes in political solution to the conflict but government was indulging in harassing the innocent people of the state in the name of counter-insurgency operations.

It also confessed its involvement in 5 March land mine blast in Dhemaji district, meant to target a CRPF vehicle. A local commander of the ULFA told a daily on phone: "It was just the beginning of a fresh round of attacks". The security agencies had already warned of the ULFA offensive in the run-up to "Sainik Divas" it observes every year on 16 March.

One of the main reasons for failure of the Goswami initiative was insistence of ULFA, before the start of the talks, on the release of 5 of its jailed leaders: Bhimkanta Buragohain, Ramu Mech, Mithinga Daimary, Pradip Gogoi and Pranati Deka.

Action Against ULFA: Defence Minister: 20 Mar 2007

Defence Minister AK Antony told the Lok Sabha on 20 Mar 2007 that "during the last two and a half month, the security forces have launched counter-insurgency operation against the outlawed ULFA and as a result 33 of their ultras were killed and 114 injured".[67]

Birthday Musings: 7 Apr 2007

On 7 Apr 1979, five likeminded youngmen met at the historic Rangghar, an amphitheatre of the erstwhile Ahom royalty in Sibsagar district of eastern Assam. After hours of confabulations on the lawn of the two-storeyed oval-shaped pavillion, the five men conceived the idea of "liberating the State from colonial clutches of Indian imperialism" through armed struggle.

Today 28 years down the line, the ULFA is not only dubbed as an outlawed terrorist outfit by New Delhi, the group has also graduated to become one of the most dreaded separatist organisations in India's North-East.

The rest is the history already narrated in some detail in this chapter. The outfit refuses to concede that it has lost much-claimed popularity with the Assamese, who seem to here rejected the idea of sovereignty, the central plank of ULFA's constitutional architecture.

It is only the ego of its leaders, Rajkhowa and Barua, particularly of the latter, that comes in the way of its holding direct talks with New Delhi. The latest offer of unconditional talks came from Assam Chief Minister Tarun Gogoi on 27 Mar 2007. Two days later, ULFA through its Chairman snubbed the Government, declaring in an e-mailed statement: "We are not mad to sit for unconditional talks after having lost 10,000 of our freedom fighters in our struggle for independence. The offer of unconditional talks is not acceptable to us."

Let us end, wishing a better sense to the ULFA leadership than reflected in the e-mailed statement.

NOTES

1. Cited by B.C. Verghese, 1997.
2. Dhekiyal Phukan (1829-89), became Sub-Assistant Commissioner in 1850. A friend and admirer of the Baptist Mission in Assam, he regularly wrote for the first Assamese journal, *Orunodoi*. It was largely due to his efforts that Assamese was restored as the official and Court language of Assam in 1873. He had pleaded this cause in his memorandum to Moffat-Mills in 1853.
3. Guha, 1977.
4. Kanaklal Barua (1872-1940), a law graduate, became an Extra Assistant Commissioner in 1900. Later, elected member of Assam's Legislative Council, he was appointed Minister for Local Government. Actively associated with historical research, he served as a member of the Indian Historical Records Commission.

5. Kamala Kanta Bhattacharyya (1855-1936) was the Editor of Assam Hitashi and actively involved in the National Movement; was known for his radical views.
6. Lakshmikant Bezbarua (1864-1938) belonged to the family of personal physicians to the Ahom Kings. Easily the most prolific and influential Assamese writer (novels, plays, short stories and satirical pieces) of modern period, he is known as *Sahityarthi*. He was determined to establish Assamese language (and literature) in its own right, with a rich literary tradition of its own; and engaged in a long debate with those who thought otherwise. He married the grand-daughter of Devendranath Tagore, Prajnasundari Devi.
7. Chandra Sudhir, *Economic and Political Weekly*, Vol. XVII, No. 32, 7-8-1982.
8. Misra, Udayon, 2000.
9. Ambaikagiri Roy-Choudhury (1885-1967) joined the Anarchist Group in 1904 and was interned at Barpeta. He edited *Chetna* from 1918. He was jailed for a year for his joining the Non-Cooperation Movement. He was a front-ranking writer in Assamese.
10. The Cabinet Mission Plan had provided for the division of British Indian provinces into three Groups A, B and C. Group C was to consist of Bengal and Assam. It was an obvious mismatch between the two constituent provinces when it came to taking decisions by a majority in the Group's Legislature, whose membership configuration is given below:

Group C States

		Members	
	General	*Muslim*	*Total*
Bengal	27	33	60
Assam	7	3	10
Total Members	34	36	70

The table shows clearly that Bengal as a political entity and the Muslims as a religious entity, were in a win-win situation. Hence the fears of the Assamese, a hapless minority on all counts.

11. *Ibid.*
12. Misra, Udayon, 2000.
13. See n. 10.
14. Saiyid Muhammad Saadhullah Khan, in all, headed five ministries in Assam at different times during the April 1937-February 1946 period. An Assamese Muslim, he is seen as largely responsible for the large-scale entry and settlement into Assam of Bengali Muslim immigrants from the then (East) Bengal. His "Grow More Food" plan during the World War II was dubbed by Lord Wavell as "Grow More Muslims" plan, in his Diary. In just one year (1939-40), his Government settled Muslim immigrants on 100,000 bighas of land in the Brahmaputra Valley. He understandably supported the Grouping

Plan of the Cabinet Mission, "which would have handed over Assam to Bengal and erase the borders between the two for an unchecked flow of immigrants".

15. Bhuyan, A.C., ed, Political History of Assam, Vol. III, 1978; cited, Misra, Udayon, 2000.
16. Sanjoy Hazarika, 1994, cited by Dinesh Kotwal of IDSA, in his "Contours of Assam Insurgency" in *Strategic Analysis,* March 2001.
17. It was his failure to keep this promise that compelled ULFA's Publicity Director to publicly ask people to boycott, at the pain of death, 1998 Parliamentary Elections (*The Outlook*, 23-2-98). Was it because of this call that Mahanta's AGP did not get a single seat in this Election as well as the one held in October 1999.
18.. Incidentally, it is the same K.P.S. Gill who was once the bete noire of the AASU agitationists, heading the Assam Police as he did during the Agitation, but by that time had become a national hero for turning Punjab back from the brink. But by that time, Mahanta was past the mid-course of his second tenure and no more a political green horn as he obviously was during his first tenure (1996-2001) as Assam's Chief Minister.
19. Why Mahanta did not emulate the simple and straightforward decision of his counterpart in J and K, Farooq Abdullah, who took over the direct command of a similar unified structure in his State, was not comprehensible to the men in uniform, fighting insurgency in the North-East.
20. From published sources and the SF releases.
21. Union Home Minister Indrajit Gupta supplied the information in Lok Sabha on 14 May 1997.
22. Documents seized from the Bodo militants disclosed this information.
23. Earlier Mcneill and Magor; now owned by the BM Khaitan group.
24. They were S.M. Kidwai, then GM, TTL and his deputy, Hamid Haq.
25. For fuller details, see *India Today* of 20-10-1997, *The Outlook* of 27-10-1997, *Indian Express* of 5-10-1997, *The Frontline* of 28 November 1997 and *Sunday Observer* of 21-9-1997.
26. In a self-serving advertisement in the Press, the Government claimed credit for surrender of 4516 ultras, belonging to ULFA (2781), BdSF (1735) and DNSF, etc. (*Hindustan Times,* 28-10-1995). "The Government sanctioned a total of Rs. 3121 lakh for their rehabilitation under 100 per cent margin money schemes.... 876 jobs have also been provided."
27. There were heart-rending scenes at village Nij-Juluki in Nalbari district. The names of 5-member family of ULFA Publicity Secretary Mithinga Daimary (real name Dipak Das) gunned down by SULFA were: Dipak's brother, Dharnidhar Das, a popular doctor in the locality, his pregnant wife Runjyoti, Dipak's mother Phuleshawari, and his sister Latika. Dipak's father was away at his daughter's house (*The Outlook*] 31-8-1998).
28. There was a precedent of a BSF battalion being raised from the ranks of ex-Naga rebels. It gave an excellent account of itself.

29. *The Hindu*, 3-4-1999.
30. *The Frontline*, 4-6-1999.
31. *The Hindu*, 24-4-1999.
32. *Hindustan Times*, 15-11-1999.
33. Gen Sinha in an interview with *The Frontline* issue dated 27-8-1999.
34. *The Frontline*, 27-8-1999.
35. *Ibid.*
36. Barun Das-Gupta, *Hindustan Times*, 15-8-2000.
37. Mahanta had been invited by the Corps Commander for the surrender ceremony for 51 militants held at Tezpur on 24 July 1998. Choosing to be absent, he sent his senior minister Z.N. Sharma to stand in for him. Pray, who was this Minister? He is the same personage against whom Army had registered a FIR in October 1997. What was Mahanta trying to convey through his absence? Again, why should he detail of all ministers in his cabinet Z.N. Sharma to represent him? Again, perhaps, it is not so subtle a message to the Army!
38. 315 of these have been rehabilitated, Mahanta told the press at Shillong on 23 January 2000 (*The Hindu*, 24-1-2000).
39. This is the BSF figure; cited by Dinesh Kotwal in his IDSA Paper dated 18-11-2000.
40. Barua gave interview to the *Asamiya Pratidin*: cited by Samudra Gupta Kashyap in *Indian Express*, 3-1-2001.
41. *Hindustan Times*, 18-1-2001.
42. The existence of Manipuri settlements in Bangladesh, especially in Sylhet district, had helped to establish these links. Reports indicated that the "hide-outs and training camps of the Manipuri insurgents exist in Srimangal, Bhanugarh and Dhamai areas, close to one another. Interrogation reports of arrested ULFA activists, some of which have been published, confirm these facts.
43. It was around the time (1992) when ULFA Chairman had written to Prime Minister Rao offering talks but carefully prefaced schedule for the talks and an eventual deal got bogged down subsequently.
44. *The Frontline*, 11-2-1994.
45. Unable to explain his participating in public protest against his own Government, Mazumdar simply replied: "Governor's speech at Bongaigaon has left me with no other alternative" whatever that might mean!
46. *Times of India* 19-12-2000.
47. Against this report of the respected *Frontline* fortnightly, the so-called national daily, *Hindustan Times*, mentions Paresh Barua's house being in Tinsukia district. This much for the care and attention the 'venerable' press brings to bear on a matter of fact concerning the location of the house of

very important—if not the most important, which perhaps he is—ULFA leader!

48. In this regard, it might be apt to mention here that ULFA had received a big jolt earlier in the year with the arrest of top leader Chitra Dehengia and the busting of its Central Publicity Office in a mid-night swoop on 7-8 January (2000) in Shillong.
49. Gen Sinha's interview to the *Assam Tribune* of 24-4-2000.
50. He was addressing the IAS officers course at the India International Centre, cited by Dinesh Kotwal, in his IDSA Paper dated 18 November 2000.
51. *Assam Tribune*, 8-9-2000.
52. *Hindustan Times*. 8-6-2002.
53. Cited by *The Outlook*, 20-4-1998.
54. Passing through Kolkata on his way to Thimpu on 2 December 2001, Bhutan's Home Minister Lyonpo Thinley Gyamtsho told *Frontline* (4-1-2002) that ULFA alone had 9 camps in Southern Bhutan. ULFA had agreed to close 4 of the camps by December 2001. "At the other 5, they will reduce the s]trength by now and eventually close them as well."
55. *The Frontline*, 4-1-2002.
56. *The Hindu*, 8-12-2001.
57. *The Hindu*, 14-6-2002.
58. *Indian Express*, 12-7-2002.
59. *Hindustan Times*, 5-6-2002.
60. *Indian Express*, 1-4-2002.
61. *Indian Express*, 7.11.2006.
62. *Ibid.*
63. Verghese K. George, *Indian Express*, 7.11.2006.
64. Rahul Singh and Rahul Karmakar (*Dinjan*, Tinsukia/Guwahati), *Hindustan Times*, 12 Jan 2007.
65. Manoj Anand, *Asian Age*, 23 Mar 2007.
66. Editorial, *The Statesman*, 25 Jan 2007.
67. All India Radio, 21 Mar 2007.

5

Bodos : Struggle for Bodoland

"Bodos are presently running one of the oldest ethnic movements in Assam." It has had a chequered history since its very inception: sometimes intense, then rather quiescent, and yet again, occasionally lapsing into horribly violent phase, before returning to a comparatively peaceful mode. But in the recent times, somewhere along the way the Movement has spawned militant outfits to further its cause, which are BdSF, BLT and NDFB. But to the dismay and chagrin of all concerned, the last-mentioned has developed into a virulently secessionist movement. This Chapter traces the history of Bodoland Movement and acts of terrorism by these outfits.

Bodos in History

The Bodo "problem" and subsequent insurgency is of comparatively recent origin. Since the 1970s, sections of this ethnic group have been "trying to regain the old glory when the Bodos ruled the valley unchallenged for centuries".

For a proper perspective on the issue, it is necessary to know the past of the Bodos, and their present economic, social, political, linguistic and cultural condition, compared to other tribal groups in the region.

Belonging to the great Mongoloid stock, the Bodos are often known as Kacharis, particularly among the non-Bodos,. But they themselves prefer the term 'Bodo'. The term 'Bodo' is a genus of large number of ethnic communities like the Boros, Boro-Kacharis, Sonowal-Kacharis, Thangal-Kacharis, Deuries, Rabhas, Tiwas, Misings, Mechs, Dimasas, Hojais, Karbis and the Barmans (of Cachar). But presently the term generally embraces the Bodos, the Boro-Kacharis and the Mechs.

They had once established a prosperous kingdom, centred round Dimapur. Under pressure from the neighbouring rulers, the capital had to be shifted to Maibong (in North Cachar district), and finally to Khaspur (in Cachar district). The historians aver that this kingdom belonged to the Dimasa-

Kacharis, rather than to the Bodos. In the pre-historic times (Mahabharata period, to be specific), the Kacharis are credited to have established two kingdoms in the Brahmaputra Valley, viz, Bana's at Sonitpur and Narakasur's at Pragjyotishpur. The Koch-Rajbongshis, who later demanded a ST status, once had established a kingdom covering Western Assam and Northern Bengal areas, but they refuse to be identified with the Bodo-Kacharis, any more.

It is admitted today that the Bodos once were a prosperous, cultured and distinct identity (nationality). In the past, their language was fairly advanced, with a strong grammatical base. Even up to the 1960s, it was known as dowan (spoken language alone). The strength of Bodo kingdom and their language can be judged by the fact that the Bodo names of the places and rivers survived the influence of the six-century long Ahom rule. The scholars hold that the Aryans and the Bodos (of the Mongoloid stock) have borrowed from each other and enriched each other in the fields of religious beliefs, cultures and languages. So the mythological war of Hari-Hara and the Rig Vedic Sukta 191/10 are indicative of the amalgamation of the two races, some kind of a melting pot phenomenon.

The majority of Bodos is still Hindu. They nurture a feeling of having been exploited and discriminated against by the so-called Assamese society, a justification for their movement for a separate state.

The Bodos and Aryans are not autochthonous communities. But the former claim they are the first comers, and hence entitled to a better share of land and resources.

The supremacy the Bodos enjoyed could not be sustained for the last few centuries. The sociologists ascribe this decline to the family-based rice-liquor consumption, rendering them less energetic, complacent and fatalistic. Consequently, the men-folk lost their work-culture. The ethnic resurgence among them in the recent years is attributed to the realisation that such liquor consumption has been their social enemy. So the youth has been forsaking it. This single point analysis is rather narrowly focused. There are other reasons for the political consciousness, compelling them to seek a place for themselves under the sun, which are summed up below:

1. There has been widespread expansion of educational institutions among them. Census data show that the literacy among the tribals (and the Bodos are their major segment) rose from 18 per cent in 1961 to 49.14 per cent in 1991; and the comparative figures for males were 28.39 per cent and 59.82 per cent, and for females 6.64 per cent and 38.99 per cent. This rate of spread of literacy among them is higher than the state average.

2. The Bodo Sahitya Sabha and Tribal Sangha played an important part to usher in an era of revivalism and self-regeneration, knitting them into a united community.
3. Restoring the Bodo language to a place of pride, and making it medium of education for the Bodo children. It made them conscious of their cultural heritage.
4. Scholarly research restored intrinsic glory to the Bodo history and their past achievements became better known. The British scholars had made great contributions in this field. The discovery and study of the historic fort at Dimapur is a shining example of this contribution.
5. The demographic concentrations of the Bodos in certain parts, spread in the large areas of the State, proved their strength. The population clustering of the Bodos on the north bank of the Brahmaputra could be cited in this connection. The Bodos are seen in all districts of the State, but are essentially concentrated in the area between the rivers Sankosh in Kokrajhar and Dhubri districts and the Orang in the Darrang district. This area is constituted by the districts wholly or partly—of Kokrajhar, Bongaigaon, Barpeta, Nalbari (northern parts), Kamrup (Rangia subdivision), and Darrang (northern parts). There is a total of 23 Development Blocks where the tribal population is more concentrated.[1] Of the total of 2494 villages, with tribal population, there are 300 with 100 per cent tribal population and 821 with predominantly tribal population between 50 and 100 per cent.
6. Starting with the mid-19th century, outsiders started entering Assam. From the early years of the 20th century, tribal lands started coming under pressure of these outsiders, particularly the migrants from the then East Bengal, later East Pakistan, and now Bangladesh. They would occupy vast vacant areas—Khasland, VGR, PGR, or Forest Land in these tracts and settle there. A large number of foreigners were settled on the tribal land under politico-religious considerations, as by Assam's Saadullah Ministry's policy of rehabilitating Bengali agriculturist Muslims there under the garb of Grow More Food campaign during World War II. Obviously, there was resentment at the tribals losing control on their own land. To reassure the tribals, the British had instituted the Inner Line system in the 1870s and in the late 1940s, Assam passed legislation constituting the Tribal Belts and Blocks. All such measures failed to eliminate the threat to the tribal identity as perceived by the Bodos, and their organisations came to the conclusion that Bodo autonomy was the answer to their problems. Hence the Movement.

Having briefly mentioned the environs that generated ethnic and political consciousness among the Bodos to revive their old glory, a look into their distant past should be of interest. They are one of the original settlers of the Brahmaputra Valley, and are reputed to have brought settled agriculture to the Region as also introduced silk weaving to it. They obviously had a glorious past, with a kingdom over the Brahmaputra Valley, down to North Bengal, Cachar Hills, Sylhet and Tripura. They had their colonies near the streams, water (di, being their word for it), hence the Bodo names like Dikhu, Diphu, Dihang, Dibru and also Tista or Dista: Grierson also mentions about Mech rule, in Pragjyotishpur for over 4000 years which began to decline by the 11th century AD. Bodos are most important Indo-Mongoloid people in East India who marked their physical presence over the entire land mass of Assam (barring eastern parts inhabited by Kuki-Chins, and Khasi and Jaintia Hills) and North and East Bengal. Being of Tibeto-Burman origin, they belong to Tibeto-Chinese Linguistic stock. The Indo-Mongoloids were known to the Vedas, Mahabharata, Ramayana, Kalika Purana, and Yogini Tantra and Kirata, who find prominent mention in the Epics.[2]

They came from areas like China, Tibet, Mongolia and Siberia, but Rev Sydney Endle thinks they are the autochthons of Assam. They ruled under different rulers at different points in time, that is, Kiratas, Asuras, Mlech and Danavas. In the comparatively recent historical times, Bodo kingdom was at zenith during the reign of Koch King Nar Narayan (1540-84). It was after the assassination of Raja Govind Chandra in 1832 that the last Bodo kingdom (in Cachar) was extinguished, with its annexation by the British. It was following this 'demise' that the Bodos started feeling marginalized, and were submerged under other hegemonies. So, not only do they have a proud past, the present Bodo Movement for autonomy (and even sovereignty, as by NDFB) has an ancient ancestry. "Militancy among the Bodos has its roots in the paternalistic attitude of the Assamese Caste Hindu elite", was the more recent cause.

Origin of the Bodo 'National' Identity

It was replacement of Assamese with Bengali in schools and courts in 1937 by the British at the 'instigation' of its Bengali officials that really hurt the 'national' pride of the Assamese. It was during the long protest and agitation against this decision that saw the beginning of rise of the Assamese middle class which finally saw their language restored to its rightful place in 1873. The year 1838 saw the establishment of literary society like the Assamiya Bhasa Unnati Sadhani Sabha which later metamorphosed into Assam Sahitya Sabha (ASS), the harbinger and upholder of the Assamese nationalism, that is, Assamiya identity, which remained unchallenged till about 1920s. There were no dissenting voices. It was the educated elite which led the way in this happy harmony. First graduate among the Bodos of Goalpara, Rup Nath

Brahma, was not only a minister in 1938 Assam Ministry but also was to become President of the History Section of ASS in 1956. Obviously, the Bodos were a part of the happy family till a particular point in time, and the issue of separate identity was not central to their educated elite which was rather taken up with social issues. The idea of separate identity gains importance somewhere in the 1930s-1940s period. The birth of Bodo Sahitya Sabha (BSS) was the culmination of the identity issue. The Bodo elite was well aware and deeply conscious of the ethno-consolidating role of Bodo language.

The large-scale import of outsiders to work the tea gardens of Assam—the tea gardens in Upper Assam alone needed 5,27,000 labour in the opening years—has had far-reaching implications in the history of Assam that is plaguing the state till date. The Bodos today are locked in deadly conflict with the descendants of these importees, for preserving their identity. Perhaps it was to establish this identity that the Bodos exhibited their inclination for the Roman script since 1884 when they came in contact with the missionaries; and particularly since the publication of an authentic monograph. The Kacharis, in 1911 by Endle wherein he narrated some Bodo folk tales in Roman script with analogous English translation. And that inclination played a crucial role in fostering and sustaining the Bodo movement in the post-Independence India, based on and informed as it is by the emphasis on their separate identity.

Birth of Brahmaism. The beginning of the 20th century, is significant because of the emergence of the Bodo middle class, though meagre in number, they had certain level of formal education. During the British rule, the middle class grew from the external compulsion of conquest and the need for playing a role, even, if subservient, in the conqueror-conquered relationship at several strategic but still comparatively minor points. But more importantly, there was also an external factor at play. It was the Vedic Movement under the guidance of Kalicharan Brahmachari in 1907. It saw the growth of a small middle class among the adherents of the new faith who adopted the suffix 'Brahma after their name. Born Kalicharan Mech in April 1860 at Kazagaon in Dhubri Sub-division, he was the preceptor and leader of the Brahma Movement, dedicating his life for the upliftment of his backward community. The opening of the East Bengal State Railway branch line from Calcutta to Dhubri in 1902 facilitated his frequent trips to Calcutta whence he came in contact with Srimat Param Hansa Sibnarayan Swamy who finally initiated him in 1907. Thus it was that Kalicharan Mech became 'Brahma' and also started preaching the tenets of Brahmaism. He emphasised that education was a must for socio-economic upliftment of Bodos. The establishment of a Bodo hostel at Dhubri was a natural step and expectedly, it became a centre for Bodo intellectuals. In 1919 was formed the Bodo Chhatra Sanmelan.

Finally, the Bodo Mahasanmelan became the main platform for activities of Bodo intellectuals, Jadavchandra Khokhlary being its first President.

Mahasanmelan's third conference adopted certain measures for social reforms: (1) Bride price lowered to Rs. 51. (2) Restrictions on women going to market removed. (3) Marriage by capture banned. More importantly, over 3000 youngmen took the oath to abide by such injunction. People were encouraged to take to trade and business in agricultural produce. Kalicharan organised the Brahma Company. Trade relations were developed with Bengal. The attempt first and last among the Bodos failed.

The position of the areas and tribes declared 'backward' under Section 52(A) of Government of India Act, 1919 was to be examined by the Simon Commission which had called the representatives of the Primitive and Backward Tribes to Shillong on 4 January 1929 for submitting their memoranda on the subject. Bodo leaders' aspirations to be identified as a separate 'nation' were manifest in the memorandum submitted by the Plains Tribals of Assam in 1929, and it is the year some analysts feel the modern Bodo movement may have started from. Here are some important points from the memorandum:

1. "In spite of our glorious past, we are not getting our due. We oppose mixed electorate because of which we have no representatives in the Legislative Council.
2. "In spite of our large numbers, all advantages of reforms are being enjoyed by a Brahmin, a Kshatriya, or a Sudra.
3. "Of the four seats for Assam in Central Legislature, one is earmarked for Muslims and three for non-Muslims; one out of the latter must be reserved for Bodos.
4. "We oppose the merger of Goalpara into Bengal. We Bodos can by no means call ourselves other than the Assamese.[3]
5. "We demand compulsory primary education.
6. "We must get share of political power through representation in the Council as also in local bodies.[4]
7. "Historically and traditionally, the Bodos stood on a very high level and socially, they enjoyed splendid isolation. But educationally and politically, they are backward, having fallen on evil days.
8. "Indians are fit for self-Government. Dyarchy is unworkable.... The provincial autonomy should be granted immediately."

MOVEMENT FOR IDENTITY

Bodo Movement : Phase I : 1930-67

Bodo elite, growing with the post-1919 Act reforms, had developed a political mind during the 1920s but failed to make any tangible gains for some years. In their 1929 Memorandum, they blamed the existing stratification in the Hindu society for their problems. Andrew Clow, Governor of Assam (1942-46), was making the same point, perhaps with some bias: "The Assamese, both caste Hindus and Muslims, professed solicitude for the tribes, but neither had studied the question nor any real sympathy with them. The feeling of deprivation among these communities thus fostered the growth of local organisations, i.e., the Kachari Sanmilan, Koch Rajbongshi Sanmilan, Chutia Sanmilan, Muttock Association, etc. throughout the Province. Initially, they all functioned independently...., but in 1933 joined hands to form All Assam Plains Tribes League (AAPTL, TL for short)."

In 1933, TL held its first session at Nagaon under the Presidentship of Jadav Chandra Khokhlari. Bhimbar (B.B.) Deuri attended the session, first time entering the direct politics. The same year, Deuri community was recognised as one of the Plains Tribes of Assam. The 1935 Act proved the turning point for the Plains Tribals of Assam, as five seats were reserved for them in the State Legislative Assembly under it. B.B. Deuri became a prominent spokesman of the Plains Tribals. By now tribal land was coming under serious onslaught from the immigrants, and also to an extent, from the local non-tribal traders, businessmen, and moneylenders. TL was fighting desperately against this occupation of their land by non-tribals. TL had joined the Saadullah-led Assam United Party Government[5] in 1937, but revolted against his pro-immigrants policies. When consequently, the Congress formed its first Ministry in September 1938 under G.N. Bordoloi after Saadullah's resignation[6], the TL made an agreement with it, as Bordoloi's proposals for protective system for tribal belts, known as Line System, to safeguard the tribal lands against encroachment by the immigrants, earned their approval. But when Bordoloi resigned in the wake of Britain joining World War II, Saadullah again succeeded to win the support of TL leaders on 10 March 1940 and formed his third Government in Assam,[7] agreeing to abide by the Line System. But his pro-immigrants policy and handling of the Line System caused anxiety amongst the tribals. The total rupture came when Saadullah supported the Cabinet Mission Plan of including Assam with Bengal in Group C. Tribals opposed it vehemently: "We are culturally more akin to Assamese than Bengalis." At fifth session of TL at Mangaldoi, they withdrew support from Muslim League. Both Rupnath and Deuri joined the Congress Party in July 1946, under an agreement. The TL stood transformed into Tribal Sangh (TS), a socio-cultural organisation. The well-meaning Assam Land and Regulation (Amendment) Act of 1947 created 33 reserved belts and blocks in Assam to protect the tribal lands against alienation and encroachment by the outsiders. But unfortunately, the Act proved inadequate for the intended purposes. The widening hiatus between the Congress and non-Congress Bodo leaders became glaringly painful when the former nominated Dharnidhar Basumatari for the Lok Sabha seat. It was perhaps first attempt by political parties at dividing the tribals, which was to become a pattern in the later years. Bodo leaders became painfully aware that if their joining hands with the Muslim League and Congress from time to time during pre-1947 India had gained them nothing, the experience was no different in the Independent India. They were convinced that the Congress Party failed to show sufficient urgency to keep its promise of safeguarding the interests of the tribals. They regretted the conversion of the TL into. TS, as the move had frozen the Bodo political activities for two decades till 1967 when they created the Plains Tribal Council of Assam (PTCA). To PTCA goes the credit of being the first Bodo organisation to demand Bodo autonomy, a separate homeland for Bodos, howsoever nebulous the concept at that stage! Side by side stood the Bodo intellectuals, already engaged in raising the community (identity) consciousness among them. They had (already) established a Brahma Boarding School at Dhubri and founded the Bodo Club which proved to be the mother of Bodo Sahitya Sabha (BSS), established in 1952. BSS was to play a vanguard role in awakening and fostering self-respect and identity consciousness among the Bodos in the decades to come.

Bodo Movement: Phase II : 1967-87

In the face of persistent demand for autonomy by various groups, Prime Minister Indira Gandhi offered to reorganise Assam on the basis of a federal structure on 13 January 1967. The Assam students opposed it but the ABSU formed on 15 January 1967 welcomed the move and in fact, wanted a homeland for Bodos in the plains of Assam. It was in fact with active support of ABSU that the PTCA was formed on 27 February under Presidentship Modoram Brahma, to formulate a suitable response to Mrs Gandhi's proposal. Subsequently, PTCA demanded an autonomous region in the shape of a UT, called Udayachal for Plains Tribals of Assam including Bodos. On 19 May 1968, BSS demanded introduction of Bodo as medium of instruction upto Secondary stage. The demand was conceded, effective 23 September 1968. Thus, not only PTCA, mostly led by the Bodos, was the first to seek autonomy in 1967,[8] the Bodos themselves were the first to win the case for their language to be media of instruction in 1968. Here lies the rub and an important fact of political life: The language is a potent weapon in the hands of communities to further their political cause including exclusivity, separatism and even secession. And Bodos had learnt their lesson from the Assamese themselves who had launched a long agitation against the decision of the British to replace Assamese by Bengali in 1837 in courts and administration. 35-year struggle by the Assamese compelled the British Government in Assam to restore Assamese in the Courts in 1872, and in education department a year later. Coerced by the Assam Sahitya Sabha, Assam Government passed the Official Language Bill of 1960, under which Assamese was declared the sole official language of state. Some analysts feel this declaration led to the unraveling of composite Assam, which ended only with the Parliament passing the North-Eastern States (Reorganisation) Bill 1971. With it, the Region stood divided into 5 States and two Union Territories—Assam being just one among the Seven. But this did not stop the PTCA in its tracks. It stood by its demand for the UT status in 1972, and in the same year BSS launched a movement for Roman script for Bodo language. When PTCA held its session at BACinadi on 20 April 1973, the Assamese press and politicians, sensing a threat to Assam's integrity, accused the Plains Tribals of "getting money from CIA". Incensed by the charge, the Bodo leaders were more firmly set on their demand. On 9 October 1973, Assam's Plains and Hill leaders met Mrs Gandhi in Guwahati and pressed their case for UT and Roman script. In April 1975, she offered Devnagri script and it was accepted by the BSS and ABSU. With the language issue out of the way, the movement for Udayachal (as a UT) was intensified.

The Emergency (1975-77) put a freeze on all activity, and when it was lifted, PTCA entered into an alliance with Janata Party on 4 June 1977 to contest forthcoming Parliamentary Elections. The PTCA won only one (Kokrajhar) seat but enough votes otherwise to win recognition from the Election Commission as a regional party. In the 1983 elections for the Sixth Assembly, it won four seats of the nine contested and joined the Golap Borbora Coalition Ministry, with Samar Brahma Choudhury becoming (Cabinet) Minister for Forests. The 1985 Elections saw a set back for PTCA, with only Charan Narzary returning to Assembly and Samar Brahma Choudhury to Lok Sabha. When the latter demanded Autonomous Region for the Plains Tribals, not the UT, ABSU staunchly opposed it, wanting nothing short of UT. PTCA was on a down slide thence on. After 1985 Elections, it got split into PTCA and PTCA-P (Progressive), the latter advocating Mishing Bodoland. This election put AGP, political face of AASU, into power. So then on, ABSU was fighting its battles with its one-time comrades-in-arms of the 1979-85 anti-foreigners movement.

For a while in 1984, there appeared on the horizon United Tribals Nation Liberation Front (UTNLF). Expectedly, it spawned United Bodo National Liberation Front (UBNLF). Both the outfits disappeared gradually as the ABSU became more effective.

Surprisingly, signing of Assam Accord on 15 August 1985 did not bring peace to the State. If the Bodos and Karbis were demanding Bodoland and an autonomous state within Assam (later UT), the ULFA wanted outright Independence. It should be interesting to see what led to the Bodoland demand. It was not the issue of identity crisis to begin with, but the language that stirred the Bodo heart, which in turn was impelled by the State Government's decisions in 1960 (Official Language Bill) and 1972 (Assamese as Medium of Instructions Bill). But the Bodos got what they wanted in 1968 (Bodos as the medium of instruction) and 1975 (Hindi script). But these very successes goaded them to other demands. PTCA had been demanding only UT status, but with its decline post-1985 elections, leadership devolved on the Bodos. The urges and aspirations of the ethnic Bodos were the underlying cause, and the apparent success of the youthful AASU in its Movement, had further fired their immigration. Later, it was a question of upping the ante. If Assam students could, why not the Bodo students?

Bodo Movement : Phase III : 1987-93

Formed in 1967, the ABSU Movement took a new turn with the election of Upendra Nath (Upen) Brahma as its President in 1987. He had impressive academic attainments: Physics Honours graduate, MSc in Physics, and Law student of Guwahati University. Till a certain stage, ABSU was supporter and part of the AASU Agitation and Upen, as a student of Cotton College, Guwahati, had closely seen and studied the AASU leaders in action. He now led ABSU Movement on same lines, becoming its moving force. Bodo elite turned to him. They had observed with dismay the Assamese 'Chauvinism' under their 'caste Hindu leaders'. Within a year, Brahma's ABSU gained near complete hold, kind of 'civil hegemony', over large sections of Bodo society. This obviously alarmed the UTNLF and AGP. With its policies and fiasco in 1985 polls, PTCA had been marginalized. Brahma and his ABSU became the prime movers of the Bodo Movement.

Brahma decided to launch a democratic mass revolution on the Gandhian non-violent ways on 2 March 1987; aimed at a separate State of Bodoland by 1990, dividing Assam on 50:50 basis. It was to be a Bodoland within Indian union, not within Assam. ABSU presented a memorandum to Governor B.N. Singh and Chief Minister Mahanta on 1 April 1987, containing a 92-point charter of demands.[9] They raised a volunteer force under Phukan Ch. Baro as Chairman and Anchula Gwra Bodosa as Convener for this peaceful movement, which did not remain so for long.

On 19 June, ABSU held a huge Bodo rally at the Judges Field, Guwahati its first for a separate state. The returning students were attacked by mobs, when a Sujit Narzari was killed, becoming the first Bodo martyr to the cause. The ABSU had by then got the support of the Mishings, Deuris, Lalungs and Rabhas, convincing them "that the separation would help all of us". This single death put the ABSU on an agitationists path, well and truly, as the following events show:

1. 21 July. Public protest through mass hunger strikes and mass religious prayers; followed by oath-taking sessions.

2. 27 August. 12-hour tribal area bandh and 24-hour National Highway blockade at Lailangpara, near Rowta Chirali in Darrang district.
3. During August, large-scale arrests of ABSU activists.
4. 9 September. State-wide ABSU 'band' attracted suppressive measures by AGP Government and AASU.
5. 24-25 September. 36-hour tribal area bandh.

The year 1987 saw 15-phases of ABSU Movement. The same year it also draw some support, even if indirect, from UMF, Congress (I), UTNLF and Lok Dal (B). May be, they all wanted to spite the AGP. The United Reservation Movement's Council, floated by the foursome, launched a padayatra, starting from Dhubri and Sadiya, and the two columns converged on Guwahad to hold a protest rally at the Judges Field.

The year 1988 saw more phases of the agitation. (1) 27 April. 72-hour Assam bandh: 20th Phase: ABSU starts losing faith in democratic ways. (2) 21 May. ABSU holds joint meeting with All Assam Koch-Rajbongshi Kshatriya Sanmilani (AAKRKS) to garner support for their movement. (3) 4 June. 180-hour Rail Roko bandh, accompanied by bomb blasts. Violence was in the air. (4) Mahanta holds talks with Brahma. No results. (5) July. All Cachar-Karimganj Students Union (ACKSU) and All Assam Minorities Students Union (AAMSU) extended support to ABSU, as they too were opposed to the process of Assamisation pursued by AGP Government. This show of unity riled the Government and Assamese in general. (6) 28 August. Joint meeting of ABSU, ACKSU and AAMSU. They worked out a common programme of 50-hour Rail Roko in Assam (for September) and further bandhs and Rail Rokos (for October). (7) September-October. All Assam Tribals Students Union (AATSU) and Tribal Students Federation (TSF) also declared their support for ABSU. The Movement was now entering (perhaps, had already entered) a militant phase.

The formation of a new Bodo body, Bodo People's Action Committee (BPAC), was an important landmark of the year 1988, with the aim of mobilizing all people in Bodoland. Actually, it adopted militant practices, viz, armed training for its cadres, and acquisition of arms and ammunition, of which there was plenty, particularly of local manufacture variety. BPAC thus turned out to be an armed wing of ABSU, Brahma Group, its main faction; the other was led by Ramsiary. BPAC adopted terrorist methods not only against the non-tribals living in the mixed population villages of Dhubri, Kokrajhar, Barpeta, Nalbari, Darrang and Sonitpur districts but also against the political rivals like BPTC, which though in decline, still claimed the support of all Plains Tribals, including Bodos.

Thus by 1988, ABSU (Brahma) had emerged as a force to reckon with. An eminent Assamese had put it aptly: "Presently, the ABSU is ruling the roost in the tribal areas as did AASU in Brahmaputra Valley during the Assam Movement, 1979-85."[10]

In March 1988, BPAC and ABSU had started movement for a separate Bodoland on the North Bank, spread from River Sankosh to Sadiya, over an area of 25,478 km^2, with a population of 4.47 million with 51 per cent Bodo majority. They had two additional demands: (1) Creation of two autonomous districts of Neelachal and Lalung on the South Bank. (2) Notification as STs of Bodo-Kachari groups living in Karbi Anglong district. They wanted Bodoland to be created as a UT initially, being elevated to statehood subsequently. When reminded of lack contiguity in the proposed State, they promptly pointed out to the precedent of Goa, Daman and Deo. This detail was essential to follow the contours of the demand and the movement to attain it. The demand[11] touched the ten districts of Assam: Dhubri, Kokrajhar, Bongaigaon, Barpeta, Nalbari, Kamrup, Darrang, Sonitpur, Lakhimpur and Dhemaji; with a total population of 11,238,965 as per 1991 Census, against Assam's total of 22,294,565. Bodoland was sought to be created out of these ten districts.

The 19-22 December Bashbari conference was another landmark of 1988, as ABSU and BPAC had gathered on a public platform for the first time, and also because it was attended by other organisations like the TSF, ACKSU, TUJS, Tripura Sundari Nari Bahini (TSNB) and All Jharkhand Students Union (AJSU). An important decision it took was to suspend 89 demands from the 92-point charter mentioned above, leaving only three political demands; the most important being creation of Bodoland as a full-fledged state. Mahanta categorically ruled out any "further fragmentation of Assam", and Prime Minister Rajiv Gandhi concurred. So fat was in the fire! ABSU charged PTCA[12] and AGP Government of conspiracy to crush 2-year old Bodo Movement.

ABSU had suspended the Movement on 30 October 1988 "to create peaceful atmosphere for discussions". All the tribal organisations of Assam convened a conference on 16-17 January 1989 to analyse political situation, under the chairmanship of Samar Brahma Choudhury. The participants were disturbed over the violence in state. ABSU and UBNLF chose to stay away. Expectedly, ABSU resumed its agitation in February 1989.

Before resuming the chronology of the Movement, a brief mention of some of the memoranda submitted by its protagonists should be of interest:

1. Earliest memorandum dated 20 May 1967 by PTCA was to President Zakir Hussain. It was signed by various PTCA leaders, viz; Biruchan Doley, BSc, LLB, President; Samar Brahma Chaudhury BA, Vice-President; Charan Narzary, MA, LLB, General Secretary, and Praful

Kumar Bhabara, BA (Hons) and Ajit Kumar Basumatari, both Joint Secretaries. They had attached following documents with the memorandum:

(a) Agreement between AAPTL and Assam Congress of 10 September 1939, Shillong.

(b) Agreement between AAPTL and Assam Muslim League, signed with Sir Saadullah, then Prime Minister of Assam.

(c) Memorandum of 20 March 1947, by Assam Tribal League submitted to the Constituent Assembly of India and Supplement submitted to its Minority Advisory Committee.

(*d*) Memorandum by *Assam Tribal Sangh* before U.N. Dhebar, Chairman, Scheduled Areas and STs Commission of India, 1960-61.

2. ABSU leaders presented on 22 January 1987 a number of documents to the Government to justify UT status for the Plains Tribals on North Bank for "all-round security and development of Bodos".

3. The Memorandum dated 23 August 1987 demanding 50:50 division of Assam. It had a list of 53 Questions and Answers, couched in rhetorical flourish!

4. ABSU presented their case in a booklet (perhaps, 'pamphlet', or even 'tract' would be better word to describe it) dated 10-11-1987 to the President, Prime Minister, and Home Minister. All manner of condemnation, and criticism were handed down to the Assamese people for their acts of commission and omission. At the end, it was signed as under:

GWJW NTH WNG[13]

Sincerely Yours

New Delhi
Date 10-11-87

For and on behalf of ABSU
Upender Nath Brahma
President, ABSU
Rabi Ram Brahma
General Secretary

1989

There were two long bandhs: for 120 hours on 16 February and 175 hours on 2 March.

During the year, terrorist activities in Kokrajhar district were on the increase. Meanwhile, the emergence of Congress(I) Ministries in Tripura, Meghalaya, Nagaland, Mizoram, Manipur and Arunachal had changed the political landscape in the North-East. AGP Government itself was tottering due to violent depredations committed by ULFA and BdSF, and the Party was being wracked by internal squabbling. The opposition to the Movement was rising. Abdul Muhib Mojumdar, Dy Leader, Congress Legislature Party, wrote to Rajiy Gandhi on 29 January, asking him to concede to the ABSU in Assam a Darjeeling-type disposition in West Bengal. The Government had held two abortive talks (26 June 1988 and 11 January 1989) with ABSU, the latter being represented by its Shillong-based Vice-President, Pradeep Kumar Daimary.

BdSF Appears on the Scene

Meanwhile, the BdSF had come into prominence. For record, it was constituted on 3 October 1986 at Odal Khasibari village in Darrang district, "to liberate the Mongoloid-dominated Indo-Burma Region. Like ULFA, it was a secessionist outfit, having no use for peaceful means. A year later, failing to get its demands acceded to, the frustrated Bodo leadership started preparing for a bitter battle. It raised Bodo Volunteer Force (BVF) under Prem Singh (P.S.) Brahma, as its military chief. Now there were two Bodo armed outfits, and an internecine conflict was inevitable. The ULFA stepped in to help its rival BdSF under Ranjan Daimary; and it later joined hands with the KIA (in Burma) and the NSCN(I-M). This hostility between the two Bodo outfits was to dog the movement for long, and entailed a heavy human cost.

It is relevant to mention here that the Bodos had been exposed to elements of the guerrilla tactics as far back as 1962 when the Special Security Bureau (SSB), established in the wake of Sino-Indian war, set up training camps at Halflong, Chakrata, etc.[14] Typical of the Indian political ethos, its opponents later accused the Congress of building up the BdSF through Central Intelligence Agencies as a counter to both ULFA and the AGP. And the Forum for Restoration of Civil Liberties, in a letter to the Prime Minister, said so in so many words:

1. "RAW was involved in Bodo agitation, and supplying weapons to them. They were targeting only *Assamese* and *Assam Police*, none others.

2. "SSB was imparting training to the ABSU extremists.

3. "SFF (Special Frontier Force) was directly involved in conducting bomb attacks in different parts of *Northern Assam*.... 'SFF was a secret agency of the Cabinet Secretariat and its most recruits were *Tibetans* and *Khampas*.' They were inducted into Assam to help Bodo extremists, and they resembled them.... *Assam* Police seized large quantities of explosives whose sophisticated variety showed that the source of supply could only be the Government."

The Forum did not disclose the source of such serious allegations, against the State and its agencies and the latter did not react as is the practice in such cases. This is the liberty run riot, indeed! But one wonders if the democracies can afford, or even survive, such unbridled freedom to malign it in the name of freedom of expression and criticism.

The Talks Begin: August 1989

The first round of talks between the Government of India and ABSU was held on 28 August 1989; by this time, ABSU and PTCA were 'enemies'. Ram Vilas Paswan represented New Delhi at the Second Round on 25 October 1989. It decided to set up a Joint Committee representing the Central and State Governments and ABSU.

The ABSU leadership suffered a big blow when its President, Upen Brahma died young on 1 May 1990. He was succeeded by Sanchuma Khunggur (S.K.) Bwiswmauthiary (also spelt 'Bwismutiary').

The 8th round of talks was held on 11 September 1990, extended up to the 13th. The tripartite Meet decided to set up a 3-member expert committee to demarcate the Bodo areas. When Paswan visited Kokrajhar on 21 October, he was invited to address a 20-lakh strong Bodo rally at Debargaon-Balagaon, whence he was presented a memorandum by ABSU.

Now we enter the period when people got tired of the agitation and the tribal economy, because of the bandhs and rasta roko, was coming to be shattered. "The Central Intelligence Agencies found the AGP Government behind the activities of the AGP." By the end of the 1980s frustration was setting in as evidence of intimidation, extortions, kidnappings and killings had generated anti-Movement sentiment. On the other hand, ABSU and BPAC complained of alienation early 1991. By then, political entities in the field were PTCA, PTCA(P) UTNLF, UBNLF, ABSU and BPAC.

The 3-member Experts Committee under Dr. Bhupinder Singh, IAS, was set up on 25 February 1991 when Assam was still under President's Rule. It submitted its report on 30 March 1992, recommending creation of two Autonomous Councils. The larger one was to be on the western central side, with a population of 1.07 million, predominantly Bodo, with some Rabhas and Sonwals, covering Bodo concentrations in the districts of Dhubri, Kokrajhar. Barpeta, Nalbari, Kamrup and Darrang. The second Autonomous Council, after an intervening gap, to be set up on the eastern side, was to cover the districts of Dhemaji, Lakhimpur and Sonitpur, and consists of Mishings (315,000) and Deuris. ABSU and PTCA rejected the Report. About this time, March 1992, BdSF, raised in October 1986, marked its presence on the violence stakes, killing 6 people including a pregnant woman, in mid-March. It signified recrudescence of Bodo violence after a fairly long lull in 1991. Since it is in the nature of extremist movements to breed more militant bodies, the emergence of the more violently inclined BdSF was no surprise, because of the failure of the Government-ABSU/BPAC talks to produce results, and "inordinately long time taken by the Committee to study the population patterns in the Region and suggest the nature of autonomy for the Plains Tribals". The absence of reliable Census data because of the cancellation of the 1981 Census operations under the AASU threat might have rendered Committee's work more difficult and time consuming. Because of the lack of results from the talks and "inordinate delay in Report", it was natural for people to become frustrated and restive, which eroded the influence of ABSU and BPAC among the people, creating conditions conducive for ascendance of more militant outfits like BdSF. The Bodo movement's history had such precedents. An older, milder organisation like the PTCA, which had reigned supreme for two decades (1967-85) had to yield ground after mid-1980s to ABSU, which modeling itself on AASU, had appeared out of the blue to take charge of the Movement. The PTCA was on the downslide ever since, in particular, after the murder of its well-known leader Samar Brahma Choudhury in August 1992.

By the time the Committee submitted its Report (March 1992), the Congress Government under Saikia was in power, after trouncing Mahanta's AGP in the June 1991 Assembly Poll. After the Bodo leaders rejected the Report, Saikia invited them for fresh talks, where they demanded 4443 villages in nine districts. Some more meetings saw them adding another 209 villages with some Bodo population, and 1035 villages which, as per official records, had no Bodo population at all. Many ding-doing battles later, the Bodo Accord was signed on 20 February 1993. The critics commented: "violence was officially rewarded with the signing of the Accord". The Accord did not solve the Bodo problem, in fact it complicated it further. The Bodo leaders insisted that the Memorandum of 10 November 1987, earlier submitted to Government of India, be made a part of the Bodo Accord. Having allowed it to be attached to the Bodo Accord, on the insistence of the 'intelligent' (or 'clever') Bodo leaders, the Assam and Central Governments would not be able to extricate themselves from the ramifications flowing from the contents of the 1987 Memorandum, as would be seen later. It makes an interesting reading, even if its reasoning may not be too plausible on certain aspects, figures in some cases highly exaggerated, and some parts or statements even incomprehensible. The Memorandum is attached as Appendix at the end of this chapter in a condensed version, but without doing any violence to the over-all integrity of its contents or their essential import. The condensed version is in the original language of the Memorandum.

Bodo Movement Phase IV: February 1993 to End-2000

The 1987 Memorandum was signed by S.K. Bwismutiary and Rabi Ram Brahma. The 1993 Accord was also signed by the Chairman of the BPAC, in addition to these two original signatories. For Assam Government, it was signed by the Additional Chief Secretary, 'in the presence of Rajesh Pilot, Union Minister of State for Home and Chief Minister Saikia. It was obviously signed in a hurry, as at that time neither was the Bodo areas delimited nor its boundary delineated. And these lacunae were to prove its undoing.

On 7 March 1993, Bodoland Autonomous Council (BAC) was inaugurated at a public rally in Kokrajhar. 11 Bodo militants, led by Prem Singh (P.S.) Brahma, Chief of Bodo Volunteer Force (BVF), surrendered with their weapons before Saikia and Pilot. About 2000 followed suit in the coming days. On 8 April, BdSF militants abducted Bolin Bordoloi, TTL executive, and demand a ransom of Rs. 15 crore (He was released 11 months later, night 1-2 March 1994). Bodoland Executive Council (BEC) members were sworn-in on 20 May by Assam's Home Secretary, at Kokrajhar; S.K. Bwismutiary as Chief Executive Member (CEM) and P.S. Brahma as Executive Member (EM); the latter was No. 2 in the BEC. There were two other EMs.

BdSF denounced the Bodo Accord in a statement on 25 May. It bode ill for it. On 1 June, Garla Botha Basumatiary was elected President of the ABSU. The new ABSU Executive dissolved the BPAC and BVF. Bodoland People's Party (BPP) launched at a convention (2-3 July) in Kokrajhar, with S.K. Bwismutiary as President; it signs an agreement on political understanding with Assamese Congress (I). On 12 July, the Bodoland Legislative Party (BLP) is divided on a decision of Assam Government—entrusting Senior Ministers the responsibility to 'look after' the interests of nine constituencies which had returned the Bodo Movement—supporters in June 1991 Poll. "The wily Saikia is already at work."

5 October 1993. Widespread communal riots in Kokrajhar and Bongaigaon districts, leaving 19 dead, almost all of them Muslim. 30,000 fled their homes, seeking shelter in camps. Was it ethnic cleansing, as the riots came in the midst of the apprehensions on the delimitation of the BAC area? Assam Government announces an All-Party Committee to delineate the BAC area on 14 October 1993. After Saikia survives a no-confidence motion on 15 October, the Committee is dissolved. They were obviously playing games (The BLP had supported the no-confidence motion).

Now came the crunch. On 28 October, Assam Government announces unilaterally that the BAC will include 2570 villages. Bwismutiary denounced the decision. He quits as CEM on 16 November. On 20th P.S. Brahma is appointed CEM of the interim BEC. Elections to a Regular BEC was to be held by 20 November, but was not held. The Bodo leadership was obviously split by Saikia's Congress.

On 10 December, Assam Government issues notification, demarcating boundary of the BAC territory, with an area of 5,186 km^2 and 2570 villages. The BAC area was spread across 29 Assembly Constituencies, but the 10 km wide belt in the north touching the international border with Bhutan was not included in it. It had population of 21,37,445, of "which only 38 per cent were the Plains Tribals. Only 1110 villages of its 2570 total enjoyed the tribal majority. All this was bound to spell trouble, at least in future. The 62 per cent non-Bodos were bound to fear the consequences, and they were not wrong as the later events were to prove. Denouncing the notification, ABSU demanded inclusion of the border belt as also additional 515 villages in the BAC.

On 28 December, State Government reconstituted the interim BEC, further marginalising the Bwismutiary faction including R.R. Brahma, former General Secretary of the ABSU under both Upen Brahma and Bwismutiary and one of the signatories to the 1987 Memorandum and 1993 Accord. Thus ended the year 1993, with the ABSU having scored a kind of victory, but badly split subsequently, perhaps consequently.

At 4-6 March 1994 session at Guwahati, Bodo Sahitya Sabha revives its demand for Roman script for their language. BdSF continues abductions and violence: 8 policemen killed in an ambush in Barpeta district on 10 January; 7 persons from 'one community' shot dead in Bongaigaon district; and a tea estate owner abducted. Majority of BLP supports Saikia Government; two dissidents formed a splinter, New BLP, on 4 April.

This is summary of the happenings and mishappenings in the post-Accord one year. Now some other details, BAC was to be a 40-member body: of which 30 were to be reserved for STs; 35 to be elected, and 5 nominated. BAC Bill was introduced in the Assembly on 5 April 1993. Koch-Rajbongshi Community was against the Accord and wanted 'right of self-determination' (to opt out of BAC) because, as it put it, "BAC's 18 lac will include 12 lac who are Koch-Rajbongshis". Its immediate demand was for ST status for itself.[15] The BAC Act, duly passed by the Assembly, was gazetted on 14 May 1993. Then on, Bodo Accord became a football, with P.S. Brahma assuming pro-Saikia stance and Bwismutiary resigning and leading hardline faction against the Accord and Saikia Government. Subsequently, it was a dance of death and destruction as much between the two Bodo outfits as against the unarmed common citizens. If the BPP, ABSU and Bwismutiary wanted more and more villages/areas to be added to the BAC, their opponents, led by BdSF, set their gaze at secession. Bodo Accord was flawed from the beginning. Its signing was hurried through, more because of the game of one-up-manship between the Union Home Minister (S.B. Chavan) and his Deputy, Minister of State (Pilot), and not because of its intrinsic soundness. Saikia later 'claimed' he had warned Pilot against it as the crucial matter of the BAC area had not been settled; and "Pilot however refused to listen and told me the draft had Prime Minister Rao's blessings".

BdSF was on the violent trajectory, 1994 onwards. In the communal riots in May-July 1994, many villages were razed to ground, forcing 5,400 refugees into 26 camps. One such camp was attacked in Barpeta, leaving 52 dead and 113 injured. Coming in the wake of similar carnage in October 1993, it seemed to be aimed at ethnic cleansing. Muslims were the initial target of the Bodo fury, though in the later years, Hindu settlers of East Bengal origin also came to grief. Alarmed by the wanton violence, Army was called out. It launched Operation Karanti in July 1994 against the BdSF in Barpeta district. Its goal eventually was to free the 2.837 km^2 Manas Wildlife sanctuary from the clutches of the BdSF, which had held sway over its vast jungle for the last 8 years. The insurgents had free run over the sanctuary, were operating from the safety of their camps inside Bhutan. Army could not go all out against the terrorists in the sanctuary not only because of its terrain and thick jungle but because of its proximity to the porous and unmanned 400 km border with Bhutan. When chased, they used the sanctuary as a safe passage to reach the hills of Bhutan, out of Indian Army's reach. Still Army had acted vigorously against the militants who had not only killed over 20 officers and men of the Forest Department over the last few years, but also looted large quantity of ivory stored at the Forest office of Barh Bari in Manas. Moving into the Manas on 26 July, 2 days after the Barpeta massacre, the troops had rounded up over 120 BdSF ultras in Phase 1. In the next phase, another 95 were in the BAC, with large quantity of RDX and IEDs.

Acting unilaterally again, Assam Government added 112 villages more to the BAC area. Their total reached 2682, including 2570 announced initially in October 1993. ABSU resented unilateralism; wanted inclusion of all the 515 villages demanded earlier, as also of the border belt; and announced fresh programme of action November 1995 onwards.

Now the situation was worse for peace in the area, which was the prime objective and reason for signing the Accord in the first place. In February 1993, when it was signed, the Bodo Accord was widely hailed as a model for resolving several ongoing sub-nationalist movements in Assam and elsewhere in the North-East. But by October 1995, less than three years from the initial euphoria, the model was not only frayed at the edges, it also looked like a sure recipe for disaster. While the Bodo insurgents had rejected the Accord out of hand, the moderates too got disillusioned by mid-1995 at its tardy implementation. If the moderate leadership was divided down the line by this time, the fault surely lay with themselves, the protagonists of the Bodoland, for allowing themselves to be manipulated by the crafty politicians and State Government. If the ABSU was threatening to revive its original demand for a separate State on the North Bank in 1995, it was to be understood in terms of competitive radicalism of various Bodo groups. The State Government displayed an element of ad hocism in its handling of the Bodo problem, conceding things in driblets, and unilaterally. As per the mutual understanding the election to the BAC was to be held within 6 months of the formation of the Interim BEC (which was done on 20 May 1993). The deadline, 20 November 1993, came and went, without anybody caring or remembering. It has been described above how S.K. Bwismutiary was marginalized, and P.S. Brahma made the GEM in 1993. When P.S. Brahma threatened to withdraw support from the Saikia Government in 1995, posing a direct threat to its life, the 'wily' Chief Minister lost no time to announce holding of elections to the 40-member BAC for 31 October 1995. And in turn, ABSU's above mentioned threat to resume agitation had something to do with these elections 'announced' by Saikia. Known as "sly politician", he forgot all about 31 October elections once he fortified his position with his customary manipulative skills. But why blame Saikia if the credulous Bodo leaders allow themselves to be taken for a ride, or to use a blunt expression, allow them to be fooled, time and again by such self-serving politicians? Nothing illustrates the ironic twists in the situation better than the 16 October 1995 *Times of India* Editorial:

> "When the Bodo leaders made a demand for a separate State during the AGP regime, it was seen by many as counter-weight to the muscle acquired by the AASU. Such is the irony of politics that the AGP today faces a 'social boycott' by AASU and there is no love lost between the Congress and moderate Bodo leaders. If the AASU leaders have fallen out with the brethren, so have ABSU leaders with the Congress, once their strong supporters. While the implementation of both Assam and Bodo has left much to be desired, Mr Saikia has established a record of sorts by granting autonomy to other ethnic groups like Rabhas Karbis, Lalungs and Mishings."

One may ignore Saikia's wiliness, but he certainly can and must be accused of the original sin of permitting himself, a senior Congress leader and Chief Minister of a State, to be bamboozled and coerced into consenting to an Accord, which he knew, very well, would explode in his face because of its inbuilt flaws and infirmities, by a junior but enthusiastic Central Minister just because "it has the approval of the Prime Minister". If he is (was) credited with near-success with ULFA by enticing large number of its cadres into surrender, he is also blamed for not trying hard enough with BdSF for "some ulterior purposes". But all said and done, he did receive overtures for talks from the BdSF in June 1995. Majority of Bodos are Hindus, only 25-40 per cent being Christians who are better educated. The leadership and cadres are Christians who started exerting themselves after the failure of largely Hindu advance guard leadership to show results."[16] "The BdSF is largely recruited from around Udalguri and any communal polarization could further complicate matters."

BdSF was in mood to resile from its stand. In a statement it issued on its 9th Foundation Day on 3 October 1995, it asserted that "It is still committed to armed struggle to secure right of self-determination for Bodos.... It does not accept the Bodo Accord." Obviously, given such hardline positions, no peace could be espied on the horizon. As if to make the point, 7 Bengalis and 1 Bodo were killed violently on 9 October at Kalaiga on the eve of a public rally by a pro-Congress youth group.

The Year 1996 : Bodo-Santhal Violence

There were violent Bodo-Santhal clashes in May 1996. The Bodos claimed the discovery of bodies of three Bodo girls from "a jungle outside the Adivasi (Santhal) village of Satyapur under Gossaigaon PS in Kokrajhar district on 10 May and "burning of several Bodo houses on the night of 10/11 May" (as alleged by Amrit Lal Basumatari, former MLA and former MP) caused these riots. The District Administration insisted that the clashes began only on 15 May, the day AGP Government was sworn-in,[17] and continued for 5 days. Four members[18] of Adivasi Council of Assam claimed that the attackers were Bodos armed with modern weapons, which should be seized. The Bodoland State Movement Committee (BSMC) leader Pramila Rani Brahma, cited Intelligence reports about some Santhal boys arrested in West Bengal trying to procure arms, after "getting armed training in camps". By July, the riots had spread to Dhubri district from Kokrajhar.[19] It was a worst Bodo-Santhal riots,[20] which spread over 2,500 km^2, devastated 75 villages on both sides, rendered 200,000 people homeless, and left 100 dead. "7,000 Santhals fled to West Bengal".[21]

BLTF blew up RCC bridge at Rakholduli in Bongaigaon district on 27 December, cutting off road link between the Region and rest of the country. They planted IEDs in the Brahmaputra Mail; consequent explosions near Sesapani station in Kokrajhar district destroyed 3 coaches and left over 30 dead.

BdSF[22] claimed 98 lives in 1996. It was reported to be the armed wing of the NDFB. "By mid-1990s, it had redesignated itself as the Bodoland Army."

Towards the end of the 1996, BSMC Chairman, S.K. Bwismutiary, and ABSU Vice-President, Anil Basumatary, appealed for a cease-fire between the

Bodo groups. Curiously, then came ULFA, asking BdSF and newly formed BLTF to stop the fratricidal clashes that would benefit only Indian State machinery".[23]

Bodo militant groups killed 260 persons in 1996.[24]

1997: Bodo Militants Continue the Killings

Some of the important cases of sabotage and killings are listed here: (1) Bodo militants caused 42 deaths between January and 7 May 1997.[25] (2) On 9 June, Chief Minister Mahanta had narrow escape when an IED-caused explosion missed his car by a few yards, near the Kamakhya Hill in Guwahati. He was on his way to the office from airfield. The fact that he had returned from Delhi a day before his scheduled date shows how the state apparatus has been penetrated/compromised. There was greater cause for concern. 300-metre wire connected to the IED was laid over the telegraph poles in part and dug underground the rest of its length. It should have been there for days, if not weeks, before it was actuated by a subversive who had ensconced himself in a hut amongst the rest of the inhabitants of the colony. Neither the wire nor the subversive were ever noticed. (3) Rail track blasts on 1 January and 13 August. (4) On 12 and 15 August, 29 non-tribals, mainly Santhals and Bengalis gunned down. The Bengali Tiger Force (BTF) answered by killing Bodos on the 17th. (5) From 1 to 20 July, 17 Army men killed in attacks and IED explosions, launched by NDFB (experts in IED use), NSCN(I-M) and ULFA. Most daring assault was on a Brigade Headquarters under 57 Mtn Div.[26] (6) During 17 June-23 August, 30 Army men including one Brigadier, one Colonel and one Captain, were killed in 10 ambushes laid by ULFA and NDFB separately.

26 July 1997. ABSU Rally at Guwahati. In a memorandum to Assam Governor, Loknath Mishra, ABSU President, Urkhao Gwra Brahma demanded tripartite talks, because "three-year experiment with BAC has failed". People's Democratic Front (PDF), till then for an Autonomous Council, announced: "It is no more for Council as the Government had failed to finalise BAC before June 1997 and Guwahati High Court has ordered State Government not to include in the BAC villages with less than 50 per cent Bodo population. PDF also join in demand for Bodoland" (*Times of India* 27-7-1997).

21 August 1997. State Cabinet decides to demarcate the BAC boundary and hold BAC elections in December 1998. ABC rejects both the proposals as "the BAC experiment has already failed".

September 1997. The United Front Government at the Centre, convinced that previous Government had acted unwisely in the matter, convened this Tripartite Meet, inviting BSMC, ABSU, PDF, Bodo Sahitya Sabha (BSS) and All Bodo Women's Welfare Federation (ABWWF). Representing the hawkish face of BSMC, its Chairman, one time moderate and former President of ABSU,

S.K. Bwismutiary reverted to demanding a full-fledged state of Bodoland, practically embracing the entire area of present Assam north of the Brahmaputra, and creation of two autonomous districts of Neelachal and Lalung. Hearing the extreme voices, the Government proposed setting up a Joint Working Group (JWG) to renegotiate the entire Bodo Accord. JWG was still-born as the Government and Bodo Groups failed to agree on its terms of reference.

To stop fratricidal killings among the Bodo outfits, which had gone on during 1996 and 1997 in Nalbari, Kamrup, Darrang districts, Peace Committees were set up in several districts, comprising representatives of ABSU, BSMC, PDF and BSS.

1998: Events and Incidents

Tripartite Talks: May (25-26) 1998. 50 Bodo leaders from ABSU, BPAC, BSS, ABWWF, All Bodo Employees Federation, etc. attended the Meet, which ended in a deadlock as Bodos insisted on Bodoland State. The Centre and Assam Government urged them to reduce Bodo-Jharkhandi Santhal tensions, which had claimed 50 lives recently. The situation was becoming explosive as the Santhal youth had raised Bisa Commando Force (BCF) and Adivasi Cobra Militant Force" (ACMF) to counter BLTF and NDFB attacks on the Santhal villages. The Meet failed" to address an important issue about the status of Koch-Rajbongshis, second largest group in BAC area, next only to the Bodos. The community, treated as part of the OBC Conglomerate till then, had been agitating for ST status. Soon after the meet ended, BLTF unleashed an orgy of violence. In a span of 3 days in June (2-4), it blew up four road bridges on NH-31 and a rail bridge between Chautara and Gossaigaon, 250 km from Guwahati. Not aimed at killing civilians, they wanted to cut off the North-East from the mainland. Besides the shift in strategy, violence was also a warning to BLTF rival, NDFB which was inclined to respond to efforts of George Fernandes (an activist Minister in the March 1998-April 1999 Vajpayee Government) to bring it to the negotiations table.

Meanwhile, Surojit Mitra, a lawyer who had been able to get the bail for militants with an unerring regularity, had become an overground link with the Bodo outfit. He was shot dead in Guwahati on 13 June 1998, "soon after he came into limelight for arranging a 45-minute telephonic talks between the secessionist NDFB and Fernandes, during the latter's recent visit to Assam". NDFB reportedly shot the mediator for crowing about his "achievement" publicly.[27]

Tripartite Talks of November 1998. Besides the three parties, the Government also invited non-Bodo groups for the meet on Bodoland, making it a "quadripartite talks". Its opponents said the creation of BAC itself was a mistake because Bodos were not in a majority in the area; and Bodos were divided into two rival groups, one demanding a separate State and other a separate Nation (Adivasi Council of Assam). Another non-Bodo group, Gossaigaon Anchalik Committee, an earlier supporter of Bodoland, told the meet they no longer supported the demand as the Bodos had committed heinous crimes in the BAC area. The BAC, headed by its Interim Chairman, Kaneshwar Narzary, had its own demands: (1) Rs. 25 crore for construction of a capital complex. (2) Army should raise a separate Bodo Regiment. The PDF, having a majority of MLAs in Bodo areas, demanded that the talks for Bodoland (they called it Boro Hadot) be held at the Home Minister's level.

Violence Continue. Between April 1997-March 1998, there were 11 cases of track sabotage and 92 Rail Roko and bandh calls. "The things are no better for the year 1998-99 so far" (*The Outlook*, 13-7-1998).

1999: Events and Incidents

In March 1999, Mahanta added another 259 villages to 2682 (original 2570 plus initial addition of 112) already under the BAC. Total now stood at 2941. The notification dated 2 April 1999 asserted that "2941 villages included now were, close to their original demand of 3031". The practice of conceding; demands in driblets seemed to proving a bane rather than balm for the troubled situation, whetting, rather than quenching the thirst. So fully aware how the State Governments surrendered before their violence at successive stages, all Bodo outfits rejected the notification. ABSU President, U.G Brahma said: "347 villages included in the 1996 notification excluded now.... Actually, 356 more villages, as also Rupsi Airport in Dhubri district and Bongaigaon Refinery, should have been included. Manas National Park also excluded, dividing BAC area into two.... We will launch Bodoland State agitation." BSMC MP, S.K. Bwismutiary: "Notification is 2 years too late.... Bodoland should, include area from the Sankosh to Sadiya, in addition to 32 Revenue Circles in the south." PDF General Secretary Gangadhar Ramchiary: "We will not compromise on Bodoland."

BAC challenged the 2 April 1999 notification in Supreme Court. The petition admitted on 1 October said "the Assam Government has issued the Notification, unilaterally deleting 347 villages from BAC area without consulting it, as required under the BAC Act.

Violence Continues. (1) One Army major and 7 Bodo ultras killed in an encounter when 11 Sikh raided a NDFB hide-out in jungles of Bishwanath Chariali Reserve Forest, bordering Arunachal Pradesh, in Assam's Sonitput district. (2) PDF President G.B. Basumatari shot at and injured by NDFB ultras in Kokrajhar district.

The leaders of BLTF (Ranjan Daimarv and D.R. Nabla) and NDFB (Hagrama Basumatari) met on 30 May and decided to make peace and put an end to internecine clashes between their outfits. BLTF wants Bodoland within India and NDFB a sovereign Bodo nation.[28]

After April 1999 Notification, there was no initiatives from the Centre, mainly because the Vajpayee Government fell that month and new Government (again under Vajpayee) took over in October only, after passing through the Kargil crisis (May-July) and an extended election process (July-October).

2000 AD: BLTF Comes Round

No tripartite or quadripartite meeting was convened possibly because they had produced no results in the past. But the new Government achieved a major breakthrough by making BLT agree to a cease-fire. The ground rules for suspension of operations between the SF and BLT were framed after a tripartite meeting between representatives of the MHA, Assam Government and BLT (led by its Vice-Chairman Chumang Brahma), and announced on 29 March. Operations were suspended effective 15 March for 6 months. The suspension was renewed for another 6 months in September 2000. Some analysts believed the NDFB would follow suit.

Intra-Bodo Differences and Violence

The BAC petition, admitted by the Supreme Court on 1 April 1999, says "80 lakh Bodos living on the North Bank for centuries were a neglected lot." But the bigger if bitter truth is that they are a divided and fractious lot. The division among them might have existed earlier too, but it became worse after they tasted power with the formation of provisional BAC in 1993.

The BLT cease-fire with the Government in March 2000 might not have brought it any closer to NDFB, but a fragile peace held between the two since the beginning of that year. But it broke down when Bineshwar Brahma, President of the BSS, was killed on 19 August at Guwahati by a suspected NDFB ultra. Brahma, a Senior Manager with the FCI, was arguably the tallest figure among the Bodo writer-intellectuals, fervently advocating reunification of Bodo political formations to achieve his ultimate aim of a separate Bodoland. Two days after his killing, Bodo MLA, Mohini Basumatary was killed, possibly in retaliation, by suspected BLT cadres triggering fears of another round of fratricidal clashes between the rival Bodo factions. The worst BLT-NDFB clash came on 12 December which left 9 BLT militants dead.

Basumatari belonged to the then 4-year old Party called PDF which the Intelligence claimed was the overground face of the banned NDFB. Likewise, BLT is said to be the protege of ABSU. Since 1996, when PDF won 7 seats to the Assembly, the two Bodo factions (PDF, NDFB vs ABSU-BLT) had been at loggerheads. "For the last 6 months, the Bodo social leaders and elders have been engaged in bringing unification between the two opposing groups", wrote *The Outlook* of 4 September 2000. Brahma, a highly respected intellectual and leading the unity move, had made good progress in this direction. This worried the NDFB, and hence his elimination. Brahma after all was an intellectual and a man of ideas—so more dangerous for NDFB than the BLT's bullets.

Not only are the NDFB (demanding sovereign, Bodo state) and BLT (wanting Bodoland within India) are poles apart, their political wings, PDF and ABSU, are also divided on political issues, the main among them being linguistic; viz the choice of script for Bodo language, hanging fire for years. It has undergone several changes in the last three decades. In the early 1960s, Roman was the chosen script. Then Devnagri was adopted. Now, a section of the Bodos mainly Christians and followers of NDFB and its political wing, PDF favour re-introduction of Roman script. Bineshwar Brahma, a leading litterateur and intellectual, was opposed to any more changes, "because the language was suffering due to constant alterations". ABSU, the leading Bodo group, spearheading the Bodoland Movement, is also for Devnagri script. So another reason for the elimination of Brahma could be to silence a strong and well-respected advocate of the Devnagri. Adds BLT Publicity Chief Daimary Mainao: "As far as May 1999, NDFB Chief had threatened to kill Brahma if he failed to accept Roman script for Bodo."

After the twin killings, "Kokrajhar and other Bodo areas have witnessed a string of killings".[29] ABSU President had then issued a warning: "If the Centre does not step in immediately, we may have Kashmir-like situation in Bodo areas.... With fratricidal killings likely to rise."[30]

The BLT-NDFB acrimony got accentuated with the former entering into a cease-fire agreement with the Government in March 2000, and it spelt into the neighbouring Arunachal as they started taking shelter in its border areas. "In December 2000, the Centre has deployed 18 additional companies of the CRPF in 17 districts of Assam and prohibitory order under Section 144 of the CrPC has also been imposed along the states border with Arunachal Pradesh."

The End-2000 Situation

Eight years past the signing of the February 1993 Bodo Accord, the situation was no better. In fact, it was back to the violent pre-Accord days. The moderate Bodos were dissatisfied, demanding addition of many more villages and areas to the jurisdiction of the BAC. The two Bodo armed outfits were engaged in bloody battles. The Bodos were still voicing their oft-repeated grievances; to cite Sansuma Khunggur Bwismutiary, the lone Bodo MP (March 2000): "Considering that the Bodos are indigenous people or Assam, they could have been accorded due status at national or state level.... But even our language is not incorporated in the 8th Schedule.... Though a bill was passed in 1984 to make Bodo an Associate Language (in Assam), it has not been implemented so far."

What is the picture on the other side of the fence? A large number of villages and populations, led by the Koch Rajbongshis, the (second) largest community after the Bodos, were unhappy at their incorporation in the BAC area. They want referendum on the issue, which is totally unacceptable to the Bodos. It is the minority dictating terms, considering that the Bodos constitute 38 per cent of the population in the BAC area. The situation is pregnant with future troubles. To add to the woes of the common people, for the first time, the ethnic Bengalis and Santhals have raised outfits like the BTF etc. to counter the depredations committed by the Bodo militants.

The UMFA President, Golam Osman, submitted a memorandum to the PMO on 12 December 2000, "opposing 100 per cent reservation for the indigenous people in Parliament and State Assembly, declaring it to be violative of the Assam Accord".

In the given scenario, the peace does not seem to have a chance in the Region; at least not in the near future. Not only that elections for the regular BAC have not been held as such in spite of repeated promises, the finalisation of the BAC area itself is subjudice as the Interim BAC has submitted a petition to the Supreme Court in 1999.

TOWARDS BTC

Now a brief look at the situation during the years 2001 and 2002.

Violence Continues

With the BLT observing cease-fire since March 2000, NDFB has continued the blood-letting of innocents, mostly non-Bodos. After lying low for over six months, it killed 31 people (all Bihari and Bengali settlers) in two incidents in latter half of January 2002: 13 on the 15th in two villages (Sikarjhar inside Manas Park, and Doulajhar, under Bijni PS, 35 km away) on the Indo-Bhutan border (Bongaigaon district); and 18 on the 22nd in Jangalbari village under Udalguri PS (Darrang district). In both cases, the ultras crossed over from their hide-outs in Southern Bhutan, and crossed back after carrying out the killings. The NDFB, with at least 15 camps just across the border, "has adopted the hit-and-run tactic in the last 3-4 years" (*The Outlook*, 4-2-2002). Further outrages: (1) 4 injured in an IED blast in Kanchenjunga Express at Alokjhar in Kokrajhar district, on 5 April. (2) A 12-hour *bandh* by ABSU on 14 April to protest the killing of its Education Secretary, Khwamkhawmban Boro, on 12 April. (3) Two NDFB cadres killed in an encounter in Sonitput district on 9 May. (4) Five ultras killed in Darrang and Nalbari districts on 22 and 23 May. (5) Two ultras killed in Satgharia village in Darrang district, on 25 August. (6) On 27 October, NDFB ultra gathered 31 villagers from Datgiri-Hatisar (in Kokrajhar district) on Indo-Bhutan border, in the open area and gunned them down. 21 died on the spot, all non-Bodos (Earlier, NDFB had killed 9 non-Bodos in a relief camp at a forest village near Kokrajhar, on 14 July).[31]

"Perhaps the most horrifying aspect of the gruesome 27 October killing of 21 non-Bodos is that such outrages have become chillingly routine exercise."[32] In a significant coincidence, there was a mortar attack in the high security area of Dispur capital complex in Guwahati on the 27 October evening, within hours of massacre on the Assam-Bhutan border, by suspected ultras of ULFA, which has close links with NDFB; both outfits have bases in Bhutan. The NDFB, around since 1987, is one of the more potent militant outfits in the Region, with considerable striking power. It is the group that has seen the least number of desertions and surrenders among the North-East outfits; so very little intelligence is available on it. It seems to be intent to thwart the formation of the BTC under the Sixth Schedule.

Is BTC the Solution?

March 2000 BLT-Assam Government cease-fire agreement was a landmark in the strife-torn Region. A year after this agreement, Mahanta and Bodo representatives, led by Bodo tribal MP S.K. Bwismutiary, held high level deliberations presided over by Home Minister Advani, on 28-30 March 2001. The idea of an alternative structure to replace the BAC[33] was apparently mooted soon after the cease-fire, and was accepted at this March 2001 Meet. The Autonomous Region under the Sixth Schedule, to be carved out of Assam, was to be called Bodo Territorial Council (BTC). Mahanta, replying to a question on the planned Autonomous Region, said on 29 March 2001: "There are already four autonomous regions existing in the state." The Bodos also demanded liberal financial package spread over the next 10 years for Infrastructural development, inclusion of the Bodo language in the 8th Schedule of the Constitution and setting up of a Central University in the Bodo area. The creation of the new BTC with four co-terminus district was an important feature of the agreement. At least 10 rounds of tripartite talks have preceded the Home Minister's discussions (with Assam Government and BLT). Advani also held separate discussions with Mahanta and Bodo groups. "The pact will be finalized after assembly polls" (due in May 2001).[34] Another long-standing Bodo demand has urged upon the Government to take steps to include the Bodos living in the areas of other autonomous councils in the ST list.

Assam Government gave its nod to the formation of the BTC, in February 2002 and asked the Centre to amend the 6th Schedule for the purpose. This consent provoked more opposition than expected, with several non-Bodo groups threatening to launch agitation against it. Leading the opposition is the Sanmilita Janagoshthiya Sangram Samiti (SJSS), an umbrella body of 18 non-Bodo groups which said "non-Bodo population in the proposed area has been totally marginalized". Samiti convener Phani Medhi said: "...Gogoi's Congress Government has simply ignored the interests of the non-Bodos living in the proposal area; they will have to live under fear.... Several villages with no Bodo population have been included in the proposed BTC area.... Government has succumbed to the pressure from a Bodo armed group (read, BLT), and non-Bodos would also not hesitate from resorting to violence...." On the other hand, BLT Chairman Hagram Basumatari welcomed the move and wanted the Government to prove its sincerity by getting the Constitution suitably amended for an early creation of the BTC.

An All-Party Meeting convened by Assam Government on 20 March 2002, attended by BJP, AGP, CPI, CPI(M) and JD(U), resolved that the boundary of BTC be finalised on the basis of the 1999 Notification on the boundary of the BAC. The ABSU immediately rejected the All-Party recommendation, asserting that in that case there would be no different between the existing BAC and proposed BTC. ABSU President Rabiram Narzary wanted inclusion of 155 more villages in addition to those already notified in 1993 and later in 1999. The Government had included 2570 villages when BAC was initially created in 1993, and added another 112 in 1995. In 1999, AGL Government added 632 villages in the BAC which were located in the 10 km belt on the Assam-Bhutan border, but simultaneously struck off the names of 371 villages located on the southern boundary of the BAC area. With the Centre negotiating the issue with the BLT since early 2001, the Bodo groups favouring a solution under the 6th Schedule of the Constitution, are demanding (mid-2002) the inclusion of these 371 villages, apart from including 155 more beyond the Pachnoi River, which is the eastern boundary of the existing BAC area.

From early 2002, the Bodos started complaining against the delay in setting up BTC. On 23 April, Mishing Brahma, recently elected unopposed to Rajya Sabha as a consensus candidate of four opposition parties (including AGP and BJP), and ABSU Adviser, condemned the delay when the proposal was cleared by the Cabinet Sub-Committee and an All-Party Meeting at the state level in February. He threatened to revert to their earlier demand of statehood. On 16 May, BLT Chairman H. Basumatari threatened "to withdraw from the talks if the issue is not decided within this month". On 16 June, BLT General Secretary Derhachat Basumatari threatened to revive the agitation if the Government continued to delay the creation of BTC.

At the 4 July 2002 tripartite meeting, attended by the representatives of the Centre, State (Chief Minister Tarun Gogoi) and Bodos and presided over by Advani, Assam Government formally agreed to the creation of the BTC. Unlike the BAC, which was set up simply as an "administrative authority within the state of Assam under a scheme", the BTC is to be constituted under the provisions of the 6th Schedule. This will entail an amendment to the 6th Schedule, which was applicable initially to "the hill tribes of Assam", and which today covers only two Hill districts of Assam. The 4 July Meeting also decided to set up an expert committee, comprising officials of Centre and the State, to draft "a modified form" of the 6th Schedule, for the purpose, and which would also safeguard the rights (status and even safety) of the non-Bodos living within the BTC area covering issues of land ownership, inheritance rights, and their role in the BTC polity. Gogoi told the Press after the Meet: "After consulting all parties, State Government had agreed to grant 126 villages in addition to these proposed under the 1999 Notification which carved out the BAC formed in 1993.... But the Bodos were demanding 101 more villages for the BTC area.... There would be 3070 villages falling in the BTC area, where Bodo population would be about 33 per cent.... Bodo would be included in the 8th Schedule and Koch-Rajbongshis would be included in the ST list."

Despite the consensus reached so far, formidable hurdles still remain in the path of creation of the BTC. For NDFB, avowedly committed to a "sovereign Bodoland", any accommodation with BLT is out of question. Its Chairman explicitly rejected the BTC. Then SJSS, comprising 18 non-Bodo groups, dominated by the Koch-Rajbongshis, are opposed to any form of greater political autonomy for the Bodos. There are reports, denied by SJSS leaders, that the combine is closely linked with ULFA. If that is true, ULFA, which has acknowledged links with the NDFB, would also have some kind of links with an outfit whose objectives run contrary to even moderate Bodo nationalist aspirations.

SJSS (Sanmilita Jangosthiya Sangram Samity) alleges that the creation of the BTC would turn the non-Bodo people into "second class citizens, and give the Bodos the opportunity to oppress us". Their fears got worse when the NDFB, BLT,[35] etc. demanded that Bodoland be liberated. The militants raised the slogan "Liberated Bodoland is for Bodos only", and since 1994, they have been drawing up an Action plan to "cleanse" Bodo villages of non-Bodo settlers, including Hindu and Muslim Bengalis from former East Pakistan and Adivasi groups like Santhals, Oraons, Mundas and Rajbansis, to change the ethnic composition of the areas (In fact, Adivasis settled in Assam during the days of the Raj). As the militant groups know that the Bodos in the BAC area do not constitute more than 30 per cent of the total population of about 30 lakh, they need to evacuate non-Bodos in order to dominate the Region. Massacres, arson and land-grabbing by Bodo militants forced thousands of non-Bodos to flee their villages and take shelter in the camps set up by the Government. Currently (mid-2002), over 100,000 non-Bodos were sheltered in 21 camps in Kokrajhar, Goalpara, Bongaigaon and Dhubri. The non-Bodos are painfully conscious of the fate that awaits them when the Bodos get their BTC.

Another complicating factor is the decision of the State Government to concede the demand of two communities to be classified as STs—Koch-Rajbongshis, who belong ethnically to the Bodo-Kachari stock, though they have become 'detribalised', and the Adivasis. "The case of Koch-Rajbongshis is interesting in that the process of de-tribalisation which generations of them have gone through, and re-tribalisation, which some of them are now seeking, are among the unobserved constants in the process of social change in Assam."[36] Rather surprisingly, their demand for ST status is strongly opposed by the Bodo leadership.

Since the Bodo Accord, ethnic tension has been prevailing in the BAC area, covering nearly 2,300 km^2 in Kokrajhar, Bongaigaon, Barpeta, Nalbari, Darrang, Mangaldoi and Sonitpur districts on the Northern Bank. Bodo leaders wanted 515 more villages in the BAC, and later in the proposed BTC, because the area, they claimed, was contiguous. Then the Saikia Government rejected the demand as the Bodos formed less than 2 per cent of their population. The Bodos will not only be a minority in the BTC area, "constituting about 38 per cent of it total population", they will be reduced to a hopeless minority in the predominantly Adivasi areas. The BLT attacks earlier, and by the NDFB presently (early 2000's) on the non-Bodo settlements, especially those of the Adivasis (the preferred nomenclature for those who were once known as Tea Garden Labour and ex-Tea Garden Labour) had racial cleansing as their objective. It was no surprise that All Assam Tea Tribe Students Association called for a 24-hour state-wide Bandh on 11 November 2002 to oppose the inclusion of tea tribal dominated areas in the proposed BTC under the 6th Schedule, and demand security to non-Bodos—in the Bodo dominated areas, besides 60 per cent reservation of Government jobs for tea tribes.

The creation of BTC under 6th Schedule raises other issue that have a bearing on the broader tribal politics of the region. The privileges and benefits enjoyed by the tribes under 6th Schedule are jealously guarded by them. Hence, any move to extend the provisions of the 6th Schedule to the plains tribes (Bodos in this instance) is bound to find resistance from those who are exclusively covered by these provisions. Indeed, one of the three major demands of the Bodoland agitation, the demand for the recognition of the Bodo Kacharis of Karbi Anglong as a ST in that district, in effect their inclusion in the 6th Schedule, was resisted by the leadership of the Autonomous State Demand Committee (ASDC), the dominant political party in that district throughout the Bodoland Agitation. Bodoland Accord does not even refer to this demand, though it refers to the "scheduling and de-scheduling of the SCs and STs residing within the Bodo areas". Ironically, as mentioned above, the BLT is demanding ST status for the Bodos residing in Karbi Anglong, but oppose the demand of the Koch-Rajbongshis in the proposed BTC area for the very same ST status.

If the non-Bodos were apprehensive about their rights and status in the BTC, the Bodos themselves are not buoyant about the future of the BTC, which is yet to be formed. Although the ongoing talks between the BLT and the Centre have made progress, the Bodo people fear that Assam Government would let them down in the creation of BTC. After all, "it was after 14 rounds of talks since March 2000 between the BLT and the Centre that a Sub-Committee was to be formed to prepare the proposals for the formation of the BTC for consideration by the Centre and Assam Government (The Sub-Committee cleared the proposal for formation of BTC in February 2002). "The current mood of the Bodo people and organisations is reminiscent of the situation that prevailed before the signing of Bodo Accord on 20 February 1993 between the Centre and the ABSU. Although the Accord paved the way for the formation of the BAC, it failed to put an end to the Bodo militancy in the State.[37] Some Bodo leaders are skeptical about the fate of the BTC: Will it go the BAC way? Perhaps, excessive pessimism is uncalled for.

APPENDIX

Why Separate Bodo State?

(Memorandum dated 10 November 1987)[38]

Population Pattern of Assam

The population census of 1971 was vague, and far from truth. Correct figures of tribes cannot be determined from this Census. Some tribes or sections of them, who used to speak Assamese or told it as their mother-tongue, were included as Assamese speaking people. Lakhs of tribals were dropped out from their respective tribes through administrative (intentional) manoeuvring but included in the general Assamese people.

On the basis of Linguistic Survey of India and comparative study of 1971 census and also from the local studies in various districts and sub-divisions of Assam, populations in Assam can be estimated as follows in 1986. Of course, correctness cannot be claimed as exact but amounts to approximation.

Population of Assam as in 1986 (Established)

Total	2,25,00,000
Muslims	40,00,000
Bengalis	33,00,000
Tribals	64,00,000
Others	88,00,000

Composition of Others

Tea-garden Workers and Family Members; Santal/Munda etc.

Adibasis	25,00,000
Nepalis	6,00,000
Rajbongshis	5,00,000
Others (General)	52,00,000
Total Non-Tribal Population	1,61,00,000
Percentage of Tribal Population	28.5

Plains Tribals of Assam

1. Barmans of Cachar	6. Lalungs
2. Boro Kacharis	7. Meches
3. Deoris	8. Miris
4. Hojais	9. Rabhas
5. Kacharis including Sonowals	

According to 1961 census, total population of these Plains Tribals was 9,56,858, which works out to 9.06 per cent of Assam's population.

Break-up of Tribal Population of Assam

Adibasis	25,00,000
Boro	40,00,000
Miri (Mishing)	6,00,000
Rabha (Koch)	4,00,000
Mikir (Karbi)	6,00,000
Sonowal Kochari	2,00,000
Deori Kachari	1,50,000
Dimasa Kochri	1,50,000
Kuki	15,000
Borman (Kochari)	15,000
Garo	15,000
Naga Tribe	10,000
Khasi Jayantia	10,000
Hwar-man, Hojang and others	35,000
Total Tribal Population in Assam	64,00,000

District-wise Break-up of Boro Population in Assam

Kokrajhar	6,00,000
Dhubri	3,00,000
Goalpara	3,35,000
Barpeta	4,00,000
Nalbari	4,50,000
Kamrup	3,50,000
Pragjyotishpur	10,000
Darrang	5,00,000
Sonitpur	4,00,000
Lakhimpur	4,00,000
Nagaon	1,00,000
Karbi Anglong	1,00,000
Jorhat	50,000
Sibsagar and Dibrugarh	5,000
Total Boro Population in Assam	40,00,000

Population of Linguistic Bodo Group of People of Assam

Boro Kachari	40,00,000
Rabha	4,00,000
Sonowal	2,00,000
Lalung	2,00,000
Deori	1,50,000
Dimasa	1,50,000
Barman	15,000
Garo	15,000
Hajong and Hojai Kachari	20,000

Chutiyas and Moran Kacharis—completely Assamised and as such their figures could not be known.

Total Bodo Groups Population in Assam:—51,50,000.

Here difference between terms Bodo and Boro is obvious. Boro includes mainly the purely Boro-speaking people although some sections of them might have forgotten their Boro language. But the term Bodo refers to all Kachari or Bodo Groups of people such as Boro Rabhas, Koch Mech, Garo Sonowal, Lalung, Deori, Dimasa, Soraniya, Barman, Hojai, Hajong, Tripuri (Tipperah), Chutiya and Moran whose languages are very close to Boro or Bara. That is why languages of those Kachari clans are known as Bodo Group languages and those tribes are known as Bodos as a whole.

Rajbongshis are not included here, as they speak Assamese. Undoubtedly they are Hinduised Bodo Mongoloids. They are also of same stock of Bodo but after adoption of Hinduism, *i.e.* Vaishnavism, they have totally forgotten Bodo language. Now they speak Assamese.

Total Boro and Mech Population: State- and Country-wise

States:	Assam	40,00,000
	West Bengal	40,000
	Meghalaya	30,000
	Nagaland	15,000
	Arunachal	2,000
Countries:	Nepal	10,000
	Bangladesh	5,000
	Bhutan	2,000
	Total Boro and Mech Population	41,04,000

As regard the terms Boro and Mech, there is no difference between the two. Of course, the Boros of Nagaland, Jalpaiguri of West Bengal and that of Northern part of erstwhile Goalpara district of Assam are sometimes known as Mech, but there is no difference in their language. Mech is nothing but bad name given to Bodos by the neighbouring non-Bodos.

Total Population of Linguistically Bodo Group of People: State- and Country-wise

States:	Assam	51,50,000
	Tripura	7,00,000
	Meghalaya	5,00,000
	West Bengal	40,000
	Nagaland	15,000
	Arunachal	2,000
Countries:	Nepal	10,000
	Bangladesh	5,000
	Bhutan	2,000
	Total Bodo Group of Population	64,24,000

Bodos are the largest tribe in the Plains of Assam and their Bodo language is of Tibeto-Burmese Family. From above, it is obvious that the Bodos are the great nationality spread in extensive areas around the world.

Area of Proposed Union Territory

	Present Area (Sq km)	*Area to be included in the Union Territory (Sq km)*	
Districts (9)			
Kokrajhar	4,716.5	4,716.50	
Lakhimpur	5,646.4	5,646.4	
Dhubri	2,745.5	1,372.5	
Goalpara	2,843.5	710.8	
Barpeta	3,307.3	1,653.6	
Nalbari	2,022.8	1,111.4	
Kamrup	4,625.9	1,155.2	
Darrang	3,465.3	2,752.3	
Sonitpur	5,255.2	4,204.2	
Sub-Divisions (2)			
Majuli	1,241.0	1,241.0	
Sodia (Sadiya)	914.0	914.0	
Union Territory	Total	25,478.1	(A)
Assam Total		78,523.0	(B)

1. If Union Territory conceded, Assam's remaining area will be	B-A	53,044.9 sq km (C)
2. Area of two Hill (Karbi Anglong 10,331 km^2 and NC 4,890 km^2) districts		15,222.0 sq km (D)
3. If the Hill Districts too go their own army, Assam's remaining area will still be	C-D	37,822 km^2 (E)
4. Total Tribal Area (Proposed)	A+D	40,700.1 km^2
5. Area of Cachar (Undivided)		6,962.0 km^2 (F)
6. Worst case scenario, if Cachar too gets away, the rump state will still be	E-F	30,860.9 km^2

Assam will still be second largest in North-East, next only to Arunachal Pradesh. Hence no question of impossibility of further division of Assam can arise.

(It goes to the credit of Bodo leaders that they did not leave any one in doubt about their concept of the proposed Bodoland. They seem to have diligently dotted their i's and crossed their t's.)

Union Territory was to be created by joining the entire areas of Kokrajhar and Lakhimpur districts and Majuli and Sadiya sub-divisions and Northern parts of Dhubri, Barpeta, Nalbari, Goalpara, Kamrup, Dartang and Sonitpur districts. Southern boundary will lie near Rupshri, neighbouring parts to the North of Bilasipara, Jogighopa, Barpeta, Howli, Pathsala, Nalbari, Rangia, Barhata Chirali, Mangoldoi, Tezpur, Biswanatha Chirali, while these towns will remain in Assam. In the North, boundary will be Bhutan and Arunachal Pradesh; in the East will be Arunachal Pradesh and Assam; and in the West, will be West Bengal.

The area of proposed Union Territory extends from Sankosh River (near Srirampur) in the West to Mazbat/River Pasnoi (near Sadiya) in the East. It will span 700 km East to West and 36 km average from North to South.

Population of Proposed Union Territory: 1986

1.	Population of Present Assam	2,25,00,000
2.	Population of proposed Union Territory	61,37,914
	Tribal Population in Union Territory	42,96,000
	Non-Tribal Population in Union Territory	18,41,914
	Percentage of Tribal Population	70
	Percentage of non-Tribal Population	30
3.	Remaining Population in Rest of Assam	1,63,61,086
	Area of Rest of Assam	53,044.9 km^2
4.	Density in Rest of Assam	308 per sq km
	Density in Proposed Union Territory	241 per sq km

Tribe-wise Population in Proposed Union Territory

Boros	33,50,000
Mishing	5,00,000
Rabhas	1,41,000
Sonowals	1,00,000
Deoris	1,00,000
Garos	5,000
Karbis	40,000
Lalung	60,000
Total Tribal Population in Union Territory	42,96,000

Memorandum of Settlement

Bodoland Accord

20-2-1993

Sd/- Sd /-

S.K. Bwismutiary K.S. Rao

President, ABSU — Additional Chief Secretary
Government of Assam

Sd /- — Sd /-

Rabi Ram Brahma — Subhash Basumatari

General Secretary — Chairman, BPAC

In the Presence of:

Rajesh Pilot, Minister of State, Ministry of Home Affairs, Government of India

Hiteswar Saikia

Chief Minister, Assam

They get the BTC

07 Feb. 2003. Contours of the final shape of the BTC emerged when the senior Bodo leader and Rajya Sabha MP Urkhaw Gwra Brahma told the press *(Exp.,* 8-2-03) that the BLT and Guwahati "have agreed on a 46-seat BTC of which 30 would be reserved for the STs, 5 for non-tribals, 5 open and 6 to be nominated by the Assam Government. Only the last category needs more discussion." BLT spokesman Mainao Daimary assured this formula would safeguard the interests of the non-Bodos in the BTC.

10 Feb. 2003. Ending a decade-long insurgency, Hagrama Basumatary, Chairman of the secessionist BLT, signed a Tripartite Agreement with the Centre (R.C.A. Jain, Secretary, Border Management, MHA) and State Government (Chief Secretary P.K. Dutta), for the creation of the BTC which would abolish the existing Bodo Autonomous Council (BAC) formed as a result of the 20-2-1993 Tripartite Agreement. The Memorandum of Settlement (MOS) was signed in the presence of Deputy PM Advani, Chief Minister Tarun Gogoi, and the two MoS in the MHA—I.D. Swami and Harin Pathak.

The MoS gives the community: (1) A University. (2) Inclusion of Bodo language in the 8th Schedule. (3) Besides Kokrajhar, three new districts of Udalguri, BACsa and Chirang. (4) More autonomy to the proposed Bodoland Territorial Area District (BTAD) under the Sixth Schedule (39 Departments had been transferred to it within a month of its constitution). (5) A Rs. 100-crore annual allocation. (6) BTC to have (said the sources) 3082 villages "beyond the Pasnoi river, Bijni town, areas around Dhaligaon, Shrirampur and Orang and Manas National Parks" *(Frontline* 14-3-03). (7) A centrally funded Central Institute of Technology.

The damper on the celebrations came not only from the fierce opposition to the Accord from the rival Bodo outfit of the NDFB, but also from the SJSS, a conglomeration of 18 non-Bodo groups, who announced a 100-hour bandh in western Assam, starting 14 February.

There are many other contentious issues flowing from or impinging upon the creation of the BTC. An angry mob of the *Koch-Raiboneshis* (KRs) ransacked (4-8-03) the BJP office, Guwahati, demanding ST status for the KRs. After all, they are aware that a Constitution Amendment Bill tabled in the Lok Sabha on 1-8-03 to give more autonomy to the Bodos in the BTC under the 6th Schedule "is likely to be passed smoothly with the support of the BJP and Congress". The KRs have been demanding the ST status for long, and the Bodos are stoutly opposed to it for they know—and are afraid—that once granted this demand, they (the Bodos) would be reduced to a 'helpless' minority—given the past experience in the North-East! Getting ST status by the KRs would only be the first step to demand an ADC for themselves within the BTC, and eventually to a UT, if not a full-fledged state. Hence the Bodo fears, and opposition, even when "the Union Tribal Affairs Minister has already informed Parliament that KRs are not 'eligible' to be enlisted as ST". In the North-East, mere ministerial assertions do not put a full stop to any issue. After all, the Sixth Schedule, exclusively crafted for benefit of the Hill Tribes of Assam, was being bent/extended/stretched "at that very time" to confer its benefits to a Plains Tribe (read 'Bodo') of Assam. It was a question of the abil ty of a particular group to put 'requisite' pressure—peacefully or otherwise—on the State and the Centre. The KRs apart, there are other problems in implementing the BTC.

The clause 8 of the 10-2-03 BTC MoU says the Centre would "sympathetically" consider the inclusion of Bodo-Kacharis living in the Karbi-Anglong (KA) and North-Cachar Hills Autonomous Council areas as ST-H (Hills), because the Bodos remonstrate that while they are recognised as ST in the Plains, why not in these two Hill districts. But the Karbis and North Cacharis, enjoying this status in the two Hills, have been up against this demand of the Bodos. On 24-7-03, an ASDC delegation led by Jayanta Rongpi, MP, submitted a memorandum to the Dy PM Advani urging him "not to disturb the ST-H list at the time of creating the BTC." The BJP is in a fix. The Congress and the ASDC, arch enemies in the two Hill districts, joined hands not only to oppose clause 8 of the BTC accord but the BTC Bill itself.) Things do not end up here. The Kukis, claiming to be 35,000 strong in the KA district, are demanding, as discussed earlier, a Kuki Autonomous Regional Council there under the Sixth Schedule. Otherwise, loudly proclaim their two representative outfits (The Reorganisation and Confederation of Kukis and its armed wing, KRA): "We will fight till the last drop of our blood." The strong opposition of the non-Bodo communities, led by the SJSS, has been mentioned above. It is obvious there is nothing known as final solution to anything in the North-East!

Now a word on the all-important issue of population mix and the territory of the proposed BTC. It is obvious that the BTC, like the earlier BAC, falls well short of the original demand for a full-fledged separate state of Bodoland, articulated rather provocatively in their March 1987 assertion: "Divide Assam fifty-fifty." The rhetoric notwithstanding, it is worth stating that the Bodo people are one, if not the largest, of the eight Plains Tribal people of the Brahmaputra valley of Assam (nine if we include the Barak Valley districts), let alone the rest of the plains tribal people who themselves are deeply divided on the issue.

The difficulties faced by the authorities in giving practical shape to the Feb. 2003 Accord can be understood by a single fact that it took them 9 months after signing of the MoS to issue Notification for Constitution of the BTC. But it was not surprising as certain things were left unsaid, uncertain, or vague in the MoS. "There is still some lack of clarity about the total area of the BTC, the total number of villages and towns that will come within that area, its total population and more importantly, its ethnic mix" (M.S. Prabhakara, *Frontline,* 05-12-03). Rather broadly, this 'ethnic mix' comprises, apart from the Bodo population, the caste Hindu Assamese who historically belong to the same ethnic block as the Bodos, Adivasis and the immigrant Muslim Communities, each one of which is "apprehensive about the political and economic consequences of a formal acknowledgement of Bodo hegemony in areas which they view, equally, as their home". Such issues left unclarified is bound to impinge upon the functioning of the yet-to-be formed BTC.

As for the territory of the BTC, which will comprise of four new contiguous districts—Kokrajhar, Baksa, Udalguri and Chirang—on the North bank of the Brahmaputra, it is being carved out of the 8 districts of Assam. Dhubri, Kokrajhar, Bongaigaon, Barpeta, Nalbari, Kamrup, Darrang and Sonitpur. The area of these 8 districts is about 27,100 Sq km, 35 per cent of Assam's total area. The area of the BTC works out to 40 per cent of the said 27,100 Sq km area.

Again, there was no finality about the number of villages that were to fall within the territory of the BTC, at the time of signing of the 10-2-03 MoS. Indeed, wrangling over this issue was one of the factors that delayed the issuing of the Notification. As per the MoS, BTC was to comprise 3082 villages. The addition of 55 other villages, demanded by the BLT, was to be discussed further. Consequent to the post-Accord negotiations, a further 13 villages (or a further 25 villages, says another report) would be included in the BTC area, thus bringing the total in the BTC area (as of end 2003) to 3095 (or 3102). Further discussions on the inclusion of the remaining 82 (or 70) villages were to follow the formation of the Interim Territorial Council. Such vagueness and imprecision is understandable.

Some of the important towns to be included in the BTC area are Kokrajhar, the Bodo heartland as it were and the home of the earlier Bodo autonomist/ nationalistic assertion, the major part of Bongaigaon, including the refinery and petro-chemical complex, Bijni, Sidli, Tamalpur and Udalguri—the last another historical seat of Bodo autonomist/nationalistic assertion.

Now for the population of the BTC area, and more critically, its 'population mix' "The MoS wisely, and perhaps unavoidably, remains silent on this crucial question." In the late 1980s, the Bodo leaders claimed that in Assam alone Bodo population was 40 lakhs, an understandable exaggeration. The 1991 Census records the total Bodo population in Assam at 12,67,015 that includes the Bodos living outside the BTC area. The total ST and Bodo populations in the 8 districts relevant to us are indicated in the table below:

District	*Total Population*	*ST Population*	*Bodo Population*
Dhubri	13,32, 475	32,260	22,628
Kokrajhar	8,00, 659	3,29,461	3,18,432
Bongaigaon	8,07, 423	1,41,542	1,33,904
Barpeta	13,85,659	1,10,452	1,03,413
Nalbari	10,16,390	1,79,641	1,47,690
Kamrup	20,00,071	2,14,340	1,12,796
Darrang	12,98,860	224,957	1,89,962
Sonitpur	14,24,287	1,52,498	1,02,369
Total	1,00,65,924	13,85,151	11,39,194

The table shows the total Bodo population in the 8 districts amounts to a little over 11 per cent of their total population. Earlier we have seen that Bodos in the BAC (now BTC) area accounted for about 38 per cent of its total population.

It all started with the BLT, "the most dreaded militant outfit with a 1,000 strong cadre", announcing early 2000 its decision to bid "farewell to arms", and signing a cease-fire agreement with the Centre on 29 Mar. 2000. A day after signing this agreement, the BLT leaders organised a public meeting at Debargaon near Kokrajhar to apprise the public of the cease-fire accord.

BTC Boundary. A contentious issue was resolved 25-6-02 when an All-Party Meeting convened by Tarun Gogoi agreed to extend the eastern boundary of the proposed BTC beyond the Pachnoi River, the existing BAC boundary (*HT* 26-06-02).

BTC Cleared—Longlast

The Assam Government issued a notification authorising the Constitution of the BTC nine months after the signing of the 10-02-03 Accord. The notification was delayed, especially because of the contentious issue of demarcation of the Council's territory. The final hurdle was cleared 31 Oct. 2003 when the Government agreed to include 25 more villages to the BTC territory, taking the total number of the villages to 3,108. The Notification also declared the BTC as covered under the 6th Schedule.

While the ABSU, BLT and other Bodo groups welcomed the development, the SJSS expectedly called for a 100-hour bandh from the day the BTC assumed office.

Protection of Non-Tribals in the BTC Area

The Lok Sabha passes two Constitution Amendment Bills 8-8-03 unanimously. The 99th Amendment Bill protects the rights of the non-tribals in the newly elected BTC in Assam. Dy PM Advani told the House that the decision to establish the BTC was taken after 21 rounds of tripartite talks. He also said "no change will take place in the boundaries of the North-Eastern States despite pressure from certain quarters".

The 94th Amendment Bill empowers the Government to set up a separate National Commission for Scheduled Tribes (NCST) by bifurcating the existing National Commission for Scheduled Castes (NCSC). The minister for Tribal Affairs. Jewel Oram said the proposed NCST would comprise a chairperson and two other members and the "NCSC shall have a chairperson, vice-chairperson, and three other members".

The 99th Amendment would also entitle the Boros and Boro-Kacharis residing in Assam, including in the BATD, the benefits of the ST status.

They Lay Down Arms

6 Dec. 2003. Cheers from the massive crowd rent the air at the Banergaon Mini-Stadium in the Bodo heartland of Kokrajhar as the first 100 BLT cadre waving white flags entered the ground in the five Tata mobile pick-ups. Then came 2,500 rebels in their jungle fatigues, led by their Chief Hagrama Basumatary, who has reverted to his original name Hagrama Mahillary after returning to the ways of peace. He lowered the BLT flag, hoisted the white flag, and then led the rebels in laying down arms "before chief Minister Gogoi in what is the biggest ever surrender ceremony in the history of the North-East insurgency" (*Week*, 21-12-03). Mahillary also announced the dissolution of the BLT.

BLT Chief Becomes the CEM

7 Dec. 2003. A day after the surrender, a 12-member Interim Executive Council (IEC) of the BTC, headed by Mahillary is sworn in at the Gauhati University Campus. Dy PM Advani, who was the chief guest, said the event was "the happiest in his political career".

The elections to the BTC, under Article 14 of the MoS "are to be held within 6 months of the constitution of the IEC", which under the given conditions, meant before 7 June 2004.

Bodo in the 8th Schedule

Even as the Lok Sabha passed the Constitution Amendment Bill 22-12-03 to include the Bodo language in the 8th Schedule, S.K. Bwismutiary, the sole representative of the newly-raised BTC, stood up and waved (The Government also included Santhali, Maithili and Dogri in the 8th Schedule). Presently, there are 18 languages in the 8th Schedule.

The Convulsions on Way to the BTC Elections

ABSU announced 11-4-05, a month before the elections to the BTC fixed for 13 May, the launch of a new political party including all Bodo socio-political groups, at a convention to be held at Kokrajhar on the 12th. The aim, said Rabiram Narzary, former ABSU President, was to ensure that non-Bodos do not wield power in the BTC. Accordingly, the Bodoland People's Progressive Front (BPPF).

Formed on the 12-4-05, the BPPF stood split by the first week of May 2005, with the former BLT leaders and cadre in one camp and the erstwhile ABSU leaders in the other. The cracks appeared at the Kokrajhar Headquarters of the BTC when several leaders of the disbanded BLT filed nominations against BPPF President Rabiram Narzary and several other official candidates. The quarrel took a serious turn when the present BTC chief Mohillary extended open support to his former comrade-in-arms, Mono Kumar Brahma, the rebel candidate against Narzary in Banargaon Constituency.

Confusion prevailed when the voters saw Narzary and Rajya Sabha MP U.G. Brahma sharing one platform to address election rallies and Mohillary campaigning for the rebel candidates. These leaders had worked together for the Bodo cause till the other day.

"Mohillary and four other official BPPF candidates have already won the election uncontested. The trouble could be traced to the time when Mohillary and two Bodo MPs (Brahma and Bwismutiary) were elected members of the BPPF's policy-making body. The Mohillary group saw in Narzary a potential rival for the top post of the CEM of the BTC. A formal disclaimer from the Narzary that he was not interested in becoming CEM or Dy CEM, was seen as a patch-up effort by the party" (*Hindu,* 7-5-05).

NDFB GRABS THE HEADLINES

The BLT decision to foresake violence and its talks with authorities leading to Feb. 2003 Accord and subsequent issues of creating the BTC and thereafter the elections for the Council had kept the outfit in the news for long years. Now some news about its equally potent rival, the NDFB, and its decision to jump on the centre stage.

Some Incidents Involving NDFB

28-4-03, NDFB demands Rs. 5 lakh annually from the NHPC (National Hydel Power Corporation) on the clear undertaking that it would not disturb its functioning.

Too many leaders in the BAC during Nov. 2002-Apr. 2003. The outlawed outfit suffered another major blow when the Kolkata police arrested two of its cadres including the founder member Sunil Brahma in the city on 29 Apr. 2003. Brahma from Darrang district, is the former Organising Secretary of the outfit and was also in charge of its cadres in North Bengal and Sikkim, as also its bases in Garo Hills in West Meghalaya. It was in Nov. 2002 that its General Secretary Gobinda Basumatary was arrested from a train at Rangiya, while its Vice-President Dhiren Boro was arrested in Gangtok on 1 Jan. 2003. The NDFB, sidelined following the BTC Accord by the BLT and operating primarily from its hide-outs/bases in Bhutan, "is now left with only two top leaders at the decision-making level", Chairman Ranjan Daimary and Publicity Secretary B. Erakdao.

Is it Demoralisation?

The return of senior NDFB leader Bijoy Boro to Guwahati in the end-July 2004 was another blow to the outfit, and the analyst were undecided: was it a surrender or arrest? The incident was seen as a major development on the insurgency front in Assam, after all, NDFB was the only major outfit left in the jungles. "Disillusionment with the struggle and particularly the leadership of Ranjan Damnary led to the arrest or surrender of senior leaders like Gobinda Basumatary, Dhiren Boro, and Finance Secretary Nileshwar Basumatary" (Rajee Sharma, *Tribune,* 17-10-04). With the fate of another senior leader, B. Erakdao, unknown, the sudden appearance of the Chairman's Chief Assistant and NDFB's arms procurer, Bijoy Boro and Benu Boro in Guwahati, had set the tongues wagging: "Are they abandoning the sinking ship one by one?" It was a pertinent query for two reasons: (1) of the three outfits in Bhutan, it suffered the most in terms of casualties and loss of arms. It was nearly wiped out in operation. All-Clear in Dec. 2003, leaving it a moribund and almost defunct. The remaining 200-strong armed cadre was entirely Bangladesh-based, at its Boyalcharri base in Khagracharri district of the CHT. Its only intact formation, 3rd Battalion, too was headquartered there. So, its ability to carry out insurgency-related operations is severely limited. (2) The total support by the Bodos for the BTC signed by the BLT seemed to be the undoing of the morale of its leadership. Some analysts feel it might itself go in for the face saving negotiations with the Government.

Presently, only a handful of senior leaders like Susranga, 'Army Chief', his Deputy Dinthilang, and Maj Rava Gothal, 3rd Battalion Commander, "Cluster around Daimary in Bangladesh (October 2004)". Two houses in Dhaka and the Boyalcharri base provide safe havens for the rump leadership. Given his hopeless situation, Daimary seemed to be in no hurry to initiate dialogue with the Government. His optimism possibly stems from his faith in the continued Dhaka support, and help from the old benefactor ULFA to sail through the choppy waters.

By way of show of force, the NDFB in coordination with ULFA organised violence in Assam during 2-5 Oct. 2004, killing 40 persons and injuring another 106. "They are obviously not a spent force yet."

Still Wanted by Interpol

NDFB chief is still on the "Wanted List" of the Interpol which issued a notice against P.P. Nabla, alias Ranjan Daimary in 1997. Here is Interpol profile of Nabla: "A post-graduate in political science, has undergone rigorous arms training and is also well-versed in guerrilla warfare. He is the man who conspired with the NSCN to mount an armed movement to cede Assam from the Indian Union."

NDFB Chief in Uranium Plot?

Two men in possession of a kilogram of semi-processed Uranium were arrested in Guwahati on 17 Apr. 2005. The seized uranium was suspected to have been stolen/smuggled out of Meghalaya. The police sent it for tests to a laboratory, suspecting the consignment to be of Uranium-235 which can be used for preparing low-grade explosives. The sources stated the processing technology of semi-processed uranium is available only with the state.

The trap was laid after the reports that the two persons were carrying RDX but actual catch turned out to be the Uranium. The Intelligence discovered on the 19th that certain Chinese agencies had assigned two crucial tasks to Ranjan Daimary: (1) To transfer dollar funds to Singapore, (2) Uranium smuggling from Meghalaya (*AA,* 20-4-05).

NDFB Comes on Board

Daimary's (or Nabla's) 30 Sept. 2004 statement offered cease-fire effective 15 October. Talking tough, Gogoi said on 25 October that he would not soften his Government's stand against the outfit. After consulting the MHA, he "has sent a letter to Nabla, now in Bangkok, to let him know the names of his representatives to begin talks for a negotiated settlement". In an equally tough report, through the NDFB spokesperson S. Sanjarang, it accused Assam of derailing peace process, and added: "We would not talk to Assam Government. Centre should not equate BLT with NDFB. We are also against talks on the modalities adopted during the talks with the BLT.... NDFB has nothing to do with the BTC Accord. ABSU must understand that our ceasefire declaration was sincere and honest, aimed at resolving the conflict peacefully and democratically...our talks will be based on our principles and ideology. When we meet Indians, certainly we will talk on our historical and legitimate rights."

The NDFB said on 16 April 2005: "In view of continuation of our talks with New Delhi to formalise the cease-fire and to formulate the modalities of talks, the NDFB has extended the cease-fire for another 6 months? The initial 6-month unilateral cease-fire of the NDFB had lapsed on 15 April (*AA*, 17-4-05).

The formal cease-fire agreement between the NDFB and New Delhi, signed on 24 May 2005 marked the end of 19-year long violent movement by the outfit (The 6-year armed struggle by the BLT had ended with the 10 Feb. 2003 BTC Accord). The MHA sources said the bilateral "Cease-fire would be effective from 1 June. The NDFB has been on a unilateral cease-fire mode since 15 Oct. 2004. The outfit agreed to hand over a list of its cadres as well as its weapons, and also set up a joint cease-fire monitoring group, comprising of equal representation from the Central and State Governments and NDFB.

Formed on 3 October 1986 as BdSF in Odla Khasibari village, off Udalguri town near the foothills of Bhutan, at the initiative of Ransaigra Nabla Daimari alias Ranjan Daimary, it changed its name to NDFB on 18 April 1993 and has a current cadre strength of 700 men. Over 1,000 cadres have surrendered in phases since 1992 while about 300 died in clashes with the SF (Another source put its cadre strength around 2,000). It has bases in Myanmar and Bangladesh, and temporary bases in Arunachal. It is active in Nalbari and Dhubri areas (*Exp.*, 25 and 26 May 2005).

17-06-05. A peace rally was organised by the All-Bodo Peace Forum at Udalguri which was attended by thousands of Bodos in traditional attire who welcomed the cease-fire agreement that came into effect on 1-6-05 for a period of one year and pledged their support to the peace process. Forum chairman Moniram Mochahari wanted support of the masses for meaningful dialogue. The Rally, witnessing an unprecedented gathering of more than 40,000 people, was addressed by leaders of various North-East organisations including Harangse Sangtam, President Naga Hoho, Artrex Shimray, Chief Adviser, NESO (North-East Students Organisation), Kanaksen Deka, Assam Sahitya Sabha and U.G Brahma, Rajya Sabha MP.

Same day (17-06-05), a 12-member NDFB delegation led by General Secretary Govinda Basumatari (alias B. Swmkhwr) attended the meeting of Cease-fire Monitoring Group, presided over by Rajiv Agarwal, JS, MHA, which discussed the setting up of designated camps for the NDFB cadres and other formalities relating to the implementation of ground rules of the Agreement. The NDFB informed the Centre and Guwahati that it had about 2,000 cadres.

Here is its General Secretary talking to the press at Udalguri, Darrang district, as reported by the *Hindu* of 20-6-05: "NDFB will hold peace talks on the basis of its original demand for a 'sovereign Boroland'.... Our ideology is liberation of Boroland, to have free Boro nation.... We will submit a 'Memorandum of Settlement' to the Centre on the issue. We want to liberate

Boroland, from the Indian expansionism and occupation. If the legitimate demand was turned down by the Centre, the NDFB would have no option but to resume its struggle." The bluster and rhetoric are understandable.

OCTOBER 2005 SITUATION: AN UNEASY CALM

After years of bloodshed, there is a relative calm in Assam's Bodo heartland after the signing of the NDFB cease-fire effective 1 June 2005. After the BLT signed BTC Accord on 10-2-03, its cadres laid down their arms. But the return of the armed youth to the mainstream has disturbed the equilibrium of Bodo politics, and triggered a power struggle between various organisations, representing the state's largest Plain tribe. If the 13 May 2005 elections to the BTC divided the BPPF into two factions led by the former ABSU leaders and former BLT leaders, the analysts are apprehensive of a more serious conflict between the BLT and NDFB rebels in the days to come. Particularly so, when the results of the NDFB dialogue with the Centre and their implications for the existing BTC set-up are not yet clear.

The BTC elections had witnessed group clashes between the two factions, who are ruling the present council in an unhappy cohabitation. The huge turn out at the 17 June Rally persuaded the feuding BPPF leaders to close ranks lest the NDFB wean away their supporters. They are worried that the NDFB will play an important role in the next Assembly poll due in May 2006. They have not forgotten the role played by the now defunct People's Democratic Front (PDF), a political party raised on behest of the NDFB, which secured control of the BAC for the support its MLAs gave to the then ruling AGP. The NDFB could revive the PDF, especially as it has all the time to do so, since the cease-fire is in force. There is also worry on another front: The non-Bodo parties, national and regional, might cause dissensions/splits in the Bodo parties, and thus gain a foothold in the BTC affairs.

For now, all eyes are set on the Assembly polls. And the Bodos could play a major role in deciding the outcome in 12 seats in the BTC area, which in turn could affect the formation of the State Government. This can happen only if they do not allow the outsiders to play any role on their turf for sectional or party gains. While the formal negotiations between the NDFB and the Centre are unlikely to reach a decisive phase before the Assembly polls, the NDFB and its arch rivals, the ABSU, the former BLT and their allied factions are likely to engage in a turf war before the polls to position themselves favourably to gain the support of the Bodo masses for these subsequent polls. It should not be forgotten that all major political parties certainly will woo the Bodo leaders to retain or capture power at Dispur.

WILL THERE BE FRATRICIDAL 'WAR' ONCE AGAIN IN BODO LAND?

Ever since the Bodo Liberation Tigers (BLT) struck a second Bodo Accord with the Centre and Assam Government in 2003 and became ruling entity in

Bodoland Territorial Council (BTC), there was always fears lurking in the minds of the analysts and congnescenti that the rival secessionist outfit, National Democratic Front of Bodoland (NDFB), still fighting for its objective and waiting in the wings, will not find it easy to accept, much less welcome, the development which resulted in its marginalisation among its constituency, the Bodos concentrated in the BTC area. The latest spark that could ignite the conflagration between the cadres of the NDFB and erstwhile BLT now dissolved came on 26 and 31 Mar. 2007. Before going into its details, a bit of history.

The first Bodo Accord was signed by the All Bodo Students Union (ABSU) in 1993 as a result of which the Bodoland Autonomous Council (BAC) came into existence. The agitation, talks and other development leading to its creation has been delineated in detail earlier in this chapter. The BLT was disbanded and its cadres came overground with the signing of the second Bodo Accord and creation of BTC subsequent to the disbandment of the erstwhile BAC. Ever since its formation, former cadres of the BLT are in power in BTC. Meanwhile, the NDFB entered into a ceasefire agreement with the Centre on 24 May 2005.

The agreement came into effect on 1 June of the same year (2005) and some armed NDFB cadres along with some top leaders moved from their hide-outs in jungles into designated camps set up by the Government in BTC areas. The Centre had set a 31 Mar. 2007 deadline for the outfit to submit its charter of demands, but it replied that was no need for such a charter as its demand for a "sovereign Bodoland" was well known to the centre. The deadlock on this issue has persisted, with the talks nowhere on the horizon. The rivalry between the two Bodo groups is understandable as the NDFB wants a share of the pie in BTC—in simple terms, a share of power to rule the Bodoland.

Now to the cause of latest trouble. The question that analysts are asking: Is the Bodo heartland (read, area under BTC) bracing for a fresh bout of fratricidal clashes between the NDFB and the BLT which has disbanded in 1993 but whose former militants rule the BTC. The spark for the latest turf war came from an attack on an NDFB camp at Medaghat in lower Assam's Baksa district on 26 Mar. 2007. Two NDFB militants were killed and three others injured. The NDFB alleged that the attack was launched by the former BLT militants. Refuting the accusation, BTC Chief Executive Member (CEM) and the former BLT Chief Hagrama Mahillary ascribed the incident to the anger among the general public, as it was fed up with the NDFB's extortion drive in violation of the ceasefire agreement.

The Medaghat attack was followed by the killing of a personal security officer (PSO) of a BTC Executive Member (EM) at Kumarikata bazar under Tamilpur police station limits of the same district on 31 March. The unidentified gunman also snatched away the PSO's service pistol. Now the roles stood reversed. Blaming the incident on the NDFB, Mohillary challenged the rival militant group to a gun battle. The NDFB, on the other hand, accused Mohillary's BPPF (Hagrama)—Bodoland People's Progressive Front (Hagrama)—through a pamphlet, of raising a new militant outfit called Bodoland Royal Tiger Force (BRTF). The NDFB charged that arms training was being imparted to the BRTF cadres in remote areas of Baksa, Kokrajhar and Chirang district. It also accused the former BLT rebels of trying to provoke the NDFB into pulling out of the ceasefire and warned "our patience may run out."

The situation in Bodoland is tense as neither of the two groups seems to be interested in reconciliation despite appeals by organisations like the Bodo Sahitya Sabha (BSS). On 1 Apr. 2007, the BPPF (Hagrama) launched a campaign urging businessmen not to buckle under the NDFB's "extortion demands." Not to be outdone, the NDFB too launched peace rallies.

It is obvious that the NDFB is keen to conclude an early peace with New Delhi. It is only after that peace agreement that it can make bid to claim some political space in Bodoland politics at first, and subsequently at Guwahati. It is equally obvious that the former BLT rebels are in no mood to yield any political space to its rival. It is worth remembering that the BPPF (current *avtar* of the disbanded BLT) is not only ruling party in the BTC but is also a partner of the ruling Congress in Guwahati. The recent elections (early 2007) to the State Assembly has only confirmed the importance the BPPF has for the ruling Congress led by Chief Minister Tarun Gogoi. He needs Hagrama's support to continue in the seat of power.

So to put it honestly, the rivalry betweeen the two outfits is being seen as the fallout of the dealy in the talks between the Centre and NDFB. The former BLT rebels are apprehesive of such talks as they can result in an accord that will enable their rivals to claim share of power both at the BTC, and then at the state level! Can the NDFB be blamed if they are convinced that its rival is coming in the way of start of these talks, one way or the other? It may even be seeing the 26 March attack in the same light.

There is another cause for worry for the BPPF. While the talks with New Delhi remain elusive, the NDFB leaders have been moving out of camps and making fervent appeal to the public to support the cause of a "sovereign Bodoland." The BPPF (Hagrama) was not worried so long as the NDFB campaign was confined to the outfit's traditional stronghold in Udalguri. But the NDFB slowly began moving into Kokrajhar, hoping to exploit the rivalry and consequently tug-of-war between the BPPF factions, led by the former BLT leaders and former ABSU President, Rabiram Brahma. This foray by the NDFB into Kokrajhar, considered a bastion of the erstwhile BLT, has obviously worried the present BTC rulers.

To the further consternation of the BPPF (Hagrama), the BPPF (Rabiram) and other Bodo organisations such as the ABSU, Bodo Women's Justice Forum, and the All Bodo Peace Forum have condemned the attack on the NDFB designated camp and rallied behind the outfit (Sushanta Tulukdar, *The Hindu*, 4 Apr. 2007).

The fight for political space in the Bodoland heartland can prove fatal to the much-desired peace there, because the two diametrically opposite forces could relapse into the days of the fratricidal clashes of 1998-2000. The only hope for the ordinary Bodo people seem to be an early intervention by New Delhi and Guwahati. The best way is for the Centre to invite the NDFB for talks. Any further dilly-dallying could result into an unimaginable tragedy for Bodos, and Assam itself.

NOTES

1. Kailash Sharma, *Bodo Insurgency in Assam,* in B. Pakam (ed), *Insurgency in North-East India,* 1997.
2. G.P. Singh (1967) has an interesting detail about Kirata King Naraka of Pragjyotisha. He was a foster child of Raja Janaka of Videha and an ancestor of King Bhagadatta. Naraka reputedly came to Pragjyotisha at 16 as a political adventurer, prior to the commencement of *Kaliyuga,* roughly in 3102 BC in pre-Mahabharata War period.
3. This was in response to the demand by some Bengali-speaking sections of Goalpara for merging it with Bengal (The refrain, of course, is different today: Bodos are not Assamese). Memorandum of the Bodo Community of Goalpara was drafted by Srijut Jadav Chandra Khokhlari of Assam Kachari Jubok Sanmeloni.
4. Local Boards were created in Assam for the purpose of managing affairs of local interest.
5. Rev J.J.M. Nichols-Roy of Progressive Nationalist Party and Rupnath Brahma, a Bodo, were the ministers in the 1937 Ministry.
6. Prior to this resignation, Saadullah had two stints as Muslim League Chief Minister of Assam.
7. Rupnath Brahma, a Bodo, again joined this Government of Saadullah.
8. Some elite groups among the Ahoms espoused separatism with the formation of Ujoni Assam Rajya Parishlid (UARP) in 1967, demanding the Ahom State in Upper Assam, comprising (undivided) districts of Sibsagar, Lakhimpur and Dibrugarh. But the demand petered out by 1978 with the merger of UARP with the Janata Party.
9. ABSU was rather good in presenting memoranda. In 1872-83 period, it had presented a large number to India's Presidents, Prime Minister and Home Ministers.
10. It was B.K. Kakati, former Editor, *Assam Tribune.*
11. Plains Tribals leaders under the banner of AAPTL had played a crucial role during 1937-47 period, voicing the demand for autonomy for all the Plains

Tribals. The AAPTL was converted into a socio-cultural organisation, Tribal Sangh, under the 1947 agreement with the Congress Party, entrusting to its care the political interests of the Plains Tribals of Assam. When they found the Congress not doing anything for their problems, the Plains Tribal leaders regretted the wasted 20 years and decided to revive their own efforts under a new organisation, PTCA, in 1967. But after it faired poorly in 1985 elections, PTCA was edged off the Centre stage, with the ABSU and then BPCA taking over reins for sectarian movements, exclusively for the Bodos, their rhetoric to the contrary, notwithstanding! In the coming years, PTCA was almost marginalised.

12. On PTCA's role in the past, see n. 11 above.
13. It has not been possible to determine the identity of this signature. One wonders if this is the transliteration of the Bodo name.
14. Hazarika, 1994.
15. The community was then represented by Kshatriya Sanmilani, whose President was Sri Phani Medhi.
16. Ahmed, Syed Zuberi, 1995.
17. Was it a macabre coincidence? Five years ago, the day after the Saikia Ministry was sworn-in (1 July 1991), 14 persons, mostly Assam officials and ONGC employees, including a Soviet national, Sergei Gretchenko, working with Coal India were abducted from Marghareta by ULFA. Eight of these were exchanged for captured ULFA insurgents, the fate of the rest being unknown. The body of the Soviet expert was subsequently found in a jungle.
18. Their names: Mathius Tudi, Simon Suren, Latindra Suren and Bodon Hasda.
19. *Times of India,* 15-8-1996.
20. The 1983 riots in Assam Valley, consequent to an ill-fated election that brought Saikia to power for the first time, was a bigger catastrophe. It was a mockery of poll process. Clashes spread across the valley. Over 300 people were killed, many of them immigrant Muslim settlers, especially at Nellie. There were also Bodo-Assamese clashes at Gohpur, Upper Assam, and attacks on Hindu Bengali settlers. ABSU's poll boycott call was too strong. Several polling booths reported no voting. Again for record, in the 1994 riots, the Muslim settlers were the main targets.
21. In a sense, these riots also had a political angle. Bodos had asked Santhals to vote for the BSMC candidates in the recent Assembly Poll, but they voted for the AGP candidate, Rajendra Mushahary (who won and was made a Cabinet Minister). The Bodo reaction to the 'defiance' was obviously not long in the coming, concluded some analysts.
22. BdSF, formed on 3 October 1986, had grabbed the headlines when it carried out a major strike in a Tea Club in Dhekiajuli in 1990.
23. NSCN(I-M) had helped and guided Paresh Barua set up ULFA in April 1979.
24. Home Minister Inderjit Gupta informs Rajya Sabha on 14 May 1997.
25. *Ibid.*
26. *The Hindu,* 23-7-1997.
27. For details, *See India Today,* 29-6-1998.
28. *See The Hindu,* 15-6-1999.

29. *The Outlook*, 4-9-2000.
30. Pity of the situation for the common, innocent and unarmed Bodos is that one Bodo outfit does not blench from aiding and abetting a third party to inflict violence on them, just to spite its rival. This is exactly what happened, as described earlier, when to avenge the killings of 29 Bengali and Santhal settlers by the NDFB, the BTF killed 12 Bodos on 17 April 1997, with the tacit support of the BLT! The-tacit understanding between the BTF and BLTF has a history of sorts. The BTF, still in its infancy, came to the notice of Assam Government through newspaper reports in May 1997. Deemed then as "only a gang of extremists having links with the BLTF", the SF were asked to zero in on its Chairman, Rabin Das. The BTF might have surfaced later, but its leaders had come in contacts with the BLTF in their earlier *avataras* in 1994, when the Saikia Government was in power. An organisation called Bodoland Autonomous Council Coordinating Committee (BAC-CC) was floated to represent all communities living in the Bodo-dominated areas, including the Bengalis. Its convener was ABSU leader, Prem Singh Brahma, who later (1996-97) spearheaded the activities of the BLTF. Members of the Bengali Yuba Chhatra Parishad (YCP) who were on the BAC-CC, became close to Brahma. The young leaders of YCP of those earlier days later organised BTF. Having known its leaders since 1994, Brahma took BTF under his wings; equipped them with automatic weapons and explosives; and helped them with donations. This very proximity of BTF to BLTF earned for it the wrath of the latter's underground rival, NDFB, which was suspected to have been responsible for the killings of the Bengalis.
31. *The Frontline* 22-11-2002, *Outlook* 4-2-2002, *Hindu* 22-4-2002, *Hindustan Times* 6-4-2002, *Indian Express* 17 and 23 January; 2 and 5 May 2002.
32. An anguished M.S. Prabhakaran in *The Hindu* 22-11-2002.
33. The Bodoland Accord of 20 February 1993 (which gave birth to the BAC) was supposed to bring to an end the 6-year long agitation that was formally launched in March 1987. The Bodo agitationists' war cry—divide Assam 50:50—and the all-too-evident hostility to and alienation from the larger Assamese Society of which many Bodo people consider themselves a part, encapsulated the Bodo nationalistic aspirations as articulated by the ABSU leadership. Relevant in this context are facts that Mahanta's AGP was ruling Assam when the agitation was launched and Saikia Congress was in power when the Accord was signed. Both the political parties, which held power alternately since the Assembly elections of 1983, have drawn their own inferences and sought to make political capital out of these undeniable pacts.
34. *Hindustan Times* 31-3-2001.
35. BdSF was formed on 3 October 1986, and it later came to be known as NDFB. The BLT split away from NDFB in June 1996. After four years of its own violent activities, BLT concluded a cease-fire with the AGP Government in March 2000.
36. *The Frontline* 2-8-2002.
37. *The Frontline* 24-5-2002 and 22-11-2002.
38. The excerpts from this Memorandum are produced verbatim for their information value and for intrinsic thinking of the Bodo leaders, unvarnished and unpretentious.

6

Bangladeshi Immigrants : Will they Carve One More Pakistan Out of India?

The subject of Bangladeshi migrants have been troubling India for a long time. Because of its implications for the nation's security a detailed examination is called for.

Migrants All

Most of the population groups in the North-East either have their roots outside India or have migrated to the region from different parts of Indian Hinterland. In the pre-British era major population flows were from the east of the region: from south-west China and Upper Burma, and beyond. During and after the colonial rule, there was a large scale influx of Bengali-speaking people, followed by Nepalese and the tribal people from Central India and Bihar. The British administrative structures and economic ventures absorbed Bengali clerks and officials and the Central Indian tribal people and the Bihar labourers were absorbed in the tea gardens and oil fields.[1]

Assam has been receiving in-migration from outside its boundaries since time immemorial.[2] But in the modern times, the problem started with the take-over of Assam in 1826. But what made matters worse was the situation that preceded and existed at the time of take-over. The Moamaria insurrections (1769-75), the subsequent civil wars caused by the princely conspiracies and mutual suspicions, and lastly and worst of it all, the Burmese invasion, conquest and consequent occupation had devastated an already collapsing polity, leaving the land destitute and practically depopulated. It was not only a case of forlorn hope but also of a forlorn landscape, with despoiled villages and wretched society, or whatever was left of it. "When the British took over Assam, there was nothing known as law and order." This should explain why they needed people from outside to run the administration of their newly-acquired territory, the subordinate civil servants from Bengal, familiar with the British revenue and other Governmental systems. Then as the British started restoring economic and political situation in Assam, the manpower was required or imported to restart and develop road and rail communications and inland water-ways. The largest influx was caused for the need to open and work the tea gardens. The decision to develop Assam on the modern lines by launching industrial enterprises like coal mining, oil installations, saw mills, etc. yet again required manpower beyond its borders. "Therefore at progressive stages, the Chinese, Baluchis, Bengalis, Biharis, and tribal labour from middle India was imported or flocked to avail of the new opportunities."[3]

Marwari merchants organized extensive trade network to provide essential supplies and services. Bengali agriculturists, mostly Muslims, Nepalese graziers, Punjabi handimen, ex-servicemen and other settlers added to the throng. Thus a demographic transformation of Assam and to an extent, the entire North-East, had begun. That this huge influx was to cause ethnic, religious, racial and social tensions of the stupendous proportions in course of time could not be foreseen at that stage. But that the disturbing and far-reaching consequences of a Muslim deluge in particular could be foreseen by a British official by 1931,[4] decades before the actual explosion, is a testimony of and a tribute to the foresightedness generally associated with the country he belonged to. The AASU Anti-foreigners agitation of the late 1970s had its origins in these population transfers. The issue is still alive, and as sensitive and emotional even today.[5]

Import of Labour: Its Physical Dimensions

To revert to the situation following the Burmese occupation of Assam, Anglo-Burmese war, and the British take over, there was hardly any cultivation, and complete disruption and chaos were facts of life. To make matters worse, the floods, famines, and diseases like Kala Azar, Cholera and Malaria had added to the devastation of the land and the people. This was the situation that stared the new (British) rulers in their face in 1826. The problems were stupendous. The vast tracts of waste land and jungle needed to be resettled. Assam's upper classes lacked the wherewithals to undertake this task as their *paiks* and slaves had deserted them (The British had banned slavery). The need to import labour was self-obvious. Meanwhile, the Daflas, Miris, Abors, Khamtis and Singphos were pressing on the plains, "taking advantage of the vacuum and absence of an effective civil authority. This added urgency to a desperate situation, compelling the British authorities to offer land grants and incentives to attract settlers from Bengal, essentially Muslim agriculturists.

By mid-19th century, tea plantations had started coming up. They needed mostly unskilled labour. By 1900, more than one million acres of land were committed to the tea gardens, but a mere one-third of this acreage had been planted. This fast expanding tea acreage demanded increasing number of garden labour which the local populace was unwilling or unable to supply. This naturally led to a regular inflow of workers from outside Assam; mainly from Bihar (the Jharkhand areas), and some from Orissa, (the then) CP (Central Provinces), UP and (the then) Madras Presidency (mainly, Andhra areas). Here are two estimates of figures for migrant tea garden labour, set apart by a period of mere 20 years—signifying tripling of the labour force in this short space.

Year	*Labour Force*
1891	4,25,000
1911	13,00,000

Because the transit to Assam by river was slow, Sir Henry Cotton, Governor of Assam ordered "speedy completion of the Assam-Bengal Railway and the Eastern Bengal Railway. That is how large-scale immigration, including that of Muslims, started. What is the situation some of these labour communities face today? About 45 per cent of it, the *adivasis,* whose forefathers were brought by the British in the 19th century from Jharkhand to work in the tea gardens, are considered foreigners! Most tribes oppose their inclusion in the list of STs because of fear that they will compete for the few jobs available to them under the reservation quota.

Muslim Agriculturists: Welcome to begin with?

Some analysts aver that the Bengali migrants, particularly Muslim farmers, made substantive contribution to the agricultural development of Assam. Initially their hard work which improved the agricultural economy of the state, was appreciated but in the subsequent decades when they started affecting the land rights and the livelihood of the indigenous people, the resentment started. The 1911 Census Report described these migrant farmers as "hardy and prolific cultivators, working their way northwards. The people are accustomed to the risk arising from the diluvian and devastating floods which other cultivators are unwilling to face." But when the influx began to undermine the interest of indigenous people, things went sour. The 1931 Census Report contained a perceptive observation by the Census Commissioner, C.S. Mullan: "In the 30 years since the beginning of the Century, millions of migrants from across Assam's border had settled quietly in the Province which would affect the Assamese society more profoundly than did the Muslim invasions of the past...and its consequences would be impacting the Assamese polity for long years to come."[6]

The new entrants created acute economic and social problems since the mid-1930s as they started settling down in the forest land, particularly in the tribal areas. Forcible occupation, purchase, mortgage etc. paved the way for the land alienation of the indigenous population, as also the problem of landlessness. Unplanned clearance of the forest led to the problem of the soil erosion in the hills and consequent floods in the plains. Trade and commerce were monopolised by the more enterprising capital-owning migrants, and the modern professions too were cornered by the better qualified among them. Presence of a large number of migrants shook the foundations of the Assamese social structure and created the sons-of-the-soil solidarity among them. The percentage of the Assamese speaking population considerably declined while the share of the Bengali-speaking populace rose in direct proportion. In certain parts of state, the immigrant population constituted more than 70 per cent of the total population and in the *char* (river islands) area, 90 per cent are immigrants.[7] During the years 1901-1991, in terms of population growth Assam became the fastest growing region in the entire sub-continent. The table on next page shows the growth of the Assamese population against the backdrop of the overall growth of Indian population.

The demographic changes resulted in acute conflicts over language, education and employment policies, leading to the Assamese fear of being overwhelmed demographically, culturally, and economically by the migrants. "Scholars have noted that mass movements in a traditionally insular area invited linguistic, ethnic and religious strife. Settlement of an alien population leads to battle over resources, particularly land."[8] The consequent tension manifested itself in different forms, ranging from political agitation, violent struggle to militant activities and insurgencies. As a result, the AASU agitation (1979-85) against the presence of "foreigners" has fuelled the conflict throughout the region. Insurgents of various hues have cited the unchecked migration as the prime reason for their 'struggle' against the established order. The term 'foreigners' began to strike an emotional chord in the Assamese breast as it evoked the frightening images of the (Muslim) hordes from a neighbouring country (Bangladesh), entering the state and forcibly occupying their lands!

Migrants and National Security

Till the recent years, migration and security were considered distinct subjects for academic studies and political discourse. Analysts and scholars focused generally on defence strategy and power relations between the states. Preserving the territorial integrity of the State and stability of the Government in the face of the external and internal military threats were considered a matter of "high politics", while migration was considered "Low politics". However in the recent years there is a growing recognition that migration does not involve only human and personal security and human rights issues but also has internal and international security implications. Migration has now come to be considered one of the "new security threats" and Myron Weiner has treated population flows as an independent rather than as a dependent variable of his security analysis. He identified five categories of situations where migrants/refugees may be perceived as a security threat.[9] In view of the surge of Islamic fundamentalist violence in various situations and regions, the presence of Bangladeshi Nationals in large numbers in India (Assam and other States) of both legal and illegal variety, is a cause of concern for the Indian security establishment.

Comparative Rates of Population Growth: India and Assam 1901-1991

Year	*Population (1901-1991)*		*Growth Percentage*	
	India Assam	*Annual India Assam*	*Decaded India Assam*	*Progressive Growth Rate over 1901 (%)*
1901	23,83,96,327	—	—	—
	32,89,680	—	—	—
1911	25,20,93,390	.56	5.75	5.75
	38,48,617	16.99	169.9	16.99
1921	25,13,21,213	-0.03	-0.31	5.42
	46,36,980	20.48	204.8	40.95
1931	27,89,77,238	1.04	11.00	17.02
	55,60,371	19.91	199.1	69.02
1941	31,86,60,580	1.33	14.22	33.67
	66,94,790	20.40	204.0	103.50
1951	36,10,88,090	1.25	13.31	51.47
	80,28,856	19.92	199.2	144.06
1961	43,92,34,771	1.96	21.51	84.85
	1,08,37,329	34.97	349.7	229.43
1971	54,81,59,652	2.20	24.80	129.94
	1,46,25,152	34.95	349.5	344.57
1981*	68,33,29,097	2.22	24.66	186.64
	1,80,41,248	23.35	233.5	448.41
1991**	84,39,30,861	2.11	23.50	254.00
	2,24,14,322	24.23	242.3	581.35

* In 1981, census was not conducted in Assam. Based on 1971 census and 1991 census figures, the population of Assam as on 1 March 1981 has been interpolated.

** The Indian population reached the 1 billion mark on 11 May 2000, according to an official release.

Most states in the North-East are waging wars against their foreigners: viz, Assam against the Muslims from Bangladesh and the non-Assamese outsiders from other parts of India; Arunachal against the Chakmas, Hajongs and Tibetans; Mizoram against the Chakmas from Bangladesh and Chins from Myanmar; Tripura tribals against the immigrant Bengalis; immigrant Manipur against the Chins; and Meghalaya, against the outsiders of all descriptions including the Bangladeshis. The indigenous inhabitants and some scholars have a point when they assert that the economic and security implications of the mass migration into the region have not been adequately addressed as yet. The measures to check infiltration from across the borders have not been successful. The continued flow of the refugees into the region has only compounded the picture. What is even more galling to the states in distress is that the anti-infiltration measures undertaken by them are not only proving inadequate but are also being resented by the very nation that has been the main source of this migration. In December 1988 foreign minister of Bangladesh Abdus Samad Azad declared that his Government was opposed to any Indian move to fence the border, because he said rather ominously, "It is not in the interest of the improvement of bilateral ties between two neighbours."[10] It is curious logic, indeed, the ties will improve only if India continues to allow the migration from his country.

Bengali Dominance: How did it happen?

Here are different perceptions of the Bengali influx. After 1911, large number of Mymensinghia (Muslim) cultivators moved into Assam. C.S. Mullan, Census Superintendent, puts it succinctly in his 1931 Census Report: "where there is waste land, thither flock Mymensinghias.... In a silent invasion, half a million persons had transported themselves from Bengal to Assam over the preceding 30 years." Mullan suggests the flood gates opened about 1906, the year immediately after that landmark event of Bengal Partition of 1905 when Assam was joined with East Bengal to create the province of East Bengal and Assam. If the Bengali nationalists saw the Partition as a British ploy to weaken their struggle for independence, the Assamese saw it as an attempt by the Muslim leaders to push large number of their co-religionist into Assam and occupy the so-called "vacant agricultural lands". But the local British officials had their own perspective on the issue : "these migrants have cultivated land lying uncultivated, and in the process generated a sense of competition among the lethargic local (Assamese) population.... With the increase in the local produce, Assam had favourable balance of trade."

But for the Assamese opinion, it was a facetious reasoning, as the result was not an unmixed blessing. The dividend from tea was repatriated to London; the Marwaris sent money outside the state; and the tea labour sent remittances home. What was the net result?

Men were coming in

Money was going out!

So how did the common Assamese gain?

In fact, besides the doubtful economic gains, the growing immigration was perceived by the Assamese as a threat to their identity and culture. They feared domination of the Assamese life by the ethnic Bengalis. So it was not only a question of Bengali Muslims forcing out the Assamese Hindus from their lands, it was also the fear of the Bengali Hindus edging out the latter from the government, educational, commercial and trading institutions that caused consternation among the Assamese.

These fears had foundations in the very early years of the British take over, when they imported the Bengalis for manning the subordinate services and for running the day-to-day administration on the British pattern that had prevailed in Bengal since 1765. As a result, the Bengalis came to dominate the administration in the Province sooner than later. The worst manifestation of this domination was the decision in 1839 to declare Bengali the official vernacular in Assam, accepting the argument of the Bengali officials and scholars that Assamese was but a dialect of Bengali. Their own language yielding place to a foreign language in their own Province deeply hurt the Assamese pride. (It was only as a result of sustained agitation that Assamese was restored to its rightful place in 1873.) But this was not the only cause for the hurt feelings and perception of injustice to the Assamese. Assamese grievances on in-migration and language were aggravated as a result of political structuring, as Assam on take over was tagged to Bengal Province as a mere division under a commissioner. The mischief was undone only in 1874 when Assam was freed from the apron strings of Bengal in 1874, and created as a separate Chief Commissioner's Province. Even this eclat did not come as an unmixed bliss, because on its creation, the incorporation of Sylhet district with Assam had started a 'war' of valleys, Surma versus Brahmaputra; and this war had Bengali versus Assamese cultural overtones since Sylhet was a predominantly Muslim district. Even this celebration of less than ideal (and flawed) separate identity did not last beyond three decades, as Assam was merged into Eastern part of Bengal to create a United Province in 1905, as mentioned above. An ill-disguised communal divide, the decision was annulled in December 1911, restoring the *status quo ante* effective 1 April 1912. But it did not end the War of Valleys, as the assertive and better off Surma Valley continued competing politically and culturally at every turn with its bigger but not so advanced Brahmaputra rival. And the unceasing immigration continued evoking fears and suspicions in the Assamese mind because the predominantly-Muslim district of Sylhet continued to be part of Assam.

The two decisions mentioned above had done permanent damage to the social, cultural and political fabric of the Assamese society. The transfer of large Bengali population to the so-called *Vacant* forest lands, particularly during the time when Assam was part of the United Province of East Bengal and Assam (1905-12) has been touched upon above. As for the second, putting Bengali-speaking Sylhet district under Assam in 1874 has its own consequences, essentially unhappy and unfortunate for Assam. The 1931 Census indicated that there were only 1,61,000 Assamese speakers in Assam against the huge majority of 4,76,000 speakers of Bengali language. (The linguistic balance must have been even more violently disturbed against the Assamese language when Assam in 1905 was joined with East Bengal to form a United Province, and remained so till 1912.) It should be apt here to mention relevant facts of history which are on record. When the then Congress Premier of Assam, G.N. Bordoloi, met Viceroy Lord Wavell on 1 April 1946, he denounced the theory that there were many large tracts of uncultivated land in his province to be colonized. Even more significantly, he conveyed to Wavell that Assam was prepared to hand over Sylhet to Bengal since it was too much of a political liability, with serious implications for Assam's future.[11]

To revert to the chronology, from 1920 onwards the Assamese interest were sought to be safeguarded by the Line System; but that was often breached through by corruption and connivance. The same fate overtook the parallel efforts to safeguard the tribal lands by demarcating a series of tribal belts and blocks. The colonists, mostly Bengali Muslims, were settling on the Crown waste land. "The Assamese respond was rather timid and ineffective, Assam lost out to a flood of migrants, Bengali and Muslim."

The situation only worsened in 1920s and 1930s because of the Muslim League's communal politics. In the second half of the 1930s, the migration not only continued unabated, it was in fact encouraged by various non-Congress Ministries headed by Mohammad Saadullah Khan,[12] under the official garb of "Grow more food" campaign to boost the war effort.[13] In a moment of candour, the then Viceroy of India, Lord Wavell (1944-47) was constrained to dub this campaign as "Grow more Muslims" campaign.[14] But a British civil servant had seen it coming much earlier. C.S. Mullan, already quoted partly, with an insight rare in his counterparts of today, had made a perceptive observation in the Census Report of 1931.[15]

> "In fact the way they have seized upon the vacant areas in Assam Valley, seems almost uncanny, without tumult, without fuss, without undue trouble to the district revenue staff, a population which must amount to over half a million has transferred itself from Bengal to Assam Valley during the last 25 years, an event which seems likely to alter permanently the whole future of Assam and destroy more fully than did the Burmese invaders of the 1820s, the whole structure of the Assamese culture and civilisation."[16]

So what the Burmese invasions and occupation of the early 19th centuries and the repeated Muslim invasions of the earlier centuries could not do with all the violence inherent in their endeavours, "These silent invaders have done from within and apparently", as Mr Perceptive wrote in 1931, "without any undue trouble" to any one. Not surprisingly, the Assamese are still paying for that influx—or "invasion", as it has been called so often—, and there seems to be no way out either. The AASU movement of the late 1970s that shook Assam (and India) directly flowed from that influx. And to imagine, a British official foresaw it as early as 1931. An Urdu poet puts it all so aptly and eloquently, "history stands testimony to the fact that people suffer for centuries for an error made in a moment".

Bordoloi Saves Assam for India

The Assamese cannot be blamed for being paranoid about the Bengali domination. They have historical reasons to be apprehensive of the dangers, starting with the examples already cited above. Then came the Cabinet Mission Plan of 16 May 1946. Having already seen the machinations of Saadullah and Muslim League in the 1930s, this plan simply convinced the Assamese that the Muslim League was bent upon absorbing Assam within Bengal. It was a foretaste of things to come. The plan placed Assam in Group C with Bengal. The Group's Constituent Assembly was to have 36 Muslim Seats and 34 General Seats, which was obviously reflective of the communal balance in the zone. The majority community would certainly dictate terms with this composition. Some critics have harshly castigated the Congress Party for having been eager to accept this plan, goaded solely by an urge to ascend to power (even at the cost of) sacrificing Assam in the process. It was a valiant fight put up by Bordoloi, with active and unstinted support from Gandhiji that saved the day for Assam, and India, as the Congress ultimately rejected the plan. Had the plan gone through, the Assamese have no doubt that they would have been reduced to a hopeless minority in their own home, "overwhelmed by the torrential flood of Muslims from Bengal". This was not an imaginary fear. Even a known well-meaning Muslim leader, a professed liberal, Mujib-Ur-Rehman, had written in his *East Pakistan: Its People, Determination and Economics*, 1946:

> "Because East Pakistan must have sufficient land for its huge population and Assam will give it full scope for expansion, and because Assam has abundant forest and mineral resources like coal, petroleum, etc. East Pakistan must include Assam to be financially and economically strong."

In view of the above, Assamese fears about the Muslim immigrants are well founded indeed!

In fact, some analysts opine that having failed to have their way with the Cabinet Mission Plan, Bangladeshis are now trying to achieve the same end by exporting Muslim to Assam through all possible means.

Is the situation regarding the exploding numbers in Bangladesh any better today, 57 years after Mujib wanted Assam as a lebensraum for his East Pakistan? Far from it. Not to speak of any possibility of its reaching stabilization levels, the Bangladeshi population is almost spinning out of control. Here is the population growth since 1947:

Bangladesh Population

Year	*Population (Millions)*
1947	42 (at Partition)
1971	75 (at its Independence)
1993	119.80
1998	130.70
2001	135.60

Its density of population at 909 per Sq km is highest in the world, and "there is no effective family planning programme in place, barring some individual efforts which are frowned upon by the clerics". The 1991 Census Report reveals the birth rate at 31.6 per 1000. Out of a total of 2,28,00,000 fertile women 68.18 or 1,50,00,000 refuse to practice any kind of family planning methods. Unchecked growth is leading to a land crises, apparent from the fact that there was only 0.20 acre of land per head in 1992, "and it would be near zero by early decades of 21st century".[17]

1947-Partition-Induced Influx and India's Unilateral Generosity

Assam came into its own in 1947, with the shedding of Bengali (Muslim) dominated Sylhet district, and spanning of the entire North-East, bar Manipur and Tripura Princely states. Not for a moment should one forget that Assam was hobbled at its birth with the unpleasant legacy of large migrant population already within its borders and what was worse, the cataclysmic events of 1947 had only increased the pace and size of the in-migration exponentially. Assam was up against the deluge of migrants. An early amendment of Assam Land Revenue Regulation in 1947 redefined a series of 10 Tribal Belts and 23 Tribal Blocks to protect the plains Tribes (of Assam) from losing more traditional lands and forests "to the continuous onrush of these immigrant hordes".

The Partition itself had generated movement both ways to regulate which the Permit system was introduced in July 1948. The Indo-Pak Passports came into effect from 15 October 1952. An important fact of history needs a mention here. Undoubtedly, there was movement in both directions after the Partition. But in the subsequent period, an asymmetry developed in the overall situation as far as the total number of refugees who remained in India (Assam) and

East Pakistan (East Bengal) were concerned. In the years following the partition a large number of refugees who had gone to East Pakistan returned to Assam to claim their property, taking advantage of the laxity of laws and humane conditions that prevailed there, but no such reverse flow took place as far as the Hindus, who had come into Assam were concerned, as will be seen hereafter.

Articles 5, 6 and 7 of the Indian Constitution were subjected to a wide interpretation to keep the doors open for the people (Muslims] returning to Assam from East Pakistan. The provisions of Article 7 in particular were exploited by unscrupulous elements involved in the business of not only helping the East Pakistanis to return to Assam, but also claiming their properties. The Indian Citizenship Act of 1955 could not help stem the return tide either, as it had provisions for conferring citizenship by registration after due inquiry by the district collectors. The process was well-intentioned but it was subjected to elastic interpretations under allurement or duress.

The whole process was vitiated by an unspoken fiction embodied in the Nehru-Liaquat Pact of 1950, following the communal violence in the eastern parts of the sub-continent, leading to the mass exodus of the minorities both ways. Since the violence had erupted two years after the partition, it was believed the refugees would return to their homes once calm returned. Unlike the western region of India where the exchange of population was deemed final and the abandoned assets were declared evacuee property to be used for payment of compensation to the incoming refugees; the Nehru-Liaquat Pact stipulated that the Eastern Refugees returning home by 31 December 1950[18] would get back their properties (This provision itself was in relaxation of another law as will be seen shortly). This opened a veritable Pandora's box for the harassed Assamese authorities. In the Eastern side, compensation on the western India model was never paid,[19] though refugee relief was doled out for years for various fancy schemes like the Dandakaranya project. In these circumstances, the Citizenship Act, Rules and Registration notwithstanding, it was an absolute conundrum to determine who was a foreigner. India, Assam in particular, was to pay a heavy price for this original sin. And to wit, this came about—or rather, was brought about by doing violation to Article 7 of the Constitution which prescribed a cut-off date not later than 17 July 1948 for migrants from Pakistan, with a very elastic provision for granting citizenship by registration thereafter. The Nehru-Liaquat Pact pushed the datum line back to the end of 1950, as mentioned above. The Indian generosity did not end with this extension.[20] More of it was to follow. The reasons? Some feel it was a case of unrequitted love; others dub it as capitulation before the hard-headed Pakistan blackmail; and his more inveterate critics blame it on his (Nehru's) infatuation with his self-image of a great, liberal world statesman! So, speaking in the Parliament on 27 July 1962, he admitted that "the infiltration from (East) Pakistan has continued but much of it took place in the first five years of Independence when the border was not adequately guarded.... Probably it will be difficult now to deal with the illegal immigrants who came before 1952, we may therefore fix 1952 as the date of our inquiry."[21] As was only to be expected and could have been anticipated with a little study and examination of the patterns of immigration and certain insight, the influx continued, punctuated by a flurry of diplomatic notes.

Indian Parliament passed the Immigrants (Expulsion from Assam) Act in 1950 which implicitly draw a distinction between the Hindu refugees (victims of the anti-Hindu violence in Pakistan) and illicit Muslim migrants (driven by land hunger as hitherto). It was repealed in 1957 because of political compulsions or whatever, and there followed another major relaxation that directly led to the abandonment of Indian, essentially Assam's interest. The Indira-Mujib Pact of 1972 tacitly provided that Bangladesh would not be held responsible for the persons who had illegally migrated to India (read, Assam) before the birth of the new Republic on 25 March 1971.

Some argued that the virtual invitation to the Hindu refugees from East Pakistan to settle and seek jobs in India under the 1950 Act was responsible for the 'alarming' influx of Hindu refugees during 1951-71 period. The critics are only partially right, because the Act stood repealed in 1957.

The Government of India launched a Reversion of Immigrants from Pakistan (RIP) scheme in 1964 and financed a special Assam police force to strengthen the border control. The force was simply allowed to waste away, and Assam Government was accused of not following the West Bengal law regarding official sanction for transfer of immovable property to any foreigner. Though some foreigners were caught and expelled under the Foreigners (Tribunal) Order 1964, but the lenient attitude towards the continuing illegal influx continued both in West Bengal and Assam, particularly in the latter as it was still sparsely populated compared to the former, and hence the favoured destination for the illegal immigrants, rather infiltrators.

The whole issue has wider implications that impinge upon our electoral politics, and hence on the Indian polity? And in a wider context, on India's national security itself. The analysts have alleged corruption at different levels and sinister machinations of vested interest of certain political parties, desirous of building up their vote banks and to promote their electoral fortunes. This indeed was playing havoc with the national security for personal, party, or sectarian gains. To take the process to its logical end, vigorous campaigns were mounted to have the "illegal immigrants" included in the electoral rolls. An honest and impartial scrutiny by the concerned officials in this respect and protests by certain political parties and forces were immediately ascribed to communal bias, and even more reprehensibly, as denial of justice to the minorities (read Muslims). No wonder, the student leader P.K. Mahanta was to later denounce the "inclusion of foreigners in the electoral rolls as a nefarious form of political conversion which emboldened unscrupulous elements to pass off foreigners as minorities and allege communal bias against those seeking their repatriation". What is even more blatantly reprehensible is that any attempt to delete the names of illegal immigrants from the rolls and their subsequent expulsion from India raises ever louder howls in the name of "protection of minorities' rights" and humanitarian grounds. An average Indian is rather amused to see the protagonists using the plural "minorities" when, in fact, they are invariably espousing the cause of only single predominant minority from the erstwhile East Pakistan, now Bangladesh. May be the niceties of political discourse and delicacy of the issue pregnant with implications beyond the national frontiers demand the fine print. But speaking cynically, the employment of less than forthright terminology in such political discourse is outright chicanery and evasion of truth! Perhaps it is only proper that the last word on the issue should rest with the man (P.K. Mahanta 1986) who was in the thick of anti-foreigners agitation in Assam:[22]

> "Indian citizenship has been put in a melting pot in Assam. The effect of Partition, wrong and misplaced notion of national interest, obligations under international treaties, (not even presented in parliament); and above all, a convenient interpretation of humanitarian considerations, in clear derogation of lawful rights of bonafide citizens residing in Assam, and formation of a sub-nationality having a distinct culture and heritage; all those have entered into an unholy alliance to promote the vested interests of groups of persons to subjugate and trample (on) the rights of the people of Assam."[23]

Optimism of a Pakistan Leader

It is pertinent that M.A. Jinnah's Private Secretary Moinal Haque Choudhury told him, "I shall present Assam to you on a platter."

Z.A. Bhutto in his book, *Myths of Independence,* referring to the dispute between India and Pakistan, wrote: "one nearly as important as Kashmir dispute is that of Assam and several districts adjoining East Pakistan... To these East Pakistan has very good claims. Even a Pro-India President of Bangladesh like Sheikh Mujib-ur-Rehman had once said 'East Pakistan must have sufficient land for its huge population and Assam will give it full scope for expansion.' It has also to be noted that next to Kashmir, Assam is the state with the highest percentage of Muslim population in India. It can thus be seen that Assam is a potential flash point in India's relations with her neighbours."

After independence the influx of illegal migrants from East Pakistan and now from Bangladesh has continued unabated.[24] This influx is due primarily to economic reasons. With a 2.2 per cent rate of growth of population, Bangladesh is a Malthusian night-mare. The density of population in Bangladesh is 987 per Sq km as against 289 in Assam. The per capita income of Bangladesh is only Rs. 1,700 per year, which is half the per capita income of Assam.

AASU Movement: Demands, Course and Consequences

The AASU had been protesting the presence of foreigners in Assam and demanding their expulsion, since the mid-1970s. The agitation meant a series of strikes and bandhs, some often turning violent. The publication of electoral rolls for the by-elections to the Mangaldoi Parliamentary Constituency in 1978 proved a flash point, with the AASU concluding that its demand for stemming the tide of foreigners into the state and their exclusion from the rolls had not been taken seriously either by the Central Governments (Indira Gandhi's and post-Emergency Morarji Desai's) or by the Janta Party's at Guwahati. Thus this by-election triggered a demand for weeding out the foreigners from the rolls, which was conceded. Soon after the exercise was started, it became subject of stay order with the rivals claiming large scale detection of foreigners, on the one side, and harassment and victimisation of genuine Indian nationals, on the other. Needless to say, the subject of contention in almost all cases were the Muslims from Bangladesh. Frustrated by the stay order, AASU became even more determined on the issue. When the Lok Sabha was dissolved due to internal dissonance in Janata Party it demanded state-wide revision of the electoral rolls for the 1980 General Elections. Conceding the demand, Chief Election Commissioner ruled that the 1977 Electoral Rolls be treated as the base and deletions and additions be determined through objections and applications, respectively. The Assamese saw the decision as a *volte-face,* even betrayal, as they had wanted an earlier date as base line, and launched a huge agitation. AASU and AAGSP staged massive street demonstrations, more than 3 million people reportedly by courting arrest between 12-17 November 1979. Seeing the situation spinning out of control President's Rule was imposed on the volatile State on 12 December 1979. Before that, of the 400,000 objections filed, 250,000 had been disposed of. The process, if it had continued, would have produced practical result. But alas, it was cut short.

The nation went through the 1980 General Elections. But the agitation aroused such passions in Assam that no polls could be conducted there except in the Bengali dominated Barak Valley (Cachar) area, a fact which only exacerbated the acrimony between the two rival valleys. Consequently the anti-socials targeted the Bengalis in Brahmaputra Valley, which led to the communal violence. The fat was truly in the fire. AASU finding no solution, was on the war path, and launched an oil embargo to stop flow of Assam's oil from Duliajan to Nunmati and Barauni refineries. It created inter-state tensions, and West Bengal and Tripura Governments protested the anti-Bengali character of the agitation. Targeting of Bengalis led Prime Minister Indira Gandhi to dub the Assam movement as a RSS ploy, a usual tactic by then of the non-BJP Parties caught in difficult situations. Politics had vitiated an emotive issue. AASU was invited to Delhi for talks that proved abortive.

Given these developments, the base of movement began to erode by end-1980, with Muslims, Leftists, Bengalis and even tribals beginning to move away. The powerful students organization, AASU split vertically, with the Muslims forming their own All Assam Minority Students Union (AAMSU). For the next two years, there were acts of mindless violence, bomb blasts, and killings, culminating in a determined effort to disrupt the conduct of February-March 1983 Assam Assembly Elections. Over 1600 culverts and bridges were destroyed (Government figures). Arguably the most violent election any where,[25] it climaxed in the Nellie massacre—a macabre saga of inhuman brutality. "The Lalung (Tiwa) tribals were 'instigated' to set upon the immigrant Muslims, who had settled 'stolen' their lands." Over 1200, including women and children, fell to the mob fury. In series of eruptions in Darrang and Lakhimpur districts, the Muslims, Bengali Hindus, and Bodos were principal victims.

The violent anti-foreigners agitation continued two years after Nellie, ending up only with the tripartite 15 August 1985 Assam Accord whose major terms were:

1. The bone of contention in the main was the cut off date for determination and deportation of foreigners. AASU was for 1952 and Government for 1971, compromise being struck on 1961, 1-1-1961 being the base date. Again AASU (and its junior partner AAGSP) had sought disenfranchisement of immigrants who came to India in the 1961-71 period; but it was restricted to 10 years.[26]
2. Early elections to Assam Assembly.
3. The post-1971 immigrants were to be deported.
4. Setting up of third oil refinery.
5. Reopening the sick paper mills.
6. Establishing an IIT and a Central University in the State.

Consequences of this agitation and violence flowing from it are summed up here:

1. It crippled the state administration and its economy. Some aver the agitation and its progeny put the state's economy back by half a century.

2. The turbulence it spawned is not yet over, the thread having been picked up by ULFA, regarded as AASU's even more violent child. Bodos and some others have learnt a lesson or two from the AASU book.
3. It deepened the distrust between different communities of Assam: between Hindus and Muslims; tribals and non-tribals; and Assamese and Bengalis.
4. Some critics blame AASU as the progenitor of electoral violence in Assam.

The students came to power in 1985 Elections. As will be seen shortly their two stints in power failed to solve the problem/issue that had brought them to power. The critics asked cynically: was the AASU agitation meant to merely replace the professional politicians with the Student politicians?

It should also be noted that AASU was not the first to ring the alarm bells against the foreigners, though they were the first to do it violently. Politically-conscious Assamese had formed the Assam Protection Association to safeguard the interest of the indigenous Assamese (Plains people and the Hill men) threatened by the hordes of immigrants. The Assamiya Sanrankshni Sabha had warned Nehru in its 1937 Memorandum: "unless the Congress Party bails out Assam from the danger of extinction of Assamese race, the Assamese intelligentsia will favour secession".

Students in Power

Their first Ministry (1985-90) could depart no more than 900 foreigners. Another analyst says "they could not detect more than 347 foreigners in all the five years they were in power; and what was more mortifying, they could not deport even one of these 347 by June 1990". What was worse, during this period, an armed insurrection under ULFA gained such a menacing strength that the Mahanta Ministry had to be dismissed in November 1990. This exit, in fact an indignity, was caused not only by lack of political experience but also by the infighting for power and pelf, the fell disease generally the politicians are believed to be heir to!

The Assembly Polls, after a stint of President's Rule returned Saikia and Congress to power. During his regime (1991-96), ULFA grew even stronger, in collaboration with the NSCN and the BdSF. But what came as a shock to AGP and the people at large was Saikia's assertion in 1994 "that there is not a single illegal migrant in Assam". This was indeed surprising in view of Prime Minister Narasimha Rao's speech at a public rally in Guwahati in July 1992. The sober and scholarly Rao, recognizing the legitimacy of the students grievances, had declared *inter alia*: "The Center was prepared to amend the IMDT Act.... The illegal migration of foreigners into Assam and their permanent residence here had caused a serious situation in the State." This was a remarkable stand taken by the All-India President of the ruling party in Assam where the Congress was accused of practicing vote bank politics with the help of the immigrant community, and tacitly encouraging its in-migration.

The second AGP Government came to power in May 1996. In its Election manifesto, the "AGP had promised that the Army would be withdrawn, black laws repealed, and people of Assam given the right of self-determination."[27] "When the AGP took over, in a bizarre development, the Chief Secretary and the DGP of Assam deserted their posts and left Assam overnight." Initially the new Government was reluctant to adopt tough measures against the ultras. By August 1997, violence had climbed to its zenith: A brigadier and two colonels had been killed in Guwahati; Mahanta himself had escaped death narrowly: the explosions had occurred in trains, notably the Brahmaputra Mail; the Bodos went on a killing spree to achieve ethnic cleansing; and consequently, after massacre of 700 non-Bodos, over 200,000 (mainly Santhals) had sought safety in refugee camps. It was then that the unified command was set up. Mahanta was reluctant to head it, unlike his counterpart in Kashmir Farooq Abdullah.

Its second stint (1996-2001) in power also did not fair any better. It blamed the opposition and the IMDT Act for its inability to detect and deport foreigners. "The idealist Students have failed the people", seemed to be the verdict after their 10 years in power. The infighting had intensified in the second stint. Allegation's of 'unabated influx', this time from its own parent organization, AASU, continued to be made, despite the construction of border roads and fencing, with watch towers, under the terms of 1985 Accord. Did it point out to the lack of commitment to the cause under exigencies of power?

The most telling comment on the AASU agitation and its success is that the organization accused Mahanta, its one-time and longest-serving President, "of betraying its agitation against the Bangladeshi migrants". He was branded "the greatest traitor the State has ever seen". He took no steps to get the IMDT Act repealed, said Samujjal Bhattacharya on 21 August 2002 *(Indian Express,* 22-08-2002).

AASU Agitation and the STs

Because of its composition, ideology, and causes it was fighting for, the "Silent Coalition" against the Assam Movement included 'old' and 'new' Muslims, and 'yellow' and 'black' tribals, as categorized by Moin-ul-Hussain (1983). He avers the yellow (plains) tribals, autochthons of Brahmaputra Valley, registered a decline in terms of percentage to the total population from 22.5 per cent in 1872 to 10.70 per cent in 1971. Explanation? They were Sanskritised, consequently Assamised, and finally accepted Assamese as the medium of instruction. Of the total ST population of 1.6 million (1971) in

Assam—Bodos, Rabhas, Tiwas, Mishings (Miris), Sonwals (Kacharis) and Deoris, being the most numerous plains tribes, in that order, and the Karbis, Dimasas, and other hill tribes—only 1.1 million were recorded as speakers of Tribal languages in 1971 Census.

The tribal identity and livelihood were always tied to land and forests. A steady erosion of their rights had already taken place due to the encroachment of their land by the immigrants. The tribal belts and blocks were also under attack over the years due to several reasons, including demands of development. All this had caused serious discontent among the tribals. It was not a recent happening either, having started by the early years of 20th century. There was always simmering anger below the impassive tribal exterior. The Nellie massacre, unimaginable in its horror, was an erruption of this anger and grievance, in a manner of speaking.

The tea garden labour, mostly from Jharkhand, was in the category of STs till 1947 when they were de-scheduled by Assam Government, these black tribals became Assamiya, a cultural rather than a territorial category. In 1961 Census, of 1.7 million tea tribals, all but 208,000 had returned Assamese as their language, the figure going up to 384,000 by 1971. Other languages spoken by them were Oriya, Santhali, Munda, Oraon, Telegu, etc.

The plains tribals supported the AASU movement since it espoused the protection of the reserve forests and vacant Government waste lands against encroachment by the foreigners. Later on, some difference cropped up between the two. Particularly after the AGP formed the Government in 1985. Sections of tribal population voiced their fears of being absorbed by the much larger Assamese society, worried about the loss of their ethnic identity, others complained of discrimination in the field of economic development. The grievances ran deep enough to compel the Bodos to demand a separate Bodoland, the reasons for which were embedded no doubt, in the pre-movement days. The 1960 Language Bill perhaps had given birth to the idea.

The IMDT Act and its Politics

The AGP Government ascribed its inability to determine and deport the foreigners to the machinations of the opposition parties, the hurdles put up by the vested interests, and in the main, to the existence of the IMDT Act. The AGP had become aware of it during its first Government (1985-90) and wanted the repeal of the Act. It maintained that stance while in opposition (1991-96). The political observers noticed a shift in its stance when the party returned to power in 1996. Now follows the story depicting the venal politics around this Act, and the games various parties are playing on the question of its repeal. "It is obvious that for their short-term gains, they all are ignoring the nation's security interests."

Prime Minister Rao was the first to promise to amend or repeal this Act at a public rally in Guwahati in July 1992 as it was coming in the way of dealing with the serious issue of foreigners in Assam. During his week long visit to the Region in October 1996, Deva Gowda publicly revealed that independent surveys had detected over 3.75 lakh illegal immigrants in Assam, as against a mere 1400 detected by the tribunals set up under ihe IMDT Act. He announced that the Act would be repealed as it was loaded in favour of the illegal immigrants. On his return to Delhi, he developed cold feet in the face of opposition from the left and Congress, the two crutches his UF Ministry survived on. "For the Left, illegal immigrants constitute an unassailable vote bank." "The Congress would not antagonize its mincuity vote bank by supporting the repeal of the Act." Their critics assert these two parties would not countenance even an amendment of the Act, not to speak of its repeal, to safeguard their 'constituencies'. Now read the account of the meeting of the Home Ministry's Consultative committee on 11 November 1996 presided over by the Home Minister and CPI Stalwart, Inderjit Gupta. Congress opposed the move on the ground that it (repeal) would lead to undue harassment of genuine citizens. G.M. Banatwala of IUML, expectedly, criticized the decision and asked Gupta to review it. The Left Parties, serious opponents of the move, did not attend the meeting. Gupta was in an embarrassing position, because the State (Assam) unit of his Party, CPI, was for tough measures against the aliens, while its "national leadership was worried that the repeal would have an adverse impact on the minority community in West Bengal and harm it politically". Acting adroitly, Gupta ended the meeting,[28] leaving it to the Parliament to take the decision on the issue. The farce did not end here. The AGP, a constituent of the ruling UF at the centre, was doing a tight rope dance of its own. On the one hand, Mahanta wanted the Act scrapped, but he could ill afford to alienate the Muslims who formed a large chunk of his vote bank, on the other. Still worse, his own Ministry was propped up by a political party (UPPA) that stoutly espoused the cause of the immigrants.

Given these contrarieties, the UF found itself in a cleft stick over the question of bringing the issue before the Parliament in its winter session 1996. The ensuing debate would only expose its internal fissures. But its worst fears arose from the scenario where it would be opposed by its supporting parties and supported by its confirmed opponent, the BJP—the party was pariah of the Indian politics of the time and no one wanted to touch it even with a barge pole. The UF was mortally scared of the spectacle of being found in the company of the BJP, only Party which openly sought the repeal of the Act. It is a different matter though that the Deva Gowda Ministry fell before they came to crossing this embarrassing bridge.

The hypocrisy of it all was too glaring to be missed at the said meeting. While divergent views were expressed on the IMDT Act,[29] members from all parties expressed serious concern over the continuous infiltration by the foreigners into the North-East. This indeed is the bane of Indian politics—politicians and political parties placing their party, sectarian, and even personal interests above those of the nation's.

AGP's silence and ambivalence on the Act during its second Government was understandable. In the May 1996 Assembly polls, the party had won over two dozen seats in western Assam which has a large concentration of Muslims. But interestingly, and expectedly, the AGP started making appropriately shrill noises against the illicit immigrants as soon as the parliamentary poll was announced in May 1999. It asked the Central Election Commissioner to "ensure the deletion of names of 3.75 lakh illegal immigrants from the Electoral Rolls before the polls".

The fact is that, notwithstanding all the sound and fury, the Act remains on the statute book. Some analysts fear another bout of violence as and when it is repealed. What are the main reasons the proponents of its repeal offer to support their case?

1. Under the Act, a foreigner is defined as the one who entered India (Assam etc.) from across the border after 25 March 1971, exempting all others who entered before that date. Further, the Act which came into force on 15 October 1983 does not cover those who have been identified as foreigners under other Acts like the Passport Act, 1967, Foreigners Act, 1946 and the Immigrants (Expulsion from Assam) Act, 1950.
2. It is applicable to Assam only and overrides all other Acts mentioned above. Thus if a foreigner enters any other part of India, he can be prosecuted under the foreigners Act. But if he enters Assam, he cannot be booked under that Act as the IMDT Act makes it redundant.
3. The process of identification under the IMDT Act is rather cumbersome. Unlike the laws in other countries, including UK, where the onus lies with the accused to prove that he is not a foreigner, this Act charges the complainant with this responsibility.
4. The Complainant/accuser must be living within 3 km of the place where the illegal immigrant is staying. The complaint can be made only on prescribed form that cost Rs. 25 and must be accompanied by a sworn affidavit of two persons.
5. As for the procedures, the Tribunals refer the cases to the investigating Agencies before whom the complainant is called to prove that so-and-so is a foreigner.

It is a complex issue not only because the humans and human emotions are involved in it. There were instances when even in case where expulsion had been ordered, it rarely took place. Though the IMDT Act needs to be repealed, but there are parties who feel replacing it with a tougher one may not be the solution "as that would only open the flood gates for harassment of the innocent Muslims". They suggest the solution lies in Permit System that allows the Bangladeshis to work here for a specific period.

At a tripartite (Centre, Assam Government and AASU) meeting at New Delhi on 1 July 1999, the AASU demanded a discussion on the contentious Citizenship Act. This demand assumes significance in the light of AASU's long-standing plea for the repeal if the IMDT Act, 1983. Having announced its decision to do away with the Act, the Vajpayee Government during its second coming (March 1998) could not push the necessary legislation through Parliament due to an ambiguous stand of the Congress Party on the issue. Incidentally, a Cabinet Note over the repeal of this Act had been awaiting clearance for some months when the Vajpayee Government fell on 17 April 1999.

It is worth noting that the Vajpayee Government could not get the Act repealed even after its third coming (October 1999) though it is running in its fourth year (2003), for the reasons of a divided polity, as mentioned above. In any case, no one—an individual or a political party—seems to be interested in its repeal any more. Interestingly, Mahanta kept repeating his Government's public stand till he was out of power in 2001 Assembly Polls. In a 'live chat' in the *Times of India* on 19-1-2001, he says "The problem remains as it is and we are trying our level best to stop infiltration from Bangladesh.... But the issue now is that the IMDT Act is the main hurdle to detect and deport infiltrators from the state."

One of the example of discrimination by New Delhi cited by the Assamese is the enactment of this very IMDT Act for detecting and deporting foreigners in/from Assam. While the Foreigners Act was deemed adequate for this very purpose for the rest of the country, what was the need and urgency for this special enactment for Assam only, which made it well-nigh impossible to deport any illegal immigrant to his/her country of origin? What was the meaning and implication of the new enactment?

Put simply, it means that a Bangladeshi illegal migrant coming into West Bengal, Bihar or any other State of the union has to be identified and dealt with by the State, but in Assam the onus of identifying an illegal immigrant has been shifted to the shoulders of the common citizen. Why has the Indian State abdicated is elementary responsibility of determining and deporting a foreigner from the sacred soil of India?

In December 2000, a delegation of the United Minority Front of Assam called on Home Minister L.K. Advani and cautioned him against the move to scrap the IMDT Act, saying that, "it would plunge the State into more turmoil".[30]

Speaking at a public meeting at Nagaon 25 February 2001, and referring to the controversial act, Advani said "The BJP is in favour of scraping it."

How the issue has been politicized was clear from the way Prime Minister Vajpayee's statement offering work permit to Bangladeshi migrants, during the election campaign for Assam Assembly in May 2001 was criticized. The Congress said it was meant to garner votes, made as it was three days before the polling. The Communists said it was meant to deny the voting rights to the migrants. The Shiv Sena said it was against the national interest "and was a deviation from the BJP's stand when it had been in opposition" (*Indian Express,* 8-5-2001).

Indigenous Assamese: Meaning, Implications and Controversies

The 10 April 2000 Centre-AASU representatives meeting in Guwahati evolved this definition of indigenous people of Assam:

"Those whose names figure in the 1951 National Register of Citizens (NRC) and their descendants. And for the seven districts of Assam where the NRC is not available, the Electoral Rolls of 1952 would be taken as the basic documents."

"This once again propelled the murky politics of citizenship in the State to the center stage."[31] The critics were up in arms. The Assam accord already provides March 25, 1971 as the cut-off date for deletion and deportation of illegal foreign migrants. By fixing new cut-off dates of 1951 (NRC) and 1952 (Voter List) in the new definition, the Centre seems to have pushed back the cut-off date by another 20 years. The minorities say it would work against the interests of the post-Partition migrants and the riot-affected people from parts of Assam who had fled to East Pakistan only to return later. To wit, 3,00,000 Muslims from western Assam, who had fled in 1950, returned to Assam under the Nehru-Liaquat Pact signed later that year. They were returning in batches till about 1952, by which time the exercise of preparing the NRC of 1951 as well as the Voters List of 1952 was over. Therefore the names of these absentee Muslims did not figure in these two documents. The definition has further implications.

At the biannual tripartite talks, held alternatively at New Delhi and Guwahati[32] to ensure the implementation of the 1985 Accord, AASU has lately been voicing demand for cent per cent reservation of seat for the "indigenous" people of Assam in the local bodies, assembly and parliament. The press reports suggested in May 2000 that "the demand has already been accepted".[33] The AASU holds that its demand for reservation stems from clause 6 of the 1985 accord.

In the State, with the complex population composition, AASU's demand for 100 per cent reservation for "indigenous" people, not for "Assamese" people, opened a veritable Pandora's box, evoking a sharp reaction from different segments of the people; viz plains tribals, hill tribals, religious and linguistic minorities etc. The new definition of "indigenous" has made matters worse. It seems, the critics aver, the "indigenous" Assamese have learned no lessons from the consequences that followed from the precipitate action of passing the Language Bill of 1960, namely, the vivisection of Assam. AASU must pause and cognitate if they are not creating sense of insecurity among the minority groups and thereby reinforcing the resolve of Bodos, Rabhas, Karbis, Kacharis, etc. for separate states of their own.

In-Migration: Dimension and Implications

After the Indian Independence, it was the Muslim immigration that became the cause of greater concern to the Assamese because of its religious, political and socio-economic ramifications, and it is quite understandable that it caused serious controversy between its supporters and opponents. The former were accused of making political capital out of the immigrant population, using them as vote bank to gain, to retain, and stay in power; and the latter are obviously chauvinistic, out to disrupt the harmony of Assam, supported by the communal forces. The identity of either side is well-known.

There are various views about the extent of illegal migration into Assam. The large increase in Assam's population in the inter census period of 1951-1961 (34.98 per cent against overall Indian average of 21.6 per cent) was cited as proof of the extent of the influx. It is rebutted by the argument that due to 1950 communal riots, Muslims had fled Assam and consequently the 1951 was an undercount. Those who had fled, returned and were counted in 1961—hence the seemingly large increase. The official version views the matter in perspective. The Census of India 1961, Paper No. 1 of 1963 estimated "that the missing persons of 1951 and their progeny would account for 2,75,000 Muslims enumerated in Assam in 1961. The balance 'excess' decadel growth was a result of illicit immigration." This aspect of increase in Muslim population in Assam was also analysed and well documented in another study of comparative demographic patterns in Assam and Tripura on the one hand and East Pakistan on the other, based on the 1961 Census figures of India and Pakistan. "The population deficit of specific East Pakistan districts in relation to national population trends was found to indicate a neat fit with the corresponding excess noticed in the adjacent regions of Assam, West Bengal and Tripura."[34]

Interestingly, in this game of the figures, different sets of the same are bandied about to prove or disprove a position, depending upon the presenter. The number and composition of the 1961-71 influx are even more contentious. The Home Minister informed the AASU delegation in 1980 that 9,67,000 immigrants had entered Assam during 1961-71; 2,14,000 being displaced person (DPs) in the wake of 1965 Indo-Pakistan War and subsequent communal riots. The break down of the remaining 7,53,000 illicit immigrants was given as below:

Hindus	631,000	Christians	30,000
Buddhists	65,000[35]	Muslims	27,000

A sympathetic Muslim academic on the other hand, feels that the Muslims are unduly castigated on the issue. He says, like the Chinese, all of whom were rounded up and dispatched from Upper Assam during the 1962 War, Muslims in Assam also became victims of prejudice and discrimination. He cites Census data showing that the percentage of Muslims in total population of Assam has remained virtually unchanged.

Year	*Percentage of Muslims*
1951	25.68
1961	25.30
1971[36]	24.56

The influx of illicit land-seeking immigrants from East Pakistan (Bangladesh) into Assam had started in 19th century, but assumed serious dimensions since 1947. But matters came to a head in the latter half of the 1970s through a combination of circumstances. Assam had shrunk[37] politically and newly emerging Assamese middle class encountered lack of economic opportunities. Shakdher, CEC, addressing the Chief Electoral Officers of states at Ooty on 4 October 1978 had painted a grim picture of situation caused by the immigration. He expressed concern about large scale inclusion of foreign nationals in the electoral rolls and castigated political parties for demanding that the names of such immigrants be included in the rolls. The result will be some foreign nationals taking part in our electoral processes, which will directly impinge our sovereignty. AASU and AGP estimates of infiltrators in Assam, if accurate, are rather disturbing.

Illegal Infiltrators in Assam

Year	*Number*
1961	10,00,000
1971	23,00,000
1979	35,00,000
1981	50,00,000

Even as sober and senior a journalist as B.G. Verghese wrote in 1980 that 1.80 million foreigners had already been enrolled (by 1980, that is), "representing as much as 20 per cent of the Assamese registered voters. The problem no one doubted was the Bangladeshi Muslims in Assam."

The high percentage of Muslim population in Assam has always worried the Assamese cognoscenti. The Cabinet Mission statement of May 1946 for Assam had 34,42,479 Muslims against 67,62,254 non-Muslims (based on 1941 Census). So Muslims were 33 per cent of Assam's population in 1941. When Muslim majority Sylhet district voted itself out in 1947, this percentage dropped. It was 24.03 per cent in 1971, still high for the concerned Assamese. It climbed to 28 per cent in mid-1990s. It is also a fact that Muslim population as a percentage of India's total has been on the increase, as seen here:

Increasing Trend in the Growth of Muslim Population in India

Sl. No.	*Year*	*Percentage of Muslim Population*
1.	1951	9.9
2.	1971	10.8
3.	1981	11.3
4.	1991	12.12

But more alarming declaration came from the AASU at Dibrugarh in July 1992, that "the ethnic Assamese were only 31.70 per cent in Assam". It set the alarm bells ringing. It was obvious that the ethnic Assamese formed a majority in Brahmaputra Valley only.

Here are official figures from the Census of India Report, released in mid-1995, giving religious break up of the country. It says the Muslim population of Assam had recorded a growth of 77.42 per cent during 1971-91 period. The percentage of the Muslims to the total population of the State ("where the 'indigenous' people are living under constant fear of being outnumbered by the Bangladeshi migrants, both Hindus and Muslims") has gone up from 24.56 per cent in 1971 to 28.47 per cent in 1991. The Hindu population of the State on the other hand, shows a decline from 72.51 per cent of the total population to 67.13 per cent during the same period (*Indian Express,* 25-7-1995). The 'alarming' statistics failed to draw any comments from political parties bar the BJP which saw in the increase a vindication of its claim about unabated influx of Muslims from Bangladesh. The party analyses this continuing influx as a sinister design by Bangladesh, helped by Pakistan ISI, to incorporate Assam "through other means", to create either a greater Bangladesh or a separate Muslim nation in India's North-East! The party and some other critics ascribes the silence of non-BJP parties on the dangers to India's integrity "to their dependence on the illegal immigrant for their hold on power". The latter, in turn, blame the BJP for practicing "communal politics".

The other six States in the Region have also recorded a high growth rate of Muslim population. "Mizoram primarily a Christian State, for instance has shown a massive 105.80 per cent rise, while Nagaland came second with 74.84 per cent increase during 1971-91." Hindus, on the other hand, have registered declining trends of growth within three States Manipur, Meghalaya and Mizoram.

The district-wise figures in Assam are even more telling in this regard. The 1991 Census Report revealed that while the Hindus constituted more than 70 per cent in 12 of the 23 districts, the Muslims were 50 per cent or more in four districts. Yet again, 10 out of 23 districts presently have more than 30 per cent Muslim population. *See* the table below:

Muslim Population (Over 30 per cent) in 10 Districts of Assam (1991 Census Report)

Sl. No.	*District*	*Total Population*	*Muslims Total*	*(%)*
1.	Dhubri	1,325,653	9,38,789	70.46
2.	Barpeta	1,382,715	7,76,974	56.18
3.	Hailakandi	448,506	2,46,016	54.8
4.	Goalpara	661,801	3,32,275	50.18
5.	Karimganj	825,551	4,06,706	49.2
6.	Nagaon	1,892,087	8,93,322	47.19
7.	Marigaon	640,376	2,89,835	45.3
8.	Cachar	1,215,952	4,19,150	34.5
9.	Bongaigaon	806,472	2,64,393	32.74
10.	Darrang	1,286,633	4,15,859	31.01

The AASU asserts it is an unnatural and unusual increase, and expectedly ascribes it to illegal immigration. It is significant that most of these districts are either contiguous to Bangladesh, closer to it, or located in Lower Assam.

The 1991 Census figures for 5 border districts of West Bengal have also shown an unusual increase in the Muslim population (Relevant table is given later under West Bengal heading).

Demographically, Assam has not only seen faster growth against the Indian average, it in fact has been the fastest growing area in the sub-continent. Its population has grown by 676 per cent from 3.3 million in 1901 to 22.3 million in 1991, comparative figures for India being 354 per cent: 238.4 million in 1901 and 843.9 million in 1991. Even when the growth rate was nearly static for all India during 1911-21, it was as high as 20.48 per cent for Assam

(Census Report). Had Assam's population increased at the same rate as the rest of India between 1901 and 1991, that is 354 per cent, then Assam's population would have been 14.9 million rather than 22.3 million, a whopping increase of 7.4 million. Here is what, in the words of Myron Weiner (*sons of the soil, 1978*), the presence of these migrants has done to Assam and the Assamese:

> "It has shaken the foundation of Assamese social structure and created solidarity among the Assamese even while generating cleavages between the indigenous Assamese and the indigenous tribals. It has influenced the educational, social, and economic aspiration of countless Assamese, determined their central political cognizance...(it has) given rise to powerful assimilationist and nativist sentiment and backlash separatist agitation, to massive conflict over languages, education and employment policy."

> (The growth rate statistics were as menancing and phenomenal in Tripura too, where the population over the last 100 years has registered 20-fold increase. The cause as in Assam was largely due to a great influx of refugees from Bangladesh. The detail are discussed in Tripura Section.)

This demographic 'aggression' caused disquiet among both the plains and hills, adversely affecting their land and livelihood. The tribals in particular were the worst sufferers, because the expansion of the plough and the increase in the number of Bengali tenants, mainly the Muslims, progressively alienated them from their land. It was the increasing marginalisation of the tribal communities which first gave rise to the militancy in the state, that later crossed into insurgency, ala the Bodo community, and to an extent the Naga tribes. It was this internal dissonance that provided a cause and an opportunity to the intelligence agencies like the ISI to indulge in geopolitical machination in India, posing a serious threat to its security and sovereignty.

Baljit Rai, retired DGP, who served in the area, warns the nation about the perils of illegal immigration, quoting alarming figures/facts, in his book, *Demographic Aggression against India: Muslim Avalanche from Bangladesh.*

> "The 6 districts of West Bengal (24-Parganas, South and North Nadia, Murshidabad, Maldah, and West Dinajpur), 4 districts of Bihar (Purnea, Katihar, Kishanganj and Araria) and 10 districts of Assam (Dhubri, Barpeta, Hailakandi, Goalpara, Karimganj, Nagaon, Marigaon, Cachar, Bongaigaon, Darrang) have become extensions of Bangladesh.

> "Hindu presence in Bangladesh has been systematically and assiduously decimated from 28 per cent of population in 1947 to less than 10 per cent in 1991.

"With a few honourable exceptions, the national media has applied total censorship and failed to highlight the gravity of the problem; with some newspapers going out of their way to support the cause of the infiltrators.

"In contrast, Bangladeshi journalists and intellectuals are far more open, honest, and forthright in staking the claim to Lebensraum in North-East India to unload their excess population. *The Hindu* journalists in India, on the other hand, appear to be supine and strangely inclined to be somnolent. Not many of them have come out of their secular cocoon to contest or refute the irrational territorial claims made by the Bangladeshi intellectuals."

Home Minister Gupta told the Lok Sabha on 3 December 1991 that there were one lakh Bangladeshi nationals in Delhi, with 9,561 Pakistan nationals overstaying. The figure for West Bengal was 5.87 lakh and for Rajasthan, 25,000.

But the figure cited for West Bengal is nowhere near the reality. T.V. Rajeswar, Governor West Bengal (1991-92) and ex-Director, IB, asserts that "not more than 20 per cent of the illegal flow is checked". The figure of 5.87 lakh, on this basis, shoots to 29.35 lakh. The State Government declared "about 28 lakh Bangladeshi nationals entered the State between 1972 and 1988 of whom 5 lakh stayed back". This was till 1988!

Significantly, Government gave no figures for illegal immigrants in Assam/ North East, an issue on which an entire movement was launched. It be noted that Bangladesh asserts "none of its nationals are staying outside its boundaries, certainly not in India". But what the Indians must note with concern is the repeated statements in Bangladesh about India's North-East being its Lebensraum. The popular perception in that country is that at the time of Partition "it was cheated off the whole of India's North-East, in particular, Assam, which has always been viewed as its natural expanding space. The continued migration from Bangladesh to Assam over the years is to be seen and understood" in the context of the "strong hope" expressed in that country that the "historical injustice" done to it would ultimately be corrected. Bhutto and Mujib have already been quoted in this context. Now read an intellectual justification for the same view, by Sadiq Khan who honestly, openly articulated his perception in the 18 October 1991 issue of the Dhaka *Weekly Holiday*:

"Along the new international order, there should also be a world demographic order, with its globalised manpower market.... There is no reason why regional and international cooperation could not be worked out to plan and execute population movements and settlements to avoid critical demographic pressures in pockets of high concentration.... A natural outflow of population pressure (in Bangladesh) is very much on the cards and will not be retainable by barbed wire or border patrol

> measures. The natural trend of population overflow from Bangladesh is towards the sparsely populated lands of the South-East in the Arakan side and to the North-East in the seven sisters side, of the Indian Sub-continent."[38]

The author Khan leaves no one in doubt about the policy and intentions of Bangladesh. Is it any surprise that the Assam leaders have often alleged that despite the 1985 Assam Accord and subsequent construction of border roads and fencing, and 'patrol measures', there has been no effective check on migration from Bangladesh?

A specialist on the subject, Sanjay Hazarika,[39] did an exhaustive Case study, "Bangladesh and India's North-East: factors behind the flow," and after studying the figures he gathered from various sources, including Dhaka-based Institute of Development Studies, came to certain conclusions, summed up here:

> "Taken in its entirety, the migration from East Pakistan or Bangladesh has resulted in the creation of a Sub-nation with the size of population of Australia.... A population of 10 to 13 million has moved lock, stock and barrel from its roots and set up new homestead in another neighbouring nation. It has moved illegally, without proper visas, passports, or any other documents worth the name. And settled into new nation with ironically, the documents that most nations give to their nationals, *viz* voting rights, ration cards, property deeds."[40]

Their helplessness against the illegal immigrants, and the inability of the Governments at New Delhi and Guwahati to undo the preposterous situation because of venality of Indians who sell themselves for a few coins, have turned large sections of the Assamese and tribals in North-East inveterate anti-outsiders as well. Often it seems the Bengalis in Assam, Marwaris in Dispur, Sylheti Bengalis in Mizoram, Chakmas in Arunachal Pradesh, and non-tribals in Bodo areas are as un-welcome, as are the foreigners. This hopelessness of their situation leads to frustration which results in periodic violence against the outsiders: the violent anti-Bengali agitation in 1960; campaign for deletion of names of foreigners from electoral rolls in February 1983; and Nellie tragedy when "7000 Bengali Muslim settlers were done to death". They fear going the Tripura way where the tribals, who were in majority till 1950, were gradually reduced to a minority in their own home by the Bengali immigrants. Are not their occasional "Chauvinistic" excesses justified, they ask? The Assamese elite often reminds the critics: "Between 1911-41, the Muslim population in Assam nearly quadrupled, during the days of the Raj."

Assam's destiny was intertwined with that of Bengal since the 1826 take over by British due to a variety of reasons, administrative, political and economic till the defining year of 1947. In this period, a major threat to its cultural and political identity came from a kind of demographic invasion, mostly by landless Muslim agriculturists and labour, drawn by prospects of working on uncultivated Government and tribal wasteland as also in tea gardens. C.S. Mullan's remarks in 1931 Census Report about "This migration of half a million population will destroy...the whole structure of Assamese culture and civilisation" has been quoted earlier. The 1947 partition did not seem to make any difference so far as the migration—the silent invasion—was concerned. The Census Commissioner R.B. Vaghai, echoing Mullan, one of his famous predecessors, wrote in the 1951 Census Report: "I have seen hundreds of persons coming in and settling in Assam and their hunger for land was so great that they frequently encroached on government reserves and lands belonging to local people."

A Muslim Nation in the North-East?

To some the fear of a Muslim nation emerging in India's North-East is highly over-blown. Others feel the fear is not entirely unfounded. May be, a discussion of the issue is called for. The concerned Assamese point to the long-standing plan of the Islamic leaders, both religious and political, to grab North-East, at least a major part of it, to convert it into Lebensraum for the burgeoning population of East Pakistan, now Bangladesh. Their plan is simple, as the former see it: "first, swamp the land with the migrant population upsetting the demographic balance in favour of the Muslims. Then up the ante by loudly or vociferously complaining against the injustice and discrimination against them (Muslims), inflaming unrest, and subsequently the secessionist sentiment among the impressionable Muslim youth to act as the vanguard of the Islamic Jehad. The rest of course would follow."

The people who fear the denouement have their own arguments. The study of the border belt of West Bengal yield some telling even disturbing statistics. 20-40 per cent villages in these districts are said to be predominantly Muslims. This trend, concentration of minority community, including Bangladeshi immigrants, in these villages, has resulted in the majority community moving into the urban centres, looking for security. Then comes to one's mind Lin Piao's classic theory of villages surrounding, and then overwhelming the cities.

The border districts of West Bengal mentioned above have a population of 27 million (1991). With one million people of Bihar's Kishanganj, it totals to 28 million—of which 17 million are Muslims—concentrated in this belt. A concerned MOD official chips in: "Proceed through the Siliguri corridor and add western districts of Lower Assam, and a more sensitive area in Asia is difficult to imagine, surrounded as it is by not-so-friendly neighbours." An analyst completes the nightmare: "A few thousand vociferous but misguided civil rights activists protesting this or that decision of the Government, or alternatively, a dozen anti-national subversives, aided and abetted by the ISI and bent upon disrupting peace, can disrupt or paralyse the communication links through this corridor cutting off the entire North-East from rest of the country." The scary scenario pushes into one's "attention what Kissinger wrote in his *The White House Years*, 1971 :

> "The inevitable emergence of Bangladesh which we postulated, presented India with fierce long-term problems. For Bangladesh in fact was East Bengal separated only by religion from India's most fractious and most separatist State, West Bengal. They shared language, tradition, culture, and above all, a volatile national character. Whether it turned nationalist or radical, Bangladesh would over time accentuate India's centrifugal tendencies. It might set a precedence of creation of other Muslim States, carved this time out of India. Once it was independent, its Muslim heritage would eventually lead to rapprochement with Pakistan."

Should not some Indian analysts descry potential threat to India's security on its eastern marches? Some starry-eyed scholars who saw Bangladesh as a nation under perpetual debt of gratitude to India are already wiser by now, seeing the ground realities. India-bashing is a popular sport of opposition parties, and the ruling party cannot even dare to be seen as overtly pro-India even if demanded by its national interest. Bangladesh like Pakistan, has already declared itself as an Islamic Republic. One part of the Kissinger Prophesy, the two drawing closer, is nearly through. It is time the Indians start worrying about the second emergence of a Muslim nation. But the stark reality is that the vote bank politics of various political parties in West Bengal and Assam make them insensitive, even oblivious, to such dangers!

To make matters worse, some recent reports suggest that "six border districts of Assam too have turned into Muslim-majority one". AGP's second spell (1996-2001) in power was truly indicative of the games the parties play to remain in power. Its Ministry survived with the active support of a religious party which vehemently espouses the cause of the immigrants, legal or otherwise. Can one imagine a more preposterous compromise to stick to power? No wonder, his critics accused Mahanta of softening his stance on expulsion of illicit immigrants.

What is the number of Bangladeshi immigrants in India in absolute terms? Unofficial estimates put the figure at 15 million: West Bengal 7 million, Assam 5 million, Bihar 2 million, and the rest in metropolitans like Delhi, Mumbai, etc. The official figures speak of 10 million. Whatever the correct figures, it is high enough to alarm the strategic analysts, as it has geo-political implications for India's internal and external security interests. Well-meaning individuals have periodically made efforts to acquaint the nation with the serious nature of the issue, as described earlier. Some effective measures devised to undo the damage had to be abandoned because of partisan politics. The flawed Nehru-Liaquat Pact, 1950 had enabled large numbers of East Pakistan's nationals to return to Assam and claim Indian citizenship. To undo the mischief, New Delhi enacted the Immigrants (Expulsion from Assam) Act the same year, and "consequently 6 lakh such immigrants were pushed backed into East Pakistan". The Empire struck back. The furore raised by certain political parties and their strident camp followers compelled the Government to repeal the Act in 1957. The MHA, in consultation with Assam and West Bengal, approved in 1963 the Prevention of Infiltration programme, as proposed by B.N Mullick, Director IB. During the next two years, about 150,000 illegal immigrants were repatriated to East Pakistan. This scheme too was given up in 1967 for reasons mentioned above.

The 1971 war pushed 10 million refugees into India. The 1972 Indira-Mujib Pact noted that about 7 million of mem had returned; and of the rest, those who entered India prior to 25 March 1971 were to be allowed to stay in India. It was a case of misplaced generosity. Why should a nation be allowed to wash its hands off its own nationals, just because it has had a regime change?

To determine the dimension of the problem, West Bengal Governor suggested in June 1989 and again in January 1990 to conduct a Census of Immigrants in his State. The same was to follow in Assam and Bihar. Again, politics intervened and the idea was dropped. The political class is simply not serious over this issue which poses a direct threat to our security. Bangladesh itself conducted a Census of Bihari Muslims in March 1992 prior to their planned repatriation to Pakistan. Indians must recognize the seriousness of the issue, remembering how a mere 7 lakh immigrants in East Europe had generated so much consternation there. Why do we forget how bigger and more prosperous nations zealously guard their borders against the aliens: US against Haitians and Chinese boat people; Australia against unfortunate refugees fleeing from China, Vietnam, and of late, Afghanistan, and Bangladesh itself from Rohingyas.

And pray, what price Indian generosity? Bangladesh blatantly denies presence of any of their nationals in India? Worse, some of their scholars (Sadiq Khan quoted above) are brazenly making a case for India's North-East (essentially Assam) providing a Lebensraum for their burgeoning numbers! Their Finance Minister tells the press in Dhaka on 15 April 1993: "If the issue of Ganga water was not solved, it might force their people in future to migrate to India." By citing a set of comparative density of population figures (given below), some analysts almost seem to be offering a sinister suggestion that Assam is the obvious destination for the Bangladeshi immigrants.

State		*Density Per Sq km*
Assam	-	286
West Bengal	-	767 (highest in India)
Bangladesh	-	849 (Perhaps, highest in the World)
India	-	273

The Muslim leaders in Assam seem occasionally intent on adding fuel to the fire. "The BJP and AASU in Barpeta, Lower Assam are up in arms over a speech by a Gogoi Minister," says a story in the *Indian Express* of 3-1-2003. At a Panchayat Election Campaign meeting "last Thursday, Ismail Hussain, Minister of State for Irrigation, had said that the Congress was all for Muslims and Assam would one day become a Muslim land". Was it a Freudian slip or a statement of intent?

If political class has been remiss in this regard, the Census Commissioners and CEC, have done their duty by the nation, warning against the foreigners vitiating the nation's electoral processes, thus not only fringing its sovereignty but also posing a threat to its security. More gratifying is a realistic view of the judiciary on the issue, as will be seen shortly.

West Bengal Situation: Is it any better?

As migration effects West Bengal also, a brief examination of the situation there is called for, even if the ruling CPM-combine continues to claim it to be "a haven of peace and tranquility". The June 1999 blast at New Jalpaiguri Railway station, killing 85 people and injuring many more, shattered the myth of a safe haven. The arrest of two ULFA insurgents next day from Siliguri and subsequent investigations based on the interrogation and intelligence reports disclosed considerable ISI penetration in the state. Earlier the Top Secret May 1999 military intelligence Report on the Internal Security situation in the 28-km wide Siliguri Corridor had disclosed that "Muslim fundamentalist organisations with ISI support are having a field day by encouraging changes in the demographic pattern of the area." India's IB put the increase in Muslim population in or around Siliguri area at an astounding 150 per cent in the past 7 years (1991-98) against 30-40 per cent in other Muslim dominated belts in the State. Far away from the hot zones of Kashmir, Punjab, and even Coimbatore, Siliguri Corridor and area beyond in West Bengal "have today become, starting early 1990s, the newest and most preferred playground of the LSI" (cited in the *Outlook* of 2-8-1999). This is not the first time that the evidence of activities of the ISI muddying India's insurgency waters in the North-East has washed up; it really started with it helping Phizo with a fake passport to travel to England from East Pakistan, in 1956.

But what should cause deep concern to India is ISI's rising presence in West Bengal in the recent years, helped by its 2187 km long porous border with Bangladesh along ten districts. Says Ranbir Samaddar, a political Scientist: "Unchecked infiltration has created an alarming phantasm among the locals' fears of Lebensraum. Free and easy passage of ISI agents, ready to exploit the discontent and sense of insecurity among the sections of the local Muslim population in the post-Babri Masjid demolition scenario." Laments an Intelligence officer: "West Bengal is a sitting duck for the ISI...the border is porous.... It is difficult to identify Bangladeshi nationals; and worse, political parties and administration abet infiltration, and are passive." Here follow some statistics that should worry the Indians, starting with two border districts neighbouring the Siliguri corridor.

Population Trends: Two Border Districts of West Bengal

(Figures in percentage)

S.l. No.	*Item*	*Jalpaiguri*		*Murshidabad*	
		1981	*1991*	*1981*	1991
1.	Total Population	22.14	28.02	36.97	47.40
2.	Hindu Population	87.50	84.42	41.15	38.37
3.	Muslim Population	8.75	10	58.67	61.39

Now some data from the Census and Intelligence Report (cited in *The Outlook* of 2-8-1999):

1. Nearly 10 million Bangladeshis, most of them infiltrators, have entered India and overstayed, with proper papers. Disconcerting pointers have been available for a long time now.
2. The 1981 Census revealed that in the eight border districts of West Bengal the population has grown by 30 per cent during 1971-81 whereas the remaining districts registered growth rate below 20 per cent.
3. During 1981-91, the Muslim population in West Bengal grew by 36.89 per cent as against the national average of 32.76 per cent.
4. Here are revealing figures about the contrasting trends in the percentage of Hindu and Muslim communities in the total population of West Bengal, taken from two enumerations, held 20 years apart.

Percentage of Hindu and Muslim Population in West Bengal

Sl. No.	*Community*	*1971 (Percentage)*	*1991 (Percentage)*
1.	Hindus	78.12	74.71
2.	Muslims	20.46	23.61

5. Infiltrators have mostly settled in the districts of Jalpaiguri, Darjeeling, North and South Dinajpur, Malda, Murshidabad and Nadia. While the over all growth of population in the State during 1971-91 has been 47.9 per cent, it was much higher in the five border districts as shown here:

Growth in 5 Border Districts of West Bengal: 1971-91

Sl. No.	*District/State*	*Growth of Population between 1971-1991 (Percentage)*
1.	Jalpaiguri	53.00
2.	West Dinajpur[41]	57.70
3.	Malda	59.00
4.	Murshidabad	67.00
5.	Nadia	63.24
6.	West Bengal	47.90

Radical Muslim Organisations: A State Home Ministry Top Secret document lists seven such outfits functioning in the State. Five of them are:

1. Jamait-e-Islami-e-Hind (JEI-Hind). A "fanatical Communal organisation", having bases in almost all districts, particularly the border districts, and in the districts of North Bengal, bar Darjeeling.
2. Jamait-Ahle-Hadis. Established in 1906, this fundamentalist outfit is funding the setting up of a Jamia Rahamania (Muslim University) in Dhulian, Murshidabad. It operates from 1 Marcus Street, Kolkata and has strong bases in North 24 Parganas and South Dinajpur districts.
3. Students Islamic Organisation (SIO). Set up in 1981, it supports the self-determination for the Kashmiris, and is run from 14, Alimuddin Street, Kolkata, a few houses away from the ruling CPI(M)'s sprawling headquarters. The SIO is "trying to get closer to the SCs and STs; and has 2000 members."
4. Students Islamic Movement of India (SIMI). Founded April 1997, it is in touch with other Muslim outfits and such ultra Left groups as "students belonging to Santosh Rana group of CPI(ML)". It also has links with the dreaded Islamic Chharra Shibir, the radical students wing of the JEI-Bangladesh and operates out of Kolkata and a dozen other districts.
5. Tablighi Jamat. Drawing ideological guidance from the Mecca-based pan-Islamic organisation Rabita-e-Alam-Islam (world Muslim League),

this outfit is attempting to unite the Muslims to counteract any attack on Islam by the VHP, RSS and other Hindu fundamentalist groups.

What should be more alarming is the plethora of Intelligence reports revealing the illegal border crossings by members of these outfits, networking with the radical Islamic groups in Bangladesh, and the latter pledging them funds and arms. Some examples:

1. A number of people from Islamgarh in North Dinajpur district walked over to Panchagarh in Bangladesh to attend the 2-day Islamic conference convened by the Jamaat-e-Islami (JEI).
2. A JEI meet decided that the trainees in their district units would be provided archery and fire-arms training and *lathikhela* (stick-wielding) "for encountering opponents during riots and for self-defence".
3. In December 1997, Abul Kasham and Abdul Raut, members of the JEI-Hind and residing in the northern outskirts of Kolkata, crossed over to Bangladesh to attend a JEI District conference. There they pledged arms and ammunition from India to the Bangladesh JEI before the local municipal elections and gave a call for removing Hasina's Awami League Government from power.
4. There have been a number of meetings "between JEI functionaries and members of West Bengal-based radical Muslim outfits in the past two years" (1998-99). The state intelligence listed "56 such important meetings" during the year 1996-97 alone.

A Weekly'[42] quoting Home Ministry files and Intelligence reports gives the following information about the dangers ahead:

1. A dozen mosques under construction in the State without any permission.
2. "The ISI is cultivating hostile and hardline Islamic groups in State in the absence of any rebel formations," says a South-Asia Security analyst.
3. Then there are post-Jalpaiguri explosion Intelligence reports worrying the security agencies. The Army has identified villages with "curious" population mix, in and around Siliguri that provide safe haven for the ISI operatives. Chapra is one such village, 55 km from Siliguri, with a population of 25,000, the nerve centre for "illegal border trade and fake currency racket of Saudi *Riyals* and other currencies". There is Islampur, a town 70 km from Siliguri, with a population of 1 lakh, a known "stronghold and hub of ISI functionaries". The town has a skewed demographic mix: some 2,000 Pushto and Baluchi settlers from Afghanistan, engaged in moneylending and ("suspected ISI

activists"); 6,000 Iranians who settled here in the late 1960s, "all of them without any vital documents and involved in narcotics smuggling;" and some Saudis who "indulge in smuggling and other illegal activities".

4. There are ostensibly educational institutions suspected of sheltering ISI activists and agents. Two names:

   (a) Tauhid Education Trust, Mahadabad. The Army intelligence warned about the Trust which is imparting religious education, preserving Islamic, religious scripts, and "maintaining vigil on anti-Islamic activities". Its boy's hostel has 650 students and 500 day scholars, and 60 teachers, including some foreigners. The girls hostel has 500 residents and 25 teachers. "The Trust is funded with financial assistance from various gulf countries." The Trust, geostrategically located near the porous borders of Bangladesh and Nepal, "could encourage subversive acts around the Siliguri Corridor and be used for launching a religious movement". Its chairman, Maulvi Abdul Salafi, is reportedly "a person of doubtful credentials". The Army Intelligence believes the Maulvi and his Trust are instrumental in propagating Muslim fundamentalism in the guise of educational and welfare institutions, by providing shelter to illegal Muslim foreigners who enter India, and thus contributing to Islamisation of the area.

   (b) Al-Jamiatul Rahaman Islamic Viswavidyalaya in Dhulian area of Murshidabad, a shadowy educational institution, is also under suspicion. Since 1987, some 50,000 people "attend a huge religious congregation, held every year, to raise funds for this University", which has received permission under the Foreign Contributions Regulations Act for foreign contribution's amounting to Rs. 1,03,500 from the Islamic Development Bank, Jeddah, Saudi Arabia.

The analysts aver that it is obvious from the foregoing that West Bengal faces as serious a threat from the influx and infiltration of the foreigners as the beleaguered Assam "but the Marxist Parties seem to be least concerned". The obvious question is: Does this veneer of non-challance come from ideological moorings or is it born of the less-exalted reasons of vote bank politics and sectarian interests? The Left Front's management of the ISI threat seems to be abysmal. "The Marxist Parties have abetted infiltration in the border districts openly, arranged food and shelter to bolster their vote bank." An Army intelligence report comments matter-of-factly: "the local administration has apparently turned a blind eye to the problem". Here is the summary of criticism against the Left and its Government:

"No one has ever heard the Communists led by the venerable Joyti Basu ever voicing their concern on the issue of Muslim influx from across the borders. The Left Front has not even discussed the issue within the four constituent parties or the Government. There has been an avalanche of Intelligence reports landing at the table of the state's Home Minister Buddhadev Bhattacharya for the last few years, but it was only recently (June 1999) that he could bring himself to admit during a visit to Murshidabad that 'there are a lot of ISI operatives here'. It is not only that the religion is a holy cow even for the Marxists but the minority community also belongs to the same class; hence the reluctance of the four Left Parties' Ruling Combine to initiate any counter measures to stem the rot even after the admission by a senior Minister and No. 2 in the Government pantheon, Bhattacharya (now Chief Minister), about the threat from the ISI."

Debabrata Bandopadhyay, Director, State Intelligence, wrote the Weekly, was more honest and forthcoming in his assessment: "the threat of ISI is really serious in West Bengal. The Region has become a fertile ground for them." Will the powers-that-be stir themselves to take some positive measures? The answer, going by their track record, could possibly be a resounding 'No'.

Figures of increase in percentage terms in some of the West Bengal Assembly Constituencies bordering Bangladesh between the years 1961 and 1991 are unusually high.

Percentage Growth in Some West Bengal Assembly Constituencies for 1961-91

Sl. No.	*Constituency*	*Percentage Increase 1961-91*
1.	Islampur (in West Dinajpur district)	88.89
2.	Karandighi	113.83
3.	Goalpokhar	96.01
4.	Maldah	115.50
5.	Murshidabad	69.57
6.	Bahrampur	74.62
7.	Kishanganj	79.40
8.	Karimpur	95.85

"The BSF deployed to check infiltration across the border has its hands tied up. The request for personnel is not met adequately and the pressure from local panchayats dominated by the leftist cadres has made the situation worse. The Panchayat head and the cadres, arrange the ration cards for the infiltrators and get their names included in the voters lists. Other benefits too are given to them to build solid and reserve vote banks. This wide scale malpractice is dangerous to the national security."[43]

Equally significant are the 1991 Census figures on the percentage of Muslim population for the five border districts of West Bengal given in the table below:

Muslim Population: Border Districts of West Bengal (1991)

Sl. No.	*District*	*Muslim Population (Percentage)*
1.	24-Parganas (North and South)	56
2.	Nadia	48
3.	Murshidabad	52
4.	Malda	54
5.	Islampur Sub-Division (of West Dinajpur)	60

An English Daily describes the running feud between the Ruling CPM Party and the State Election Department on the eve of the 1999 Parliamentary Poll that shows the attitude of the Party and its Government towards these immigrants:

"With the Voters Lift being revised in the state, the infiltration issue has revived with an apparently inflated number of new applicants awaiting inclusion in the list.... The differences between the CPM and Election Department have opened up the issue. While the tight-lipped Department did nothing but released the cold figures about the aspiring applicants, CPM has already refused to accept that infiltration could be a factor contributing to the increase.... The Department has already spotted areas in the border districts where the increase is almost 19.67 percent.... It is not that some at least in the CPM are not worried about the increase in the number of voters. For the first time during the Left Front's 22-year rule, when the Party's politburo members met Chief Electoral Officer (CEO), Jahwaar Sircar, they complained about 'Various irregularities' in the process of revision of the Voters List.... The CPM blamed the "communalist and fascist forces for trying to include the bogus and underage voters in the final List. But it ruled out the possibility of the Bangladeshi infiltration.... CEO Sircar said, 'We take this rise very seriously and have to gear up our machinery for inquiry and screening process.... The Final List has to be prepared by 21 July'."[44]

A weekly reported that DGBSF, Parkash Singh, before his retirement, had informed the MHA by a letter that "the infiltration has reached an alarming stage in West Bengal and the North-East States" and warned that if proper measures were not taken "to tackle "the infiltration and insurgency in the North-East, the entire area would very soon, plunge into a Kashmir-like situation". Excerpts from the letter:

> "Compared to other states, the border districts of West Bengal have recorded an alarming rise in Bangladeshi infiltration. From 1983 to 1993, the No. of names in the voters list of these districts has risen from 7 to 14 per cent. When the leftists came to power in 1977, the State Assembly voters totalled 2,60,32,989. The figure reached 4,25,08,579 in 16 years, an increase of 53.28 per cent."[45]

Crescent classroom. Murshidabad district in West Bengal has the 'distinction' of being a part of Pakistan for two days from 15 August to 17 August 1947, when the Radcliff Award which respected demography but not geography was amended bilaterally. The district reverted to India as it is the link between North and South (West) Bengal but its dominant Muslim population (64 per cent in 2001) makes it a socio-cultural island of sorts. The neighbouring Malda district too has a large Muslim population "but Murshidabad is more of a fanatic oddity in a State not much given to stand off along communal lines". Barua Rahamani Education Society (BRES) is spearheading a drive to purity education as the syllabi of the Government run *Madrasas* lack Koranic contents and Arabic literature. BRES, an organisation of Islamic leaders with strong Saudi Arabian ties and founded in 1993, has already opened 109 madrasas in the State (including 35 in Murshidabad, 22 in Malda and 10 each in Birbhum, north Dinajpur and Nadia. Over 40,000 attend the BRES classes and the number is growing. It is not the number that is worrying but the BRES's almost totally communal syllabus. A book on economics tells the students that the chief sources of national income is the divine act of "expropriating the property of the vanquished enemy". A history text justifies the destruction of the Somnath Temple because: "The Pandits and Brahmins of Gujarat began a conspiracy and turned the Temple into the Centre of political activities." BRES is flush with Arab funds. "In West Bengal now, as in Afghanistan in 1980s, fundamentalism gets a boost when Marxists are out to prove their secular credential" (*India Today*, 25-6-2001; *Crescent Classroom* by Sumit Mitra).

Government Wakes up to the Danger: Long Last

CPM-dominated Government of West Bengal has shown awareness about the seriousness of immigration problem for the first time in its quarter-of-a-century rule in the State. Excerpts from the *Indian Express* of 17-6-2002:

> "The Central Agencies (including BSF) on vigil along the 1,150 km. border with Bangladesh in Southern West Bengal are planning a demographic mapping of the five districts to investigate the profiles of Bangladeshi settlers.... Writers Building is now more vocal than ever on the 'new menace of infiltration by fundamentalist-cum-terrorists from Bangladesh.... State's hardening stand on infiltration.... Besides the mapping, the Agencies may propose an investigation into Bangladeshis' overstaying their visas in nine districts and Kolkata. The Agencies set up after the

recent spurt in population in South Dinajpur, Nadia, Murshidabad and North 24 Parganas districts, that did not match the state's population growth rate.... A census report suggests the average growth rate in these districts is a little over 4.27 per cent unlike the rest of the state.... For example, in south Dinajpur and Malda, the figures are 22 per cent and 25 per cent compared with the state's 18 per cent."

Consequences of Unchecked Migration

Do the following seven tables reflect the consequences of continued, unchecked, un-interrupted (or is it politically-connived at) influx of the foreigners on the three States of India?

Percentage Growth of Population between 1991 and 2001 in Assam Districts Bordering Bangladesh

District	*Muslims*	*Non-Muslims*	*Total*
Dhubri	29.5	7.1	22.9
Goalpara	31.7	14.4	23.0
Hailakandi	27.2	13.3	20.9
Karimganj	29.4	14.5	21.9
Cachar	24.6	16.0	18.9

Percentage Growth of Population between 1991 and 2001 in Four other Districts of Assam

District	*Muslims*	*Non-Muslims*	*Total*
Barpeta	25.8	10.0	18. 9
Nagaon	32.1	11.3	22.2
Marigaon	27.2	16.3	21.2
Darrang	28.9	9.6	15.8

Percentage Growth of Population between 1991 and 2001 in Districts of West Bengal

District	*Muslims*	*Non-Muslims*	*Total*
South 24 Parganas	34.2	11.5	20.8
North 24 Parganas	23.0	22.6	22.7
Nadia	21.9	18. 8	19.5
Murshidabad	28.4	16.4	23. 8
Malda	30.7	19.4	24.7
Kolkata	19.0	0.7	3.9
South & North Dinajpur	31.9	22.7	26.1
Jalpaiguri	31.3	20.4	21.5
Cooch Behar	18.5	12.8	14.2
Total West Bengal	25.9	15.3	17.8

Muslims as Percentage of Population in Districts of Assam

	1991	*2001*
Districts bordering Bangladesh		
Dhubri	70.4	74.3
Goalpara	50.2	53.6
Hailakandi	54.8	57.6
Karimganj	49.2	52.3
Cachar	34.5	38.1
Four other Districts		
Barpeta	56.1	59.4
Nagaon	47.2	51.0
Marigaon	46.0	47.6
Darrang	32.0	35.6
Total Assam	28.4	30.9

Muslims as a Percentage of Total Population in Districts of West Bengal

District	*1991*	*2001*
South 24 Parganas	29.9	33.2
North 24 Parganas	24.2	24.2
Nadia	24.9	25.4
Murshidabad	61.4	63.7
Malda	47.5	49.7
Kolkata	17.7	20.3
South & North Dinajpur	36.8	38.4
Jalpaiguri	10.0	10.8
Cooch Behar	23.4	24.2
Total West Bengal	23.6	25.2

Percentage Growth of Population between 1991 and 2001 in Districts of Bihar

District	*Muslims*	*Non-Muslims*	*Total*
Kishanganj	35.2	25.0	31.71
Araria	36.1	32.4	34.0
Purnea	44.1	30.8	35.4
Katihar	39.7	25.4	31.1

Muslims as Percentage of Population in Districts of Bihar

District	*1991*	*2001*
Kishanganj	65.8	67.6
Araria	40.5	41.2
Purnea	34.5	36.7
Katihar	39.9	42.5

Source for these 7 tables: Arun Shourie, *Ind. Exp.* of 09-10-04.

The *TOI* of 22 May 2005 is making no revelation when it says the demography of some of the border districts of West Bengal is changing because of the illegal immigration from across the Bangla border. In some places, like Malda and Murshidabad, the border is demarcated by rivers and the fencing is not yet complete, making it near impossible to control the immigration.

A common complaint against the immigrants is that they come in search of jobs and get ration cards easily with the help of the politicians. Friends in villages near the border provide shelter. It is easy to identify a Bangladeshi in the North-East but not so in West Bengal because of the common language. Here is data from three districts from the 2001 Census.

Districts	*2001 Population (Percentage)*	
	Hindus	*Muslims*
Malda	49	49
North Dinajpur	52	47
Murshidabad	36	64

Floating Migrants in Tripura

Sharing an 856 km border with Bangladesh, Tripura has a different type of infiltration problem: A large floating Bangladeshi population crosses the border at daybreak for work and returns home at sunset. Sources say Agartala has 5000 Bangladeshis located just 2 km from the border (Can they be called the NRIs, rather, [NRTs], non-resident Tripuris?). They go for 'work' each morning—men are mostly rickshaw-pullers; women, maids; and even the children as rag-pickers—and return the evening. Says Arunaday Saha of Tripura University matter-of-factly: "Cheap labour ignores all boundaries. I do not see any human-face in this cross border movement, I see only the economics." The cheap labour makes them an acceptable, even welcome, commodity!

Illegal Bangladeshis: Detailed Distribution

The MHA has estimated the state-wise distribution of these immigrants as on 31 Dec. 2002 (*The Week*, 16-2-03). *See* table here:

Illegal Bangladeshis in India: Distribution

State	*Number*	*State*	*Number*
Arunachal Pradesh	1,080	Mizoram	39
Assam	67,00,300	Nagaland	79,800
Bihar	6,41,390	Orissa	41,670
Gujarat	150	Punjab	345
Haryana	800	Rajasthan	3,390
Himachal Pradesh	25	Tripura	4,44,867
J&K	480	Uttar Pradesh	34,867
Karnataka	15	West Bengal	76,80,122
Madhya Pradesh	950	Andaman and Nicobar	4,050
Maharashtra	28,089	Delhi	5,02,345
Meghalaya	40,510	Total	1,62,05,284

National Commission for Minorities (NCM) Raises Alarm

15 Feb. 2005. The NCM said there was an "abnormally high" growth of Christian population in the North-East and this could be due to illegal Bangladeshi Muslim migrants reporting themselves as Christians. Its Chairman Trilochan Singh told reporters while the population of Christians had remained the same at 2.3 per cent for 1991 and 2001 but scientific analysis of the 2001 Census data showed its "abnormally high" growth particularly so in the districts bordering Bangladesh. Nagaland, Mizoram and Meghalaya "have the highest percentage of Christians at 90 percent, 87 per cent, and 70.3 per cent respectively", Singh said (*HT, TOI*, 15-2-05).

8 June 2005. The NCM is worried that unchecked influx of Bangladeshis into the North-East could upstage the dominance of tribal communities and lead to their losing reservations in legislatures and Parliament. In his letter to Chairman, Delimitation Commission, Justice Kuldip Singh, Trilochan Singh asked the commission to devise 'special provisions' to ensure continued political representation to the tribal communities. He also points out that such an influx has affected the life and culture of tribals who are a majority in the Region.

The reason—or, is it provocation—behind the consternation of the NCM that impelled it to write this letter is the recent analysis conducted by Prof Ashish Bose, Chairman of the NCM's Experts Committee, on the Census 2001 data on the religions (*Express* 9-6-05).

Panic in Upper Assam: April-May 2005

"On 12 April 2005 when Assam was celebrating the Rongali Bihu festival, youths at Bihutoli in Chiring (Siring), Chapori (Saproi) locality of Dibrugarh town were busy planning an economic blockade of Bangladeshis" (*TOI*, 22-05-05). These youths set up the Siring Sapori Yuva Mancha (SSYM) and launched a campaign on 24 April, asking locals not to employ Bangladeshis or give them shelter. Gathering storm, the campaign spread to other parts of Upper Assam, taking on Communal Colours. It triggered alarm bells from Guwahati to Delhi. The Assembly poll due in less than a year, the issue took a political hue, all the three major players, Congress, BJP and AGP, exploiting it for partisan ends.

The SSYM had a 4-point agenda: do not employ illegal migrants for household work; do not travel in vehicles driven by them; do no business with them; and do not rent out houses to them. Said an activitst: "We saw a massive increase in the number of illegal Bangladeshi labourers in Dibrugarh in the last one year." By mid-May many Bangladeshis left, and the movement had spread to three other Upper Assam districts of Sibsagar, Jorhat and Golaghat. The SSYM circulated leaflets and sent SMS. Panic stricken, the immigrants working as rickshaw-pullers, domestic help, and brick-kiln labour fled these districts to the safety of the five immigrant-dominated districts of Dhubri, Goalpara, Kokrajhar, Marigaon and Nagaon.

That a little-known group could generate so much insecurity shows how fragile the peace is. Only 500 people had left, said the Dibrugarh DC, H.N. Borah. But the Intelligence put the figure at 6,000 though the local sources claimed 15,000 had fled. Mindful of the polls in 2006, Gogoi ordered the probe into the exodus.

Deportation of Foreigners: Problems

What is the record of both the Congres; and AGP Governments? Here is a set of figures from the national dailies. During the 1986-93 period, the Police picked up 2,87,000 as suspected foreigners and referred them to the Screening Committees, composed of the Deputy Commissioners and Superintendents of Police of the districts concerned. As required under the IMDT Act, these Committees were required to refer these cases to the Tribunals, constituted for the purpose. "These Tribunals are pathetically short of staff and Government of India are reluctant to make up the shortages", an official laments. Consequently the Tribunals could identify only 9,000 of the 2,87,000 suspects as foreigners. Of these 9,000 only 876 could be deported! And most of the deportees, in any case, re-entered India (Assam), and then, it was business as usual, say the analysts.

If the long-winded procedures both administrative and judicial hamper the deportation of illegal migrants, the party politics muddies the waters further, as the whole issue gets enmeshed in the political 'minority versus majority' polemic.

The issue was in focus at the Chief Ministers' conference of the North-Eastern States in Delhi on September 28, 1992. At the 1995 Dhaka SAARC meet the Prime Ministers of India and Bangladesh agreed to sort out the issue. But there has been no movement since.

Now a brief account of what came out of Maharashtra Government's (BJP-Shiv Sena) efforts in 1997-98 to deport the illegal immigrants from Mumbai. The issue generated immense hear between Mumbai and Kolkata, not surprising for those "well acquainted with the tactics and political character of the CPM and Leftists of all hues". The West Bengal Government was accused of "disrupting the deportation by evoking the Bengali sentiments and by adopting the 'unfederal' behaviour; thus not only stopping the process but also enhancing the morale of the illegal immigrants". It was the Right verses the Left. As during the AASU Movement, the Communists dubbed the BJP-Sena Government not only as Anti-Muslim but also as Anti-Bengali. The latter saw it as a deliberate move to defame it as communal and accused the CPM-Conumnunist of reinforcing their support base among the illicit migrants staying in West Bengal. "They have secured their vote bank, even if in the process, they have served the cause of Bangladesh." One cannot blame Dhaka if it sees in this Sena-CPM polemics an endorsement of their official stance that there is not a single Bangladeshi in India.

Most astounding statements on the issue reportedly came from Chief Minister Basu: "What is the point in deporting when they are sure to return to India sooner rather than later!" The critics have called it a surrender ro vested and sectarian interests. Now examine a defiant statement by Feroze Sheikh, born to Bangladeshi parents in Mumbai: send me back and I will return with 10 more!" (Asian records 22-1-1999). The valid question that cries for an answer is: "Is this defiance the cause of Basu's postulation— rather, an outcry of despair—or its effect?"

The problem of Bangladeshi nationals staying illegally in Delhi is of long vintage. "It assumed serious proportions of late as they have become key players in the Capital's soaring crime graph" (*Times of India,* 9-6-2000). The police was asked to identify them and initiate proceedings for their deportation. A police officer laments: "It is a highly challenging task as they look no different from Indians and speak the same language. Most of them have 'proper' ration cards. If the identification is difficult, deportation is even more so, as the issue becomes play-thing in the hands of the political parties for electoral considerations. Police sources assert the number of illegal immigrants run into "several lakhs".

In the wake of happenings in Kashmir and ISI activities in various parts of India, these foreigners have become a security risk; particularly so after terror struck the Indian Parliament and the US Twin Towers.

As for Home Minister's statement about one lakh Bangladeshi nationals in Delhi, the news weekly "Dhaka Courier" in its issue of 6-12 September 1991 carried an account with names and photographs of "more than 1,50,000 Bangladeshis who have found a home in Delhi".[46]

Now a set of official figures to see the difficulties involved in deportation. Till 1993, expulsion notices were served on a total 5018 illegal migrants, of whom 1186 were extradited. However, during the same period 16,334 fresh immigrants, including the 908 're-infiltrators', were discovered. How difficult, even frustrating, is the task for the agencies involved in executing it?

Here is an economist (1991) re-emphasizing the point made above: "Influx will always remain a fact here. Assam's population density is 287 per km^2 as compared to Bangladesh's 800 and people keep crossing into India."

But long last the nation does not seem to bc accepting, this counsel of despair. Home Minister Advani announced on January 7, 2003 that "orders have been issued to the States to identify and deport 15 million illegal Bangladeshi immigrants and 11,500 Pakistanis who have overstayed illegally". The issue has assumed seriousness because these illicit immigrants pose a threat to Indian security. The MHA has decided to issue to the Indian citizens (in the 13 States, in the first instance) the Multi-Purpose National Identity Card (MNIC) to provide credible individual identification system, as also to act as a deterrent against future illegal immigration (*Times of India,* 8-1-2003). The issue of MNIC to all Indians would cost Rs. 5000 crore (*Indian Express,* 13-1-2003). Will it succeed, is yet to be seen?

Advani's directive of "throwing out" the illegal foreigners (essentially, 15 million Bangladeshis and 15,000 Pakistanis) will not be easy to execute. It is easy to see "why" in the official record of Assam, thc State probably worst affected in the country because of the Bangladeshi influx. It has been able to expel only a 1501 since the signing of the Assam Accord in 1985. Number who may have crept in during the same period? Records show that in those 17 years, Assam has pushed back over 22,500 Bangladeshis as they attempted to cross over. Infiltration has been a problems for long, but more serious since Independence. Over 2,00,000 people were deported from Assam under the provisions of the Foreigners Act between 1952 and 1984, till the Assam Accord was signed. The deportees number over 1,74,000 during the 1952-66; 69,000 during 1967-73; and 5,148 during 1973-84. Interestingly, after the State Congress Government (with Centre too under it) enacted the controversial IMDT Act in 1983, the number of Bangladeshis detected and deported from Assam started coming down. Enters AGP President Brindaban Goswami. "This in itself is enough to prove that the IMDT Act was specifically passed by the Congress to safeguard the interest of the Bangladeshi infiltrators...we have been demanding the repeal of the same." The BJP too has been demanding the same and its President M. Venkaiah Naidu urged Prime Minister Vajpayee on January 11, 2003 to have the Act scrapped. He said: "Illegal and large scale of Bangladeshis into India is not a Hindu-Muslim question, but one that is directly linked to our national unity, security and economy." But the Congress regime in Assam is opposed to the scrapping of the Act, as it feels the Act safeguards Muslims against discrimination and harassment in the name of deporting Bangladeshi immigrants. "It is also a fact well-known by now that illegal Bangladeshi migrants are in a commanding position in as many as 36 assembly constituencies of Assam apart from being in a majority in four of the States' 23 districts" (Samudra Gupta Kashyap in *Indian Express,* 14-1-2003).

Assam Governor, Lt Gen (Retd) S.K. Sinha, had blown the whistle in his November 1997 Report to the Union President about the dangers posed to the Nation's integrity by these immigrants, expressing the fears this "majority" population (in bordering areas would soon demand merger of these areas with Bangladesh. Some excerpts from the 42-page Report:

> "....Unless the border fencing in the North-East, especially Assam, is done seriously, country's security is in danger. As important as the Kashmir issue is, the one involving the influx of the Bangladeshis, for this might first lead to a demand for merger of the North-Eastern border areas with Bangladesh, and ultimately lead to a situation when Dhaka would cut off the Region from the rest of the country.... The demographic pattern in the Region has already changed, reducing the indigenous population to a minority.... The Muslim population of Assam rose by 77.42 per cent during 1971-91, compared to 41.89 per cent for the Hindus; the All-India increase in Muslim population for that period being only 55.04 per cent...(We are aware of) How Pakistan leaders and pro-Pakistan leaders of pre-Independence days made consistent efforts to include Assam and adjoining areas in Pakistan, and same efforts are being carried out by Bangladesh in later years. The political parties are guilty of indirectly encouraging infiltration to build up their solid vote bank, an allegation constantly voiced by AASU since 1979.... C.S. Mullan wrote in 1931 that within 30 years, Sibsagar would remain the only district in the State where 'the Assamese will remain a majority'. This prophecy is well on its way to becoming true as reflected by the present demographic pattern of Assam. The IMDT Act, 1983 must be repealed immediately as instead of curbing influx, it was only helping infiltrators. That only 9,955 persons have been identified under this Act proved how ineffective it has been" (cited by Samudra Gupta Kashyap in *Indian Express,* 17-12-1998).

There is no doubt that illegal migration has adversely affected not only the political situation in the State, to the detriment of India's national security, but also the livelihood of the common Assamese. Writes M.K. Shukla (from Lanka in Nagaon district) in *Hindustan Times* of 28 September 1999: "The indigenous tribals of the villages in the south-eastern parts of Nagaon Parliamentary Constituency have lost out even the limited labour market to Bangladeshi infiltrators." He was only confirming a minor specificity of the larger reality, Governor Sinha had sketched in his report; *viz,* Nagaon had acquired the 'distinction' of being a Bangladeshi majority district, similar to the far away districts of Dhubri, Goalpara, Karimganj and Hailakandi.

" Governor Sinha told *The Hindu* (17-7-2000): "The people felt enraged over illegal migration and at losing their identities.... I have sent a report on it.... The centre is evolving its response to some of the points...." If Advani's 'directive' of 7 January 2003 to expel foreigners from the country is the response, it should be welcome, even if belated by five years!

As for expulsion from metropolitans like Mumbai, Delhi, etc. the situation is very serious. Instead of decrease in immigration the numbers are adding up. "Silently, without local authorities noticing, the population of Bangladeshis in Mumbai's Golibar enclave has swelled, by some estimates, to about 20,000 in just two years (2000-02)", says J. Dey in *Indian Express,* 14 January 2003. Expulsion is an uphill task, indeed.

Is Deportation Impossible—nearly?

"Taking a U-turn on its resolve to deport at least 3,000 Bangladeshi migrants every month, India is likely to tone down the exercise very soon", the *Indian Express* of 28-4-05 informs us. "Earlier this week", the MHA decided a rethink on this policy, as it felt the deportation exercise was "un-implementable". Some realisation this, about a serious security issue that has plagued the nation since its very birth 50 years ago!

The decision will have a serious impact on the states like Assam, Nagaland, Maharashtra and West Bengal whose Chief Ministers had voiced serious concern over the free run the illegal migrants were having in their states, at the recent Chief Ministers conference in New Delhi presided over by Prime Minister Manmohan Singh. West Bengal Chief Minister Buddhadev Bhattacharya had even sought Central intervention, alleging that the Pak ISI was making use of the porous border.

What is the reason behind this give-up, though the MHA would like to term it as 'rethink', even if in reality it is 'surrender' to an unreasonable, blustering, and overbearing neighbour. One of the key reasons that forced a rethink, the MHA officials would like us to believe, was BDR's persistent denial to take back the Bangladeshi migrants. "Once the BDR denies to accept the illegal migrants, there is very little India can do", a senior officer tells the *Express.* Assuming superior airs of morality and humanism, he further pontificates: "Though the BSF can be asked to push back the illegal migrants, the Ministry feels it is an 'inhuman practice' and will not be encouraged under any circumstances." So India will accept all comers. Even mighty USA and powerful European nations do not follow such a "liberal" and "humane" policy towards migrants from smaller nations, forget about a nation of 180 million people and still adding to its numbers. Will some one ask this MHA worthy what happens to over 320 million Indians who are still living below the poverty line? More importantly, is India governed by bureaucracy? Where, pray, is the political leadership? Or, may be, the latter is speaking through the former. As an analyst says, the Ministry, in line with the Congress-led UPA Government stand, is now treating the issue of illegal migrants as a "human problem". "Sources indicated that the parameters of the new policy will be sketched out later this month" (April 2005). "Well, we are waiting."

Tripura Fencing: Revisited

Fencing on Tripura border has its own share of problems. At the 3 May 2005 high level meeting at the MHA, the NSA, M.K. Narayanan had advocated the need to go ahead with the fencing between the Zero Line and 150 yards on Tripura-Bangladesh border, even though strongly opposed by Dhaka. The BDR is against fencing in this particular area of about 200 km, claiming that some of the 938 villages in this region are in their territory. Even though India rejects this claim, there is some dispute on the issue.

Inadequacies of Anti-Infiltration Measures

How effectual have been the administrative and political measures against the influx of the foreigners, illegal or otherwise, so far? Can physical measure really deter a determined infiltrator from entering a neighbouring country? The *charlands,* the islands formed between different channels of the Brahmaputra, get submerged when the mighty river is in spate during monsoons. This is worst of the times for population who inhabit these islands as they move from *one charland* to another in country boats. Their thatched houses are washed away by the turbulent waters. The river has no respect for the international boundaries nor do the people in the rainy season. It is the most opportune time for the infiltration and smuggling as the distributaries of the rivers increase manifold and the goods can be carried to remote villages in boats on either side of the border. But more worrisome is the smuggling of human beings.

The BSF men charged with the duty of guarding these borders shift to the boats and establish floating outposts in the heart of the river when the border outpost are submerged. Of the 126 km Assam-Bangladesh border, that the two BSF Battalions are required to guard, about (25 + 46) 71 km is riverine, for which they have a water Wing.[47]

Equally difficult is the task of protecting the sanctity of the land border on the North-Eastern Frontier because of thick vegetation in the submontane terrain. "It is the continuous infiltration of the Bangladeshis over the past 5 decades which is of immense concern. Political persecution of the minorities in that country and the economic compulsion of the majority have forced thousands to sneak into India."[48] Checking such infiltration is a near impossible task without active support from the local population. Since the populations on either side of the border have same socio-economic and religio-ethnic composition, information is rarely offered voluntarily to the BSF, laments an officer of the force. Lack of communication and an open border make the task even more difficult. It was because of these problems that the Assam Accord of 1985 had provisions for construction of border fencing and roads. But the implementation has been slow. "It took all of 7 years after the Accord to complete a mere 30 km of fencing and 52 km of road against a total of 72 km of road and fencing proposed under it."

The situation was even worse in Meghajaya, where out of 168 km of road and fencing proposed to be laid, only 50 km and 33 km of these two respectively were completed till 1992.

In December 1988, Bangladesh Foreign Minister Abdus Samad Azad declared that his Government was opposed to any Indian move to fence the borders and added rather ominously: "It is not in the interest of the improvement of the biliteral ties between the two neighbours. It is not a good omen for bilateral ties and also not conducive to present initiatives on the creation of a South Asia Free Trade Area."[49] It is rather a curious logic, the Foreign Minister telling India that unless it continues to allow the migration from the very country which is its major source, the relations between the two neighbours would deteriorate!

The progress on construction of road-cum-fencing project, launched in 1987 as an anti-infiltration measure under the 1985 Assam Accord, has been rather halting and tardy. While India shares 4096-km-long border with Bangladesh, only 852 km of fencing has been completed so far (2002), at the cost of Rs. 139.79 crore. The worst hit is the Assam portion, 262 km long, of which only 149 km has been fenced so far in a period of 15 years. The work on construction of roads too is progressing at a snail's pace, with only 2539 km against a total border length of 4096 km having been completed in these 15 years. The government's ambitious project to fence the Indo-Bangladesh international border to halt illegal infiltration will take another 5 years to be realized. "The border fence project has entered phase 2 with the Government estimating a sum of Rs. 847 crore for the 2,429.5 km, the date for completion being fixed at 2007."[50]

The fencing work again hit a road block in May-July 2005 with Bangladesh stoutly opposing any construction within 150 yds of the zero line. BDR are known to firing and shelling the BSF-led construction parties engaged in the task. Taking a U-turn on its decision to continue border fencing despite protests from Bangladesh, "the MHA has suspended fencing 3 May 2005 along 212 patches where villages on the Indian side stretch upto the international boundary". Home Minister Patil, explaining the change in stance, sources said, wanted the CCS, the MEA, and the PM to take a view on the issue as the consequences of fencing this 4,000 km border were not limited to his Ministry only. Patil issued the suspension orders even as the BSF and section of officials urged that fencing be continued.

The BSF and BDR have an informal agreement on not having defensive structures within 150 yds of the *"Zero* Line". Adhering to this would mean leaving out 254 Indian villages, with a population of 65,000, outside the fence. The MHA made a power-point presentation to Patil in the presence of M.K. Narayjm, N.S.A., Neelam Deo, JS (Bangladesh), MEA; Home Secretary, V.K. Duggal; and the DGBSF. This meeting assumed great significance coming as it did a day after the MOD released its Annual Report, slamming Bangladesh for being "insensitive and unresponsive" to India's Security concerns.

There was contention in July 2005 with India demanding that it must erect the fence closer to the Zero Line where topography compels it to do so and Bangladesh insisting "No fencing within 150 yds of this Line". The problem becomes acute where the two differ on the demarcation of the boundary. Thus is the fencing work "has hit a road-block at two points in Tripura and one in West Bengal".

The MHA is determined to complete the fencing by 2006 (as Patil announced recently), "as the detection and deportation of the infiltrators has failed to address the problem". The infiltration is going on unabated along the porous Bangla border. The areas from where bids are made include 24 Parganas, Nadia, Murshidabad, Malda, and Dakshin West Bengal; Dubri in Assam; and Gokul Nagar and Udaipur in Tripura. "The BDR is supporting infiltration."

K. Natwar Singh, during his 2-day Aug. (6-7) 2005 visit to Dhaka, told the press: "A strong fence was useful for both sides to achieve their common objectives of ensuring peace and tranquilty and facilitating interaction between two friendly people while doing their utmost to prevent illegal cross border activity." He was obviously alluding to a sharp increase in cross-border criminal activity, including illegal trade in arms and explosives, counterfeit currency, trafficking in narcotics, women and children (*Tribune, AA* of 3 and 4 May, 1 and 8 Aug., all 2005).

Census 2001: Portentous Fall-out for Ethnic Assamese

As the February 2001 Census got underway the perennial fears of the Assamese and other ethnic communities being swamped by religious and linguistic aliens loomed large in Assam. During the month-long operations the focus was on the Muslims in Assam, most of whom had migrated from Bangladesh along with many Bengali Hindus. The fears that the Census 2001 would show a drop in the Assamese populations are not unfounded. Assamese comprised 60.89 per cent of the State's populations in 1971 Census. But 20 years later, in 1991 Census, this percentage fall to 57.29, while that of the Bengalis rose by almost 4 per cent to 21.5 per cent.

Besides the continuing influx of the Bangladeshis, other reasons, given by the demographers for this fall in the Assamese population during the 1971-91 period, are:

1. Movement for a separate Bodoland state had peaked by 1991 and ABSU had advocated against Bodo-speaking population enlisting themselves as Assamese.
2. But a major factor was the decision of many neo-Assamese to revert to this original Bengali Language following an anti-minorities wave in the 1980, marked by the Nellie massacre.

Maulana Abdul Haq, President of Jamiat-Ulema-e-Hind (Assam), said before the census 2001, "There is no reason why the settlers should not call themselves Assamese as they have been doing since 1981." Bengali Hindu organisation like the All Assam Bengali Yuva Chhatra Federation also wanted the Bengali-speaking residents of the State to mark them as Assamese. Whether these exhortations would change the situation for better for the Assamese can be seen after the results of 2001 Census are published, but under the given circumstances, it seems unlikely. The Rabhas are likely to follow the lead given by the Bodos, as the too are demanding a self-ruled territory.

ISI and Extremist Outfits: Nexus in Assam

The ISI with its tentacles spread all over the North-East, is creating disaffection in the Region with the help of extremist elements among the foreigners. It is sponsoring and funding several militant or terrorists outfits to foster anti-India sentiment in the area. Muslim Liberation Tigers of Assam (MLTA) is the leading Muslim extremist outfit which threatened (1995) to create a separate Islamic state in Assam. "Propped up and funded by Iran and some West Asian countries," some of the extremist outfits are listed here:

1. Muslim Voluntary Force (MVF)
2. Students Islamic Movement of India (SIMI)
3. Islamic Revolutionary Force (IRF)
4. Islamic United Liberation Army (1ULA)
5. Assam Minorities Liberation Army (AMLA)

6. Minorities United Liberation Front of Assam (MULFA)
7. Muslim Liberation Front of Assam (MLFA)
8. Special United Reform Army of Assam (SURAA)
9. Islamic Revolutionary Army (IRA)
10. Saddam Bahini (SB)
11. Islamic Sevak Sangh (1SS)
12. Minority Liberation Tigers of Assam (MLTA)
13. Muslim Liberation Tigers of Assam (MULTA)[51]
14. Islamic Liberation Army of Assam (ILAA)

With the help and guidance of the ISI, these outfits are smuggling into Assam arms not only from Bangladesh, but also through Burma from countries beyond it. Ostensibly, they claim to safeguard the interests of the Muslims in Assam, the long-term aim is to destabilise Assam, North-East, and then India in that order. The ISI's nexus with NSCN(I-M) is a given, and the latter's tie up with outfits like ULFA, PLA and Bangladesh Security Forces provides it a safe corridor to Cox Bazar port centre for global narco-terrorist combine. As several Islamic countries reportedly give grants to them, these outfits are never short of funds.

This Pan-Islamic slant to the foreigners issue in Assam gives it a more sinister dimension, which gets flagrantly dangerous for India's security because of the flip-flop attitude of certain political formations towards these infiltrators. "It should be a cause of concern that in 56 out of 126 Assembly constituencies in Assam, the Muslim migrants and their sympathizers had become decisive actors by 1995." Intelligence reported in 1995-96 that "all the 17 JEI MPs of Bangladesh hailing from its borders districts are playing subtle if sinister role in this dangerous anti-India plan". Besides the 14 outfits mentioned above, there are 24 others operating clandestinely. "There are plans to bring all of them under one umbrella organisation, ala 32 separatist groups functioning under the rubric of the APHC in Kashmir.

The MVF, the largest militant group with 500 cadres derives its sustenance from a powerful Agar lobby of Hojjai. MVF and other groups like IRF, MULFA, MLTA, etc., keep adding to their cadres through dubious means, as also from outfits like the SIMI and certain district units of JEI Hind.[52] ISI was using the *Pasban*, a front of the JEI, and Jamaat-ul-Fuqra, as conduit for funds etc. to the Muslim groups in Assam.

Another view holds that the *modus operandi* of these militant outfits is reminiscent of the Muslim League plan of 1947, mooted at Dhaka, "to lay siege of Assam through means devious, violent or otherwise, and to grab it for Pakistan". After all one should not forget that in 1946 the Cabinet Mission had placed Assam and Bengal in group C.

Even Bangladesh made some ostensibly helpful noises occasionally. In November 1998, India and Bangladesh agreed to enforce the 1991 Agreement on illegal immigrants, with the latter pledging that no one would be allowed to use its soil for anti-India activities. But there was little to show in practical terms for such statements pregnant with pious intent.[53]

The Issue Reaches Supreme Court

Whatever be the shenanigans of the political class on the emotive issue that simultaneously impinges on the national security, the nation's highest Court was more pragmatic, when it ruled in March 1993 that possession of a ration card and figuring in the Voters List did not confer any privilege on a suspected foreigner. Seeing the inaction of various Governments since Independence on the issue, it reached the Supreme Court through Public Interest Litigation (PIL) route. On 20 September 1999, its 3-Judge bench admitted a public interest petition from the All India Lawyers Forum, seeking repatriation of the Bangladeshi migrants illegally staying in India. The Petitioner, P.P. Saxena, Forum's President, alleged that about 1 crore Bangladeshis had illegally infiltrated four North-Eastern States—Assam, Tripura, Meghalaya and Manipur—and West Bengal, causing severe constraints on the limited resources of these States. He sought directions to the authorities for their repatriation.[54]

The Court granted 8 weeks time to the Centre to file a comprehensive affidavit dealing with the issue relating to the illegal Bangladeshi migrants in these five States. The court observed that this was a serious matter and the Central Government should take steps to stop this illegal infiltration as it was threatening to change the demography of these States.

The Assam Government in its affidavit, had stated that a total of 4,05,267 illegal migrants were detected in the region between 1952 and 1999, of which 3,47,689 were deported. "In the recent past, there appeared to be a close nexus between the illegal migrants and the fundamentalist organisations on the one hand, and between fundamentalist organisations and Pakistan's ISI, on the other. The State suggested repeal of the IMDT Act, 1983 in view of the impediments in detection and deportation of migrants. "It also suggested intensification of BSF patrolling in border areas by reducing the distance between the border posts, high-tech communication facilities using satellites and issuance of multipurpose photo identity cards in the border villages."

The Tripura Government informed the Court it had pushed back 1,43,188 illegal migrants since 1971. The migration from Bangladesh had a devastating effect, virtually engulfing the indigenous tribal communities who were previously enjoying majority.

The West Bengal stated that it had suggested to the Centre to introduce changes in the Foreigners Act to strengthen the power of the enforcing agencies and to streamline the procedure for deporting Bangladeshis.

The Supreme Court's concern about the unabated migration of Bangladeshis and asking the Government to make "honest" and "serious" attempt to stop the influx assume importance since they posed a threat to India's security.

Proving the point that political and sectarian consideration takes precedence over national interest, three months after coming into power in Assam, the Saikia Government of the Congress party, has sought the Supreme Court's permission to withdraw the former (AGP) Government's affidavit favouring repeal of the IMDT Act. Even though the Congress Government's fresh affidavit said the "Act is not aimed at protecting the interests of Bangladeshis as perceived by the former AGP Regime," the data adduced by it proved the contrary:

> "16 Tribunals constituted under the Act, are dealing with the cases from 23 districts. Tribunals have initiated inquiries on the basis of 3,29,905 complaints, but they could only declare 10,353 persons as illegal migrants. However, only 1494 persons (among these 10,353) could be deported from the State."[55]

Even after being declared illegal migrants under the Act, their actual deportation was not possible, the fresh affidavit said, because the Bangladesh Government refused to accept them without verifying their Bangladeshi nationality.

Supreme Court Hands out a Tough Verdict

12 July 2005. The Supreme Court struck down as unconstitutional the IMDT Act, 1983. The 3-Judge (CJ R.C. Lahoti, JJ G.P. Mathur and P.K. Balasubramanyan) Bench, declaring the 1983 Act and the Rules framed thereunder in 1984 as *ultra vires* of the Constitution, directed that all tribunals constituted under the IMDT Act adjudicating the cases for identification of illegal migrants from Bangladesh cease to function with immediate effect, and these cases would stand transferred to tribunals under the Foreigners Act. The petition filed by the AGP M.P. Sarbananda Sonowal, and now allowed by the Court, had said the Act was only encouraging vote bank politics without addressing the mammoth problem of illegal migrants. The reaction to the judgement was on expected lines: AGP, ASSU rejoice; BJP, Shiv Sena welcomed it; Congress, Left, and the minorities dismayed."

The Court verdict says, *inter alia:* "Local people reduced to minority status, face external pressure.... Bangladeshis took Assam land.... The Act encouraged infiltration in Assam.... It boosted Assam Muslim population.... Assam facing aggression...." It pans Centre on the IMDT Act....

Mamta Banerji alleged "the CPM has packed 8 border districts of West Bengal with illegal migrants. These districts have collectively gained 18 Assembly seats". The Leader of Opposition Advani, speaking in the Lok Sabha, said: "The illegal immigration was the 'biggest disaster' and the 'biggest threat to national security'. The Government must gracefully accept the verdict. Why did it appoint the Group of Ministers (GOM)?"

If Gogoi rushed to New Delhi, the Centre appointed a GOM to study the verdict. The critics alleged its aim was to nullify the verdict (*Hindu, Exp., TOI, HT*—13 and 14 July 2005).

Are the Illegal Immigrants Vitiating India's Electoral Processes?

It is an unfortunate situation where a nation does not seem to be concerned about non-Indians, and that too illegal immigrants from a neighbouring country, participating in its electoral process and consequently dictating the results in not-too-insignificant number of constituencies. Mamta Banerji may not be altogether off the mark when she alleges that the CPM has packed 8 border districts in her state with illegal migrants. The Chief Election Commissioners (CEC) in the past did warn the nation against the foreigners vitiating our national elections. L.K. Advani's warning about the "Illegal immigration being biggest threat to our security" is too self-obvious to need further comment. The then CEC B.B. Tandon certainly seemed to be exercised on this count.

Tandon said 14 December 2005 that "almost 1.5 lakh voters on the (Assam) State's electoral rolls are of 'doubtful' nature". This is after the 'D' category figures have come down in the past few years. "The inclusion of the names of the Bangladeshi infiltrators in the State's electoral rolls has remained a major issue for more than three decades now and the Election Commission had in the early 1990s directed the state election officials in Assam to mark as 'D' (D for doubtful) as many as 3.75 lakh voters on the ground that the citizenship status of these voters was doubtful, and suspected to be Bangladeshi infiltrators" (*Express* 15-15-05). The Foreigners Tribunals have, over the years, examined several such names and made revisions. The 1.5 lakh is obviously the latest revised figure in 'D' category as mentioned by the CEC, and he made it clear that these people whose names figure in the State's electoral rolls would not be allowed to cast votes in the forthcoming (2006) State Assembly elections.

Assam has been vociferous about deportation of these Bangladeshis for long decades. They had launched a strident Anti-Foreigners Agitation (1979-85) on the issue. West Bengal has only recently, perhaps after the change in the chief ministership, raised alarm about the illegal immigrants in the state.

Non-Left spectrum of the political parties are demanding the CEC conduct "free and fair" poll in the West Bengal in 2006 a la the 2005 Bihar Assembly Elections.

Supreme Court Admits Another Petition on the Issue

10 Dec. 2004, a 3-Judge Bench (CJ R.C. Lahoti, JJ G.P. Mathur and P.P. Naolekar) admitted a PIL petition by Image India Foundation, expressing concern over the alarming growth of Bangladeshi immigrants in the country, especially in West Bengal and five North-Eastern states. It alleged that the Government of India was ignoring several reliable reports by the Army and others, that if effective measures were not taken to stem the tide, the demography of the Region would change, leading to the possibility of a demand for 'Brihad (Greater) Bangladesh' in the future (*AA,* 11-12-04).

The IMDT Act: Impregnable till Highest Court Acted

The Act came into force in 1983 when Anti-Foreigners agitation was at its peak. The 1985 Accord mentions certain difficulties in implementing the provisions of the 1983 Act as brought out by the AASU.

20 Sep. 1990. The AASU for the first time demands the repeal of the Act. March 1992, the AGP repeats the demand. Now a brief chronology of events to show how this important issue was dealt by all concerned:

1. *11 Aug. 1997.* The Centre accept that the results achieved under the Act have been very poor. The AASU President stated at the meeting that the former Prime Minister during his visit to Assam had informed the AASU that the decision to repeal the Act had already been taken.
2. *6 Apr. 1998.* At a tripartite meeting, the MHA officials inform that the AASU request for the repeal of the Act would be put up to the new Government for decision.
3. *23 Sep. 1998.* At this meeting, the AASU was informed that the repeal of the Act was "under the active consideration of the Government".
4. *Feb.* 1999. In his address to Parliament, the President says the repeal of Act "was under active consideration of the Government".
5. *18 Mar. 1999.* Tripartite meet again. The MHA repeats the "under active consideration" assurance.
6. *1 July 1999.* The AASU urged that an ordinance be issued to repeal the Act.
7. *Mar. 2000.* Sarbananda, erstwhile President of AASU filed a writ petition in the Supreme Court. Avoiding details of how the colours of the Governments kept changing at Guwahati (AGP to Congress) and New Delhi (NDA to UPA), and with the stand and stance on the question of repeal of the IMDT Act, suffice it to say that the course of the Sarbananda petition went through tortuous turns and twists before the Supreme Court delivered its judgement on 12-07-05.

Are Only Some Governors Patriotic?

"The (Assam) Congress Government is in crisis over the Report sent by the Governor, Mr (Lt Gen) Ajai Singh to the MHA regarding the huge and unchecked infiltration across the border", says *HT* 14-4-05. The report comes at a time when Chief Minister Gogoi was yet to come out of the open threat hurled at him by Jamiat-Ulema-e-Hind President Maulana Asad Madani when he was attending the Jamiat's rally at Guwahati on 3 Apr. 2005. The threat: "The Jamiat will overthrow his Government if its demands like the job reservation for Muslims and seats in the Lok Sabha and the Assembly were not met within 6 months."

The Report says Assam's border with Bangladesh was one of the world's most fluid borders "with 6,000 Bangladeshis daily crossing it and a large number of them illegally settling here, thus threatening the demographic character of Assam". Such a huge influx could lead to setting up of bases of the Pak ISI and international terrorist outfit's like the Al Qaida.

An analyst avers that Madani's threat, and now the Governor's Report "are certainly going to help the BJP and the AGP to charge Gogoi of appeasing the Muslims". The Congress is the only major party opposed to the repeal of the IMDT Act, only applicable in Assam, which others feel comes in the way of deporting illegal migrants to Bangladesh.

The Report is seen as the vindication of the stand of the political parties like the BJP, Shiv Sena, AGP, etc. and organisations like the AASU, All India Lawyers Forum for Civil Liberties, and individuals like Sarbananda—some of whom had petitioned the Supreme Court for striking down the IMDT Act on the ground that it has failed in its aim of checking illegal immigration, and instead, it proved a shield for 20 lakh Bangladeshis, settled in the border districts. Governor Ajai Singh is not the first to paint a grim picture on this issue, as a former Governor, Lt Gen SK Sinha, presently Governor of J & K, had also sent a similar report to the President, saying how the influx has turned Lower Assam into a Muslim majority area. Sinha had also said the settlement of huge proportion of foreigners in the border districts, posed a grave threat to the security and integrity of the nation. As is their wont, the Congress and the Communists had accused Sinha of raking up communal passions but Ajai Singh's Report "has also said that the demographic changes due to illegal migration are eroding the social and religious fabric" of Assamese Society (*Tribune*, 4-5-05). The sanctuaries of the Bangladeshi population, "mushrooming in the border districts of Assam will provide trans-border support for the secessionist and separatist insurgency movements in our state". Sinha too had voiced the same fears, though worded differently. Interestingly, the Governments at the Centre and Guwahati had taken different stands, depending on the party in power there. Is it indicative of the typical

Indian 'condition' (or syndrome) where the party interests comes before the demands of national security?

These are not the only Governors who chose to be the whistle blowers when the nation's security is relegated to second position. Two more come to mind: (l) Lt Gen VK Nayar who resigned as Manipur Governor when his report to the President that his Chief Minister was colluding with the insurgents was ignored. (2) T.V. Rajeshwar, West Bengal Governor, too had warned the Centre about the threat posed to the nation by this unchecked influx. It may be a mere coincidence that the three are Armymen and the fourth a Policeman. In contrast, another set of Three Governors in the very recent past (of Jharkhand, Goa and Bihar) come to mind who are generally believed to have failed to defend the Constitution they are sworn to do. So, there are Governors and Governors! Why are only some Governors patriotic enough to do their duty by the Indian Constitution?

Current Situation : Post-Jul 2005 Supreme Court Verdict

Some Important Related Issues

The Supreme Court on 12 Jul 2005 striking down as unconstitutional the IMDT Act 1983 was a seminal judgement; for some, may be historic. The Bench declared the 1983 Act and the Rules framed there under in 1984 as *ultra vires* of the constitution and directed that all tribunals constituted under the IMDT Act adjudicating the cases for identification of illegal migrants from Bengladesh cease to function with immediate effect, and these cases would stand transferred to the tribunals under the Foreigners Act.

Some of the events/decisions starting with this judgement itself are noted hereafter.

- 12 Jul. 2005. Supreme Court strikes down the IMDT Act 1983 as unconstitutional.
- The Supreme Court had directed that "all cases pending before the tribunals under the IMDT Act shall stand transferred to the tribunals constituted under the Foreigners (Tribunals) Order, 1964, and shall be decided in the manner provided in the Foreigners Act. The very first thing the MHA did after the declaration of the Court's judgement was to issue two notification.
- Notification One : Called the Foreigners (Tribunals) Amendment Order, 2006, under which the Foreigners (Tribunals) order, 1964, was made applicable to the whole of India except Assam.
- Notification Two : Called the Foreigners (Tribunals for Assam) Order, 2006, under which a new set of laws was created exclusively for Assam.
- Under the Foreigners (Tribunals) Amendment order, 2006, as well as the Foreigners (Tribunals) order, 1964, the onus of proving citizenship was on the suspected 'foreigner'. But under the Foreigners (Tribunals

for Assam) Order, 2006, the onus of proof was on the complainant, as under the struck down MDT Act, 1983. Opponents of the order issued under Notification Two argued that all the objectionable provisions of the IMDT Act 1983 struck down by the Supreme Court were brought back by the Executive.

- 5 Dec. 2006. As was to be expected, the Supreme Court scrapped the Foreigners (Tribunals for Assam) Order 2006, which was brought through a gazette notification after the Supreme Court struck down controversial I MDT Act, 1983 on 12 Jul 2005. The Bench declared the impugned order of 2006 as "unreasonable and issued in an arbitrary exercise of power". It also directed the centre to constitute within four months a sufficient number of tribunals under the 1964 Order to effectively deal with foreigners who have illegally come from Bangladesh or are residing in Assam.
- 30 Jan 2007 : "Halt the delimitation process" An all-party delegation from Assam, led by Assam Assembly speaker Tanka Bahadur Rai met Home Minister Patil and demanded that the delimitation process should immediately be stopped in the State until the National Register of Citizens is completed. Other members of the delegation were : Prithibi Majhi and Sarat Borkotoky (both Congress), Chandra Mohan Patowary (AGP); Parimal Shukla Baidya (BJP); Drupad Borgohain (CPI); and Parameshwar Brahma (BPPF).

The Delimitation Commission is now demarcating boundaries of parliamentary constituencies in the State based on the 2001 Census figures.

Many political parties feel that for detection of foreigners in Assam, the update of the NRC on the basis of 1971 voter list is important.

Reactions to Supreme Court Rulings of Jul 2005 and Dec 2006

The Supreme Court order of Dec. 2006, quashing the Foreigners (Tribunals for Assam) Order, 2006 issued by the ruling UPA has expectedly evoked mixed reactions in Assam More importantly, it has brought centre stage the politics of migration.

The judgement has been hailed by the influential AASU and the major Opposition parties, the AGP and the BJP. The AGP felicitated its MP from Dibrugarh, Sarbananda Sonowal, who was one of the petitioners who had challenged the impured 2006 Order, along with Charan Deka a BJP leader. Incidentally, Sonowal had also filed a petition challenging the erstwhile IMDT Act 1983, which was struck down by the Supreme Court in July 2005.

It may be of interest to know that the Bench imposed an examplary cost of Rs. 25,000 to be paid to the petitioners, Sarbananda and Charan Deka, who challenged the controversial 2006 Order.

Minority (Muslim) bodies on the other hand expressed fears that in the absence of adequate legal protection, genuine Indian citizens may be harassed by the police. All Assam Minority Students Union (AAMSU) called for a State-wide 12 hour bandh, which was marred by incidents of stone-throwing by bandh supporters in some pockets of northern Assam. After the Supreme Court had struck down the IMDT Act, 1983, Muslims had demanded an amendment to the Foreigners Act 1964; they also wanted the amended law to be applicable throughout the country. These demands became vociforous after Dec. 2006 ruling.

What is the main striking point? While under the IMDT Act 1983, the onus lay on the complainant to prove that the accured person was not an Indian citizen, under the Foreigners Act the onus is on the person who faces the complaint to prove that he or she is an Indian citizen and not a foreigner. The AASU, AGP and BJP objected to the Foreigners (Tribunals in Assam) Order, because it shifted the onus of proof back to the complainant and thus came in the way of detecting and deporting "foreigners". The three parties also contend that there cannot be two laws on the same subject : one for Assam and the other for the rest of the country.

After the latest (Dec. 2006) ruling, Congress led coalition government of Assam rushed to pacify the Muslim Community with Chief Minister Tarun Gogoi promising measures to ensure no one was harassed or made to feel insecure. But the Assam United Democratic Front (AUDF) was cynical, accusing the State Government of "deceiving the minorities" in the name of protecting them. The AUDF was formed after the IMDT Act was struck down in Jul 2005 and it represented itself as a replacement for the Congress as the protector of the minority interests. The latest ruling has provided it more fuel to attack the Congress, accusing it of deliberately leaving some legal loop-holes while issuing the two notifications, one for Assam and the other for rest of the country, with the ulterior motive of winning the support of minorities in the Assembly polls.

The AUDF criticism was also echoed by the Char Chapori Sahitya Parishad (CCSP), Assam. Its President Hafiz Ahmad repeats allegations of the AUDF that Congress had intentionally left the loopholes to pose as saviours of Muslims once the 2006 Order is struck down. The CCSP says the Foreigners Act gives the police enormous powers, which are often abused. It cites figures to prove their point. Before the promulgation of the IMDT Act, 210,446 Muslims were driven out of Assam between 1952 and 1971 without trial and without any opportunity to defend their status. It again says that 192,339 people mere deported from the State between 1972 and 1983 in a similar manner.

Obviously, there is a wide chasm between the stands taken by the Muslim bodies/political parties and the parties like the AASI, AGP and BJP. But all of them agreed that once the National Register of Indian Citizens (NRIC) in Assam is updated on the basis of the electoral rolls of 1971 and photo identity cards are issued, the problem may be solved once for all. At a tripartite meeting on 5 May 2005 which was attended by Prime Minister Manmohan Singh, Home Minister Shivraj Patil and Chief Minister Gogoi, it was decided that the NRIC would be updated with the names of all persons who had settled in Assam before 25 Mar 1971, and their dependents.

While the issue of detection and deportation of foreigners in Assam has been mired in legal battles the entire affair has taken a heavy toll on the State exchequer. The Assam Government spent Rs. 400 crore on detection and deportation of foreigners in the past 21 years after the signing of the Assam Accord in 1985. And what did all this achieve? During all these years, only 2,221 illegal Bangladeshi immigrants have been expelled. The State Minister, Implementation of the (1985) Assam Accord, Dr. Bhumidhar Barman disclosed these figures in the Assembly on 12 Dec. 2006. The opponents of the IMDT Act claim that these meagre figures only prove their point that this Act came in the may of Assam expelling the illegal migrants to the country they came from. It will be of interest to know how many "illegal foreigners" are expelled will be expelled now that the impuned Act is out of the way.

Barman also informed the Assembly the same day that the Government did not have the exact number of illegal immigrants living in Assam at present.

Influx Continues in Different Form : BSF Confirms : Nov. 2006

It is difficult to put a number to the immigrants who cross over from Bangladesh to India every day.

On 28 Nov 2006, BSF, DG AK Mitra, however, came up with a tally of Bangladeshi nationals who entered India with valid documents during the past five years through the integrated check-posts and never returned. The figure for such Bangladeshis, officially shown "missing" in records, amounts to a whopping 1.5 lakh.

Mitra believes, like so many other analysts, Indian and foreign, that it is the eastern region, and not Jammu and Kashmir, which could become a problem area in the future. "No one knows where they (1.5 lakh Bangladeshis) went!"

Intelligence agencies had sounded an alert when a dozen Pakistani nationals walked through the Wagah border in 2005 to watch cricket matches and disappeared. It prompted security agencies to slash the cricket visas during the recent (2006) matches, and scaled up the survillance.

Mitra, who ordered increased vigil along the India-Bangladesh border in view of the political development (during the days of the care-taker government) in Dhaka and the impending polls, suspects that some of those who entered India legally would have been involved in anti-India activity.

"They must have come for something." He admitted that his force could not stop illegal cross-overs from Bangladesh.

Mitra's serious concern was that every terror attack trail led to Bangladesh. Initially, it was economic migration, but of late investigation into various terror strikes in the hinterland has revealed that the Bangladesh border was freely being used by militants to enter India. That makes the illegal migration problem a little more serious. He was briefing the media at New Delhi ahead of the Raising Day of the BSF on 1 December (Alok Tikku, *Hindustan Times,* 29 Nov 2006).

Analysts find a pattern in the infiltration by terrorist and insurgent groups from the eastern border. Insurgents from the North-East entered India through North Bengal; those using Bangladesh as an entry point into Jammu and Kashmir or other parts usually took the South Bengal route.

When asked if the Khaleda Zia Government supported the anti-India outfits, his reply : "It is 'safe presumption' to make as the BNP has been in alliance with the JEI and the Islamic Oikya Jote, both rabidly anti-India."

BANGLADESHIS IN INDIA : A POTENT THREAT TO NATIONAL SECURITY

Bangladeshi migrants/entrants/infiltrators are a serious threat to India's strategic interests and national security and unfortunately the subject has not received the attention it deserves in informed circles and security community, not to speak of the political and academic establishment. Only a few commentators have dilated upon the subject in the past, and some of them only in passing. 'Political correctness' is the main reasons for the journalists, academics and strategic analysts shying away from the 'sensitive' issue. In India, any subject impinging upon its "minority community" in any way is rather 'no go' area.

The author distinctly remembers a senior journalist (and son of an eminent journalist of the yore) waxing eloquent on the danger posed to India's security and integrity by the Bangladeshi immigrants in India—mostly illegal—who are already a majority in more than a dozen districts bordering the international frontier (with Bangladesh) in the states of Assam and West Bengal. This was at the India International Centre, New Delhi sometimes in 1990s. Listening intently to his passionate concerns for nation's security and integrity because of this continuing ingress—some call it silent invasion—the author addressed an innocuous, even innocent, question to this senior journalist : "I can clearly see your concerns on the issue, but I have never seen any article by you on the subject in any newspaper. Why have not you written one?" His reply stunned me : "I can't even think of doing so. I shall straight-way be called a (Hindu) communalist!"

The issue of Bangladeshi (and earlier East Pakistani, and still earlier East Bengali) infiltration has been discussed above in some detail from its inception in mid-19th century till end of the 20th century. What follows are the events of the last decade or so, relevant to the subject, preceded by a brief summary to put the issues in perspective.

The influx of illegal migrants has continued unabated for decades by now, and as a result the security scenario in India's North-East has registered a palpable change for the worse with an estimated 12 million Bangladeshis having infiltrated since 1971. The situation has reached such as alarming stage that Bangladeshi migrants are in a position to influence results of elections in about 32 percent of constituencies[56] in Assam. The IB estimates put the number of illegal immigrants way back in 1998 at 1.1 crore with the largest concentration in Assam and West Bengal.

It must be recognised that the impact of this huge illegal immigration into Assam has been far-reaching, and profound. If from 1891 till Independence (1947), its population grew at around 20 per cent per decade, the corresponding figure is presently pegged at a harrowing 53 per cent.

The Bangladeshi politicians and academics alike are brazen enough to deny any illegal immigration into India, essentially Assam and West Bengal. One of its Prime Minister smugly announced on the Indian soil during an official visit that there is not a single illegal Bangladeshi in India!" But the data compiled by demographers at the Bangladesh Institute of Development Studies reveal that nearly 3.5 million people disappeared from East Pakistan between 1951 and 1961 probably as a result of partition while another 1.5 million may have have entered India between 1961 and 1974.

That is not all. There is more to come. Astonishingly, a quarter of the 10 million refugees who came to India to escape the killings and hardships during[57] the war of Liberation never returned. Inexplicably, we Indians are indeed keen to keep the horrible fact under wraps. It is obvious that the Indian policy makers are yet to decipher the threat to Indian security from this massive illegal foreign population entrenched in the North-East. The growth of multiple Islamist organisations in the North-East and their metastatis are only making India's security concerns even more acute, assest the analysts.

It is a matter of grave concern that even after the Group of Ministers' comprehensive report on reforming the National Security System viewed seriously the large scale illegal migration and its serious implications for the internal security in the eastern theatre during the NDA regime, the nation is yet to see through the problem that is assuming an alarming proportion every passing day.

Bangladesh Terrorists Eye Border Areas of Assam

There are reports of Jamiat-ul-Mujahideen Bangladesh (JMB) regrouping itself since mid-2006. It adopted a new name for itself Kital Fi Sabilillah (KFS) which translates into "establishment of Islamic rule." It appears to be working in a more scientific way—concentrating into areas where it has strength. It has divided this area into five commands with established leadership hierarchy, ideological indoctrination and arms training camps.

The Indo-Bangladesh border remains highly porous even after parts of it has been fenced, and it is a haven for smugglers from both sides. Not only illegal infiltration continues having started in 1820s with the British take-over of Assam, a large quantities of illegal arms and ammunition too enters India most of which are for criminal activities but considerable quantities supplement the arsenals of radical Indian terrorists for a 'right' price.

JMB Chief Sheikh Abdur Rahman confessed that first JMB foreign unit was set up in Murshidabad district of West Bengal in 2001. Presently it is under re-vamp to prepare it to provide strategic depth for terrorist activities of the JMB during 2007 elections. Murshidabad is a strategic centre for the activities of SIMI and Jamat-ul-Islam-e-Hind and is a traditional conservative Muslim stronghold—making it attractive for JMB across the border.

JMB is eyeing border area of Assam to consign it a role similar to the one for Murshidabad, namely, to provide strategic depth to the terrorist activities during the 2007 Bangladesh poll. It is emboldened by the reports that the MULTA in Assam's bordering area is increasingly linking up with the JMB in Sylhet.

Assam's border areas would yield more fertile ground to the JMB since its six Muslim-majority border districts have already put forward a demand that these be constituted into a separate state.

Regrouping of the JMB and its plans for the 2007 elections period are portentrous development for India at geo-strategic level, and for Assam at local level as it immediately threatens its integrity.

So, as far as India is concerned, these developments portend a hot winter in Bangladesh. India cannot remain complacent and unruffled if Bangladesh sinks into turmoil in the course of the 2007 elections. Assam will face crisis situation if the JMB violence forces large-scale exodus of Bangladeshis into border areas of Assam, where, by then, JMB would have already pushed enough activists of its own to make further trouble. Assam is already facing threat of disintegration consequent to demand for a separate Bodoland and for UT status by two Hill Districts. The Muslim-majority districts, abetted by the Muslim extremists and JMB activists, will bc third entity vociferously voicing for further vivisection of Assam.

NOTES

1. Sabri Bandopadhyay and Debesh Chakraborty, *Migration to the North-Eastern Region and Problems of Security* in Sanjukta Bhattacharya and Rochana Das (ed), *Perspectives on India's North-East,* 1998.

2. See Chapter 1.
3. Verghese, 1997.
4. *See* notes 6 and 15 below.
5. As soon as the General Election to Indian Parliament were announced by the Election Commission in June of that year, AASU demanded the deletion of nearly 5 lakh foreigners from the Electoral Rolls of the State, terming them as "illegal immigrants".
6. This profound and far-sighted observation by C.S. Mullan has been quoted appreciatively as often as it has been deprecated as a mischievous British ploy to divide the Hindus and Muslims, depending upon the identity and proclivity of the analyst.
7. Goswami, A. and Gogoi, T.K., "Immigration and Demographic Transformation of Assam, 1901-71", in B.L. Adbi (ed), *North-East Region: Problems and Prospects of Development* (Chandigarh CRRID), 1984, cited by Sri Radha Datta in *Strategic Analysis,* March 2000, monthly publication of the IDSA.
8. Sanjay Hazarika, "Insurgency in North-East India" in B. Pakem (ed), *Insurgency in North-East India,* 1997.
9. Weiner, Myron, *Security, Stability and International Migration, in International Security,* Volume 17, No. 3, Winter 1992-93, pp. 91-126.
10. Assam Recorder, 21-1-1999, p. 27856.
11. Luckily for it, Sylhet went out of Assam, minus its Karimganj Subdivision, on 15 August 1947.
12. Saadullah led three Ministries in Assam consequent to the elections held in 1937, under the provisions of Government of India Act, 1935.
13. Guha, Amalendu, 1977.
14. Wavell, *Viceroy's Journal.*
15. Excerpts from the 1931 Census Report, cited by Guha, Amalendu, 1977.
16. An ultra liberal, leftist academic, who has found nothing right with any post Narasimha Rao (1991-96) Governments in power since 1996 and would go to any lengths to liberate them, and support any anti-India resolutions on the nuclear issue at the UN or any other international fora which condemns the NDA Government's Nuclear Policy, recently dubbed Mullan's insightful 1931 observations as "mischievous" without explaining why in a 1998 article in an equally BJP-phobic fortnightly, published from the South.
17. The data cited here is from a Bangladesh Family Planning Department booklet of November 1994.
18. Critics of Nehru accused him and Indian officialdom of not learning from the history of unchecked influx of immigrants into Assam for the last 50 years and more. This provision should never have been written into the Pact. It left the door ajar for the subsequent mischief. Not only large number of people returned to Assam but Pakistan made use of the provision for propaganda purposes. To make matter worse, and as should have been anticipated, there was hardly any reverse flow out of Assam.
19. It should be a subject of an interesting and rewarding inquiry by a scholar or an eminent judge to determine the reason for such a decision in the East. Because of a proper decision in the west, the refugees from the West Pakistan

were able to stort afresh from scratch and made a success of it generally, many even rising to the very top in the fields of their chosen endeavour. On the other hand, why the refugees in the East were kept on doles and for years, rendering them mendicants, is beyond comprehension. Most remained refugees for years on end, fewer ever rising to positions of eminence in any sphere of life. Given equal chances, they should have fared as well, if not better, than their brethren in the west. Or, does the whole thing have to do with the different character traits of the Punjabis and the Assamese or Bengalis? One does not know the answer.

20. It is easy to see that the Indian generosity in this provision and in subsequent relaxations is informed by the humanitarian considerations but is bereft of the hard-nosed realities of political calculus. Not only was it never reciprocated by Pakistan, but it was also made a butt of wild and unsubstantiated accusations by that country. The price of all this generosity of Delhi was, of course, paid by the already hard-pressed Assam.
21. Cited by Verghese 1996.
22. Cited by Verghese 1996.
23. This is Mahanta, enjoying the first flush of power, after taking over in (end) 1985, and obviously, the idealism and sincerity of his convictions are still to desert him. But he certainly could not be comfortable with such thoughts today, having failed to have achieved his goals during his two stints as Chief Minister. The issue, detection and expulsion of foreigners, on which they had mounted a 7 years agitation, remains where it was before he assumed the reins of power in 1985: UNRESOLEVED and SIMMERING! The foreigners expelled by him during his 10-year stint in power, did not cross three figures. During his second stint, the chair mattered more than the mission!
24. Lt Gen (Retd) SK Sinha, PVSM, Governor of Assam, Insurgency in Assam, the *USI* Journal, July-September 1998.
25. These elections, boycotted and actively or violently opposed by AASU and AAGSP, were an unmitigated disaster. It left 3-5,000 people dead.
26. A serious charge the critics laid at their door was the students' agreeing to 1971 as the cut-off date (with minor concessions), the very formula offered to them by Indira Gandhi five-year back which they had haughtily spurned. The unsaid but clearly implied accusation was they had unnecessarily plunged Assam into five years of violence, destruction and disruption.
27. Lt Gen (Retd) SK Sinha, Governor Assam, in his lecture at the USI, New Delhi on 29 July 1998, excerpted in the *USI* Journal, July-September 1998.
28. For details of this meeting, see *Times of India* of 13-11-1996. Other related information is culled from its issue dated 2-2-1997.
29. It was reported that it was UPPA's Abdul Mohib Majumdar who had conceptualized the IMDT Act of 1983 in the first place, and had got it later incorporated in the 1985 Assam Accord.
30. *Times of India* 13-12-2000.
31. *Hindu* of 24-4-2000; Wasbir Hussain, *Of Natives and Aliens.*
32. September 1998 and September 1999 talks were held at Guwahati; and the March 1999 and May 2000 rounds were at New Delhi.
33. Barun Das Gupta, *The Hindu*, 28-5-2000.

34. Verghese, B.C., et al., 1980; Hussain, M., 1993.
35. They are the unfortunate Chakmas displaced by the Kaptai Dam in the Chittagong Hills Tract.
36. No Census was taken in Assam in 1981, and the 1991 Census omitted all denominational figures for states.
37. Nagaland had become a separate state in 1963. In January 1972, Meghalaya (with Manipur and Tripura) achieved statehood and Mizoram and Arunachal Pradesh got UT status. Assam had "lost" all these territories in less than a decade.
38. Cited in *Times of India* 5-12-1991.
39. Sanjay Hazarika worked for the *New York Times* in the first half of the 1990s and carried out this study for the American Academy of Art and Science, Toronto University.
40. This speaks volumes for the value system of some Indians and their sense of and regard for nation's interests. They provide all these documents to the illicit immigrants for a consideration, enabling them to get Indian Citizenship overnight. It is a crying shame. The counterparts and partners-in-crime of these anti-national Indians are the political parties and other entities who vehemently espouse the cause of there illicit immigrants (turned "Indian nationals") and thwart all efforts at their deportation.
41. The West Dinajpur district was divided into two districts of North and South Dinajpur, effective 1 April 1992.
42. *The Outlook,* 2-8-1999.
43. Saikat Neogi, "Bangladesh Infiltration into West Bengal," in the *Organizer Weekly,* 14-4-1994.
44. The story headed, *List revision rakes up infiltration issue,* datelined Calcutta is by Santanu Bannerjee, *Indian Express,* 2-6-1999.
45. Cited by Saikat Neogi, in his, "Bangladeshi Infiltration into West Bengal," *The Organiser Weekly,* 14-4-1994.
46. Cited in *Times of India,* 5-12-1991.
47. Surinder Awasthi, *Times of India,* 23-1-1992.
48. An official cited by Awasthi, n. 47.
49. Asian Records, 22-1-1999, p. 27856.
50. Samudra Gupta Kashyap, "Indo-Bangla Border still a free-way for all," *Indian Express* 5-6-2002.
51. Some intelligence Reports suggest that the outfits at sers 12 (MLTA) and 13 (MULTA) are different names of the same outfit.
52. A report in *Assam Daily* of 5-2-1995.
53. *Times of India,* 23-11-1998.
54. *The Hindu,* 21-9-1999.
55. Syed Liaquat Ali, *Hindustan Times,* 10-8-2001.
56. Seema Sangupta, *The Pioneer*, 19 Jan. 2007.
57. *Ibid.*